THE OXFORD BOOK OF THE
SUPERNATURAL

D. J. Enright is a distinguished poet and critic and the editor of
several anthologies including *The Oxford Book of Death* (1983), *The
Faber Book of Fevers and Frets* (1989), and *The Oxford Book of
Friendship* (1991, with David Rawlinson). A new volume of his
Selected Poems was published in 1990, and his most recent poetry
collection is *Old Men and Comets* (1993).

THE OXFORD BOOK
OF THE
SUPERNATURAL

Chosen and edited by

D. J. ENRIGHT

Oxford New York

OXFORD UNIVERSITY PRESS

1995

Oxford University Press, Walton Street, Oxford OX2 6DP

Oxford New York
Athens Auckland Bangkok Bombay
Calcutta Cape Town Dar es Salaam Delhi
Florence Hong Kong Istanbul Karachi
Kuala Lumpur Madras Madrid Melbourne
Mexico City Nairobi Paris Singapore
Taipei Tokyo Toronto
and associated companies in
Berlin Ibadan

Oxford is a trade mark of Oxford University Press

Selection and editorial material © D. J. Enright 1994

First published by Oxford University Press 1994
First issued as an Oxford University Press paperback 1995

British Library Cataloguing in Publication Data

Data available

Library of Congress Cataloging in Publication Data
The Oxford book of the supernatural / chosen and edited by
D. J. Enright.
p. cm.
Includes bibliographical references and index.
1. Supernatural. I. Enright, D. J. (Dennis Joseph), 1920–
133—dc20   BF1999.094   1994   93-32896
ISBN 0-19-283203-4

1 3 5 7 9 10 8 6 4 2

Printed in Great Britain by
Biddles Ltd
Guildford and King's Lynn

CONTENTS

EDITOR'S NOTE

UNLESS otherwise indicated, dates attached to extracts are of first publication. In the case of material from other languages, when no translator is indicated the editor is responsible for the English version.

The editor is obliged to the following for help of various kinds, intentional or inadvertent: Chris Baldick (*The Oxford Book of Gothic Tales*, 1992), Jonathan Barker, Shirley Chew, Ernst de Chickera, Richard Dalby (E. F. Benson: 'The Recent "Witch-Burning" at Clonmell'), Madeleine Enright, Gabriel Fitzmaurice, Christopher Frayling (*The Face of Tutankhamun*, 1992), Ann Geneva, Gerry Keenan, Koh Tai Ann, Jeremy Lewis, Judith Luna (Oxford University Press), Dorothy McCarthy, Maurice Marsh, Douglas Matthews (The London Library), Iona Opie and Moira Tatem (*A Dictionary of Superstitions*, 1989), David Rawlinson, Betty Robson, Jeffrey Burton Russell, Jacqueline Simms, Emma Spina, ffiona Swabey, Jane Turner.

D. J. E.

'Sir, to leave things out of a book, merely because people tell you they will
not be believed, is meanness.'

SAMUEL JOHNSON, Boswell's *Life*, 21 March 1772

'Ay, but there's this in it,' said the landlord. 'There's folks, i' my opinion,
they can't see ghos'es, not if they stood as plain as a pikestaff before 'em.
And there's reason i' that. For there's my wife, now, can't smell, not if
she'd the strongest o' cheese under her nose. I never see'd a ghost myself;
but then I says to myself, "Very like I haven't got the smell for 'em." And
so, I'm for holding with both sides; for, as I say, the truth lies between
'em.'

GEORGE ELIOT, *Silas Marner*, 1861

'How am I to fear the absolutely non-existent?' said Hurree Babu, talking
English to reassure himself. It is an awful thing still to dread the magic
that you contemptuously investigate—to collect folklore for the Royal
Society with a lively belief in all Powers of Darkness.

RUDYARD KIPLING, *Kim*, 1901

> To communicate with Mars, converse with spirits,
> To report the behaviour of the sea monster,
> Describe the horoscope, haruspicate or scry, . . .
>   release omens
> By sortilege, or tea leaves, riddle the inevitable
> With playing cards, fiddle with pentagrams
> Or barbituric acids, or dissect
> The recurrent image into pre-conscious terrors—
> To explore the womb, or tomb, or dreams; all these are usual
> Pastimes and drugs, and features of the press:
> And always will be, some of them especially
> When there is distress of nations and perplexity
> Whether on the shores of Asia, or in the Edgware Road.

T. S. ELIOT, 'The Dry Salvages', 1941

ASSORTED APPARITIONS

O NE thing is certain, that the supernatural has this in common with nature: you may drive it out with a pitchfork, but it will constantly come running
back. And in a variety of shapes, whether blood-curdling, enigmatic, comfort-
ing, or plain funny. Sometimes, it has to be said, it assumes a tedious or
dispiriting guise, as a number of the contributors to this book complain; the
classic formulation here is 'There needs no ghost, come from the grave, to tell
us this.' Even so, we shall see, there remains room for pleas and intimations,
explication and exculpation. Like God, the supernatural moves in a mysterious
way its wonders and banalities to perform: which is an old, infuriating apolo-
gia, one that has been put to base purposes, but one all the same that cannot
be indisputably refuted. As Maeterlinck said, the Unknown is 'even more
unknown than that which we think we know'.

The hunger to believe in things supernatural is matched only by the compulsion to disbelieve. Believers and disbelievers can be equally entrenched,
equally predictable, and equally boring in their confident claims and counter-
claims. The ever credulous and the unremittingly incredulous resemble two
political parties forever nagging each at the other. If there were a third party,
one would vote for it. But there is a third party, or loose association of third
parties, as I hope this anthology will show by presenting material in which,
touchingly, grotesquely, eerily, or frighteningly, the supernatural and the natural
meet and ignite, illuminating our deepest anxieties and hopes. For the supernatural impinges on the natural in the latter's most sympathetic aspects and in
its most deplorable, in love and longing, in concupiscence and cupidity, in the
urge to help and the desire to destroy.

I have interpreted the term 'supernatural' liberally, and have made no
attempt in the selecting and arranging of material to distinguish between fact

(or what is advanced as such) and fiction (or what is offered as such), for the simple reason that it would be impossible to do so. My role has been that of a seeker, who gives due weight to Samuel Johnson's view that the subject, despite scoffers, frauds, and dupes, is still 'one of the most important that can come before the human understanding'; and my attitude, in as far as I can judge, while hardly extending as far as Blake's Proverb of Hell, that 'everything possible to be believed is an image of truth', approximates to that of a character in Robertson Davies's *Murther & Walking Spirits* (1991) who holds that matters of the spirit require 'a fine credulity about everything, kept in check by a lively scepticism about everything'. When his interlocutor objects that this doesn't get you anywhere, he replies: 'Oh, but it does. It keeps you constantly alert to every possibility. It is a little understood aspect of the Golden Mean.'

The opening section is a miscellany of apparitions, ancient and modern, and a review of haunted houses or localities, along with such accessories as an armchair and a coat-hanger. Of reputedly haunted houses, John Aubrey suggested in the late seventeenth century that tales of this sort might be put about by tenants with the aim of keeping the rent down, thus echoing Pliny's story of the dwelling in Athens rented cheaply by the philosopher Athenodorus and expeditiously restored to order, and anticipating the news item concerning a council house reproduced on p. 471. The section ends with some accounts of poltergeists, or in plain English, ghosts who kick up a racket.

In each case the choice has been huge, and I have sought to take those instances which are either conveniently representative or else of some peculiar interest. Or perhaps just those which have for one reason or another captured my fancy.

~

We learn from this exhaustive study of selected narratives: first, that a large majority of apparitions appear at or near the death of the deceased person; second, that apparitions are seen in any light from dawn to daylight, sometimes at night with a luminosity of their own; they appear in any house, ancient or quite modern, and are seen by persons of every type, quite independently of their health, temperament, or intellectual capacity; and, third, that apparitions are seen not only by individuals at odd moments and places, but, unless one's mind is closed entirely to human testimony, ghosts of a more persistent type are associated with certain localities and houses.

SIR ERNEST BENNETT, *Apparitions and Haunted Houses: A Survey of Evidence*, 1939; the selected narratives came from a very large number received by the Society for Psychical Research

A characteristic of apparitions, which has given rise to some confusion, not to say ridicule, is that the central figure does not appear alone. It appears with clothes on; and people have asked whether, in addition to believing in ghosts, they are expected to believe in ghostly skirts and ghostly trousers! The answer supplied by the evidence is quite definite. They are not only expected to believe in ghostly skirts and trousers, but also in ghostly hats, sticks, dogs, horses, carriages, doors, curtains—anything, in fact, with which a human being is commonly surrounded. The difficulty in accepting these things is not really a difficulty at all. It arises from a false conception of what an apparition is.

G. N. M. TYRRELL, *Apparitions*, 1943

Plutarch in his *Life of Theseus* relates how many combatants at Marathon, fighting against the Medes, saw the Spirit of Theseus, who had died many a long year before, in arms rushing on in front of them against the Barbarians. Wherefore the Athenians were moved to honour him as a demi-god. Pausanius [Greek geographer, 2nd century AD] in his *Attica* also writes of Marathon that even four hundred years after the battle: 'At this spot every night you may hear horses neighing and men fighting. To go on purpose to see the sight never brought good to any man; but with him who chances to light on it unwittingly and by accident the spirits are not angry.' . . .

In another work, the *De Sera Numinis Vindicta*, Plutarch tells how Pausanius [Spartan general, 5th century BC], being at Byzantium, sent to fetch by force a maiden named Cleonice, of an honourable house and rare beauty, in order that he might enjoy her. But night having fallen when she was brought to him, he awoke suddenly—for he had been toasting her in full cups of wine—and half-dazed with sleep and the fumes of wine he imagined that some assassin had entered his bedchamber to slay him, and so great was his alarm that in the confusion he ran her through with his sword. From that self-same hour he was haunted by her ghost, a pale bleeding figure which crooned softly so he only might hear:

Keepe thou thy selfe upright, and justice see thou feare,
For woe and shame be unto him, that justice donne doth beare.

And since this phantom appeared to him every night he was at last obliged to
go to the temple of Heracleia, where they evoke the souls of the dead, and here,
after the customary sacrifices of propitiation and the funeral libations, he
caused the spirit of Cleonice to be summoned. When she appeared she said
that very soon after his return to Sparta he would be freed from his troubles,
and indeed no sooner had he reached his country than he died.

FR. NOËL TAILLEPIED, *A Treatise of Ghosts*, 1588; tr. Montague Summers

Brutus. Let me see, let me see; is not the leaf turned down
    Where I left reading? Here it is, I think.
        He sits and reads
        Enter the Ghost of Caesar
    How ill this taper burns! Ha! Who comes here?
    I think it is the weakness of mine eyes
    That shapes this monstrous apparition.
    It comes upon me. Art thou any thing?
    Art thou some god, some angel, or some devil,
    That mak'st my blood cold, and my hair to stare?
    Speak to me what thou art.
Ghost. Thy evil spirit, Brutus.
Brutus.   Why com'st thou?
Ghost. To tell thee thou shalt see me at Philippi.
Brutus. Well; then I shall see thee again?
Ghost. Ay, at Philippi.
Brutus. Why, I will see thee at Philippi then.
    Exit Ghost
    Now I have taken heart, thou vanishest.
    Ill spirit, I would hold more talk with thee.

WILLIAM SHAKESPEARE, *Julius Caesar*, 1599; Caesar's ghost appeared again to
Brutus, on the eve of Brutus's defeat at the battle of Philippi

It is not miraculous, that the masculine spirit of Marcus Brutus, surrounded
by darkness and solitude, distracted probably by recollection of the kindness
and favour of the great individual whom he had put to death to avenge the

wrongs of his country, though by the slaughter of his own friend, should at length place before his eyes in person the appearance which termed itself his evil Genius, and promised again to meet him at Philippi. Brutus' own intentions, and his knowledge of the military art, had probably long since assured him that the decision of the civil war must take place at or near that place; and, allowing that his own imagination supplied that part of his dialogue with the spectre, there is nothing else which might not be fashioned in a vivid dream or a waking reverie, approaching, in absorbing and engrossing character, the usual matter of which dreams consist.

SIR WALTER SCOTT, *Letters on Demonology and Witchcraft*, 1830

The last Battle fought in the North of Ireland between the Protestants and the Papists [1650] was in Glinsuly near Letterkenny in the County of Donegall. Veneras the Popish Bishop of Clogher, was General of the Irish Army; and that of the Parliament Army Sir Charles Coot. They pitch'd their Tents on each side the River Suly. And the Papists constantly persist in it to this very day, that the Night before the Action, a Woman of uncommon stature all in white appeared to the said Bishop, admonished him not to cross the River first to assault the Enemy, but suffer them to do it, whereby he should obtain the Victory. That if the Irish took the water first to move towards the English, they should be put to a total rout, which came to pass. Ocahan, and Sir Henry O Neal, who were both kill'd there, saw severally the same Apparition, and disswaded the Bishop from giving the first onset, but could not prevail upon him. In the mean time I find nothing in this Revelation, that any common Soldier might not conclude without extraordinary means.

Near the same place a party of the Protestants had been surpriz'd sleeping by the Popish Irish, were it not for several Wrens that just wakned them by dancing and pecking on the Drums as the Enemy were approaching. For this reason the wild Irish mortally hate these Birds to this day, calling them the Devils Servants, and killing them where ever they catch them: They teach their Children to thrust them full of Thorns: You'll see sometimes on Holidays a whole Parish running like mad-men from Hedg to Hedg a Wren-hunting.

JOHN AUBREY, *Miscellanies*, 1696

Enter Ghost
Hamlet. Angels and ministers of grace defend us!
    Be thou a spirit of health, or goblin damn'd,

Bring with thee airs from Heaven, or blasts from Hell,
Be thy intents wicked or charitable,
Thou com'st in such a questionable shape
That I will speak to thee. I'll call thee Hamlet,
King, father, royal Dane: Oh, answer me,
Let me not burst in ignorance; but tell
Why thy canoniz'd bones hearsèd in death
Have burst their cerements, why the sepulchre
Wherein we saw thee quietly inurn'd,
Hath op'd his ponderous and marble jaws,
To cast thee up again? What may this mean?
That thou, dead corse, again in còmplete steel,
Revisit'st thus the glimpses of the Moon,
Making night hideous? and we fools of nature,
So horridly to shake our disposition,
With thoughts beyond the reaches of our souls?
Say, why is this? wherefore? what should we do?

                    Ghost beckons Hamlet

.   .   .   .

Hamlet. Where wilt thou lead me? Speak; I'll go no further.
Ghost. Mark me.
Hamlet.   I will.
Ghost.   My hour is almost come,
    When I to sulphurous and tormenting flames
    Must render up myself.
Hamlet.   Alas poor ghost!
Ghost. Pity me not, but lend thy serious hearing
    To what I shall unfold.
Hamlet.   Speak, I am bound to hear.
Ghost. So art thou to revenge, when thou shalt hear.
Hamlet. What?
Ghost.   I am thy father's spirit,
    Doomed for a certain term to walk the night;
    And for the day confin'd to fast in fires,
    Till the foul crimes done in my days of nature
    Are burnt and purg'd away. But that I am forbid
    To tell the secrets of my prison-house,
    I could a tale unfold, whose lightest word
    Would harrow up thy soul, freeze thy young blood,

Make thy two eyes, like stars, start from their spheres,
Thy knotted and combinèd locks to part,
And each particular hair to stand an end,
Like quills upon the fretful porpentine.
But this eternal blazon must not be
To ears of flesh and blood . . .

SHAKESPEARE, *Hamlet*, 1600–1

In the year 1772, a certain parishioner of Sainte-Mandé, named Loiseaut, being at church, believed that he saw an extraordinary person kneeling close by him; this was a very swarthy man, whose only garment was a pair of coarse worsted drawers. His beard was long, his hair woolly, and about his neck there was a ruddy circular scar. He carried a book, having the following inscription emblazoned in golden letters: *Ecce Agnus Dei*.

Loiseaut observed with astonishment that no one but himself seemed aware of this strange presence, but he finished his devotions and returned home, where the same personage was awaiting him. He drew nearer to ask who he was and what might his business be, when the fantastic visitor vanished. Loiseaut retired to bed in a fever and unable to sleep. The same night he found his room illuminated suddenly by a ruddy glow; he sprang up in bed, believing that the place was on fire; and then on a table in the very centre of the room he saw a gold plate, wherein the head of his visitor was swimming in blood, encompassed by a red nimbus. The eyes rolled terribly, the mouth opened, a strange and hissing voice said: 'I await the heads of kings, the heads of the courtesans of kings; I await Herod and Herodias.' The nimbus faded and the sick man saw no more.

Some days after he had recovered sufficiently to resume his usual occupations. As he was crossing the Place Louis XV, a beggar accosted him and Loiseaut, without looking, threw a coin into his hat. 'Thank you,' said the recipient, 'it is a king's head; but here,' and he pointed towards the middle place of the thoroughfare, 'there will fall another, and it is that for which I am waiting.' Loiseaut looked with astonishment towards the speaker and uttered a cry when he recognized the strange figure of his vision. 'Be silent,' said the mendicant; 'they will take you for a fool, as no one but yourself can see me. You have recognized me, I know, and to you I confess that I am John the Baptist, the Precursor. I am here to predict the punishment which will befall the successors of Herod and the heirs of Caiaphas; you may repeat all that I tell you.'

ÉLIPHAS LÉVI, *The History of Magic*, 1859; tr. Arthur Edward Waite

Here you have an old woman dead, one that, it may be, has hid a little money in the orchard or garden; and an apparition, is supposed, comes and discovers it, by leading the person it appears to, to the place, and making some signal that he should dig there for somewhat; or a man is dead, and having left a legacy to such and such, the executor does not pay it, and an apparition comes and haunts this executor till he does justice. Is it likely an angel should be sent from heaven to find out the old woman's earthen dish with thirty or forty shillings in it? or an angel should be sent to harass this man for a legacy of perhaps five or ten pounds? and as to the Devil, will any one charge Satan with being solicitous to have justice done? they that know him at all, must know him better than to think so hardly of him.

Who then must it be? and from whence? To say it is the soul or ghost of the departed person, and that he could not be at rest till the injured person be righted, is advanced upon no principle that is agreeable to the Christian doctrine at all; for if the soul is happy, is it reasonable to believe that the felicity of heaven can be interrupted by so trivial a matter, and on so slight an occasion? if the soul be unhappy, remember the great gulf fixed; there is no room for us to believe that those miserable souls have any leisure or liberty to come back upon earth on an errand of such a nature.

In a word, there is nothing but difficulty in it on every side: apparitions there are, we see no room to doubt the reality of that part; but what, who, or from whence, is a difficulty which I see no way to extricate ourselves from, but by granting that there may be an appointed, deputed sort of stationary spirits in the invisible world, who come upon these occasions, and appear among us; which inhabitants or spirits (you may call them angels if you please), bodies they are not, and cannot be, neither had they been ever embodied; but such as they are, they have a power of conversing among us, and particularly with spirits embodied, and can by dreams, impulses, and strong aversions, move our thoughts, and give hope, raise doubts, sink our souls today, elevate them tomorrow, and many ways operate upon our passions and affections; may give intimations of good or evil; but cannot, through some unknown restraint upon their power, go any further, speak any plainer, or give the least assistance to us, no, not by counsel or direction to guide us or tell us how to act for our own preservation.

I have a story by me of a gentleman who carried on a secret and criminal conversation with a certain lady, and having made an assignation to meet the lady, was met at the place by an apparition of his own mother; she said nothing, she did not offer to speak, nor did he at first know it to be an apparition. The gentleman walks about in the field near a house where he had appointed the lady to meet; the apparition walked about likewise, and he takes it to be a woman in ordinary, as any woman might be seen to walk up and down in the same field or walk.

By and by the woman or lady appointed comes, he meets her, and goes forward to salute her; the apparition shows itself just behind the lady, and looks him full in the face; he starts back from the lady, and instead of kissing her, cries out, and asks her, who's that behind her? she turns about, but sees nobody, nor he neither; which frights them both.

He fancies it to be an imaginary vapour, having no faith at all in apparitions, and offers to go up to the lady again; and behold, he sees the apparition just behind her again, the face standing just so as to look over the lady's shoulder, and stare just upon him; he cries out again, and knows it to be his mother, who, it seems, was dead; and in crying out again, he adds, My mother! at which it vanishes.

Had this apparition any occasion to speak? was it not rebuke enough to look him in the face? Even in common affairs a look from the eye of one who has authority to reprove, is sometimes more effectual than the reproof, if it was given in words at length.

Suppose this spectre to regard him not with a threatening aspect, but with a countenance of pity, of a maternal reprehension, a reproof urging shame and reproach, like that of Solomon, *What, my son! what, the son of my vows; my son be seen embracing a strumpet!* The man went away, says my story, filled with confusion; as no question indeed but he would.

Here was no need of speech; the look was a lash, and a reproof sufficient; the man would hardly meet there any more, if he would meet the same lady any more, and it is very likely he never did.

DANIEL DEFOE, *The Secrets of the Invisible World Disclos'd; or, The History and Reality of Apparitions*, 1727

That the Cock Lane Ghost became a *cause célèbre* was due less to any striking occurrences than to the keen interest taken by persons of social or intellectual consequence.

In late 1759 Mr and Mrs Kent, William and Frances (known as Fanny), took lodgings at the house of Richard Parsons in Cock Lane, West Smithfield. The two were not actually married, because Kent's first wife had died in childbirth and Fanny was her sister, and hence fell within the prohibited degrees. On 2 February 1760 Fanny died, apparently of smallpox. Thereafter noises and scratchings were heard in the house for which no natural cause could be found. It was put about that they came from Fanny's spirit, and her message, delivered by the simple method of one knock to signify yes and two knocks for no, was to the effect that she had died of poison administered by William Kent, to whom she had left all her possessions (as he had willed everything he owned, which was much more, to her). It should be mentioned that there was bad blood between Kent and Parsons, the latter declining to repay a modest sum lent by the former. The knocking was always heard in the vicinity of Parsons's young daughter, Elizabeth; indeed the spirit seemed to follow her about. Large audiences, including ladies and gentlemen of fashion, gathered expectantly in the room where Elizabeth lay tucked into bed. The press had a field-day.

A committee was formed of 'gentlemen eminent for their rank and character', including Dr Johnson, 'for the examination of the noises supposed to be made by a departed spirit, for the detection of some enormous crime'. The examination took place on 1 February 1762. Nothing happened, and Johnson drew up a report which was approved by the other members. It concluded: 'It is therefore the opinion of the whole assembly, that the child has some art of making or counterfeiting particular noises, and that there is no agency of any higher cause.' Subsequently it was observed that Elizabeth was able to slip out of her bonds, and a wooden board was found in her bed. Mr and Mrs Parsons, together with three others, including the credulous rector of a nearby church, were accused of 'conspiracy to take away William Kent's life'. They were found guilty, and fined or sentenced to fairly short terms of imprisonment. The laying of the ghost provided further material for poets, balladeers, actors, and artists in satirical vein.

> Summarized from various reports; see pp. 472, 508-9, 523-4, in the present book. Douglas Grant gives a full account in *The Cock Lane Ghost*, 1965

This brought on the chapter of romance, national peculiarities, fetches, second-sights, etc. etc.; in the latter of which, both Lord Erskine and the Duchess of G—— acknowledged their belief. I could not avoid expressing some surprise that such persons should give way to the influence of such irrational superstition. The duchess was displeased, and said, 'I don't like to see young ladies setting themselves above their superiors, and giving in to free thinking. I never knew any one cry down what is called superstition, but those who have no religion.'

It was in vain that 'I rose to explain' . . . Her grace related a very curious and romantic tale of second-sight in her own family, which amused, if it did not convert me—while the affecting manner in which it was told, left no doubt as to the sincerity of the relator.

'I also,' said Lord Erskine, 'believe in second-sight, because I have been its subject. When I was a very young man, I had been for some time absent from Scotland. On the morning of my arrival in Edinburgh, as I was descending the steps of a close, on coming out from a bookseller's shop, I met our old family butler. He looked greatly changed, pale, wan, and shadowy, as a ghost. "Eh! old boy," I said, "what brings you here?" He replied, "To meet your honour, and solicit your interference with my lord, to recover a sum, due to me, which the steward at our last settlement did not pay." Struck by his looks and manner, I bade him follow me to the bookseller's, into whose shop I stepped back; but when I turned round to speak to him, he had vanished.

I remembered that his wife carried on some little trade in the old town. I remembered even the house and the flat she occupied, which I had often visited in my boyhood. Having made it out, I found the old woman in widow's mourning. Her husband had been dead for some months; and had told her on his death-bed, that my father's steward had wronged him of some money, but that when Master Tom returned, he would see her righted. This I promised to do, and shortly after fulfilled my promise. The impression was indelible; and I am extremely cautious how I deny the possibility of such "supernatural visitings" as those which your grace has just instanced in your own family.'

Either Lord Erskine did, or did not, believe this strange story; if he did, what a strange aberration of intellect!—if he did not, what a stranger aberration from truth! My opinion is, that he *did* believe it.

LADY MORGAN, *The Book of the Boudoir*, 1829

A noble lady did nothing but read and pray and let her farm run down without lifting a finger. After she died, she 'walked', and now she shared in all the work . . . The new owner asked her why she was there, and she answered 'Everyone is born to work, and since I neglected this in life I must do it now as a punishment.'

People often saw the pastor here walking at midnight with a book under his arm, and going into the church. When asked why he did it he replied, 'I walk now while I am alive so I don't have to do it when I am dead.'

Old people in Skalmstrup . . . said that every year on one holiday, I think it was St Martin's Eve, they could hear a woman who stood and beat clothes down by a spring where they got water for the nearest houses. That spring was at the end of the village and it is still there. They could stand in their doors and hear her at work very clearly, but no one dared go down. The story is that she had washed clothes there on a holiday, and now she must stand there and do it until doomsday.

Where I was born there was a ghost who couldn't be dealt with because it was so old—none of the good folk there knew its language and so nothing could be done about it.

> EVALD TANG KRISTENSEN, *Danish Legends*, 'from the oral tradition', 1897; tr. Joan Rockwell

Some souls seem to be condemned to wander for rather unimportant sins. Such was Molly Lee, of Burslem, who haunted the streets of that town because she had given short weight and sold watered milk in her lifetime. Her constant appearances, carrying her milk-pail on her head and confessing her sins, so distressed the townspeople that six clergymen met in the church to lay the troubled spirit—in a pig-trough, according to the story told to Miss Burne, but actually in an old stone coffin. She was finally laid, 'but,' the narrator added, 'three of the parsons died of it and the other three had a big job to get over it. That's true, that is; for I've been over to Burslem churchyard myself on purpose to see the pig-trough, and I stood and put my foot in it.'

> CHRISTINA HOLE, *Haunted England*, 1940; the reference is to Charlotte Sophia Burne: *Shropshire Folk-Lore*, 1883

Don John. Poh! Poh! Heaven is not so strict as you imagine; and, if at all times when Men—
         Ghost in the Form of a Woman veil'd
Sganarel (seeing the Ghost). Ah! Sir, 'tis Heaven that Speaks to you, 'tis a Warning it gives you.
Don John. If 'tis Heaven that gives me Warning, it must speak plainer, if it wou'd have me understand it.
Ghost. Don John has but one Moment longer to lay hold on the Mercy of Heaven, and if he Repents not now, his Destruction is determin'd.
Sganarel. D'ye hear, Sir?
Don John. Who is that dares talk so? Methinks I shou'd know that Voice.
Sganarel. Ah! Sir, 'tis a Ghost, I know it by its Stalking.

Don John. Ghost, Fantom, or Devil, I'll see what it is.

   The Ghost changes Shape and represents Time with his Scythe in his Hand

Sganarel. Oh! Heaven, d'ye observe, Sir, that change of Shape?

Don John. No, no, nothing is capable of impressing a Terror upon me, I'll try with my Sword whether 'tis Body or Spirit.

   The Ghost vanishes the Instant Don John pushes at it

Sganarel. Ah! Sir, yield to so many Proofs, and repent immediately.

Don John. No, no, come what will, it shall never be said I was capable of Repentance. Come, follow me.

      The Statue of the Governor

Statue. Don John, you gave me your Word Yesterday to come eat with me.

Don John. Yes; where shall we go?

Statue. Give me your Hand.

Don John. There 'tis.

Statue. Don John, Obstinacy in Wickedness brings on a fatal Death; and rejecting the Favours of Heaven opens a way to its Thunder.

Don John. Oh Heavens! What do I feel? An invisible Flame scorches me, I can bear it no longer, my whole Body is a burning Fire-brand. Oh!

   Loud Thunder and great Flashes of Lightning fall on Don John, the Earth opens and swallows him: and Flames burst out from the Place where he descended.

           MOLIÈRE, *Dom Juan*, 1665; tr. anon., 1739

[He] took me aside that he might say—'I hope you never invoke spirits—that is a very dangerous thing to do. I am told that even the planetary spirits turn upon us in the end.' I said, 'Have you ever seen an apparition?' 'O, yes, once,' he said. 'I have my alchemical laboratory in a cellar under my house where the Bishop cannot see it. One day I was walking up and down there when I heard another footstep walking up and down beside me. I turned and saw a girl I had been in love with when I was a young man, but she died long ago. She wanted me to kiss her. O no, I would not do that.' 'Why not?' I said. 'O she might have got power over me.' 'Has your alchemical research had any success?' I said. 'Yes, I once made the elixir of life. A French alchemist said it had the right smell and the right colour' (the alchemist may have been Éliphas Lévi, who visited England in the 'sixties, and would have said anything) 'but the first effect of the elixir is that your nails fall out and your hair falls off. I was afraid that I might have made a mistake and that nothing else might happen, so I put

it away on a shelf. I meant to drink it when I was an old man, but when I got
it down the other day it had all dried up.'

W. B. YEATS, *The Trembling of the Veil*, 1922; concerning the Revd W. A.
Ayton, a fellow member of the Hermetic Order of the Golden Dawn, whom
Yeats described as 'the most panic-stricken person I have ever known'

[Theodore] Dreiser said that when he was living in New York, on West Fifty-
seventh Street, John Cowper Powys came occasionally to dinner. At that time
Powys was living in this country, in a little town about thirty miles up the
Hudson, and he usually left Dreiser's place fairly early to catch a train to take
him home. One evening, after a rather long after-dinner conversation, Powys
looked at his watch and said hurriedly that he had no idea it was so late, and
he would have to go at once or miss his train. Dreiser helped him on with his
overcoat, and Powys, on his way to the door, said, 'I'll appear before you, right
here, later this evening. You'll see me.'

'Are you going to turn yourself into a ghost, or have you a key to the door?'
Dreiser laughed when he asked that question, for he did not believe for an
instant that Powys meant to be taken seriously.

'I don't know,' said Powys. 'I may return as a spirit or in some other astral
form.'

Dreiser said that there had been no discussion whatever during the evening
of spirits, ghosts or visions. The talk had been mainly about American publishers
and their methods. He said that he gave no further thought to Powys's promise
to reappear, but he sat up reading for about two hours, all alone. Then he
looked up from his book and saw Powys standing in the doorway between the
entrance hall and the living-room. The apparition had Powys's features, his
tall stature, loose tweed garments and general appearance, but a pale white
glow shone from the figure. Dreiser rose at once, and strode towards the ghost,
or whatever it was, saying, 'Well, you've kept your word, John. You're here.
Come on in and tell me how you did it.' The apparition did not reply, and it
vanished when Dreiser was within three feet of it.

As soon as he had recovered somewhat from his astonishment Dreiser
picked up the telephone and called John Cowper Powys's house in the country.
Powys came to the phone, and Dreiser recognized his voice. After he had heard
the story of the apparition, Powys said, 'I told you I'd be there, and you oughtn't
to be surprised.' Dreiser told me that he was never able to get any explanation
from Powys, who refused to discuss the matter from any standpoint.

W. E. WOODWARD, *The Gift of Life*, 1947

Richard de la Mare: Among his favourites was certainly Thomas Hardy, who I think influenced him to some extent and who was a friend of his as well.

Robert Robinson: Did he share Hardy's interest in death?

de la Mare: Well, in a curious way he did, yes. He felt it was the great adventure at the end of your life and that it was something in a way to be looked forward to—as a great adventure. I mean he firmly believed in some sort of life after death, I haven't any doubt about that at all.

Robinson: I'm very addicted to his ghost stories and I think of the grotesque Seaton's Aunt and the appalling Mr Bloom . . . Did anything ever happen in real life of a vaguely occult nature?

de la Mare: Well yes. I wouldn't use the word occult but perhaps telepathic would be the better word to use. More than once, yes. There was one occasion I remember vividly because I was involved in it personally. We were going to look at antique shops. He collected furniture and china to some extent, in a rather desultory way; but it was an amusing thing to do, to go and look at antique shops, and very often I would go with him. This particular day, we got on our coats ready to go when a friend turned up who wasn't expected and whom he didn't particularly want to see but he felt he must stay and talk to; and we were prevented from going—and he was disappointed. Well, that afternoon two other friends of his went to this particular shop that he visited regularly and while they were looking in the window the wife suddenly ran away from the shop in some sort of distress and her husband went after her and said, 'What on earth's the matter?' And she said, 'Well, I'm worried about Mr de la Mare because I could see him in the shop, but he wasn't there because I could see a bureau through him . . .'

From the transcript of an interview on BBC Radio 4 on 25 April 1973, the centenary of the birth of Walter de la Mare

Father Melchior [de Flavin] tells [1563] of another apparition, a ghost who appeared some forty years ago in circumstances that came under his personal knowledge. In the town of Saint-Pons near Narbonne, there died suddenly a scholar, who was, alas! unshriven and in a state of sin. This youth appeared on the morrow of his funeral to a close friend of his, a scholar likewise, whom he begged to go on his behalf to Rodez and crave absolution from the holy Bishop. His friend at once set out, and as he made his way through the mountain passes, dangerous to tread and slippery with snow, his dead friend went with him, guiding his steps and conversing with him, although he saw no man. The ghost, indeed, led him safely over the snow and ice, and when he was come to

Rodez he obtained a full absolution from the Bishop, the Blessed François. On his return the ghost again companioned with and conducted him with careful steps. As is the Catholic custom in such a case absolution was given to the dead body, and the Spirit then took leave of his friend with many tender expressions of gratitude, promising to pray for and assist him.

TAILLEPIED, *A Treatise of Ghosts*

As Mrs Agnes Kelly of Fartown, Huddersfield, drove her car into a sharp bend, the glare of oncoming headlights picked out the figure of a young, fair-haired boy. Horrified, she swung the steering wheel over as the boy's freckled face loomed up in front of the windscreen. That single act probably saved her life. She crashed into a parked car, but suffered only shock. As she waited for an ambulance, she anxiously asked a policeman, 'Have I killed the boy?' But there was no boy.

A court heard, in January 1981, that what Mrs Kelly saw as she took the bend in Somerset Road, Huddersfield, was a vision of an eight-year-old child, who had been knocked down and killed by a car on the same spot many years before. After the case she said, 'But for that vision I am sure I would have driven straight into the car coming up the hill towards me. I most probably would have been killed.'

TERENCE WHITAKER, *Yorkshire's Ghosts and Legends*, 1983

In 1979 the mind's survival of death was even recognized in an American courtroom. The occasion was the trial of a man named Allan Showery for the murder of a Filipino nurse, Teresita Basa. She was stabbed to death in her apartment in Evanston, Illinois, on 21 February 1977. Medical evidence indicated that the 48-year-old nurse had let a man into her apartment and that he had encircled her neck from behind in a Japanese half nelson and rendered her unconscious: then he had stripped her and stabbed her between the ribs with such force that the knife went right through her . . .

Two weeks later, in the Edgewater Hospital where Teresita Basa had worked, one of her colleagues remarked to another Filipino, a respiratory therapist named Remy Chua, 'Teresita must be turning in her grave. Too bad she can't tell the police who did it.' And Remy Chua replied seriously, 'She can come to me in a dream. I'm not afraid.' Later that day, as she was dozing in the locker room, Remy Chua opened her eyes to see Teresita Basa standing in front of her. She ran out of the room in a panic.

Remy Chua began to dream of the murder and of the killer, whom she then recognized as a black hospital orderly named Allan Showery. And one day, as she lay on her bed, a voice spoke through her mouth saying, 'I am Teresita Basa. I want you to tell the police . . .' The voice spoke in Tagalog, the native language of the Philippines. Her husband heard the words although Remy Chua remembered nothing when she recovered from her trance. They decided to do nothing about it. Two weeks later 'Teresita' came back and spoke through Remy Chua's mouth again, this time naming her killer as 'Allan'. A few days later she named him as Allan Showery, and said he had stolen her jewellery and given it to his girlfriend—she even gave the telephone number of someone who could identify the jewellery. She claimed that 'Al' had come to fix her television and killed her.

Finally the Chuas called the police. They were unconvinced and it was several days before they questioned Showery, who admitted promising to repair Teresita's television but claimed he had simply forgotten. However when the police questioned Showery's live-in girlfriend Yanka and asked her if he had ever given her jewellery, she showed them an antique ring that he had given her as a 'belated Christmas present'. The police called the number that Mrs Chua had spoken in her trance and two of the victim's cousins came to the station and identified the ring as Teresita's. They also identified some other jewellery that had belonged to her. Faced with this evidence Showery broke down and confessed.

At the trial in January 1979 the defence argued that the case should be dismissed on the grounds that the evidence had been—apparently—provided by a ghost, and implied that ghosts were untrustworthy. Judge Frank W. Berbero overruled the objection. But the jury obviously had its doubts and confessed to being hopelessly deadlocked. At a second trial a month later, however, Showery changed his plea to guilty and was sentenced to fourteen years in prison.

COLIN WILSON, *Beyond the Occult*, 1988

> The loud wind never reached the ship,
> Yet now the ship moved on!
> Beneath the lightning and the Moon
> The dead men gave a groan.
>
> They groaned, they stirred, they all uprose,
> Nor spake, nor moved their eyes;
> It had been strange, even in a dream,
> To have seen those dead men rise.

The helmsman steered, the ship moved on;
Yet never a breeze up-blew;
The mariners all 'gan work the ropes,
Where they were wont to do;
They raised their limbs like lifeless tools—
We were a ghastly crew.

The body of my brother's son
Stood by me, knee to knee:
The body and I pulled at one rope,
But he said nought to me.

'I fear thee, ancient Mariner!'
Be calm, thou Wedding-Guest!
'Twas not those souls that fled in pain,
Which to their corses came again,
But a troop of spirits blest:

For when it dawned—they dropped their arms,
And clustered round the mast;
Sweet sounds rose slowly through their mouths,
And from their bodies passed.

Around, around, flew each sweet sound,
Then darted to the Sun;
Slowly the sounds came back again,
Now mixed, now one by one.

Sometimes a-dropping from the sky
I heard the sky-lark sing;
Sometimes all little birds that are,
How they seemed to fill the sea and air
With their sweet jargoning!

And now 'twas like all instruments,
Now like a lonely flute;
And now it is an angel's song,
That makes the heavens be mute.

.   .   .   .

I woke, and we were sailing on
As in a gentle weather:
'Twas night, calm night, the Moon was high;
The dead men stood together.

All stood together on the deck,
For a charnel-dungeon fitter:
All fixed on me their stony eyes,
That in the Moon did glitter.

The pang, the curse, with which they died,
Had never passed away:
I could not draw my eyes from theirs,
Nor turn them up to pray.

And now this spell was snapt: once more
I viewed the ocean green,
And looked far forth, yet little saw
Of what had else been seen—

Like one, that on a lonesome road
Doth walk in fear and dread,
And having once turned round walks on,
And turns no more his head;
Because he knows, a frightful fiend
Doth close behind him tread.

But soon there breathed a wind on me,
Nor sound nor motion made:
Its path was not upon the sea,
In ripple or in shade.

It raised my hair, it fanned my cheek
Like a meadow-gale of spring—
It mingled strangely with my fears,
Yet it felt like a welcoming.

Swiftly, swiftly flew the ship,
Yet she sailed softly too:
Sweetly, sweetly blew the breeze—
On me alone it blew.

Oh! dream of joy! is this indeed
The light-house top I see?
Is this the hill? is this the kirk?
Is this mine own countree?

SAMUEL TAYLOR COLERIDGE, from 'Rime of the Ancient Mariner', 1798. By wantonly killing an albatross the mariner has brought a curse on the ship, which is becalmed; the curse is lifted only when without thinking he blesses the creatures of the sea

The same face: the very same. Marley in his pigtail, usual waistcoat, tights and boots; the tassels on the latter bristling, like his pigtail, and his coat-skirts, and the hair upon his head. The chain he drew was clasped about his middle. It was long, and wound about him like a tail; and it was made (for Scrooge observed it closely) of cash-boxes, keys, padlocks, ledgers, deeds, and heavy purses wrought in steel. His body was transparent; so that Scrooge, observing him, and looking through his waistcoat, could see the two buttons on his coat behind . . .

Scrooge fell upon his knees, and clasped his hands before his face.

'Mercy!' he said. 'Dreadful apparition, why do you trouble me?'

'Man of the worldly mind!' replied the Ghost, 'do you believe in me or not?'

'I do,' said Scrooge. 'I must. But why do spirits walk the earth, and why do they come to me?'

'It is required of every man,' the Ghost returned, 'that the spirit within him should walk abroad among his fellow-men, and travel far and wide; and, if that spirit goes not forth in life, it is condemned to do so after death. It is doomed to wander through the world—oh, woe is me—and witness what it cannot share, but might have shared on earth, and turned to happiness!'

Again the spectre raised a cry; and shook its chain and wrung its shadowy hands.

'You are fettered,' said Scrooge, trembling. 'Tell me why?'

'I wear the chain I forged in life,' replied the Ghost. 'I made it link by link, and yard by yard; I girded it on of my own free-will, and of my own free-will I wore it. Is its pattern strange to *you*?'. . .

'Oh! captive, bound, and double-ironed,' cried the phantom, 'not to know that ages of incessant labour, by immortal creatures, for this earth must pass into eternity before the good of which it is susceptible is all developed! Not to know that any Christian spirit working kindly in its little sphere, whatever it may be, will find its mortal life too short for its vast means of usefulness! Not to know that no space of regret can make amends for one life's opportunities misused! Yet such was I! Oh, such was I!'

'But you were always a good man of business, Jacob,' faltered Scrooge, who now began to apply this to himself.

'Business!' cried the Ghost, wringing its hands again. 'Mankind was my business. The common welfare was my business: charity, mercy, forbearance, and benevolence were, all, my business. The dealings of my trade were but a drop of water in the comprehensive ocean of my business!'

It held up its chain at arm's length, as if that were the cause of all its unavailing grief, and flung it heavily upon the ground again.

CHARLES DICKENS, *A Christmas Carol*, 1843

I did not believe in ghosts. Or rather, until this day, I had not done so, and whatever stories I had heard of them I had, like most rational, sensible young men, dismissed as nothing more than stories indeed. That certain people claimed to have a stronger than normal intuition of such things and that certain old places were said to be haunted, of course I was aware, but I would have been loath to admit that there could possibly be anything in it, even if presented with any evidence. And I had never had any evidence . . .

But out on the marshes just now, in the peculiar, fading light and desolation of that burial ground, I had seen a woman whose form was quite substantial and yet in some essential respect also, I had no doubt, ghostly. She had a ghostly pallor and a dreadful expression, she wore clothes that were out of keeping with the styles of the present-day; she had kept her distance from me and she had not spoken. Something emanating from her still, silent presence, in each case by a grave, had communicated itself to me so strongly that I had felt indescribable repulsion and fear. And she had appeared and then vanished in a way that surely no real, living, fleshly human being could possibly manage to do. And yet . . . she had not looked in any way—as I imagined the traditional 'ghost' was supposed to do—transparent or vaporous, she had been real, she had been there. I had seen her quite clearly, I was certain that I could have gone up to her, addressed her, touched her.

I did not believe in ghosts.

What other explanation was there?

'Jennet Humfrye gave up her child, the boy, to her sister, Alice Drablow, and Alice's husband, because she'd no choice. At first she stayed away— hundreds of miles away—and the boy was brought up a Drablow and was never intended to know his mother. But, in the end, the pain of being parted from him, instead of easing, grew worse and she returned to Crythin. She was not welcome at her parents' house and the man—the child's father—had gone abroad for good. She got rooms in the town. She'd no money. She took in sewing, she acted as a companion to a lady. At first, apparently, Alice Drablow would not let her see the boy at all. But Jennet was so distressed that she threatened violence and in the end the sister relented—just so far. Jennet could visit very occasionally, but never see the boy alone nor ever disclose who she was or that she had any relationship to him. No one ever foresaw that he'd turn out to look so like her, nor that the natural affinity between them would grow out. He became more and more attached to the woman who was, when all was said and done, his own mother, more and more fond, and as he did so, he began to be colder towards Alice Drablow. Jennet planned to take him away, that much I do know. Before she could do so, the accident happened, just as you heard. The boy . . . the nursemaid, the pony trap and its driver . . . And there was the boy's little dog too. That's a treacherous place, as you've found out to your own cost. The sea fret sweeps over the marshes suddenly, the quicksands are hidden.'

'So they all drowned.'

'And Jennet watched. She was at the house, watching from an upper window, waiting for them to return.'

I caught my breath, horrified.

'The bodies were recovered but they left the pony trap, it was held too fast by the mud. From that day Jennet Humfrye began to go mad.'

'Was there any wonder?'

'No. Mad with grief and mad with anger and a desire for revenge. She blamed her sister who had let them go out that day, though it was no one's fault, the mist comes without warning . . . Whether because of her loss and her madness or what, she also contracted a disease which caused her to begin to waste away. The flesh shrank from her bones, the colour was drained from her, she looked like a walking skeleton—a living spectre. When she went about the streets, people drew back. Children were terrified of her. She died eventually. She died in hatred and misery. And as soon as ever she died the hauntings began. And so they have gone on.'

'What, all the time? Ever since?'

'No. Now and again. Less, these past few years. But still she is seen and the sounds are heard by someone chancing to be out on the marsh.' . . .

'Well, Mrs Drablow is dead. There, surely, the whole matter will rest.'

But Mr Daily had not finished. He was just coming to the climax of his story.

'And whenever she has been seen,' he said in a low voice, 'in the graveyard, on the marsh, in the streets of the town, however briefly, and whoever by, there has been one sure and certain result.'

'Yes?' I whispered.

'In some violent or dreadful circumstance, a child has died.'

'What—you mean by accident?'

'Generally in an accident. But once or twice it has been after an illness, which has struck them down within a day or a night or less.'

'You mean any child? A child of the town?'

'Any child.'

SUSAN HILL, *The Woman in Black*, 1983

Presently . . . the tramp overtook a boy who was stooping to light a cigarette. He wore no overcoat, and looked unspeakably fragile against the snow. 'Are you on the road, guv'nor?' asked the boy huskily as he passed.

'I think I am,' the tramp said.

'Oh! then I'll come a bit of the way with you if you don't walk too fast. It's a bit lonesome walking this time of day . . . I'm eighteen,' he said casually. 'I bet you thought I was younger.'

'Fifteen, I'd have said.'

'You'd have backed a loser. Eighteen last August, and I've been on the road six years. I ran away from home five times when I was a little 'un, and the police took me back each time. Very good to me, the police was. Now I haven't got a home to run away from.'

'Nor have I,' the tramp said calmly.

'Oh, I can see what you are,' the boy panted; 'you're a gentleman come down. It's harder for you than for me.' The tramp glanced at the limping, feeble figure and lessened his pace.

'I haven't been at it as long as you have,' he admitted.

'No, I could tell that by the way you walk. You haven't got tired yet. Perhaps you expect something the other end?'

The tramp reflected for a moment. 'I don't know,' he said bitterly, 'I'm always expecting things.'

'You'll grow out of that,' the boy commented. 'It's warmer in London, but it's harder to come by grub. There isn't much in it really . . . Last night I took a lease of a barn for nothing and slept with the cows, and this morning the farmer routed me out and gave me tea and toke because I was little. Of course, I score there; but in London, soup on the Embankment at night, and all the rest of the time coppers moving you on.'

'I dropped by the roadside last night and slept where I fell. It's a wonder I didn't die,' the tramp said. The boy looked at him sharply.

'How do you know you didn't?' he said.

'I don't see it,' the tramp said, after a pause.

'I tell you,' the boy said hoarsely, 'people like us can't get away from this sort of thing if we want to. Always hungry and thirsty and dog-tired and walking all the time. And yet if anyone offers me a nice home and work my stomach feels sick. Do I look strong? I know I'm little for my age, but I've been knocking about like this for six years, and do you think I'm not dead? I was drowned bathing at Margate, and I was killed by a gipsy with a spike, he knocked my head right in, and twice I was froze like you last night, and a motor cut me down on this very road, and yet I'm walking along here now, walking to London to walk away from it again, because I can't help it. Dead! I tell you we can't get away if we want to.'

The boy broke off in a fit of coughing, and the tramp paused while he recovered.

'You'd better borrow my coat for a bit, Tommy,' he said, 'your cough's pretty bad.'

'You go to hell!' the boy said fiercely, puffing at his cigarette; 'I'm all right. I was telling you about the road. You haven't got down to it yet, but you'll find out presently. We're all dead, all of us who're on it, and we're all tired, yet somehow we can't leave it . . . I don't know, I don't know—' He lurched forward suddenly, and the tramp caught him in his arms.

'I'm sick,' the boy whispered—'sick.'

The tramp looked up and down the road, but he could see no houses or any sign of help. Yet even as he supported the boy doubtfully in the middle of the road a motor car suddenly flashed in the middle distance, and came smoothly through the snow.

'What's the matter?' said the driver quietly as he pulled up. 'I'm a doctor.' He looked at the boy keenly and listened to his strained breathing.

'Pneumonia,' he commented. 'I'll give him a lift to the infirmary, and you, too, if you like.'

The tramp thought of the workhouse and shook his head. 'I'd rather walk,' he said.

The boy winked faintly as they lifted him into the car.

'I'll meet you beyond Reigate,' he murmured to the tramp. 'You'll see.' And the car vanished along the white road.

All the morning the tramp splashed through the thawing snow, but at midday he begged some bread at a cottage door and crept into a lonely barn to eat it. It was warm in there, and after his meal he fell asleep among the hay. It was dark when he woke, and started trudging once more through the slushy roads.

Two miles beyond Reigate a figure, a fragile figure, slipped out of the darkness to meet him.

'On the road, guv'nor?' said a husky voice. 'Then I'll come a bit of the way with you if you don't walk too fast. It's a bit lonesome walking this time of day.'

'But the pneumonia?' cried the tramp aghast.

'I died at Crawley this morning,' said the boy.

RICHARD MIDDLETON, from 'On the Brighton Road', 1912

It is not often that one finds an empty cinema, but this one I used to frequent in the early 1930s because of its almost invariable, almost total emptiness. I speak only of the afternoons, the heavy grey afternoons of late winter; in the evenings, when the lights went up in the Edgware Road and the naphtha flares, and the peep-shows were crowded, this cinema may have known prosperity. But I doubt it . . .

I remember I went in one afternoon and found myself quite alone . . . I hoped the girl would soon leave her job and come in. I sat almost at the end of a row with one seat free as an indication that I felt like company, but she never came. An elderly man got entangled in the curtain and billowed his way through it and lost himself in the dark. He tried to get past me, though he had the whole cinema to choose from, and brushed my face with a damp beard. Then he sat down in the seat I had left, and there we were, close together in the wide dusty darkness.

The flat figures passed and repassed, their six-year-old gestures as antique as designs on a Greek coin. They were emotional in great white flickering letters, but their emotions were not comic nor to me moving. I was surprised when I heard the old man next to me crying to himself—so much to himself and not to me, not a trace of histrionics in those slow, carefully stifled sobs, that I felt sorry for him and did not grudge him the seat. I said:

'Can I do anything?'

He may not have heard me, but he spoke: 'I can't hear what they are saying.'

The loneliness of the old man was extreme; no one had warned him that he would find only silent pictures here. I tried to explain, but he did not listen, whispering gently, 'I can't see them.'

I thought that he was blind and asked him where he lived, and when he gave an address in Seymour Terrace, I felt such pity for him that I offered to show him the way to another cinema and then to take him home . . . But no! He wouldn't move. He said that he always came to this cinema of an evening, and when I said that it was only afternoon, he remarked that afternoon and evening were now to him 'much of a muchness'. I still didn't realize what he was enduring, what worse thing than blindness and age he might be keeping to himself.

Only a hint of it came to me a moment after, when he turned suddenly towards me, brushing my lips with his damp beard, and whispered.

'No one could expect me to see, not after I've seen what I've seen', and then in a lower voice, talking to himself, 'From ear to ear.'

That startled me because there were only two things he could mean, and I did not believe that he referred to a smile.

'Leave them to it,' he said, 'at the bottom of the stairs. The black-beetles always came out of that crack. Oh, the anger', and his voice had a long weary *frisson*.

It was extraordinary how he seemed to read my thoughts, because I had already begun to comfort myself with the fact of his age and that he must be recalling something very far away, when he spoke again: 'Not a minute later than this morning. The clock had just struck two, and I came down the stairs, and there he was. Oh, I was angry. He was smiling.'

'From ear to ear,' I said lightly, with relief.

'That was later,' he corrected me, and then he startled me by reading out suddenly from the screen the words, 'I love you. I will not let you go.' He laughed and said, 'I can see a little now. But it fades, it fades.'

I was quite sure then that the man was mad, but I did not go. For one thing, I thought that at any moment the girl might come and two people could deal with him more easily than one; for another, stillness seemed safest. So I sat very quietly, staring at the screen, and knew that he was weeping again beside me, shivering and weeping and shivering. Among all the obscurities one thing was certain, something had upset him early that morning.

After a while he spoke again . . . I caught the words 'serpent's tooth' and guessed that he must have been quoting scripture. He did not leave me much longer in doubt, however, of what had happened at the bottom of the stairs, for he said quite casually, his tears forgotten in curiosity:

'I never thought the knife was so sharp. I had forgotten I had had it reground.'

Then he went on speaking, his voice gaining strength and calmness: 'I had just put down the borax for the black-beetles that morning. How could I have guessed? I must have been very angry coming downstairs. The clock struck two, and there he was, smiling at me. I must have sent it to be reground when I had the joint of pork for Sunday dinner. Oh, I was angry when he laughed: the knife trembled. And there the poor body lay with the throat cut from ear to ear', and hunching up his shoulders and dropping his bearded chin towards his hands, the old man began again to cry.

Then I saw my duty quite plainly. He might be mad and to be pitied, but he was dangerous.

It needed courage to stand up and press by him into the gangway, and then turn the back and be lost in the blind velvet folds of the curtains which would not part, knowing that he might have the knife still with him. I got out into the grey afternoon light at last, and startled the girl in the box with my white face. I opened the door of the kiosk and shut it again behind me with immeasurable relief. He couldn't get at me now.

'The police station,' I called softly into the telephone, afraid that he might hear me where he sat alone in the cinema, and when a voice answered, I said hurriedly, 'That murder in Seymour Terrace this morning.'

The voice at the other end became brisk and interested, telling me to hold the line, and then the seconds drummed away.

All the while I held the receiver I watched the curtain, and presently it began to shake and billow, as if somebody was fumbling for the way out. 'Hurry, hurry,' I called down the telephone, and then as the voice spoke I saw the old man wavering in the gap of the curtain. 'Hurry. The murderer's here,' I called, stumbling over the name of the cinema and so intent on the message I had to convey that I could not take in for a moment the puzzled and puzzling reply: 'We've got the murderer. It's the body that's disappeared.'

GRAHAM GREENE, from 'All But Empty', 1947

∾

There is no end to the old houses, with resounding galleries, and dismal state-bedchambers, and haunted wings shut up for many years, through which we may ramble, with an agreeable creeping up our back, and encounter any number of ghosts, but (it is worthy of remark perhaps) reducible to a very few general types and classes; for, ghosts have little originality, and 'walk' in a beaten track. Thus, it comes to pass, that a certain room in a certain old hall, where a certain bad lord, baronet, knight, or gentleman, shot himself, has certain planks in the floor from which the blood *will not* be taken out. You may scrape and scrape, as the present owner has done, or plane and plane, as his father did, or scrub and scrub, as his grandfather did, or burn and burn with strong acids, as his great-grandfather did, but, there the blood will still be— no redder and no paler—no more and no less—always just the same. Thus, in such another house there is a haunted door, that never will keep open; or another door that never will keep shut; or a haunted sound of a spinning-wheel, or a hammer, or a footstep, or a cry, or a sigh, or a horse's tramp, or the rattling of a chain. Or else, there is a turret-clock, which, at the midnight hour, strikes thirteen when the head of the family is going to die; or a shadowy, immovable black carriage which at such a time is always seen by somebody, waiting near the great gates in the stable-yard. Or thus, it came to pass how Lady Mary went to pay a visit at a large wild house in the Scottish Highlands, and, being fatigued with her long journey, retired to bed early, and innocently said, next morning, at the breakfast-table, 'How odd, to have so late a party last night, in this remote place, and not to tell me of it, before I went to bed!' Then, every one asked Lady Mary what she meant? Then, Lady Mary replied, 'Why, all night long, the carriages were driving round and round the terrace, underneath my window!' Then, the owner of the house turned pale, and so did his Lady, and Charles Macdoodle of Macdoodle signed to Lady Mary to say no more, and every one was silent. After breakfast, Charles Macdoodle told Lady Mary that it was a tradition in the family that those rumbling carriages on the terrace betokened death. And so it proved, for, two months afterwards, the Lady of the mansion died. And Lady Mary, who was a Maid of Honour at Court, often told this story to the old Queen Charlotte; by this token that the old King always said, 'Eh, eh? What, what? Ghosts, ghosts? No such thing, no such thing!' And never left off saying so, until he went to bed.

DICKENS, from 'A Christmas Tree', 1850

Houses of any antiquity in New England are so invariably possessed with spirits that the matter seems hardly worth alluding to. Our ghost used to heave deep sighs in a particular corner of the parlour, and sometimes rustled paper, as if he were turning over a sermon in the long upper entry—where nevertheless he was invisible, in spite of the bright moonshine that fell through the eastern window. Not improbably he wished me to edit and publish a selection from a chest full of manuscript discourses that stood in the garret. Once, while Hillard and other friends sat talking with us in the twilight, there came a rustling noise as of a minister's silk gown, sweeping through the very midst of the company, so closely as almost to brush against the chairs. Still there was nothing visible. A yet stranger business was that of a ghostly servant-maid, who used to be heard in the kitchen at deepest midnight, grinding coffee, cooking, ironing—performing, in short, all kinds of domestic labour—although no traces of anything accomplished could be detected the next morning. Some neglected duty of her servitude, some ill-starched ministerial band, disturbed the poor damsel in her grave and kept her at work without any wages.

NATHANIEL HAWTHORNE, from 'The Old Manse', 1846

All houses wherein men have lived and died
    Are haunted houses. Through the open doors
The harmless phantoms on their errands glide,
    With feet that make no sound upon the floors.

We meet them at the doorway, on the stair,
    Along the passages they come and go,
Impalpable impressions on the air,
    A sense of something moving to and fro.

There are more guests at table, than the hosts
    Invited; the illuminated hall

Is thronged with quiet, inoffensive ghosts,
  As silent as the pictures on the wall.

The stranger at my fireside cannot see
  The forms I see, nor hear the sounds I hear:
He but perceives what is; while unto me
  All that has been is visible and clear.

We have no title-deeds to house or lands;
  Owners and occupants of earlier dates
From graves forgotten stretch their dusty hands,
  And hold in mortmain still their old estates.

The spirit world around this world of sense
  Floats like an atmosphere, and everywhere
Wafts through these earthly mists and vapours dense
  A vital breath of more ethereal air.

HENRY WADSWORTH LONGFELLOW, from 'Haunted Houses', 1858

The present recess from business affords you leisure to give, and me to receive, instruction. I am extremely desirous therefore to know your sentiments concerning spectres, whether you believe they actually exist and have their own proper shapes and a measure of divinity, or are only the false impressions of a terrified imagination? . . .

There was at Athens a large and spacious, but ill-reputed and pestilential house. In the dead of the night a noise, resembling the clashing of iron, was frequently heard, which, if you listened more attentively, sounded like the rattling of fetters; at first it seemed at a distance, but approached nearer by degrees; immediately afterward a phantom appeared in the form of an old man, extremely meagre and squalid, with a long beard and bristling hair, rattling the gyves on his feet and hands. The poor inhabitants consequently passed sleepless nights under the most dismal terrors imaginable. This, as it broke their rest, threw them into distempers, which, as their horrors of mind increased, proved in the end fatal to their lives. For even in the day time, though the spectre did not appear, yet the remembrance of it made such a strong impression upon their imaginations that it still seemed before their eyes, and their terror remained when the cause of it was gone. By this means the house was at last deserted, as being judged by everybody to be absolutely uninhabitable; so that it was now entirely abandoned to the ghost. However, in hopes that some tenant might be found who was ignorant of this great calamity which attended it, a bill was put up, giving notice that it was either to be let or sold.

It happened that Athenodorus the philosopher came to Athens at this time, and reading the bill ascertained the price. The extraordinary cheapness raised his suspicion; nevertheless, when he heard the whole story, he was so far from being discouraged, that he was more strongly inclined to hire it, and, in short, actually did so. When it grew towards evening, he ordered a couch to be prepared for him in the fore-part of the house, and after calling for a light, together with his pen and tablets, he directed all his people to retire within. But that his mind might not, for want of employment, be open to the vain terrors of imaginary noises and apparitions, he applied himself to writing with all his faculties. The first part of the night passed with usual silence, then began the clanking of iron fetters; however, he neither lifted up his eyes, nor laid down his pen, but closed his ears by concentrating his attention. The noise increased, and advanced nearer, till it seemed at the door, and at last in the chamber. He looked round and saw the apparition exactly as it had been described to him: it stood before him, beckoning with the finger. Athenodorus made a sign with his hand that it should wait a little, and bent again to his writing, but the ghost rattling its chains over his head as he wrote, he looked round and saw it beckoning as before. Upon this he immediately took up his lamp and followed it. The ghost slowly stalked along, as if encumbered with its chains; and having turned into the courtyard of the house, suddenly vanished. Athenodorus being thus deserted, marked the spot with a handful of grass and leaves. The next day he went to the magistrates, and advised them to order that spot to be dug up. There they found bones commingled and intertwined with chains; for the body had mouldered away by long lying in the ground, leaving them bare, and corroded by the fetters. The bones were collected, and buried at the public expense; and after the ghost was thus duly laid, the house was haunted no more.

PLINY THE YOUNGER (*c*.62–*c*.112), letter to Lucius Licinius Sura; tr. William Melmoth, rev. W. M. L. Hutchinson

Moreover it is well known to all men, that harlots, and whooremongers, have practised their wickednesse a long season under this cloake and pretence, persuading their family, that walking Spirites haunt the house, least they shoulde be taken with the deede dooing, and that they might enjoy their desired love. Many times such bugges have been caught by the magistrats, and put to open shame. Theves likewise under this colour have many times robbed their neighboures in the night time, who supposing they heard the noyse of walking Spirites, never went about to drive the theeves away.

> Louis Lavater, Swiss Protestant priest, *Of Ghostes and Spirites Walking by Night*, 1570; tr. R.H.

Towards the end of 1715 a maidservant, new to the household of the Reverend Samuel Wesley of Epworth, heard mysterious groans from the dining-room. The groans were followed by knockings and similar disturbances in other parts of the house. Sometimes the noises were like bottles being clashed together, or a man trampling up and down stairs, or the gobbling of a turkey cock, but usually they sounded like knockings, three or four blows at a time. Mrs Wesley thought they might be caused by rats and having heard of rats being driven out by the sounding of a horn, she had a horn blown loudly in each room in turn for half a day. The uproar so antagonized 'Old Jeffrey' [nickname given by Miss Emily Wesley] that he began to knock in the daytime too, sometimes with extreme violence. The goblin, or poltergeist, was easily angered: by the hunting-horn, of course, but also by Samuel Wesley rebuking him as 'a deaf and dumb devil' for troubling innocent children, and telling him to come to his study, if he had anything to say. 'Old Jeffrey' took him at his word, and Wesley was the only person actually pushed by him. He would sometimes answer knock for knock, but more than a simple pattern puzzled him. He was seen twice; once in shape like a badger and again like a white rabbit, with its ears back and its scut up straight. John Wesley was away at school when these happenings took place, but he was later to draw up and publish an account of them. He credited them, of course, implicitly, and would have echoed his father's comment at the time, that though Providence's design in permitting 'Old Jeffrey' might not be understood, 'secret things belong to God', and wisdom and duty were 'to prepare seriously for all events'.

> Douglas Grant, *The Cock Lane Ghost*. Emily Wesley explained the phenomena as revenge for her father's recent sermons 'against consulting those that are called cunning men', the local wizards. John Wesley later attributed them to his father's broken vow to desert his mother unless and until she (a Jacobite) recognized the Prince of Orange as king. He ended his account thus: 'Several gentlemen and clergymen now earnestly advised my father to quit the house. But he constantly answered: "No, let the devil flee from me; I will never flee from the devil." But he wrote to my eldest brother at London to come down. He was preparing to do so when another letter came, informing him that the disturbances were over, after they had continued from the 2nd of December to the end of January'

Of John Wesley, he said, 'He can talk well on any subject.' BOSWELL: 'Pray, Sir, what has he made of his story of a ghost?' JOHNSON: 'Why, Sir, he believes it; but not on sufficient authority. He did not take time enough to examine the girl. It was at Newcastle, where the ghost was said to have appeared to a young woman several times, mentioning something about the right to an old house, advising application to be made to an attorney, which was done; and, at the same time, saying the attorney would do nothing, which proved to be the fact. "This," says John, "is a proof that a ghost knows our thoughts." Now (laughing), it is not necessary to know our thoughts, to tell that an attorney will sometimes do nothing. Charles Wesley, who is a more stationary man, does not believe the story. I am sorry that John did not take more pains to inquire into the evidence for it.' MISS SEWARD (with an incredulous smile): 'What, Sir! about a ghost?' JOHNSON (with solemn vehemence): 'Yes, Madam: this is a question which, after five thousand years, is yet undecided; a question, whether in theology or philosophy, one of the most important that can come before the human understanding.'

JAMES BOSWELL, *The Life of Samuel Johnson*, 15 April 1778

In 1814 I was appointed keeper of the Crown Jewels in the Tower, where I resided with my family until my retirement in 1852. One Saturday night in October, 1817, about 'the witching hour', I was at supper with my then wife, our little boy, and her sister, in the sitting-room of the Jewel House, which—then comparatively modernized—is said to have been 'the doleful prison' of Anne Boleyn, and of the ten bishops whom Oliver Cromwell piously accommodated therein . . . The room was, as it still is, irregularly shaped, having three doors and two windows, which last are cut nearly nine feet deep into the outer wall; between these is a chimney-piece projecting far into the room, and (then) surmounted with a large oil picture. On the night in question the doors were all closed; heavy and dark cloth curtains were let down over the windows, and the only light in the room was that of two candles on the table . . . I sate at the foot of the table, my son on my right hand, his mother fronting the chimney-piece, and her sister on the opposite side. I had offered a glass of wine and water to my wife, when, on putting it to her lips, she paused and exclaimed, 'Good God, what is that?' I looked up, and saw a cylindrical figure like a glass tube, seemingly about the thickness of my arm, and hovering between the ceiling and the table. Its contents appeared to be a dense fluid, white and pale azure, like to the gathering of a summer cloud, and incessantly rolling and mingling within the cylinder. This lasted about two minutes, when it began slowly to move *before* my sister-in-law, then following the oblong shape of the table, before my son and myself; passing *behind* my wife it paused for a moment over her right shoulder (observe, there was no mirror opposite to her in which she could then behold it). Instantly she crouched down, and, with both hands, covering her shoulder, she shrieked out, 'Oh, Christ! it has seized me.' Even now, while writing, I feel the fresh horror of that moment. I caught up my chair, struck at the wainscot behind her, rushed upstairs to the other children's room . . . Neither my sister-in-law nor my son beheld this 'appearance' . . . I am bound to add that shortly before this strange event some young lady residents in the Tower had been, I know not wherefore, suspected of making phantasmagorical experiments at their windows, which, be it observed, had no command whatever on any windows in my dwelling. An additional sentry was accordingly posted so as to overlook any such attempt. Happening, however, as it might, following hard at heel the visitation of my household, one of the night sentries at the Jewel Office was, as he said, alarmed by a figure like a huge bear issuing from underneath the door. He thrust at it with his bayonet, which stuck in the door, even as my chair dinted the wainscot. He dropped in a fit, and was carried senseless to the guardroom. His fellow-sentry declared that the man was neither asleep nor drunk, he himself having seen him the moment before awake and sober. Of all this I avouch nothing more than that I saw the poor man in the guardhouse prostrated with terror, and that in two or three days the fatal result, be it of fact or fancy, was that he died. Let it be understood that to *all* which I have herein set forth *as seen by myself*, I absolutely pledge my faith and my honour.

EDMUND LENTHAL SWIFTE, *Notes and Queries*, September 1860

In March 1920 I was appointed Vicar here, my vicarage being a very old building from pre-Reformation times. One evening in June 1920 at 5.30 I was crossing the bridge opposite my dining-room window and happened to look over to this window and was surprised to see an old gentleman sitting at my table in the room as if writing. He looked up and, catching sight of me, seemed to glide away towards the door, and was seen no more. My housekeeper was out; I hurried to the front door and took out my key and as I was inserting it suddenly felt that my first impression of an intruder in the flesh was wrong and that what I had seen was supernatural. However, I searched the house but found no one. A fortnight or so after this I was making my first call as the new Vicar on a lady in the parish, and while waiting for her to appear in the drawing-room, saw a photo on her wall of my ghost, and, on inquiring whose photo it was, was informed that it was that of the old Vicar, who had been here forty-four years. He had at this time been dead for twenty-six years. I told her of my vision and I was not at all disturbed, though it was my first vision of anything of the kind. He has never been seen by me again.

> Statement sent to Sir Ernest Bennett by the vicar of a Cornwall parish, March 1934

'Are you ready?'

'I am ready, Mister Jarsper. Let the old 'uns come out if they dare, when we go among their tombs. My spirits is ready for 'em.'

'Do you mean animal spirits, or ardent?'

'The one's the t'other,' answers Durdles, 'and I mean 'em both.' . . .

They enter, locking themselves in, descend the rugged steps, and are down in the crypt. The lantern is not wanted, for the moonlight strikes in at the groined windows, bare of glass, the broken frames for which cast patterns on the ground. The heavy pillars which support the roof engender masses of black shade, but between them there are lanes of light. Up and down these lanes, they walk, Durdles discoursing of the 'old 'uns' he yet counts on disinterring, and slapping a wall, in which he considers 'a whole family on 'em' to be stoned and earthed up, just as if he were a familiar friend of the family. The taciturnity of Durdles is for the time overcome by Mr Jasper's wicker bottle, which circulates freely;—in the sense, that is to say, that its contents enter freely into Mr Durdles's circulation, while Mr Jasper only rinses his mouth once, and casts forth the rinsing.

They are to ascend the great Tower. On the steps by which they rise to the Cathedral, Durdles pauses for new store of breath. The steps are very dark, but out of the darkness they can see the lanes of light they have traversed. Durdles seats himself upon a step. Mr Jasper seats himself upon another. The odour from the wicker bottle (which has somehow passed into Durdles's keeping) soon intimates that the cork has been taken out; but this is not ascertainable through the sense of sight, since neither can descry the other. And yet, in talking, they turn to one another, as though their faces could commune together.

'This is good stuff, Mister Jarsper!'

'It is very good stuff, I hope. I bought it on purpose.'

'They don't show, you see, the old 'uns don't, Mister Jarsper!'

'It would be a more confused world than it is, if they could.'

'Well, it *would* lead towards a mixing of things,' Durdles acquiesces: pausing on the remark, as if the idea of ghosts had not previously presented itself to him in a merely inconvenient light, domestically, or chronologically. 'But do you think there may be ghosts of other things, though not of men and women?'

'What things? Flower-beds and watering-pots? Horses and harness?'

'No. Sounds.'

'What sounds?'

'Cries.'

'What cries do you mean? Chairs to mend?'

'No. I mean screeches. Now, I'll tell you, Mister Jarsper. Wait a bit till I put the bottle right.' Here the cork is evidently taken out again, and replaced again. 'There! *Now* it's right! This time last year, only a few days later, I happened to have been doing what was correct by the season, in the way of giving it the welcome it had a right to expect, when them town-boys set on me at their worst. At length I gave 'em the slip, and turned in here. And here I fell asleep. And what woke me? The ghost of a cry. The ghost of one terrific shriek, which shriek was followed by the ghost of the howl of a dog: a long dismal howl, such as a dog gives when a person's dead. That was *my* last Christmas Eve.'

'What do you mean?' is the very abrupt, and, one might say, fierce retort.

'I mean that I made inquiries everywheres about, and that no living ears but mine heard either that cry or that howl. So I say they was both ghosts; though why they came to me, I've never made out.'

'I thought you were another kind of man,' says Jasper, scornfully.

'So I thought, myself,' answers Durdles with his usual composure; 'and yet I was picked out for it.'

DICKENS, *The Mystery of Edwin Drood*, 1870, left unfinished

The Professor said: 'Very few people ever see ghosts, because they are local-ized. Now Passenham is a good locality for ghosts, near Stony Stratford. They have more ghosts there than rate-payers.'

'All these supernatural stories,' said the Countess coldly, 'boil down to hearsay in the end. Even the Holy Ghost has always struck me as being a great deal less definite than the other members of the Trinity. Have you ever seen one of the creatures yourself?'

'At Passenham I attended a sort of concert with several of them. Ghosts are fond of music, and will go anywhere to hear it.'

'Did you actually see one?'

'No,' replied the Professor with reluctance . . .

'I was trying to explain about Passenham,' explained the Professor. 'It lies low and flat, on the banks of the Ouse. The Ouse is a very haunted stream really, as you can imagine from its name . . . Music and mists. The village lies there by the riverside, flat and secluded. It has very few inhabitants now; live inhabitants, I mean, for the dead ones come and go in the mist. Mist into mist, they throng the bridle paths and saunter between the hedgerows. The man who drives the new maids out from Stony Stratford to the big house always says to them, as he drops them at the door, "I'll be back for you in a month, miss. They never stay longer than that." Indeed, the only man not frightened of ghosts is old Fowley the sexton. He, when the spirits are more than usually troublesome in November, has been known to walk down the village street brandishing a scythe and exclaiming to the white air: "I'll larn 'em to come a-plaguing decent people, what have been at the trouble of burying on 'em." . . .

But the ghosts are friendly, of course. Not so much friendly as sociable. They seem to have a liking for company, just as all people do in mists. The fog makes you feel lonely, cut off from your fellow beings, so that when you do see a figure looming up out of the silence it is natural to fall into step beside him. The old sexton would often find somebody walking at his shoulder, but he never paid much heed. He had a kind of acquaintance with them, I suppose, having rumbled the earth down on to most of their coffins. In fact, old Fowley treated them very much like rabbits: a nuisance if they got into the garden and nibbled the vegetables, but nothing more. On the whole the ghosts were respectful towards Fowley. He ignored them in rather a pointed way, and this made them feel inferior. It is galling to be cut by anybody, and to be positively sent to Coventry, as he had done with all the shire ghosts, must have made them feel very small beer. The only time Fowley was ever frightened himself—and then it was more a case of being startled—was on a Sunday night in December. He was verger and general factotum, and he was ringing the church bell for service. He had a lanthorn with him in the belfry, and it blew out, for it was a stormy night. He let go the bell rope to light the lanthorn, and the bell went on ringing. This surprised him, so he took hold of the rope again in the dark: but there was a hand under his own on the rope, a skeleton hand, rather frigid and slippery, and a faint musty smell in the belfry.'

T. H. WHITE, from 'Soft Voices at Passenham', written in the 1930s

. . . the following little story of what occurred here during the War, when our house was turned into a hospital for wounded men.

We had beds here for two hundred and fifty wounded. The Bishop of

Winchester, Dr Talbot, was our chaplain, a Father Robo looked after the Roman Catholics, and the Dissenting Minister from Farnham attended to the Nonconformists. I always made a point of sending the Roman Catholics in to the church at Farnham for Mass, but the little room that used to be my sitting-room was also turned into a chapel for the use of those who were unable to make the journey. Father Robo could come here as often as he liked. He always had lunch with us in the Staff Room and we became great friends.

One Easter he told me that he wanted to have High Mass in my little sitting-room. This had never previously been allowed in a house belonging to Church of England people, but he had obtained permission for the service from the Pope, in recognition of what we had done for the Roman Catholic wounded.

It had always been supposed that the Abbey was haunted by the ghost of a Cardinal, whom some declared they had seen walking about the place. He was one of those who had been buried in the old Cistercian building and should have been prayed for in perpetuity. He frequently appeared in the large draw-ing-room, where we had eighteen beds for the wounded. They and the nurses continually saw him; and this happened when they were all together, so that the apparition could not be explained away as proceeding from the imagination of a single person. The general belief was that the Abbey was under a curse, as having been the property of the Church and stolen from her.

The priest had invited me to be at Mass that Easter morning and conse-quently I heard the address which he gave to the men after it was over. He told them that he had had a message from the Pope through the Archbishop of Westminster (Cardinal Bourne). His Holiness had sent word that, in appreciation for what we had done for his flock, he had removed the curse from Waverley Abbey; that we were to pray for the Cardinal, which thereupon we did, after which his soul would rest in peace. This happened seven or eight years ago, and since that day the Cardinal has not been seen again.

I was in Rome last April. The present Pope knows all about the story and graciously sent for me to have an audience with him, which I much appreciated.

> 'The Cardinal at Waverley Abbey': a story sent to Lord Halifax in 1925 by Mrs Anderson, the then owner of Waverley Abbey, which was founded in 1128, as the first Cistercian establishment in England

It is certain that evil may attach itself to possessions, to jewellery and gems, to objects of value and objects of comparatively no worth, to pictures, to mini-atures and photographs, and, almost especially perhaps, to articles of furniture.

It may not be unfitting to give a striking example of this, as I have read and am very well assured is both recent and true. A young couple, who live in a small but ancient coast town in Devonshire, after a courtship unmarred by any cloud, were married. The husband, who was about twenty-five years old, had worked with one firm for seven years, bearing a remarkably steady reputation. They spent a brief honeymoon in London, and then returned to their new home. One night, about a fortnight later, the young fellow came home completely intoxicated. His bride was aghast. The next day he was truly penitent, reproaching himself most bitterly. It was the first time that he had ever drunk to excess and he was usually content with just one glass of beer. About a month later they brought him home dead drunk. After this he was miserable and full of remorse. A few weeks later the same thing happened, he again got hopelessly drunk. His wife privately had recourse to a 'wise woman' whom she consulted on the case. This sibyl came to the house and at once pointed to a certain piece of furniture, a large old-fashioned armchair, which had been given to the young couple as a wedding present, and in which the husband usually sat of an evening. 'This is the trouble,' said the wise woman. 'It is all wrong. If you take my advice you will break it up and burn it.' The wife forthwith burned the chair, and after that all went well. The husband never showed the slightest inclination to drink. The history of the chair was traced. It had once belonged to a butcher who was a hardened drunkard, and who in a delirious fit had killed himself whilst sitting in it.

> MONTAGUE SUMMERS, *The Werewolf*, 1933; the 'striking example' was drawn from an article by T. C. Bridges, 'Unlucky Possessions', in *Occult Review*, March 1927

Before I retired, my mother and my sister would ask me to look under the beds, in the fireplaces, behind the doors, to visit the staircases, the passages and adjoining corridors. All the castle legends, of thieves and ghosts, were returning to their minds. People were convinced that a certain Comte de Combourg, with a wooden leg, dead for three centuries, appeared at certain times, and that he had been encountered on the big staircase of the turret; on occasion his wooden leg would walk around on its own, accompanied by a black cat.

A few years earlier, my sisters, very young then, had found themselves alone at Combourg with my father. One night they were reading together about the death of Clarissa [in Samuel Richardson's novel]. Already very upset by the details of this death, they hear clearly footsteps on the stairs leading to their apartment. Terrified, they blow out their light and fling themselves into their beds. Someone is approaching; someone reaches the door of their bedroom; someone stops, as if to listen; then someone turns into a secret staircase communicating with my father's room. After a little time, someone comes back; someone crosses the antechamber again, and the sound of the retreating steps is lost in the depths of the castle.

On the following day, my sisters did not dare to speak; they were afraid that the ghost, or the thief, might have been my father, wanting to surprise them. He put them at ease by asking whether they had heard anything. He told them that someone had knocked at the wicket of the secret staircase leading to his room, and would have broken in but for a chest that happened to be standing against the door. Awaking with a start, he had seized his pistols, for he was armed at all times. The noise having ceased, he supposed he had been mistaken, and he went back to sleep.

Another time, during a December evening, my father was writing, alone, by the fireplace at the end of the great hall. A door opens behind him; he turns his head and catches sight of a sort of tall goblin, with a face black as ebony, rolling its haggard eyes. M. de Chateaubriand seizes from the fire the tongs used to shift the elm logs. Armed with the red-hot tongs, he rises and walks towards the black apparition, which goes out, slips through the shadows, and fades into the night.

> FRANÇOIS RENÉ DE CHATEAUBRIAND, *Mémoires d'outre-tombe*, written between 1809 and 1848

The Blake family who held Renvyle House before me, having taken it over from a member of the Clan O'Flaherty, Princes of Iar Connaught, left a ghost behind them to resent newcomers. It resented Yeats of the second sight even more. At least it could make its displeasure manifest to him by more than the sounds and strange happenings, which by me might have been attributed to the noise and movements of Atlantic gales . . .

'Willie,' said his wife one evening, 'do not leave me to dress alone. I do not want to see that face again looking out from the glass.' . . .

'What face?' I asked.

But I was not answered. Yeats and his wife left the room. I was resigned to being treated as uninitiated, but my friends looked at one another. Evan Morgan, a Cymric Celt, from immemorial Wales, felt the supernatural at once.

'You never told me about this,' he complained, all alert.

Now, you cannot ask a man to meet a ghost, because ghosts are not to be counted on.

'I did not care to talk about it,' I said. 'I thought that Yeats . . .'

I could not say—'If you met Yeats you met enough of faery, as much as I am ever likely to meet.' I implied that it was far more in Yeats's province than mine, and, that being so, the omission was not mine wholly. But he was not quite satisfied. My hospitality fell short of the necromantic.

After dinner there were very few in the library—in fact only Seymour Leslie and one or two. Evidently something was going on. Seymour could not be left out when anything exciting was taking place. He left the room to investigate. I lolled in front of the fire, hoping that something, no matter what provided it was exciting, might occur. A maid brought me a note.

'Take your friend Leslie away from us. He is a regular vortex of evil spirits.' It was in unmistakable and distinguished calligraphy. Good Lord! What is this? There must be a seance in full blast going on somewhere and Seymour has butted in . . . crestfallen, Leslie returned.

'What's up?'

'They are all at it. Lord Conyngham, Yeats, Mrs Yeats and a fourth. They are getting after the ghost.'

'But how?'

'I just looked in to one of the rooms. Lord Conyngham was at the Ouija board. When I appeared, everyone stopped. Yeats said significantly, "We cannot go on until we hear what Mr Leslie wants." That meant that I was politely asked to go.' . . .

'I for one shall not butt in,' I said. 'I don't hold with seances. I am not sensitive enough.' Winds moaned reprovingly in the chimney. 'I was kicked out of the Hermetic Society on the only evening I went with George Moore to see what it was all about. Let us have a smoke.' . . .

'Seances,' I said, with the authority of one who makes a premise suit his needs, 'usually last many hours. There are people in the next room. Would you care to make a fourth at bridge?'

I knew that Evan Morgan was in the drawing-room with half-a-dozen friends, who saw Shelley plain in him with his long, white open neck, high forehead, chestnut hair, and aquamarine eyes. I hoped that their company would prevent Seymour from spoiling what, if left to itself, would prove to be one of the most interesting psychological experiments in our country. A ghost which had been felt first hand by me and many others. None of your 'I-heard-for-a-fact-from-a-friend' ghosts, but one I had heard myself, and two of us had *seen*.

As the folding doors closed behind the reluctant Seymour, 'Evan is psychic,' I called after him. A moment later, I was left alone . . .

I believe in ghosts: that is, I know that there are times, given the place which is capable of suggesting a phantasy, when those who are sufficiently impressionable may perceive a dream projected as if external to the dreamy mind: a waking dream due both to the dreamer and the spot . . .

Suddenly! Was that a scream! There, it shrieks out again! Now what the devil? . . . Lights are moving on the stairs of the west wing. Frightened friends in their nighties peer out, but someone is running towards me.

'Quick! Evan is dying!'

'Where is he?'

'In that room there!'

Evan was being supported on a chair by two ladies. His face was deathly pale and his head had fallen forwards. Seymour was hopping in front of him saying, 'Don't take it so seriously, old man!' A table had fallen on its side, presenting a cool shield of green baize.

'What's all this about?' I demanded.

'Evan suddenly became hysterical.'

His pulse was racing. He was but semi-conscious.

'What on earth were you doing?'

'We were holding our own little seance, and just as we were getting results Evan got the jigs or something rather like them.' . . .

'Leave him to me and run to get some brandy.' . . .

His body was smooth as marble: heart firm: no aspirin about. I could not understand the collapse. Presently he broke out in a cold perspiration. Slower pulse, breathing audible.

'What did they do to you, Evan?'

'The ghost!' he gasped, and tore at his open collar.

'The ghost? What ghost?'

'Seymour sent me into the haunted room to raise the ghost, but when it came it transferred into me all the thoughts by which he was obsessed before he went mad.'

'Now really, Morgan, you know very well that there is no ghost; no ghost anyway here who is insane.'

'It was Seymour's seance. Yeats was having one . . .'

'I know. Quite.' A rival seance! . . .

'Seymour heard that Yeats spent hours in the haunted room. "Now it's up to you," he said. I went in about 12.30, and after they had locked the door . . .'

'Locked the door?'

'Yes. Locked me in . . . I felt a strange sensation. A sensation that I was all keyed up just like the tension in a nightmare, with the terror added that nightmares have. Presently I saw a boy, stiffly upright, in brown velvet with some sort of shirt showing at his waist. He was about twelve. Behind the chair he stood, all white-faced, hardly touching the floor. It seemed that if he came nearer some awful calamity would happen to me. I was just as tensed up as he was: nightmare terrors; twingling air; but what made it awful was my being awake. The figure in brown velvet only looked at me, but the atmosphere in the room vibrated. I don't know what else happened. I saw his large eyes. I saw the ruffles on his wrists. He stood vibrating just as I was vibrating. His luminous brown eyes reproved me. He looked deeply into my eyes. Then, oh then! . . . Oh, God! . . .'

'Old fellow, you know I am solid enough and all damned spirits steer clear of me. Don't talk about it any more. What about a large one and a spot of soda?'

'I must, I simply can't go on until I tell you.'

'Yes, but don't weep because Seymour sent you into the worst-furnished room in the house.'

'Yes, but let me tell you. The apparition lifted his hands to his neck, and then, all of a sudden, his body was violently seized as if by invisible fiends and twisted into horrible contortions in mid air. He was mad! I sympathized for a moment with his madness and I felt myself at once in the electric tension of Hell. Suicide! Suicide! Oh, my God! He committed suicide in this very house.'

I'll 'commit' Seymour when I go downstairs, I determined.

At 2 a.m. Yeats appeared.

'She should be down any moment now,' he said casually. 'Yes, she should be here presently if all goes well.'

But where was she, Mrs Yeats?

It transpired that the ghost had communicated with Yeats through automatic writing. He objected to the presence of strangers in the house. But he was in for a course of adjuration he little expected from the Archimandrite Yeats.

1. You must desist from frightening the children in their early sleep.
2. You must cease to moan about the chimneys.
3. You must walk the house no more.
4. You must not move furniture or horrify those who sleep near by.
5. You must name yourself to me.

Now, Yeats could never have guessed that it was the custom of the Blake family to call their sons after the Heptarchy. And yet he found it out and the ghost's particular name. I had never gleaned it from the local people, though I lived for years among them.

The troubled spirit promised to appear in the ghost room to Mrs Yeats, as he was before he went mad sixty years ago . . .

Presently Mrs Yeats appeared, carrying a lighted candle. She extinguished it, and nodded curtly to her husband. 'Yes. It is just as you said.'

What was? we all wondered.

After a whispered consultation Yeats announced:

'My wife saw a pale-faced, red-haired boy of about fourteen years of age standing in the middle of the north room. She was by the fireside when he first took shape. He had the solemn pallor of a tragedy beyond the endurance of a child. He resents the presence of strangers in the home of his ancestors. He is Athelstone Blake. He is to be placated with incense and flowers. Lord Conyngham!'

With grace, and saving presence of mind, Lord Conyngham presented flowers and his collection of scent bottles to Mrs Yeats.

OLIVER ST JOHN GOGARTY, *As I Was Going Down Sackville Street*, 1936

Because there is safety in derision
I talked about an apparition,
I took no trouble to convince,
Or seem plausible to a man of sense,
Distrustful of that popular eye
Whether it be bold or sly.
Fifteen apparitions have I seen;
The worst a coat upon a coat-hanger.

 I have found nothing half so good
As my long-planned half solitude,
Where I can sit up half the night
With some friend that has the wit
Not to allow his looks to tell
When I am unintelligible.
Fifteen apparitions have I seen;
The worst a coat upon a coat-hanger.

When a man grows old his joy
Grows more deep day after day,
His empty heart is full at length
But he has need of all that strength
Because of the increasing Night
That opens her mystery and fright.
Fifteen apparitions have I seen;
The worst a coat upon a coat-hanger.

W. B. YEATS, 'Apparitions', 1938

9 November 1934

Then I went to luncheon with Virginia [Woolf], who gave me an imitation of Yeats telling her why he was occult. He has been confirmed in this theory because he saw a coat-hanger emerge from his cupboard and travel across the foot of his bed; next night, it emerged again, clothed in one of his jackets; the third night, a hand emerged from one of the cuffs; the fourth night—'Ah, Mrs Woolf, that would be a long story; enough to say, I finally recovered my potency.'

HAROLD NICOLSON, *Diaries and Letters 1930–1939*, ed. Nigel Nicolson, 1966

Even though they had to crowd the other rooms, none of the young women would sleep in it. Accustomed to nestling with a bedful of siblings and grannies, they fitted their privacy tighter rather than claim the haunted room as human territory. No one had lived in it for at least five years, not since a series of hauntings had made its inhabitants come down with ghost fear that shattered their brains for studying. The haunted ones would give high, startled cries, pointing at the air, which sure enough was becoming hazy. They would suddenly turn and go back the way they had come. When they rounded a corner, they flattened themselves fast against the building to catch what followed unawares moving steadily forward. One girl tore up the photographs she had taken of friends in that room. The stranger with arms hanging at its sides who stood beside the wall in the background of the photograph was a ghost. The girl would insist there had been nobody there when she took the picture. 'That was a Photo Ghost,' said my mother when the students talked-story. 'She needn't have been afraid. Most ghosts are only nightmares. Somebody should have held her and wiggled her ears to wake her up.'

My mother relished these scare orgies. She was good at naming—Wall Ghost, Frog Spirit (frogs are 'heavenly chickens'), Eating Partner. She could find descriptions of phenomena in ancient writings—the Green Phoenix stories, 'The Seven Strange Tales of the Golden Bottle', 'What Confucius Did Not Talk About'. She could validate ghost sightings.

'But ghosts can't be just nightmares,' a storyteller protested. 'They come right out into the room. Once our whole family saw wine cups spinning and incense sticks waving through the air. We got the magic monk to watch all night. He also saw the incense tips tracing orange figures in the dark— ideographs, he said. He followed the glow patterns with his inkbrush on red paper. And there it was, a message from our great-grandfather. We needed to

put bigger helpings and a Ford in front of his plaque. And when we did, the
haunting stopped immediately.'

'I like to think the ancestors are busier than that,' my mother said, 'or more
at rest. Yes, they're probably more at rest. Perhaps it was an animal spirit that
was bothering your house, and your grandfather had something to do with
chasing it off.' After what she thought was a suitably tactful pause, she said,
'How do we know that ghosts are the continuance of dead people? Couldn't
ghosts be an entirely different species of creature? Perhaps human beings just
die, and that's the end. I don't think I'd mind that too much. Which would
you rather be? A ghost who is constantly wanting to be fed? Or nothing?'

> MAXINE HONG KINGSTON, *The Woman Warrior*, 1976; concerning a haunted
> room in the women's dormitory at the To Keung School of Midwifery,
> Canton, *c*.1933

On the stairs I met a tenant from the same floor.

'Going out again, you bounder?' he asked, pausing with his legs astride two
steps.

'What can I do?' I said, 'I've just had a ghost in my room.'

'You say that with the same sort of distaste as if you'd found a hair in your
soup.'

'You jest. Mark my words, though: a ghost is a ghost.'

'Very true. But what if one doesn't believe in ghosts in the first place?'

'You don't think I believe in ghosts, do you? But how does not believing in
them help me?'

'Very simple. You no longer need be frightened when a ghost actually
appears.'

'Yes, but that's only the incidental fear. The actual fear is fear of what
causes the phenomenon. And that fear there's no getting rid of. I possess a
really splendid example of the genre.' In sheer nervousness I started searching
through all my pockets.

'But having no fear of the phenomenon itself you could safely have interrogated it as to its cause!'

'You've obviously never spoken to a ghost. You'll never get a straight
answer out of one of them. Talk about vacillation! These ghosts seem to doubt
their own existence even more than we do, which given their fragility is hardly
surprising.'

'I've heard one can feed them up, though.'

'You heard correctly. One can. But who's going to?'

'Why not? If it's a female ghost, for example,' he said as he swung himself up to the top step.

'Aha,' I said. 'But even then there's no future in it.'

FRANZ KAFKA, from 'Unhappiness', 1913; tr. J. A. Underwood

I have recently finished a novel about a haunted house . . . The first thing that happened was in New York City; we—my husband and I—were on the train which stops briefly at the 125th Street station, and just outside the station, dim and horrible in the dusk, I saw a building so disagreeable that I could not stop looking at it; it was tall and black and as I looked at it when the train began to move again it faded away and disappeared. That night in our hotel room I woke up with nightmares, the kind where you have to get up and turn on the light and walk around for a few minutes just to make sure that there is a real world and this one is it, not the one you have been dreaming about; my nightmares had somehow settled around the building I had seen from the train. From that time on I completely ruined my whole vacation in New York City by dreading the moment when we would have to take the train back and pass that building again. Let me just point out right here and now that my unconscious mind has *been* unconscious for a number of years now and it is my firm intention to keep it that way. When I have nightmares about a horrid building it is the horrid building I am having nightmares about, and no one is going to talk me out of it; that is final. Anyway, my nervousness was so extreme, finally, that we changed our plans and took a night train home, so that I would not be able to see the building when we went past, but even after we were home it bothered me still, colouring all my recollections of a pleasant visit to the city, and at last I wrote to a friend at Columbia University and asked him to locate the building and find out, if he could, why it looked so terrifying. When we got his answer I had one important item for my book. He wrote that he had had trouble finding the building, since it only existed from that one particular point of the 125th Street station; from any other angle it was not recognizable as a building at all. Some seven months before it had been almost entirely burned in a disastrous fire which killed nine people. What was left of the building, from the other three sides, was a shell. The children in the neighbourhood knew that it was haunted.

I do not think that the Society for Psychical Research would accept me as a qualified observer; I think, in fact, that they would bounce me right out the door, but it seemed clear to me that what I had felt about that horrid building was an excellent beginning for learning how people feel when they encounter the supernatural. I have always been interested in witchcraft and superstition,

but have never had much traffic with ghosts, so I began asking people everywhere what they thought about such things, and I began to find out that there
was one common factor—most people have never seen a ghost, and never want
or expect to, but almost everyone will admit that sometimes they have a
sneaking feeling that they just possibly *could* meet a ghost if they weren't
careful—if they were to turn a corner too suddenly, perhaps, or open their
eyes too soon when they wake up at night, or go into a dark room without
hesitating first.

Well, as I say, fiction comes from experience. I had not the remotest desire
to see a ghost. I was absolutely willing to go on the rest of my life without ever
seeing even the slightest supernatural manifestation. I wanted to write a book
about ghosts, but I was perfectly prepared—I cannot emphasize this too
strongly—I was perfectly prepared to keep these ghosts wholly imaginary . . .

By then it was abundantly clear to me that I had no choice; the ghosts were
after me. In case I *had* any doubts, however, I came downstairs a few mornings
later and found a sheet of copy paper moved to the centre of my desk, set
neatly away from the general clutter. On the sheet of paper was written DEAD
DEAD in my own handwriting. I am accustomed to making notes for books, but
not in my sleep; I decided that I had better write the book awake, which I got
to work and did.

SHIRLEY JACKSON, from 'Experience and Fiction', a lecture, 1958

[In 1920] Jung met a real ghost—in England, of course . . . He spent several
weekends in a country house in Buckinghamshire which a friend had recently
rented. During several nights he heard all sorts of noises—the dripping of
water, rustlings, knockings, which increased in intensity until, during the fifth
weekend, he thought somebody was knocking at the wall with a sledge-hammer.
'I had the feeling of a close presence. I opened my eyes with an effort. Then
I saw lying next to my head on the pillow, the head of an old woman whose
right eye, wide open, was staring at me. The left half of her face, including the
eye, was missing. I leapt out of bed and lit a candle.' Thereupon the head
vanished. Later on, Jung and his host discovered that the whole village knew
the house was haunted. It was torn down soon after.

ARTHUR KOESTLER, *The Roots of Coincidence*, 1972

Somewhere in England where there are books and pictures and plays and shop
windows to look at, and thousands of men who spend their lives in building up

all four, lives a gentleman who writes real stories about the real insides of people; and his name is Mr Walter Besant. But he will insist upon treating his ghosts—he has published half a workshopful of them—with levity. He makes his ghostseers talk familiarly, and, in some cases, flirt outrageously with the phantoms. You may treat anything, from a Viceroy to a Vernacular Paper, with levity; but you must behave reverently towards a ghost, and particularly an Indian one.

There are, in this land, ghosts who take the form of fat, cold, pobby corpses, and hide in trees near the roadside till a traveller passes. Then they drop upon his neck and remain. There are also terrible ghosts of women who have died in childbed. These wander along the pathways at dusk, or hide in the crops near a village, and call seductively. But to answer their call is death in this world and the next. Their feet are turned backwards that all sober men may recognize them. There are ghosts of little children who have been thrown into wells. These haunt well-kerbs and the fringes of jungles, and wail under the stars, or catch women by the wrist and beg to be taken up and carried. These and the corpse-ghosts, however, are only vernacular articles and do not attack Sahibs. No native ghost has yet been authentically reported to have frightened an Englishman; but many English ghosts have scared the life out of both white and black.

Nearly every other station in India owns a ghost. There are said to be two at Simla, not counting the woman who blows the bellows at Syree dak-bungalow on the Old Road; Mussoorie has a house haunted of a very lively Thing; a White Lady is supposed to do night-watchman round a house in Lahore; Dalhousie says that one of her houses 'repeats' on autumn evenings all the incidents of a horrible horse-and-precipice accident; Murree has a merry ghost, and now that she has been swept by cholera, will have room for some sorrowful ones; there are Officers' Quarters in Mian Mir whose doors open without reason, and whose furniture is guaranteed to creak, not with the heat of June but with the weight of Invisibles who come to lounge in the chairs; Peshawar possesses houses that none will willingly rent; and there is something—not fever—wrong with a big bungalow in Allahabad. The older Provinces simply bristle with haunted houses, and march phantom armies along their main thoroughfares.

RUDYARD KIPLING, from 'My Own True Ghost Story', 1888

Visiting Versailles in 1901, Miss Moberly, Principal of St Hugh's, Oxford, and Miss Jourdain, later Vice-Principal, found themselves in the Petit Trianon gardens apparently during the presence there of Marie Antoinette, possibly on 5 October 1789.

Both of us have inherited a horror of all forms of occultism. We lose no opportunity of preaching against them as unwholesome and misleading; because they mostly deal with conditions of physical excitement, and study of the abnormal and diseased, including problems of disintegrated personality which present such close analogy to those of insanity. We have the deepest distrust in, and distaste for, stories of abnormal appearances and conditions. We find narratives of *revenants* unconvincing, and studiously avoid (as utterly lowering) all spiritualistic methods of communication with the dead. We have never had the curiosity, or the desire, to help in the investigations of psychical phenomena.

At the time Miss Jourdain thought that there was something unusual about the place and was puzzled . . . Miss Moberly put her feeling of oppression down to some physical fatigue in herself . . . After some days, when Miss Moberly was writing an account of the expedition, she thought it over with care, and realized that her sensations had not been caused by fatigue, but had produced fatigue. She became convinced that the oppression had been due to some unusual cause in the place itself, and instantly turned to Miss Jourdain and said so. Miss Jourdain agreed. We then discussed the man by the kiosk and the running man, but said that there was much besides which had caused dreamy depression. Miss Moberly returned to her letter and wrote down: 'We both think that the Petit Trianon is haunted.' . . .

Miss Jourdain, in her story, used the words 'uncanny' and 'eerie' to describe her feelings, but they did not mean that she had the least idea at the time that any of the people encountered were unreal or ghostly; this was still more true of the scenery.

Nothing unusual marked the lady sitting on a low seat on the grass immediately under the north terrace. I remember recognizing that her light-coloured skirt, white fichu, and straw hat were in the present fashion, but they struck me as rather dowdy in the general effect. She was so near us that I looked full at her, and she bent slightly forward to do the same.

I never doubted that we had both seen her, and three months after was astonished to hear that Miss Jourdain had not done so. That sounds simple to others, to ourselves it is inexplicable. Miss Jourdain had seen the plough, the cottage, the woman, and the girl, which I had not; but she is generally more observant than I, and there were other things to look at. At this moment there was nothing to see on the right, and merely a shady, damp-looking meadow on the left, and the lady was sitting in front of the house we had come to see, and were both eagerly studying. The lady was visible some way off. We walked side by side straight up to her, leaving her slightly on the left hand as we passed up the steps to the terrace, from whence I saw her again from behind, and noticed that her fichu had become a pale green.

The fact that she had not been seen at a moment when we were both a little exercised by our meeting with the men—one looking so unpleasant, and the other so unaccountably and infectiously excited—made a deep impression.

In the following winter we heard the legend of the Queen having been occasionally seen sitting in front of the house in the English garden, but of this we have no further proof . . .

In the summer of 1908 we read the *Journal* of Madame Éloffe (the Queen's modiste). She says that during the year 1789 the Queen was extremely economical, and had very few dresses made. Madame Éloffe repaired several light, washing, short skirts, and made, in July and September, two green silk bodices, besides many large white fichus. This agrees exactly with the dress seen in 1901. The skirt was not of a fresh white, but was light coloured—slightly yellowish. The white fichu in front seemed to have an edge of green or gold, just as it would have appeared if the white muslin, or gauze, was over green . . . The straight edge in front and the frill behind had often puzzled me, but in Madame Éloffe's illustrations of the fashions at that time there are instances of the same thing. There is in the book a coloured picture of the green silk bodice.

CHARLOTTE ANNE ELIZABETH MOBERLY and ELEANOR FRANCES JOURDAIN, *An Adventure*, 1911

'I hear the piano playing—
   Just as a ghost might play.'
'—O, but what are you saying?
   There's no piano today;
Their old one was sold and broken;
   Years past it went amiss.'
'—I heard it, or shouldn't have spoken:
   A strange house, this!

I catch some undertone here,
   From some one out of sight.'
'Impossible; we are alone here,
   And shall be through the night.'

'—The parlour-door—what stirred it?'
     '—No one: no soul's in range.'
'—But, anyhow, I heard it,
          And it seems strange!

Seek my own room I cannot—
     A figure is on the stair!'
'—What figure? Nay, I scan not
     Any one lingering there.
A bough outside is waving,
     And that's its shade by the moon.'
'—Well, all is strange! I am craving
          Strength to leave soon.'

'—Ah, maybe you've some vision
     Of showings beyond our sphere;
Some sight, sense intuition
     Of what once happened here?
The house is old; they've hinted
     It once held two love-thralls,
And they may have imprinted
          Their dreams on its walls?

They were—I think 'twas told me—
     Queer in their works and ways;
The teller would often hold me
     With weird tales of those days.
Some folk can not abide here,
     But we—we do not care
Who loved, laughed, wept, or died here,
          Knew joy, or despair.'

THOMAS HARDY, 'The Strange House (Max Gate, AD 2000)', 1914

A Miss Broke, a niece of our host, told me a curious story. A few years ago there was a lady living in Ireland—a Mrs Butler—clever, handsome, popular, prosperous, and perfectly happy. One morning she said to her husband, and to any one who was staying there, 'Last night I had the most wonderful night. I seemed to be spending hours in the most delightful place, in the most enchanting house I ever saw—not large, you know, but just the sort of house one might live in one's-self, and oh! so perfectly, so deliciously comfortable. Then there was the loveliest conservatory, and the garden was so enchanting! I wonder if anything half so perfect can really exist.'

And the next morning she said, 'Well, I have been to my house again. I must have been there for hours. I sat in the library: I walked on the terrace; I examined all the bedrooms: and it is simply the most perfect house in the world.' So it grew to be quite a joke in the family. People would ask Mrs Butler in the morning if she had been to her house in the night, and often she had, and always with more intense enjoyment. She would say, 'I count the hours till bedtime, that I may get back to my house!' Then gradually the current of outside life flowed in, and gave a turn to their thoughts: the house ceased to be talked about.

Two years ago the Butlers grew very weary of their life in Ireland. The district was wild and disturbed. The people were insolent and ungrateful. At last they said, 'We are well off, we have no children, there's no reason why we should put up with this, and we'll go and live altogether in England.' So they came to London, and sent for all the house-agents' lists of places within forty miles of London, and many were the places they went to see. At last they heard of a house in Hampshire. They went to it by rail, and drove from the station. As they came to the lodge, Mrs Butler said, 'Do you know, this is the lodge of my house.' They drove down an avenue—'But this *is* my house!' she said.

When the housekeeper came, she said, 'You will think it very odd, but do you mind my showing *you* the house: that passage leads to the library, and through that there is a conservatory, and then through a window you enter the drawing-room,' &c., and it was all so. At last, in an upstairs passage, they came upon a baize door. Mrs Butler, for the first time, looked puzzled. 'But that door is not in my house,' she said. 'I don't understand about your house, ma'am,' said the housekeeper, 'but that door has only been there six weeks.'

Well, the house was for sale, and the price asked was very small, and they decided at once to buy it. But when it was bought and paid for, the price had been so extraordinarily small, that they could not help a misgiving that there must be something wrong with the place. So they went to the agent of the people who had sold it and said, 'Well, now the purchase is made and the deeds are signed, *will* you mind telling us why the price asked was so small?'

The agent had started violently when they came in, but recovered himself. Then he said to Mrs Butler, 'Yes, it is quite true the matter is quite settled, so there can be no harm in telling now. The fact is that the house has had a great reputation for being haunted; but you, madam, need be under no apprehensions, for you are yourself the ghost!' On the nights when Mrs Butler had dreamt she was at her house, she—her 'astral body'—had been seen there.

AUGUSTUS J. C. HARE, *The Story of My Life, Second Part*, 1900

My father told me that within a week after his father's death he slept in the dead man's bed, earnestly desiring to see his ghost, but no ghost came. 'You see,' he said, 'ghosts do not generally come to imaginative people.'

HALLAM TENNYSON, *Alfred Lord Tennyson: A Memoir, by His Son*, 1897

One need not be a Chamber—to be Haunted—
One need not be a House—
The Brain has Corridors—surpassing
Material Place—

Far safer, of a Midnight Meeting
External Ghost
Than its interior Confronting—
That Cooler Host.

Far safer, through an Abbey gallop,
The Stones a'chase—
Than Unarmed, one's a'self encounter—
In lonesome Place—

Ourself behind ourself, concealed—
Should startle most—
Assassin hid in our Apartment
Be Horror's least.

The Body—borrows a Revolver—
He bolts the Door—
O'erlooking a superior spectre—
Or More—

EMILY DICKINSON (1830–86), 'One need not be a Chamber'

~

LITHOBOLIA, or the Stone-throwing Devil. Being an Exact and True account (by way of Journal) of the various actions of infernal Spirits or (Devils Incarnate) Witches or both: and the great Disturbance and Amazement they gave to George Walton's Family at a place called Great Island in the Province of New Hampshire in New England, chiefly in throwing about (by an Invisible hand) Stones, Bricks and Brick-Bats of all Sizes, with several other things, as Hammers, Mauls, Iron-Crows, Spits and other domestic Utensils, as came into their Hellish Minds, and this for the space of a Quarter of a Year.

By R.C. Esq., who was a sojourner in the same Family the whole Time and an Ocular Witness of these Diabolick Inventions. The Contents hereof being manifestly known to the Inhabitants of that Province and persons of other Provinces, and is upon record in his Majestie's Council-Court held for that Province.

Printed and are to be sold by E. Whitlock, near Stationers-Hall, 1698.

> Title-page of pamphlet, *Lithobolia*, possibly by Richard Chamberlain

Mr *John Mompesson* of *Tedworth*, in the County of *Wilts*, being about the middle of *March*, in the year 1661 . . . hearing a Drum beat there, he inquired of the Bailiff of the Town, at whose House he then was, what it meant. The Bailiff told him, that they had for some days been troubled with an idle Drummer, who demanded Money of the Constable by vertue of a pretended Pass, which he thought was counterfeit . . .

[The drum was confiscated, and deposited in Mr Mompesson's house.] When he was got back to Bed, the noise was a Thumping and Drumming on the top of his House, which continued a good space, and then by degrees went off into the Air.

After this, the noise of Thumping and Drumming was very frequent, usually five Nights together, and then it would intermit three. It was on the outsides of the House, which is most of it Board. It constantly came as they were going to sleep, whether early or late . . .

It returned in a ruder manner than before, and followed and vext the youngest Children, beating their Bedsteds with that violence, that all present expected when they would fal in pieces. In laying Hands on them, one should feell no blows, but might perceive them to shake exceedingly. For an hour together it would beat, *Round-heads and Cuckolds*, the *Tat-too*, and several other points of War, as well as any Drummer. After this, they should hear a scratching under the Childrens Bed, as if by something that had Iron Tallons. It would lift the Children up in their Beds, follow them from one Room to another, and for a while haunted none particularly but them . . .

During the time of the knocking, when many were present, a Gentleman of the Company said, *Satan*, if the Drummer set thee to work, give three knocks and no more, which it did very distinctly and stopt. Then the Gentleman knockt, to see if it would answer him as it was wont, but it did not. For further trial, he bid it for confirmation, if it were the Drummer, to give five knocks and no more that night, which it did, and left the House quiet all the night after . . .

Another night strangers being present, it purr'd in the Childrens Bed like a Cat, at which time also the Cloaths and Children were lift up from the Bed, and six Men could not keep them down: hereupon they removed the Children, intending to have ript up the Bed. But they were no sooner laid in another, but the second Bed was more troubled than the first. It continued thus four hours, and so beat the Childrens Leggs against the Bed-posts, that they were forced to arise, and sit up all night. After this it would empty Chamber-pots into their Beds, and strew them with Ashes, though they were never so carefully watcht. It put a long piked Iron into Mr *Mompesson*'s Bed, and into his Mothers a naked Knife upright. It would fill Porrengers with Ashes, throw every thing about, and keep a noise all day . . .

The Drummer was tryed at the Assizes at *Salisbury* upon this occasion. He was committed first to *Gloucester* Gaol for stealing, and a *Wiltshire* Man coming to see him, he askt what news in *Wiltshire*? The Visitant said, he knew of none. No, saith the Drummer! do not you hear of the Drumming at a Gentlemans House at *Tedworth*? That I do enough, said the other. I, quoth the Drummer, I have plagued him (or to that purpose) and he shall never be quiet, till he hath made me satisfaction for taking away my Drum. Upon Information of this, the Fellow was tryed for a Witch at *Sarum* . . .

The fellow was condemned to Transportation, and accordingly sent away; but I know not how ('tis said by raising storms, and affrighting the Seamen) he made a shift to come back again. And 'tis observable, that during the time of his restraint and absence the House was quiet, but as soon as ever he came back at liberty, the disturbance returned. He had been a Souldier under *Cromwel*, and used to talk much of Gallant Books he had of an odd Fellow, who was counted a Wizzard.

JOSEPH GLANVILL, *Saducismus Triumphatus: or, Full and Plain Evidence concerning Witches and Apparitions*, 1681

. . . to the Trinity-house at London, where, among others, I find my Lord Sandwich and Craven and my Cosen Rogr Pepys and Sir Wm Wheeler . . . Both at and after dinner we had great discourses of the nature and power of Spirits and whether they can animate dead bodies; in all which, as of the general appearing of spirits, my Lord Sandwich is very scepticall. He says the greatest warrants that ever he had to believe any, is the present appearing of the Devil in Wiltshire, much of late talked of, who beats a drum up and down; there is books of it, and they say very true. But my Lord observes that though he doth answer to any tune that you will play to him upon another drum, yet one tune he tried to play and could not; which makes him suspect the whole, and I think it is a good argument.

SAMUEL PEPYS, *Diary*, 15 June 1663

When the family returned [from church, Sunday, 10 March 1850] the front door was standing wide open, and the furniture was strewn about the place in disorder. Nothing, however, had been stolen, and a gold watch in a conspicuous position had been left undisturbed . . . Everything was out of place. Moreover in the principal bedroom 'a sheet was found spread over the bed outside the counterpane, and beneath this were a nightgown and chemise laid out with the arms folded across the breast, with stockings placed in a position to represent, as it seemed, a corpse disposed as is usual before placing it in the coffin'. Similar tricks were renewed next morning, and on that day the visible movement of furniture and other objects began. 'An umbrella, standing in the hall, leaped a distance of at least twenty-five feet. Dr Phelps saw the movement, and knows there was no perceptible agency by which the motion was produced. A bucket standing at the head of the stairs was thrown into the entry below.' Smaller articles such as nails, forks, knives, spoons, bits of tin, iron and keys were thrown from different directions about the house . . .

Several times during the day, loud noises, like someone pounding with an axe or some heavy substance on the floor, were heard in different parts of the house, and several times the loud poundings terminated with a frightful scream.

These and similar incidents were renewed hundreds of times. As the days went by and the news of these strange happenings circulated, numbers of people came to witness them. They could find no solution, but were agreed that neither the children nor the servant had any hand in their production. The mediumistic power seemed to centre mainly in the boy Harry aged twelve, but also in his sister Anna, who was four years older. On one occasion when Harry was taken for a drive by his father, twenty stones were thrown at intervals into the carriage. At times he was violently caught up from the ground until his head nearly struck the ceiling; once he was thrown into a cistern of water, and once also he was tied up and suspended from a tree. Under the eyes of a clergyman visitor the boy's trousers 'were rent from the bottom upwards, higher than the knee, and were literally torn to ribbons an inch or more wide'. . . .

There were also written communications which suddenly appeared in unsuspected places, some of them bogus letters couched in facetious terms and signed with the names of neighbouring ministers. Dr Phelps in fact averred that, when writing alone in his study, he had for a minute turned his back to the table, and on resuming his task found written in large letters, the ink still wet, upon the sheet before him: 'Very nice paper and very nice ink for the devil.' But the most bizarre of all the reported manifestations was the following:

On 16 March, soon after breakfast, two or three 'images' appeared in the middle room; soon again another, followed by others still, numbering in all eleven or twelve. They were formed of articles of clothing, found about the house, stuffed to resemble the human figure. A lady's dress would be stuffed in some cases with a muff; again with a pillow, and sometimes with other dresses; a bonnet and shoes were aptly placed to complete the figure. These all but one represented females in the attitude of devotion, some having Bibles or prayer books placed before them. One formed of Mrs Phelps's dress so much resembled the real that the little boy, scarce three years old, coming into the room with his sister, whispered: 'Be still, Ma is saying prayers.'

HERBERT THURSTON, SJ, *Studies* (Dublin), March 1928; material concerning Dr Phelps, a Presbyterian clergyman in Stratford, Connecticut, drawn from *Modern Spiritualism, Its Facts and Fanaticisms*, Boston 1855, by E. W. Capron, an acquaintance of Dr Phelps

I now pass on to another Irish case of which I heard soon after the disturbances broke out [in 1877], and was able to visit the spot while the Poltergeist was still active, so that I was an eye-witness of many of the occurrences ...

The place was a hamlet called Derrygonnelly, about nine miles from Enniskillen, and the cottage was some two miles further on. A more lonely spot could hardly be found in this country. Across the bog that lay before us rose the huge limestone cliffs of Knockmore, crowned by an escarpment of over-hanging rock. The cottage itself was hidden in the hollow of a field, and no other house could be seen anywhere.

The household consisted of a grey-headed farmer who had recently lost his wife, and a family of four girls and one boy, the youngest about ten years of age, and the eldest, Maggie, round whom the disturbances arose, about twenty years old. The cottage had the usual large kitchen and dwelling-room, with earthen floors in the centre, and a smaller room opening from each side. In one of them Maggie and the girls slept on a large, old-fashioned four-post bed. The noises, rappings and scratches generally began after they had retired, and often continued the whole night through. Rats, of course, were first suspected; but when objects began to move without any visible cause, stones to fall, candles and boots repeatedly thrown out of the house, the rat theory was abandoned and a general terror took possession of the family. Several neighbours urged them to send for the priest, but they were Methodists, and their class leader advised them to lay an open Bible on the bed. This they did in the name of God, putting a big stone on the top of the volume; but the stone was lifted off by an unseen hand, and the Bible placed on top of it. After that 'it', as the farmer called the unseen cause, moved the Bible out of the room and tore seventeen pages right across. Then they could not keep a light in the house, candles and lamps were mysteriously stolen, or thrown out. They asked their neighbours' help, and here I quote the old farmer's words: 'Jack Flanigan came and lent us his lamp, saying he would engage the devil himself could not steal it, as he had got the priest to sprinkle it with holy water.' 'But that,' the old man said, 'did us no good either, for the next day it took away that lamp also.' They were forced to keep their candles in a neighbour's house some way off, and fetch them at night, and keep them lighted . . .

The following night we made another visit . . . When we were about to leave some two hours later, the farmer was distressed that we had not 'laid the ghost', and I asked him what he thought it was. He replied:

'I would have thought, sir, it do be fairies, but them late readers and knowledgeable men will not allow such a thing, so I cannot tell what it is. I only wish, sir, you would take it away.' . . .

Before leaving—it was now past midnight—the farmer implored us not to go without ridding him of this pertinacious poltergeist. So I asked my clerical friend to read a few words of scripture and offer up a prayer. He did so, choosing appropriate passages from our Lord's ministry to the possessed, and a suitable prayer. It was a weird scene, the children were in bed, but not asleep, in the inner room, the farmer and Mr Plunkett seated by the kitchen fire, Mr Close seated on a stool at the open bedroom door, I holding a lighted candle for him, and seated just within the bedroom. The noises were at first so great we could hardly hear what was read, then as the solemn words of prayer were uttered they subsided, and when the Lord's Prayer was joined in by all, a profound stillness fell on the whole cottage. The farmer rose from his knees with tears streaming from his eyes, gratefully grasped our hands, and we left for our long midnight drive back to Enniskillen.

I am afraid this does not sound a very scientific account, but it is a veracious one.

Subsequent correspondence, and reports from Mr Plunkett, showed that the poltergeist had fled from that night onwards, until some curious visitors, after reading my published description [*Dublin University Magazine*, December 1877], had gone to the farmer's cottage, and tried to bring it back again. It

came, they said, feebly and furtively, but whether genuine or Maggie's Irish
desire to please the visitors, I have no means of knowing.

SIR WILLIAM BARRETT, *Proceedings* of the Society for Psychical Research, Vol.
25, 1910

It is undoubtedly true that some of the most famous poltergeist cases have
involved adolescents who have just reached puberty. The Esther Cox case,
which became famous as 'the Amherst Mystery', took place in Nova Scotia in
1878. It began when twenty-two-year-old Esther escaped an attempted rape by
her boyfriend, who then fled the area. Esther became depressed and disturbed.
One night her bedclothes began flying around the room, her pillow inflated,
then she herself began to swell like a balloon. There was a loud explosion and
she 'deflated'. As she lay there an invisible hand scratched on the wall above
her bed, 'Esther, you are mine to kill.' . . . This poltergeist continued to persecute Esther for several months: furniture moved around, fires were started
spontaneously and metal objects stuck to her as if she were a magnet. When a
barn caught fire and Esther was jailed for arson the manifestations suddenly
ceased.

I told him [Guy Playfair] I was writing a book on the poltergeist and asked his
opinion. He frowned, hesitated, then said, 'I think it's a kind of football.'
'Football!' I wondered if I'd misheard him: 'A football of energy. When people
get into conditions of tension, they exude a kind of energy—the kind of thing
that happens to teenagers at puberty. Along come a couple of spirits, and they
do what any group of schoolboys would do—they begin to kick it around,
smashing windows and generally creating havoc. Then they get tired and leave
it. In fact the football often explodes, and turns into a puddle of water.'
  'So you mean a poltergeist is actually a spirit?'
  'That's right. I'm not saying there's not such a thing as spontaneous psycho-
kinesis. But most poltergeists are spirits.'

WILSON, *Beyond the Occult*

Haunted for twelve months and more by a mischievous spirit—called a
Poltergeist—driven almost to a state of distraction, threatened with a lunatic
asylum, and then cured by the help of a band of spirit Indians, is the extraordinary experience of the nineteen-year-old Gwynneth Morley, who lives with

her widowed mother at Keighley, and who was employed in the spinning mills of Messrs Hay and Wright . . .

Day by day the amazing manifestations of her tormenting spirit were noted down. [She had been brought to London, to work as a housemaid for Mr Hewet McKenzie, of the British College of Psychic Science.] In between the new and full moon the disturbances were worse. Everything in the room in which Gwynneth happened to be would be thrown about and smashed. Tables were lifted and overturned, chairs smashed to pieces, bookcases upset, and heavy settees thrown about.

In the kitchen of Holland Park the preparation of meals, when Gwynneth was about, was a disconcerting affair. Bowls of water would be spilt and pats of butter thrown on the floor.

On another occasion when Gwynneth was in the kitchen the housekeeper, who was preparing some grapefruit for breakfast, found that one half had disappeared and could be found neither in the kitchen nor in the scullery. She got two bananas to take its place, and laid them on the table beside her; immediately the missing grapefruit whizzed past her ear and fell before her and the bananas vanished. Some ten minutes later they were found on the scullery table.

All this time Gwynneth was being treated by psychic experts. Every week the girl sat with Mr and Mrs McKenzie and others. It was found that she was easily hypnotized, and that tables moved towards her in the circle.

At other times during the cure the Poltergeist seemed to accept challenges. One night after a particularly exciting day, Mrs Barkel [a medium, in touch with a 'Professor J.' and a band of Indians 'on the other side'] magnetized her head and quietened her, and Mrs McKenzie suggested that she should go to bed, saying 'Nothing happens when you get into bed.' Going up the stairs a small table and a metal vase crashed over, and a little later a great noise of banging and tearing was heard in Gwynneth's room. When Mrs McKenzie went into the room it looked as if a tornado had swept over it.

After an active spell from June 21 to June 25 the spirit behaved itself until July 1, when the girl had a kind of fit. Suddenly she fell off her chair with her hands clenched. They laid her on a bed, and she fell into another fit. She gripped her own throat powerfully.

Since that evening she has had no further attacks, nor have there been any disturbances.

> *Sunday Express*, 11 October 1925; quoted in Montague Summers: *The History of Witchcraft and Demonology*, 1926, where Summers comments: 'The girl should have been exorcized by a trained and accredited exorcist. These amateurs neither know nor even faintly realize the harm they may do, the dangers they encounter'

A few yards from the house there was a clothes-line, on which there were hanging four dishcloths. Three heavy iron saucepans sailed through the air, hit the dishcloths, and fell to the ground. Evidently they had taken to the air without due preparation, for their lids were scattered on the ground below them . . .

'Is this what you call a poltergeist?' I asked Mamma. We had read about them in books by Andrew Lang.

'Yes, Rose,' said Mamma, her voice quivering with indignation, 'you see I am right, supernatural things are horrible.'

I was a little frightened, but not much; and I tried to remain imperturbable, because I assumed that the supernatural took this coarse form in Constance's house because she lived among common people, and I had no desire to be impolite by drawing attention to her circumstances.

'If you are old-fashioned enough to eat soup in the middle of the day,' said Constance, 'I have still some of the turkey broth, and I was thinking of frying some Christmas pudding, and there are tangerines. Oh, my dear, it has been so dreadful. There is a thing called the Society of Psychical Research—oh, watch the dresser, it's starting again.'

Out in the pantry, a jug fell off a shelf and was smashed to pieces on the floor. Through the open door we were showered with small pieces of coal. Outside a tattoo was banged on the side of a saucepan, louder and louder, so that for the time being it was useless to talk.

When the din had died away my mother breathed indignantly, looking about her with a curled lip. 'The lowest of the low.'

'The dregs,' agreed Constance, 'but this Society, it made everything so much worse. They seemed to think poor Rosamund had something to do with it. They followed her about as if she were a pickpocket, they questioned me about her as if she were a bad child, though it happens just as much when she is not in the house or anywhere near it, and though the wretched things are harder on her than on anyone, they drag the clothes off her bed at night.'

'It is always terribly hard on the children,' sighed Mamma.

'Rosamund, come at once, your cousin Rose is here,' called Constance, and then, as a very loud crash came from the kitchen, went back into the house . . .

. . . a pack of demons were skylarking within a couple of yards of me. For though no more saucepans had come out to assault the clothes-line, someone was throwing about a number of pots and pans inside the house.

'There's one thing,' said Rosamund, coming to a halt. 'They never hurt us. They just break things and spoil things, so that we have to spend our lives mending and washing.' Thus she managed to say 'Don't be afraid', without making it plain that she had noticed I was afraid, as for the last few moments, finding I had a mob of spectral monsters between my Mamma and me, I certainly had been, though not to the degree that an adult would have been . . .

Mamma and Constance were sitting at the table, their faces contorted as by neuralgic pain, while a flour-dredger, a tin-tray, and a spiky cloud of kitchen cutlery were thrown into the room through the other door, forks striking spoons, knives clashing on knives. But as soon as Rosamund and I entered the kitchen all this possessed ironmongery suddenly became quiet. Each fork, each spoon, knife, the flour-dredger and the tray, wavered slowly downwards and softly took the ground, after the meditative fashion of falling leaves. There they lay and stirred no more, nor were ever to stir again in all the known history of that house. To drive out the evil presence it had been needed simply that we four should be in a room together, nothing more.

'We're lucky, don't you think? We know more than the other girls at school. We have mothers that are wonderful. I can see your mother is like mine, better than anyone else's. And we have a great advantage over the other girls at school, we have been through things they haven't. They don't have demons in the house, and so long as you can get rid of them it gives you a great advantage to know there are such things. I think we'll always be lucky. Don't you? Don't you?'

REBECCA WEST, *The Fountain Overflows*, 1957

Mr Lusty himself had written almost as soon as I arrived in London to say how delighted he was with, 'What we are all anticipating will be a long and extremely successful association', and it seemed that no one could be happier with a publisher and perhaps a publisher with an author, until Mr Lusty and I met.

Though I would not claim to be psychic, now and again I have been subjected to an 'interference' which transcends the ordinary; it has always been difficult to know whether it should be fought or taken as a warning.

Mr Lusty asked me to lunch with him at the Jardin des Gourmets. I had been all morning with Jimmie Simon at the House of Lords where Lord Simon was presiding over the Court of Appeal. I had to leave before the end, needing to wash and go to the lavatory before my lunch date, but the Peeresses' cloakroom was closed so that I arrived at the Jardin des Gourmets in rather dire need, only to be told that the cistern in the ladies' room had suddenly exploded and the room was out of action. I was too shy to insist I must be taken somewhere else and went through the lunch in agony.

Mr Lusty—he is now Sir Robert . . . was more than kind and understanding to me but the poltergeist manifestation persisted; after that luncheon he suggested that next time we needed to see each other I should come to 26 Bloomsbury Street which, as he says in his autobiography, 'should have been safe but as she (RG) arrived the ancient lavatory cistern of the house shattered into small pieces'.

It was not only explosions; Michael Joseph published a long poem of mine, *In Noah's Ark*. I read proof; Jon read proof; Mr Lusty read proof as did his copy editor, yet when the book was printed, words had been left out or distorted, lines had been reversed, paragraphs were missing. The whole edition had to be withdrawn.

In an effort to end this 'nonsense' as I tried to call it, the following summer I gave a small luncheon for Mr Lusty at the Colony, asking an Indian friend and his wife who, I thought, would particularly charm him. It was a hot day, hot as only a city can be, and I had ordered an iced fruit cup—white wine with fruit, cucumber and watercress in it. Mr Lusty was talking happily to glamorous Cuckoo Chaudhuri, when the big glass jug with its silver top was placed on the table. As he laughed with her, there was a loud crack, a bang, and the jug exploded over the table, festooning them both with pieces of ice, watercress, pineapple and cherries.

After that we decided, perhaps with mutual relief, to part.

RUMER GODDEN, *A House with Four Rooms*, 1989

Bemused police confessed yesterday that they have little idea how to deal with the Christmas spirits who allegedly assaulted a baby and a dog at a house in Westcliff-on-Sea, Essex.

Officers were called to tackle the ghostly presences by neighbours roused by the sound of Martin Rivers struggling with a poltergeist.

He explained yesterday that an evil spirit invaded the house in Gainsborough Drive, threw his son Daniel out of bed, moved furniture and attacked the dog. Neighbours woken by screams, wails and barking confirmed that the noises were spine-chilling.

A police spokesman said that the claims were taken seriously. Officers had made sure that the man and baby were all right.

He said: 'We are keeping an eye on the premises. But apart from offering humanitarian help there is not much we can do. Arresting a ghost is a bit tricky.'

'Poltergeist raid puzzles detectives', *The Times*, 10 December 1990

Throughout dinner, the old, old woman spoke about poltergeists. The meal was a long one. I tried to envy her for her experiences. Why didn't any poltergeist ever come to me? I tried to change the topic, out of pure defiance. She wouldn't let go. A telephone book had moved, moved from the spot. Shoes had been gathered on a bed. I found this poor. I would have preferred a poltergeist confusing the names and addresses in the telephone book, for I can give the thing a simple little kick all by myself. But I was downright embarrassed for the shoes gathered on the bed. Why hadn't they all gone strolling in different directions? I didn't care to listen. The poltergeist was unimaginative. The old, old woman, sensing my disappointment, began to speak of other things. I finally left her, she was tired. It took hours for me to realize that she herself was the poltergeist. She was preparing for her future career. She was talking about her plans.

ELIAS CANETTI, dated 1951, in *The Human Province*, 1973; tr. Joachim Neugroschel

LOVING REVENANTS

T HE calling back of the dead, or the desirability of so doing, is a ticklish question, it is said in *The Magic Mountain*, and we may wonder which is the more grievous, not being able to call them back or not being able to want to do so. Such were the thoughts of the inmates of the Sanatorium Berghof, gathered in seance. Seemingly the spirit of the young soldier Joachim, Hans Castorp's cousin, materializes, looking much as he did during his final illness, but oddly dressed and wearing what resembled an army cooking pot upside-down on his head. All Castorp can do is whisper, 'Forgive me', perhaps for summoning him gratuitously, for frivolous purposes, perhaps for ensnaring him with the soldier's prayer from Gounod's *Faust* played on the gramophone. To be conjured up could well arouse resentment in any spirit, though none was visible in the mild-eyed, friendly gaze of Joachim.

When the initiative is left to the dead, we might sympathize with the character in Margaret Oliphant's novel, that the wonder is that they could ever be kept away. Yet the thought that the dead can observe the living, undeterred by walls and curtains, is discomfiting: 'one short hour' of communication, in Tennyson's words, will suffice; and preferably at our convenience. We are beset by conflicting and disparate emotions: we wish devoutly, we are awfully embarrassed. In some verses from *In Memoriam* Tennyson does his best to allay such fears:

> Do we indeed desire the dead
>   Should still be near us at our side?
>   Is there no baseness we would hide?
> No inner vileness that we dread?

'I wrong the grave with fears untrue,' he continues, 'there must be wisdom with great Death':

Be near us when we climb or fall:
Ye watch, like God, the rolling hours
With larger other eyes than ours,
To make allowance for us all. ·

That these visitors rarely convey a message of much overt significance has
found its reasons. What motivates them rather than the delivery of some
urgent intelligence is the natural desire to glimpse their children, their loved
ones, to revisit places where they lived or worked (a pantry, a library, an altar),
returning, in the words of Hardy's poem, to where the living person 'found life
largest, best'. Such appearances are more for the sake of the revenant, then.
In the case of Mr D.'s dream (p. 335), it may have been the dead youth's wish
to clear himself promptly of the imputation of suicide, if not to spare the
feelings of someone who had been good to him.

If it was given to a child to experience the Aberfan disaster in advance, why
didn't adults foresee it? 'Does our unknown guest speak an unknown language?' Maeterlinck asks. A voice tells the mother: 'Turn the mattress'; it's
a small matter and she is busy, so she doesn't bother. If the voice had only
added: 'And then remove the matches you will find there', the child would not
have been burned to death. If the voice may not interfere with the future—by
completing the sentence it 'would be destroying in the womb the very event
which it is foretelling'—why does it say anything at all? Hard question. Are
hints and half measures allowed, but not specific unmistakable instructions?
The dilemma spirits apparently experience has something in common with a
law met in science fiction: that space explorers must not interfere with the
customs of any other life forms they encounter, however alien. Judging by the
simple morality of *Star Trek*, tactful little adjustments are to be condoned,
though nothing as extreme as colonization: rather as in the case, reported in
the first volume of the *Journal* of the Society for Psychical Research (1885), of
a Captain MacGowan in Brooklyn, who had promised his two sons that he
would take them to a theatre, and booked seats there. On the day he heard a
voice repeating 'Do not go to the theatre; take the boys back to school.' This
so worried him that finally he cancelled the plan, much to the boys' disgust.
The future was not pre-empted in that the theatre burned down the same
night, and 300 people died against three saved. Thus Sir William Barrett, after
his death, explained that communication was always permissible 'so long as it
is not allowed to interfere with the spiritual, the mental and physical development of the individual while on earth'. It remains essential that our freedom of
action, including the freedom to choose not to turn a mattress, shall be preserved.

If the dead are not to suffer from observing the living they will truly need
larger and other eyes than ours. In Rider Haggard's story 'Only a Dream'

(1920), a man on the eve of his second marriage muses thus: 'Poor dead wife, I wonder if there are any doors in the land where you have gone through which you can creep out to look at me tonight? I hope that there are none. Death must indeed be a hell if the dead can see and feel and take measure of the forgetful faithlessness of their beloved.' But in the majority of the pieces in this section no theological doctrine or moral principle is at issue, no demands are made by either party, nothing of tremendous significance is given or taken. All that happens is an exchange of recognition, of tacit greetings, between the living and the dead.

∼

A shadow flits before me,
Not thou, but like to thee:
Ah Christ, that it were possible
For one short hour to see
The souls we loved, that they might tell us
What and where they be.

ALFRED, LORD TENNYSON, *Maud,* 1855

Why should it be a matter of wonder that the dead should come back? The wonder is that they do not. Ah! that is the wonder. How one can go away who loves you, and never return, nor speak, nor send any message—that is the miracle: not that the heavens should bend down and the gates of Paradise roll back, and those who have left us return. All my life it has been a marvel to me how they could be kept away.

MARGARET OLIPHANT, *A Beleaguered City,* 1879

April 26, 1752, being after 12 at Night of the 25th.
O Lord! Governour of heaven and earth, in whose hands are embodied and departed Spirits, if thou hast ordained the Souls of the Dead to minister to the Living, and appointed my departed Wife to have care of me, grant that I may enjoy the good effects of her attention and ministration, whether exercised by

appearance, impulses, dreams or in any other manner agreeable to thy Government. Forgive my presumption, enlighten my ignorance, and however meaner agents are employed, grant me the blessed influences of thy holy Spirit, through Jesus Christ our Lord. Amen.

> SAMUEL JOHNSON, in Boswell's *Life*. Boswell comments, 'What actually followed upon this most interesting devotion by Johnson, we are not informed; but I, whom it has pleased GOD to afflict in a similar fashion to that which occasioned it, have certain experience of benignant communication by dreams'

Allow me to call your attention to a circumstance which seems to me very curious. In the first place, it decided my future life, and, besides that, its circumstances were not ordinary ones.

In 1867 (I was then twenty-five) on December 17th, I went to bed. It was nearly eleven o'clock, and as I undressed I sat down and began thinking. My thoughts were fixed on a young girl I had met during my last vacation at the sea-bath of Trouville. My family knew hers quite intimately, and Martha and I became very fond of each other. Our marriage was on the eve of being arranged when our two families quarrelled, and it had to be given up. Martha went to Toulouse, and I returned to Grenoble. But we continued to love each other so sincerely that the young girl refused other offers for her hand.

That evening, December 17, 1867, I was thinking about all this, when the door of my room opened softly, and, almost noiselessly, Martha entered. She was dressed in white, with her hair streaming over her shoulders. Eleven o'clock struck—this I can confidently assert, for I was not sleeping. The vision drew near me, leaned lightly over me, and I tried to seize the young girl's hand. It was icy cold. I uttered a cry, the phantom disappeared, and I found myself holding a glass of cold water in my hand. This may have given me the sensation of cold. But, observe, I was not asleep, and the glass of water had been standing on the *table de nuit* at my side. I could not sleep that night. *On the evening of the next day I heard of the death of Martha, at Toulouse, the night before, at eleven*. Her last word had been, 'Jacques!'

This is my story. I may add that I have never married. I am an old bachelor, but I think constantly of my vision. It haunts my sleep.

> JACQUES C., in Camille Flammarion: *The Unknown*, 1900; Flammarion was an eminent French astronomer

Myers records one such case concerning a Mr Akhurst, who was deeply in love with a certain lady. She married another man, Mr Clark, but that Akhurst remained in love with her was clear enough when he visited her and her husband about two years later. He left them to go to Yorkshire and Mrs Clark did not hear from him again. Not quite three months later her baby was born, and shortly afterwards, very early one morning he 'appeared' to her as she was feeding the baby. 'I felt a cold waft of air through the room,' she reported, 'and a feeling as though somebody had touched my shoulder . . . Raising my eyes to the door (which faced me) I saw Akhurst standing in his shirt and trousers looking at me, when he seemed to pass through the door.'

Mr Clark corroborated that his wife had told him of her vision later the same morning but that he had dismissed it as nonsense. She had, however, persisted and had said that Akhurst had been wearing only his shirt and trousers. On enquiry they learnt that ten weeks earlier Akhurst had been found dead clad in shirt and trousers, having taken an overdose of chloral.

> ROSALIND HEYWOOD, *The Sixth Sense: An Inquiry into Extra-sensory Perception*, 1959. The reference is to F. W. H. Myers: *Human Personality and Its Survival of Bodily Death*, 1903; Myers was one of the founding members of the Society for Psychical Research in 1882

This tale may be explained by those who know how souls are made, and where the bounds of the Possible are put down. I have lived long enough in this India to know that it is best to know nothing, and can only write the story as it happened.

Dumoise was our Civil Surgeon at Meridki, and we called him 'Dormouse', because he was a round little, sleepy little man. He was a good Doctor and never quarrelled with any one, not even with our Deputy Commissioner who had the manners of a bargee and the tact of a horse. He married a girl as round and as sleepy-looking as himself. She was a Miss Hillardyce, daughter of 'Squash' Hillardyce of the Berars . . .

A honeymoon in India is seldom more than a week long; but there is nothing to hinder a couple from extending it over two or three years. India is a delight-ful country for married folk who are wrapped up in one another. They can live absolutely alone and without interruption—just as the Dormice did. Those two little people retired from the world after their marriage, and were very happy. They were forced, of course, to give occasional dinners, but they made no friends thereby, and the Station went its own way and forgot them; only saying, occasionally, that Dormouse was the best of good fellows though dull. A Civil Surgeon who never quarrels is a rarity, appreciated as such.

Few people can afford to play Robinson Crusoe anywhere—least of all in India, where we are few in the land and very much dependent on each other's kind offices. Dumoise was wrong in shutting himself from the world for a year, and he discovered his mistake when an epidemic of typhoid broke out in the Station in the heart of the cold weather, and his wife went down. He was a shy little man, and five days were wasted before he realized that Mrs Dumoise was burning with something worse than simple fever, and three days more passed before he ventured to call on Mrs Shute, the Engineer's wife, and timidly speak about his trouble. Nearly every household in India knows that Doctors are very helpless in typhoid. The battle must be fought out between Death and the Nurses minute by minute and degree by degree. Mrs Shute almost boxed Dumoise's ears for what she called his 'criminal delay', and went off at once to look after the poor girl. We had seven cases of typhoid in the Station that winter and, as the average of death is about one in every five cases, we felt certain that we should have to lose somebody. But all did their best. The women sat up nursing the women, and the men turned to and tended the bachelors who were down, and we wrestled with those typhoid cases for fifty-six days, and brought them through the Valley of the Shadow in triumph. But, just when we thought all was over, and were going to give a dance to celebrate the victory, little Mrs Dumoise got a relapse and died in a week, and the Station went to the funeral. Dumoise broke down utterly at the brink of the grave, and had to be taken away.

After the death Dumoise crept into his own house and refused to be comforted. He did his duties perfectly, but we all felt that he should go on leave, and the other men of his own Service told him so. Dumoise was very thankful for the suggestion—he was thankful for anything in those days—and went to Chini on a walking-tour. Chini is some twenty marches from Simla, in the heart of the Hills, and the scenery is good if you are in trouble. You pass through big, still deodar forests, and under big, still cliffs, and over big, still grass-downs swelling like a woman's breasts; and the wind across the grass, and the rain among the deodars say—'Hush—hush—hush.' So little Dumoise was packed off to Chini, to wear down his grief with a full-plate camera and a rifle. He took also a useless bearer, because the man had been his wife's favourite servant. He was idle and a thief, but Dumoise trusted everything to him.

On his way back from Chini, Dumoise turned aside to Bagi, through the Forest Reserve which is on the spur of Mount Huttoo. Some men who have travelled more than a little say that the march from Kotegarh to Bagi is one of the finest in creation. It runs through dark wet forest, and ends suddenly in bleak, nipped hillside and black rocks. Bagi dak-bungalow is open to all the winds and is bitterly cold. Few people go to Bagi. Perhaps that was the reason why Dumoise went there. He halted at seven in the evening, and his bearer went down the hillside to the village to engage coolies for the next day's march. The sun had set, and the night-winds were beginning to croon among the rocks. Dumoise leaned on the railing of the verandah, waiting for his bearer to return. The man came back almost immediately after he had disappeared, and at such a rate that Dumoise fancied he must have crossed a bear. He was running as hard as he could up the face of the hill.

But there was no bear to account for his terror. He raced to the verandah and fell down, the blood spurting from his nose and his face iron-grey. Then he gurgled—'I have seen the Memsahib! I have seen the Memsahib!'

'Where?' said Dumoise.

'Down there, walking on the road to the village. She was in a blue dress, and she lifted the veil of her bonnet and said—"Ram Dass, give my salaams to the Sahib and tell him that I shall meet him next month at Nuddea." Then I ran away, because I was afraid.'

What Dumoise said or did I do not know. Ram Dass declares that he said nothing, but walked up and down the verandah all the cold night, waiting for the Memsahib to come up the hill, and stretching out his arms into the dark like a madman. But no Memsahib came, and, next day, he went on to Simla cross-questioning the bearer every hour.

Ram Dass could only say that he had met Mrs Dumoise, and that she had lifted up her veil and given him the message which he had faithfully repeated to Dumoise. To this statement Ram Dass adhered. He did not know where Nuddea was, had no friends at Nuddea, and would most certainly never go to Nuddea, even though his pay were doubled.

Nuddea is in Bengal, and has nothing whatever to do with a Doctor serving in the Punjab. It must be more than twelve hundred miles south of Meridki.

Dumoise went through Simla without halting, and returned to Meridki, there to take over charge from the man who had been officiating for him during his tour. There were some Dispensary accounts to be explained, and some recent orders of the Surgeon-General to be noted, and, altogether, the taking-over was a full day's work. In the evening Dumoise told his locum tenens, who was an old friend of his bachelor days, what had happened at Bagi; and the man said that Ram Dass might as well have chosen Tuticorin while he was about it.

At that moment a telegraph-peon came in with a telegram from Simla, ordering Dumoise not to take over charge at Meridki, but to go at once to Nuddea on special duty. There was a nasty outbreak of cholera at Nuddea, and the Bengal Government being short-handed, as usual, had borrowed a Surgeon from the Punjab.

Dumoise threw the telegram across the table and said—'Well?'

The other Doctor said nothing. It was all that he could say.

Then he remembered that Dumoise had passed through Simla on his way from Bagi; and thus might possibly have heard first news of the impending transfer.

He tried to put the question and the implied suspicion into words, but Dumoise stopped him with—'If I had desired *that*, I should never have come back from Chini. I was shooting there. I wish to live, for I have things to do . . . but I shall not be sorry.'

The other man bowed his head, and helped, in the twilight, to pack up Dumoise's just opened trunks. Ram Dass entered with the lamps.

'Where is the Sahib going?' he asked.

'To Nuddea,' said Dumoise softly.

Ram Dass clawed Dumoise's knees and boots and begged him not to go. Ram Dass wept and howled till he was turned out of the room. Then he wrapped up all his belongings and came back to ask for a character. He was not going to Nuddea to see his Sahib die and, perhaps, to die himself.

So Dumoise gave the man his wages and went down to Nuddea alone, the other Doctor bidding him goodbye as one under sentence of death.

Eleven days later he had joined his Memsahib; and the Bengal Government had to borrow a fresh Doctor to cope with that epidemic at Nuddea.

> KIPLING, 'By Word of Mouth'; the tale's first publication, in the *Civil and Military Gazette* (Lahore) of 10 June 1887, brought letters from readers who believed it to be a true account and claimed to know the couple in question

. . . somewhere about 3 a.m. I woke in my sleep and there she was beside me in actuality of being: not remembered, not evoked, not a sense of presence. *Actual*.

I was sitting in the kitchen and she standing beside me, in a cotton shirt and grey trousers, looking down on me, with love, intimately, ordinarily, with her look of tantalizing a little, her easy amorous look. She was within touch of my hand. I looked at her and felt the whole force of my love for her, its amazement, a delighted awe, entrancement, rapture. We were familiar, ourselves to ourselves. I was withheld from speaking. I looked. I gave myself. I loved with my whole being. No words occurred to me. I knew I must not try to touch her, and I was wholly an embrace of her. And then without ending, it was at an end. I was conveyed into another layer of sleep.

> SYLVIA TOWNSEND WARNER, unpublished diaries, 24 September 1972; quoted in Claire Harman: *Sylvia Townsend Warner*. Valentine Ackland died on 9 November 1969

My spirit will not haunt the mound
    Above my breast,
But travel, memory-possessed,
To where my tremulous being found
    Life largest, best.

My phantom-footed shape will go
    When nightfall grays
Hither and thither along the ways
I and another used to know
    In backward days.

> HARDY, 'My Spirit Will Not Haunt The Mound', 1914

Two Persons (Ladies) of Quality, (both being not long since Deceased,) were intimate Acquaintance, and lov'd each other entirely: It so fell out, that one of them fell sick of the Small-Pox, and desired mightily to see the other, who would not come, fearing the catching of them. The Afflicted at last dies of them, and had not been buried very long, but appears at the others House, in the Dress of a Widow, and asks for her Friend, who was then at Cards, but sends down her Woman to know her Business, who in short, told her, *She must impart it to none but her Lady*, who, after she had receiv'd this Answer, bid her Woman have her into a Room, and desir'd her to stay while the Game was done, and she would wait on her. The Game being done, down Stairs she came to the Apparition, to know her Business; *Madam*, says the Ghost, turning up her Veil, (and her Face appearing full of the Small-Pox;) *You know very well, that You, and I, lov'd entirely; and your not coming to see me, I took it so ill at your Hands, that I could not rest till I had seen You, and now I am come to tell you, that you have not long to live, therefore prepare to die; and when you are at a Feast, and make the Thirteenth Person in Number, then Remember my Words*; and so the Apparition vanish'd. To conclude, she was at a Feast, where she made the Thirteenth Person in Number, and was afterwards asked by the Deceased's Brother, *whether his Sister did appear to her as was reported?* She made him no answer, but fell a Weeping, and died a little time after. The Gentleman that told this Story, says, That there is hardly any Person of Quality but knows it to be True.

Athenian Mercury, June 1695; cited by Aubrey: *Miscellanies*

There is some little incongruity in this story too, which renders it inconsistent, not with the Devil only, but even with the nature of a spirit or apparition: as 1. Why should the apparition come when the lady was engaged and could not speak to her? as if she, being a ghost or spirit, as we vulgarly express it, did not know what she was doing, as well as where she was. 2. How does her taking ill the living lady's not visiting her oblige her to come and give her this kind notice of her death: I took it so ill at your hands, that I could not rest till I had seen you? . . .

It seems more rational to be as I have read the story, that the ghost should say thus: Though I took it very ill at your hands that you would not come to see me, yet I could not rest till I had seen you, to tell you that you have not long to live, and that you should prepare, &c. This is much better sense, and more agreeable to the nature of the thing; for certainly coming in that manner to give the lady notice of the approach of her end, and to counsel her to prepare accordingly, must be allowed to be an act of kindness, not of resentment, and a testimony of the affection that was between them; and therefore her taking it ill that she had not been to visit her in her illness, could not rationally be given as a reason for it.

But as to the apparition itself, since it could not be the soul of the deceased lady, and, for the reasons above [it not being very suitable to his disposition, and less to his design], was not likely to be the Devil, or, I may venture to say positively, was not the Devil, what then was it? I answer with a question: what could it be but a good angel, or angelic spirit, from the invisible world, sent with a message of goodness, and a merciful notice of her approaching death; that she might receive a due caution, preparing her mind, and turning her thoughts to a proper meditation upon so serious a subject?

DEFOE, *The Secrets of the Invisible World Disclos'd*; regarding the story 'of which Mr Aubrey has given us the last relation'

An old man, well liked but considered eccentric, lived alone in a cottage. He had never married. Falling sick, he sent for his only relatives, a widowed sister-in-law and her son. One day, while they were at his bedside, and he was sleeping, a white butterfly flew into the room and settled on his pillow. Several times the nephew drove it away with a fan, but it always returned. Finally he chased it into the garden and then into the cemetery of a nearby temple. There it hovered obstinately, and he began to think it might be an evil spirit. He saw it fly towards a tomb, and disappear. The tomb was of someone called Akiko, who had died at the age of eighteen, fifty years before. Moss had gathered, but fresh flowers lay there.

Returning to the house, the young man found that his uncle had died, peacefully, a smile on his face. He told his mother of what had happened in the cemetery.

'Ah,' she said, 'then it must have been Akiko . . .'

'But who was Akiko?'

'When he was young, your uncle was betrothed to a lovely girl called Akiko, the daughter of a neighbour. She died of consumption just before they were to be married. Your uncle swore never to marry, and built this cottage beside the cemetery in which she was buried. Every day during the fifty years that followed he prayed at her grave. But he never spoke of it. The white butterfly was Akiko's soul—at last she came to fetch him.'

Japanese tale

> . . . but surely the dead must walk again.
> They stroll most oddly in and out of
> small corners of your being, optical blips.
> They go with an awkward gait, like foreign changelings
> through the edges of a crowd or down the block.
>
> It is at random seasons when the mind
> is full at ease that my father, roundshouldered,
> shuffles along to wait for lights to change
> or my tall son shambles down the footpath
> in a woollen cap, relentlessly unfashionable
> and quiet as a cloud.
>
> What do they want?
> Can they be translated?
>
> Space-time is no longer their medium;
>   they inhabit
> antipodes of the radiant fair dinkum,

post-Heisenberg, transphysical, post-Planck,
taunting us all with quips of antimatter.
They are black holes punched in the modern world.
They have been resurrection.
                              They are Dreaming
and we the dream they paint their names across
in grey and lavender and thunderblue,
photocopies of Krishna passing
by Lasseter's reef; or somebody
behind us on the back road to Emmaus,
footsteps in the dust.
                              I would not have it
any other way.
                    They walk on by.

                    CHRIS WALLACE-CRABBE, 'Trace Elements', 1992

In the afternoon [shortly after the writer's daughter Sally had died, in 1958], my friends went out for a walk, leaving me behind to rest. As all bereaved people know, grief is inexpressibly tiring; and I was thankful to fling myself down on my bed and be alone; thankful too that in spite of feeling prostrated with fatigue I was still in a frail state of mental calm. A blackbird was pouring forth his whole being just beyond my window; and from where I lay I could see elm tops moving against an intensely blue sky in billowing masses of unearthly greens and golds.

Suddenly, a clear high-pitched vibration, like the twang of a harp-string, crossed my ears. I thought: 'This again . . . what is it?'—remembering that I had heard it before, very soon after the news came: in fact, that it had preceded that sensation of being 'lifted by the Breath'. But this time, instead of being transitory, the sound settled into a strong, rising and sinking hum like the sound of a spinning top. At the same time a sort of convulsion or alarum struck me in the heart centre, followed by a violent tugging sensation in this region. As if attached to an invisible kite string that was pulling me out, out, upwards, upwards, I began to be forcibly ejected from the centre of my body. I heard myself moan, felt a torrent of tears pour down my face, distinctly remarked to myself that this was like some very peculiar birth process; registered phenomenal occurrences deep inside my head: it seemed that my eardrums were being plucked—literally plucked and shaken—as if they were closed doors that must be shaken loose: my hearing was being freed, I suppose, and it was a difficult yet painless process. Then the humming faded out, and the song of the black-bird swelled, swelled, as if it was being stepped up a hundredfold. Never could I have imagined notes of such wild, piercing purity and sweetness. For a while I did hear that bird—I must have heard him—with liberated ears.

I was drifting and floating now . . . but where, and for how long? There is no way of telling. Perhaps for only a few seconds of earth time. A passage of symphonic music, jubilant, penetrating, vigorous, crossed and receded from me like a wave. Was I picking up, suprasensibly, from the ether, an actual performance going on somewhere at that moment? There was certainly no gramophone or radio switched on in the house . . . Whatever I heard seemed at once familiar and unknown. As I write, I can recall its melodic outline, but I cannot recognize it.

Now I was with Sally. She was behind my left shoulder, leaning on it. Together we were watching Patrick [P. J. Kavanagh, Sally's husband]. His face, only his face, confronted us: it was clearly recognizable but the whole scale of it was altered, expanded; and it was self-luminous, and transformed by an expression of dreaming beatitude. He was (we both knew) starting on a journey. I said: 'Aren't you going with him?' 'No,' she said, 'he's got to go alone.' I said: 'I expect he's going to D.' (one of his closest friends, at that time a novitiate in the Dominican Order). Again she said: 'No'; and added: 'He'll go to Auntie Peg.' This is the name by which my sister Beatrix, the actress, is known to all her nephews and nieces. I am anxious not to make hard and fast interpretations. All I want to say is that, in those early days, I held to the entirely erroneous supposition that Patrick might decide to retire from a world become intolerable. It never occurred to me that he might choose to become an actor, as well as a writer . . . However, two years after his return from Java, he suddenly decided to throw up his job in a publisher's office and joined the Salisbury Repertory Theatre: thus, as one might say, 'going to Auntie Peg!'

Patrick's lit face vanished, but Sally and I remained together, wordlessly communicating. More than anything, it was like laughing together, as we always did laugh; like sharing the humour of a situation: his going off without her in some sort of state of disarray and unpreparedness . . . She made some characteristic joke (I can't define it) about the muddle of his packing. I did not see her. I had the unaccountable impression that she was hiding her face, that I was forbidden to look round. There was no light, no colour, no external scenic feature: only close embrace, profound and happy communion; also the strongest possible impression of her individuality.

Then, with no shock or sense of travelling, I was back in my body, awake, cheerful as if I had just replaced the receiver after one of our long gossiping joking conversations . . .

I looked at my watch and found that over an hour had passed. I sprang up, went to the window and looked out . . . and beheld a visionary world. Everything around, above, below me was shimmering and vibrating. The tree foliage, the strip of lawn, the flower-beds—all had become incandescent. I seemed to be looking through the surfaces of all things into the manifold iridescent rays which, I could now see, composed the substances of all things. Most dramatic phenomenon of all, the climbing roses round the window-frame had 'come alive'—the red, the white. The beauty of each one of them was fathomless,—a world of love. I leaned out, they leaned towards me, as if we were exchanging love. I saw, I *saw* their intensity of meaning, feeling.

ROSAMOND LEHMANN, *The Swan in the Evening*, 1967

There was one who was perfect, who had
faults doubtless, but they were for God
to see, not for us who loved her, though whatever
I think of her is usually mixed with my
own falling short. But sometimes I see her
as she was, nothing to do with me:

as sometimes a cloud leaves the sun alone
and every leaf on a tree is a plate for light,
the tree become solely itself, and stays itself
though another cloud crosses and it goes dull again,
its secret kept; puzzled at by the eyes
of one who wants it always to stay gilded,
isolated, amazing: resentful of its patience,
obscuringly angered he only sometimes sees.

P. J. KAVANAGH, 'Sometimes', 1974

'Who knocks?' 'I, who was beautiful,
   Beyond all dreams to restore,
I, from the roots of the dark thorn am hither,
   And knock on the door.'
'Who speaks?' 'I—once was my speech
   Sweet as the bird's on the air,
When echo lurks by the waters to heed;
   'Tis I speak thee fair.'

'Dark is the hour!' 'Ay, and cold.'
   'Lone is my house.' 'Ah, but mine?'
'Sight, touch, lips, eyes yearned in vain.'
   'Long dead these to thine . . .'

Silence. Still faint on the porch
   Brake the flames of the stars.
In gloom groped a hope-wearied hand
   Over keys, bolts, and bars.

A face peered. All the grey night
   In chaos of vacancy shone;
Nought but vast sorrow was there—
   The sweet cheat gone.

WALTER DE LA MARE, 'The Ghost', 1918

Hereto I come to view a voiceless ghost;
   Whither, O whither will its whim now draw me?
Up the cliff, down, till I'm lonely, lost,
   And the unseen waters' ejaculations awe me.
Where you will next be there's no knowing,
   Facing round about me everywhere,
     With your nut-coloured hair,
And gray eyes, and rose-flush coming and going.

Yes: I have re-entered your olden haunts at last;
   Through the years, through the dead scenes I have tracked you;
What have you now found to say of our past—
   Scanned across the dark space wherein I have lacked you?
Summer gave us sweets, but autumn wrought division?
   Things were not lastly as firstly well
     With us twain, you tell?
But all's closed now, despite Time's derision.

I see what you are doing: you are leading me on
   To the spots we knew when we haunted here together,
The waterfall, above which the mist-bow shone
   At the then fair hour in the then fair weather,
And the cave just under, with a voice still so hollow
   That it seems to call out to me from forty years ago,
     When you were all aglow,
And not the thin ghost that I now fraily follow!

Ignorant of what there is flitting here to see,
   The waked birds preen and the seals flop lazily;
Soon you will have, Dear, to vanish from me,
   For the stars close their shutters and the dawn whitens hazily.
Trust me, I mind not, though Life lours,
   The bringing me here; nay, bring me here again!
      I am just the same as when
Our days were a joy, and our paths through flowers.

HARDY, 'After a Journey', 1914

Where art thou, my beloved Son,
Where art thou, worse to me than dead?
Oh find me, prosperous or undone!
Or, if the grave be now thy bed,
Why am I ignorant of the same
That I may rest; and neither blame
Nor sorrow may attend thy name? . . .

I look for ghosts; but none will force
Their way to me: 'tis falsely said
That there was ever intercourse
Between the living and the dead;
For, surely, then I should have sight
Of him I wait for day and night,
With love and longings infinite.

WILLIAM WORDSWORTH, from 'The Affliction of Margaret ———', 1807

At this time of Mr Donne's and his wife's living in Sir Robert's house, the Lord Hay was by King James sent upon a glorious embassy to the then French King, Henry the Fourth; and Sir Robert [Drury] put on a sudden resolution to accompany him to the French court, and to be present at his audience there. And Sir Robert put on as sudden a resolution to subject Mr Donne to be his companion in that journey. And this desire was suddenly made known to his wife, who was then with child, and otherwise under so dangerous a habit of body, as to her health, that she professed an unwillingness to allow him any absence from her; saying, *Her divining soul boded her some ill in his absence*; and therefore desired him not to leave her. This made Mr Donne lay aside all thoughts of the journey, and really to resolve against it. But Sir Robert became restless in his persuasions for it, and Mr Donne was so generous as to think he had sold his liberty, when he received so many charitable kindnesses from him; and told his wife so; who did therefore with an unwilling willingness give a faint consent to the journey, which was proposed to be but for two months; for about that time they determined their return. Within a few days after this resolve, the Ambassador, Sir Robert, and Mr Donne left London, and were the twelfth day got all safe to Paris. Two days after their arrival there, Mr Donne was left alone in that room, in which Sir Robert, and he, and some other friends had dined together. To this place Sir Robert returned within half an hour; and as he left, so he found, Mr Donne alone; but in such an ecstasy, and so altered as to his looks, as amazed Sir Robert to behold him; insomuch that he earnestly desired Mr Donne to declare what had befallen him in the short time of his absence. To which Mr Donne was not able to make a present answer: but, after a long and perplexed pause, did at last say, 'I have seen a dreadful vision since I last saw you: I have seen my dear wife pass twice by me through this room, with her hair hanging about her shoulders, and a dead child in her arms: this I have seen since I saw you.' To which Sir Robert replied, 'Sure, sir, you have slept since I saw you; and this is the result of some melancholy dream, which I desire you to forget, for you are now awake.' To which Mr Donne's reply was, 'I cannot be surer that I now live, than that I have not slept since I saw you: and I am as sure, that at her second appearing she stopped, and looked me in the face, and vanished.'—Rest and sleep had not altered Mr Donne's opinion the next day; for he then affirmed this vision with a more deliberate, and so confirmed a confidence, that he inclined Sir Robert to a faint belief that the vision was true.—It is truly said, that desire and doubt have no rest; and it proved so with Sir Robert; for he immediately sent a servant to Drury-house, with a charge to hasten back, and bring him word, whether Mrs Donne were alive; and, if alive, in what condition she was as to her health.—The twelfth day the messenger returned with this account— That he found and left Mrs Donne very sad, and sick in her bed; and that, after a long and dangerous labour, she had been delivered of a dead child. And, upon examination, the abortion proved to be the same day, and about the very hour, that Mr Donne affirmed he saw her pass by him in his chamber.

IZAAK WALTON, *The Life of Dr John Donne*, 1640

There lived a wife at Usher's Well,
　　And a wealthy wife was she;
She had three stout and stalwart sons,
　　And sent them o'er the sea.

They hadna been a week from her,
　　A week but barely ane,
When word came to the carlin wife   *old woman*
　　That her three sons were gane.

They hadna been a week from her,
　　A week but barely three,
When word came to the carlin wife
　　That her sons she'd never see.

'I wish the wind may never cease,
　　Nor fashes in the flood,   *troubles*
Till my three sons come hame to me,
　　In earthly flesh and blood!'

It fell about the Martinmas,
　　When nights are lang and mirk,
The carlin wife's three sons came hame,
　　And their hats were o' the birk.   *birch*

It neither grew in syke nor ditch,   *marsh*
　　Nor yet in ony sheugh;   *trench*
But at the gates o' Paradise
　　That birk grew fair eneugh.

'Blow up the fire, my maidens,
　　Bring water from the well;
For a' my house shall feast this night,
　　Since my three sons are well.'

And she has made to them a bed,
　　She's made it large and wide,
And she's ta'en her mantle her about,
　　Sat down at the bedside.

Up then crew the red, red cock,
　　And up and crew the gray;
The eldest to the youngest said,
　　''Tis time we were away.'

The cock he hadna craw'd but once,
　　And clapp'd his wings at a',

When the youngest to the eldest said,
   'Brother, we must awa'.

'The cock doth craw, the day doth daw',
   The channerin' worm doth chide;   *fretting*
Gin we be miss'd out o' our place,   *If*
   A sair pain we maun bide.'

'Lie still, lie still, but a little wee while,
   Lie still but if we may;
Gin my mother should miss us when she wakes,
   She'll go mad ere it be day.'

'Fare ye weel, my mother dear!
   Fareweel to barn and byre!
And fare ye weel, the bonny lass
   That kindles my mother's fire!'

ANON., 'The Wife of Usher's Well'

A soldier shows an old couple a monkey's paw, mummified, which he has brought back from India. 'It had a spell put on it by an old fakir, a very holy man. He wanted to show that fate ruled people's lives, and that those who interfered with it did so to their sorrow.' The owner of the paw can obtain three wishes from it. Reluctantly, the soldier gives it to the husband, who wishes for £200. The next day the couple's only son is killed at work, caught in the machinery and horribly mangled. The employer offers £200 in compensation. Ten days after the son's burial, the wife persuades her husband to make his second wish: that their son should be alive again.

A third knock sounded through the house.

'*What's that?*' cried the old woman, starting up.

'A rat,' said the old man in shaking tones—'a rat. It passed me on the stairs.'

His wife sat up in bed listening. A loud knock resounded through the house.

'It's Herbert!' she screamed. 'It's Herbert!'

She ran to the door, but her husband was before her, and catching her by the arm, held her tightly.

'What are you going to do?' he whispered hoarsely.

'It's my boy; it's Herbert!' she cried, struggling mechanically. 'I forgot it was two miles away. What are you holding me for? Let go. I must open the door.'

'For God's sake don't let it in,' cried the old man, trembling.

'You're afraid of your own son,' she cried, struggling. 'Let me go. I'm coming, Herbert; I'm coming.'

There was another knock, and another. The old woman with a sudden wrench broke free and ran from the room. Her husband followed to the landing, and called after her appealingly as she hurried downstairs. He heard the chain rattle back and the bottom bolt drawn slowly and stiffly from the socket. Then the old woman's voice, strained and panting.

'The bolt,' she cried, loudly. 'Come down. I can't reach it.'

But her husband was on his hands and knees groping wildly on the floor in search of the paw. If he could only find it before the thing outside got in. A perfect fusillade of knocks reverberated through the house, and he heard the scraping of a chair as his wife put it down in the passage against the door. He heard the creaking of the bolt as it came slowly back, and at the same moment he found the monkey's paw, and frantically breathed his third and last wish.

The knocking ceased suddenly, although the echoes of it were still in the house. He heard the chair drawn back, and the door opened. A cold wind rushed up the staircase, and a long loud wail of disappointment and misery from his wife gave him courage to run down to her side, and then to the gate beyond. The street lamp flickering opposite shone on a quiet and deserted road.

W. W. JACOBS, from 'The Monkey's Paw', 1902

An earthly nourrice sits and sings,   *nurse*
    And aye she sings, 'Ba, lily wean!
Little ken I my bairn's father,
    Far less the land that he staps in.'

Then ane arose at her bed-fit,   *feet*
    An' a grumly guest I'm sure was he: *grim*
'Here am I, thy bairn's father,
    Although that I be not comèlie.

I am a man, upo' the lan',
    An' I am a silkie in the sea;   *seal*
And when I'm far and far frae lan',
    My dwelling is in Sule Skerrie.'

'It was na weel,' quo' the maiden fair,
    'It was na weel, indeed,' quo' she,

'That the Great Silkie of Sule Skerrie
   Suld hae come and aught a bairn to me.'   *owned*

Now he has ta'en a purse of goud,   *gold*
   And he has pat it upo' her knee,
Sayin', 'Gie to me my little young son,
   An' tak thee up thy nourrice-fee.

An' it sall pass on a simmer's day,
   When the sin shines het on evera stane,
That I will tak my little young son,
   An' teach him for to swim his lane.   *by himself*

An' thu sall marry a proud gunner,
   An' a proud gunner I'm sure he'll be,
An' the very first schot that ere he schoots,
   He'll schoot baith my young son and me.'

ANON., 'The Great Silkie of Sule Skerrie'

Children love to listen to stories about their elders when *they* were children; to stretch their imagination to the conception of a traditionary great-uncle, or grandame whom they never saw. It was in this spirit that my little ones crept about me the other evening . . .

. . . they looked up, and prayed me not to go on about their uncle, but to tell them some stories about their pretty dead mother. Then I told how for seven long years, in hope sometimes, sometimes in despair, yet persisting ever, I courted the fair Alice W———n; and, as much as children could understand, I explained to them what coyness, and difficulty, and denial meant in maidens— when suddenly, turning to Alice, the soul of the first Alice looked out at her eyes with such a reality of re-presentment, that I became in doubt which of them stood there before me, or whose that bright hair was; and while I stood gazing, both the children gradually grew fainter to my view, receding, and still receding till nothing at last but two mournful features were seen in the utter-most distance, which, without speech, strangely impressed upon me the effects of speech: 'We are not of Alice, nor of thee, nor are we children at all. The children of Alice called Bartrum father. We are nothing; less than nothing, and dreams. We are only what might have been, and must wait upon the tedious shores of Lethe millions of ages before we have existence, and a name'—and immediately awaking, I found myself quietly seated in my bachelor armchair, where I had fallen asleep.

CHARLES LAMB, from 'Dream-Children', 1822

He was on his way from his bachelor flat to the club, a man of middle age with a slight stoop, and an expression of face firm yet gentle, the blue eyes with light and courage in them, and a faint hint of melancholy—or was it resignation?— about the strong mouth. It was early in April, a slight drizzle of warm rain falling through the coming dusk; but spring was in the air, a bird sang rapturously on a pavement tree. And the man's heart wakened at the sound, for it was the lift of the year, and low in the western sky above the London roofs there was a band of tender colour.

His way led him past one of the great terminal stations that open the gates of London seawards; the birds, the coloured clouds, and the thought of a sunny coast-line worked simultaneously in his heart . . . Upon the wet pavement, where the street lamps already laid their network of faint gold, he saw, perhaps a dozen yards in front of him, the figure of a little boy.

The boy, for some reason, caught his attention and his interest vividly. He was dressed in Etons, the broad white collar badly rumpled, the pointed coat hitched grotesquely sideways, while, from beneath the rather grimy straw hat, his thick light hair escaped at various angles. This general air of effort and distress was due to the fact that the little fellow was struggling with a bag packed evidently to bursting point, too big and heavy for him to manage for more than ten yards at a time. He changed it from one hand to the other, resting it in the intervals upon the ground, each effort making it rub against his leg so that the trousers were hoisted considerably above the boot. He was a pathetic figure.

'I must help him,' said the man. 'He'll never get there at this rate. He'll miss his train to the sea.' For his destination was obvious, since a pair of wooden spades was tied clumsily and insecurely to the straps of the bursting bag.

Occasionally, too, the lad, who seemed about ten years old, looked about him to right and left, questioningly, anxiously, as though he expected some-one—someone to help, or perhaps to meet him. His behaviour even gave the impression that he was not quite sure of his way. The man hurried to overtake him . . .

'It's too big for you, my boy,' he said, recovering himself with a jolly laugh; 'or, rather, you're not big enough—yet—for it—eh! Where to, now? Ah! the station, I suppose?' And he stooped to grasp the handles of the bulging bag, first poking the spades more securely in beneath the straps . . .

But the man, swaying sideways, nearly lost his balance. He had calculated automatically the probable energy necessary to lift the weight; he had put this energy forth. He received a shock as though he had been struck, for the bag had no weight at all; it was as light as a feather. It might have been of tissue-paper, a phantom bag. And the shock was mental as well as physical. His mind swayed with his body.

'By jove!' cried the boy, strutting merrily beside him, hands in his pockets. 'Thanks most awfully. This *is* jolly!' . . .

But the man was troubled. The face reminded him, as he gazed, of many children, of children he had loved and played with, both boys and girls, his Substitute Children, as he had always called them in his heart . . . Then, suddenly, the boy came closer and took his arm. The sweet human perfume of a small, deeply loved, helpless and dependent little life rose past his face.

He suddenly blurted out: 'But, I say, this bag of yours—it weighs simply nothing!'

The boy laughed—a ring of true careless joy was in the sound. He looked up.

'Do you know what's in it? Shall I tell you?' He added in a whisper: 'I will, if you like.'

But the man was suddenly afraid and dared not ask.

'Brown paper probably,' he evaded laughingly; 'or birds' eggs. You've been up to some wicked lark or other.'

The little chap clasped both hands upon the supporting arm. He took a quick, dancing step or two, then stopped dead, and made the man stop with him. He stood on tiptoe to reach the distant ear. His face wore a lovely smile of truth and trust and delight.

'My future,' he whispered. And the man turned into ice.

They entered the great station. The last of the daylight was shut out. They reached the ticket-office. The crowds of hurrying people surged about them. The man set down the bag. For a moment or two the boy looked quickly about him to right and left, searching, then turned his big blue eyes upon the other with his radiant smile:

'She's in the waiting-room as usual,' he said. 'I'll go and fetch her—though she *ought* to know you're here.' He stood on tiptoe, his hands upon the other's shoulders, his face thrust close. 'Kiss me, father. I shan't be a second.'

'You little beggar!' said the man, in a voice he could not control; then, opening his big arms wide, saw only an empty space before him.

He turned and walked slowly back to his flat instead of to the club; and when he got home he read over for the thousandth time the letter—its ink a little faded during the twelve intervening years—in which she had accepted his love two short weeks before death took her.

ALGERNON BLACKWOOD, from 'The Little Beggar', 1924

XCII

If any vision should reveal
   Thy likeness, I might count it vain
   As but the canker of the brain;
Yea, tho' it spake and made appeal

To chances where our lots were cast
   Together in the days behind,
   I might but say, I hear a wind
Of memory murmuring the past.

Yea, tho' it spake and bared to view
   A fact within the coming year;
   And tho' the months, revolving near,
Should prove the phantom-warning true,

They might not seem thy prophecies,
   But spiritual presentiments,
   And such refraction of events
As often rises ere they rise.

XCIII

I shall not see thee. Dare I say
   No spirit ever brake the band
   That stays him from the native land
Where first he walk'd when claspt in clay?

No visual shade of some one lost,
   But he, the Spirit himself, may come
   Where all the nerve of sense is numb;
Spirit to Spirit, Ghost to Ghost.

O, therefore from thy sightless range
   With gods in unconjectured bliss,
   O, from the distance of the abyss
Of tenfold-complicated change,

Descend, and touch, and enter; hear
    The wish too strong for words to name;
    That in this blindness of the frame
My Ghost may feel that thine is near.

TENNYSON, *In Memoriam*, 1850

Highclere Castle, Newbury, November 8th, 1894

On Saturday, October, 1893, I was in Berlin with Lord Carnarvon. We went to a theatre together and returned before midnight. I went to bed, leaving, as I always do, a bright light in the room (electric light). As I lay in bed I found myself looking at an oleograph which hung on the wall opposite my bed. I saw distinctly the face of my father, the Maharajah Duleep Singh, looking at me, as it were out of this picture; not like a portrait of him, but his real head. The head about filled the picture frame. I continued looking and still saw my father looking at me with an intent expression. Though not in the least alarmed, I was so puzzled that I got out of bed to see what the picture really was. It was an oleograph commonplace picture of a girl holding a rose and leaning out of a balcony, an arch forming a background. The girl's face was quite small, whereas my father's head was the size of life and filled the frame.

I was in no special anxiety about my father at the time, and had for some years known him to be seriously out of health; but there had been no news to alarm me about him.

Next morning (Sunday) I told the incident to Lord Carnarvon.

That evening, late on returning home, Lord Carnarvon brought two telegrams into my room and handed them to me. I said at once, 'My father is dead.' That was the fact. He had had an apoplectic seizure on the Saturday evening at about nine o'clock, from which he never recovered, but continued unconscious and died on the Sunday, early in the afternoon. My father had often said to me that if I was not with him when he died he would try and come to me.

VICTOR DULEEP SINGH

I can confirm Prince V. Duleep Singh's account. I heard the incident from him on the Sunday morning. The same evening, at about 12 p.m., he received a telegram notifying him of his father's sudden illness and death. We had no knowledge of his father's illness. He has never told me of any similar previous occurrence.

CARNARVON

Journal of the Society for Psychical Research, Vol. 6, 1894; the Maharajah died on 22 October 1893

Cardan [Gerolamo Cardano, 1501–76, mathematician, inventor of cardan universal joint] says that while he was living at Pavia, looking down one day on his hands, he was much alarmed to see on his right forefinger a spot of red. During the evening he received a letter from his son-in-law, apprising him that his son had been imprisoned and was expressing an ardent desire to see him at Milan, as he had been *condemned to death*. The red mark continued to spread for fifty-three days, by which time it had reached the tip of the finger and was the colour of blood. When his son had been executed the red mark grew smaller; the day after his death it had almost entirely disappeared, and two days later no trace of it could be found.

FLAMMARION, *The Unknown*

It is calm work, remembering their names
In a house of geraniums and white stucco,
Looking at death and looking at the sea,
Salt on the wind filming its weather eye.

Each photograph is purest ectoplasm,
Part of the way lights crease the window-sill,
A teacup's ring is glimmered on the table,
Kind thoughts lie pencilled in a Fairy Book.

But all these wishes, all these visitations?
'I know she was with me on the day she died.'
Sheet-lightning: air stuck in sultry vapours
That she dispersed with a particular joy.

And other, simpler wraiths who keep their patience
As we arrange a mystery about them,
Who, if we find them voices, only say:
'We were; you are. Why should you ask for more?'

The dead are anything that sighs in millions:
The tossing flower-heads of Queen Anne's Lace,
Moths trawling the dark, those waifs of snow
Flocked against glass, formations of the night

Which grows towards us: ghosts talking of ghosts,
Compounded of old walls, old bones, old stories,
Watching an inch of sun slip to the West,
Playing the revenant to this house and garden

Sleepy with cats down a remembered lane
Where unaccustomed eyes look cleanly through us;
Pity our grey hair, unfamiliar pauses,
Our tongues which trip so lightly over our graves.

PETER SCUPHAM, 'A House of Geraniums', 1986

In 1867 his only sister, aged eighteen, to whom he was very attached, died of
cholera in St Louis, Mo. In 1876, as a commercial traveller, he had 'drummed'
the city of St Joseph, Mo., and was in his hotel room, cheerfully writing out
the orders he had received, when he became conscious of his sister, sitting on
his left, one arm resting on the table. 'She appeared as if alive. Her eyes looked
kindly and perfectly naturally into mine. Her skin was so lifelike that I could
see the glow or moisture on its surface.' As he moved towards her, she vanished. He took the next train home and told his parents of what had occurred.
His father was inclined to ridicule him. But when he spoke of a bright red line
or scratch on the right-hand side of his sister's face, his mother 'rose trembling
to her feet and nearly fainted away'. 'With tears streaming down her face, she
exclaimed that I had indeed seen my sister, as no living mortal but herself was
aware of that scratch, which she had accidentally made when adjusting something about her head while in the casket.' The mother was pained to think she
had marred her daughter's features, and had carefully obliterated traces of the
slight scratch with the aid of powder: she had never mentioned this to anyone
before. She died a few weeks later.

F.G., Boston, 11 January 1888; drawn from his account as given in Sir Ernest
Bennett: *Apparitions and Haunted Houses*

Wandering into dreams
My loved and lost ones shake
My cool agnostic ways.
He: 'Look how I see again.'
'Let's take that ferny walk
We promised ourselves,' she says.

Then from the battleground
My brother saunters in
Unscarred by fear or flame.

'How's that for a dare?' he laughs,
Almost as though war's waste
Were a mad schoolboy game.

Unnerving presences!
In the heart-thumping dark
Waking, I'm called to choose.
Bold memory? Or a glimpse
Of some bright meeting-place,
Religion's good news?

As first light edges round
Curtains still closely drawn
I drowse between world and wraith:
Dawn-stirrings, a clamant bird,
And those voices that'll baffle my day
Like a kind of faith.

J. C. HALL, 'A Kind of Faith', 1985

The Apparition of the Ghost of Major George Sydenham, *to Captain* William Dyke, *taken out of a Letter of Mr* James Douch *of* Mongton, *to Mr* Jos. Glanvill.

. . . I have it from the Worthy and Learned Dr *Tho. Dyke*, a near Kinsman of the Captain's, thus: Shortly after the Major's Death, the Doctor was desired to come to the House, to take care of a Child that was there sick, and in his way thither he called on the Captain, who was very willing to wait on him to the Place, because he must, as he said, have gone thither that Night, though he had not met with so encouraging an Opportunity. After their arrival there at the House, and the Civility of the People shewn them in that Entertainment, they were seasonably conducted to their Lodging, which they desired might be together in the same Bed; Where after they had lain a while, the Captain knockt and bids the Servant bring him two of the largest and biggest Candles lighted that he could get. Whereupon the Doctor enquires what he meant by this? The Captain answers, you know, Cousin, what Disputes my Major and I have had touching the Being of a God, and the Immortality of the Soul. In which Points, we could never yet be resolved, though we so much fought for, and desired it. And therefore it was at length fully agreed between us, That he of us that dyed first, should the third Night after his Funeral, between the Hours of Twelve and One, come to the little House that is here in the Garden, and there give a full Account to the Surviver touching these Matters, who should be sure to be present there at the set time, and so receive a full Satisfaction. And this, says the Captain, is the very Night, and I am come on Purpose to fulfil my Promise. The Doctor disswaded him, minding him of the Danger of following those strange Counsels, for which we could have no Warrant, and that the Devil might, by some cunning Device, make such an Advantage of this rash Attempt, as might work his utter Ruine. The Captain replies, that he had solemnly engaged and that Nothing should discourage him . . . To that Purpose he sets his Watch by him, and as soon as he perceived by it, that it was half an hour past Eleven, he rises, and taking a Candle in each Hand, goes out by a back Door, of which he had before gotten the Key, and walks to the Garden-house, where he continued two Hours and an half, and at his Return declared that he neither saw nor heard any thing more than what was usual. But I know, said he, that my Major would surely have come, had he been able.

About six Weeks after the Captain rides to *Eaton*, to place his Son a Scholar there when the Doctor went thither with him. They lodged there at an Inn, the Sign was the *Christopher*, and tarried two or three Nights, not lying together now as before at *Dulverton*, but in two several Chambers. The Morning before they went thence, the Captain stayed in his Chamber longer than he was wont to do before he called upon the Doctor. At length he comes into the Doctor's Chamber, but in a Visage and Form much differing from himself, with his Hair and Eyes staring, and his whole Body shaking and trembling. Whereat the Doctor wondring, presently demanded, What is the Matter, Cousin Captain? The Captain replies, I have seen my Major. At which the Doctor seeming to smile, the Captain immediately confirms it, saying, if ever I saw him in my Life I saw him but now. And then he related to the Doctor what had passed, thus: This Morning after it was light, some one comes to my Beds side, and suddenly drawing back the Curtains, calls *Cap. Cap.* (which was the Term of Familiarity that the Major used to call the Captain by) to whom I replied, What my Major? to which he returns, I could not come at the Time appointed, but I am now come to tell you, *That there is a God, and a very Just and Terrible one, and if You do not turn over a New Leaf* (the very Expression as is by the Doctor punctually remembred) *You will find it so.* (The Captain proceeded) On the Table by, there lay a Sword, which the Major had formerly given me. Now after the Apparition had walked a Turn or two about the Chamber, he took up the Sword, drew it out, and finding it not so Clean and Bright as it ought, *Cap. Cap.* says he, *this Sword did not use to be kept after this Manner, when it was mine.* After which Words he suddenly disappeared.

In Glanvill: *Saducismus Triumphatus*

Lord Byron used sometimes to mention a strange story, which the commander of the packet, Captain Kidd, related to him on the passage [between Falmouth and Lisbon, in July 1809]. This officer stated that, being asleep one night in his berth, he was awakened by the pressure of something heavy on his limbs, and, there being a faint light in the room, could see, as he thought, distinctly, the figure of his brother, who was at that time in the naval service in the East Indies, dressed in his uniform, and stretched across the bed. Concluding it to be an illusion of the senses, he shut his eyes and made an effort to sleep. But still the same pressure continued, and still, as often as he ventured to take another look, he saw the figure lying across him in the same position. To add to the wonder, on putting his hand forth to touch this form, he found the uniform, in which it appeared to be dressed, dripping wet. On the entrance of one of his brother officers, to whom he called out in alarm, the apparition vanished; but in a few months after he received the startling intelligence that on that night his brother had been drowned in the Indian seas. Of the supernatural character of this appearance, Captain Kidd himself did not appear to have the slightest doubt.

THOMAS MOORE, *Letters and Journals of Lord Byron*, 1830

We were lying off Victoria [Cameroons]. I had gone down to my cabin thinking to write some letters. I drew aside the door curtain and stepped inside and to my amazement I saw Wilfred sitting in my chair. I felt shock run through me with appalling force and with it I could feel the blood draining away from my face. I did not rush towards him but walked jerkily into the cabin—all my limbs stiff and slow to respond. I did not sit down but looking at him I spoke quietly: 'Wilfred, how did you get here?' He did not rise and I saw that he was involuntarily immobile, but his eyes which had never left mine were alive with the familiar look of trying to make me understand; when I spoke his whole face broke into his sweetest and most endearing dark smile. I felt no fear—I had not when I first drew my door curtain and saw him there; only exquisite mental pleasure at thus beholding him. All I was conscious of was a sensation of enormous shock and profound astonishment that he should be here in my cabin. I spoke again. 'Wilfred dear, how can you be here, it's just not possible . . .' But still he did not speak but only smiled his most gentle smile. This not speaking did not now as it had done at first seem strange or even unnatural; it was not only in some inexplicable way perfectly natural but radiated a quality which made his presence with me undeniably right and in no way out of the ordinary. I loved having him there: I could not, and did not want to try to understand how he had got there. I was content to accept him, that he was here with me was sufficient. I could not question anything, the meeting in itself was complete and strangely perfect. He was in uniform and I remember thinking how out of place the khaki looked amongst the cabin furnishings. With this thought I must have turned my eyes away from him; when I looked back my cabin chair was empty . . .

I felt the blood run slowly back to my face and looseness into my limbs and with these an overpowering sense of emptiness and loss . . . I wondered if I had been dreaming but looking down I saw that I was still standing. Suddenly I felt terribly tired and moving to my bunk I lay down; instantly I went into a deep oblivious sleep. When I woke up I knew with absolute certainty that Wilfred was dead.

> HAROLD OWEN, *Journey from Obscurity*, Vol. III, 1965; Wilfred, Harold's brother, had been killed on the Western Front several weeks earlier

Sorley's relationships and attempts to communicate did not end with his death at the battle of Loos on 13 October—at least according to one of his friends. There is a curious story related by A. A. Milne in 'Land and Water' (5 December 1918), which Milne believed to be true. It concerned Sorley's friend, Walter Ogilvie Field, who had been in Sorley's house, C1, at Marlborough. Field had left school two years before Sorley for Trinity College, Oxford. His degree was interrupted by the war, which he entered at the outset. Field, who was described by a contemporary as 'eccentric, voluble and lovable', had an equally odd appearance. Tall and thin, he talked in a high-pitched voice and walked with his head well back in an effort to balance a pair of pince-nez on a nose manifestly unsuited to them. To crown his oddity in the eyes of the world, he had also acquired an interest in spiritualism . . .

Shortly after Sorley's death in October 1915, while Field was home on leave, he had called on the Sorley family and been invited to choose a memento of his dead friend. He had chosen Sorley's stick. According to Field, during the following night Sorley had talked to him and told him how glad he was that Field had his stick. 'That stick will do great things for you,' he said; 'it will save the lives of many of your battalion.' During his remaining four days' leave, Field told everybody he knew in London of this remarkable communication with the dead. To the friends who saw him off, his last remark was: 'Look out for news of the old stick', waving it gleefully at them.

Two days later everyone in Field's battalion had heard that his new stick was going to save their lives and had frankly scoffed at him. However, Field soon had a chance to prove his conviction.

The battalion, which was involved in a new offensive, was being held up by a German machine-gunner a hundred and fifty yards from their line. The company commander was at his wits' end, and a number of men had already been killed by him, when Field, tucking Sorley's stick securely under his left arm, and adjusting his pince-nez with his right, strolled serenely towards the machine-gunner. He carried no revolver, his steel helmet was on the back of his head, but for some inexplicable reason he was not hit. Once he reached his goal, he withdrew the stick from the crook of his left arm and, in a friendly way, hit the machine-gunner over the head with it. The German collapsed and Field dragged him back to the British trench by his coat collar. 'Well,' he said when he reached the company commander, 'and what about the jolly old stick *now*?' Field firmly believed that Sorley's stick had not only saved the lives of many men that day but that it had also brought him unscathed through the entire war.

JEAN MOORCROFT WILSON, introduction to *The Collected Letters of Charles Hamilton Sorley*, 1990

Of nearness to her sundered Things
The Soul has special times—
When Dimness—looks the Oddity—
Distinctness—easy—seems—

The Shapes we buried, dwell about,
Familiar, in the Rooms—
Untarnished by the Sepulchre,
The Mouldering Playmate comes—

In just the Jacket that he wore—
Long buttoned in the Mould
Since we—old mornings, Children—played—
Divided—by a world—

The Grave yields back her Robberies—
The Years, our pilfered Things—
Bright Knots of Apparitions
Salute us, with their wings—

As we—it were—that perished—
Themself—had just remained till we rejoin them—
And 'twas they, and not ourself
That mourned.

EMILY DICKINSON, 'Of nearness to her sundered Things'

MAGIC AND MAGICIANS, POSSESSION AND EXORCISM, SPELLS

In its beginnings science was barely to be distinguished from magic; what it involved was an arcane search for knowledge that might well be forbidden: any attempt at a cure for sickness could be seen as presumptuous interference with the will of God, who, if he had intended us always to be well, would never have created disease. Even now we say of a medicine (and of other things) that 'it worked like magic'; not that it worked like science. The spirits invoked by Dr Dee in a passage which follows convey medical and dietary advice ('beware of raw fruit'), and also hold out large promises—'unto him that judgeth truly, what secret is hidden?'—of a Faustian kind, though wrapped in pious-sounding language.

'If magic is to be defined as the employment of ineffective techniques to allay anxiety when effective ones are not available,' Keith Thomas has written, 'then we must recognize that no society will ever be free from it.' Most of us have our innocuous forms of protective magic, often called superstitions: touching wood, crossing fingers, counting magpies, and such ritualistic compulsions as contriving to take a specific number of steps to arrive at a particular spot (in Dr Johnson's case, to reach a door by what Boswell called a 'sort of magical movement'). Such practices do for some people allay whatever anxieties they are associated with, and are comparable to the actions in which, as A. E. Waite says concerning the ritual observances attached to magic, 'an inherent virtue was supposed to reside'.

In his lively, irreverent essay on devils, excerpts from which are printed in a later section, Shelley characterizes thus the Gadarene swine of St Luke, chapter 8: 'These were a set of hypochondriacal and high-minded swine, very unlike any others of which we have authentic record; they disdained to live, if they must live in so intimate a society with Devils, as that which was imposed on them, and the pig-drivers were no doubt confounded by so heroical a resolution.' Shelley was not always so rational in his thinking or acting.

'I sometimes forget,' Yeats wrote to a friend in a tone of lordly astonishment, real or assumed, 'that the word "magic" which sounds so familiar to my ears has a very outlandish sound to other ears.'

~

An intending Magus shall be discreet and faithful; he shall never reveal what he has been told by a spirit. Daniel was commanded to set a seal on several matters; Paul was forbidden to reveal what he beheld in his ecstasy. The importance of this ordination cannot be exaggerated.

The ceremonial part of magic, with its direfully potent formulae and its excess of grotesque ritual observance, was accredited in the past with an absolute value. It will be seen that an inherent virtue was supposed to reside in certain words and acts—a principle which is at the basis of all superstitious observance. Now, the actual and demonstrable value of ceremonial magic is of two kinds. It produced an exaltation in the operator which developed the latent faculties of his interior being; and the atmospheric conditions required for success in all classes of mystical experiments were produced by its perfumes and incense. As human imagination is ever open to the same classes of impressions, and as modern psychology is equally dependent for success on atmospheric and other conditions, Ceremonial Magic should be as potent in its effect today as at any period of antiquity.

ARTHUR EDWARD WAITE, *The Occult Sciences*, 1891

You will remember that Albertus Magnus, after describing minutely the process by which spirits may be invoked and commanded, adds emphatically that the process will instruct and avail only to the few—that *a man must be born a magician!*—that is, born with a peculiar physical temperament, as a man is born a poet. Rarely are men in whose constitution lurks this occult power of the highest order of intellect—usually in the intellect there is some twist, perversity, or disease. But, on the other hand, they must possess, to an astonishing degree, the faculty to concentrate thought on a single object—the energetic faculty that we call *will*. Therefore, though their intellect be not sound, it is exceedingly forcible for the attainment of what it desires.

I will imagine such a person pre-eminently gifted with this constitution and its concomitant forces. I will place him in the loftier grades of society. I will suppose his desires emphatically those of the sensualist—he has, therefore, a strong love of life. He is an absolute egotist—his will is concentrated in himself—he has fierce passions—he knows no enduring, no holy affections, but he can covet eagerly what for the moment he desires—he can hate implacably what opposes itself to his objects—he can commit fearful crimes, yet feel small remorse—he resorts rather to curses upon others than to penitence for his misdeeds. Circumstances, to which his constitution guides him, lead him to a rare knowledge of the natural secrets which may serve his egotism. He is a close observer where his passions encourage observation, he is a minute calculator, not from love of truth, but where love of self sharpens his faculties—therefore he can be a man of science.

I suppose such a being, having by experience learned the power of his arts over others, trying what may be the power of will over his own frame, and studying all that in natural philosophy may increase that power. He loves life, he dreads death; he *wills to live on*. He cannot restore himself to youth, he cannot entirely stay the progress of death, he cannot make himself immortal in the flesh and blood; but he may arrest for a time so prolonged as to appear incredible, if I said it, that hardening of the parts which constitutes old age. A year may age him no more than an hour ages another. His intense will, scientifically trained into system, operates, in short, over the wear and tear of his own frame. He lives on. That he may not seem a portent and a miracle, he *dies* from time to time, seemingly, to certain persons. Having schemed the transfer of a wealth that suffices to his wants, he disappears from one corner of the world, and contrives that his obsequies shall be celebrated. He reappears at another corner of the world, where he resides undetected, and does not revisit the scenes of his former career till all who could remember his features are no more. He would be profoundly miserable if he had affections—he has none but for himself. No good man would accept his longevity, and to no men, good or bad, would he or could he communicate its true secret.

EDWARD GEORGE BULWER-LYTTON, from 'The Haunted and the Haunters', 1859

When thou art come into the land which the Lord thy God giveth thee, thou shalt not learn to do after the abominations of those nations.

There shall not be found among you any one that maketh his son or his daughter to pass through the fire, or that useth divination, or an observer of times [soothsayer], or an enchanter, or a witch,

Or a charmer, or a consulter with familiar spirits, or a wizard, or a necromancer.

For all that do these things are an abomination unto the Lord: and because of these abominations the Lord thy God doth drive them out from before thee.

Deuteronomy 18

Within the navel of this hideous wood,
Immured in cypress shades, a sorcerer dwells,
Of Bacchus and of Circe born, great Comus,
Deep skilled in all his mother's witcheries,
And here to every thirsty wanderer
By sly enticement gives his baneful cup,
With many murmurs mixed, whose pleasing poison
The visage quite transforms of him that drinks,
And the inglorious likeness of a beast
Fixes instead, unmoulding reason's mintage
Charactered in the face; this have I learnt
Tending my flocks hard by i' th' hilly crofts
That brow this bottom glade, whence night by night
He and his monstrous rout are heard to howl
Like stabled wolves, or tigers at their prey,
Doing abhorrèd rites to Hecate
In their obscurèd haunts of inmost bow'rs.
Yet have they many baits and guileful spells
T' inveigle and invite th' unwary sense
Of them that pass unweeting by the way.

JOHN MILTON, *Comus*, a masque presented in 1634

Whatever Cypselus had left undone, by killing and banishing, Periander [his son] completed. One day he stripped all the Corinthian women, on account of his own wife Melissa [whom he had killed]: for when he sent messengers to the Thesprotians on the river Acheron, to consult the oracle of the dead respecting a deposit made by a stranger, Melissa having appeared, said that she would neither make it known, nor tell in what place the deposit lay, because she was cold and naked; for that there was no use in the garments in which he had buried her, since they had not been burnt: and as a proof that she spoke truth, she added, that Periander had put his bread into a cold oven. When this answer was brought back to Periander, for the token was convincing to him, since he had lain with Melissa after her death, he immediately, on receiving the message, made proclamation that all the women of Corinth should repair to the temple of Juno. They accordingly went, as to a festival, dressed in their best attire; but he having privately introduced his guards, stripped them all alike, both the free women and attendants; and having collected them [their clothes] together in a pit, he invoked Melissa, and burnt them. When he had done this, and sent a second time, the phantom of Melissa told in what place she had laid the stranger's deposit.

HERODOTUS (*c*.480–*c*.425 BC), *History*; tr. Henry Cary

There lived in the City of Legions in our time a Welshman called Melerius, who, under the following circumstances, acquired the knowledge of future and occult events. Having on a certain night, namely that of Palm Sunday, met a damsel, whom he had long loved, in a pleasant and convenient place, while he was indulging in her embraces, suddenly, instead of a beautiful girl, he found in his arms a hairy, rough, and hideous creature, the sight of which deprived him of his senses, and he became mad. After remaining for many years in this condition, he was restored to health in the Church of St David's through the merits of the saints. But having always an extraordinary familiarity with unclean spirits by seeing them, talking with them, and calling each by his proper name, he was enabled through their assistance to foretell future events . . . The spirits appeared to him usually on foot, equipped as hunters, with horns suspended from their necks, and truly as hunters not of animals, but of souls. He particularly met them near monasteries and monastic cells; for where rebellion exists, there is the greatest need of armies and strength. He knew when anyone spoke falsely in his presence, for he saw the Devil, as it were, leaping and exulting on the tongue of the liar. If he looked on a book faultily or falsely written, or containing a false passage, although wholly illiterate he would point out the place with his finger. Being questioned how he could gain such knowledge, he said he was directed by the demon's finger at the place. In the same manner, entering into the dormitory of a monastery, he indicated the bed of any monk not sincerely devoted to religion . . . If the evil spirits oppressed him too much, the Gospel of St John was placed on his bosom, when, like birds, they immediately vanished; but when the book was removed, and the History of the Britons by Geoffrey Arthur was substituted in its place, they instantly reappeared in greater numbers, and remained a longer time than usual on his body and on the book.

> GIRALDUS CAMBRENSIS (*c.*1146–*c.*1220), *The Itinerary of Wales*; tr. Sir Richard Colt Hoare. Geoffrey of Monmouth's *History* was commonly regarded as unreliable; it proved a rich source for poets and dramatists

The necromancer . . . wished me to bring with me a little boy of pure virginity. I chose one of my shop-lads, who was about twelve years old, and invited Vincenzio Romoli again; and we also took a certain Agnolino Gaddi, who was a very intimate friend of both . . . Now the necromancer began to utter those awful invocations, calling by name on multitudes of demons who are captains of their legions, and these he summoned by the virtue and potency of God, the Uncreated, Living, and Eternal, in phrases of the Hebrew, and also of the Greek and Latin tongues; insomuch that in a short space of time the whole Coliseum was full of a hundredfold as many as had appeared upon the first occasion. Vincenzio Romoli, together with Agnolino, tended the fire and heaped on quantities of precious perfumes. At the advice of the necromancer, I again demanded to be reunited with Angelica. The sorcerer turned to me and said: 'Hear you what they have replied; that in the space of one month you will be where she is?' Then once again he prayed me to stand firm by him, because the legions were a thousandfold more than he had summoned, and were the most dangerous of all the denizens of hell; and now that they had settled what I asked, it behoved us to be civil to them and dismiss them gently. On the other side, the boy, who was beneath the pentacle, shrieked out in terror that a million of the fiercest men were swarming round and threatening us. He said, moreover, that four huge giants had appeared, who were striving to force their way inside the circle . . .

The necromancer appealed for my support, entreating me to stand firm by him, and to have asafoetida flung upon the coals . . . I looked at Agnolino Gaddi, whose eyes were starting from their sockets in his terror, and who was more than half dead, and said to him: 'Agnolo, in time and place like this we must not yield to fright, but do the utmost to bestir ourselves; therefore, up at once, and fling a handful of that asafoetida upon the fire.' Agnolo, at the moment when he moved to do this, let fly such a volley from his breech, that it was far more effectual than the asafoetida. The boy, roused by that great stench and noise, lifted his face a little, and hearing me laugh, he plucked up courage, and said the devils were taking to flight tempestuously. So we abode thus until the matin-bells began to sound. Then the boy told us again that but few remained, and those were at a distance. When the necromancer had concluded his ceremonies, he put off his wizard's robe, and packed up a great bundle of books which he had brought with him; then, all together, we issued with him from the circle, huddling as close as we could to one another, especially the boy, who had got into the middle, and taken the necromancer by his gown and me by the cloak . . . The necromancer assured me that, often as he had entered magic circles, he had never met with such a serious affair as this . . . Engaged in this conversation, we reached our homes, and each one of us dreamed all that night of devils.

Benvenuto Cellini (1500–71), Life; tr. John Addington Symonds

Dr Dee consults the spirits
March 2, 1584

Madimi. I answer your inward man. I am come again.

Edward Kelley. She is bigger than she was.

Mad. I am a little grown.

John Dee. As concerning a medicine for my Ague, I would gladly . . . And as concerning the wife of my dear friend, the Lor . . .

Mad. I pray you, bear with me at this time: I am as willing to answer you (when light cometh again) as you to ask me. You may consider of many things, I can answer them briefly. Such blessing as my Mother bestoweth on me, such I give you.

E. K. She smileth.

J. D. God grant that his good Creatures may smile on me.

Mad. . . . When you know me well, you will find, I have been very charitable.

E. K. She goeth away naked; her body being besprent with blood; at the least that side of her toward [me].

J. D. Laudetur Deus Trinus & unus, nunc & in sempiterna seculorum secula. Amen . . .

Mad. Thus sayeth my Mother. Beware of wilde hony, and raw fruit: The one clarified, the other ripened may become good. Those that know not wine become drunken, but to such as know it, it bringeth health. Even so, this Doctrine. For, unto him that it is tasted, being ripe, or . . . or becometh comfort, and the Key of a pr . . . But unto him that tasteth it wildly, and . . . Worketh sorrow. Your knowledge is not *to have*, but to *learn to* . . . So that you may be, both having and learned. Small are the Treasures of this world, in respect of the wisdom that judgeth NATURE. For unto him that judgeth truely, what secret is hidden? Those that seek the world shall be contemned of it: But he that flieth from her, shall use her as a slave, or as the second mother doth her daughter. Notwithstanding, of my self, I will be more appliable unto you, then you shall be followers of me. For, for that *cause am I become childish*. Therefore cease: He is truely wise, that sayeth, God knoweth at all times what we have need of. Be not tempters. Be patient . . .

E. K. Now she is gone, as a mighty tall woman.

October 2, 1584

Dee. I beseech you for God his sake, & *per viscera misericordiae Altissimi*, that you would declare unto us a certain remedy of my wife her disease, &c.

Gabriel. When thy wife was a milkie substance, growing by the perfection of the place and *influence radical, (which onely, is the gift of the Sun)* then, was not the Matrix, or bag of Nature (wherein she encreased) perfect, or of sufficient *retention*: By reason of a feaver going before the conception: So that, the Angelical administration, generally containing, the vessel of life, for the proportion of the world, entred by force of their Order immediately, before the inward parts, were established in their nutriment and proportion.

Which is the cause, that the second vessel, and lowest of nature (for, your terms I must use) is so thin, and tyed short, that it is not able to keep in, or retain, the simile and quidditie of her own substantial being *and feed*.

Wherefore, when the rest of her digestions (according to her age and natural strength) fulfil their offices, by degree to be received into *that receptacle*; then, doth the force of nature quail: and by the subtilty of the principle, or *matter ejected* . . . the guts and passages, are offended and scalded with an intemperate heat . . .

Behold now, being *faetive*, and the force of heat drawn to the nutriment of the Creature; moreover the other part Active compelled into a nearer place, by the *impediment of imagination*, bringeth great danger now, by reason that Nature is become very weak, and not able to make excremental expulsion.

But dost thou think that there is a remedy to this disease?

Dee. Yea verily, through the wisdom and mercies of the Highest.

Gab. I have taught the disease; I will go and see if there be a remedy . . . Come again after Diner.

Dee. We had been sent for to diner, twice or thrice before. So we went. *Misericordiae Dei sint super nos. Amen* . . .

Gab. Take pure wheat, a pinte: one Pheasant-Cock alive, an eleven ounces of Masculine Amber (which is the white Amber) an ounce and a quarter of Turpentine.

Dee. Of washed Turpentine?

Gab. Turpentine that is washed loseth his vertue. Break the Cock in pieces with a pestel, (his feathers pluckt off) pound the Amber small. Put all this into a gallon of red wine.

Dee. May we take the red wine of this Country?

Gab. I. Distill them, with a fire of the second heat. Still it again the second time, (the feces being cast away) And adde something more to the fire, so that it be a quarter toward the third. Let her fast forty hours from meat: And let her divide the Medicine into three parts. The first part, let her drink (being milk-warm) by little and little. The second part, let her make a sawce of, for five or six meales. The last part, let her use in Abscondita: *And she shall have health.*

Dee. I beseech you, in how many dayes compass would you have this to be done?

Gab. It is no question: the necessity of the thing teacheth.

Dee. As concerning the Infant, what state is it in?

Gab. Shut thy mouth: Seek not.

Dee. I am contented. As concerning a Pheasant-Cock, I know not how or where to get it.

Gab. All the creatures of the world, else, help not. I have taught, take you care.

> *A True and Faithful Relation of Dr John Dee and Some Spirits.* In his preface to the first printing of 1659 M. Casaubon states that the original manuscript, written by Dr Dee, had long been buried in the earth before a copy was made by hand. Madimi was a spirit in the shape of 'a pretty girle', and Gabriel was identified as 'the man of God' who appeared to Daniel (8: 16). Dee (1527–1608) was a mathematician, geographer, alchemist, and astrologer; Edward Kelley: his assistant

John Hume. Jesu preserve your royal Majesty!

Duchess of Gloucester. What say'st thou? Majesty! I am but Grace.

Hume. But, by the grace of God, and Hume's advice,
Your Grace's title shall be multiplied.

Duch. What say'st thou, man? Hast thou as yet conferr'd
With Margery Jourdain, the witch of Eie,
With Bolingbroke, the cunning conjurer,
And will they undertake to do me good?

Hume. This they have promis'd me, to show your Highness
A spirit rais'd from depth of under ground,
That shall make answer to such questions
As by your Grace shall be propounded him.

Hume. Come, my masters; the Duchess, I tell you, expects performance of your promises.

Bolingbroke. Master Hume, we are therefore provided: will her ladyship behold
and hear our exorcisms?

Hume. Ay, what else? Fear you not her courage.

Boling. I have heard her reported to be a woman of an invincible spirit: but it
shall be convenient, Master Hume, that you be by her aloft, while we be
busy below; and so, I pray you, go, in God's name, and leave us. Mother
Jourdain, be you prostrate, and grovel on the earth; and let us to our work.

Duch. Well said, my masters; and welcome all. To this gear, the sooner the
better.

Boling. Patience, good lady; wizards know their times:

Deep night, dark night, the silent of the night,

The time of night when Troy was set on fire,

The time when screech-owls cry, and ban-dogs howl,

And spirits walk, and ghosts break up their graves;

That time best fits the work we have in hand.

Madam, sit you, and fear not: whom we raise

We will make fast within a hallow'd verge.

> *Here do the ceremonies belonging, and make the circle; Bolingbroke reads,*
> Conjuro te, *&c. It thunders and lightens terribly; then the Spirit riseth.*

Spirit. Adsum.

Margery Jourdain. Asnath!

By the eternal God, whose name and power

Thou tremblest at, answer that I shall ask;

For till thou speak thou shalt not pass from hence.

Spir. Ask what thou wilt. That I had said and done!

Boling. [*Reads*] 'First, of the King, what shall of him become?'

Spir. The duke yet lives that Henry shall depose;

But him outlive, and die a violent death.

Boling. 'Tell me what fate awaits the Duke of Suffolk.'

Spir. By water shall he die and take his end.

Boling. 'What shall betide the Duke of Somerset?'

Spir. Let him shun castles:

Safer shall he be upon the sandy plains

Than where castles mounted stand.

Have done, for more I hardly can endure.

Boling. Descend to darkness and the burning lake:

False fiend, avoid!

> *Thunder and lightning. Exit Spirit.*

> SHAKESPEARE, *2 Henry VI, c.*1590. Eleanor Cobham, Duchess of Gloucester,
> was charged in 1441 with conspiring to bring about the death of Henry VI.

She had employed the clerk Bolingbroke, with others, to look into the future for her. This was interpreted as an enquiry into the length of the King's life and thus a conspiracy to destroy him (in favour of her husband's succeeding him). Treason was denied; but Bolingbroke was hanged, drawn, and quartered, and Margery Jourdemayne, known as the Witch of Eye (the Manor of Eye-next-Westminster), was burnt at Smithfield. The Duchess spent the rest of her life in prison. In Shakespeare's play, John Hume is a priest

The Master, in a sneering manner, requested that the great enchanter might have his own way ... The room was darkened; the friar went into a small alcove, and, by the help of a magic lanthorn, a thing never before seen in Scotland, he raised up a tremendous and horrid figure on the wall. It was of gigantic size; its eyes, lips, and paws moved; and its body was thrown into various contortions.

All were in breathless silence on the appearance of this extraordinary shade; but among the darkling group there was distinctly heard one whose breathing was frequently cut short, as if something had been choking him, or seizing him by the throat.

After the apparition had gone through its various evolutions, all apparently at the further end of the apartment, it fixed its eyes, clenched its teeth, and, stretching forth its claws, it appeared to make a spring forward at the party.

'Aih! L——d be here!' cried Charlie in a trumpet voice, and threw himself flat down behind the rest. Hearing that some of them laughed at the fright he had got, he ventured to speak and expostulate a little; but no curiosity could induce him to raise his face from the floor, or open his eyes again while the friar's exhibition continued ...

The friar went on with his phantasmagoria. The figure, after giving a shiver or two, was parted into three, all of the same form and size, but all making different motions, and different contortions of feature. The three were afterwards parted into six, which, among other grotesque feats, danced a reel, and, on running thro' it, every one threw itself heels-over-head. The group of onlookers laughed outright at this, notwithstanding their astonishment, and called to Charlie to look. But he would not move his face from the earth ...

When the friar had concluded this feat, he put out his small lanthorn, took the machinery out of it, concealing it beneath his ample frock, and again opened all the windows ...

The friar's associates looked at the lanthorn, examining it with curious eyes, but perceived nothing about it which could in any way account for the apparition they had seen. Master Michael Scott did not deign to ask a sight of it, but paced over the floor in sullen and thoughtful mood. The seneschal stood fixed to the spot on which he had witnessed the phenomenon, with his heavy unmoving eyes turned towards his master. He seemed dubious whether he was vanquished or not. The Master at length spoke, addressing the friar:

'I hope, right worshipful Primate, this is not the extent of your knowledge and power in the sublime art of divination? The whole is only a delusion—a shadow—a phantom, calculated to astonish women or children. I acknowledge it to be ingenious; still it is nothing. You multiplied your shadows, turning three into six; now, if I turn three men into six living, breathing, substantial beings, will you acknowledge yourself outdone?'

'Certes, I will,' said the friar.

'Away, then, with deception,' said the Master: 'What I do, I do in the open eye of day.—Stand forth three of you.'

'Master Michael Scott, I'll tell you what it is,' said Charlie, 'I solemnly protest against being parted into twa.'

'You shall neither suffer nor feel the least inconvenience by the change, brave yeoman,' said the Master; 'therefore be not afraid, but stand forth.'

Charlie hung his head to one side in a deep reverie, till at length his countenance lightened up by degrees, his features opening into a broad smile.

'I'll tell you what it is, Sir Knight,' said he, 'if you will assure me that baith o' us shall be as stout and as wight chaps as I am mysel e'en now, gude faith, I dinna care though ye mak me into twa, for my master the warden's sake. If you could double an army that gate, it wad be a great matter . . . Nane o' your cutting and cleaving, however, Sir Knight. Nane o' your imps wi' their langkail gully knives again.'

Charlie stepped up the floor, and took his stand with his back at the wall, to await doggedly this multiplication of himself. Tam soon joined him: but there was a hard contest between Gibbie and the poet, both of whom were rather personal cowards, and both alike averse to such experiments. The former was at length obliged to yield . . .

Michael stamped thrice with his heel, and spoke some words in an unknown tongue, in a low muttering tone; but some of them heard the sounds of Prig, Prim, and Pricker. There was a momentary confusion in the apartment. A darkening haze flashed over it, and blinded the eyes of men for a short space; the floor gave a shake, as if it had sunk down a little,—and there stood two of each of the three friends, so completely alike that no one knew who was who.

No scene could be more truly ludicrous than the one which now ensued; each man turned to his prototype, and the looks of confusion and astonishment in both being the same, the beholders were seized with irrepressible laughter.

Charlie felt his legs, thighs, and ribs, if they remained the same as before. The other boardly personage in the same shape followed his example, and added, 'Gude faith, the like o' this I saw never!'

'You may weel say't,' said the other; 'But let me see if you can draw that lang sword as weel an' as cleverly as I can do.'

'Gude Lord, hear til him!' said the first: 'He's speaking as he were the true Charlie Scott himsel! Speak ye, friend: Were you me before this! That is, did you ride with the warden over the border?'

'I am sure if you were there, I never saw you before,' said the second speaker; 'But I dinna ken what I am saying; for the truth is I dinna comprehend this.'

With that they again gazed at each other, and looked over their shoulders, as if they would not have cared to have fled from one another's presence.

With every pair the scene was much the same. Tam was so much astonished that he turned to his second self, cowered down, leaning his hands upon his knees, and made a staunch point at him. The other took precisely the same posture, so that their long noses almost met . . .

'Friend, I canna say but ye're very like me,' said Gibbie to his partner; 'But, though nane o' us be great beauties, ye look rather the warst o' the twae.'

'It brings me a-mind o' a story I hae heard my mother tell,' said the other, 'of a lady and her twa Blackamores'—

'What the deil, man!' exclaimed the first; 'Did your mother tell that story too?'

'Ay; wha else but she tauld it? I say my mother, auld Effy Blakely of the Peatstacknowe.'

'Eh?—She your mother? It is gayan queer if we be baith ane after a'! for I never had a billy [brother].'

'Primate of Douay, so celebrated for thy mighty enchantments, how thinkest thou of this?' said the Master.

'That thou hast done what no man could have done beside,' said the friar; 'and that thy power even surpasseth that of the magicians of Egypt, and of those of the countries in the lands of the east. But in one thing my power is even as thy power. Dost thou know that I could have prevented thy charm, and put a period to thy enchantment at my will and pleasure?'

'It is not the power of prevention that we are trying,' said the Master. 'Suffer my servants to do their work, as I shall suffer thine, and we shall then see who are most punctually obeyed, and who shall perform the greatest works. Only, if I prevail in all things, you will surely have the generosity to acknowledge that my master is greater than thine?'

'Wo be unto me if such a confession proceed out of my lips!' said the friar:

'Who can be greater than he who builded the stories of heaven, and laid the foundations of this earth below; who lighted up the sun, sending him abroad in brightness and in glory, and placed the moon and the stars in the firmament on high? Who is greater than he who hath made the mountains to stand, the seas to roll, and the winds to blow? who hath not only made the souls of men, but all the spirits of the upper and nether world—'

'Peace, thou maniac!' cried the Master, interrupting the friar, in a voice that made him leap from the floor: 'Comest thou here to babble treason against the master whom I serve, and the mighty spirits with whom I am in league? Do what thou canst do, and cease from speaking evil of dignities. What knowest thou of the principalities and powers that inhabit and rule over the various regions of the universe? No more than the mole that grovelleth beneath the sward.—What further canst thou do in proof of thy profound art?'

'Behold with thine eyes, O thou who accountest thyself the greatest among the children of men!' said the friar, with a waggish air; 'that I will but speak the word, and the mountains shall be rent asunder, and the tops of the everlasting hills stand in opposition.'

> JAMES HOGG, *The Three Perils of Man: War, Women and Witchcraft*, 1822.
> A contest between Michael Scott, 13th-century Scottish scholar, alchemist, astronomer, and reputed magician, and (the friar) Roger Bacon, philosopher and scientist, popularly considered a necromancer because of his interest in chemistry and alchemy

Fryer Bacon reading one day of the many Conquests of England, bethought himselfe how he might keepe it hereafter from the like Conquests, and to make himselfe famous hereafter to all posterities: This (after great study) he found could be no way so well done as one; which was to make a head of Brasse, and if he could make this head to speake (and heare it when it speakes) then might he be able to wall all England about with Brasse. To this purpose he got one Fryer Bungey to assist him, who was a great Schollar and a magician, (but not to be compared with Fryer Bacon): These two with great study and paines so framed a head of Brasse, that in the inward parts thereof there was all things (like as is in a naturall mans head): this being done, they were as farre from perfection of the worke as they were before, for they knew not how to give those parts that they had made motion, without which it was impossible that it should speake: Many bookes they read, yet could not finde out any hope of what they sought, so that at the last they concluded to raise a spirit, and to know of him that which they could not attaine to by their owne studies. To do this they prepared all things ready and went one evening to a wood thereby, and after many ceremonies used, they spake the words of conjuration, which the Devill straight obeyed and appeared unto them, asking what they would? Know, said Fryer Bacon, that we have made an artificiall head of Brasse, which we would have to speake, to the furtherance of which we have raised thee; and being raised, we will here keepe thee, unlesse thou tell to us the way and manner how to make this Head to speak. The Devill told him that he had not that power of himselfe: beginner of lyes (said Fryer Bacon) I know that thou dost dissemble, and therefore tell it us quickly, or else we will here bind thee to remaine during our pleasures. At these threatnings the Devill consented to doe it, and told them, that with a continuall fume of the six hotest Simples it should have motion, and in one moneth space speake, the Time of the moneth or day he knew not; also he told them, that if they heard it not before it had done speaking, all their labour should be lost: they, being satisfied, licensed the Spirit for to depart.

Then went these two learned Fryers home againe, and prepared the Simples ready, and made the fume, and with continuall watching attended when this Brasen head would speake: thus watched they for three weekes without any rest, so that they were so weary and sleepy, that they could not any longer retaine from rest: then called Fryer Bacon his man Miles and . . . intreated Miles that he would watch whilest that they sleep, and call them if the Head speak . . . Miles, to keepe him from sleeping, got a Tabor and Pipe, and being merry disposed, sung this Song to a Northren tune . . .

With his owne Musicke, and such songs as these spent he his time, and kept from sleeping; at last, after some noyse the Head spake these two words, *Time is*. Miles hearing it to speake no more, thought his Master would be angry if he waked him for that, and therefore he let them both sleepe, and began to mocke the Head in this manner: Thou Brazen-faced Head, hath my Master tooke all this paines about thee, and now dost thou requite him with two words . . . if thou can speake no wiser, they shall sleepe till doomes day for me . . .

After halfe an hour had passed, the Head did speake againe, two words, which were these: *Time was*. Miles respected these words as little as he did the former, and would not wake them, but still scoffed at the Brasen head, that it had learned no better words, and had such a Tutor as his Master . . . Thus Miles talked and sung till another halfe hour was gone, then the Brazen-head spake againe these words: *Time is past*: and therewith fell downe, and presently followed a terrible noyse, with strange flashes of fire, so that Miles was halfe dead with feare: at this noyse the two Fryers awakened, and wondred to see the whole roome so full of smoake, but that having vanished, they might perceive the Brazen-head broken and lying on the ground: at this sight they grieved, and called Miles to know how this came. Miles halfe dead with feare, said that it fell downe of it selfe, and that with the noyse and fire that followed he was almost frighted out of his wits: Fryer Bacon asked him if he did not speake? Yes (quoth Miles) it spake, but to no purpose. I'll have a Parret speake better in that time that you have beene teaching this Brazen-head. Out on thee villaine (said Fryer Bacon) thou hast undone us both, hadst thou but called us when it did speake, all England had bin walled round about with Brasse, to its glory and our eternall fames . . . Thus that great worke of these learned Fryers was overthrown (to their great griefes) by this simple fellow.

ANON., *The Famous History of Fryer Bacon*, late 16th-century tale; earliest extant printing 1627

Durtal looked at the astrologer. His head was still shaped like a sugar loaf, his hair a dirty brown, the colour of hydroquinone and ipeca powder, his eyes were those of a frightened bird, his fingers beringed and enormous, his manner solemn and ingratiating, his voice sacerdotal. But his complexion had become almost fresh, his skin smooth, and his eyes clearer and brighter, since his return from Lyon.

Durtal congratulated him on the success of the cure.

—It was high time for me to resort to Dr Johannès' good care, for I was very low. Since I do not possess the gift of clairvoyance and did not know of any extra-lucid cataleptic who might inform me of Canon Docre's clandestine preparations, I could not avail myself of the law of countersigns and the reverse stroke.

—But, des Hermies asked, supposing that through the agency of a flying spirit you could have known of the priest's operations, how would you have foiled them?

—Well, when you know the time and place of the attack, the law of countersigns consists in forestalling it by running away from the house, which bewilders and repels the poison-bearer; or by announcing, half an hour in advance: Here I am, strike! The object of this last device is to expose the liquids to the air and thus paralyse the power of the assailant. In Magic, every action, once known, is lost. As for the reverse stroke, a warning is necessary if you are to turn the spells back on the one who is casting them before you are struck yourself.

So I was sure I would die. One day had passed since the spell was cast on me; two more days in Paris and I was dead.

—Why two days?

—Because anyone affected by the operation of Magic has only three days to seek protection. After this, the harm is very often incurable. Therefore, when Docre told me he was condemning me to death on his own authority, and when two hours later I began to feel very ill, I did not hesitate to pack my bag and leave for Lyon.

—And there? asked Durtal.

—There I saw Dr Johannès. I told him about Docre's threat and about my sickness. He simply answered: 'This priest knows how to clothe the most virulent poison in the most terrible sacrilege; the fight will be hard, but I shall defeat him.' And he called at once for a clairvoyant, a lady who lives in his house.

He put her to sleep, and on his orders she described the nature of the spell cast on me. She reconstructed the scene; she actually saw me being poisoned by the menstrual blood of a woman who had been fed with consecrated bread, stabbed through, and drugs cunningly measured and mixed into her food and drink. This sort of spell is so terrible that Dr Johannès is the only thaumaturge in France to dare attempt the cure.

Finally the Doctor told me: 'You can be cured only by an inviolable Power. There is no time to spare, we must at once turn to Melchizedek's sacrifice of glory.'

Then he set up an altar, made of a table, a wooden tabernacle in the shape of a little house topped with a cross, encircled under the pediment, like a clock face, by the round shape of the Tetragrammaton. Then he had the silver chalice, the unleavened bread, and the wine brought to him. He robed himself in his priestly habit, put on his finger the ring which had received the supreme benediction, and began to read the prayers of the sacrifice from a special missal.

Almost at once the clairvoyant cried: 'Here are the spirits invoked for the maleficence, who bore the poison on the orders of the master of incantations, the Canon Docre.'

As for me, I sat near the altar. Dr Johannès placed his left hand on my head and, stretching the other hand towards the sky, he begged the Archangel Michael to assist him. He adjured the glorious legions of the Swordsmen and the Invincibles to overpower and chain up the evil spirits.

I could feel some relief; the sensation of stifling which had tormented me in Paris was lifting.

Dr Johannès continued to read his prayers; then, when it was time for the prayer of warding off, he took my hand, placed it on the altar, and cried three times: 'Let the designs of the author of iniquity who worked the spell against you be destroyed; let any resumption by Satanic means be trodden underfoot;

let all attacks against you be made null and void; let all your enemy's maledictions be turned into benedictions from the highest of the eternal hills; let his potions of death be transmuted into ferments of life . . . and let the Archangels of Sentences and Punishments decide upon the fate of the miserable priest who put his faith in the works of Darkness and Evil!

As for you, you are freed. Heaven has cured you: let your heart give ardent thanks to the Living God and Christ Jesus in the name of the glorious Virgin Mary.'

Then he offered me the unleavened bread and the wine. I was indeed saved.

JORIS-KARL HUYSMANS, *Là-bas*, 1891

On the table in Mr Abney's study certain papers were found which explained the situation to Stephen Elliott when he was of an age to understand them. The most important sentences were as follows:

'It was a belief very strongly and generally held by the ancients—of whose wisdom in these matters I have had such experience as induces me to place confidence in their assertions—that by enacting certain processes, which to us moderns have something of a barbaric complexion, a very remarkable enlightenment of the spiritual faculties in man may be attained: that, for example, by absorbing the personalities of a certain number of his fellow creatures, an individual may gain a complete ascendancy over those orders of spiritual beings which control the elemental forces of our universe.

'It is recorded of Simon Magus that he was able to fly in the air, to become invisible, or to assume any form he pleased, by the agency of the soul of a boy whom, to use the libellous phrase employed by the author of the *Clementine Recognitions*, he had "murdered". I find it set down, moreover, with considerable detail in the writings of Hermes Trismegistus, that similar happy results may be produced by the absorption of the hearts of not less than three human beings below the age of twenty-one years. To the testing of the truth of this receipt I have devoted the greater part of the last twenty years, selecting as the *corpora vilia* of my experiment such persons as could conveniently be removed without occasioning a sensible gap in society. The first step I effected by the removal of one Phoebe Stanley, a girl of gypsy extraction, on March 24, 1792. The second, by the removal of a wandering Italian lad, named Giovanni Paoli, on the night of March 23, 1805. The final "victim"—to employ a word repugnant in the highest degree to my feelings—must be my cousin, Stephen Elliott. His day must be this March 24, 1812.

'The best means of effecting the required absorption is to remove the heart from the *living* subject, to reduce it to ashes, to mingle them with about a pint of some red wine, preferably port. The remains of the first two subjects, at least, it will be well to conceal: a disused bathroom or wine-cellar will be found convenient for such a purpose. Some annoyance may be experienced from the psychic portion of the subjects, which popular language dignifies with the name of ghosts. But the man of philosophic temperament—to whom alone the experiment is appropriate—will be little prone to attach importance to the feeble attempts of these beings to wreak their vengeance on him. I contemplate with the liveliest satisfaction the enlarged and emancipated existence which the experiment, if successful, will confer on me: not only placing me beyond the reach of human justice (so-called), but eliminating to a great extent the prospect of death itself.'

Mr Abney was found in his chair, his head thrown back, his face stamped with an expression of rage, fright, and mortal pain. In his left side was a terrible lacerated wound, exposing the heart. There was no blood on his hands, and a long knife that lay on the table was perfectly clean.

M. R. JAMES, from 'Lost Hearts', 1904

An unwholesome curiosity, an outburst of perverted affection, the result of my horrible loneliness, filled me with a passionate desire to try to re-establish contact with my wife and child, for I loved them both. How was I to do this now that legal proceedings for a divorce were in progress? Perhaps some extraordinary happening, a common misfortune, like being struck by lightning, involved in a fire or a flood . . . in a word, some catastrophe that might serve to reunite two hearts, the sort of thing that happens in novels, where enemies join hands by a sickbed. Of course, the very thing! An attack of illness. Small children are always falling ill for one reason or another. A mother's tender heart always exaggerates the danger: a telegram, and that would be that.

I was quite unversed even in the simplest forms of magic, but some fatal instinct whispered in my ear what I must do to the portrait of my beloved little daughter, the one person who was later to be my only consolation in a damnable existence.

In the spring . . . I had a letter from the children of my first marriage, telling me that they had been seriously ill and had had to go to hospital. When I compared the date they mentioned with the date of my experiment in bewitchment I was seized with horror. By playing with those mysterious powers out of pure folly I had given the reins to my evil desires, but they, guided by the hand of the Unseen, had struck at my own heart.

> AUGUST STRINDBERG, *Inferno*, 1897; tr. Mary Sandbach. In his introduction to the translation F. L. Lucas explains that, while Strindberg wished illness on his daughter Kerstin (by his second wife, Frida Uhl) in Austria, it was his children by his first wife Siri von Essen, in Finland, who fell ill: 'the telepathic rays got misdirected?'

The Samoans tell how two young wizards, passing a house where a chief lay very sick, saw a company of gods from the mountain sitting in the doorway. They were handing from one to another the soul of the dying chief. It was wrapped in a leaf, and had been passed from the gods inside the house to those sitting in the doorway. One of the gods handed the soul to one of the wizards, taking him for a god in the dark, for it was night. Then all the gods rose up and went away; but the wizard kept the chief's soul. In the morning some women went with a present of fine mats to fetch a famous physician. The wizards were sitting on the shore as the women passed, and they said to the women, 'Give us the mats and we will heal him.' So they went to the chief's house. He was very ill, his jaw hung down, and his end seemed near. But the wizards undid the leaf and let the soul into him again, and forthwith he brightened up and lived.

> SIR JAMES FRAZER, *The Golden Bough*, 1890 onwards

One day as Sir Francis Drake was playing at Kales [ninepins] on Plymouth Hoe he had news that a foreign fleet was sailing into the harbour. He finished his game and then took a hatchet and ordered a large block of wood to be brought to him. He chopped this up into small pieces and threw them into the sea with magic words. As they touched the water each one became a fire-ship and sailed against the foreign fleet so that it was utterly destroyed.

> MRS A. E. BRAY, *Traditions, Legends, Superstitions and Sketches of Devonshire on the Borders of the Tamar and the Tavy*, 1838

Rabbi Arié lived to the age of one hundred and fifty, in full vigour of body and spirit, and he was ninety when he undertook to build a golem.

To build a golem is in itself not an enterprise of great account, and many have attempted it. In fact, a golem is little more than a nothing: it is a portion of matter, or rather of chaos, enclosed in human or animal semblance; it is in short a simulacrum, and as such it is good for nothing—indeed it is something essentially suspect and to stay away from, for it is written that 'you shall not make graven images and shall not worship them'. The golden calf was a golem: so was Adam, and so are we . . .

Now, Arié was not a blasphemer, and had not set himself the task of creating a second Adam. He did not intend to build a man, but rather a *po'el*, or shall we say a worker, a strong, faithful servant and not too discerning: in short, what in his Czech language is called a robot.

So Rabbi Arié-Lion began his work with a serene spirit, in the cellar of his house on Broad Street: the clay was brought to him at night by two disciples, together with water from the Moldau, and coal to feed the fire in the kiln. Day by day, actually night by night, the golem was taking shape . . .

He was a giant, and his figure was human from the waist up. There is a reason for this too: the waist is the frontier, only above the waist is man made in God's image, whereas below it he is a beast . . . His arms were gnarled and strong as oak branches; his hands nervous and bony, Arié had patterned them on his own. The face was not truly human, but rather leonine, because anyone bringing succour must inspire fear and because Arié had wanted to sign his name . . .

At the decisive moment, when it became a matter of infusing into the servant's leonine skull the three principles of movement, which are the Nous, the Epithymia and the Thymos, Arié destroyed the letters of the first two and wrote on a parchment only those of the third; underneath he added, in large letters of fire, the symbols of God's ineffable name, rolled up the parchment and slipped it into a silver case. Thus the golem had no mind, but he had courage and strength, and the faculty of coming to life only when the case with the Name was slipped between his teeth.

Arié was not disappointed by his servant . . . For many years he was a valid defender of the Prague community against high-handed injustice and violence. Several exploits of his are told: how, all by himself, he barred the way to a platoon of Turkoman warriors who intended to force the White Gate and plunder the ghetto; how he thwarted the plans for a slaughter by capturing the true perpetrator of a murder that the emperor's henchmen tried to disguise as a ritual murder; how, again by himself, he saved the store of grain in the warehouse from a sudden and disastrous flood of the Moldau river.

Now there came a day (it was in fact a Friday) on which the rabbi had taken the golem into his own house . . . He assigned to him a pile of small chunks of wood to chop, lifted one of his arms and put the axe into his hand . . . He tarried so long that he did not notice that something was happening, indeed had already happened outside the window, in the air of Broad Street, in the hazy sky of Prague: the sun had set, the sabbath had begun.

When he did notice, it was too late. Arié tried in vain to stop his servant in order to extract the Name from his mouth: the golem eluded him, swept him away with hard arms, turned his back to him. The rabbi, who had never touched him before, came to know his inhuman weight, and a hardness like that of a rock: like a pendulum the golem swung back and forth in the small room and chopped wood on top of wood, so that the fragments sprayed all the way to the beams in the ceiling. Arié hoped and prayed that the golem's fury would cease when the pile of logs was finished; but at that point the giant bent over, creaking in all of his joints, picked up the hatchet, and with the hatchet he stormed away until dawn, shattering everything around him, the furniture, the drapes, the windows, the dividing walls, even the safe with the silver and the shelves of holy books.

Arié sought shelter under the staircase, and there he had the ease and time to meditate over a terrible truth: nothing brings one closer to madness than two contradictory orders. In the golem's stony brain was written, 'You shall faithfully serve your master: you shall obey him like a corpse'; but there was also written the entire Law of Moses, which had been transmitted to him with every letter of the message from which he had been born, because every letter of the Law contains all the Law. Thus in him was also written, 'You shall rest on the sabbath: you shall do no work whatsoever on it.' . . .

When Saturday's dawn shone through the broken windows and there was nothing left to break in the rabbi's house, the golem stopped as though exhausted. Arié approached him fearfully, he reached out a hesitant hand and extracted from his mouth the silver capsule that contained the Name.

The monster's eyes darkened and did not light up again. When evening came, and the sad sabbath was over, Arié tried in vain to call him back to life so that he would help him, with the orderly strength of the past, and tidy up his devastated home. The golem remained immobile and inert, similar by now in everything to a forbidden and hateful idol, an obscene man-beast of reddish clay chipped here and there by his own frenzy. Arié touched him with one finger and the giant fell to the ground and was shattered.

> PRIMO LEVI, from 'The Servant', 1977; tr. Raymond Rosenthal. In one legend the word EMET, 'Truth', is inscribed on the golem's forehead. The golem grows so tall that his master cannot reach him. He asks the golem to help him with his shoes, and when the golem bends down, the rabbi erases the first letter of the word, leaving MET, 'Death'. The golem turns to dust

Has everybody heard of Doctor Dee, the magician, and of the black speculum or mirror of cannel coal, in which he could see at will everything in the wide world, and many things beyond it? If so, I may introduce myself to the readers in the easiest manner possible. Although I cannot claim to be a descendant of Doctor Dee, I profess the occult art to the extent of keeping a black mirror, made exactly after the model of that possessed by the old astrologer. My speculum, like his, is constructed of an oval piece of cannel coal, highly polished, and set on a wooden back with a handle to hold it by. Nothing can be simpler than its appearance; nothing more marvellous than its capacities— provided always that the person using it be a true adept. Any man who disbelieves nothing is a true adept. Let him get a piece of cannel coal, polish it highly, clean it before use with a white cambric handkerchief, retire to a private sitting-room, invoke the name of Doctor Dee, shut both eyes for a moment, and open them again suddenly on the black mirror. If he does not see anything he likes after that—past, present, or future—then let him depend on it there is some speck or flaw of incredulity in his nature; and the sad termination of his career may be considered certain. Sooner or later, he will end in being nothing but a rational man.

I, who have not one morsel of rationality about me; I, who am as true an adept as if I had lived in the good old times ('the Ages of Faith', as another adept has very properly called them), find unceasing interest and occupation in my black mirror. For everything I want to know, and for everything I want to do, I consult it. This very day, for instance (being in the position of most of the other inhabitants of London, at the present season), I am thinking of soon going out of town. My time for being away is so limited, and my wanderings have extended, at home and abroad, in so many directions, that I can hardly hope to visit any really beautiful scenes, or gather any really interesting experiences that are absolutely new to me. I must go to some place that I have visited before; and I must, in common regard to my own holiday interests, take care that it is a place where I have already thoroughly enjoyed myself, without a single drawback to my pleasure that is worth mentioning.

Under these circumstances, if I were a mere rational man, what should I do? Weary my memory to help me to decide on a destination, by giving me my past travelling recollections in one long panorama—although I can tell by experience that of all my faculties memory is the least serviceable . . . As a true adept, I know better than to give myself any useless trouble of this sort. I retire to my private sitting-room, take up my black mirror, mention what I want— and, behold! on the surface of the cannel coal the image of my former travels passes before me, in a succession of dream-scenes. I revive my past experiences, and I make my present choice out of them, by the evidence of my own eyes; and, I may add, by that of my own ears also—for the figures in my magic landscapes move and speak!

WILKIE COLLINS, from 'My Black Mirror', 1863

I worked also at acquiring the power of invisibility. I reached a point when my physical reflection in a mirror became faint and flickering. It gave very much the effect of the interrupted images of the cinematograph in its early days. But the real secret of invisibility is not concerned with the laws of optics at all; the trick is to prevent people noticing you when they would normally do so. In this I was quite successful. For example, I was able to take a walk in the street in a golden crown and a scarlet robe without attracting attention.

I thought it polite to impress them [Algerians] with my majesty as a Magician. With this object I took [Sir Richard] Burton's hint that a star sapphire was universally venerated by Moslems, and having bought a very large and fine specimen of this stone in Ceylon and made it into a ring with a gold band of two interlaced serpents, I found that Burton was right. I had merely to exhibit this ring to command the greatest possible respect. On one occasion, in fact, a quarrel in a coffee shop having developed into a sort of small riot, and knives being drawn, I walked into the scrimmage and drew sigils in the air with the ring while intoning a chapter of the Koran. The fuss stopped instantly, and a few minutes later the original parties to the dispute came to me and begged me to decide between them, for they saw that I was a saint . . .

I soon saw that [Victor] Neuburg with his shambling gait and erratic gestures, his hangdog look and his lunatic laugh, would damage me in the estimation of the natives. So I turned the liability into an asset by shaving his head except for two tufts on the temples, which I twisted up into horns. I was thus able to pass him off as a demon that I had tamed and trained to serve me as a familiar spirit. This greatly enhanced my eminence. The more eccentric and horrible Neuburg appeared, the more insanely and grotesquely he behaved, the more he inspired the inhabitants with respect for the Magician who had mastered so fantastic and fearful a genie.

I went on with my magical and other work; in particular, I invented a practice which has proved very useful. Its object is to prevent mosquitoes from biting one. The method is: to love them. One reminds oneself that the mosquito has as much right to his dinner as a man has. It is difficult to get the exact shade of feeling and more so to feel it. One begins by lying defenceless against the enemy and sternly repressing the impulse to wave, to slap and to scratch. After a little perseverance, one finds that the bites no longer become inflamed; and this preliminary success is soon followed by complete protection. They will not bite one at all.

ALEISTER CROWLEY (1875–1947), *The Confessions of Aleister Crowley: An Autohagiography*

~

The people of Bali, an island to the east of Java, have periodical expulsions of devils upon a great scale. Generally the time chosen for the expulsion is the day of the 'dark moon' in the ninth month. When the demons have been long unmolested the country is said to be 'warm', and the priest issues orders to expel them by force, lest the whole of Bali should be rendered uninhabitable. On the day appointed the people of the village or district assemble at the principal temple. Here at a crossroad offerings are set out for the devils. After prayers have been recited by the priests, the blast of a horn summons the devils to partake of the meal which has been prepared for them. At the same time a number of men step forward and light their torches at the holy lamp which burns before the chief priest. Immediately afterwards, followed by the bystanders, they spread in all directions and march through the streets and lanes crying, 'Depart! go away!' Wherever they pass, the people who have stayed at home hasten by a deafening knocking on doors, beams, rice-blocks, etc., to take their share in the expulsion of devils. Thus chased from the houses, the fiends flee to the banquet which has been set out for them; but here the priest receives them with curses which finally drive them from the district. When the last devil has taken his departure, the uproar is succeeded by a dead silence, which lasts during the next day also. The devils, it is thought, are anxious to return to their old homes, and in order to make them think that Bali is not Bali but some desert island, no one may stir from his own premises for twenty-four hours. Even ordinary household work, including cooking, is discontinued . . . Most people still stay at home, striving to while away the time with cards and dice.

FRAZER, *The Golden Bough*

When I was on an expedition to Mount Elgon (East Africa) in 1925–26, one of our water-bearers, a young woman who lived in a neighbouring kraal, fell ill with what looked like a septic abortion with high fever. We were unable to treat her from our meagre medical supplies, so her relatives immediately sent for a *nganga*, a medicine-man. When he arrived, the medicine-man walked round and round the hut in ever-widening circles, snuffing the air. Suddenly he came to a halt on a track that led down from the mountain, and explained that the sick girl was the only daughter of parents who had died young and were now up there in the bamboo forest. Every night they came down to make their daughter ill so that she should die and keep them company. On the instructions of the medicine-man a 'ghost-trap' was then built on the mountain path, in the form of a little hut, and a clay figure of the sick girl was placed inside it together with some food. During the night the ghosts went in there, thinking to be with their daughter. To our boundless astonishment the girl recovered within two days. Was our diagnosis wrong? The puzzle remained unsolved.

> CARL GUSTAV JUNG, from 'The Psychological Foundations of Belief in Spirits', 1920; tr. R. F. C. Hull

Pa Daoud had prepared his *mise en scène*; a few jars covered with yam leaves, a large bunch of flowers adorned with artificial birds of plaited palm, and, on a brass tray, a pot of incense and bowls of rice. He waved away the lamp. The spirits detest its smell of kerosene and its too emphatic light. Three little tapers flickered in the darkness.

A pinch of incense on the hot embers which Ngah has just brought in. The smoke mounts in a thin vertical column, and Pa Daoud contemplates it, motionless, awaiting the first omen. In a moment or two it bends gently towards him in a faint compliance. Then, with both his hands the wizard breaks the shaft of smoke, gathers it into the palms of his hands and slowly inhales it. The smoke seems to intoxicate him. He sways slightly and his triple shadow flickers on the wall.

The incense had bowed towards him; that means that an invisible being accepts his offering and consents to help him.

'Peace on thee, Tanju!' chants Pa Daoud.

> 'I know thy name and whence thou camest
> Thou art impure but sanctified
> Born of the mucus from Muhammad's eyes
> When he fled from Mekkah
> In the dust of the desert
> Guided by an infidel
> Closing his eyes that were blind from weeping . . .'

Nothing impresses the spirits so much as to hear themselves reminded of their origin. It deprives them of the mysterious prestige which they fancy they enjoy among human beings. And when he who addresses them adds to this proof of mastery allusions to the sacred texts that betray a true servant of Allah, they are completely in subjection.

Pa Daoud knows how to profit by this feeling without abusing it. He picks up the bunch of flowers, holds it out to the smoke, which he then blows downwards on to the blossoms.

> 'Come into thy garden of delight
> Full of perfumes and of birds
> Created by Allah
> Offered by my brother Smail
> Accept this garden of delights
> Show me the sickness of my brother Smail.'

All that is asked of this spirit is a diagnosis; and he will indicate it by the disposition of some grains of roasted rice sprinkled over some water in a jar. The grains float, and the sorcerer bends over them; for a long while he watches them in silence.

'I see that it is invisible,' murmurs Daoud at last.

And turning towards us, he adds:

'It is a *badi*.' . . .

A *badi* is not a demon, it is something more impersonal, a malignant entity that inhabits all living things, animals, plants, stones, and smoke . . . It might almost be described as a fluid essence, a power of obsession. Thus, it is the *badi* that passes from the eyes of the tiger and the snake into the eyes of their victims, that glares malignantly from the face of a passer-by, and casts a shadow over the daylight; it is the *badi* that gleams in the rays of the setting sun, in the heavy hour of fear. But an attempt to define it destroys the intuition of what it is. Suffice it to say that there are degrees in the immaterial domain, and that if the demons are evil beings, the *badi* is merely a potentiality, like the germ of an evil deed.

Pa Daoud's body now sways with a movement recalling the dance of the cobra beset by enemies, alert, elastic, with menace and fear in its cold eyes. Then the lips begin to move. Magic formulae, to be more effective, must come from far away, they must find inspiration in the deep places of the mind, just as the breath that shoots the arrow from a blowpipe must come from deep down in the lungs. The words hover, as yet unuttered, on the magician's quivering lips. Then comes the voice, hoarse at first, but soon incisive as an arrow. But not one of us can understand the meaning of those hissing sounds . . . Against his impalpable adversary the sorcerer calls to his aid occult allies in a sphere where inarticulate words are understood. Thus, when thunder growls, the dog's troubled eyes seek comfort in the eyes of man.

The strange sounds grow insensibly more distinct, until they could, it seems, be written down in the letters of our alphabet. Among them are Arabic words, and I recognized some names. Pa Daoud was invoking the four Archangels: Israfil, master of the elements, Azrail, master of animate beings, Mikail, who feeds and fertilizes, Jibrail, who instructs. He returns once more to Israfil, the furthest and most transcendent, the ultimate Archangel who can still hear the prayers of men; beyond is silence, and the will of Allah.

Emboldened by these Great Ones, the sorcerer stands up and calls upon the *badi* in harsh tones. He speaks in Malay, and it matters little whether the *badi* understands or even hears; the appeal is made articulate, and the sacred frenzy will act through the aid of the protecting powers.

> 'O *Badi*! O *Badi*! O *Badi*!
> Enter into this bunch of leaves
> Absorb the sap of these leaves
> The seven antidotes of these leaves
> Return to the places from which thou camest
> In the water that flows and trickles
> In the wind that passes and does not return
> In the red abysses of the earth
> To the herbless plains
> To the shoreless seas
> To the stretchless spaces
> By the virtue of La-ilaha-illa-llah . . .'

In a hand that no more trembles he holds out the bunch of leaves to the purifying incense, and then sweeps it seven times over Smail's stiffened body from the head to the feet. The *badi* must go forth and the frightened soul must now return. The body must not remain untenanted, or it would fall into decay. Pa Daoud summons the soul with the word the Malays use to call their chickens: *Kur*! *Kur*!

'*Kur*! *Semangat*! Come, soul of Smail bin Bangka! Come ye seven souls! . . . Come, bird, come, little one, come, shadowy one . . .' And indeed, at that very moment, the body quivers under the tickling twigs, and suddenly the soul returns. The soul? I should say seven shrieking souls . . . We sprang up, ready to help. But the sorcerer swept us aside with an arm that cut like a lash, and, bending over Smail, gripped him by the head, glared into his eyes, and screamed; screamed louder even than the sick man, without taking breath. There they crouched like two dogs baying at death. And then they both fell back exhausted.

HENRI FAUCONNIER, *The Soul of Malaya*, 1930; tr. Eric Sutton

One such occurrence related to the servants' quarters in a European house-hold. It was alleged that a Chinese houseboy had hanged himself from a beam on the veranda three years previously. Several persons claimed to have seen his ghost. The reputation reached such proportions that no servants could be persuaded to live there. Eventually a young Cantonese girl agreed to stay provided the ghost was laid by a Chinese *dang-ki* [medium]. The ceremony was arranged for a Saturday afternoon. The cult promoters and assistants arrived in a lorry with much of the temple's portable equipment, including the image of the 'Great Saint'. A temporary altar was set up inside the room the girl was going to occupy, complete with the image, swords, whips, flags, candles, incense and fruit offerings. An Eight Trigram flag was planted outside the building and all washing was removed from the clothes-line in the vicinity.

The earlier part of the *dang-ki*'s performance was identical with the proce-dure followed in his own temple. He went into a trance in a chair placed near the doorway, ate burning incense sticks and cut his tongue to daub blood on charm papers. A white cockerel was then produced. Holding the bird and a horsehair whip in his right hand, and a bundle of flags and a willow whisk in his left hand, the *dang-ki* began a perambulation of the block in which the room was situated.

Preceded by an assistant hurling salt and rice into the air, and another cracking an exorcizing whip at every corner of the building, the *dang-ki* pranced his way down the line of servants' quarters, past the garage at the back, and returned once more to his altar. Here he cut the cockerel's throat and sprinkled the blood on charm papers. One of these, together with the willow whisk, was fastened to the lintel of the door.

There was then a long conference between the *dang-ki* and his assistants. The *shen* [spirit] informed them that the real cause of the trouble was not the man who hanged himself, but several unsatisfied ghosts who had been killed by the Japanese [during the occupation]. This being so, it was impossible to lay them completely. But any evil effect that they might have could be counter-acted by suitable offerings.

The servant girl who was to occupy the room was called in and instructed to make offerings to the hungry ghosts on the first and fifteenth of every month, and throughout the whole of the Seventh Moon. She was then made to kneel down in front of the altar while an Eight Trigram flag was held over her head and the *dang-ki* made a stamp mark on her back as a special protection.

The immediate consequence of the rites was somewhat unfortunate. As soon as they had ended, the whole grounds were found to be surrounded by a strong posse of armed police who had arrived on the scene in response to a telephone complaint from a nearby resident concerning the unprecedented noise of drums and gongs in a predominantly European area. The puzzled Indian inspector had to be reassured that there had been no breach of the peace in the legal sense, and that such noise as there was would not be repeated.

It must also be recorded that the servant girl disappeared next day and was never seen by the householders again. It appears that she was more scared by the rites of exorcism than by the ghost. The promoters of the cult commented rather disgustedly that she was a modern kind of girl who had never been properly instructed in her religious devotions.

ALAN J. A. ELLIOTT, *Chinese Spirit-Medium Cults in Singapore*, 1955

And they [Jesus and his disciples] arrived at the country of the Gadarenes, which is over against Galilee.

And when he went forth to land, there met him out of the city a certain man, which had devils long time, and ware no clothes, neither abode in any house, but in the tombs.

When he saw Jesus, he cried out, and fell down before him, and with a loud voice said, What have I to do with thee, Jesus, thou Son of God most high? I beseech thee, torment me not.

(For he had commanded the unclean spirit to come out of the man. For oftentimes it had caught him: and he was kept bound with chains and in fetters; and he brake the bands, and was driven of the devil into the wilderness.)

And Jesus asked him, saying, What is thy name? And he said, Legion: because many devils were entered into him.

And they besought him that he would not command them to go out into the deep.

And there was there an herd of many swine feeding on the mountain: and they besought him that he would suffer them to enter into them. And he suffered them.

Then went the devils out of the man, and entered into the swine: and the herd ran violently down a steep place into the lake, and were choked.

When they that fed them saw what was done, they fled, and went and told it in the city and in the country.

Then they went out to see what was done; and came to Jesus, and found the man, out of whom the devils were departed, sitting at the feet of Jesus, clothed, and in his right mind: and they were afraid.

Luke 8

A nun did eat a lettuce without grace or signing it with the sign of the cross, and was instantly possessed. Durand relates that he saw a wench possessed in Bononia with two devils, by eating an unhallowed pomegranate, as she did afterwards confess, when she was cured by exorcisms. And therefore our papists do sign themselves so often with the sign of the cross, that the demon may not dare to enter, and exorcize all manner of meats, as being unclean or accursed otherwise.

ROBERT BURTON, *The Anatomy of Melancholy*, 1621

Upon a certain day, one of the Nuns, going into the garden saw a lettuce that liked her, and forgetting to bless it before with the sign of the cross, greedily did she eat it: whereupon she was suddenly possessed with the devil, fell down to the ground, and was pitifully tormented. Word in all haste was carried to Equitius [abbot in the province of Valeria], desiring him quickly to visit the afflicted woman, and to help her with his prayers: who as soon as he came into the garden, the devil that was entered began by her tongue, as it were, to excuse himself, saying: 'What have I done? What have I done? I was sitting there upon the lettuce, and she came and did eat me.' But the man of God in great zeal commanded him to depart, and not to tarry any longer in the servant of almighty God, who straightways went out, not presuming any more to touch her.

ST GREGORY THE GREAT, *Dialogues*, 593; tr. P.W.

For all the Christians of an earlier day, 'speaking with tongues' was an extraordinary grace, a gratuitous gift of the Holy Spirit. But it was also (such is the strangely equivocal nature of the universe) a sure symptom of possession by devils . . . In 1598, for example, Marthe Brossier made a great name for herself by exhibiting the symptoms of possession. One of these symptoms—a thoroughly traditional and orthodox symptom—consisted in going into convulsions every time a prayer or an exorcism was read over her. (Devils hate God and the Church; consequently they tend to fly into a rage every time they hear the hallowed words of the Bible or the prayer book.) To test Marthe's paranormal knowledge of Latin, the Bishop of Orléans opened his Petronius and solemnly intoned the somewhat unedifying story of the Matron of Ephesus. The effect was magical. Before the first sonorous sentence had been completed, Marthe was rolling on the floor, cursing the Bishop for what he was making her suffer by his reading of the Sacred Word. It is worth remarking that, far from putting an end to Marthe's career as a demoniac, this incident actually helped her to go forward to fresh triumphs. Fleeing from the Bishop, she put herself under the protection of the Capuchins, who proclaimed that she had been unjustly persecuted and made use of her to draw enormous crowds to their exorcisms.

ALDOUS HUXLEY, *The Devils of Loudun*, 1952

I accost you, damned and most impure spirit, cause of malice, essence of crimes, origin of sins, you who revel in deceit, sacrilege, adultery, and murder! I adjure you in Christ's name that, in whatsoever part of the body you are hiding you declare yourself, that you flee the body that you are occupying and from which we drive you with spiritual whips and invisible torments. I demand that you leave this body, which has been cleansed by the Lord. Let it be enough for you that in earlier ages you dominated almost the entire world through your action on the hearts of human beings. Now day by day your kingdom is being destroyed, your arms weakening. Your punishment has been prefigured as of old. For you were stricken down in the plagues of Egypt, drowned in Pharaoh, torn down with Jericho, laid low with the seven tribes of Canaan, subjugated with the gentiles by Samson, slain by David in Goliath, hanged by Mordecai in the person of Haman, cast down in Bel by Daniel and punished in the person of the dragon, beheaded in Holofernes by Judith, subjugated in sinners, burned in the viper, blinded in the seer, and discountenanced by Peter in Simon Magus. Through the power of all the saints you are tormented, crushed, and sent down to eternal flames and underworld shadows . . . Depart, depart, wheresoever you lurk, and never more seek out bodies dedicated to God; let them be forbidden you for ever, in the name of the Father, the Son, and the Holy Spirit.

> Form of exorcism, Gallican liturgy, 8th-century MS; tr. Jeffrey Burton Russell, who adds, 'The scrutinies also included the "exsufflation", in which the priest blew into the candidate's face. A standard part of many liturgies from the fourth century, the exsufflation showed contempt for the demons and was believed to drive them away; it was much like the desert fathers' practice of hissing or spitting at demons. The priest also touched the catechumen's ears with spittle, again to show contempt for the Devil but also because spittle has healing properties'

On Tuesday, February 29th, 1820, when religious service was concluded in Windmill-Hill Chapel, J. LOSE, the stepfather of J. EVENS, came to me, and said,

'Sir, my boy wishes you would come and pray with him.' Is he sick? After a little hesitation, he said, 'He is worse than sick; I can compare his case to none but that of the child mentioned in the gospels, whose father brought him to Jesus Christ, that he might cast out of him the evil spirit, which sometimes threw him into the water, and sometimes into the fire, that he might destroy him. This appears to be the case with my boy: he has made several attempts to go into the water, and into the fire.'

I immediately went with him to his house, and saw the boy. He was between nine and ten years old,—rather tall for his age.

His conduct when under the influence of his disorder, was extremely various. At one time he would be violently convulsed, and in a few seconds, begin all manner of whimsical frolicks. He would halt like a lame beggar;—strut like mock majesty;—would chase and scratch like a dog;—run like a rabbit;—and walk like a crab; would face and claw, like a tiger meeting a foe;—and run about like a cat catching flies;—would beat the air like a boxer;—and fly at the door like a fury;—would dance about with all sorts of attitudes, odd, awkward, and elegant. Sometimes he appeared pleased; at others, grievously vexed. Frequently he would perform dangerous manoeuvres, and take care not to hurt himself; and often he would make violent efforts to accomplish his own destruction. Sometimes as harmless as a kitten at play, and sometimes as dangerous as an angry cur. It is impossible to give an adequate description of his singular conduct; his terrible shrieks; his piteous cries; and his horrible looks.

On Friday, April 14th, I was again called in to assist his mother . . . Perceiving him to be so furiously violent, I found it necessary to throw him down upon his back, to sit upon his knees, and cautiously to hold his arms, so that he should neither strike, nor scratch, nor bite me . . . I then addressed the evil spirit. He was all attention in an instant. He began to talk inwardly, without using his lips or tongue, the sound coming through his nose. There was no difficulty in understanding his meaning, especially as there was a great deal of significance in his looks and gestures. He said, with a majestical air, 'What brings you here?' and made motions for me to go home. I replied, 'I come, in the name of the Lord, to see if I can do any good to this poor lad, to help the family, and to oppose your troubling them.' He frowned and growled dreadfully, and began to spit in my face. Again I tried whether he knew what was addressed to him in mind only, without any visible sign whatever. Closing my lips, and looking steadily in the lad's face, I said in thought, and in thought only, to the evil spirit, 'I command thee, in the name of our Lord Jesus Christ, to come out of him.' He gave his usual significant looks, and said through his nose, '*I won't!*' Again, with the same caution to keep my lips close, and to guard my countenance, I said in spirit, 'But God Almighty shall compel you to go.' He struggled, and frowned, and angrily cried through his nose, *'He can't.'* I said, in the same merely mental way, 'But he can and will.' He again repeated angrily and aloud, 'He can't.'

Sunday, April 16th, was a day of furious rage and great tribulation. His stepfather took up the hymn-book to read, and the boy attacked him, like a furious tiger. It was with great difficulty he could be held. My assistance was requested, and I went in to help the family. The boy was unusually strong and violent. He spoke through his nose, as from his stomach, without using his tongue or lips; and much conversation passed between him and some of the family, in this way. The boy's mind was suspended in its operations, as in a dead sleep, and the evil spirit used the body. The father said, 'Thou shalt not reign here, to the annoyance of all the family.' The spirit answered violently and repeatedly, 'I will.' 'Thou shalt not,' said the father. 'But I will,' said the demon. Father, 'God shall drive thee out.' Demon, 'He can't.' Father, 'God is almighty.' Demon, 'So am I.' Father, 'God can do all things.' Demon, 'So can I.' Father, 'There is one thing thou canst not do, thou canst not save sinners.' Demon, 'Don't want to', &c.

> JAMES HEATON, *The Extraordinary Affliction and Gracious Relief of a Little Boy*, 1822

In March 1895 Bridget Cleary, aged 26, of Clonmel in Co. Tipperary, was stabbed, burned, and eventually killed, by a group of nine people, her husband, father, friends and neighbours. They believed they were saving her soul by expelling an evil spirit which had possessed her body. The charge of murder brought against them was subsequently changed to one of manslaughter.

It appears from evidence given at the committal that Bridget Cleary, in consequence of certain nervous, excited symptoms which she had exhibited, was forced to swallow certain herbs, was beaten and burned, and was repeatedly asked the question, 'In the name of God, are you Bridget Cleary?' During this treatment she received the injuries of which she died, but it is, I think, quite clear that the men neither wished nor meant to kill her. All the witnesses, who on important points entirely corroborated each other, agreed in saying that the object of this treatment was to drive out from her body the fairy which had taken possession of it, and which exhibited its presence by her nervous disorder. The woman's own soul would then be able to return. This is not, then, a case of witch-burning at all.

We find that in many savage tribes the priests or sorcerers are the only doctors . . . In Western Australia, the doctor or sorcerer used to run round and round his patient, shouting as loud as he could, in order to frighten the possessing spirit away . . . Again, the Hottentots of the Cape of Good Hope used to shake, jolt, and pummel a dying man in a final effort to drive the spirit of disease out of him. But invariably, as time advances, these demons, originally malignant, and treated as enemies, to be got rid of by force and hostility, are found to be amenable to gentler means. In New Guinea, for instance, we find that the doctors used to paint their patient all over with bright colours, in order to please the spirit which possessed him, and induce him to come out. He is still malignant, but can be approached in a friendly manner . . . Now, all the details of the death of Bridget Cleary point to the earliest stage in such beliefs, when the possessing spirit was thought to be purely malignant and had to be forcibly ejected.

After her death they were influenced by an entirely distinct and different superstition, one that is commoner to the country, less primitive, and more elaborate. They had been unable to completely satisfy themselves that the soul of the woman had returned to her body, and they fell back on the hope that they had killed, not Bridget Cleary, but a changeling which had been substituted for her. In neither case was murder present to their minds, for in the first stage their design was to bring her soul back to her body, and in the second they believed, and still seem to believe, that it was not she who was dead.

E. F. BENSON, from 'The Recent "Witch-Burning" at Clonmel', *The Nineteenth Century*, June 1895

To lay the lorn spirit, you o'er it must pray,
And command it, at length, to be gone far away,
And in Wookey's deep hole,
To be under control,
For the space of seven years and a day.

If it then return, you must pray and command
By midnight
By moonlight
By death's ebon wand,
That to Cheddar cliffs now it departeth in peace,
And another seven years its sore troubling will cease.

> If it return still,
> As, I warn you, it will,
> To the Red Sea for ever
> Command it; and never
> Or noise more or sound
> In the house shall be found.

ANON., 18th-century poem; Wookey Hole, a cave in the Mendip Hills, Somerset. Theo Brown (*The Fate of the Dead*, 1979) remarks that variant names are 'Ochie-hole' and 'Ochy's dreadful hole'. The Red Sea was traditionally believed to be extremely deep, if not bottomless, and an entrance into hell

Mr Lyde's ghost: he was an old Salcombe family and at first appeared in the Orchard, then every year he grew a cockstride nearer and sat on the road gate. Six ministers were called to lay him but they could not and next year he got into the cellar and next sat down to dinner with them. Then they rode wildish up to Paccombe for Mr George Cornish who came with a small Bible but laid him at once. The reason why the others could not was that it takes an Oxford clerk to lay a bad ghost. It was fine to hear Mr Cornish tell him he was in Hell and lay him. Next day to make sure they drove a donkey cart up to Pepperell's field with his things and laid him with gravel for fifty years in a pit. Some are only bound with sand, but they generally work free, and have then to be bound with bricks.

JOHN BASTIN, a contemporary parishioner, in J. Y. Anderson-Morshead: *Salcombe Regis Parish Documents*, MS, Exeter City Library. The ghost may have been Thomas Lyde, who died in 1824

Barbara Rieger, of Steinbach, aged ten, in 1834, was possessed by two spirits, who spoke in two distinctly different male voices and dialects; one said he had formerly been a mason, the other gave himself out for a deceased provisor; the latter of whom was much the worse of the two. When they spoke, the child closed her eyes, and when she opened them again, she knew nothing of what they had said. The mason confessed to have been a great sinner, but the provisor was proud and hardened, and would confess nothing. They often commanded food, and made her eat it, which when she recovered her individuality, she felt nothing of, but was very hungry. The mason was very fond of brandy, and drank a great deal; and if not brought when he ordered it, his raging and storming was dreadful. In her own individuality, the child had the greatest aversion to this liquor. They treated her for worms and other disorders, without the slightest effect; till at length, by magnetism, the mason was cast out. The provisor was more tenacious, but, finally, they got rid of him, too, and the girl remained quite well.

CATHERINE CROWE, *The Night-Side of Nature*, 1849

Sinne-eaters

In the County of Hereford was an old Custome at Funeralls, to hire poor people, who were to take upon them all the Sinnes of the party deceased . . . The manner was that when the Corps was brought-out of the house and layd on the Biere, a Loafe of bread was brought out, and delivered to the Sinne-eater over the corps, as also a Mazar-bowle of Maple full of beer, which he was to drinke up, and sixpence in money, in consideration whereof he tooke upon him (*ipso facto*) all the Sinnes of the Defunct, and freed him or her from Walking after they were dead. This custome alludes (me thinkes) something to the Scapegoate in the old Lawe. *Leviticus*, cap. xvi verses 21, 22. 'And Aaron shall lay both his hands on the head of the live goate, and confesse over him all the iniquities of the Children of Israel, and all their transgressions in all their sins, putting them upon the head of the goat, and shall send him away by the hand of a fitt man into the wildernesse. And the goat shall beare upon him all their iniquities, unto a land not inhabited: and he shall let the goat goe into the Wildernesse' . . .

In North-Wales, the Sinne-eaters are frequently made use of; but there, in sted of a Bowle of Beere, they have a bowle of Milke.

JOHN AUBREY, *Remaines of Gentilisme and Judaisme*, begun 1688

Some of the natives of Borneo and Celebes sprinkle rice upon the head or body of a person supposed to be infested by dangerous spirits; a fowl is then brought, which, by picking up the rice from the person's head or body, removes along with it the spirit or ghost which is clinging like a burr to his skin.

In Travancore, when a Rajah is dangerously ill and his life is despaired of, a holy Brahman is brought, who closely embraces the King, and says, 'O King! I undertake to bear all your sins and diseases. May your Highness live long and reign happily.' Then the sin-bearer is sent away from the country, and never allowed to return.

FRAZER, *The Golden Bough*

The Major was coming down the street, bowling like a hoop and howling like a wolf. He rolled along the gutter smiting the kerb as he spun, shoulder, hip and thigh, springing now to his feet, now flinging himself backwards in a somersault, shrieking the while that the devil had sent his fiends to fetch him.

'The *loup-garou*,' said Valentine.

'DTs,' said Mrs O'Connor. She leapt down the steps and grabbed him as he came opposite Dancing Master House. ' 'Old 'is legs,' she directed Aunt Irene. 'Valentine, nip roun' Peabody Buildin's and look for a pram, 'n' when you've foun' one fin' out 'oose it is and make 'er give you the baby's orange juice. Tell 'er it's a matter of life 'n' deaf. 'S the only fing,' she told Aunt Irene as they grappled with the writhing foaming Major. 'Concentrated orange juice's the nex' bes' thing to scurvy grass, 'n' we got no scurvy grass.' . . .

'Shut up, you silly ole sod,' she directed the Major. 'Siddown.'

'What's he saying?' asked Aunt Irene.

' 'E says the sky's black wiv devils,' translated Mrs O'Connor after a moment.

'But they're pigeons,' objected Aunt Irene. 'Filthy dirty pigeons.'

'They *look* like pigeons,' corrected Mrs O'Connor, briefly lifting a hand from the Major to cross herself with it.

Aunt Irene looked up at the sky involuntarily. 'Surely *you* don't think they're devils?' she asked.

'I'm not sayin',' said Mrs O'Connor guardedly. 'Only some funny fings 'ave bin 'appenin', 'n' all I'll say is—devils don't bovver in this manner in the ornery way 'cos everyone 'ere's wicked enough already. They mos'ly spend their time in monasteries temptin' monks. They're idle, devils are—they don' do nuffin' they don' 'ave to . . .' She lowered her voice and leaned over the Major to tell Aunt Irene in confidence that they only appeared when taunted by the presence of perfect goodness. 'Like flies roun' an 'oney pot,' she concluded.

'Well, *I* don't know,' said Aunt Irene. 'I think *you* must've been drinking. I can't understand a word you say.'

'Lotsa people don't,' observed the sibyl complacently, 'on'y I'm a'ways right.'

ALICE THOMAS ELLIS, *The 27th Kingdom*, 1982

Arise Evans [b. 1607, prophet] had a fungous Nose, and said, it was reveal'd to him, that the King's Hand would Cure him: And at the first coming of King Charles II into St James's Park he Kiss'd the King's Hand, and rubb'd his Nose with it; which disturb'd the King, but Cured him. Mr Ashmole told me.

AUBREY, *Miscellanies*

A purely magical verse which makes no claim to religious inspiration was used for burns in 1920 by a herbalist in the East End of London. His method was to breathe three times on the burnt place and say:

> Here come I to cure a burnt sore.
> If the dead knew what the living endure,
> The burnt sore would burn no more.

This man's many patients in East London asserted that he always stopped the pain immediately and that no scar afterwards remained, however bad the original injury.

CHRISTINA HOLE, *Witchcraft in England*, 1945; citing *The Times*, 12 April 1920

The evil eye is dreaded by Malays. Not only are particular people supposed to be possessed of a quality which causes ill-luck to accompany their glance (the *mal'occhio* of the Italians), but the influence of the evil eye is often supposed to affect children, who are taken notice of by people kindly disposed towards them. For instance, it is unlucky to remark on the fatness and healthiness of a baby, and a Malay will employ some purely nonsensical word, or convey his meaning in a roundabout form, rather than incur possible misfortune by using the actual word 'fat'. '*Ai bukan-nia poh-poh gental budak ini?*' ('Isn't this child nice and round?') is the sort of phrase which is permissible.

Journal of the Straits Branch of the Royal Asiatic Society, 1878–99

> Holy Water come and bring;
> Cast in Salt, for seasoning:
> Set the Brush for sprinkling:
> Sacred Spittle bring ye hither;
> Meale and it now mix together;
> And a little Oyle to either:

Give the tapers here their light,
Ring the *Saints-Bell*, to affright
Far from hence the evill Sp'rite.

In the morning when ye rise
Wash your hands, and cleanse your eyes.
Next be sure ye have a care
To disperse the water farre.
For as farre as that doth light,
So farre keepes the evill Spright.

Hang up Hooks and Sheers to scare
Hence the Hag, that rides the Mare,
Till they be all over wet
With the mire and the sweat:
This observ'd, the Manes shall be
Of your horses, all knot-free.

ROBERT HERRICK, 'The Spell', 'Another Charme', 'Another Charme, for Stables', 1648

Come, butter, come!
Come, butter, come!
Peter stands at the gate,
Waiting for a buttered cake.
Come, butter, come!

Charm to be used when churning milk, attributed to the 16th-century Scottish witch, Agnes Sampson, an associate of Agnes Tompson (see pp. 151–2)

Many strange spells are effected by the means of a dead man's hand—chiefly to produce butter in the churn. The milk is stirred round nine times with the dead hand, the operator crying aloud all the time, 'Gather! gather! gather!' While a secret form of words is used which none but the initiated know.

Another use is to facilitate robberies. If a candle is placed in a dead hand, neither wind nor water can extinguish it. And if carried into a house the inmates will sleep the sleep of the dead as long as it remains under the roof, and no power on earth can wake them while the dead hand holds the candle.

LADY WILDE ('Speranza', mother of Oscar Wilde), *Ancient Legends, Mystic Charms, and Superstitions of Ireland*, 1887

Very occasionally, on our walks, Grandma would tell me things about Wales: about the great cart-horses who died of heart trouble from toiling to and fro up the steep cliff road all their lives; and how, as a child, she had walked to church along the sands. And she told me about her relations; of one young cousin in particular, who had never thrived but sat by the fire instead of going to school with the other children, not growing an inch. There was nothing the matter with him, simply that he did not thrive. In the end, the mother had sent for an old lady from the Isle of Anglesey, thought to be a witch. She came, and with her little instrument (which in my imagination took the form of a ticket-collector's punch) nipped the lobe of the boy's ear. Then she returned home. From that day on, the bewitched one had begun to grow, and was now (said Grandma) a fine man with a family.

WINIFRED BEECHEY, from 'The Duke of Wellington, and Jane', 1991

'What's to do with Polly?'

'It's what *inna* to do with the child,' says Missis Beguildy. 'First she got the chin-cough and now she's got the ringworm. She's always got summat. He's put her in a chair with a string of roasted onions round her neck, and I'm sure I cried quarts getting em ready. Dunna you ever be wife to a wizard, Prue. It's like what it says in the good book, and I wish I could go to church Christian and hear it, it be like it says, "I die daily." Ah, it's like that, being wife to a wizard. If it inna onions it's summat else. I'm sure I near broke my neck fetching bletch from the church bells for this very child, to cure the chick-pox, the maister being a deal too bone-idle to fetch it himself.' . . .

Mother always said the mill children were measly because the water-fairy in the pool under the mill-race put her eye on their mother afore they were born, but Gideon said it was because they were fed on the flour the rats got into, and Missis Beguildy said it was because they sent em to Beguildy to be cured . . .

Just then Beguildy popped his head in, and looking dreamily at his missus said—

'I want some May butter.'

'May butter! You met as well ask for gold. How dun you think I've got any May butter, nor June nor July butter neither, when we sell every morsel of butter we make almost afore it be out of the churn, and never taste naught but lard?'

'I'm bound to have May butter or the charm wunna work,' says Beguildy in his husky voice.

'What be it for?'

'To fry the mid bark of the elder and cure the chin-cough.'

'Well, for all the butter, May or December, as she'll get in our place, she may die of the chin-cough!' shouts Missis Beguildy. And with that, a loud roaring came from the inner chamber, because poor Polly thought she was at death's door.

'Go and read in your old books, and find summat easier,' says Missis Beguildy. 'I've summat better to think of than charms.'

MARY WEBB, *Precious Bane*, 1924. 'Bletch': (black) grease from bells, believed to cure ringworm

A Gentlewoman having sore eies, made hir mone to one, that promised hir helpe, if she would follow his advise: which was onelie to weare about hir necke a scroll sealed up, whereinto she might not looke. And she conceiving hope of cure thereby, received it under the condition, and left hir weeping and teares, wherewith she was woont to bewaile the miserable darkenesse, which she doubted to indure: whereby in short time hir eies were well amended. But alas! she lost soone after that pretious jewell, and thereby returned to hir woonted weeping, and by consequence to hir sore eies. Howbeit, hir jewell or scroll being found againe, was looked into by hir deere friends, and this onelie posie was conteined therein:

> The divell pull out both thine eies,
> And etish* in the holes likewise.

Whereby partlie you may see what constant opinion can doo, according to the saieng of *Plato*: If a mans fansie or mind give him assurance that a hurtfull thing shall doo him good, it may doo so, &c.

* Spell the word backward, and you shall soone see this slovenlie charme or appension.

REGINALD SCOT, *The Discoverie of Witchcraft*, 1584

Sor Asdrubale ... believes that if only you lay a table for two, light four candles made of dead men's fat, and perform certain rites about which he is not very precise, you can, on Christmas Eve and similar nights, summon up San Pasquale Baylon, who will write you the winning numbers of the lottery upon the smoked back of a plate, if you have previously slapped him on both cheeks and repeated three Ave Marias. The difficulty consists in obtaining the dead men's fat for the candles, and also in slapping the saint before he have time to vanish.

'If it were not for that,' says Sor Asdrubale, 'the Government would have had to suppress the lottery ages ago—eh!'

VERNON LEE, from 'Amour Dure', 1890

It had to happen. Just when Cameroon's victory over Argentina might have laid to rest the witch doctor jibe that seems to follow African countries, along comes the Cameroon doctor to put the record straight.

Pierre Tsala Mbala gave due credit to the team's skill, but then said witch doctors and sorcerers might have given the players a psychological edge. 'You cannot explain victories by magic. But the magic is a little something extra for the players psychologically,' he said. 'I'm sure some players have amulets in their luggage and that is no problem, it is not dangerous.'

The little something extra is restricted. Witch doctors are forbidden from treating players and are not allowed to rub magic potions on limbs or hand out special elixirs because of the possibility of banned drugs being involved. But the doctor maintains that there is nothing wrong with players seeking advice, predictions or good-luck charms from them.

The last time the claws of witchcraft emerged in football was in November when several Zimbabwean players were banned for life after urinating on the field before a match.

The Times, 12 June 1990, 'World Cup Notebook: Unearthly forces rally to the call'

WITCHCRAFT

T HE Devil, too, moves in a mysterious way, in his case to perform his wickedness, judging by the incompetence, meagre ambitions, and ludicrous effects of those he chooses as his servants. That a poor old woman like Elizabeth Sawyer, abandoned by God and mocked by men, should turn to Satan for some small revenge on her persecutors would not be surprising. What is surprising, as Reginald Scot points out, is that in exchange for the certainty of having their souls burn in hell and the likelihood of having their bodies burn on earth, these supposed witches did not ask for 'all worldly felicity and pleasure'. Faust expected no less, but then, he was an educated man. And, Scot continues, if what the witch-hunters say about their horrendous powers is true, why haven't the witches managed to destroy them and all the magistrates as well?

There is more reason to believe that such witch-finders and inquisitors as Matthew Hopkins and the authors of the *Malleus Maleficarum* were truly the Devil's servants. The *Malleus Maleficarum* is a repulsive document, insufficiently relieved by what seem to us its patent absurdities, such as the etymology of the word *femina*. It was the practice of inquisitors to probe a suspect's body with needles, and if at any spot no blood was drawn and no pain caused, this indicated the presence of the Devil's mark and thus proved guilt. According to French sources, such was the zeal of some examiners in the early seventeenth century that they used retractable needles or blades which didn't pierce the skin and therefore caused no pain and drew no blood.

In the extracts which follow whys and wherefores are given for the predominance of women in witchcraft, the fundamental reason, of course, having to do with Eve, who bewitched Adam and then betrayed him: the Devil got on better with women from the very start. God had Adam's ear, leaving him to pass on as much as he thought fit to Eve in language suited to her; and, as if by a division of labour, Satan had the ear of Eve to whisper in. Éliphas Lévi (or Lévy, alias Alphonse Louis Constant, a professor of theology who left the priesthood and published occult works under this pseudonym) said much the same thing in other terms: 'Women are superior to men in sorcery because they are more easily transported by excess of passion'; the old accusation lurks here, that women are insatiable; unlike men, they never shoot their bolt. Naturally there are exceptions, Dr Fian for one, transported by the passion of lust, and cleverly and aptly undone by the girl's mother; she was herself a witch, we are told, and therefore received no credit.

Talking of Scottish witches, the brisk and sensible Mrs Lynn Linton remarked on the irony that 'the land of the Lord should have been the favourite camping-ground of Satan, that the hill of Zion should have had its roots in the depths of Tophet'. The irony, if irony it is, is an ancient one, and a modern one too. (And irony extends to Reginald Scot's sturdy defence of so-called witches: it has been said that his detailed exposés had the contrary effect of increasing disquiet on the subject, and he certainly exacerbated the wrath of King James.) Witches, persons claiming to be witches, exist nowadays, and so does persecution, though in accord with the spirit of the age it is rarely these innocuous individuals who are persecuted. (The self-proclaimed witch mentioned later really couldn't expect to keep his job as a church organist, not even today.) Persecution is made of sterner stuff. Joan of Arc's death, says the Earl of Warwick in Shaw's play, is 'a political necessity which I regret but cannot help'; and preferably it shouldn't be a heroical death on the battlefield.

Faith of whatever kind needs heresy to help define itself; the community needs aliens and opposites to keep itself warm and self-righteous; divided we stand more firmly; we all, individually or in mass, require a scapegoat at one time or another; tolerance of the 'other' is a delicate plant. Today we express incredulous horror at this hounding of befuddled women and dotty men, but we should not deceive ourselves that we could never behave in a comparable way. In *The Devils of Loudun*, Aldous Huxley notes that it is plain to see how all the evils of religion can flourish in the absence of any belief in the supernatural. 'Self-styled humanists will persecute their adversaries with all the zeal of Inquisitors exterminating the devotees of a personal and transcendent Satan.' So it goes on. The relative is turned into the absolute, political bosses into gods, and all those who dissent into devils incarnate. And 'when the current beliefs come, in their turn, to look silly, a new set will be invented, so that the immemorial madness may continue to wear its customary mask of legality, idealism and true religion'.

The first Witch was *Proserpine*, and she dwelt halfe in heaven and halfe in hell: halfe witches are they that pretending anie Religion, meddle halfe with God, and halfe with the divell . . . In another kinde witches may be said to meddle halfe with God and halfe with the Divell, because in their Exorcismes they use halfe Scripture and halfe blasphemie.

THOMAS NASHE, *The Terrors of the Night*, 1594

Philomathes. Permit mee I pray you to interrupt you one worde, which yee have put mee in memorie of, by speaking of Women. What can be the cause that there are twentie women given to that craft [witchcraft], where ther is one man?

Epistemon. The reason is easie, for as that sexe is frailer then man is, so is it easier to be intrapped in these grosse snares of the Devill, as was over well proved to be true, by the Serpents deceiving of *Eva* at the beginning, which makes him the homelier with that sexe sensine [since then].

JAMES I (JAMES VI of Scotland), *Daemonologie*, 1597; written against the 'damnable opinions' of Reginald Scot, who denied the reality of witchcraft

As for the first question, why a greater number of witches is found in the fragile feminine sex than among men; it is indeed a fact that it were idle to contradict, since it is accredited by actual experience, apart from the verbal testimony of credible witnesses. And without in any way detracting from a sex in which God has always taken great glory that His might should be spread abroad, let us say that various men have assigned various reasons for this fact, which nevertheless agree in principle . . .

For as regards intellect, or the understanding of spiritual things, they seem to be of a different nature from men . . . it should be noted that there was a defect in the formation of the first woman, since she was formed from a bent rib, that is, a rib of the breast, which is bent as it were in a contrary direction to a man. And since through this defect she is an imperfect animal, she always deceives . . . And it is clear in the case of the first woman that she had little faith; for when the serpent asked why they did not eat of every tree in Paradise, she answered: Of every tree, etc.—lest perchance we die. Thereby she showed that she doubted, and had little faith in the word of God. And all this is indicated by the etymology of the word; for *Femina* comes from *Fe* and *Minus*, since she is ever weaker to hold and preserve the faith.

> JAKOB SPRENGER and HEINRICH KRÄMER, *Malleus Maleficarum* ('Hammer of the Witches'), *c.*1486. Written at the behest of Pope Innocent VIII, a 'textbook' by two German inquisitors on the identification and punishment of witches; tr. Montague Summers, who speaks of the work as the most important and authoritative in the whole vast literature of witchcraft, with its 'seemingly inexhaustible wells of wisdom'

For my part, I have ever believed and do now know, that there are Witches: they that doubt of these, do not onely deny *them*, but Spirits; and are obliquely and upon consequence a sort not of Infidels, but Atheists. Those that to confute their incredulity desire to see apparitions, shall questionless never behold any, nor have the power to be so much as Witches; the Devil hath them already in a heresie as capital as Witchcraft.

SIR THOMAS BROWNE, *Religio Medici*, written *c.*1635

Thou shalt not suffer a witch to live.

Exodus 22

Now Samuel was dead, and all Israel had lamented him, and buried him in Ramah, even in his own city. And Saul had put away those that had familiar spirits, and the wizards, out of the land.

And the Philistines gathered themselves together, and came and pitched in Shunem: and Saul gathered all Israel together, and they pitched in Gilboa.

And when Saul saw the host of the Philistines, he was afraid, and his heart greatly trembled.

And when Saul enquired of the Lord, the Lord answered him not, neither by dreams, nor by Urim [means of divination], nor by prophets.

Then said Saul unto his servants, Seek me a woman that hath a familiar spirit, that I may go to her, and enquire of her. And his servants said to him, Behold, there is a woman that hath a familiar spirit at En-dor.

And Saul disguised himself, and put on other raiment, and he went, and two men with him, and they came to the woman by night: and he said, I pray thee, divine unto me by the familiar spirit, and bring me him up, whom I shall name unto thee.

And the woman said unto him, Behold, thou knowest what Saul hath done, how he hath cut off those that have familiar spirits, and the wizards, out of the land: wherefore then layest thou a snare for my life, to cause me to die?

And Saul sware to her by the Lord, saying, As the Lord liveth, there shall no punishment happen to thee for this thing.

Then said the woman, Whom shall I bring up unto thee? And he said, Bring me up Samuel.

And when the woman saw Samuel, she cried with a loud voice: and the woman spake to Saul, saying, Why hast thou deceived me? for thou art Saul.

And the king said unto her, Be not afraid: for what sawest thou? And the woman said unto Saul, I saw gods ascending out of the earth.

And he said unto her, What form is he of? And she said, An old man cometh up; and he is covered with a mantle. And Saul perceived that it was Samuel, and he stooped with his face to the ground, and bowed himself.

And Samuel said to Saul, Why hast thou disquieted me, to bring me up? And Saul answered, I am sore distressed; for the Philistines make war against me, and God is departed from me, and answereth me no more, neither by prophets, nor by dreams: therefore I have called thee, that thou mayest make known unto me what I shall do.

Then said Samuel, Wherefore then dost thou ask of me, seeing the Lord is departed from thee, and is become thine enemy?

. . . for the Lord hath rent the kingdom out of thine hand, and given it to thy neighbour, even to David:

Because thou obeyedst not the voice of the Lord, nor executedst his fierce wrath upon Amalek, therefore hath the Lord done this thing unto thee this day.

Moreover the Lord will also deliver Israel with thee into the hand of the Philistines: and tomorrow shalt thou and thy sons be with me: the Lord also shall deliver the host of Israel into the hand of the Philistines.

Then Saul fell straightway all along on the earth, and was sore afraid, because of the words of Samuel: and there was no strength in him; for he had eaten no bread all the day, nor all the night.

1 Samuel 28

We find that the *Devil by the Instigation of the Witch at Endor appeared in the Likeness of the Prophet Samuel*. I am not ignorant that some have asserted that, which, if it were proved, would evert this Argument, *viz.* that it was the true and not a delusive *Samuel* which the Witch brought to converse with *Saul*. Of this Opinion are some of the Jewish Rabbies and some Christian Doctors and many late Popish Authors . . . But that it was a *Daemon* representing *Samuel* has been evinced by learned and Orthodox Writers . . . only let me add, that the Witch said to *Saul, I see Elohim,* i.e. *A God* (for the whole Context shows, that a single Person is intended) *Ascending out of the Earth,* 1 Samuel 28: 13. The Devil would be Worshipped as a God, and *Saul* now, that he was become a *Necromancer,* must bow himself to him. Moreover, had it been the true *Samuel* from Heaven reprehending *Saul,* there is great Reason to believe, that he would not only have reproved him for his sin, in not executing Judgment on the *Amalekites;* as in Verse 18. But for his Wickedness in consulting with Familiar Spirits: for which Sin it was in special that he died, 1 *Chronicles* 10: 13.

> INCREASE MATHER (father of Cotton Mather, see p. 174), *Cases of Conscience Concerning Evil Spirits Personating Men,* 1693

. . . the Spirit who appeared to Saul is explicitly and precisely named Samuel, and if it had been the devil in a feigned shape who manifested himself, some other phrase would have been found. Nay, the text would surely have informed us of the deceit . . . Further, the Bible relates that the Spirit said: *Why hast thou disturbed my rest, that I should be brought up?* If it had been the devil in feigned shape who appeared, certes, he would not have reproached Saul for having invoked him, nor would he have rebuked him thus, but rather he would have been well pleased that he should have been called upon in this way, for such appeal ministers to his pride and likes him well . . . It was the true Samuel who snibbed guilty Saul.

> TAILLEPIED, *A Treatise of Ghosts*

In 1233 Gregory IX had in fact issued a bull, known as *Vox in Rama,* which . . . describes what happens when a novice is received into a heretical sect. Usually there first appears a toad, which the novice has to kiss either on the behind or on the mouth; though sometimes the creature may be a goose or a duck, and it may also be as big as a stove. Next a man appears, with coal-black eyes and a strangely pale complexion, and so thin that he seems mere skin and bone. The novice kisses him too, finding him cold as ice to the touch;

and as he does so, his heart is emptied of all remembrance of the Catholic faith. Then the company sits down to a feast. At all such gatherings a certain statue is present: and from it a black cat descends, to gather the obscene homage . . .

After songs have been sung the master asks one follower, 'What does this teach?' and receives the answer, 'The highest peace', while another adds, 'And that we must needs obey.' There follows the usual promiscuous, incestuous, often homosexual orgy; after which a man comes out from a dark corner, radiant like the sun in his upper half, but black like a cat from the waist down. The light streaming from him illumines the whole place. The master presents this man with a piece of the novice's garment, saying, 'I give you what was given me.' The shining man answers, 'You have served me well, you will serve me better still. What you have given me I leave in your care.' And then he vanishes.

This report is followed by what purports to be a summary of the heretics' doctrine. God, in their view, acted contrary to all justice when he cast Lucifer down to hell. Lucifer is the real creator of heaven; and one day he will cast God out and resume his rightful and glorious place. Then the heretics, as they hope, will attain eternal blessedness through him and with him. From this they conclude that they should avoid doing anything that is pleasing to God and should do whatever is hateful to him. This doctrinal summary confirms what one would in any case have assumed—that the toad, the cat, the pale ice-cold man and the man half radiant and half black are so many guises of Lucifer or Satan.

NORMAN COHN, *Europe's Inner Demons*, 1975

And now the reign of Matthew Hopkins, of Manningtree, gent., begins—that most infamous follower of an infamous trade—the witch-finder general of England. It was Hopkins who first reduced the practice of witch-finding to a science, and established rules as precise as any to be made for mathematics or logic. His method of proceeding was to 'walk' a suspected witch between two inquisitors, who kept her from food and sleep, and incessantly walking, for four-and-twenty hours; or if she could not be thus walked she was cross-bound—her right toe fastened to her left thumb, and her left toe to her right thumb—care being taken to draw the cords as tightly as possible, and to keep her as uneasily, and in this state she was placed on a high stool or chair, kept without food or sleep for the prescribed four-and-twenty hours, and vigilantly watched. And Hopkins recommended that a hole be made in the door, through which her imps were sure to come to be fed, and that her watchers be careful to kill everything they saw—fly, spider, lice, mouse, what not; for none knew when and under what form her familiars might appear; and if by any chance they missed or could not kill them, then they might be sure that they were imps, and so another proof be indisputably established. If neither of these ways would do, then, still cross-bound, she was to be 'swum'. If she sank, she was drowned; if she floated—and by putting her carefully on the water she generally would float—then she was a witch, and to be taken out and hung. For water, being the sacred element used in baptism, thus manifestly refused to hold such an accursed thing as a witch within its bosom . . .

The blood-money, for which he sent so many hapless wretches to the gallows (he charged twenty shillings a town for his labours), though not an exceeding bribe, as he himself boasts, was money pleasantly earned and pleasantly spent; for what man would object to travel through a beautiful country, surrounded by friends, and carrying influence and importance wherever he went, and have all his expenses paid into the bargain?

> Eliza Lynn Linton, *Witch Stories*, 1861. Hopkins is said to have been chiefly responsible for the execution of some 200 'witches' in the eastern counties. He published *The Discovery of Witches* in 1647 and was in the same year 'discovered' as himself a sorcerer and hanged. Samuel Butler wrote of him in *Hudibras* (1663): 'Who after proved himself a witch, And made a rod for his own breech'

Meroe had a certain lover whom, by the utterance of one only word, she turned into a beaver because he loved another woman beside her, and the reason why she transformed him into such a beast, is that it is his nature, when he perceives the hunters and hounds to draw after him, to bite off his members and lay them in the way, that the pursuers may be at a stop when they find them, and to the intent that so it might happen unto him (because he fancied another woman) she turned him into that kind of shape. Likewise she changed one of her neighbours, being an old man and one that sold wine, in that he was a rival of her occupation, into a frog, and now the poor wretch swimming in one of his own pipes of wine, and being well nigh drowned in the dregs, doth cry and call with croakings continually for his old guests and acquaintance that pass by. Likewise she turned one of the advocates of the Court (because he pleaded and spake against her) into a horned ram, and now the poor ram doth act advocate. Moreover she caused the wife of a certain lover that she had, because she spake sharply and wittily against her, should never be delivered of her child, but should remain, her womb closed up, everlastingly pregnant, and according to the computation of all men, it is eight years past since the poor

woman began first to swell, and now she is increased so big that she seemeth
as though she would bring forth some great elephant.

APULEIUS (born *c.*125), *The Golden Ass*; tr. William Aldington, rev. S. Gaselee

In 1527, a great number of women were accused in Navarre of the practice of
sorcery, through the information of two girls, one of eleven, the other only of
nine years old . . . We are assured by the historian who has recorded these
events (don Prudencio de Sandoval) that the commissioner took one of the
witches and offered her pardon if she would perform before him the operation
of sorcery, so as to fly away in his sight. To this proposal she agreed, and
having obtained possession of the box of ointment which was found upon her
when arrested, she went up into a tower with the commissioner, and placed
herself in front of a window. She began by anointing with her unguent the
palm of her left hand, her wrist and elbow, and by rubbing it under her arm,
and on the groin and left side. She then said with a loud voice, 'Art thou
there?' All the spectators heard a voice in the air replying, 'Yes, I am here.'
The woman then began to descend the wall of the tower with her head
downwards, crawling on her hands and feet like a lizard; and when she was
halfway down, she took a start into the air, and flew away in view of all the
spectators, who followed her with their eyes till she was no longer visible. The
commissioner offered a reward to anybody who would bring her back, and two
days afterwards she was brought in by some shepherds who had found her in
the fields. When asked by the commissioner why she did not fly away far
enough to be out of the reach of her pursuers, she said that 'her master' would
not carry her further than three leagues, at which distance he left her in the
field where the shepherds found her.

THOMAS WRIGHT, *Narratives of Sorcery and Magic*, 1851

Besides the sonne of this Mother Smith, confessed that his mother did keepe
three Spirites, whereof the one called by her Great Dicke, was enclosed in a
wicker Bottle: The seconde named Little Dicke, was putte into a Leather
Bottle: And the third termed Willet, she kepte in a Wolle Packe. And thereupon the house was commaunded to be searched. The Bottles and Packe were
found but the Spirites were vanished awaie.

A Detection of damnable driftes, practized by three Witches arraigned at
Chelmisforde in Essex, at the late Assises there holden, which were executed in
Aprill 1579, 1579

Item, the said Doctor did also confesse that he had used means sundry times to obtain his purpose and wicked intent of the same Gentlewoman, and seeing himselfe disapointed of his intention, he determined by all waies he might to obtaine the same, trusting by conjuring, witchcraft and Sorcery to obtaine it in this manner.

It happened this gentlewoman being unmarried, had a brother who went to schoole with the said Doctor, and calling his Scholler to him, demaunded if he did lye with his sister, who answered he did, by meanes whereof he thought to obtaine his purpose, and therefore secretlye promised to teach him w^tout stripes, so he would obtain for him three haires of his sisters privities, at such time as he should spye best occasion for it: which the youth promised faithfullye to perfourme, and vowed speedily to put it in practise, taking a peece of conjured paper of his maister to lappe them in when he had gotten them: and thereupon the boye practised nightlye to obtaine his maisters purpose, especially when his sister was a sleepe.

But God who knoweth the secrets of all harts, and revealeth all wicked and ungodlye practises, would not suffer the intents of this divilish Doctor to come to that purpose which he supposed it would, and therefore to declare that he was heavilye offended with his wicked entent, did so woorke by the Gentle-womans owne meanes, that in the ende the same was discovered and brought to light: for she being one night a sleepe, and her brother in bed with her, suddenlye cryed out to her mother, declaring that her Brother would not suffer her to sleepe, whereupon her mother having a quick capacitie, did vehemently suspect Doctor *Fians* entention, by reason she was a witche of her selfe, and therefore presently arose, and was very inquisitive of the boy to understand his intent, and the better to know ye same, did beat him with sundry stripes, wherby he discovered the trueth unto her.

The Mother therefore being well practised in witchcrafte, did thinke it most convenient to meete with the Doctor in his owne Arte, and thereupon tooke the paper from the boy, wherein hee should have put the same haires, and went to a young Heyfer which never had borne Calfe nor gone to the Bull, and with a paire of sheeres, clipped off three haires from the udder of the Cow, and wrapt them in the same paper, which she againe delivered to the boy, then willing him to give the same to his saide Maister, which he immediatly did.

The Schoolemaister so soone as he had received them, thinking them indeede to bee the Maides haires, went straight and wrought his arte upon them: But the Doctor had no sooner doone his intent to them, but presentlye the Heyfer or Cow whose haires they were indeed, came unto the doore of the Church wherein the Schoolemaister was, into the which the Heyfer went, and made towards the Schoolemaister, leaping and dauncing upon him, and following him foorth of the church and to what place so ever he went, to the great

admiration of all the townes men of Saltpans, and many other who did beholde
the same.

ANON., *Newes from Scotland, declaring the damnable life and death of Doctor
Fian, a notable Sorcerer, who was burned at Edenbrough in January last*, 1591

Thunder. Enter the three Witches

First Witch.   Where hast thou been, sister?
Second Witch.   Killing swine.
Third Witch.   Sister, where thou?
First Witch.   A sailor's wife had chestnuts in her lap,
   And munched and munched and munched. 'Give me,' quoth I.
   'Aroint thee, witch!' the rump-fed ronyon cries.
   Her husband's to Aleppo gone, master o'the *Tiger*.
             But in a sieve I'll thither sail
             And like a rat without a tail
             I'll do, I'll do, and I'll do.
Second Witch.   I'll give thee a wind.
First Witch.   Th'art kind.
Third Witch.   And I another.
First Witch.   I myself have all the other.
             And the very ports they blow
             All the quarters that they know
             I'the shipman's card.
             I'll drain him dry as hay;
             Sleep shall never night nor day
             Hang upon his penthouse lid.
             He shall live a man forbid.
             Weary sev'n-nights nine times nine
             Shall he dwindle, peak, and pine.
             Though his bark cannot be lost,
             Yet it shall be tempest-toss'd.

SHAKESPEARE, *Macbeth*, 1606

   The owl is abroad, the bat and the toad,
     And so is the cat-o'-mountain;
   The ant and the mole sit both in a hole,
     And frog peeps out o' the fountain;

The dogs they do bay, and the timbrels play,
  The spindle is now a-turning;
The moon is red, and the stars are fled,
  But all the sky is a-burning:
The ditch is made, and our nails the spade,
With pictures full, of wax and of wool;
Their livers I stick with needles quick:
There lacks but the blood, to make up the flood.

BEN JONSON, *The Masque of Queens*, 1609; witches' charm

In Brill . . . a Muscatier one night standing centinell upon the walls, a little before day, he heard a great noise of tatling gossips, laughing and talking aloude, their voices (as he thought) came from the aire, when casting his eies about to knowe whence this prodegie might proceed: he might perceive a duskie cloud come sweeping close along by him, in which it seemed to him they sat that were so merrie; being first affrighted at the object, and after taking courage, he gives fire and shoots toward the cloud at randome; at the report of the musket the town is up in armes, his officers leave the court of guard and come to know the matter, he tells them an incredible discourse, which he spares not to confirme with a volley of oathes, they seeke further toward the place where he aimed his musket, and found an old woman with a bunch of keyes at her girdle and a bullet in her buttock, dropt out of the cloud, and the rest vanisht.

THOMAS HEYWOOD, *Nine Bookes of Various History, concerninge Women*, 1624

Item, the said *Agnis Tompson* confessed that the Divell being then at North Barrick Kerke attending their comming in the habit or likenes of a man, and seeing that they tarried over long, he at their comming enjoyned them all to a pennance, which was, that they should kisse his Buttockes, in signe of duetye to him: which being put over the Pulpit barre, everye one did as he had enjoyned them: and having made his ungodly exhortations, wherein he did greatlye enveighe against the King of Scotland, he received their oathes for their good and true service towards him, and departed . . .

Moreover she confessed that at the time when his Majestie was in Denmarke, she . . . tooke a Cat and christened it, and afterward bound to each parte of that

Cat, the cheefest partes of a dead man, and severall joynts of his bodie, and that in the night following the saide Cat was conveied into the midst of the sea by all these witches sayling in their riddles or cives as is aforesaide, and so left the saide Cat right before the Towne of Lieth in Scotland: this doone, there did arise such a tempest in the Sea, as a greater hath not beene seene: which tempest was the cause of the perrishing of a Boate or vessell comming over from the towne of Brunt Iland to the towne of Lieth, wherein was sundrye Jewelles and riche giftes, which should have been presented to the now Queen of Scotland, at her Majesties comming to Lieth.

Againe it is confessed, that the said christened Cat was the cause that the Kinges Majesties Ship at his comming foorth of Denmarke, had a contrary winde to the rest of his Ships, then being in his companye, which thing was most strange and true, as the Kings Majestie acknowledgeth, for when the rest of the Shippes had a faire and good winde, then was the winde contrarye and altogither against his Majestie: and further the saide witche declared, that his Majestie had never come safelye from the Sea, if his faith had not prevailed above their ententions.

Newes from Scotland

The Finnes and Laplands are acquainted well
With such-like Sp'rits, and Windes to Merchants sell,
Making their cov'nant, when and how they please
They may with prosp'rous weather crosse the seas.
As thus: they in an hand-kerchiefe fast tye
Three knots; unloose the first, and by and by
You finde a gentle gale blow from the shore.
Open the second, it encreaseth more,
To fill your sailes. When you the third untye,
Th'intemperate gusts grow vehement and hye.

THOMAS HEYWOOD, *The Hierarchie of the Blessed Angells*, 1635

The Hag is astride,
This night for to ride;
The Devill and shee together:
Through thick, and through thin,
Now out, and then in,
Though ne'er so foule be the weather.

A Thorn or a Burr
She takes for a Spurre:
With a lash of a Bramble she rides now,
 Through Brakes and through Bryars,
 O'er Ditches, and Mires,
She followes the Spirit that guides now.

 No Beast, for his food,
 Dares now range the wood;
But husht in his laire he lies lurking:
 While mischeifs, by these,
 On Land and on Seas,
At noone of Night are a-working.

 The storme will arise.
 And trouble the skies;
This night, and more for the wonder,
 The ghost from the Tomb
 Affrighted shall come,
Call'd out by the clap of the Thunder.

        HERRICK, 'The Hag', 1648

Night-fiends ride not only on horses, but also on any abbreviated representative of a horse . . . The Roman Strigas themselves rode on broomsticks. As is well known, the later witches' ride could be performed on a great variety of objects, notably pitchforks, cart-shafts and broomsticks, as well as on living objects such as horses, cats, goats, etc. When more than one witch had to be carried the companion, less refined than our modern pillion riders, rode on a pole stuck into the goat's hindquarters . . . The modern ride on a broomstick is our children's 'hobby-horse' . . . and when one remembers the psychological significance of collecting manias the metaphor 'to ride his hobby to death' is seen to be not such a distant relative of the old Night-flight on a magic staff as might at first sight appear.

    ERNEST JONES, *On the Nightmare*, 1931; for 'Strigas' see p. 207

Out of these is shaped the true *Idaea* of Witch, an olde weather-beaten Croane, having her Chinne and her knees meeting for age, walking like a bow leaning on a shaft, hollow-eyed, untoothed, furrowed on her face, having her lips trembling with the palsie, going mumbling in the streetes, one that hath forgotten her *pater noster*, and hath yet a shrewd tongue in her head, to call a drab, a drab.

SAMUEL HARSNETT, *Declaration of Egregious Popishe Impostures*, 1603

Elizabeth Sawyer. And why on me? why should the envious world
  Throw all their scandalous malice upon me?
  'Cause I am poor, deform'd, and ignorant,
  And like a bow buckled and bent together
  By some more strong in mischief than myself,
  Must I for that be made a common sink
  For all the filth and rubbish of men's tongues
  To fall and run into? Some call me witch,
  And being ignorant of myself, they go
  About to teach me how to be one; urging
  That my bad tongue—by their bad usage made so—
  Forspeaks their cattle, doth bewitch their corn,
  Themselves, their servants, and their babes at nurse.
  This they enforce upon me, and in part
  Make me to credit it . . .
  What is the name, where and by what art learn'd,
  What spells, what charms, or invocations,
  May the thing call'd Familiar be purchas'd?

Enter a Black Dog

Dog. Ho! have I found thee cursing? now thou art
  Mine own.
Sawyer.   Thine! what art thou?
Dog.   He thou hast so often
  Importun'd to appear to thee, the devil.
Sawyer. Bless me! the devil?
Dog. Come, do not fear; I love thee much too well
  To hurt or fright thee; if I seem terrible,
  It is to such as hate me. I have found
  Thy love unfeign'd; have seen and pitied
  Thy open wrongs; and come, out of my love,
  To give thee just revenge against thy foes.
Sawyer. May I believe thee?

Dog.   To confirm't, command me
  Do any mischief unto man or beast,
  And I'll effect it, on condition
  That, uncompell'd, thou make a deed of gift
  Of soul and body to me.
Sawyer.   Out, alas!
  My soul and body?
Dog.   And that instantly,
  And seal it with thy blood: if thou deniest,
  I'll tear thy body in a thousand pieces.
Sawyer. I know not where to seek relief: but shall I,
  After such covenants seal'd, see full revenge
  On all that wrong me?
Dog.   Ha, ha! silly woman!
  The devil is no liar to such as he loves ...
Sawyer. Then I am thine; at least so much of me
  As I can call mine own—
Dog.   Equivocations?
  Art mine or no? speak, or I'll tear—
Sawyer.   All thine.
Dog. Seal't with thy blood.
    She pricks her arm, which he sucks. Thunder and lightning.

    THOMAS DEKKER, JOHN FORD, and WILLIAM ROWLEY, *The Witch of Edmonton*,
    1621. 'The witch' was based on Elizabeth Sawyer, hanged for such in April
    1621

'The sin of witchcraft.' We read about it, we look on it from the outside; but
we can hardly realize the terror it induced. Every impulsive or unaccustomed
action, every little nervous affection, every ache or pain was noticed, not
merely by those around the sufferer, but by the person himself, whoever he
might be, that was acting or being acted upon, in any but the most simple and
ordinary manner. He or she (for it was most frequently a woman or girl that
was the supposed subject) felt a desire for some unusual kind of food—some
unusual motion or rest—her hand twitched, her foot was asleep, or her leg had
the cramp; and the dreadful question immediately suggested itself, 'Is anyone
possessing an evil power over me, by the help of Satan?' and perhaps they went
on to think, 'It is bad enough to feel that my body can be made to suffer
through the power of some unknown evil-wisher to me, but what if Satan gives

them still further power, and they can touch my soul, and inspire me with loathful thoughts leading me into crimes which at present I abhor?' and so on, till the very dread of what might happen . . . really brought about the corruption of imagination at last, which at first they had shuddered at. Moreover, there was a sort of uncertainty as to who might be infected—not unlike the over-powering dread of the plague, which made some shrink from their best-beloved with irrepressible fear. The brother or sister, who was the dearest friend of their childhood and youth, might now be bound in some mysterious deadly pact with evil spirits of the most horrible kind—who could tell? . . . There were others who, to these more simple, if more ignorant, feelings of horror at witches and witchcraft, added the desire, conscious or unconscious, of revenge on those whose conduct had been in any way displeasing to them. Where evidence takes a supernatural character, there is no disproving it.

ELIZABETH GASKELL, from 'Lois the Witch', 1859; the story is set in Salem, Massachusetts, in 1692

If all the divels in hell were dead, and all the witches in *England* burnt or hanged, I warrant you we should not faile to have raine, haile and tempests, as now we have: according to the appointment and will of God, and according to the constitution of the elements, and the course of the planets, wherein God hath set a perfect and perpetuall order.

I am also well assured, that if all the old women in the world were witches, and all the priests, conjurers: we should not have a drop of raine, nor a blast of wind, the more or the lesse for them. For the Lord hath bound the waters in the clouds, and hath set bounds about the waters, untill the daie and night come to an end: yea it is God that raiseth the winds and stilleth them: and he saith to the raine and snowe: Be upon the earth, and it falleth.

Alas! if they were so subtill, as witchmongers make them to be, they would espie that it were meere follie for them, not onelie to make a bargaine with the divell to throw their soules into hell fire, but their bodies to the tortures of temporall fire and death, for the accomplishment of nothing that might benefit themselves at all: but they would at the leastwise indent with the divell, both to inrich them, and also to enoble them; and finallie to endue them with all worldlie felicitie and pleasure: which is furthest from them of all other. Yea, if they were sensible, they would saie to the divell: Whie should I hearken to you, when you will deceive me? Did you not promise my neighbour mother *Dutton* to save and rescue hir; and yet lo she is hanged? Surelie this would appose the divell verie sore. And it is a woonder, that none, from the beginning of the world till this daie, hath made this and such like objections, whereto the divell could never make answer.

If it were true that witches confesse, or that all writers write, or that witchmongers report, or that fooles beleeve, we should never have butter in the chearne, nor cow in the close, nor corne in the field, nor faire weather abroad, nor health within doores . . . Or what needed such preparation of warres, or such trouble, or charge in that behalfe? No prince should be able to reigne or live in the land. For (as Danaeus saith) that one *Martine* a witch killed the emperour of *Germanie* with witchcraft: so would our witches (if they could) destroie all our magistrates. One old witch might overthrowe an armie roiall: and then what needed we any guns, or wild fire, or any other instruments of warre? A witch might supplie all wants, and accomplish a princes will in this behalfe, even without charge or bloudshed of his people.

SCOT, *The Discoverie of Witchcraft*

. . . And, wow! Tam saw an unco sight!
Warlocks and Witches in a dance:
Nae cotillion, brent new frae France,
But hornpipes, jigs, strathspeys, and reels,
Put life and mettle in their heels.
A winnock-bunker in the east,   *window-seat*
There sat Auld Nick, in shape o' beast;
A tousie tyke, black, grim, and large, *shaggy cur*
To gie them music was his charge:
He screw'd the pipes and gart them skirl, *made*
Till roof and rafters a' did dirl.   *resound*
Coffins stood round, like open presses,
That shaw'd the dead in their last dresses;
And, by some devilish cantraip sleight, *magic trick*
Each in its cauld hand held a light:
By which heroic Tam was able
To note upon the haly table,
A murderer's banes, in gibbet-airns; *irons*
Twa span-lang, wee, unchristen'd bairns;
A thief new-cutted frae a rape—   *rope*
Wi' his last gasp his gab did gape;
Five tomahawks wi' bluid red-rusted;
Five scimitars wi' murder crusted;

A garter which a babe had strangled;
A knife a father's throat had mangled—
Whom his ain son o' life bereft—
The grey hairs yet stack to the heft;
Wi' mair o' horrible and awfu',
Which even to name wad be unlawfu'.
Three lawyers' tongues, turned inside out,
Wi' lies seamed like a beggar's clout;
Three priests' hearts, rotten, black as muck,
Lay stinking, vile, in every neuk . . .

ROBERT BURNS, from 'Tam o' Shanter', 1791

The young man turned aside, but took care to watch his companion, who advanced softly along the road, until he had come within a staff's length of the old dame. She, meanwhile, was making the best of her way, with singular speed for so aged a woman, and mumbling some indistinct words, a prayer, doubtless, as she went. The traveller put forth his staff, and touched her withered neck with what seemed the serpent's tail.

'The devil!' screamed the pious old lady.

'Then Goody Cloyse knows her old friend?' observed the traveller, confronting her, and leaning on his writhing stick.

'Ah, forsooth, and is it your worship, indeed?' cried the good dame. 'Yea, truly is it, and in the very image of my old gossip, Goodman Brown, the grandfather of the silly fellow that now is. But—would your worship believe it?—my broomstick hath strangely disappeared, stolen, as I suspect, by that unhanged witch, Goody Cory, and that, too, when I was all anointed with the juice of smallage and cinque-foil and wolf's bane—'

'Mingled with fine wheat and the fat of a new-born babe,' said the shape of old Goodman Brown.

'Ah, your worship knows the receipt,' cried the old lady, cackling aloud. 'So, as I was saying, being all ready for the meeting, and no horse to ride on, I made up my mind to foot it; for they tell me, there is a nice young man to be taken into communion tonight. But now, your good worship will lend me your arm, and we shall be there in a twinkling.'

'That can hardly be,' answered her friend. 'I may not spare you my arm, Goody Cloyse, but here is my staff, if you will.'

So saying, he threw it down at her feet, where, perhaps, it assumed life, being one of the rods which its owner had formerly lent to the Egyptian Magi. Of this fact, however, Goodman Brown could not take cognizance. He had cast up his eyes in astonishment, and looking down again, beheld neither Goody Cloyse nor the serpentine staff, but his fellow-traveller alone, who waited for him as calmly as if nothing had happened.

'That old woman taught me my catechism!' said the young man; and there was a world of meaning in this simple comment.

'A grave and dark-clad company!' quoth Goodman Brown.

In truth, they were such. Among them, quivering to-and-fro, between gloom and splendor, appeared faces that would be seen, next day, at the council-board of the province, and others which, Sabbath after Sabbath, looked devoutly heavenward, and benignantly over the crowded pews, from the holiest pulpits in the land. Some affirm, that the lady of the governor was there. At least, there were high dames well known to her, and wives of honored husbands, and widows, a great multitude, and ancient maidens, all of excellent repute, and fair young girls, who trembled lest their mothers should espy them . . . Good old Deacon Gookin had arrived, and waited at the skirts of that venerable saint, his revered pastor. But, irreverently consorting with these grave, reputable, and pious people, these elders of the church, these chaste dames and dewy virgins, there were men of dissolute lives and women of spotted fame, wretches given over to all mean and filthy vice, and suspected even of horrid crimes. It was strange to see, that the good shrank not from the wicked, nor were the sinners abashed by the saints . . .

Another verse of the hymn arose, a slow and mournful strain, such as the pious love, but joined to words which expressed all that our nature can conceive of sin, and darkly hinted at far more. Unfathomable to mere mortals is the lore of fiends. Verse after verse was sung, and still the chorus of the desert swelled between, like the deepest tone of a mighty organ. And, with the final peal of that dreadful anthem, there came a sound, as if the roaring wind, the rushing streams, the howling beasts, and every other voice of the unconverted wilderness, were mingling and according with the voice of guilty man, in homage to the prince of all. The four blazing pines threw up a loftier flame, and obscurely discovered shapes and visages of horror on the smoke-wreaths, above the impious assembly. At the same moment, the fire on the rock shot redly forth, and formed a glowing arch above its base, where now appeared a figure. With reverence be it spoken, the figure bore no slight similitude, both in garb and manner, to some grave divine of the New-England churches.

'Bring forth the converts!' cried a voice, that echoed through the field and rolled into the forest.

NATHANIEL HAWTHORNE, from 'Young Goodman Brown', 1846

She was with a number of other girls, foolish and frivolous, who went to consult an old woman who had the reputation of being a witch, and who was supposed to have the power of making them see their future husbands. She said they must say their prayers backwards, perform certain incantations with water, lock their doors when they went to bed, and then they would see whom they were to marry, but they would find their doors locked in the morning.

The girl followed all the witch's directions. Then she locked her door, went to bed, and waited. Gradually, by the firelight, a young man seemed to come in—to come straight through the locked door—a young man in uniform; she saw him distinctly. He went to the end of the room and returned. As he passed the bed his sword caught in the curtain and fell upon the floor. Then he seemed to pass out. The girl fainted.

In the morning at first she thought it was a dream, but there, though her door was still locked, lay the actual sword upon the floor! Greatly aghast, she told no one, but put it away and kept it hidden. It was a terrible possession to her.

The following year, at a country-house, she met the very young man she had seen. They fell violently in love and were married. For one year they were intensely—perfectly—happy. Then her husband's regiment had to change its quarters. As she was packing up, with horror which was an instinct, she came upon the sword put away among her things. Just then, before she could hide it, her husband came in. He saw the sword, turned deadly pale, and in a stern voice said, 'How did you come by that?' She confessed the whole truth.

He was rigid. He said, 'I can never forgive it; I can never see you again'; and nothing she could say or do could move him. 'Do you know where I passed that terrible night?' he said; 'I passed it *in hell*!' He has given up three-quarters of his income to her, but she has never seen him since.

HARE, *The Story of My Life*

I stayed the night for shelter at a farm
Behind the mountain, with a mother and son,
Two old-believers. They did all the talking.

MOTHER. Folks think a witch who has familiar spirits
She could call up to pass a winter evening,
But won't, should be burned at the stake or something.
Summoning spirits isn't 'Button, button,
Who's got the button', I would have them know.

SON. Mother can make a common table rear
And kick with two legs like an army mule.

MOTHER. And when I've done it, what good have I done?
Rather than tip a table for you, let me
Tell you what Ralle the Sioux Control once told me.
He said the dead had souls, but when I asked him
How could that be—I thought the dead were souls—
He broke my trance. Don't that make you suspicious
That there's something the dead are keeping back?
Yes, there's something the dead are keeping back.

ROBERT FROST, from 'The Witch of Coös', 1923

Mrs Clapp's cottage . . . backed on to the churchyard, with a small plot of garden in the front and another at the side. There was a foul smell all round it as Mrs Clapp, who was a white witch, grew many of the herbs she needed herself. Wild arrach was one of them, the most popular remedy of all. There can have been no woman in the village who had not had recourse to it at some time, as it dealt with all ailments of the womb. It made barren women fertile, and it brought on abortions. It supported fallen wombs and cooled those that were overheated, encouraged sluggish periods and checked those that were too profuse. It was a pretty little plant to look at but it smelled like rotten fish and furthermore needed to be surrounded by large quantities of fresh dung in order to do really well . . .

She was not much use when any action was required, as in midwifery, but she was well liked and people would excuse her by saying that though she was no good in an emergency she was excellent afterwards: when the patient had either died or recovered presumably. She never tried to deceive the innocent, as many witches, even the whitest, used to do, and she really understood herbs. She had remedies for everything from the snakebites which were an everyday danger to the less dramatic toothache from which most of the population suffered drearily and spasmodically throughout their lives. She had views, too. The more white witches talked in general the more the listener came to the conclusion that everything cured anything and that anything cured everything. They spoke of no plant that would not, if necessary, provoke urine, and the bloody flux could be cleared up by any plant they cared to mention. But Mrs Clapp was selective.

PATRICIA BEER, *Moon's Ottery*, 1978; the year is 1587

'Of witches there be two sorts,' says Thomas Pickering, in his *Discourse of the damned Art of Witchcraft*, printed 1610, 'the *bad witch* and the *good witch*; for so they are commonly called. The *bad witch* is he or she that hath consulted in league with the Devill; to use his helpe for the doing of hurt onely, so as to strike and annoy the bodies of men, women, children, and cattell, with diseases and with death itselfe; so likewise to raise tempests by sea and by land, &c. This is commonly called the *binding* witch. The *good witch* is he or she that by consent in a league with the Devill doth use his helpe for the doing of good onely. This cannot hurt, torment, curse, or kill, but onely heale and cure the hurt inflicted upon men or cattell by bad witches. For as they can doe no good but onely hurt; so this can doe no hurt but good onely. And this is that order which the Devill hath set in his kingdome, appointing to severall persons their severall offices and charges. And the good witch is commonly called the *unbinding witch*.'

But the good witch, as Pickering calls her, was no better off than the bad. Indeed she was held in even greater dread, for the black witch hurt only the body and estate, while the white witch hurt the soul when she healed the body; the healed part never being able to say 'God healed me.' Wherefore it was severed from the salvation of the rest, and the wholeness of the redemption destroyed. In consequence of this belief we find as severe punishments accorded to the blessing as to the banning witches; and no movement of gratitude was dreamt of towards those who had healed the most oppressive diseases, or shown the most humane feeling and kindness, if there was a suspicion that the power had been got uncannily, or that the drugs had more virtue than common.

LYNN LINTON, *Witch Stories*

One of the leading personalities in the witchcraft revival was a retired Customs officer, Gerald Gardner, who had returned from the Far East and settled in the New Forest in Hampshire. Gardner was interested in Spiritualism and the occult and as a result joined a Rosicrucian theatre company operating in Christchurch before the war. This theatre had been founded by disciples of Annie Besant who were co-Masons and had formed a group known as the Corona Fellowship of the Rosy Cross. This was an unofficial offshoot of the Temple of the Rose Cross founded by Besant in 1912. Gardner soon discovered that several of these neo-Rosicrucians were also members of a witch coven and in 1939 he was initiated as a witch by their high priestess, an old lady called Dorothy Clutterbuck who lived in a large house in the New Forest.

In June 1940 when England faced invasion from the Nazis, Gardner claims that the high priestess of his coven called a huge gathering of witches in the New Forest where the Great Circle was erected. This was a magical ritual only performed in cases of extreme emergency. Previously it had only been raised twice before, in 1588 to combat the Spanish Armada, which was defeated not only by Drake and his ships but with the help of a great storm, and in the 1800s when it looked as if Napoleon would cross the Channel. The ritual in the forest involved raising a cone of psychic power and directing it towards the French coast with the command, 'You cannot cross the sea. You cannot cross the sea. You cannot come.' According to Gardner this ritual involved the use of the life force of the gathered covens and as a result several elderly witches died. The ritual was repeated four times and then the Elders said 'We must stop. We must not kill too many of our people.'

MICHAEL HOWARD, *The Occult Conspiracy*, 1989

Goodbye broomsticks. Farewell eye of newt. Contemporary American witches pick up the telephone and say: 'I won't be around tomorrow but my voice mail will be active.'

The voice on the answering machine belongs to Cheryl Costa, a computer programmer at a consulting firm in Washington. Outside office hours she is Lady Cassandra, a third-degree high priestess in the Alexandrian Path of Wicca.

'We're just like everyone else,' Ms Costa says. But not everyone would spend a wet Friday night performing a pagan ceremony around a makeshift altar (a wooden table) with shop-bought chocolate-chip cookies and apple juice to four-part chants wafting from a portable cassette player.

Lady Cassandra, dressed for the ceremony in a rumpled black robe and a metal tiara, is unfazed that some people find her weird. 'Strange spirituality,' she smiles, 'is better than no spirituality at all.' Therein lies the secret of pagan religion's popularity in the United States today. Many women have rejected

Judeo-Christian male domination. Yet they long for ritual in a disorderly world. Intellectuals have argued that goddess worship is the latest phase in women's rights . . .

Almost anything, except satanism, goes. Modern American witches claim not to use spells for evil at all but for what one might call willpower to chivvy fate into winking a certain way.

The prospect for financial profits in today's race for spiritual fulfilment cannot be underestimated. A publishing survey shows that the rare areas of expansion during a recession this year were dieting, feminism and the occult. Ms Costa was brought up a Catholic, but felt let down by the emphasis on heterosexuality in her church's teaching. She swapped theology for 'sheology'. Her divinity is Mother Earth. Now she and her assistant, Erica Angell, a.k.a. Kestryl, a second-degree high priestess, have launched a bi-weekly cable television programme aiming to show a variety of bewitching ceremonies. For $25 (£14.50) per person, they also run an occasional crash course in rudimentary Wicca, a paganism named after an old English word for witch.

SUSAN ELLICOTT, from 'America under a spell', *The Times*, 21 October 1991

'One knew a witch once,' the witch said reflectively, 'who built herself a cottage out of sugar and gingerbread. When one says built, one means of course she arranged for some dwarves to do it for her. Dwarves are not very intelligent but if one keeps one's eye on them they make excellent little workmen. Certainly her cottage looked a treat when they'd finished. But a person ought to have seen what happened when it rained. Dear oh dear. One has to admit the cottage did look a fright, as a person will know if she's ever dropped her birthday-cake into the bath.' . . .

'Oh dear one,' the witch said, when her laughter had blown itself out, 'here one is, laughing oneself. But a person has to have a sense of humour; otherwise life would be so dreary. Sometimes one sees a motor-car accident, or hears of a child dying of some horrid disease, and it is all one can do to raise a laugh.'

Children's books are full of food. Hansel and Gretel is about nothing but eating . . . Witches are always offering children food, which in one respect is odd, since when people ill-treat youngsters they're more likely to starve them. One traditionally associates witches not with bare cupboards, and empty tables, but with steaming cauldrons. I suppose the original sisterhood were tribal ladies who on account of their venerable years had the task of maintaining the sacred fire and stirring the communal stewpot. Cooking after all is a form of magic, because you convert food from one state to another. Into the pot goes your nasty raw meat, your eye of newt and your leg of toad, then you let it hubble-bubble for a while, giving it a good stir from time to time, prick it, pat it, mark it with b, and hey presto, out comes something hot and appetizing, like *bouillabaisse*, or *boeuf à la bourguignonne*.

RICHARD FRANCIS, *The Land Where Lost Things Go by Olive Watson*, 1990

A minister called yesterday for a church in Gloucester to be exorcized after the former organist admitted being a witch who worshipped naked in his own occult temple.

For almost six years Shaun Pickering-Merrett accompanied hymns at St Michael's Church in Tuffley, Gloucester. When he told the vicar, the Revd Tony Minchin, that he was not a Christian, Mr Minchin asked him to continue none the less.

Now that Mr Minchin is leaving the parish, however, Mr Pickering-Merrett has resigned, and the Revd John Cuthbert, a minister of another denomination, has demanded that St Michael's be exorcized. 'Witchcraft is totally incompatible with Christianity,' he said.

Mr Pickering-Merrett, 26, denies being a servant of the devil, saying he uses witchcraft to help people. His 'sacred temple' is in the spare bedroom of his Gloucester council house.

'I usually worship alone, but when the coven meets for rituals everyone is usually naked,' Mr Pickering-Merrett said. 'There is nothing sexual about it. I worship a god and a goddess, both pre-Christian. The goddess is Diana. I have named my ginger cat after her.'

ROBIN YOUNG, 'Call for exorcism at witch's church', *The Times*, 16 October 1992

Some witches use actual images of the people they wish to heal, bless or influence, but in these days it is usual to make use of photographs as aids to visualization of the subject. Some witches also use dolls to help them visualize the actual body of a person more vividly.

In the past these dolls were called 'poppets', and it was said by the persecutors of witches that they were used solely for cursing, either by sticking pins in the dolls or by mutilating them in some other way. The assumption was made that sticking pins into poppets was invariably intended to be destructive. A moment's thought, however, tells one that touching, or probing, a source of pain can well be healing. Witches may indeed have been early practitioners of acupuncture; they were certainly aware of acupressure and of the importance of using touch. Be that as it may, witches today certainly do study acupressure and the various kinds of massage . . . Therapeutic touch can be used to some extent at a distance from the sufferer by means of strong visualization, and dolls may be used in this procedure.

ROBIN SKELTON, *The Practice of Witchcraft Today*, 1988

At supper we had Dr Cullen, his son the advocate, Dr Adam Fergusson, and Mr Crosbie, advocate. Witchcraft was introduced. Mr Crosbie said, he thought it the greatest blasphemy to suppose evil spirits counteracting the Deity, and raising storms, for instance, to destroy his creatures.—JOHNSON: 'Why, sir, if moral evil be consistent with the government of the Deity, why may not physical evil be also consistent with it? It is not more strange that there should be evil spirits, than evil men: evil unembodied spirits, than evil embodied spirits. And as to storms, we know there are such things; and it is no worse that evil spirits raise them, than that they rise.'—CROSBIE: 'But it is not credible, that witches should have effected what they are said in stories to have done.'—JOHNSON: 'Sir, I am not defending their credibility. I am only saying, that your arguments are not good, and will not overturn the belief of witchcraft.' (Dr Fergusson said to me aside, 'He is right.') 'And then, sir, you have all mankind, rude and civilized, agreeing in the belief of the agency of preternatural powers. You must take evidence: you must consider, that wise and great men have condemned witches to die.'—CROSBIE: 'But an act of parliament put an end to witchcraft.'—JOHNSON: 'No, sir! witchcraft had ceased; and therefore an act of parliament was passed to prevent persecution for what was not witchcraft. Why it ceased, we cannot tell, as we cannot tell the reason of many other things.'

BOSWELL, *Journal of a Tour to the Hebrides*, entry dated 16 August 1773

Men did not cease to believe in witchcraft because the evidence was against it, but because they gradually got a vague idea that such things did not happen. It is by faith rather than by reason that we have come to disbelieve in a world of witches. As Lecky has said, 'If we considered witchcraft probable, a hundredth part of the evidence we possess would have placed it beyond the region of doubt.'

ANON., *New Statesman*, 3 April 1915; quoted by Ernest Jones, *On the Nightmare*, where he is arguing that 'both the origin and the disappearance of such beliefs as that in Witches are predominantly matters of emotion'

Devils and Angels,
Hells and Heavens

I is only proper that the Devil, in the singular and sometimes capitalized, should take pride of place here, pride being his prime quality, the mainspring of his dealings with us unfortunates. Of angels there is much less to be said. We know that they are bright still though the brightest fell, that an undetermined number of them can if required dance on the point of a needle, that (as Voltaire noted) it has not pleased God to inform us of their exact abode, and that on rare occasions they descend with momentous tidings. Mostly we envisage them listening complacently to God and making music in between. In de la Mare's poem, 'Tom's Angel', the protagonist is represented as very large in size, blue as fire, and barefooted, whereupon Tom and Polly run away and the poem ends. Like heavenly bliss, angels are too remote from our experience for us to conceive of them except in the vaguest terms. For the German mystic, Meister Eckhart (*c*.1260–1327), it was not so. He posed the question, whether the joys of the angels who dwell with us here and protect and serve us are less than those of the angels who are in eternity, and answered: No, not at all, for the work of an angel is the will of God, and if God were to command an angel to fly to a tree and pick caterpillars off it, the angel would do so readily and this, the will of God, would be its beatitude.

'Why is there a tendency to reject belief in the Devil today?' Jeffrey Burton Russell asked in 1984, with Western intellectuals and theologians expressly in mind, adding that this was all the stranger at a time 'when evil threatens to engulf us totally, when evil has already claimed more victims in this century than in all previous centuries combined'. (And we might think of the increasing number of sickening crimes which are apparently unmotivated, or motivated only by what one has to call sheer evil.) In a later instalment of his history of the Devil through the ages, he writes: '*Nullus diabolus nullus redemptor* (no Devil, no Redeemer). Believers suspected that if the Devil, the second best-known figure in Christianity, could be excised from the Christian tradition, then any other figure might be eliminated as well.'

Perhaps this consideration has been voiced most cogently, in one fashion or another, by non-Christians or by those whose beliefs are distinctly unorthodox. Flaubert wrote in a letter: 'When folk no longer believe in the Immaculate Conception, they will believe in table-turning.' (Compare Blake: 'Man must & will have Some Religion: if he has not the Religion of Jesus, he will have the Religion of Satan.') Later in the nineteenth century A. W. Schlegel declared that 'Free thinking always proceeds in the following sequence: first the Devil is attacked, then the Holy Spirit, next the Lord Christ, and finally God the Father.' And, in a passage given here, the domino effect is anticipated, jocularly or hopefully, by Shelley. Professor Russell surmises that some modern theologians have been moved by the thought that the subtraction of Devil/Evil from Christianity would 'remove barriers' and 'be ecumenical'. By the same reasoning, the subtraction of God would remove further barriers and prove even more ecumenical, truly opening the church gates to all sorts and conditions of men and women.

But the scope and potency of the Devil has always been a problem. He has had to be portrayed as a dread and subtle figure, an ever-present threat, but also as someone whom devout Christians can resist and overcome with relative ease so long as they place their trust in God. Hence no doubt, alongside fearful warnings, the many stories in which the Devil and his minions are ignominiously put to rout. When, in the castle Wartburg, Luther was assailed by a demon seeking to interrupt his translating of the New Testament, he threw his inkstand at it, and that was that. These stories may have been a way of cheering oneself up. In Aix-en-Provence in 1611, during the final stages of the trial of a male witch, a former priest who had been horribly tortured, unearthly noises were heard in the large chamber where dignitaries were gathered, ecclesiastical, political, legal, and medical. Terror spread through them; they believed that all the talk of the Devil had attracted him. The noise grew, and then ended as a black man fell into the grate. It was a sweep who had mistaken his chimney. The incident strikes us as droll, but it demonstrates the intensity of the belief in the Devil as a physical presence, incarnate.

As elsewhere, considerations of space have necessitated a somewhat spare coverage of the subject, and likewise of heavens and hells, although theological matters, including the eschatological, cannot easily, or simply cannot, be left out of any self-respecting survey of the supernatural. For a more specialized account of the arch-fiend as featured in literature, recourse may be had to Francis Spufford's anthology, *The Chatto Book of the Devil*, 1992.

A salutary note on physical representations of our old adversary, Prince of Light, Prince of Darkness, comes from J. S. Forsyth, in the early nineteenth century: 'The Ethiopians paint the devil white, to be even with the Europeans, who paint him black.'

~

But the devil said: Suffer me, and I will tell thee how I was cast down into this place, and how the Lord did make man. I was going to and fro in the world, and God said unto Michael: Bring me a clod from the four corners of the earth, and water out of the four rivers of paradise. And when Michael brought them God formed Adam in the regions of the east, and shaped the clod which was shapeless, and stretched sinews and veins upon it and established it with joints; and he worshipped him, himself for his own sake first, because he was the image of God, therefore he worshipped him. And when I came from the ends of the earth Michael said: Worship thou the image of God, which he hath made according to his likeness. But I said: I am fire of fire, I was the first angel formed, and shall I worship clay and matter? And Michael saith to me: Worship, lest God be wroth with thee. But I said to him: God will not be wroth with me; but I will set my throne over against his throne, and I will be as he is. Then was God wroth with me and cast me down, having commanded the windows of heaven to be opened. And when I was cast down, he asked also the six hundred that were under me, if they would worship: but they said: Like as we have seen the first angel do, neither will we worship him that is less than ourselves. Then were the six hundred also cast down by him with me. And when we were cast down upon the earth we were senseless for forty years; and when the sun shone forth seven times brighter than fire, suddenly I awaked; and I looked about and saw the six hundred that were under me senseless. And I awaked my son Salpsan and took him to counsel how I might deceive the man on whose account I was cast out of the heavens. And thus did I contrive it. I took a phial in mine hands and scraped the sweat from off my breast and the hair of mine armpits, and washed myself in the springs of the waters whence the four rivers flow out, and Eve drank of it and desire came upon her: for if she had not drunk of that water I should not have been able to deceive her.

The Gospel of Bartholomew, Greek text, ?5th century, Apocryphal New Testament; tr. M. R. James

We created man of dried clay, of black mud, formed into shape; and we had before created the devil of subtle fire. And remember when thy Lord said before the angels, 'Verily I am about to create man of dried clay, of black mud, wrought into shape; when therefore I shall have completely formed him, and shall have breathed of my spirit into him, do ye fall down and worship him.'

And all the angels worshipped Adam together, except Eblis [Satan], who refused to be with those who worshipped him.

And Allah said unto him, 'O Eblis, what hindered thee from being with those who worshipped Adam?'

He answered, 'It is not fit that I should worship man, whom thou hast created of dried clay, of black mud, wrought into shape.'

Allah said, 'Get thee therefore hence; for thou shalt be driven away with stones; and a curse shall be on thee, until the day of judgement.'

The devil said, 'O Lord, give me respite until the day of resurrection.'

Allah answered, 'Verily thou shalt be one of those who are respited until the day of the appointed time.'

The devil replied, 'O Lord, because thou hast led me astray, I will surely tempt them to disobedience on the earth; and I will seduce them all, except such of them as shall be thy chosen servants.'

Allah said, 'This is the right way with me.'

The Koran, 'Al-Hijr'; adapted from the translation by George Sale

And I summoned again to stand before me *Beelzeboul*, the prince of demons, and I sat him down on a raised seat of honour, and said to him: 'Why art thou alone, prince of the demons?' And he said to me: 'Because I alone am left of the angels of heaven that came down. For I was first angel in the first heaven, being entitled *Beelzeboul*. And now I control all those who are bound in *Tartarus* . . .'

I Solomon said unto him: '*Beelzeboul*, what is thy employment?' And he answered me: 'I destroy kings. I ally myself with foreign tyrants. And my own demons I set on to men, in order that the latter may believe in them and be lost. And the chosen servants of God, priests and faithful men, I excite unto desires for wicked sins, and evil heresies, and lawless deeds; and they obey me, and I bear them on to destruction. And I inspire men with envy, and murder, and for wars and sodomy, and other evil things. And I will destroy the world . . .'

I said to him: 'Tell me by what angel thou art frustrated.' And he answered: 'By the holy and precious name of the Almighty God, called by the Hebrews

by a row of numbers, of which the sum is 644, and among the Greeks it is
Emmanuel. And if one of the Romans adjure me by the name of the power
Eleêth, I disappear at once.'

Testament of Solomon, ?first century AD; tr. F. C. Conybeare

Depend upon it, that when a person once begins to think that perhaps there is
no Devil, he is in a dangerous way. There may be observed, in polite society,
a great deal of coquetting about the Devil, especially among divines, which is
singularly ominous. They qualify him as the evil spirit; they consider him as
synonymous with the flesh. They seem to wish to divest him of all personality . . . It is popular, and well looked upon, if you deny the Devil 'a local
habitation and a name'. Even the vulgar begin to scout him. Hell is popularly
considered as metaphorical of the torments of an evil conscience, and by no
means capable of being topographically ascertained. No one likes to mention
the torments of everlasting fire and the poisonous gnawing of the worm that
liveth for ever and ever. It is all explained away into the regrets and the
reproaches of an evil conscience . . .

On the other hand, Heaven is supposed to have some settled locality, and
the joys of the elect are to be something very positive. This way of talking
about a personage whose office in the mythological scheme is so important,
must lead to disbelief. It is, in fact, a proof of approaching extinction in any
religion, when its teachers and its adherents, instead of proudly and dogmat-
ically insisting upon the most knotty or unintelligible articles of their creed,
begin to palliate and explain away the doctrines in which their more believing
ancestors had shown a reverential acquiescence, and an audacious confidence.

It is commonly said that the Devil has only precisely so much power as is
allowed him by God's providence. Christians exhort each other to despise his
attacks, and to trust in God. If this trust has ever been deceived, they seem in
a poor way, especially when it is considered that God has arranged it so that
the Devil should have no inconsiderable portion of the souls of men. A pious
friend of mine tells me that she thinks that about nineteen in twenty will be
damned. Formerly it was supposed that all those who were not Christians, and
even all those who were not of a particular sect of Christians, would be
damned. At present this doctrine seems abandoned or confined to a few. One
does not well see who is to be damned, and who not, according to the fashionable creed.

PERCY BYSSHE SHELLEY, from 'On the Devil, and Devils', written 1820–1

Do we not know how great is the knowledge and experience of demons? It is certain that they have a deep knowledge of all things. For there is no Theologian who can interpret the Holy Scripture better than they; there is no Lawyer with a profounder knowledge of Testaments, Contracts and Actions; there is no physician or philosopher who better understands the composition of the human body, and the virtue of the Heavens, the Stars, Birds and Fishes, of trees and herbs and metals and stones. Furthermore, since they are of the same nature as the Angels, all bodies must obey them in respect of local motion. Again, do we not know how great is the power which God in express words has given them upon earth. The Book of Job teaches us this so plainly that there is no need of other proofs; for God even says that there is no power upon earth which may be compared with that of Behemoth.

> HENRI BOGUET, a judge in witchcraft trials in Burgundy, *Examen of Witches*, 1602; tr. E. Allan Ashwin

Be sober, be vigilant; because your adversary the devil, as a roaring lion, walketh about, seeking whom he may devour.

> 1 Peter 5

Cain. Ah! didst *thou* tempt my mother?
Lucifer.   I tempt none,
   Save with the truth: was not the tree, the tree
   Of knowledge? and was not the tree of life
   Still fruitful? Did *I* bid her pluck them not?
   Did *I* plant things prohibited within
   The reach of beings innocent, and curious
   By their own innocence? I would have made ye
   Gods: and even He who thrust ye forth, so thrust ye
   Because 'ye should not eat the fruits of life,
   And become gods as We.' Were those His words?
Cain. They were, as I have heard from those who heard them,
   In thunder.
Lucifer.   Then who was the demon? He
   Who would not let ye live, or he who would
   Have made ye live for ever in the joy,
   The power of knowledge?

> BYRON, GEORGE GORDON, LORD, *Cain*, 1821

When we speak of *The Devil*, 'tis, *A name of Multitude*; it means not *One* Individual Devil, so Potent and Scient, as perhaps a *Manichee* would imagine; but it means a *Kind*, which a *Multitude* belongs unto. Alas, the *Devils*, they swarm about us, like the *Frogs of Egypt*, in the most Retired of our Chambers. Are we at our *Boards*? There will be Devils to Tempt us unto Sensuality. Are we in our *Beds*? There will be Devils to Tempt us unto Carnality. Are we in our *Shops*? There will be Devils to Tempt us unto Dishonesty. Yea, Tho' we get into the Church of God, there will be Devils to Haunt us in the very *Temple* it self, and there tempt us to manifold Misbehaviours. I am verily perswaded, That there are very few Humane Affairs whereinto some Devils are not Insinuated . . .

'Tis to be supposed, that some *Devils* are more peculiarly *Commission'd*, and perhaps *Qualify'd*, for some Countries, while others are for others. This is intimated when in *Mark* 5: 10, the Devils *besought* our Lord much, *that he would not send them away out of the Countrey*. Why was that? But in all probability, because *these Devils* were more able to *do the works of the Devil*, in such a Countrey, than in another. It is not likely that every Devil does know every *Language*; or that every Devil can do every *Mischief*. 'Tis possible, that the *Experience*, or, if I may call it so, the *Education* of all Devils is not alike, and that there may be some difference in their *Abilities*.

COTTON MATHER, The Wonders of the Invisible World, 1693

There is no vulgar story of the devil's having appeared anywhere without a *cloven foot*. It is observable also that this infernal enemy, in graphic representations of him, is seldom or never pictured without one.

The learned Sir Thomas Browne is full on this subject of popular superstition in his 'Vulgar Errors': 'The ground of this opinion at first,' says he, 'might be his frequent appearing in the shape of *a goat*' (this accounts also for his *horns* and *tail*), 'which answers this description. This was the opinion of the ancient Christians concerning the apparition of Panites, Fauns, and Satyrs; and of this form we read of one that appeared to Anthony in the Wilderness. The same is also confirmed from expositions of Holy Scripture. For whereas it is said, Thou shalt not offer unto devils: the original word is Seghuirim, that is, rough and hairy goats, because in that shape the devil most often appeared . . .' He observes, also, that the goat was the emblem of the sin-offering, and is the emblem of sinful men at the day of judgment.

The learned and pious Mede, also, in his 'Discourses' [1642], has ventured some thoughts on this subject, as follows: 'The devil could not appear in humane shape, while man was in his integrity; because he was a spirit fallen from his first glorious perfection, and therefore must appear in such shape which might argue his imperfection and abasement, which was the shape of a beast: otherwise, no reason can be given why he should not rather have appeared to Eve in the shape of a woman than of a serpent. But, since the fall of man, the case is altered; now we know he can take upon him the shape of man. He appears, it seems, in the shape of man's imperfection, either for age or deformity, as like an old man (for so the witches say); and perhaps it is not altogether false, which is vulgarly affirmed, that the devil, appearing in human shape, has always a deformity of some uncouth member or other: as though he could not yet take upon him human shape entirely, for that man himself is not entirely and utterly fallen, as he is.'

JOHN BRAND (?1743–1806), *Observations on Popular Antiquities*, ed. Sir Henry Ellis, 1813

It should be (but it is not) unnecessary to add that a belief in angels, whether good or evil, does not mean a belief in either as they are represented in art and literature. Devils are depicted with bats' wings and good angels with birds' wings not because anyone holds that moral deterioration would be likely to turn feathers into membrane, but because most men like birds better than bats. They are given wings at all in order to suggest the swiftness of unimpeded intellectual energy. They are given human form because man is the only rational creature we know. Creatures higher in the natural order than ourselves, either incorporeal or animating bodies of a sort we cannot experience, must be represented symbolically if they are to be represented at all.

C. S. LEWIS, Preface to *The Screwtape Letters*, 1961 edition

Authors of legends, painters, sculptors, expended the best of their inventive talent in depicting Satan; and so well, or to speak more correctly, so ill did they depict him that Satan himself must have resented their efforts—though it is not likely that he sets any great store by his own beauty. There is a well-known story, told by many writers of the Middle Ages, about a painter who, having painted a certain devil uglier than fairness demanded, was by that same demon hurled down headlong from the scaffolding where he was working. Luckily for the painter, a Madonna, whom he had represented as very beautiful, thrust forth her arm from the picture and caught and upheld him in mid-air.

Thus the Devil, who fully understands such matters, succeeds, with a single temptation and oftentimes a most trivial one, in placing in the mind the first germ of sin; and this germ, aided by him, straightway takes root, grows, becomes a plant, and in a short time bears its pernicious fruits. There was a hermit who lived a most austere life and had great reputation for holiness. One day the Devil appeared before him in the semblance of an honest wight and said to him: 'You live such a lonely life; why don't you get a cock to bear you company and to rouse you betimes in the morning?' The poor hermit at first refused, then hesitated, and finally followed this advice and procured the cock. What harm in that? A cock cannot possibly be the Devil. But the cock becomes weary of living by himself and grows thinner from day to day. Then the hermit, through a sentiment of charity, provides a hen for the cock. Oh that he had never done so! The sight of certain spectacles awakens within his mind old ardours which he thought forever quenched. He becomes enamoured of the daughter of a neighbouring nobleman, a young and very beautiful girl; he sins with her; then, to escape the vengeance of her parents, he kills the girl and conceals her body beneath his couch. But the crime is discovered and the criminal is sentenced to pay the supreme penalty. While mounting the scaffold, he exclaims: 'Behold, to what an end a cock has brought me!'

A very wicked tax-gatherer, rapacious and cruel, was on his way one day to a certain village, intending to carry out there one of his customary exactions. On the road he fell in with an individual whom he speedily recognized as the Devil; it is unnecessary to add that, on recognizing him, he was anxious, for the best of reasons, to get rid of his company. They meet a man driving a pig which has given its owner so much trouble that, losing all patience, he cries out: 'The Devil take you!' Says the tax-gatherer to the Devil: 'Don't you hear him? The man is giving you his pig; go and take it.' 'No,' replied the Devil, 'he isn't giving it from his heart.' A little further on they find a mother who, exasperated at her crying child, shouts: 'May the Devil have you!' 'And why don't you take it?' exclaims the tax-gatherer. 'She isn't giving it to me from her heart,' answers the Devil, 'that's a mere figure of speech.' Meanwhile they arrive at the village, and the poor villagers, seeing their tormentor coming, cry out in chorus: 'The Devil take you! May you serve the Devil!' Quoth the Devil: 'These people are giving you to me from their hearts, therefore you are mine.' And saying no more, he seized him by the hair and carried him off.

Arturo Graf, *The Story of the Devil*, 1889; tr. Edward Noble Stone

Medieval philosophers and theologians held that evil is in its essence so horrible that the human mind, if it could realize it, must perish at its contemplation.

Such realization was by mercy ordinarily withheld, but its possibility was hinted in the legend of the *Visio malefica.* The *Visio beatifica* was, as is well known, that vision of the Deity or realization of the perfect Good which was to form the happiness of heaven, and the reward of the sanctified in the next world. Tradition says that this vision was accorded also to some specially elect spirits even in this life, as to Enoch, Elijah, Stephen, and Jerome. But there was a converse to the Beatific Vision in the *Visio malefica,* or presentation of absolute Evil, which was to be the chief torture of the damned, and which, like the Beatific Vision, had been made visible in life to certain desperate men. It visited Esau, as was said, when he found no place for repentance, and Judas, whom it drove to suicide. Cain saw it when he murdered his brother, and legend relates that in his case, and in that of others, it left a physical brand to be borne by the body to the grave. It was supposed that the Malefic Vision, besides being thus spontaneously presented to typically abandoned men, had actually been purposely called up by some few great adepts, and used by them to blast their enemies. But to do so was considered equivalent to a conscious surrender to the powers of evil, as the vision once seen took away all hope of final salvation.

JOHN MEADE FALKNER, *The Lost Stradivarius,* 1895

The greatest punishment God can inflict on the wicked, is when the church, to chastise them, delivers them over to Satan, who, with God's permission, kills them, or makes them undergo great calamities. Many devils are in woods, in waters, in wildernesses, and in dark pooly places, ready to hurt and preju-dice people; some are also in the thick black clouds, which cause hail, lightnings, and thunderings, and poison the air, the pastures and grounds. When these things happen, then the philosophers and physicians say, it is natural, ascribing it to the planets, and showing I know not what reasons for such misfortunes and plagues as ensue.

MARTIN LUTHER, *Table-Talk,* first German edition 1566; tr. William Hazlitt, jun.

If anie aske why he [the Devil] is more conversant & busie in churchyards and places where men are buried, than in anie other places, it is to make us beleeve that the bodies & soules of the departed rest entirely in his possession, and the peculiar power of death is resigned to his disposition. A rich man delights in nothing so much as to be uncessantly raking in his treasurie, to bee turning over his rustie gold everie houre: the boanes of the dead, the divell counts his chiefe treasurie, and therfore is he continually raking amongst them; and the rather he doth it, that the living which heare it should bee more unwilling to die, insomuch as after death their boanes should take no rest.

NASHE, *The Terrors of the Night*

A law student from the north of England named Briggs . . . had been to a lecture on the sin against the Holy Ghost, and had misunderstood the lecturer to say that *all* sins came into this category. Searching his conscience and discovering many faults of one kind or another, he persuaded himself that he too had committed the sin and was a reprobate whose prayers were in vain. After several unsuccessful attempts at suicide, he noticed that he was being followed by an ugly dog which would not be driven away. When preparing to jump into the Thames he saw it glaring at him 'with such terrible sparkling eyes' that he realized it was no ordinary dog, but the Devil waiting for his soul. The dog subsequently vanished and a well-meaning physician, diagnosing a case of melancholy, prescribed blood-letting and a purge. But Briggs fell into a trance, and from his lips came forth his part of a dialogue between himself and the Devil which was eagerly recorded by the godly onlookers. The Devil assaulted him with a combination of threats and promises. On the one hand he assured him that there were no pains in Hell, that there was no God, that Christ was not the Son of God, that Christ's parents were unmarried, that the Scripture was false, and that everything happened by mere nature. On the other he urged that he was damned anyway, and that he would do better to settle for his offers of a cupboard of plate, and a seductive 'painted woman' (who temptingly sang and danced before him). This discussion continued at intervals for over a fortnight (the Devil explaining that he took Sundays off to cut purses among the crowd at St Paul's Cross).

In the end Foxe was called in to conduct a special prayer-meeting to reclaim the patient. Addressing the Devil directly ('Thou most wretched serpent . . . O thou foul devil, I command thee to depart'), he engaged the spirit in fluent argument, clearly enjoying the opportunity of a joust of this kind. Satan skilfully counter-attacked by denouncing Foxe as a witch, but ultimately the patient himself was prevailed upon to command the Devil to depart in God's name, and his troubles were over.

KEITH THOMAS, *Religion and the Decline of Magic*, 1971; drawn from an account of 1574 by the puritan John Foxe, author of the *Book of Martyrs*

A man had a habit, whenever he fell, of saying: 'Devil take me.' He was advised to discontinue this evil custom, lest some day the devil should take him at his word. He promised to vent his impatience by some other phrase; but, one day, having stumbled, he called upon the devil, in the way I have mentioned, and was killed upon the spot, falling on a sharp-pointed piece of wood.

When I could not be rid of the devil with sentences out of the Holy Scripture, I made him often fly with jeering words; sometimes I said unto him: Saint Satan! if Christ's blood, which was shed for my sins, be not sufficient, then I desire that thou wouldst pray to God for me. When he finds me idle, with nothing in hand, he is very busy, and before I am aware, he wrings from me a bitter sweat: but when I offer him the pointed spear, God's Word, he flies; yet, before he goes, makes a grievous hurricane. When I began to write against the pope, and the gospel was going on, the devil set himself strongly to work, rumbling and raging about, for he would willingly have preserved purgatory at Magdeburg. There was a citizen, whose child died, for whom he refused to have vigils and masses sung. The devil played his freaks, came every night, about twelve o'clock, into the chamber where the boy died, and made a whining like a young child. The good citizen being therewith full of sorrow, knew not what course to take. The popish priests said: O, now you see how it goes when vigils are not solemnized. Whereupon the citizen sent to me, desiring my advice (for the sermon I had lately preached on this text: 'They have Moses and the prophets', had been printed, and been read by him); and I wrote to him from Wittenberg, and advised him not to suffer any vigils at all to be held, for he might be fully assured that these were merely pranks of the devil; whereupon, the children and servants in the house jeered the devil, and said: What doest thou, Satan? Avoid, thou cursed spirit, get thee gone to the place where thou oughtest to be, to the pit of hell. When the devil marked their contempt, he left off his game, and came there no more. He is a proud spirit, and cannot endure scorn.

LUTHER, *Table-Talk*

Doctor Luther said: When he could not get rid of Satan by means of the sacred Scriptures and earnest words of rebuke, he had often driven him off by a good joke, or a hearty laugh, or a biting sarcasm. As for instance, he said to him: 'Dear devil, if the blood of Christ is not enough to cover my sins, be kind enough to offer for me a word or two of prayer thyself.' . . .

Mr Jacob, the mayor of Bremen, came to Magdeburg and took up his abode at the head hotel. 'I want,' said he to his host, 'to hear this devil which is so much talked of here.' 'You shall, honoured sir, hear him this evening at eight o'clock.' Sure enough, the devil came down the chimney, breaking and overthrowing everything in his passage. 'Well, well,' said Mr Jacob, 'I have had enough of him. Let's to bed.' There were two chambers near each other. In one lay the landlady, her children and her maidservants; the other was occupied by Mr Jacob and mine host. When now Mr Jacob had gone to bed, the devil came and began to sport with him, taking away his coverlet. Mr Jacob was horrified, and fell to pray with all his might. Then the devil went into the next chamber and began to play his tricks on the women, chaffing them and running over the bedclothes, now as a troop of mice and now as a troop of rats. And as he would not cease, the hostess threw at him a certain chamber convenience, saying, 'Take that, vile wretch! and go on a pilgrimage to Rome, to worship thine idol the pope, and buy a score of indulgences at his shop! You need them all; and when you have got them, what good will they do you?' That moment the devil and his imps fled away; *quia est superbus spiritus et non potest ferre contemptum sui*; for he is a haughty scoundrel, and cannot endure contempt.

JOHN R. BEARD, DD, *The Autobiography of Satan*, 1872

His Highness did not complain in any way of the bad reputation he enjoys in every part of the world, he assured me that he was, himself, the person most concerned to abolish *superstition*, and avowed that he had never felt fear concerning his own power, except once, on the day when he had heard a preacher, more subtle than his colleagues, cry from the pulpit: 'My dear brothers, never forget, when you hear praise of the Enlightenment and its progress, that the cleverest ruse of the Devil is to persuade you that he doesn't exist!'

One shouldn't believe that the Devil only tempts men of genius. No doubt he despises fools, but he doesn't disdain their co-operation. On the contrary, he builds great hopes on them.

Look at George Sand. She is above all, and more than anything else, a *big idiot*; but she is *possessed*. It is the Devil who has persuaded her to trust to *her good heart* and *her good sense*, so that she might persuade all the other big idiots to trust to their good heart and their good sense . . .

George Sand is one of those old *ingénues* who never want to quit the boards.

I read recently a preface (the preface to *Mlle La Quintinie*) in which she claims that a true Christian cannot believe in Hell.

She has good reasons for wishing to do away with Hell.

> CHARLES BAUDELAIRE, first extract from 'Le Joueur généreux', 1864, second from *Mon Cœur mis à nu*, published posthumously in 1887

The aged, feeling premonitions of decline, are apt to look back and survey the past. If they become aware that, whatever the cause, they suffer in public opinion, they naturally take up the pen and write their own biography. Such is my condition . . .

The falsity is, that I am a personal concentration of transcendental vice, wickedness and woe. The truth which I wish to substitute is, that I am a personification of the dark side of humanity and the universe. Being, as such, an impalpable presence, I exist in every land and occupy a corner in every human heart. A reflection of the outer world of matter and the inner world of mind, I am not all dark, nor could I ever have been painted black had not theological speculation first thrown its own murky clouds over the heart of man and over the creation of God. The human soul in ruins and the world under its Maker's curse inevitably perpetuated that incarnation of Evil which theologians call the Devil or Satan. The terrific figment came the more readily into vigour, because, while a shadow from man's own baseness, it served as a substitute for his relief and a palliation of his guilt.

> Bad as he is, the Devil may be abused,
> Be falsely charged and causelessly accused,
> When men, unwilling to be blamed alone,
> Shift off on him the crimes that are their own . . .

Yet I am a power. I am a power under God, and as such I perform a task which, however unlovely and however painful, is destined to put forward God's wise and benignant purposes for the good of man . . . My origin is human, my sphere of action earthly, my final end dissolution. Evil must cease when good is universal. While, then, I cannot boast of a heavenly birth, I disown fiendish dispositions. Worse than the worst man I cannot be. I am indeed a sort of mongrel, born, bred, reared and nurtured of human fancy, folly and fraud. As such, I possess a *quasi* omnipresence and a *quasi* omniscience; for I exist wherever man exists, and, dwelling in human hearts, know all that men think, feel and do. Hence I have power to tempt and mislead, and that power, when I am in my worst moods, I am pleased to exercise.

BEARD, *The Autobiography of Satan*

The Archbishop of Heligoland believes his faith, and it makes him so unhappy that he finds it impossible to advise any one to accept it. He summons the Devil, makes a compact with him and is relieved by being made to see that there was nothing in it—whereon he is very good and happy and leads a most beneficent life, but is haunted by the thought that on his death the Devil will claim his bond. This terror grows greater and greater, and he determines to see the Devil again.

The upshot of it all is that the Devil turns out to have been Christ who has a dual life and appears sometimes as Christ and sometimes as the Devil.

SAMUEL BUTLER (1835–1902), *Notebooks*; proposed subject for a short story

Mephistopheles. Now, Faustus, what wouldst thou have me do?
Faustus. I charge thee wait upon me whilst I live,
　　To do whatever Faustus shall command,
　　Be it to make the moon drop from her sphere,
　　Or the ocean to overwhelm the world.
Meph. I am a servant to great Lucifer,
　　And may not follow thee without his leave;
　　No more than he commands must we perform.
Faust. Did he not charge thee to appear to me?
Meph. No, I came hither of mine own accord.
Faust. Did not my conjuring speeches raise thee? Speak!
Meph. That was the cause, but yet *per accidens*,
　　For when we hear one rack the name of God,
　　Abjure the Scriptures, and his Saviour Christ,
　　We fly in hope to get his glorious soul;
　　Nor will we come, unless he use such means
　　Whereby he is in danger to be damn'd.
　　Therefore the shortest cut for conjuring
　　Is stoutly to abjure the Trinity,
　　And pray devoutly to the prince of hell.

Faust. So Faustus hath already done, and holds this principle:
    There is no chief but only Belzebub,
    To whom Faustus doth dedicate himself.
    This word damnation terrifies not him,
    For he confounds hell in Elysium:
    His ghost be with the old philosophers!
    But, leaving these vain trifles of men's souls,
    Tell me what is that Lucifer thy Lord?
Meph. Arch–regent and commander of all spirits.
Faust. Was not that Lucifer an angel once?
Meph. Yes, Faustus, and most dearly lov'd of God.
Faust. How comes it, then, that he is prince of devils?
Meph. O, by aspiring pride and insolence,
    For which God threw him from the face of heaven.
Faust. And what are you that live with Lucifer?
Meph. Unhappy spirits that fell with Lucifer,
    Conspir'd against our God with Lucifer,
    And are for ever damn'd with Lucifer.
Faust. Where are you damn'd?
Meph. In hell.
Faust. How comes it, then, that thou art out of hell?
Meph. Why, this is hell, nor am I out of it.
    Thinkst thou that I, who saw the face of God,
    And tasted the eternal joys of heaven,
    Am not tormented with ten thousand hells
    In being depriv'd of everlasting bliss?
    O, Faustus, leave these frivolous demands,
    Which strike a terror to my fainting soul!
Faust. What, is great Mephistopheles so passionate
    For being deprived of the joys of heaven?
    Learn thou of Faustus manly fortitude,
    And scorn those joys thou never shalt possess.

Faust. First will I question with thee about hell:
    Tell me, where is the place that men call hell?
Meph. Under the heavens.
Faust. Ay, but whereabout?
Meph. Within the bowels of these elements,
    Where we are tortur'd and remain for ever.
    Hell hath no limits, nor is circumscrib'd

In one self place; for where we are is hell,
And where hell is, there must we ever be.
And, to conclude, when all the world dissolves,
And every creature shall be purified,
All places shall be hell that are not heaven.

Faust. Come, I think hell's a fable.

Meph. Ay, think so still, till experience change thy mind.

CHRISTOPHER MARLOWE, *The Tragical History of Dr Faustus*; earliest known
performance 1594, the year after Marlowe's death

Mephistopheles. Do you know me now? Skinny, cadaverous bitch,
    Do you know your lord and master? Why don't I
    Smash you to pieces, tell me why,
    You and your ape-familiars? Must I teach
    You some respect for my red doublet? What
    Is this cock's feather, eh? My face,
    Have I been hiding it? You learn your place,
    Old hag! Am I to name myself or not?

Witch. Oh master, pardon my rude greeting!
    But where's your cloven hoof, your horse's leg?
    And your two ravens? Sir, I beg
    To be excused!

Meph. Well, well, and so
    You are for once; it's true, I know,
    Some time has passed since our last meeting.
    Besides, civilization, which now licks
    Us all so smooth, has taught even the Devil tricks;
    The northern fiend's becoming a lost cause—
    Where are his horns these days, his tail, his claws?
    As for my foot, which I can't do without,
    People would think me odd to go about
    With that; and so, like some young gentlemen,
    I've worn false calves since God knows when.

Witch [*capering about*]. I'm crazy with excitement now I see
    Our young Lord Satan's back again!

Meph. Woman, don't use that name to me!

Witch. Why, sir, what harm's it ever done?

Meph. The name has been a myth too long.

Not that man's any better off—the Evil One
They're rid of, evil is still going strong.
Please call me 'Baron', that will do.
I'm just a gentleman, like others of my kind.
My blood's entirely noble, you will find;
My coat of arms may be inspected too.
        [He makes an indecent gesture.]
Witch [shrieking with laughter].
Ha! ha! You haven't changed a bit!
Still the same bad lad, by the looks of it!

    JOHANN WOLFGANG VON GOETHE, *Faust* Part One, 1808; tr. David Luke

At first Pope Alexander the sixth, having society with wicked spirits and devils, gave himself body and soul unto them, upon condition he might attain to the pope's seat and dignity, which they promised him and fulfilled, but he enjoyed it not long, contrary to his expectation. For he, being privily conveyed into a chamber in a certain place called Mount Cavillus, and there questioning with his demon how long he should reign pope, was answered that he should reign 11 and 8, which this holy father understood to be so many years; but he was deceived.

For after he had reigned pope 11 years and 8 months, this devil would no longer be without his prey, but straight came to the pope's court decked like a courtier, and at the pope's chamber door did knock very loudly, saying that he must needs speak with his Fatherhood. The door being opened, he came and spake with the pope, all others being bid to avoid.

But they were so earnestly talking together that many did rightly conject that they were at contention. For the pope stoutly affirmed his time not to be expired, 'for,' said he, 'I had promised me 19 years (for 11 and 8 is 19) and of these 19 years I have reigned but 11 years and 8 months.' But this courtier-like devil replied and said that he mistook his words, 'for I said not,' said he, '19 years, but I meant 11 years and 8 months, and therefore now thou must needs die.' Whereat the pope being abashed fell to entreating, but all was in vain.

    ANON., *The Examination of John Walsh . . . upon certayne Interrogatories touchyng Wytchcrafte and Sorcerye*, 1566; ed. Barbara Rosen

You see, supposedly, if you look long enough and hard enough at the glass, here, by the rose tree, you find another figure in the window. It is one of those freak things, the way in which angles and colours go together randomly forms another shape—or perhaps the maker of the window intended it to happen. The figure is of a dark man, Satan himself, naturally, who took a serpent's appearance to seduce Eve to wrongdoing . . .

A hundred years ago, the tale has it, one of the great landowning families had one young fair daughter. She was noted as wonderfully vivacious, and how she loved to dance all night at all the balls in the area . . . Well, it would seem she visited the church and saw the window, and saw the figure of Satan. She found him handsome, and, in the way of some young girls, she—do hope you are broad-minded—she fell in love with him, with the Devil himself. And she made some vow, something adolescent and messy, with blood and such things. She invited him to come in that form and claim her for a dance. And when the next ball was held, about one in the morning, a great silence fell on the house. The orchestra musicians found their hands would not move, the dancers found their feet likewise seemed turned to stone. Then the doors blew open in a gust of wind. Every light in every chandelier went out—and yet there was plenty of light, even so, to see by: it was the light of Hell, shining into the ballroom. Then a dark figure, a tall dark man, entered the room. He had come, as she requested, to claim his dance. It seems he brought his own orchestra with him. They were masked, every one of them, but sitting down by the dance floor they struck up such a waltz that no one who heard it could resist its rhythm—and yet no one in the room could move! Then he came to the landowner's daughter and bowed and asked her for the honour of partnering her. And she alone of all the company was freed from the spell. She glided into his arms. He drew her away. They turned and whirled like a thing of fire, while all the rest of the room danced in their bones to the music, unable to dance in any other way, until all their shoes, and the white dresses of the women, and the fine evening clothes of the gentlemen, were dappled inside with their blood! . . . But presently the Devil dashed his partner away through the floor. They vanished, and the demon musicians vanished, although no other there was able to regain motion until the cocks crowed. As for the girl, they found her skin—her *skin*, mark you, solely that—some days later on a hill. It had been danced right off her skeleton. But on her face, such as there was of it, was fixed a grin of agonized joy.

TANITH LEE, from 'The Devil's Rose', 1988

No one could have recognized the village of ours a little over a hundred years ago; it was a hamlet, the poorest kind of hamlet . . . In this hamlet a man, or rather a devil in human form, often made his appearance. Why he came, and whence, no one knew. He prowled about, got drunk, and suddenly disappeared as if into the air, leaving no trace of his existence. Then, behold, he seemed to have dropped from the sky again, and went flying about the street of the village . . . He would collect together all the Cossacks he met; then there were songs, laughter, and cash in plenty, and vodka flowed like water . . . He would address the pretty girls, and give them ribbons, earrings, strings of beads—more than they knew what to do with. It is true that the pretty girls rather hesitated about accepting his presents: God knows, perhaps, what unclean hands they had passed through. My grandfather's aunt, who kept at that time a tavern, in which Basavriuk (as they called this devil-man) often caroused, said that no consideration on the earth would have induced her to accept a gift from him. But then, again, how avoid accepting? Fear seized on everyone when he knit his shaggy brows, and gave a sidelong glance which might send your feet God knows whither: whilst if you did accept, then the next night some fiend from the swamp, with horns on his head, came and began to squeeze your neck, if there was a string of beads upon it; or bite your finger, if there was a ring upon it; or drag you by the hair, if ribbons were braided in it. God have mercy, then, on those who held such gifts! But here was the difficulty: it was impossible to get rid of them; if you threw them into the water, the diabolical ring or necklace would skim along the surface and into your hand.

My late grandfather's aunt said that he was particularly angry with her because she had abandoned her former tavern, and tried with all his might to revenge himself upon her. Once the village elders were assembled in the tavern, and, as the saying goes, were arranging the precedence at the table, in the middle of which was placed a small roasted lamb, shame to say. They chattered about this, that, and the other—among the rest about various marvels and strange things. Well, they saw something; it would have been nothing if only one had seen it, but all saw it, and it was this: the sheep raised his head; his goggling eyes became alive and sparkled; and the black, bristling moustache, which appeared for one instant, made a significant gesture at those present. All at once recognized Basavriuk's countenance in the sheep's head; my grandfather's aunt thought it was on the point of asking for vodka. The worthy elders seized their hats and hastened home.

Another time, the church elder himself, who was fond of an occasional private interview with my grandfather's brandy-glass, had not succeeded in getting to the bottom twice, when he beheld the glass bowing very low to him. 'Satan take you, let us make the sign of the cross over you!' And the same marvel happened to his better half. She had just begun to mix the dough in a huge kneading-trough when suddenly the trough sprang up. 'Stop, stop! where are you going?' Putting its arms akimbo, with dignity, it went skipping all about the cottage. You may laugh, but it was no laughing matter to our grandfathers.

NIKOLAI VASILIEVICH GOGOL, from 'St John's Eve', 1830; tr. C. J. Hogarth

Some of the Cabala books were chiefly concerned with sacred matters, but others, such as the *Book of Raziel* and the *Book of the Devout*, devoted much space to the powers of evil—demons, devils, imps, hobgoblins—as well as to magic. God had His kingdom, and Satan, or Asmodeus, had his own . . .

Because my brother Joshua had left the path of righteousness and denied both God and the devil, my parents often spoke of both these forces in order to overcome his arguments. If there were demons, there had to be a God. I heard countless stories of dybbuks, corpses that left their graves at night and wandered off to visit miracle workers or to attend distant fairs. Some of them forgot that they were dead and launched all kinds of business ventures or even got married. In Bilgorai, my mother's home town, there was a ritual slaughterer, Avromele, on whose window an evil spirit had been beating for weeks on end. Every evening the whole population of the town gathered in the house to listen to the invisible force knock on the pane. One could discourse with it. One asked it questions and it tapped out the answers—mainly 'yes' or 'no' but occasionally entire words according to an agreed-upon code . . . Well, and what about the girl in Krasnik who was possessed by the soul of a sinful man which in a male voice recounted the sins and abominations he had committed during his lifetime? The girl was of common stock and didn't even know the alphabet, yet the dybbuk spouted passages and quotations from the Gemara, the Midrash, and other holy books. Often, wag that he was, he transposed the sacred words so that they emerged obscene but in a way apparent only to those who were learned. I read about such demons in storybooks. They were even mentioned in the Gemara, which spoke of Jewish demons and of Gentile demons.

I lived in dread of these invisible beings. Our stairs were dark at night, and going up and down them became for me a terrible burden. I often counted the fringes on my ritual garment to see that none were missing. I mumbled incantations from the Gemara and from other sacred books. My brother Joshua laughed at me. He argued that there was no such thing as evil spirits. It was all fantasy, fanaticism. Well, but had a whole world conspired to make up the same lie? An anthology of German poetry had somehow found its way into our house. Since German is similar to Yiddish and because my eagerness to read was so great, I had learned to read German and I read Goethe's 'Der Erlkönig', Heine's poem about the Lorelei, and many other mystical poems. The whole world believed in ghosts. If it could be shown that a piece of mud in the gutter housed millions of unseen microbes, why couldn't hordes of invisible ghosts be flying around in the air? Even my astute brother couldn't come up with an answer to this question.

ISAAC BASHEVIS SINGER, from 'A Little Boy in Search of God', 1975; in *Love and Exile*

Some that are yet living with me, affirm this to be true which I will now speak of. A man of holy life there was, called Stephen, who was a Priest in the province of Valeria, nigh of kindred to my deacon Bonifacius: who, coming home upon a time from travel, spake somewhat negligently to his servant, saying: 'Come, sir devil, and pull off my hose': at which words, straightways his garters began to loose in great haste, so that he plainly perceived that the devil indeed, whom he named, was pulling off his stocking: whereat being much terrified, he cried out aloud, and said: 'Away, wretched caitiff, away: I spake not to thee, but to my servant.' Then the devil gave over, leaving his garters almost quite off. By which we may learn, that if the devil be so officious in things concerning our body, how ready and diligent he is to observe and note the cogitations of our soul.

ST GREGORY THE GREAT, *Dialogues*

There is another piece of dark practice here, which lies between Satan and his particular agents, and which they must give us an answer to, when they can, which I think will not be in haste; and that is about the obsequious Devil submitting to be called up into visibility, whenever an old woman has her hand crossed with a white sixpence, as they call it. One would think that instead of these vile things called witches being sold to the Devil, the Devil was really sold for a slave to them; for how far soever Satan's residence is off from this state of life, they have power, it seems, to fetch him from home, and oblige him to come at their call.

DEFOE, *The Political History of the Devil*, 1726

One day, when Dominick [St Dominic] was in his study, the devil so pestered him in the shape of a flea, leaping and frisking about on the leaves of his book, that he found it impossible to continue his reading: irritated at length by such unhandsome treatment, he fixed him on the very spot where he finished reading, and in this shape made use of him to find the place again. Having at last, however, released old *nick* from this demonological dilemma, he appeared to him again in his study in the guise of a monkey, and grinned so 'horribly a ghastly grin', and skipped about so, that he was more annoyed now than before. To put a stop to these monkey tricks, Dominick forthwith commanded him, the said monkey, to take the candlestick and hold it for him; this the monkey did, and Dominick made him continue holding it, until it was burnt down to the bottom of the wick, and although the monkey made a horrid noise at burning his fingers, he was forced to hold it until it was burnt out, which it did until it had burnt the devil's monkey fingers to the bone.

> J. S. FORSYTH, *Demonologia, or, Natural Knowledge Revealed: being an Exposé of Ancient and Modern Superstitions*, 1827

St Dunstan was skilled in all artefacts, and he was specially famous as a smith. He had a smithy of his own in his palace at Mayfield [in Sussex], where he often used to entertain himself with ingenious pieces of metal work. One day the Devil chose to visit him there. He had often been worsted by St Dunstan in his proper form, and knew that it was no good to try straight conclusions with him, so he assumed the appearance of a very beautiful woman, and came gliding into the cell on the pretence that he had some ghostly counsel to seek. It was not long before the lovely creature began to make amorous advances to the Saint. Whether he saw something odd in her footwear or noticed that she kept one foot always hidden we are not told, at all events St Dunstan shrewdly suspected that it was not mortal wickedness that inspired her; but he made no sign, but continued working at his forge. At length the lady sidled right up to him, and St Dunstan drew a red-hot pair of pincers out of the fire and clipped it onto her beautiful nose. At once there was a stench and shriek, and where the lady had been a hideous devil appeared with flapping wings and lashing tail; but the pincers were still firmly fixed on his nose, and St Dunstan still held the other end of them. Round and round the room he dragged the Devil, until they were both tired, and St Dunstan opened the pincers and let him fly. And with one flap of his wings the Devil fled to Tunbridge Wells, where he cooled his nose in the waters, which have had a ruddy, ochreous tinge ever since. But the very pincers that St Dunstan used are still to be seen at Mayfield Palace to witness to the tale.

> K. M. BRIGGS, *Pale Hecate's Team*, 1962

'This is how we keep the fast. But what is that compared with you, holy Father,' added the monk, growing more confident, 'for all the year round, even at Easter, you take nothing but bread and water, and what we should eat in two days lasts you full seven? It's truly marvellous—your great abstinence.'

'And mushrooms?' asked Father Ferapont, suddenly.

'Mushrooms?' repeated the surprised monk.

'Yes. I can give up their bread, not needing it at all, and go away into the forest and live there on the mushrooms or the berries, but they can't give up their bread here, wherefore they are in bondage to the devil. Nowadays the unclean deny that there is need of such fasting. Haughty and unclean is their judgement.'

'Och, true,' sighed the monk.

'And have you seen devils among them?' asked Ferapont.

'Among them? Among whom?' asked the monk, timidly.

'I went to the Father Superior on Trinity Sunday last year, I haven't been since. I saw a devil sitting on one man's chest, hiding under his cassock, only his horns poked out; another had one peeping out of his pocket with such sharp eyes, he was afraid of me; another settled in the unclean belly of one, another was hanging round a man's neck, and so he was carrying him about without seeing him.'

'You—can see spirits?' the monk enquired.

'I tell you I can see, I can see through them. When I was coming out from the Superior's I saw one hiding from me behind the door, and a big one, a yard and a half or more high, with a thick long grey tail, and the tip of his tail was in the crack of the door and I was quick and slammed the door, pinching his tail in it. He squealed and began to struggle, and I made the sign of the cross over him three times. And he died on the spot like a crushed spider. He must have rotted there in the corner and be stinking, but they don't see, they don't smell it. It's a year since I have been there. I reveal it to you, as you are a stranger.'

'Your words are terrible! But, holy and blessed Father,' said the monk, growing bolder and bolder, 'is it true, as they noise abroad even to distant lands about you, that you are in continual communication with the Holy Ghost?'

'He does fly down at times.'

'How does he fly down? In what form?'

'As a bird.'

'The Holy Ghost in the form of a Dove?'

'There's the Holy Ghost and there's the Holy Spirit. The Holy Spirit can appear as other birds—sometimes as a swallow, sometimes a goldfinch and sometimes as a blue tit.'

'How do you know him from an ordinary tit?'

'He speaks.'

'How does he speak, in what language?'

'Human language.'

'And what does he tell you?'

'Why, today he told me that a fool would visit me and would ask me unseemly questions.'

FYODOR MIKHAILOVICH DOSTOEVSKY, *The Brothers Karamazov*, 1879–80; tr. Constance Garnett

While on the subject of the Devil, I cannot omit a story told of a certain close-fisted Cornish man, whom we will call Mr Pengelly, as he is still alive. The story lost nothing in the vicar's mouth.

Mr Pengelly was very ill and like to die. So one night the Devil came to the side of his bed, and said to him: 'Mr Pengelly, I will trouble you if you please.'

'Yu will trouble me with what, your honour?' says Mr Pengelly, sitting up in bed.

'Why, just to step along of me, sir,' says the Devil.

'Oh! but I don't please at all,' replies Mr Pengelly, lying down again and tucking his pillow under his cheek.

'Well, sir, but time's up, yu know,' was the remark the Devil made thereupon; 'and whether it pleases yu or no, yu must come along of me to once, sir. It isn't much of a distance to speak of from Morwenstow,' says he by way of apology.

'If I must go, sir,' says Mr Pengelly, wiping his nose with his blue pocket-handkerchief covered with white spots, and R.P. marked in the corner in red cotton, 'why, then, I suppose yu ain't in a great hurry. Yu'll give me ten minutes?'

'What do'y want ten minutes for, Mr Pengelly?' asks the Devil.

'Why, sir,' says Mr Pengelly, putting his blue pocket-handkerchief over his face, 'I'm ashamed to name it, but I shu'd like to say my prayers. Leastwise, they couldn't du no harm,' exclaimed he, pulling the handkerchief off and looking out.

'They wouldn't du yer no gude, Mr Pengelly,' says the Devil.

'I shu'd be more comfable in my mind, sir, if I said 'em,' says he.

'Now, I'll tell yu what, Mr Pengelly,' says the Devil after a pause. 'I'd take to deal handsome by yu. Yu've done me many a gude turn in your day. I'll let yu live as long as yonder cann'l-end burns.'

'Thank'y kindly, sir,' says Mr Pengelly. And presently he says, for the Devil did not make signs of departing: 'Would yu be so civil as just tu step into t'other room, sir? I'd take it civil as I can't pray comfably with yu here, sir.'

'I'll oblige yu in that too,' said the Devil; and he went out to look after Mrs Pengelly.

No sooner was his back turned than Mr Pengelly jumped out of bed, extinguished the candle-end, clapped it in the candle-box, and put the candle-box under his bed. Presently the Devil came in, and said: 'Now, Mr Pengelly, yu're all in the dark: I see the cann'l's burnt out, so yu must come with me.'

'I'm not so much in the dark as yu, sir,' says the sick man, 'for the cann'l's not burnt out, and isn't like to. He's safe in the cann'l-box. And I'll send for yu, sir, when I want yu.'

Mr Pengelly is still alive; but let not the visitor to his farm ask him what he keeps in his candle-box, or, old man of seventy-eight though he is, he will jump out of his chair, and lay his stick across the shoulders of his interrogator. 'They du say,' said my informant, 'that Mrs Pengelly hev tried a score of times to get hold of the cann'l-end, and burn it out; but the master is tu sharp for his missus, and keeps it as tight from her as he does from the Devil.'

SABINE BARING-GOULD, *The Vicar of Morwenstow: A Life of R. S. Hawker*, 1876

I found it was not so easie to imprint right Notions in his Mind about the Devil, as it was about the Being of a God . . . I had been telling him how the Devil was God's Enemy in the Hearts of Men, and used all his Malice and Skill to defeat the good Designs of Providence, and to ruine the Kingdom of Christ in the World; and the like. 'Well,' says Friday, 'but you say, God is so strong, so great, is he not much strong, much might as the Devil?' 'Yes, yes,' says I, 'Friday, God is stronger than the Devil, God is above the Devil, and therefore we pray to God to tread him down under our Feet, and enable us to resist his Temptations and quench his fiery Darts.' 'But,' says he again, 'if God much strong, much might as the Devil, why God no kill the Devil, so make him no more do wicked?'

DEFOE, *Robinson Crusoe*, 1719

'The Devil isn't a popular figure nowadays. The people who take him seriously are few.'

'I know. How he must laugh. I don't suppose God laughs at the people who think He doesn't exist. He's above jokes. But the Devil isn't. That's one of his most endearing qualities.' . . .

Theologians have not been so successful in their definitions of the Devil as they have been in their definitions of God. The words of the Westminster Confession, painstakingly learned by heart as a necessity of Presbyterian boyhood, still seemed, after many wanderings, to have the ring of indisputable authority. God was *infinite in being and perfection, a most pure spirit, invisible, without body, parts or passions, immutable, immense, eternal, incomprehensible, almighty, most wise, most holy, most free, most absolute, working all things according to the counsel of his own immutable and most righteous will, for his own glory.* Excellent, even if one is somewhat seduced by the high quality of the prose of 1648. What else? *Most loving, most gracious, merciful, longsuffering, abundant in goodness and truth, forgiving iniquity, transgression and sin; the rewarder of those that diligently seek him* . . . What else had I been taught in that profound and knotty definition? That God was *most just and terrible in his judgements, hating all sin, one who will by no means clear the guilty.* Noble words, and (only slightly cloaked by their nobility) a terrifying concept. And why should it not be terrifying? A little terror, in my view, is good for the soul, when it is terror in the face of a noble object.

The Devil, however, seems never to have been so splendidly mapped and defined. Nor can you spy him simply by turning a fine definition of God inside out; he is something decidedly more subtle than just God's opposite.

Is the Devil, then, sin? No, though sin is very useful to him; anything we may reasonably call sin involves some personal choice. It is flattering to be asked to make important choices. The Devil loves the time of indecision.

What about evil, then? Is the Devil the origin and ruler of that great realm of manifestly dreadful and appalling things which are not, so far as we can determine, anybody's fault or the consequences of any sin? Of the cancer wards, and the wards for children born misshapen and mindless? I have had reason to visit such places—asylums for the insane in particular—and I do not think I am fanciful or absurdly sensitive in saying that I have felt evil to be palpable there, in spite of whatever could be done to lessen it.

These are evil things within my knowledge: I am certain there are worse things I have never encountered. And how constant this evil is! Let mankind laboriously suppress leprosy, and tuberculosis rages: when tuberculosis is chained, cancer rushes to take its place. One might almost conclude that such evils were necessities of our collective life. If the Devil is the inspirer and ruler of evil, he is a serious adversary indeed, and I cannot understand why so many people become jokey and facetious at the mention of his name.

ROBERTSON DAVIES, *World of Wonders*, 1975

I was once in an oratory, when Satan, in an abominable shape, appeared on my left hand. I looked at his mouth in particular, because he spoke, and it was horrible. A huge flame seemed to issue out of his body, perfectly bright, without any shadow. He spoke in a fearful way, and said to me that, though I had escaped out of his hands, he would yet lay hold of me again. I was in great terror, made the sign of the cross as well as I could, and then the form vanished—but it reappeared instantly. This occurred twice. I did not know what to do; there was some holy water at hand; I took some, and threw it in the direction of the figure, and then Satan never returned . . .

May this I have written be of use to the true servant of God, who ought to despise these terrors, which Satan sends only to make him afraid! Let him understand that each time we despise those terrors, their force is lessened, and the soul gains power over them. There is always some great good obtained; but I will not speak of it, that I may not be too diffuse. I will speak, however, of what happened to me once on the night of All Souls. I was in an oratory, and, having said one Nocturn, was saying some very devotional prayers at the end of our Breviary, when Satan put himself on the book before me, to prevent my finishing my prayer. I made the sign of the cross, and he went away. I then returned to my prayer, and he, too, came back; he did so, I believe, three times, and I was not able to finish the prayer without throwing holy water at him. I saw certain souls at that moment come forth out of purgatory—they must have been near their deliverance, and I thought that Satan might in this way have been trying to hinder their release.

Our Lord was pleased that I should have at times a vision of this kind: I saw an angel close by me, on my left side, in bodily form . . . He was not large, but small of stature, and most beautiful—his face burning, as if he were one of the highest angels, who seem to be all of fire: they must be those whom we call cherubim. Their names they never tell me; but I see very well that there is in heaven so great a difference between one angel and another, and between these and the others, that I cannot explain it.

I saw in his hand a long spear of gold, and at the iron's point there seemed to be a little fire. He appeared to me to be thrusting it at times into my heart, and to pierce my very entrails; when he drew it out, he seemed to draw them out also, and to leave me all on fire with a great love of God. The pain was so great, that it made me moan; and yet so surpassing was the sweetness of this excessive pain, that I could not wish to be rid of it. The soul is satisfied now with nothing less than God. The pain is not bodily, but spiritual; though the body has its share in it, even a large one. It is a caressing of love so sweet which now takes place between the soul and God, that I pray God of His goodness to make him experience it who may think that I am lying.

The Life of Saint Teresa of Jesus, written by herself, *c*.1562–8; tr. David Lewis

I do think that many mysteries ascribed to our own inventions have been the courteous revelations of Spirits; (for those noble essences in Heaven bear a friendly regard unto their fellow Natures on Earth;) and therefore believe that those many prodigies and ominous prognosticks, which fore-run the ruines of States, Princes, and private persons, are the charitable premonitions of good Angels, which more careless enquiries term but the effects of chance and nature.

BROWNE, *Religio Medici*

I believe that the angels are all up in arms, are putting on their harness, and girding their swords about them. For the last judgement draws nigh, and the angels prepare themselves for the combat, and to strike down Turk and pope into the bottomless pit.

LUTHER, *Table-Talk*

THESES QUAEDAM THEOLOGICAE

First, Whether God loves a lying Angel better than a true Man?

Second, Whether the Archangel Uriel *could* affirm an untruth? and if he *could*, whether he *would*?

Third, Whether Honesty be an angelic virtue, or not rather to be reckoned among those qualities which the Schoolmen term *virtutes minus splendidae et terrae et hominis participes* [virtues less splendid, partaking of the earth and of man]?

Fourth, Whether the higher order of Seraphim Illuminati ever sneer?

Fifth, Whether pure intelligences can love?

Sixth, Whether the Seraphim Ardentes do not manifest their virtues by the way of vision and theory? and whether practice be not a sub-celestial and merely human virtue?

Seventh, Whether the Vision Beatific be any thing more or less than a perpetual representment to each individual Angel of his own present attainments and future capabilities, somehow in the manner of mortal lookingglasses, reflecting a perpetual complacency and self-satisfaction?

Eighth, and last, Whether an immortal and amenable soul may not come to be condemned at last, and the man never suspect it beforehand?

LEARNED SIR, MY FRIEND,—Presuming on our long habits of friendship, and emboldened further by your late liberal permission to avail myself of your correspondence in case I want any knowledge . . . I now submit to your inquiries the above Theological Propositions, to be by you defended or oppugned, or both, in the Schools of Germany; whither, I am told, you are departing . . .

I remain

Your friend and docile Pupil to instruct . . .

LAMB, letter to Coleridge, May 1798

With these came they who, from the bord'ring flood
Of old Euphrates to the brook that parts
Egypt from Syrian ground, had general names
Of Baalim and Ashtaroth, those male,
These feminine. For Spirits when they please
Can either sex assume, or both; so soft
And uncompounded is their essence pure,
Not tied or manacled with joint or limb,
Nor founded on the brittle strength of bones,
Like cumbrous flesh; but in what shape they choose,
Dilated or condensed, bright or obscure,
Can execute their airy purposes,
And works of love or enmity fulfill.
For those the race of Israel oft forsook
Their living Strength, and unfrequented left
His righteous altar, bowing lowly down
To bestial gods . . .

'To love thou blam'st me not, for love thou say'st
Leads up to heav'n, is both the way and guide;
Bear with me then, if lawful what I ask:
Love not the heav'nly Spirits, and how their love
Express they, by looks only, or do they mix
Irradiance, virtual or immediate touch?'
      To whom the Angel, with a smile that glowed
Celestial rosy red, love's proper hue,
Answered: 'Let it suffice thee that thou know'st
Us happy, and without love no happiness.
Whatever pure thou in the body enjoy'st
(And pure thou wert created) we enjoy
In eminence, and obstacle find none
Of membrane, joint, or limb, exclusive bars;
Easier than air with air, if Spirits embrace,
Total they mix, union of pure with pure
Desiring; nor restrained conveyance need
As flesh to mix with flesh, or soul with soul.'

MILTON, *Paradise Lost*, 1667; from Book I: some among the rebel angels who
fell with Satan; from Book VIII, Adam questioning Raphael, 'the affable
Archangel'

~

The Turks tell their people of a heaven where there is sensible pleasure, but
of a hell where they shall suffer they don't know what. The Christians quite
invert this order: they tell us of a hell where we shall feel sensible pain, but of
a heaven where we shall enjoy we can't tell what.

JOHN SELDEN (1584–1654), *Table Talk*

It is in the nature of man to sympathize only with those things which relate to
him, which touch him at some point, such as misfortune, for example. Heaven,
where boundless felicity reigns, is too far above the human condition for the
soul to be strongly affected by the bliss of the elect: one can interest oneself but
little in beings who are perfectly happy. This is why poets have succeeded
better in the description of hells: at least humanity is there, and the torments
of the guilty remind us of the miseries of our life.

CHATEAUBRIAND, *The Genius of Christianity*, 1802

The ancient tradition that the world will be consumed in fire at the end of six thousand years is true, as I have heard from Hell;

For the cherub with his flaming sword is hereby commanded to leave his guard at [the] tree of life, and when he does, the whole creation will be consumed and appear infinite and holy, whereas it now appears finite & corrupt.

This will come to pass by an improvement of sensual enjoyment.

But first the notion that man has a body distinct from his soul is to be expunged: this I shall do, by printing in the infernal method, by corrosives, which in Hell are salutary and medicinal, melting apparent surfaces away, and displaying the infinite which was hid.

If the doors of perception were cleansed, every thing would appear to man as it is, infinite.

For man has closed himself up, till he sees all things thro' narrow chinks of his cavern.

WILLIAM BLAKE, *The Marriage of Heaven and Hell*, c.1793

In the spiritual world there are two great cities like London, which most of the English enter after death. I have been permitted to enter and explore the chief of the two. The centre of the city answers to the London Exchange where the merchants meet, and that is where the rulers live. In front and above this centre is the east, behind and below it is the west, on the right side is the south, and on the left the north. In the eastern quarter live those who more than others have lived a life of charity, and here there are magnificent palaces. In the southern quarter live the wise, among whom there is much splendour. In the northern quarter live those who have loved the liberty of speaking and writing; and in the western quarter live those who are zealous for the doctrine of justification by faith alone. In this quarter, on the right, is the entrance to the city, and also the way out; those who live wickedly are expelled through this gate. The clergy who live in the west, and teach the doctrine of justification by faith alone, dare not pass through the chief streets, but only through narrow alleys; for only those who are in the faith of charity are tolerated in the city . . .

The other great city, which is also called London, is not in the Christian centre, but at some distance to the north; it is the temporary abode after death of those who are inwardly evil. In the middle of it there is an open communication with hell, which from time to time swallows up certain of the inhabitants.

EMANUEL SWEDENBORG, 'The English in the Spiritual World', *The True Christian Religion*, 1771

Hell is a city much like London—
  A populous and a smoky city;
There are all sorts of people undone,
And there is little or no fun done;
  Small justice shown, and still less pity.

SHELLEY, *Peter Bell the Third*, written 1819

Here are cakes for thy body,
Cool water for thy throat,
Sweet breezes for thy nostrils,
And thou art satisfied.

No longer dost thou stumble
Upon thy chosen path,
From thy mind all evil
And darkness fall away.

Here by the river,
Drink and bathe thy limbs,
Or cast thy net, and surely
It shall be filled with fish.

The holy cow of Hapi
Shall give thee of her milk,
The ale of gods triumphant
Shall be thy daily draught.

White linen is thy tunic,
Thy sandals shine with gold;
Victorious thy weapons,
That death come not again.

Now upon the whirlwind
Thou followest thy Prince,
Now thou hast refreshment
Under the leafy tree.

Take wings to climb the zenith,
Or sleep in Fields of Peace;
By day the Sun shall keep thee,
By night the rising Star.

'The Other World', *The Egyptian Book of the Dead*, *c.*3300 BC; tr. Robert Hillyer

'There are more things in heaven and earth than are dreamed of in our philosophy', and among these may be placed that marvel and mystery of the seas, the Island of St Brandan. Those who have read the history of the Canaries, the Fortunate Islands of the ancients, may remember the wonders told of this enigmatical island. Occasionally it would be visible from their shores, stretching away in a clear bright west, to all appearance substantial like themselves, and still more beautiful. Expeditions would launch forth from the Canaries to explore this land of promise. For a time its sun-gilt peaks, and long, shadowy promontories, would remain distinctly visible, but in proportion as the voyagers approached, peak and promontory would gradually fade away until nothing would remain but blue sky above and deep blue water below. Hence this mysterious isle was stigmatized by ancient cosmographers with the name of Aprositus, or the Inaccessible. The failure of numerous expeditions sent in quest of it, both in ancient and modern days, has at length caused its very existence to be called in question, and it has been rashly pronounced a mere optical illusion, like the Fata Morgana of the Straits of Messina, or has been classed with those unsubstantial regions known to mariners as Cape Flyaway and the coast of Cloud Land.

Let us not permit, however, the doubts of worldly-wise sceptics to rob us of all the glorious realms owned by happy credulity in days of yore . . . Historians and philosophers may have their doubts, but its existence has been attested by that inspired race, the poets; who, being gifted with a kind of second sight, are enabled to discern those mysteries of nature hidden from the eyes of ordinary men. To this gifted race it has ever been a kind of wonderland. Here once bloomed, and perhaps still blooms, the famous garden of the Hesperides, with its golden fruit. Here too the sorceress Armida had her enchanted garden, in which she held the Christian paladin, Rinaldo, in delicious but inglorious thraldom, as set forth in the immortal lay of Tasso. It was in this island that Sycorax, the witch, held sway, when the good Prospero and his infant daughter, Miranda, were wafted to its shores. Who does not know the tale as told in the magic pages of Shakespeare? The island was then—

> . . . full of noises,
> Sounds and sweet airs, that give delight, and hurt not.

The island, in fact, at different times, has been under the sway of different powers, genii of earth, and air, and ocean, who have made it their shadowy abode. Hither have retired many classic but broken-down deities, shorn of almost all their attributes, but who once ruled the poetic world. Here Neptune and Amphitrite hold a diminished court, sovereigns in exile. Their ocean chariot, almost a wreck, lies bottom upward in some sea-beaten cavern; their pursy Tritons and haggard Nereids bask listlessly like seals about the rocks.

Sometimes those deities assume, it is said, a shadow of their ancient pomp, and glide in state about a summer sea; and then, as some tall Indiaman lies becalmed with idly flapping sail, her drowsy crew may hear the mellow note of the Triton's shell swelling upon the ear as the invisible pageant sweeps by.

On the shore of this wondrous isle the kraken heaves its unwieldy bulk and wallows many a rood. Here the sea-serpent, that mighty but much contested reptile, lies coiled up during the intervals of its revelations to the eyes of true believers. Here even the Flying Dutchman finds a port, and casts his anchor, and furls his shadowy sail, and takes a brief repose from his eternal cruisings.

In the deep bays and harbours of the island lies many a spellbound ship, long since given up as lost by the ruined merchant. Here, too, its crew, long, long bewailed in vain, lie sleeping from age to age, in mossy grottoes, or wander about in pleasing oblivion of all things. Here in caverns are garnered the priceless treasures lost in the ocean. Here sparkles in vain the diamond and flames the carbuncle. Here are piled up rich bales of Oriental silks, boxes of pearls, and piles of golden ingots.

WASHINGTON IRVING, from 'The Phantom Island', 1885

Saint Peter sat by the celestial gate,
   His keys were rusty, and the lock was dull,
So little trouble had been given of late;
   Not that the place by any means was full,
But since the Gallic era 'eighty-eight',
   The devils had ta'en a longer, stronger pull,
And 'a pull all together', as they say
At sea—which drew most souls another way.

The angels all were singing out of tune,
   And hoarse with having little else to do,
Excepting to wind up the sun and moon,
   Or curb a runaway young star or two,
Or wild colt of a comet, which too soon
   Broke out of bounds o'er the ethereal blue,
Splitting some planet with its playful tail,
As boats are sometimes by a wanton whale.

The guardian seraphs had retired on high,
   Finding their charges past all care below;
Terrestrial business fill'd nought in the sky
   Save the recording angel's black bureau;

Who found, indeed, the facts to multiply
 With such rapidity of vice and woe,
That he had stripp'd off both his wings in quills,
And yet was in arrear of human ills.

His business so augmented of late years,
 That he was forced, against his will, no doubt,
(Just like those cherubs, earthly ministers),
 For some resource to turn himself about,
And claim the help of his celestial peers,
 To aid him ere he should be quite worn out
By the increased demand for his remarks:
Six angels and twelve saints were named his clerks.

This was a handsome board—at least for heaven;
 And yet they had even then enough to do,
So many conquerors' cars were daily driven,
  So many kingdoms fitted up anew;
Each day too slew its thousands, six or seven,
 Till at the crowning carnage, Waterloo,
They threw their pens down in divine disgust—
The page was so besmear'd with blood and dust.

This by the way; 'tis not mine to record
 What angels shrink from: even the very devil
On this occasion his own work abhorr'd,
 So surfeited with the infernal revel,
Though he himself had sharpen'd every sword,
 It almost quench'd his innate thirst of evil.
(Here Satan's sole good work deserves insertion—
'Tis, that he has both generals in reversion.)

      BYRON, *The Vision of Judgement*, 1822

'Now that's all reasonable and right,' says I. 'Plenty of work, and the kind you hanker after; no more pain, no more suffering—'

'Oh, hold on; there's plenty of pain here—but it don't kill. There's plenty of suffering here, but it don't last. You see, happiness ain't a *thing in itself*—it's only a *contrast* with something that ain't pleasant. That's all it is. There ain't a thing you can mention that is happiness in its own self—it's only so by contrast with the other thing. And so, as soon as the novelty is over and the force of the contrast dulled, it ain't happiness any longer, and you have to get something fresh. Well, there's plenty of pain and suffering in heaven—consequently there's plenty of contrasts, and just no end of happiness.'

Says I: 'It's the sensiblest heaven I've heard of yet, Sam, though it's about as different from the one I was brought up on as a live princess is different from her own wax figger.'

'Oh, there are a lot of such things that people expect and don't get. For instance, there's a Brooklyn preacher by the name of Talmage, who is laying up a considerable disappointment for himself. He says, every now and then in his sermons, that the first thing he does when he gets to heaven, will be to fling his arms around Abraham, Isaac and Jacob, and kiss them and weep on them. There's millions of people down there on earth that are promising themselves the same thing. As many as sixty thousand people arrive here every single day, that want to run straight to Abraham, Isaac and Jacob, and hug them and weep on them. Now mind you, sixty thousand a day is a pretty heavy contract for those old people. If they were a mind to allow it, they wouldn't ever have anything to do, year in and year out, but stand up and be hugged and wept on thirty-two hours in the twenty-four. They would be tired out and as wet as muskrats all the time. What would heaven be, to *them*? It would be a mighty good place to get out of . . . Those are kind and gentle old Jews, but they ain't any fonder of kissing the emotional highlights of Brooklyn than you be. You mark my words, Mr T's endearments are going to be declined, with thanks. There are limits to the privileges of the elect, even in heaven.' . . .

'Do you think Talmage will really come here?'

'Why, certainly, he will; but don't you be alarmed; he will run with his own kind, and there's plenty of them. That is the main charm of heaven—there's all kinds here—which wouldn't be the case if you let the preachers tell it. Anybody can find the sort he prefers, here, and he just lets the others alone, and they let him alone. When the Deity builds a heaven, it is built right, and on a liberal plan.'

MARK TWAIN, *Captain Stormfield's Visit to Heaven*, 1909

If after our death they want to transform us into a tiny withered flame that walks along the paths of winds—we have to rebel. What good is an eternal leisure on the bosom of air, in the shade of a yellow halo, amid the murmur of two-dimensional choirs?

One should enter rock, wood, water, the cracks of a gate. Better to be the creaking of a floor than shrilly transparent perfection.

ZBIGNIEW HERBERT, 'Anything Rather Than an Angel', 1961; tr. Czeslaw Milosz

Vampires, Werewolves, Zombies, and Other Monsters

Does one have to be of a certain age to flinch at the casualness with which extreme displays of squalor and depravity—an advance on what was chummily known as sex 'n' violence—figure in today's world of entertainment? The Devil himself must feel things have gone a bit far.

The current fascination with the supernatural extends to its more extravagantly horrible forms, in particular vampirism. On top of books and films and even a species of televised soap opera, a secondary industry has grown up; there exists a *Consumer's Guide to Vampire Fiction*, and Devendra P. Varma, described on the jacket of *Voices from the Vaults* (1988) as a professor of English and Gothic Romance Literature at Dalhousie University in Canada, mentions the Vampire Research Center, of Elmhurst, New York, whose director has estimated that there are between eighty and a hundred vampires active in the United States. The modern revival of interest in vampires, Professor Varma says, 'chimes with the escalation of violence and terror in modern civilization and curiosity about the occult'; true, but this doesn't take us much further forward.

That interest has been around for a very long time. At the heart of the vampire myth lie two abidingly great subjects: immortality (and the price that may have to be paid for it) and eroticism (and the price sometimes paid for that). In his introduction to Bram Stoker's *Dracula* (The World's Classics, 1983) A. N. Wilson states that Stoker

reflects the very bewildered sense, still potent in a world which was (even in 1897) preparing to do without religion, that mysteries can only be fought by mysteries, and that the power of evil in human life is too strong to be defeated by repression, violence, or good behaviour . . . His classic gift was that of a mythologist. It might almost seem, to future generations, as though he had some of the qualities, popularized and vulgarized no doubt, but none the less real, of a metaphysician.

As for sex, Clive Leatherdale has drawn attention to the phallic connotations of long teeth and, in *Dracula: The Novel and the Legend* (1985), claims that a careful search of Stoker's novel brings to light 'seduction, rape, necrophilia, paedophilia, incest, adultery, oral sex, group sex, menstruation, venereal disease, voyeurism'. Perhaps it would be enough simply to adduce love bites, blood ties, and the extreme intimacy in many respects of the vampirical act and relationship.

Convention has it that male vampires prey on women and female vampires on men, thus showing themselves an embellished variety of incubus or succubus. More recently vampirism has been co-opted into current concerns and fashions, with the protagonist featuring variously as serial killer, black, lesbian (lightly prefigured in Le Fanu's 'Carmilla' of 1872), and feminist (a more general example is *What Did Miss Darrington See?: An Anthology of Feminist Supernatural Fiction*). Elaine Showalter writes (*Times Literary Supplement*, 8 January 1993): 'If Stoker's *Dracula* has been filmed over 150 times, it is because it offers a potent cultural mythology as well as a series of erotic and horrific images . . . directors have found a way to use the vampire legend to illuminate issues and styles of our own time'; with AIDS in mind, she adds that 'vampirism is a sexually transmitted disease of the blood'.

Earlier, Gabriel Ronay notes in *The Dracula Myth* (1972), the sinister Count was invoked during the Second World War as a German soldier, his fangs dripping with the blood of innocents (the extent of the identification 'can be gauged from the decision of the United States Army to issue free paperback copies of Stoker's *Dracula* to the troops serving overseas'), and then, during the Cold War, though he had once stood for the blood-sucking capitalist, he came to symbolize 'the fanatical hordes of the East' who threatened to conscript the West into their way of life. The vampire can be slotted in practically anywhere, a myth for all seasons.

Besides the causes listed by Paul Barber, and besides inheriting vampirism by being the victim of a vampire, the sins and misfortunes reckoned to lead to the condition have included some weird items: committing suicide, of course, but also working on Sundays, smoking on holy days, drinking to excess, and having sexual intercourse with one's grandmother; more innocently, those born on Christmas Day are doomed to the same fate in punishment of their mothers' presumptuousness in conceiving on the same day as the Virgin Mary. Writing in the *Dictionnaire Philosophique* about epidemics of vampirism, Voltaire states that, in the dialectic mode of the medieval scholastics, the difficulty lay in establishing whether it was the body or the soul of the vampire that feasted, and it was decided that both were involved, the 'delicate, insubstantial dishes', as it were meringues or whipped cream on fruit, went to the soul, whereas 'the roast beef' served for the body. Not all authorities have granted the vampire a soul.

Repulsive though the subject is, a character in E. T. A. Hoffmann's 'Aurelia' remarks, 'it is capable of providing a material, when dealt with by a writer of imagination possessed of some poetical tact, which has the power of stirring within us that profound sense of awe which is innate in our hearts, and when touched by the electric impulse from an unseen spirit world causes our soul to thrill, not altogether unpleasantly'. Yes, except that of late the market value of imagination and poetical tact has plummeted.

While the werewolf legend is low in sexual appeal and lacks the urbane charm of the European aristocracy, it has featured widely in folklore. The Devil, one theory has it, chose to change sorcerers into wolves rather than any other animal because of the wolf's notorious ferocity and because it symbolizes the eternal enemy of the lamb, emblem of Christ. The history of Peter Stubbe, executed in 1589 for slaughtering and devouring some sixteen people in Germany over a period of twenty-five years, is in line with the serial killings of our day.

Associated with Caribbean voodoo cults, zombies are the 'Walking Dead', and also the working dead, a source of cheap labour best employed in distant plantations lest they be recognized by friends or relatives. The story runs that *houngans* or voodoo priests, the real monsters of the piece, are wont to put their victim into a trance resembling death; after the funeral they dig up the body and administer an antidote producing partial life. Zombies have no memory of their identity, obey commands, and labour untiringly and without recompense.

There is a family likeness among most of the other 'monsters' represented here, a mix of succubus, vampire, and lamia; like witches, they are commonly female, preying on besotted men, though at times directing their attention to women, as witness Coleridge's Geraldine, who by demonic convention has to be invited into the dwelling of her intended victims, even carried over the threshold, but whose subsequent activities remain unrecorded. The type is ancient. We hear that the original Lamia was a Libyan queen loved by Jupiter and robbed of her offspring by jealous Juno, whereon she ran mad and vowed vengeance on all children. And in folklore Lilith is a demon of the night given to attacking children (akin to the Malay vampires described by W. W. Skeat, and the Roman *striges* who take the form of birds and prey on infants in the cradle: from *strix*, 'screech-owl'), while in Talmudic writings she appears as the first wife of Adam, turning up in Isaiah 34 as the 'screech owl' (Vulgate, 'lamia') who shall 'find for herself a place of rest' when the earth is devastated by the fury of the Lord. During the Walpurgis Night scene in Goethe, Mephistopheles cries, "'Tis Lilith, see!'; Faust asks, 'Who?', and his companion tells him, 'Adam's first wife is she', and warns him to beware her beautiful tresses, the sole adornment of this *belle dame sans merci*.

The monsters of myth are customarily circumscribed in their powers: vampires can operate only in darkness, and are repulsed by garlic or crucifix; witches can make us seasick but not drown us; malicious elves cannot cross running water; jinn are vulnerable to the name of Allah; lamiae can be exposed by philosophers . . . We do not care to exhibit ourselves as being utterly outwitted and hopelessly helpless; at least not in myth. It is the sleep of reason, they say, that breeds monsters. Since reason is less alert and less puissant than we like to suppose, we always have cause to fear them.

~

> In tombs of gold and lapis lazuli
> Bodies of holy men and women exude
> Miraculous oil, odour of violet.
>
> But under heavy loads of trampled clay
> Lie bodies of the vampires full of blood;
> Their shrouds are bloody and their lips are wet.
>
> YEATS, 'Oil and Blood', 1929

In general, lists of potential revenants tend to contain people who are distinguished primarily by being different from the people who make the lists. [Dagmar] Burkhart [1966], for example, gives the following categories of revenants-by-predisposition: 'the godless (people of a different faith are included here, too!), evildoers, suicides, in addition sorcerers, witches, and werewolves; among the Bulgarians the group is expanded by robbers, highwaymen, arsonists, prostitutes, deceitful and treacherous barmaids and other dishonourable people.'

Frequently people become revenants through no fault of their own, as when they are conceived during a holy period, according to the church calendar, or when they are the illegitimate offspring of illegitimate parents. Indeed, in

Romania it is reported that merely being the seventh son in a family is apt to cause one to become a revenant.

Often potential revenants can be identified at birth, usually by some abnormality, some defect, as when (among the Poles of Upper Silesia and the Kashubes) a child is born with teeth. Similarly suspicious are children born with an extra nipple (Romania); with a lack of cartilage in the nose, or a split lower lip (Russia); or with features that are viewed as bestial, such as fur down the front or back or a tail-like extension of the spine, especially if it is covered with hair (Romania). (This can actually occur, according to [Andrew] MacKenzie [1977].) And Wilhelm Hertz [1862] makes mention of a belief that a revenant is born with two hearts, one of which is dedicated to the destruction of humanity. Burkhart also mentions this and adds that this belief is most common in the Ukraine, that it applies also to witches, and that it is sometimes souls, rather than hearts, that are superabundant.

PAUL BARBER, *Vampires, Burial, and Death*, 1988

All we have to go upon are traditions and superstitions. These do not at the first appear much, when the matter is one of life and death—nay, of more than either life or death. Yet must we be satisfied; in the first place because we have to be—no other means is at our control—and secondly, because, after all, these things—tradition and superstition—are everything. Does not the belief in vampires rest for others—though not, alas! for us—on them? A year ago which of us would have received such a possibility, in the midst of our scientific, sceptical, matter-of-fact nineteenth century? . . . Take it, then, that the vampire, and the belief in his limitations and his cure, rest for the moment on the same base. For, let me tell you, he is known everywhere that men have been. In old Greece, in old Rome; he flourish in Germany all over, in France, in India, even in the Chersonese; and in China, so far from us in all ways, there even is he, and the peoples fear him to this day. He have follow the wake of the berserker Icelander, the devil-begotten Hun, the Slav, the Saxon, the Magyar . . . The vampire live on, and cannot die by mere passing of the time; he can flourish when that he can fatten on the blood of the living. Even more, we have seen amongst us that he can even grow younger; that his vital faculties grow strenuous, and seem as though they refresh themselves when his special pabulum is plenty . . . He throws no shadow; he make in the mirror no reflect . . . He has the strength of many in his hand . . . He can transform himself to wolf . . . he can be as bat . . . He can come in mist which he create . . . He come on moonlight rays as elemental dust . . . He become so small . . . He can see in the dark—no small power this, in a world which is one half shut from the light. Ah, but hear me through. He can do all these things, yet he is not free. Nay, he is even more prisoner than the slave of the galley, than the madman in his cell. He cannot go where he lists; he who is not of nature has yet to obey some of nature's laws—why we know not. He may not enter anywhere at the first, unless there be someone of the household who bid him to còme; though afterwards he can come as he please. His power ceases, as does that of all evil things, at the coming of the day . . . It is said, too, that he can only pass running water at the slack or the flood of the tide. Then there are things which so afflict him that he has no power, as the garlic that we know of, and as for things sacred, as this symbol, my crucifix, to them he is nothing, but in their presence he take his place far off and silent with respect. There are others, too, which I shall tell you of, lest in our seeking we may need them. The branch of wild rose on his coffin keep him that he move not from it; a sacred bullet fired into the coffin kill him so that he be true dead; and as for the stake through him, we know already of its peace; or the cut-off head that giveth rest. We have seen it with our eyes . . .

But he is clever. I have asked my friend Arminius, of Buda-Pesth University, to make his record; and, from all the means that are, he tell me of what he has been. He must, indeed, have been that Voivode Dracula who won his name against the Turk, over the great river on the very frontier of Turkey-land. If it be so, then was he no common man; for in that time, and for centuries after, he was spoken of as the cleverest and the most cunning as well as the bravest of the sons of 'the land beyond the forest'. That mighty brain and that iron resolution went with him to his grave, and are even now arrayed against us. The Draculas were, says Arminius, a great and noble race, though now and again were scions who were held by their coevals to have had dealings with the Evil One . . . There have been from the loins of this very one great men and good women, and their graves make sacred the earth where alone this foulness can dwell. For it is not the least of its terrors that this evil thing is rooted deep in all good; in soil barren of holy memories it cannot rest.

Bram Stoker, Dracula, 1897; Dr Van Helsing speaking

After a subject by the name of Peter Plogojowitz had died, ten weeks past—he lived in the village of Kisilova, in the Rahm District [Serbia]—and had been buried according to the Raetzian custom, it was revealed that in this same village of Kisilova, within a week, nine people, both old and young, died also, after suffering a twenty-four-hour illness. And they said publicly, while they were yet alive, but on their death-bed, that the above-mentioned Plogojowitz, who had died ten weeks earlier, had come to them in their sleep, laid himself on them, and throttled them, so that they would have to give up the ghost. The other subjects were very distressed . . . And since with such people (which they call vampires) various signs are to be seen—that is, the body undecomposed, the skin, hair, beard and nails growing—the subjects resolved unanimously to open the grave of Peter Plogojowitz and to see if such above-mentioned signs were really to be found on him. To this end they came here to me and, telling of these events, asked me and the local pope, or parish priest, to be present at the viewing. And although I at first disapproved, telling them that the praise-worthy administration should first be dutifully and humbly informed, and its exalted opinion about this should be heard, they did not want to accommodate themselves to this at all, but rather gave this short answer: I could do what I wanted, but if I did not accord them the viewing and the legal recognition to deal with the body according to their custom, they would have to leave house and home, because by the time a gracious resolution was received from Belgrade, perhaps the entire village—and this was already supposed to have happened in Turkish times—could be destroyed by such an evil spirit, and they did not want to wait for this. Since I could not hold such people from the resolution they had made, either with good words or with threats, I went to the village of Kisilova, taking along the Gradisk pope, and viewed the body of Peter Plogojowitz, just exhumed, finding, in accordance with thorough truthfulness, that first of all I did not detect the slightest odour that is otherwise characteristic of the dead, and the body, except for the nose, which was somewhat fallen away, was completely fresh. The hair and beard—even the nails, of which the old ones had fallen away—had grown on him; the old skin, which was somewhat whitish, had peeled away, and a new fresh one had emerged under it. The face, hands, and feet, and the whole body were so constituted, that they could not have been more complete in his lifetime. Not without astonishment, I saw some fresh blood in his mouth, which, according to the common observation, he had sucked from the people killed by him. In short, all the indications were present that such people (as remarked above) are said to have. After both the pope and I had seen this spectacle, while the people grew more outraged than distressed, all the subjects, with great speed, sharpened a stake—in order to pierce the corpse of the deceased with it—and put this at his heart, whereupon, as he was pierced, not only did much blood, completely fresh, flow also through his ears and mouth, but still other wild signs (which I pass by out of high respect) took place. Finally, according to their usual practice, they burned the often-mentioned body, *in hoc casu*, to ashes, of which I inform the most laudable Administration, and at the same time would like to request, obediently and humbly, that if a mistake was made in this matter, such is to be attributed not to me but to the rabble, who were beside themselves with fear.

Imperial Provisor, Gradisk District

Report of 1725, translated by Paul Barber, op. cit. The expression 'other wild signs' is thought to signify a supposed erection, a phenomenon which Barber ascribes to the bloating attendant on decomposition

The figure turns half round, and the light falls upon the face. It is perfectly white—perfectly bloodless. The eyes look like polished tin; the lips are drawn back, and the principal feature next to those dreadful eyes is the teeth—the fearful-looking teeth—projecting like those of some wild animal, hideously, glaringly white, and fang-like. It approaches the bed with a strange, gliding movement. It clashes together the long nails that literally appear to hang from the finger-ends. No sound comes from its lips. Is she going mad—that young and beautiful girl exposed to so much terror? she has drawn up all her limbs; she cannot even now say help. The power of articulation is gone, but the power of movement has returned to her; she can draw herself slowly along to the other side of the bed from that towards which the hideous appearance is coming.

But her eyes are fascinated. The glance of a serpent could not have produced a greater effect upon her than did the fixed gaze of those awful, metallic-looking eyes that were bent on her face. Crouching down so that the gigantic height was lost, and the horrible, protruding, white face was the most prominent object, came on the figure. What was it?—what did it want there?—what made it look so hideous—so unlike an inhabitant of the earth, and yet to be on it? . . .

With a sudden rush that could not be foreseen—with a strange howling cry that was enough to awaken terror in every breast, the figure seized the long tresses of her hair, and twining them round his bony hands he held her to the bed. Then she screamed—Heaven granted her then power to scream. Shriek followed shriek in rapid succession. The bedclothes fell in a heap by the side of the bed—she was dragged by her long silken hair completely on to it again. Her beautifully rounded limbs quivered with the agony of her soul. The glassy, horrible eyes of the figure ran over that angelic form with a hideous satisfaction—horrible profanation. He drags her head to the bed's edge. He forces it back by the long hair still entwined in his grasp. With a plunge he seizes her neck in his fang-like teeth—a gush of blood, and a hideous sucking noise follows. *The girl has swooned, and the vampire is at his hideous repast!*

JAMES MALCOLM RYMER, *Varney, the Vampyre*, 1845-7

The next day the formal proceedings took place in the Chapel of Karnstein. The grave of the Countess Mircalla was opened; and the General and my father recognized each his perfidious and beautiful guest, in the face now disclosed to view. The features, though a hundred and fifty years had passed since her funeral, were tinted with the warmth of life. Her eyes were open; no cadaverous smell exhaled from the coffin. The two medical men . . . attested the marvellous fact, that there was a faint but appreciable respiration, and a corresponding action of the heart. The limbs were perfectly flexible, the flesh elastic; and the leaden coffin floated with blood, in which to a depth of seven inches, the body lay immersed. Here then, were all the admitted signs and proofs of vampirism. The body, therefore, in accordance with the ancient practice, was raised, and a sharp stake driven through the heart of the vampire, who uttered a piercing shriek at the moment, in all respects such as might escape from a living person in the last agony. Then the head was struck off, and a torrent of blood flowed from the severed neck. The body and head were next placed on a pile of wood, and reduced to ashes, which were thrown upon the river and borne away, and that territory has never since been plagued by the visits of a vampire.

How they [vampires] escape from their graves and return to them for certain hours every day, without displacing the clay or leaving any trace of disturbance in the state of the coffin or the cerements, has always been admitted to be utterly inexplicable. The amphibious existence of the vampire is sustained by daily renewed slumber in the grave. Its horrible lust for living blood supplies the vigour of its waking existence. The vampire is prone to be fascinated with an engrossing vehemence, resembling the passion of love, by particular persons. In pursuit of these it will exercise inexhaustible patience and stratagem, for access to a particular object may be obstructed in a hundred ways. It will never desist until it has satiated its passion, and drained the very life of its coveted victim. But it will, in these cases, husband and protract its murderous enjoyment with the refinement of an epicure, and heighten it by the gradual approaches of an artful courtship. In these cases it seems to yearn for something like sympathy and consent. In ordinary ones it goes direct to its object, overpowers with violence, and strangles and exhausts often at a single feast.

It is the nature of vampires to increase and multiply, but according to an ascertained and ghostly law.

Assume, at starting, a territory perfectly free from that pest. How does it begin, and how does it multiply itself? I will tell you. A person, more or less wicked, puts an end to himself. A suicide, under certain circumstances, becomes a vampire. That spectre visits living people in their slumbers; *they* die, and almost invariably, in the grave, develop into vampires.

J. SHERIDAN LE FANU, from 'Carmilla', 1872

He began by calling attention to his personal appearance. 'You would hardly recognize me for the same man I was a year ago,' he said. 'I've been losing weight steadily for the last six months. I came up from Scotland about a week ago, to consult a London doctor. I've seen two . . . They don't seem to know what is really the matter with me.'

'Is your wife changed at all—physically?' interrupted Vance.

Davenant reflected. 'Changed,' he said, 'yes, but so subtly that I hardly know how to describe it. She is more beautiful than ever—and yet it isn't the same beauty, if you can understand me. I have spoken of her white complexion, well, one is more than ever conscious of it now, because her lips have become so red—they are almost like a splash of blood upon her face. And the upper one has a peculiar curve that I don't think it had before, and when she laughs she doesn't smile—do you know what I mean? Then her hair—it has lost its wonderful gloss. Of course, I know she is fretting about me; but that is so peculiar, too, for at times, as I have told you, she will implore me to go and leave her, and then, perhaps only a few minutes later, she will wreathe her arms round my neck and say she cannot live without me. And I feel that there is a struggle going on within her, that she is only yielding slowly to the horrible influence—whatever it is—that she is herself when she begs me to go, but when she entreats me to stay—and it is then that her fascination is most intense—oh, I can't help remembering what she told me before we were married, and that word'—he lowered his voice—'the word "vampire"—'.

He passed his hand over his brow that was wet with perspiration. 'But that's absurd, ridiculous,' he muttered; 'these fantastic beliefs have been exploded years ago. We live in the twentieth century.' . . .

'A curious and most interesting case,' remarked Vance when we were alone. 'What do you make of it, Dexter?'

'I suppose,' I replied cautiously, 'that there is such a thing as vampirism even in these days of advanced civilization? I can understand the evil influence that a very old person may have upon a young one if they happen to be in constant intercourse—the worn-out tissue sapping healthy vitality for their own support. And there are certain people—I could think of several myself—who seem to depress one and undermine one's energies, quite unconsciously, of course, but one feels somehow that vitality has passed from oneself to them. And in this case, when the force is centuries old, expressing itself, in some mysterious way, through Davenant's wife, is it not feasible to believe that he may be physically affected by it, even though the whole thing is sheerly mental?'

'You think, then,' demanded Vance, 'that it is sheerly mental? Tell me, if that is so, how do you account for the marks on Davenant's throat?'

This was a question to which I found no reply.

> ALICE and CLAUDE ASKEW, from 'Aylmer Vance and the Vampire', 1914; in this story husband and wife are saved from the ancestral vampire who has assumed the wife's shape

Among the numerous folk-tales about vampires is one relating to a fiend called Dekanavar, who dwelt in a cave in Armenia. He would not permit anybody to penetrate into the mountains of Ulmish Altotem or to count their valleys. Everyone who attempted this had in the night the blood sucked by the monster from the soles of his feet until he died.

At last, however, he was outwitted by two cunning fellows. They began to count the valleys, and when night came they lay down to sleep, taking care to place themselves with the feet of each under the head of the other. In the night the monster came, felt as usual and found a head. Then he felt at the other end and found a head there also.

'Well!' cried he. 'I have gone through all of the three hundred and sixty-six valleys of these mountains and have sucked the blood of people without end, but never yet did I find one with two heads and no feet!' So saying he ran away, and never more was seen in that country, but ever since people have known that the mountains have three hundred and sixty-six valleys.

> From 'Vampires in New England', *New York World*, 2 February 1896

The popular superstition about the Langsuir is thus described by Sir William Maxwell:—

'If a woman dies in childbirth, either before delivery or after the birth of a child, and before the forty days of uncleanness have expired, she is popularly supposed to become a *langsuyar*, a flying demon of the nature of the "white lady" or "banshee". To prevent this a quantity of glass beads are put in the mouth of the corpse, a hen's egg is put under each armpit, and needles are placed in the palms of the hands. It is believed that if this is done the dead woman cannot become a *langsuyar*, as she cannot open her mouth to shriek or wave her arms as wings, or open and shut her hands to assist her flight.'

The superstitions about the Langsuir, however, do not end here, for with regard to its origin the Selangor Malays tell the following story:—

The original Langsuir (whose embodiment is supposed to be a kind of night-owl) is described as being a woman of dazzling beauty, who died from the shock of hearing that her child was stillborn and had taken the shape of the Pontianak. On hearing this terrible news, she 'clapped her hands', and without further warning 'flew whinnying away to a tree, upon which she perched'. She may be known by her robe of green, by her tapering nails of extraordinary length (a mark of beauty), and by the long jet black tresses which she allows to fall down to her ankles—only, alas! (for the truth must be told) in order to conceal the hole in the back of her neck through which she sucks the blood of children! These vampire-like proclivities of hers may, however, be successfully combated if the right means are adopted, for if you are able to catch her, cut short her nails and luxuriant tresses, and stuff them into the hole in her neck, she will become tame and indistinguishable from an ordinary woman, remaining so for years. Cases have been known, indeed, in which she has become a wife and a mother, until she was allowed to dance at a village merry-making, when she at once reverted to her ghostly form, and flew off into the dark and gloomy forest from whence she came . . .

The Pontianak, as has already been said, is the stillborn child of the Langsuir, and its embodiment is like that of its mother, a kind of night-owl. Curiously enough, it appears to be the only one of these spirits which rises to the dignity of being addressed as a 'Jin' or 'Genie', as appears from the charms which are used for laying it. Thus we find in a common charm:—

> O Pontianak the Stillborn,
> May you be struck dead by the soil from the grave-mound.
> Thus (we) cut the bamboo-joints, the long and the short,
> To cook therein the liver of the Jin (Demon) Pontianak.
> By the grace of 'There is no god but God', etc.

To prevent a stillborn child from becoming a Pontianak the corpse is treated in the same way as that of the mother, i.e. a hen's egg is put under each armpit, a needle in the palm of each hand, and (probably) glass beads or some simple equivalent in its mouth.

The Pĕnanggalan is a sort of monstrous vampire which delights in sucking the blood of children. The story goes that once upon a time a woman was sitting, to perform a religious penance, in one of the large wooden vats which are used by the Malays for holding the vinegar made by drawing off the sap of the thatch-palm. Quite unexpectedly a man came in, and finding her sitting in the vat, asked her, 'What are you doing there?' To this the woman replied, 'What business have you to ask?' but being very much startled she attempted to escape, and in the excitement of the moment, kicked her own chin with such force that the skin split round her neck, and her head (with the sac of the stomach depending from it) actually became separated from the trunk, and flew off to perch upon the nearest tree. Ever since then she has existed as a spirit of evil, sitting on the roof-tree whinnying whenever a child is born in the house, or trying to force her way up through the floor on which the child lies, in order to drink its blood.

W. W. SKEAT, *Malay Magic*, 1900

Beneath the lamp the lady bowed,
And slowly rolled her eyes around;
Then drawing in her breath aloud,
Like one that shuddered, she unbound
The cincture from beneath her breast:
Her silken robe, and inner vest,
Dropt to her feet, and full in view,
Behold! her bosom and half her side—
A sight to dream of, not to tell!
O shield her! shield sweet Christabel!

Yet Geraldine nor speaks nor stirs;
Ah! what a stricken look was hers!
Deep from within she seems halfway
To lift some weight with sick assay,
And eyes the maid and seeks delay;
Then suddenly, as one defied,
Collects herself in scorn and pride,
And lay down by the Maiden's side!—
And in her arms the maid she took,
    Ah wel-a-day!
And with low voice and doleful look
Those words did say:

'In the touch of this bosom there worketh a spell,
Which is lord of thy utterance, Christabel!
Thou knowest tonight, and wilt know tomorrow,
This mark of my shame, this seal of my sorrow;
   But vainly thou warrest,
      For this is alone in
   Thy power to declare,
      That in the dim forest
   Thou heard'st a low moaning,
And found'st a bright lady, surpassingly fair;
And didst bring her home with thee in love and in charity,
To shield her and shelter her from the damp air.'

COLERIDGE, *Christabel*, Part I, written 1797

Lamiae were supposed of the aunciente people to be women having eyes to put
out or in at their plesure, or rather certaine shapes of devils, which taking on
them the shew of beautifull women, devoured children and yong men, allured
unto them with sweete inticements . . . *Lamiae* are also called *Striges*. *Striges*
(as they saye) are unluckie birdes, whiche sucke out the bloud of infants lying
in their cradles.

LAVATER, *Of Ghostes and Spirites*

      . . . a palpitating snake,
Bright, and cirque-couchant in a dusky brake.
She was a gordian shape of dazzling hue,
Vermilion-spotted, golden, green, and blue;
Striped like a zebra, freckled like a pard,
Eyed like a peacock, and all crimson barr'd;
And full of silver moons, that, as she breathed,
Dissolv'd, or brighter shone, or interwreathed
Their lustres with the gloomier tapestries—
So rainbow-sided, touch'd with miseries,
She seem'd, at once, some penanced lady elf,
Some demon's mistress, or the demon's self.
Upon her crest she wore a wannish fire
Sprinkled with stars, like Ariadne's tiar . . .

Left to herself, the serpent now began
To change; her elfin blood in madness ran,
Her mouth foam'd, and the grass, therewith besprent,
Wither'd at dew so sweet and virulent;
Her eyes in torture fix'd, and anguish drear,
Hot, glaz'd, and wide, with lid-lashes all sear,
Flash'd phosphor and sharp sparks, without one cooling tear.
The colours all inflam'd throughout her train,
She writh'd about, convuls'd with scarlet pain:
A deep volcanian yellow took the place
Of all her milder-mooned body's grace;
And, as the lava ravishes the mead,
Spoilt all her silver mail, and golden brede;
Made gloom of all her frecklings, streaks and bars,
Eclips'd her crescents, and lick'd up her stars:
So that, in moments few, she was undrest
Of all her sapphires, greens, and amethyst,
And rubious-argent: of all these bereft,
Nothing but pain and ugliness were left.
Still shone her crown; that vanish'd, also she
Melted and disappear'd as suddenly;
And in the air, her new voice luting soft,
Cried, 'Lycius! gentle Lycius!' . . .

Ah, happy Lycius!—for she was a maid
More beautiful than ever twisted braid,
Or sigh'd, or blush'd, or on spring-flowered lea
Spread a green kirtle to the minstrelsy:
A virgin purest lipp'd, yet in the lore
Of love deep learned to the red heart's core:
Not one hour old, yet of sciential brain
To unperplex bliss from its neighbour pain;
Define their pettish limits, and estrange
Their points of contact, and swift counterchange;
Intrigue with the specious chaos, and dispart
Its most ambiguous atoms with sure art;
As though in Cupid's college she had spent
Sweet days, a lovely graduate . . .

JOHN KEATS, *Lamia*, 1820; see Robert Burton, p. 359

And at last from the corpse of Rowena, Ligeia rises. Out of her death, through the door of a corpse they have destroyed between them, reappears Ligeia, still trying to have her will, to have more love and knowledge, the final gratification which is never final, with her husband.

For it is true, as William James and Conan Doyle and the rest allow, that a spirit can persist in the after-death. Persist by its own volition. But usually, the evil persistence of a thwarted will, returning for vengeance on life. Lemures, vampires.

It is a ghastly story of the assertion of the human will, the will-to-love and the will-to-consciousness, asserted against death itself. The pride of human conceit in KNOWLEDGE.

There are terrible spirits, ghosts, in the air of America.

D. H. LAWRENCE, from 'Edgar Allan Poe', 1924

If there is in the world one attested story it is that of the Vampires. Nothing is missing: procès-verbaux, certificates from Notabilities, Surgeons, Priests, Magistrates. The juridical proof is most complete. With all this, who believes in Vampires? Shall we all be damned for not having believed?

JEAN-JACQUES ROUSSEAU, *Letter to Christophe de Beaumont, Archbishop of Paris*, 1763

~

This is the *Lycanthropos*; the French call it *Garloup*: and doe believe that some wicked men can transforme themselves into Woolves and bite, and worry people and doe mischiefe to mankind: When I was at Orleans I sawe in the Hospitall there a young fellow in cure whose left Cheeke was eaten (he sayd by this *Garloup*) for sayd he had it been a woolfe he would have killed me out right and eaten me up. No doubt heretofore this opinion was in this island.

AUBREY, *Remaines of Gentilisme and Judaisme*

It also happened my Master was gone to Capua to dispatch somewhat or other: I laid hold of the opportunity, and persuaded mine Host to take an Evenings Walk of four or five Miles out of Town, for he was a stout Fellow, and as bold as a Devil. The Moon shone as bright as Day, and about Cock-crowing we fell in with a Burying-place, and certain Monuments of the Dead. My Man loitered behind me a star-gazing, and I sitting expecting him, fell a Singing and numbering them, when looking round me, what should I see but mine Host stript stark-naked, and his Cloaths lying by the Highway-side. The sight struck me every where, and I stood as if I had been dead; but he Piss'd round his Cloaths, and of a sudden was turned to a Wolf. Don't think I jest; I value no Man's Estate at that rate, as to tell a Lye. But as I was saying, after he was turned to a Wolf, he set up a Howl, and fled to the Woods. At first I knew not where I was, till going to take up his Cloaths, I found them also turn'd to Stone. Another Man would have dy'd for fear, but I drew my Sword, and slaying all the Ghosts that came in my way, lighted at last on the place where my Mistress was: I entred the first Door; my eyes were sunk in my Head, the Sweat ran off me by more streams than one, and I was just breathing my last, without thought of recovery, when my Melissa coming up to me, began to wonder why I'd be walking so late; and 'If,' said she, 'you had come a little sooner, you might have done us a kindness; for a Wolf came into the Farm, and has made Butchers work enough among the Cattle; but tho' he got off, he has no reason to laugh, for a Servant of ours ran him through the Neck with a Pitch-fork.' As soon as I had heard her, I could not hold open my Eyes any longer, and ran home by Daylight, like a Vintner whose House had been robb'd. But coming by the place where the Cloaths were turned to Stone, I saw nothing but a Puddle of Blood; and when I got home, found mine Host lying a-bed like an Oxe in his Stall, and a Chirurgeon dressing his Neck. I understood afterwards he was a Fellow that could change his Skin; but from that day forward, could never eat a bit of Bread with him, no, if you'd have kill'd me.

PETRONIUS (1st century AD), *Satyricon*; tr. William Burnaby

Tales of the marvellous and the supernatural excite interest and fear in a Malay audience, but they occasion no surprise. Malays know that strange things have happened in the past, and are daily occurring to them and to their fellows . . .

Thus the existence of the Malayan Loup Garou to the native mind is a fact and not a mere belief. The Malay *knows* that it is true. Evidence, if it be needed, may be had in plenty; the evidence, too, of sober-minded men, whose words, in a Court of Justice, would bring conviction to the mind of the most obstinate jurymen, and be more than sufficient to hang the most innocent of prisoners. The Malays know well how Haji Abdallah, the native of the little state of Korinchi in Sumatra, was caught naked in a tiger trap, and thereafter purchased his liberty at the price of the buffaloes he had slain, while he marauded in the likeness of a beast. They know of the countless Korinchi men who have vomited feathers, after feasting upon fowls, when for the nonce they had assumed the forms of tigers; and of those other men of the same race, who have left their garments and their trading packs in thickets, whence presently a tiger has emerged. All these things the Malays know have happened, and are happening today, in the land in which they live, and with these plain evidences before their eyes, the empty assurances of the enlightened European that Were-Tigers do not, and never did exist, excite derision not unmingled with contempt.

HUGH CLIFFORD, *In Court and Kampong*, 1897

The gudewife sits i' the chimney-neuk,
    An' looks at the louping flame;
The rain fa's chill, and the win' ca's shrill,
    Ere the auld gudeman comes hame.

'Oh why is your cheek so wan, gudewife?
    An' why do ye glower on me?
Sae dour ye luik i' the chimney-neuk,
    Wi' the red licht in your e'e!

'Yet this nicht should ye welcome me,
    This ae nicht mair than a',
For I hae scotched yon great grey wolf
    That took our bairnies twa . . .

'An' 'twas ae sharp stroke o' my bonny knife
    That gar'd her hand awa';
Fu' fast she went out owre the bent
    Wi'outen her right fore-paw . . .'

He's flung his pouch on the gudewife's lap,
    I' the firelicht shinin' fair,
Yet naught they saw o' the grey wolf's paw,
    For a bluidy hand lay there.

O hooly, hooly, rose she up,
    Wi' the red licht in her e'e,
Till she stude but a span frae the auld gudeman,
    Whiles never a word spak' she.

But she stripped the claiths frae her lang right arm,
    That were wrappit roun' and roun';

The first was white, an' the last was red,
    And the fresh bluid dreeped adown.

She stretchit him out her lang right arm,
    An' cauld as the deid stude he.
The flames louped bricht i' the gloamin' licht—
    There was nae hand there to see!

        GRAHAM R. TOMSON, from 'Ballad of the Werewolf', 1890

Not so very long ago, a young woman in our village married a man who vanished clean away on her wedding night. The bed was made with new sheets and the bride lay down in it; the groom said, he was going out to relieve himself, insisted on it, for the sake of decency, and she drew the coverlet up to her chin and she lay there. And she waited and she waited and then she waited again—surely he's been gone a long time? Until she jumps up in bed and shrieks to hear a howling, coming on the wind from the forest . . .

The young woman's brothers searched the outhouses and the haystacks but never found any remains so the sensible girl dried her eyes and found herself another husband not too shy to piss into a pot who spent the nights indoors. She gave him a pair of bonny babies and all went right as a trivet until, one freezing night, the night of the solstice, the hinge of the year when things do not fit together as well as they should, the longest night, her first good man came home again.

A great thump on the door announced him as she was stirring the soup for the father of her children and she knew him the moment she lifted the latch to him although it was years since she'd worn black for him and now he was in rags and his hair hung down his back and never saw a comb, alive with lice.

'Here I am again, missus,' he said. 'Get me my bowl of cabbage and be quick about it.'

Then her second husband came in with wood for the fire and when the first one saw she'd slept with another man and, worse, clapped his red eyes on her little children who'd crept into the kitchen to see what all the din was about, he shouted: 'I wish I were a wolf again, to teach this whore a lesson!' So a wolf he instantly became and tore off the eldest boy's left foot before he was chopped up with the hatchet they used for chopping logs. But when the wolf lay bleeding and gasping its last, the pelt peeled off again and he was just as he had been, years ago, when he ran away from his marriage bed, so that she wept and her second husband beat her.

        ANGELA CARTER, from 'The Company of Wolves', 1979

A man, who from his childhood had been a werewolf, when returning one night with his wife from a merry-making, observed that the hour was at hand when the evil usually came upon him; giving therefore the reins to his wife, he descended from the vehicle, saying to her, 'If anything comes to thee, only strike at it with thine apron.' He then withdrew, but immediately after, the woman, as she was sitting in the vehicle, was attacked by a werewolf. She did as the man had enjoined her, and struck it with her apron, from which it rived a portion, and then ran away. After some time the man returned, holding in his mouth the rent portion of his wife's apron, on seeing which, she cried out in terror, 'Good Lord, man, why, thou art a werewolf!' 'Thank thee, wife,' said he, 'now I am free.' And from that time he was no more afflicted.

SABINE BARING-GOULD, *The Book of Werewolves*, 1865; a Danish story

A curious tale that threaded through the town
Through greying women sewing under eaves,
Was how his greed had brought old Le Brun down,
Greeted by slowly shutting jalousies
When he approached them in white linen suit,
Pink glasses, cork hat, and tap-tapping cane,
A dying man licensed to sell sick fruit,
Ruined by fiends with whom he'd made a bargain.
It seems one night, these Christian witches said,
He changed himself to an Alsatian hound,
A slavering lycanthrope hot on a scent,
But his own watchman dealt the thing a wound.
It howled and lugged its entrails, trailing wet
With blood, back to its doorstep, almost dead.

DEREK WALCOTT, 'Le loupgarou', 1962

≈

We have the quick and the dead. But in Haiti there is the quick, the dead, and then there are Zombies.

This is the way Zombies are spoken of: They are the bodies without souls. The living dead. Once they were dead, and after that they were called back to life again . . .

Now, why have these dead folk not been allowed to remain in their graves? There are several answers to this question, according to the case.

A was awakened because somebody required his body as a beast of burden. In his natural state he could never have been hired to work with his hands, so he was made into a Zombie because they wanted his services as a laborer. B was summoned to labor also but he is reduced to the level of a beast as an act of revenge. C was the culmination of 'ba' Moun' ceremony and pledge. That is, he was given as a sacrifice to pay off a debt to a spirit for benefits received.

I asked how the victims were chosen, and many told me that any corpse not too old to work would do. The Bocor [priest of devil-worshipping cult] watched the cemetery and went back and took suitable bodies. Others said no, that the Bocor and his associates knew exactly who was going to be resurrected even before they died. They knew this because they themselves brought about the 'death'.

Maybe a plantation owner has come to the Bocor to 'buy' some laborers, or perhaps an enemy wants the utmost in revenge. He makes an agreement with the Bocor to do the work . . . After that [various rituals] the victim is a Zombie. He will work ferociously and tirelessly without consciousness of his surroundings and conditions and without memory of his former state. He can never speak again, unless he is given salt.

The most famous Zombie case of all Haiti is the case of Marie M. It was back in October 1909 that this beautiful young daughter of a prominent family died and was buried. Everything appeared normal and people generally forgot about the beautiful girl who had died in the very bloom of her youth. Five years passed.

Then one day a group of girls from the same school Marie had attended went for a walk with one of the Sisters who conducted the school. As they passed a house one of the girls screamed and said that she had seen Marie M. The Sister tried to convince her she was mistaken. But others had seen her too. The news swept over Port-au-Prince like wildfire. The house was surrounded, but the owner refused to let anyone enter without the proper legal steps. The father of the supposedly dead girl was urged to take out a warrant and have the house searched. This he refused to do at once. Finally he was forced to do so by the pressure of public opinion. By that time the owner had left secretly. There was no one nor nothing in the house. The sullen action of the father caused many to accuse him of complicity in the case. Some accused her uncle and others her godfather. And some accused all three. The public clamored for her grave to be opened for inspection. Finally this was done. A skeleton was in the coffin but it was too long for the box. Also the clothes that the girl had been buried in were not upon the corpse. They were neatly folded beside the skeleton that had strangely outgrown its coffin.

It is said that the reason she was in the house where she was seen was that the houngan [voodoo priest] who had held her had died. His wife wanted to be rid of the Zombies that he had collected. She went to a priest about it and he told her these people must be liberated. Restitution must be made as far as possible. So the widow of the houngan had turned over Marie M. among others to this officer of the church and it was while they were wondering what steps to take in the matter that she was seen by her schoolmates. Later dressed in the habit of a nun she was smuggled off to France where she was seen later in a convent by her brother.

> Zora Neale Hurston, *Tell My Horse: Voodoo and Life in Haiti and Jamaica*,
> 1938

'Adou,' I ask, 'what is a zombi?'

The smile that showed Adou's beautiful white teeth has instantly disappeared; and she answers, very seriously, that she has never seen a zombi, and does not want to see one.

'*Moin pa te janmain ouè zombi,—pa 'lè ouè ço moin!*'

'But, Adou, child, I did not ask you whether you ever saw it;—I asked you only to tell me what it is like?' . . .

Adou hesitates a little, and answers:

'*Zombi? Mais ça fai désòde lanuitt, zombi!*'

'Ah! it is Something which "makes disorder at night."' Still, that is not a satisfactory explanation. 'Is it the spectre of a dead person, Adou? Is it *one who comes back*?'

'*Non, Missié,—non; çé pa ça.*' . . .

'But are the dead folk zombis, Adou?'

'No; the *moun-mò* are not zombis. The zombis go everywhere: the dead folk remain in the graveyard. . . . Except on the Night of All Souls: then they go to the houses of their people everywhere.'

'Adou, if after the doors and windows were locked and barred you were to see entering your room in the middle of the night, a woman fourteen feet high?' . . .

'*Ah! pa pàlé ça!!*'

'No; tell me, Adou.'

'Why, yes: that would be a zombi. It is the zombis who make all those noises at night one cannot understand. . . . Or, again, if I were to see a dog that high [she holds her hand about five feet above the floor] coming into our house at night, I would scream: *Mi Zombi!*'

Then it suddenly occurs to Adou that her mother knows something about zombis.

'*Ou! Maman!*'

'*Eti!*' answers old Théréza's voice from the little out-building where the evening meal is being prepared, over a charcoal furnace, in an earthen canari.

'*Missié-là ka mandé save ça ça yé yonne zombi;—vini ti bouin!*' . . . The mother laughs, abandons her canari, and comes in to tell me all she knows about the weird word.

'*I ni pè zombi*'—I find from old Théréza's explanations—is a phrase indefinite as our own vague expressions, 'afraid of ghosts', 'afraid of the dark'. But the word 'zombi' also has special strange meanings . . . '*Ou passé nans grand chimin lanuitt, épi ou ka ouè gouôs difé, épi plis ou ka vini assou difé-à pli ou ka ouè difé-à ka màché: çé zombi ka fai ça . . . Encò, chouval ka passé,—chouval ka ni anni toua patt: ça zombi.*' (You pass along the high-road at night, and you see a great fire, and the more you walk to get to it the more it moves away: it is the zombi makes that . . . Or a horse with only three legs passes you: that is a zombi.)

'How big is the fire that the zombi makes?' I ask.

'It fills the whole road,' answers Théréza: '*li ka rempli toutt chimin-là.* Folk call those fires the Evil Fires,—*mauvai difé;*—and if you follow them they will lead you into chasms,—*ou ké tombé adans labîme.*'

And then she tells me this:

'Baidaux was a mad man of colour who used to live at St Pierre, in the Street of the Precipice. He was not dangerous,—never did any harm;—his sister used to take care of him. And what I am going to relate is true,—*çe zhistouè veritabe!*

'One day Baidaux said to his sister: "*Moin ni yonne yche, va!—ou pa connaitt li!*" (I have a child, ah!—you never saw it!) His sister paid no attention to what he said that day; but the next day he said it again, and the next, and the next, and every day after—so that his sister at last became much annoyed by it, and used to cry out: "*Ah! mais pé guiole ou, Baidaux! ou fou pou embêté moin comm ça!—ou bien fou!*" . . . But he tormented her that way for months and for years.

'One evening he went out, and only came home at midnight leading a child by the hand,—a black child he had found in the street; and he said to his sister:—

'"*Mi yche-là moin mené ba ou! Tou léjou moin té ka di ou moin tini yonne yche: ou pa té 'lè couè,—eh, ben! MI Y!*"' (Look at the child I have brought you! Every day I have been telling you I had a child: you would not believe me,—very well, LOOK AT HIM!)

'The sister gave one look, and cried out: "*Baidaux, oti ou pouend yche-là?*" . . . For the child was growing taller and taller every moment . . . And Baidaux—because he was mad—kept saying: "*Çé yche-moin! çé yche moin!*" (It is my child!)

'And the sister threw open the shutters and screamed to all the neighbours,—"*Sécou, sécou, sécou! Vini oué ça Baidaux mené ba moin!*" (Help! help! Come see what Baidaux has brought in here!) And the child said to Baidaux: "*Ou ni bonhè ou fou!*" (You are lucky that you are mad!) . . . Then all the neighbours came running in; but they could not see anything: the zombi was gone.'

> LAFCADIO HEARN, from 'The Country of the Comers-Back', 1889. Hearn lived in Martinique 1887–9, before going to Japan, where he spent the rest of his life

⁓

He seems there [in Caliban, in *The Tempest*] to have created a person which was not in Nature, a boldness which, at first sight, would appear intolerable; for he makes him a species of himself, begotten by an incubus on a witch; but this, as I have elsewhere proved, is not wholly beyond the bounds of credibility, at least the vulgar still believe it. We have the separated notions of a spirit, and of a witch (and spirits, according to Plato, are vested with a subtle body; according to some of his followers, have different sexes); therefore, as from the distinct apprehensions of a horse, and of a man, imagination has formed a centaur; so, from those of an incubus and a sorceress, Shakespeare has produced his monster. Whether or no his generation can be defended, I leave to philosophy; but of this I am certain, that the poet has most judiciously furnished him with a person, a language, and a character, which will suit him, both by father's and mother's side: he has all the discontents and malice of a witch, and of a devil, besides a convenient proportion of the deadly sins; gluttony, sloth, and lust, are manifest; the dejectedness of a slave is likewise given him, and the ignorance of one bred up in a desert island. His person is monstrous, and he is the product of unnatural lust; and his language is as hobgoblin as his person.

> JOHN DRYDEN, from 'Preface to *Troilus and Cressida*', 1679

He has come, the One who aroused the first terrors in our simple ancestors, the One who was exorcized by apprehensive priests, whom sorcerers summoned on gloomy nights, without as yet seeing him, he to whom the forebodings of earth's fleeting masters lent all the monstrous or pleasing shapes of gnomes, spirits, genii, fairies, hobgoblins. After the crude conceptions of primitive fear, men more perspicacious envisaged him more clearly. Mesmer had guessed at it and, ten years since, doctors discovered in a precise manner the nature of his power. They have played with this weapon of the new Lord, the domination of a mysterious will over the human mind become enslaved. They have called it magnetism, hypnotism, suggestion . . . what have you. I have seen them amusing themselves like thoughtless children with this horrible power! Woe betide us! Woe betide man! He has come, the . . . the . . . what name does he bear? . . . the . . . it is as if he is calling out his name to me, and I do not hear it . . . the . . . yes . . . he is calling it . . . I am listening . . . I cannot . . . repeat . . . the . . . Horla . . . I have heard . . . the Horla . . . it is he . . . the Horla . . . he has come!

Ah! the vulture has devoured the dove, the wolf has devoured the lamb, the lion has devoured the sharp-horned buffalo; man has slain the lion with the arrow, with the blade, with gunpowder; but the Horla will do unto man as we have done unto the horse and the ox: his chattel, his servant, and his food, by the might alone of his will. Woe upon us!

GUY DE MAUPASSANT, from 'The Horla', 1887

O who rides by night thro' the woodland so wild?
It is the fond father embracing his child;
And close the boy nestles within his loved arm,
To hold himself fast, and to keep himself warm.

'O father, see yonder! see yonder!' he says;
'My boy, upon what dost thou fearfully gaze?'
'O, 'tis the Erl-King with his crown and his shroud.'
'No, my son, it is but a dark wreath of the cloud.'

'O come and go with me, thou loveliest child;
By many a gay sport shall thy time be beguiled;
My mother keeps for thee full many a fair toy,
And many a fine flower shall she pluck for my boy.'

'O father, my father, and did you not hear
The Erl-King whisper so low in my ear?'
'Be still, my heart's darling—my child, be at ease;
It was but the wild blast as it sung thro' the trees.'

'O wilt thou go with me, thou loveliest boy?
My daughter shall tend thee with care and with joy;
She shall bear thee so lightly thro' wet and thro' wild,
And press thee, and kiss thee, and sing to my child.'

'O father, my father, and saw you not plain
The Erl-King's pale daughter glide past thro' the rain?'
'O yes, my loved treasure, I knew it full soon;
It was the grey willow that danced to the moon.'

'O come and go with me, no longer delay,
Or else, silly child, I will drag thee away.'
'O father! O father! now, now, keep your hold,
The Erl-King has seized me—his grasp is so cold!'

Sore trembled the father; he spurr'd thro' the wild,
Clasping close to his bosom his shuddering child;
He reaches his dwelling in doubt and in dread,
But, clasp'd to his bosom, the infant was dead.

GOETHE, 'The Erl-King', 1782; tr. Sir Walter Scott. 'Erl' was a misunder-
standing of the Danish word for 'elf'. Misunderstandings could occur on both
sides of the great divide: in Eduard Mörike's poem 'Elfenlied' (1828) an elf
hears the night-watchman crying 'Elfe!', the hour of eleven, and thinks it is
being summoned

The Ginn are said to be of pre-adamite origin, and, in their general properties,
an intermediate class of beings between angels and men, but inferior in dignity
to both, created of fire, and capable of assuming the forms and material fabric
of men, brutes, and monsters, and of becoming invisible at pleasure. They eat
and drink, propagate their species (like, or in conjunction with, human beings),
and are subject to death; though they generally live many centuries. Their
principal abode is in the chain of mountains called 'Káf', which are believed to
encompass the whole earth. Some are believers in El-Islám: others are infidels:
the latter are what are also called 'Sheytáns', or devils; of whom Iblees (that is,
Satan, or *the* devil) is the chief: for it is the general and best-supported opinion, that he (like the other devils) is a ginnee, as he was created of fire; whereas
the *angels* are created of *light*, and are impeccable. Of both the classes of ginn,
good and evil, the Arabs stand in great awe; and for the former they entertain
a high degree of respect. It is a common custom of this people, on pouring
water, &c., on the ground, to exclaim or mutter, 'Destoor'; that is, to ask the
permission, or crave the pardon, of any ginnee that may chance to be there: for

the ginn are supposed to pervade the solid matter of the earth, as well as the firmament, where, approaching the confines of the lowest heaven, they often listen to the conversation of the angels respecting future things, thus enabling themselves to assist diviners and magicians. They are also believed to inhabit rivers, ruined houses, wells, baths, ovens, and even the *latrina*: hence, persons, when they enter the latter place, and when they let down a bucket into a well, or light a fire, and on other occasions, say, 'Permission', or 'Permission, ye blessed':—which words, in the case of entering the latrina, they sometimes preface with a prayer for God's protection against all evil spirits; but in doing this, some persons are careful not to mention the name of God after they have entered (deeming it improper in such a place), and only say, 'I seek refuge with *Thee* from the male and female devils.'

The term 'efreet is commonly applied rather to an evil ginnee than any other being; but the ghosts of dead persons are also called by this name . . . There are some persons, however, who hold them in no degree of dread.—I had once a humorous cook, who was somewhat addicted to the intoxicating hasheesh: soon after he had entered my service, I heard him, one evening, muttering and exclaiming, on the stairs, as if in surprise at some event; and then politely saying, 'But why are you sitting here in the draught?—Do me the favour to come up into the kitchen, and amuse me with your conversation a little.' The civil address, not being answered, was repeated and varied several times; till I called out to the man, and asked him to whom he was speaking. 'The 'efreet of a Turkish soldier,' he replied, 'is sitting on the stairs, smoking his pipe, and refuses to move: he came up from the well below: pray step and see him.' On my going to the stairs, and telling the servant that I could see nothing, he only remarked that it was because I had a clear conscience. He was told, afterwards, that the house had long been haunted; but asserted that he had not been previously informed of the supposed cause; which was the fact of a Turkish soldier having been murdered there. My cook professed to see this 'efreet frequently after.

EDWARD WILLIAM LANE, *An Account of the Manners and Customs of the Modern Egyptians*, 1836

At dusk Alboufaki [a great camel], making a sudden stop, stamped with his foot, which to Carathis, who knew his ways, was a certain indication that she was near the confines of some cemetery. The moon shed a bright light on the spot, which served to discover a long wall with a large door in it, standing ajar, and so high that Alboufaki might easily enter. The miserable guides, who perceived their end approaching, humbly implored Carathis, as she had now so good an opportunity, to inter them, and immediately gave up the ghost. Nerkes and Cafour, whose wit was of a style peculiar to themselves, were by no means parsimonious of it on the folly of these poor people; nor could anything have been found more suited to their taste than the site of the burying-ground, and the sepulchres which its precincts contained. There were at least two thousand of them on the declivity of a hill. Carathis was too eager to execute her plan to stop at the view, charming as it appeared in her eyes. Pondering the advantages that might accrue from her present situation, she said to herself: 'So beautiful a cemetery must be haunted by ghouls! they never want for intelligence: having heedlessly suffered my stupid guides to expire, I will apply for directions to them; and as an inducement, will invite them to regale on these fresh corpses.' After this wise soliloquy, she beckoned to Nerkes and Cafour, and made signs with her fingers, as much as to say: 'Go; knock against the sides of the tombs, and strike up your delightful warblings.'

The negresses, full of joy at the behests of their mistress, and promising themselves much pleasure from the society of the ghouls, went with an air of conquest, and began their knockings at the tombs. As their strokes were repeated, a hollow noise was made in the earth; the surface hove up into heaps; and the ghouls on all sides protruded their noses to inhale the effluvia which the carcasses of the woodmen began to emit. They assembled before a sarcophagus of white marble, where Carathis was seated between the bodies of her miserable guides. The princess received her visitants with distinguished politeness; and supper being ended, they talked of business. Carathis soon learned from them everything she wanted to discover; and, without loss of time, prepared to set forward on her journey. Her negresses, who were forming tender connections with the ghouls, importuned her, with all their fingers, to wait at least till the dawn. But Carathis, being chastity in the abstract, and an implacable enemy to love intrigues and sloth, at once rejected their prayer.

WILLIAM BECKFORD, *Vathek: An Arabian Tale*, 1786

Below the thunders of the upper deep;
Far, far beneath in the abysmal sea,
His ancient, dreamless, uninvaded sleep
The Kraken sleepeth: faintest sunlights flee
About his shadowy sides: above him swell
Huge sponges of millennial growth and height;
And far away into the sickly light,

From many a wondrous grot and secret cell
Unnumber'd and enormous polypi
Winnow with giant arms the slumbering green.
There hath he lain for ages and will lie
Battening upon huge seaworms in his sleep,
Until the latter fire shall heat the deep;
Then once by man and angels to be seen,
In roaring he shall rise and on the surface die.

TENNYSON, 'The Kraken', 1830

'And ye come frae the College!' sneered Uncle Gordon. 'Gude kens what they learn folk there; it's no muckle service onyway . . . Na; the sea's like the land, but fearsomer. If there's folk ashore, there's folk in the sea—deid they may be, but they're folk whatever; and as for deils, there's nane that's like the sea deils. There's no sae muckle harm in the land deils, when a's said and done. Lang syne, when I was a callant in the south country, I mind there was an auld, bald bogle in the Peewie Moss. I got a glisk o' him mysel' sittin' on his hunkers in a hag, as gray's a tombstane. An', troth, he was a fearsome-like taed. But he steered naebody. Nae doobt, if ane that was a reprobate, ane the Lord hated, had gane by there wi' his sin still upon his stamach, nae doobt the creature would hae lowped upo' the likes o' him. But there's deils in the deep sea would yoke on a communicant! Eh, sirs, if ye had gane doon wi' the puir lads in the *Christ-Anna*, ye would ken by now the mercy o' the seas. If ye had sailed it for as lang as me, ye would hate the thocht of it as I do. If ye had but used the een God gave ye, ye would hae learned the wickedness o' that fause, saut, cauld, bullering creature, and of a' that's in it by the Lord's permission: labsters an' partans, an' sic like, howking in the deid; muckle, gutsy, blawing whales; an' fish—the hale clan o' them—cauld-wamed, blind-eed uncanny ferlies. O, sirs,' he cried, 'the horror—the horror o' the sea!'

We were all somewhat staggered by this outburst; and the speaker himself, after that last hoarse apostrophe, appeared to sink gloomily into his own thoughts. But Rorie, who was greedy of superstitious lore, recalled him to the subject by a question.

'You will not ever have seen a teevil of the sea?' he asked.

'No clearly,' replied the other. 'I misdoubt if a mere man could see ane clearly and conteenue in the body. I hae sailed wi' a lad—they ca'd him Sandy Gabart; he saw ane, shüre eneuch, an' shüre eneuch it was the end of him. We were seeven days oot frae the Clyde,—a sair wark we had had—gaun north wi'

seeds an' braws an' things for the Macleod. We had got in ower near under the
Cutchull'ns, an' had just gane about by Soa, an' were off on a lang tack, we
thocht would maybe hauld as far's Copnahow. I mind the nicht weel; a mune
smoored wi' mist; a fine gaun breeze upon the water, but no steedy; an'—what
nane o' us likit to hear—anither wund gurlin' owerheid, amang thae fearsome,
auld stane craigs o' the Cutchull'ns. Weel, Sandy was forrit wi' the jib sheet;
we couldnae see him for the mains'l, that had just begude to draw, when a' at
ance he gied a skirl. I luffed for my life, for I thocht we were ower near Soa;
but na, it wasnae that, it was puir Sandy Gabart's deid skreigh, or near hand,
for he was deid in half an hour. A't he could tell was that a sea deil, or sea
bogle, or sea spenster, or sic-like, had clum up by the bowsprit, an' gi'en him
ae cauld, uncanny look. An', or the life was oot o' Sandy's body, we kent weel
what the thing betokened, and why the wund gurled in the taps o' the
Cutchull'ns; for doon it cam'—a wund do I ca' it! it was the wund o' the
Lord's anger—an' a' that nicht we foucht like men dementit, and the niest that
we kenned we were ashore in Loch Uskevagh, an' the cocks were crawing in
Benbecula.'

'It will have been a merman,' Rorie said.

'A merman!' screamed my uncle with immeasurable scorn. 'Auld wives'
clavers! There's nae sic things as mermen.'

'But what was the creature like?' I asked.

'What like was it? Gude forbid that we suld ken what like it was! It had a
kind of a heid upon it—man could say nae mair.'

ROBERT LOUIS STEVENSON, from 'The Merry Men', 1887

On the Akasaka Road, in Tokyo, there is a slope called Kii-no-kuni-zaka,—
which means the Slope of the Province of Kii . . . Before the era of street-
lamps and jinrikishas, this neighbourhood was very lonesome after dark; and
belated pedestrians would go miles out of their way rather than mount the Kii-
no-kuni-zaka, alone, after sunset.

All because of a Mujina that used to walk there.

The last man who saw the Mujina was an old merchant of the Kyōbashi
quarter, who died about thirty years ago. This is the story, as he told it:—

One night, at a late hour, he was hurrying up the Kii-no-kuni-zaka, when he
perceived a woman crouching by the moat, all alone, and weeping bitterly.
Fearing that she intended to drown herself, he stopped to offer her any assistance or consolation in his power. She appeared to be a slight and graceful

person, handsomely dressed; and her hair was arranged like that of a young girl of good family. 'O-jochū [honourable maiden],' he exclaimed, approaching her,— 'O-jochū, do not cry like that! . . . Tell me what the trouble is; and if there be any way to help you, I shall be glad to help you.' (He really meant what he said; for he was a very kind man.) But she continued to weep,—hiding her face from him with one of her long sleeves. 'O-jochū,' he said again, as gently as he could,—'please, please listen to me! . . . This is no place for a young lady at night! Do not cry, I implore you!—only tell me how I may be of some help to you!' Slowly she rose up, but turned her back to him, and continued to moan and sob behind her sleeve. He laid his hand lightly upon her shoulder, and pleaded:—'O-jochū! —O-jochū!—O-juchō! . . . Listen to me, just for one little moment! . . . O-jochū! O-jochū!' . . . Then that O-jochū turned round and dropped her sleeve, and stroked her face with her hand;—and the man saw that she had no eyes or nose or mouth,—and he screamed and ran away.

Up Kii-no-kuni-zaka he ran and ran; and all was black and empty before him. On and on he ran, never daring to look back; and at last he saw a lantern, so far away that it looked like the gleam of a firefly; and he made for it. It proved to be only the lantern of an itinerant *soba*-seller [vendor of buckwheat noodles], who had set down his stand by the road-side; but any light and any human companionship was good after that experience; and he flung himself down at the feet of the *soba*-seller, crying out, 'Aa!—aa!!—*aa!!!*' . . .

'*Koré! koré!*' roughly exclaimed the *soba*-man, 'Here! what is the matter with you? Anybody hurt you?'

'No—nobody hurt me,' panted the other,—'only . . . *Aa!—aa!*' . . .

'—Only scared you?' queried the pedlar, unsympathetically. 'Robbers?'

'Not robbers,—not robbers,' gasped the terrified man . . . 'I saw . . . I saw a woman—by the moat;—and she showed me . . . *Aa!* I cannot tell you what she showed me!' . . .

'*Hé!* Was it anything like THIS that she showed you?' cried the *soba*-man, stroking his own face—which therewith became like unto an Egg . . . And, simultaneously, the light went out.

> HEARN, from 'Mujina', 1904, based on an old Japanese tale; the Mujina was a badger capable of changing shape

∽

Tibetans keenly desire avoiding any intercourse with the dead. Peasants use especially precise words to get rid of them. Just before the corpse is carried out of the house, a meal is served to him and an aged member of the family harangues him, in these words:

'So-and-so, listen. You are dead, be sure of that. You have nothing more to do here. Eat copiously for the last time. You have a long road to run and several mountain passes to cross. Take strength and do not return ever again.'

I heard an even stranger discourse.

After having duly told the dead man that he no longer belonged to this world and bidding him never to reappear, the orator added:

'Pagdzin. I must tell you that your house has been destroyed by fire, everything you possessed is burned. Because of a debt you had forgotten, your creditor has taken your two sons away as slaves. Your wife has left with a new husband. As it would sadden you to see all this misery, be careful not to return.'

I listened in astonishment to this extraordinary list of calamities.

'How did this series of misfortunes happen?' I asked an assistant.

'Nothing at all has happened,' he answered, smiling maliciously. 'The farm and the cattle are intact and the widow is sitting quietly at home with the sons. We invented that tale to disgust Pagdzin so that he will not think of returning to his home.'

This seemed rather a naïve stratagem for people who credit the 'spirit' with the faculty of seeing what is going on in our world.

ALEXANDRA DAVID-NEEL, *With Mystics and Magicians in Tibet*, 1919

Most Europeans who believe in an after-life draw a clear horizon-line between the worlds of the living and the dead. The pagans of the Gilbert Islands, as I knew them, imagined no such comfortable partition. The seen and the unseen made but one world for them. Their dead were helped overseas to a western paradise, it is true, but no known ritual could bind them there; only the lapse of generations could do that.

The belief was that the more recently departed could and did return. They were jealous. They wanted to see what their descendants were doing. Their skeletons or skulls were preserved in village shrines mainly for them to re-enter as they liked. If skulls at least were not kept, their ghosts would come and scream reproach by night with the voices of crickets from the palm-leaves that overhung the dwellings. And so, whether a man was pious or impious to his fathers, his house was a house forever brooded over by unseen watchers.

Not that the older folk thought of their dead only as threatening ghosts. There was love as well as fear in the ancient cult of the ancestor, and mostly the love predominated. I was looking round the waterfront of a Tarawa village one day when I came upon an old, old man alone in a canoe shed nursing a skull in the crook of his elbow. He was blowing tobacco smoke between its jaws. As he puffed, he chuckled and talked aloud: 'The smoke is sweet, grandfather—ke-e-e?' he was saying, 'We like it—ke-e-e?' He told me he was loving the skull because his grandfather—who was inside it at that moment—had been very good to him in years gone by. 'Is it not suitable,' he asked, 'for me to be good to him in return?' and answered himself at once, '*Aongkoa*! (of course!)' He went on to say he had chosen tobacco as his offering of love because, as far as he knew, there was no supply of that particular luxury in the ancestral paradise.

> ARTHUR GRIMBLE, *A Pattern of Islands*, 1952; the period is the second decade of the 20th century

He puffed away in silence for a few seconds, while I sat watching him. I had never seen a ghost smoking a pipe before, that I could remember, and it interested me.

I asked him what tobacco he used, and he replied, 'The ghost of cut cavendish, as a rule.'

He explained that the ghost of all the tobacco that a man smoked in life belonged to him when he became dead. He said he himself had smoked a good deal of cut cavendish when he was alive, so that he was well supplied with the ghost of it now.

I observed that it was a useful thing to know that, and I made up my mind to smoke as much tobacco as ever I could before I died.

> JEROME K. JEROME, from 'My Own Story', 1891

The four boards of the coffin lid
Heard all the dead man did.

The first curse was in his mouth,
Made of grave's mould and deadly drouth.

The next curse was in his head,
Made of God's work discomfited.

The next curse was in his hands,
Made out of two grave-bands.

The next curse was in his feet,
Made out of a grave-sheet.

'I had fair coins red and white,
And my name was as great light;

I had fair clothes green and red,
And strong gold bound round my head.

But no meat comes in my mouth,
Now I fare as the worm doth;

And no gold binds in my hair,
Now I fare as the blind fare.

My live thews were of great strength,
Now am I waxen a span's length;

My live sides were full of lust,
Now are they dried with dust.'

The first board spake and said:
'Is it best eating flesh or bread?'

The second answered it:
'Is wine or honey the more sweet?'

The third board spake and said:
'Is red gold worth a girl's gold head?'

The fourth made answer thus:
'All these things are as one with us.'

The dead man asked of them:
'Is the green land stained brown with flame?

Have they hewn my son for beasts to eat,
And my wife's body for beast's meat?

Have they boiled my maid in a brass pan,
And built a gallows to hang my man?'

The boards said to him:
'This is a lewd thing that ye deem.

Your wife has gotten a golden bed,
All the sheets are sewn with red.

Your son has gotten a coat of silk,
The sleeves are soft as curded milk.

Your maid has gotten a kirtle new,
All the skirt has braids of blue.

Your man has gotten both ring and glove,
Wrought well for eyes to love.'

The dead man answered thus:
'What good gift shall God give us?'

The boards answered him anon:
'Flesh to feed hell's worm upon.'

ALGERNON CHARLES SWINBURNE, 'After Death', 1862

That night I made the acquaintance of numerous demons. The Mati-Anak, a stillborn child; the Langsuyar, dead in childbirth; the Hantu Golek, that comes out of tombs, and leaps and rolls upon the ground, swathed in its shroud . . .

'Are the souls of the dead always malignant?' I asked.

'Always.'

'And yet if I were to die I should not, I think, wish anyone harm.'

Smail shrugged his shoulders.

'The Tuan is not evil, but when dead, he would smell as evil as the rest.'

'Then you believe that my soul would become a hideous demon flapping round my tomb?'

'Your soul is your soul, Tuan. It will go straight to hell. But there will be perhaps ten thousand demons round your tomb.'

'But what are the demons doing there if they are not the souls of the dead?'

'The mouse-deer asks questions of the buffalo,' said Smail. 'The Tuan is subtle. I do not know.'

I, on the contrary, had the impression of being the buffalo.

FAUCONNIER, *The Soul of Malaya*

FAIRIES AND LITTLE FOLK

By and large fairies, as the least malignant class of monsters, and their tales, as the most edifying fables, have been handed over to children; albeit one suspects that, if Sir James Barrie's law is valid, their ranks will have been much depleted in recent decades. 'Every time a child says "I don't believe in fairies" there is a little fairy somewhere that falls down dead.' According to other reports they are tougher than this suggests, and by no means invariably cosy creatures; Good Fairies are offset by Bad Fairies, and one common black mark against them is that, as gypsies were reputed to do, they carry off human young, and occasionally a more or less consenting adult. Scott describes their way of life as being quite magnificent, but only to reveal it as all mere illusion, 'fairy gold' as we say.

Irish fairies, at least at the time when Yeats and Lady Gregory drew up their classifications, were (and perhaps they still are) in good health and standing, displaying a greater variety, versatility, and characterfulness than those resident elsewhere, while nearer to our day the sprites portrayed by Sylvia Townsend Warner and Manuel Mujica Lainez run them close in these respects and surpass them in worldly sophistication, and A. L. Barker's little people are more chillingly baleful.

The theory mentioned by Hopkins, that fairies are half-fallen angels, those who consented in part to Satan's rebellion, is an appealing one. 'Because thou art lukewarm, and neither cold nor hot, I will spue thee out of my mouth.' And it accounts for their uncertain position in the hierarchy and their equivocal behaviour towards mortals.

In everyday life the Tooth Fairy lingers on here and there, and her colleagues feature in pantomime or on the top of Christmas trees, but otherwise 'Farewell, rewards and fairies', for

> who of late for cleanliness
> Finds sixpence in her shoe?

~

These *Siths*, or Fairies, they call *Sleagh Maith*, or the Good People, it would seem, to prevent the Dint of their ill Attempts (for the Irish use to bless all they fear Harme of); and are said to be of a midle Nature betuixt Man and Angel, as were Dæmons thought to be of old; of intelligent studious Spirits, and light changable Bodies (lyke those called Astral), somewhat of the Nature of a condensed Cloud, and best seen in Twilight. Thes Bodies be so plyable thorough the Subtilty of the Spirits that agitate them, that they can make them appear or disappear att Pleasure. Some have Bodies or Vehicles so spungious, thin, and desecat, that they are fed by only sucking into some fine spirituous Liquors, that peirce lyke pure Air and Oyl: others feid more gross on the Foyson or substance of Corns and Liquors, or Corne it selfe that grows on the Surface of the Earth, which these Fairies steall away, partly invisible, partly preying on the Grain, as do Crowes and Mice; wherefore in this same Age, they are some times heard to bake Bread, strike Hammers, and do such lyke Services within the little Hillocks they most haunt: some whereof of old, before the Gospell dispelled Paganism, and in some barbarous Places as yet, enter Houses after all are at rest, and set the Kitchens in order, cleansing all the Vessels. Such Drags goe under the name of Brownies.

> ROBERT KIRK, *The Secret Commonwealth of Elves, Fauns and Fairies*, 1691. In introducing an edition of 1933, R. B. Cunninghame Graham wondered if the Revd Mr Kirk 'was but a changeling from birth, a Leprechaun I think they call it, in the dialect of Erse, spoken in Ireland, and sent on earth as an ambassador from the Secret Commonwealth of Elves and Fairies, to make their ways and customs manifest to us, the grosser mortals, nurtured on beef and brose'

> *Fairy*. Either I mistake your shape and making quite
> Or else you are that shrewd and knavish sprite
> Called Robin Goodfellow. Are not you he
> That frights the maidens of the villagery,
> Skim milk, and sometime labour in the quern,
> And bootless make the breathless housewife churn,

And sometime make the drink to bear no barm,
Mislead night-wanderers, laughing at their harm?
Those that 'Hobgoblin' call you, and 'Sweet Puck',
You do their work, and they shall have good luck.
Are not you he?

Puck.   Fairy, thou speak'st aright:
I am that merry wanderer of the night.
I jest to Oberon, and make him smile
When I a fat and bean-fed horse beguile,
Neighing in likeness of a filly foal;
And sometime lurk I in a gossip's bowl
In very likeness of a roasted crab,
And when she drinks, against her lips I bob
And on her wither'd dewlap pour the ale.
The wisest aunt, telling the saddest tale,
Sometime for three-foot stool mistaketh me;
Then slip I from her bum, down topples she,
And 'Tailor' cries, and falls into a cough;
And then the whole choir hold their hips and laugh,
And waxen in their mirth, and sneeze, and swear
A merrier hour was never wasted there.

SHAKESPEARE, *A Midsummer Night's Dream*, *c.*1595; 'Tailor': 'tailer', an
exclamation on falling on one's backside

The employment, the benefits, the amusements of the Fairy court, resembled
the aerial people themselves. Their government was always represented as
monarchical. A King, more frequently a Queen, of Fairies, was acknowledged;
and sometimes both held their court together. Their pageants and court enter-
tainments comprehended all that the imagination could conceive of what was,
by that age, accounted gallant and splendid. At their processions, they paraded
more beautiful steeds than those of mere earthly parentage—the hawks and
hounds which they employed in their chase were of the first race. At their daily
banquets, the board was set forth with a splendour which the proudest kings
of the earth dared not aspire to; and the hall of their dancers echoed to the
most exquisite music. But when viewed by the eye of a seer the illusion vanished. The young knights and beautiful ladies showed themselves as wrinkled
carles and odious hags—their wealth turned into slate-stones—their splendid
plate into pieces of clay fantastically twisted—and their victuals, unsavoured

by salt (prohibited to them, we are told, because an emblem of eternity), became tasteless and insipid—the stately halls were turned into miserable damp caverns—all the delights of the Elfin Elysium vanished at once. In a word, their pleasures were showy, but totally unsubstantial—their activity unceasing, but fruitless and unavailing . . . Besides the unceasing and useless bustle in which these spirits seemed to live, they had propensities unfavourable and distressing to mortals.

One injury of a very serious nature was supposed to be constantly practised by the fairies against 'the human mortals', that of carrying off their children, and breeding them as beings of their race. Unchristened infants were chiefly exposed to this calamity; but adults were also liable to be abstracted from earthly commerce . . .

The reason assigned for this kidnapping of the human race, so peculiar to the elfin people, is said to be that they were under a necessity of paying to the infernal regions a yearly tribute out of their population, which they were willing to defray by delivering up to the prince of these regions the children of the human race, rather than their own.

SCOTT, *Letters on Demonology and Witchcraft*

Afterwards he told me how one of his children had been taken by the fairies.

One day a neighbour was passing, and she said, when she saw it on the road: 'That's a fine child.' Its mother tried to say: 'God bless it', but something choked the words in her throat. A while later they found a wound on its neck, and for three nights the house was filled with noises.

'I never wear a shirt at night,' he said, 'but I got up out of my bed, all naked as I was, when I heard the noises in the house, and lighted a light, but there was nothing in it.'

Then a dummy came and made signs of hammering nails in a coffin.

The next day the seed potatoes were full of blood, and the child told his mother that he was going to America.

That night it died, and 'Believe me,' said the old man, 'the fairies were in it.'

J. M. SYNGE, *The Aran Islands*, 1907

Romeo. I dreamt a dream tonight.
Mercutio.   And so did I.

Rom. Well, what was yours?
Mer.   That dreamers often lie.
Rom. In bed asleep, while they do dream things true.
Mer. O, then I see Queen Mab hath been with you.
   She is the fairies' midwife, and she comes
   In shape no bigger than an agate stone
   On the forefinger of an alderman,
   Drawn with a team of little atomies
   Over men's noses as they lie asleep.
   Her chariot is an empty hazelnut,
   Made by the joiner squirrel or old grub,
   Time out o' mind the fairies' coachmakers.
   Her wagon spokes made of long spinners' legs;
   The cover, of the wings of grasshoppers;
   Her traces, of the smallest spider web;
   Her collars, of the moonshine's watery beams;
   Her whip, of cricket's bone; the lash, of film;
   Her wagoner, a small grey-coated gnat,
   Not half so big as a round little worm
   Pricked from the lazy finger of a maid.
   And in this state she gallops night by night
   Through lovers' brains, and then they dream of love;
   O'er courtiers' knees, that dream on curtsies straight;
   O'er lawyers' fingers, who straight dream on fees;
   O'er ladies' lips, who straight on kisses dream,
   Which oft the angry Mab with blisters plagues,
   Because their breaths with sweetmeats tainted are.
   Sometime she gallops o'er a courtier's nose,
   And then dreams he of smelling out a suit.
   And sometime comes she with a tithe-pig's tail
   Tickling a parson's nose as 'a lies asleep;
   Then he dreams of another benefice.
   Sometime she driveth o'er a soldier's neck,
   And then dreams he of cutting foreign throats,
   Of breaches, ambuscados, Spanish blades,
   Of healths five fathom deep; and then anon
   Drums in his ear, at which he starts and wakes,
   And being thus frighted, swears a prayer or two
   And sleeps again. This is that very Mab
   That plaits the manes of horses in the night

And bakes the elf-locks in foul sluttish hairs,
Which once untangled much misfortune bodes.
This is the hag, when maids lie on their backs,
That presses them and learns them first to bear,
Making them women of good carriage.

SHAKESPEARE, *Romeo and Juliet*, *c*.1595

I may as well mention here, that the conclusion I arrived at from the observations I was afterwards able to make, was, that the flowers die because the fairies go away; not that the fairies disappear because the flowers die. The flowers seem a sort of houses for them, or outer bodies, which they can put on or off when they please. Just as you could form some idea of the nature of a man from the kind of house he built, if he followed his own taste, so you could, without seeing the fairies, tell what any one of them is like, by looking at the flower till you feel that you understand it. For just what the flower says to you, would the face and form of the fairy say; only so much more plainly as a face and human figure can express more than a flower . . . Whether all the flowers have fairies, I cannot determine, any more than I can be sure whether all men and women have souls . . .

The whole garden was like a carnival, with tiny, gaily decorated forms, in groups, assemblies, processions, pairs or trios, moving stately on, running about wildly, or sauntering hither or thither. From the cups or bells of tall flowers, as from balconies, some looked down on the masses below, now bursting with laughter, now grave as owls; but even in their deepest solemnity, seeming only to be waiting for the arrival of the next laugh. Some were launched on a little marshy stream at the bottom, in boats chosen from the heaps of last year's leaves that lay about, curled and withered. These soon sank with them; whereupon they swam ashore and got others. Those who took fresh rose-leaves for their boats floated the longest; but for these they had to fight; for the fairy of the rose-tree complained bitterly that they were stealing her clothes, and defended her property bravely.

'You can't wear half you've got,' said some.

'Never you mind; I don't choose you to have them: they are my property.'

'All for the good of the community!' said one, and ran off with a great hollow leaf. But the rose-fairy sprang after him (what a beauty she was! only too like a drawing-room young lady), knocked him heels-over-head as he ran, and recovered her great red leaf.

GEORGE MACDONALD, *Phantastes*, 1858

High in the mountains there was a place where many beautiful flowers grew, mostly peonies and camellias, sometimes to a height of ten or twenty feet. A young student named Huang, seeking quiet, built himself a little house nearby. One day he noticed from his window a young lady dressed in white, wandering among the flowers. Her loveliness pierced his heart. When he went out, she ran behind a white peony and disappeared. Later he saw her again, with another young lady who was dressed in red. But when he approached, they screamed and ran away with their skirts and long sleeves fluttering in the breeze and scenting all the air around. Huang followed, but they vanished behind some flowers.

That evening, as he was sitting over his books, he was astonished to see the white girl walk into his house. With tears in her eyes, she implored him to help her. Trying to comfort her, he took her hand and asked what was distressing her. But she seemed unable to explain, and soon she bade him farewell and left. The following day a stranger came, and was much taken with a white peony, which he dug up and carried away. Huang realized that the white girl was a flower spirit, and he was deeply saddened by what had happened. It came to his ears that the peony had lived only a few days after being moved. He went to the hole from which it had been dug up, and watered the ground with his tears. Suddenly he became aware of the young lady of the red clothes standing beside him. 'Alas,' she lamented, 'that my dear sister should be torn from me! . . . Yet the tears you have shed, sir, may perhaps prove the means of restoring her to us.'

The same night he dreamt that the red girl appeared again, and said that she too was in danger, and begged him to help her. In the morning he discovered that a new house was to be built in the neighbourhood, and the builder had ordered that a beautiful red camellia, which stood in the way, should be cut down. Huang contrived to prevent its destruction. And in the evening the red girl came to thank him, accompanied this time by her white sister. The red girl told him that the Flower God, touched by Huang's tears, had permitted the white girl to return to life. Rejoicing, Huang grasped the white girl's hand, but now his fingers passed right through it. She said, 'When I was a flower spirit I had a body, but now I am no longer a real person, only a kind of ghost as seen in a dream, although I still have my home in a white peony, beside the red camellia, my sister.'

Huang was so grieved at the loss of the white girl that he fell ill and soon died. By his own wish, he was buried next to the white peony, and before very long another white peony grew up, straight out of Huang's grave.

'The Flower Fairies', a Chinese tale; based on a version by Herbert A. Giles, 1911

True Thomas lay on Huntlie bank,
    A ferlie he spied wi' his e'e;   *marvel*
And there he saw a ladye bright
    Come riding down by the Eildon Tree.

Her shirt was o' the grass-green silk,
    Her mantle o' the velvet fyne;
At ilka tett of her horse's mane   *tuft*
    Hung fifty siller bells and nine.

True Thomas, he pull'd aff his cap
    And louted low down to his knee: *bowed*
All hail, thou mighty Queen of Heaven!
    For thy peer on earth I never did see.

O no, O no, Thomas, she said,
    That name does not belang to me;
I am but the Queen of fair Elfland
    That am hither come to visit thee.

Harp and carp, Thomas, she said,   *sing*
    Harp and carp along wi' me,
And if ye dare to kiss my lips,
    Sure of your bodie I will be.

Betide me weal, betide me woe,
    That weird shall never daunton me.   *fate*
Syne he has kissed her rosy lips   *Then*
    All underneath the Eildon Tree.

Now ye maun go wi' me, she said,   *must*
    True Thomas, ye maun go wi' me;
And ye maun serve me seven years
    Thro' weal or woe, as may chance to be.

She mounted on her milk-white steed,
    She's ta'en True Thomas up behind;
And aye whene'er her bridle rung
    The steed flew swifter than the wind.

O they rade on, and farther on—
    The steed gaed swifter than the wind—
Untill they reach'd a desart wide
    And living land was left behind.

Light down, light down now, True Thomas,
    And lean your head upon my knee;

Abide and rest a little space
  And I will shew you ferlies three.

O see ye not yon narrow road
  So thick beset with thorns and briers?
That is the path of righteousness,
  Though after it but few enquires.

And see ye not that braid, braid road
  That lies across that lily leven?   *lovely lea*
That is the path of wickedness,
  Though some call it the road to heaven.

And see not ye that bonny road
  That winds about the fernie brae?
That is the road to fair Elfland,
  Where thou and I this night maun gae.

But Thomas, ye maun hold your tongue
  Whatever ye may hear or see,
For if you speak word in Elflyn land
  Ye'll ne'er get back to your ain countrie.

O they rade on, and farther on,
  And they waded through rivers aboon the knee,
And they saw neither sun nor moon
  But they heard the roaring of the sea.

It was mirk, mirk night and there was nae stern light   *dark; star*
  And they waded through red blude to the knee;
For a' the blude that's shed on earth
  Rins through the springs o' that countrie.

Syne they came on to a garden green
  And she pu'd an apple frae a tree:
Take this for thy wages, True Thomas,
  It will give thee the tongue that can never lie.

My tongue is mine ain, True Thomas said,
  A gudely gift ye wad gie to me;
I neither dought to buy nor sell   *dare*
  At fair or tryst where I may be;   *market*

I dought neither speak to prince or peer
  Nor ask of grace from fair ladye.
Now hold thy peace, the lady said,
  For as I say, so must it be.

He has gotten a coat of the even cloth
    And a pair of shoes of velvet green;
And till seven years were gane and past
    True Thomas on earth was never seen.

ANON., 'Thomas the Rhymer'

Somewhat more courteous was a Danish boy whom an Elf-maiden met and offered drink from a costly drinking-horn one evening as he rode homeward late from Ristrup to Siellevskov. He received the horn, but fearing to drink its contents, poured them out behind him, so that, as in several of these stories, they fell on the horse's back, and singed the hair off. The horn he held fast, and the horse probably needed no second hint to start at the top of its speed. The elf-damsel gave chase until horse and man reached a running water, across which she could not follow them. Seeing herself outwitted, she implored the youth to give her back the horn, promising him in reward the strength of twelve men. On this assurance he returned the horn to her, and got what she had promised him. But the exchange was not very profitable; for with the strength of twelve men he had unfortunately acquired the appetite of twelve.

A Cornish tale relates that a farmer's boy of Portallow was one night sent to a neighbouring village for some household necessaries. On the way back he fell in with some piskies, and by repeating the formula he heard them use, transported himself with them, first to Portallow Green, then to Seaton Beach, and finally to 'the King of France's cellar', where he joined his mysterious companions in tasting that monarch's wines. They then passed through magnificent rooms, where the tables were laden for a feast. By way of taking some memorial of his travels, he pocketed one of the rich silver goblets which stood on one of the tables. After a very short stay, the word was passed to return, and presently he found himself again at home. The good wife complimented him on his despatch. 'You'd say so, if you only know'd where I've been,' he replied; 'I've been wi' the piskies to Seaton Beach, and I've been to the King o' France's house, and all in five minutes.' The farmer stared and said the boy was *mazed*. 'I thought you'd say I was mazed, so I brort away this mug to show vor et,' he answered, producing the goblet. With such undeniable evidence his story could not be any longer doubted. Stealing from a natural enemy like the King of France was probably rather meritorious than otherwise; and the goblet remained in the boy's family for generations, though unfortunately it is no longer forthcoming for the satisfaction of those who may still be sceptical.

EDWIN SIDNEY HARTLAND, *The Science of Fairy Tales*, 1890

I was with the laybrothers that week . . . Br. [Brother John] Byrne: Hockey and football are much played in Ireland and the great day is Shrove Tuesday, on which the 'merits' are awarded. A player who had greatly distinguished himself at football was that day going home when in a lonely field a ball came rolling to his feet; he kicked it, it was kicked back, and soon he found himself playing the game with a fieldfull of fairies and in a place which was strange to him. The fairies would not let him go but they did their best to amuse him, they danced and wrestled before him so that he should never want for entertainment, but they could not get him to eat, for knowing that if he eat what they gave him they would have a claim upon him he preferred to starve and they for fear he should die on their hands at last put him on the right road home. On reaching home he found a pot of stirabout on the fire and had only had time to taste a ladlefull when the fairies were in upon him and began to drag him away again. He caught hold of the doorpost and called on the saints but when he came to our Lady's name they let go and troubled him no more.

Br. Byrne even gives them on the authority of some priest a theological standing ground. They are half-fallen angels who gave a part-consent to Lucifer's sin and are in probation till the last day here on earth. Their behaviour towards men comes from envy.

I asked Miss Jones in my Welsh lesson the Welsh for *fairy*, for we were translating Cinderella. She told me *cĭpenăper* (or perhaps *cĭpernăper*, *Anglice kippernapper*): the word is nothing but *kidnapper*, moulded, according to their fashion, to give it a Welsh etymology, as she said, from *cĭpio*/to snatch, to whisk away. However in coming to an understanding between ourselves what fairies (she says *fairess* by the way for a she-fairy) and kippernappers were, on my describing them as little people 'that high', she told me quite simply that she had seen them. It was on or near the Holywell road (she indicated the spot). She was going to her grandfather's farm on the hill, not far from where Justice Williams lived, on the slope of the Rhuallt. It was a busy time, haymaking I think. She was going up at five o'clock in the morning, when she saw three little boys of about four years old wearing little frock coats and odd little caps running and dancing before her, taking hands and going round, then going further, still dancing and always coming together, she said. She would take no notice of them but went on to the house and there told them what she had seen and wondered that children could be out so early. 'Why she has seen the kippernappers' her grandmother said to her son, Susannah Jones' father.

GERARD MANLEY HOPKINS, *Journal*, 4 April 1870; 7 February 1875

The *Lepracaun*, *Cluricaun*, and *Far Darrig*. Are these one spirit in different moods and shapes? Hardly two Irish writers are agreed. In many things these three fairies, if three, resemble each other. They are withered, old, and solitary ... They dress with all unfairy homeliness, and are, indeed, most sluttish, slouching, jeering, mischievous phantoms. They are the great practical jokers among the good people.

The *Lepracaun* makes shoes continually, and has grown very rich. Many treasure-crocks, buried of old in wartime, has he now for his own.

The *Cluricaun* makes himself drunk in gentlemen's cellars. Some suppose he is merely the Lepracaun on a spree.

The *Far Darrig* (*fear dearg*), which means the Red Man, for he wears a red cap and coat, busies himself with practical joking, especially with gruesome joking. This he does, and nothing else.

The *Fear-Gorta* (Man of Hunger) is an emaciated phantom that goes through the land in famine time, begging an alms and bringing good luck to the giver.

The *Leanhaun Shee* (fairy mistress) seeks the love of mortals. If they refuse, she must be their slave; if they consent, they are hers, and can only escape by finding another to take their place. The fairy lives on their life, and they waste away. Death is no escape from her. She is the Gaelic muse, for she gives inspiration to those she persecutes. The Gaelic poets die young, for she is restless, and will not let them remain long on earth—this malignant phantom.

The *banshee* (from *ban* [*bean*], a woman, and *shee* [*sidhe*], a fairy) is an attendant fairy that follows the old families, and none but them, and wails before a death. Many have seen her as she goes wailing and clapping her hands. The keen [*caoine*], the funeral cry of the peasantry, is said to be an imitation of her cry. When more than one banshee is present, and they wail or sing in chorus, it is for the death of some holy or great one. An omen that sometimes accompanies the banshee is the *coach-a-bower* [*cóiste-bodhar*]—an immense black coach, mounted by a coffin, and drawn by headless horses driven by a *Dullahan* [headless phantom]. It will go rumbling to your door, and if you open it, according to Croker, a basin of blood will be thrown in your face. These headless phantoms are found elsewhere than in Ireland. In 1807 two of the sentries stationed outside St James's Park died of fright. A headless woman, the upper part of her body naked, used to pass at midnight and scale the railings. After a time the sentries were stationed no longer at the haunted spot. In Norway the heads of corpses were cut off to make their ghosts feeble. Thus came into existence the *Dullahans*, perhaps; unless, indeed, they are descended from that Irish giant who swam across the Channel with his head in his teeth.

YEATS, *Fairy and Folk Tales of the Irish Peasantry*, 1888

The Banshee means, especially, the woman of the fairy race, from *van*, 'the Woman—the Beautiful'; the same word from which comes *Venus*. Shiloh-Van was one of the names of Buddha—'the son of the woman'; and some writers aver that in the Irish *Sullivan* (Sulli-van) may be found this ancient name of Buddha.

As the Leanan-Sidhe was the acknowledged *spirit of life*, giving inspiration to the poet and the musician, so the Ban-Sidhe was the *spirit of death*, the most weird and awful of all the fairy powers.

But only certain families of historic lineage, or persons gifted with music and song, are attended by this spirit; for music and poetry are fairy gifts, and the possessors of them show kinship to the spirit race—therefore they are watched over by the spirit of life, which is prophecy and inspiration; and by the spirit of doom, which is the revealer of the secrets of death.

Sometimes the Banshee assumes the form of some sweet singing virgin of the family who died young, and has been given the mission by the invisible powers to become the harbinger of coming doom to her mortal kindred. Or she may be seen at night as a shrouded woman, crouched beneath the trees, lamenting with veiled face; or flying past in the moonlight, crying bitterly: and the cry of this spirit is mournful beyond all other sounds on earth, and betokens certain death to some member of the family whenever it is heard in the silence of the night.

LADY WILDE, *Ancient Legends . . . of Ireland*

> *Belinda* still her downy Pillow prest,
> Her Guardian *Sylph* prolong'd the balmy Rest.
> 'Twas he had summon'd to her silent Bed
> The Morning-Dream that hover'd o'er her Head.
> A Youth more glitt'ring than a *Birth-night Beau*
> (That ev'n in Slumber caus'd her Cheek to glow)
> Seem'd to her Ear his winning Lips to lay,
> And thus in Whispers said, or seem'd to say:
>   Fairest of Mortals, thou distinguish'd Care
> Of thousand bright Inhabitants of Air! . . .
> Know then, unnumber'd Spirits round thee fly,
> The light *Militia* of the lower Sky;
> These, tho' unseen, are ever on the Wing,
> Hang o'er the *Box*, and hover round the *Ring*.
> Think what an Equipage thou hast in Air,

And view with scorn *Two Pages* and a *Chair*.
As now your own, our Beings were of old,
And once inclos'd in Woman's beauteous Mold;
Thence, by a soft Transition, we repair
From earthly Vehicles to these of Air.
Think not, when Woman's transient Breath is fled,
That all her Vanities at once are dead:
Succeeding Vanities she still regards,
And tho' she plays no more, o'erlooks the Cards.
Her Joy in gilded Chariots, when alive,
And Love of *Ombre*, after Death survive.
For when the Fair in all their Pride expire,
To their first Elements their Souls retire:
The Sprights of fiery Termagants in Flame
Mount up, and take a *Salamander*'s Name.
Soft yielding Minds to Water glide away,
And sip, with *Nymphs*, their Elemental Tea.
The graver Prude sinks downwards to a *Gnome*,
In search of Mischief still on Earth to roam.
The light Coquettes in *Sylphs* aloft repair,
And sport and flutter in the Fields of Air.
   Know farther yet. Whoever fair and chaste
Rejects Mankind, is by some *Sylph* embrac'd:
For Spirits, freed from mortal Laws, with ease
Assume what Sexes and what Shapes they please.
What guards the Purity of melting Maids,
In Courtly Balls, and Midnight Masquerades,
Safe from the treach'rous Friend, the daring Spark,
The Glance by Day, the Whisper in the Dark,
When kind Occasion prompts their warm Desires,
When Musick softens, and when Dancing fires?
'Tis but their *Sylph*, the wise Celestials know,
Tho' *Honour* is the Word with Men below.

ALEXANDER POPE, *The Rape of the Lock*, 1714

I went across to the lame old lady. She acknowledged my coming with the prettiest of gestures possible; and, half apologetically, said, 'It is a little dull to be unable to move about on such evenings as this; but it is a just punishment to me for my early vanities. My poor feet, that were by nature so small, are now taking their revenge for my cruelty in forcing them into such little slippers.' . . .

The lame lady took up the word. 'Tonight is the night when, of all the year, this great old forest surrounding the castle is said to be haunted by the phantom of a little peasant girl who once lived hereabouts; the tradition is that she was devoured by a wolf. In former days I have seen her on this night out of yonder window at the end of the gallery. Will you, *ma belle*, take monsieur to see the view outside by the moonlight (you may possibly see the phantom-child); and leave me to a little *tête-à-tête* with your husband?'

With a gentle movement the lady with the roses complied with the other's request, and we went to a great window, looking down on the forest, in which I had lost my way. The tops of the far-spreading and leafy trees lay motionless beneath us in that pale, wan light, which shows objects almost as distinct in form, though not in colour, as by day. We looked down on the countless avenues, which seemed to converge from all quarters to the great old castle; and suddenly across one, quite near to us, there passed the figure of a little girl, with the 'capuchon' on, that takes the place of a peasant girl's bonnet in France. She had a basket on one arm, and by her, on the side to which her head was turned, there went a wolf. I could almost have said it was licking her hand, as if in penitent love, if either penitence or love had ever been a quality of wolves—but though not of living, perhaps it may be of phantom wolves.

'There, we have seen her!' exclaimed my beautiful companion. 'Though so long dead, her simple story of household goodness and trustful simplicity still lingers in the hearts of all who have ever heard of her; and the country-people about here say that seeing that phantom-child on this anniversary brings good luck for the year. Let us hope that we shall share in the traditionary good fortune.'

ELIZABETH GASKELL, from 'Curious, If True', 1865

There was once a regular student: he lived in a garret, and nothing at all belonged to him; but there was also once a regular huckster: he lived on the ground floor, and the whole house was his; and the Goblin lodged with him, for here, every Christmas Eve, there was a dish of porridge, with a great piece of butter floating in the middle. The huckster could give that, and consequently the Goblin stuck to the huckster's shop, and that was very interesting.

One evening the student came through the back door to buy candles and cheese for himself. He procured what he wanted and paid for it, and the huckster and his wife both nodded a 'good evening' to him; and the woman was one who could do more than merely nod—she had an immense power of tongue! And the student nodded too, and then suddenly stood still, reading the sheet of paper in which the cheese had been wrapped. It was a leaf torn out of an old book, a book that ought not to have been torn up, a book that was full of poetry.

'There lies more of it,' said the huckster: 'I gave an old woman a few coffee beans for it; give me three pence and you shall have the remainder.'

'Thanks,' said the student, 'give me the book instead of the cheese: I can eat my bread and butter without cheese. It would be a sin to tear the book up entirely. You are a capital man, a practical man, but you understand no more about poetry than does that cask yonder.'

Now, that was an impolite speech, especially towards the cask; but the huckster laughed and the student laughed, for it was only said in fun. But the Goblin was angry that anyone should dare to say such things to a huckster who lived in his own house and sold the best butter.

When it was night, and the shop was closed and all were in bed except the student, the Goblin came forth, went into the bedroom, and took away the good lady's tongue, for she did not want that while she was asleep; and whenever he put this tongue upon any object in the room, the said object acquired speech and language, and could express its thoughts and feelings as well as the lady herself could have done; but only one object could use it at a time, and that was a good thing, otherwise they would have interrupted each other.

And the Goblin laid the tongue upon the Cask in which the old newspapers were lying.

'Is it true,' he asked, 'that you don't know what poetry means?'

'Of course I know it,' replied the Cask: 'poetry is something that always stands at the foot of a column in the newspapers, and is sometimes cut out. I dare swear I have more of it in me than the student, and I'm only a poor tub compared to the huckster.'

Then the Goblin put the tongue upon the coffee-mill, and, mercy! how it began to go! And he put it upon the butter-cask, and on the cashbox: they were all of the waste-paper Cask's opinion, and the opinion of the majority must be respected.

'Now I shall tell it to the student!'

And with these words the Goblin went quite quietly up the back stairs to the garret, where the student lived. The student had still a candle burning, and the Goblin peeped through the keyhole, and saw that he was reading in the torn book from downstairs.

But how light it was in his room! Out of the book shot a clear beam, expanding into a thick stem, and into a mighty tree, which grew upward and spread its branches far over the student. Each leaf was fresh, and every blossom was a beautiful girl's head, some with dark sparkling eyes, others with wonderfully clear blue orbs; every fruit was a gleaming star, and there was a glorious sound of song in the student's room.

Never had the little Goblin imagined such splendour, far less had he ever seen or heard anything like it . . .

'This is an incomparable place,' said the Goblin: 'I never expected such a thing! I should like to stay here with the student.'

And then he thought it over—and thought sensibly; then he sighed, 'The student has no porridge!' And then he went down again to the huckster's shop . . .

But the Goblin could no longer sit quietly and contentedly listening to all the wisdom down there: as soon as the light glimmered from the garret in the evening, he felt as if the rays were strong cables drawing him up, and he was obliged to go and peep through the keyhole; and there a feeling of greatness rolled around him, such as we feel beside the ever-heaving sea when the storm rushes over it, and he burst into tears. He did not know himself why he was weeping, but a peculiar feeling of pleasure mingled with his tears. How wonderfully glorious it must be to sit with the student under the same tree! But that might not be—he was obliged to be content with the view through the keyhole, and to be glad of that . . . It was cold, very cold; but the little manikin only felt that when the light in the room was extinguished and the tones in the tree died away. Ha! then he shivered, and crept down again to his warm corner, where it was homely and comfortable . . .

In the middle of the night the Goblin was awakened by a terrible tumult and knocking against the window-shutters. People rapped noisily without, and the watchman blew his horn, for a great fire had broken out—the whole street was full of smoke and flame. Was it in the house itself or at a neighbour's? Where was it? Terror seized on all. The huckster's wife was so bewildered that she took her gold earrings out of her ears and put them in her pocket, that at any rate she might save something; the huckster ran up for his share-papers, and the maid for her black silk mantilla, for she had found means to purchase one. Each wanted to save the best thing they possessed; the Goblin wanted to do the same thing, and in a few leaps he was up the stairs and into the room of the student, who stood quietly at the open window, looking at the conflagration that was raging in the house of the neighbour opposite. The Goblin seized upon the wonderful book which lay upon the table, popped it into his red cap, and held the cap tight with both hands. The best treasure of the house was saved; and now he ran up and away, quite on to the roof of the house, on to the chimney. There he sat, both hands pressed tightly over his cap, in which the treasure lay; and now he knew the real feelings of his heart, and knew to whom it really belonged. But when the fire was extinguished, and the Goblin could think calmly again, why, then . . .

'I must divide myself between the two,' he said; 'I can't quite give up the huckster, because of the porridge!'

Now, that was spoken quite like a human creature. We all of us visit the huckster for the sake of the porridge.

> HANS CHRISTIAN ANDERSEN, from 'The Goblin and the Huckster'; tr. W. A. and J. K. Craigie. Andersen's tales were written between 1835 and 1872

Between the kingdoms of Paflagonia and Crim Tartary, there lived a mysterious personage, who was known in those countries as the Fairy Blackstick, from the ebony wand or crutch which she carried; on which she rode to the moon sometimes, or upon other excursions of business or pleasure, and with which she performed her wonders.

When she was young, and had been first taught the art of conjuring, by the necromancer, her father, she was always practising her skill, whizzing about from one kingdom to another upon her black stick, and conferring her fairy favours upon this Prince or that. She had scores of royal godchildren; turned numberless wicked people into beasts, birds, millstones, clocks, pumps, bootjacks, umbrellas, or other absurd shapes; and in a word was one of the most active and officious of the whole College of fairies.

But after two or three thousand years of this sport, I suppose Blackstick grew tired of it. Or perhaps she thought, 'What good am I doing by sending this Princess to sleep for a hundred years? by fixing a black pudding on to that booby's nose? by causing diamonds and pearls to drop from one little girl's mouth, and vipers and toads from another's? I begin to think I do as much harm as good by my performances. I might as well shut my incantations up, and allow things to take their natural course. There were my two young goddaughters, King Savio's wife, and Duke Padella's wife: I gave them each a present, which was to render them charming in the eyes of their husbands, and secure the affections of those gentlemen as long as they lived. What good did my Rose and my Ring do these two women? None on earth. From having all their whims indulged by their husbands, they became capricious, lazy, ill-humoured, absurdly vain, and leered and languished, and fancied themselves irresistibly beautiful, when they were really quite old and hideous, the ridiculous creatures! They used actually to patronize me when I went to pay them a visit—*me*, the Fairy Blackstick, who knows all the wisdom of the necromancers, and who could have turned them into baboons, and all their diamonds into strings of onions, by a single wave of my rod!'

So she locked up her books in her cupboard, declined further magical performances, and scarcely used her wand at all except as a cane to walk about with.

WILLIAM MAKEPEACE THACKERAY, *The Rose and the Ring*, 1855

Beauty is in the eye of the beholder. In the eye of Elfins the qualities considered to constitute beauty are slenderness, narrow hands and feet, sharp-cut features (rather small eyes are admired), arched eyebrows, the fineness of detail one associates with moths and butterflies. These canons are conditioned by Elfin build and longevity: majestic contours are irreconcilable with flight, and a *jolie-laide* countenance is likelier to remain charming over centuries than a classically moulded one. Elfins are averse to any variation from the racial type. Few of them really enjoy Ovid's 'Metamorphoses'. Above all, miscegenation with mortals is reprobated because of its probable results—corpulence, coarse skin, broad smiles, dimples, premature decay, and flat fingernails.

Wirre Gedanken was a small Elfin Kingdom, never of any importance and now extinct. In the Austrian section of Countess Morphy's 'Recipes of All Nations', *Wirre Gedanken* (translated 'Troubled Thoughts') designates a kind of fried bun; but there does not seem to be any historical connection. The Castle of Wirre Gedanken was situated in a gloomy crevice of the Harz Mountains. As it lay beneath one of the main routes to the Walpurgisnacht Festival on the Brocken, the excited screamings and hallooings of witches and warlocks flying overhead was a recurrent nuisance and a recurrent subject of conversation. There was also the plight of the marmots to be deplored. The great bonfires burned so hotly that the snow melted and seeped into the marmot burrows, prematurely wakening the harmless little animals to die of hunger and pneumonia. So Queen Balsamine declared. Compassion for marmots was the soft spot in a character otherwise so irritable and arbitrary that Balsamine survives in English folklore of the nineteenth century as the Red Queen. The castle resounded with the weeping of maidservants, the moaning of bower-women, the howls of pages under the lash. The Headsman was always at the ready— though in fact few executions took place, as Balsamine's attention was constantly diverted to a new offender and the Headsman went in fear of being blamed for striking off the wrong head. He drew a large salary and liked his comforts.

Sylvia Townsend Warner, from (1) 'Castor and Pollux', (2) 'The Blameless Triangle', *Kingdoms of Elfin*, 1977

Anyone who doesn't believe in fairies had better shut these pages here and now and throw them into the wastepaper basket, or cut them up to line his book-shelves, and very expensive that will be. Not only will he be rejecting the evident truth that nothing, absolutely nothing, is explicable in this mysterious world, but, in his antiquated Victorian scepticism (and this without disrespect to a monarch I revere), he will miss some extremely interesting things, and I am sorry for him. Of the many ways of being poor in spirit, and dismissing the earth as a dull sort of place, perhaps the stupidest is to say no to the hidden relish that gives this life its touch of magic.

As for denying the existence of fairies, good and bad, you have to be blind not to see them. They are everywhere, and naturally I have links of affection or dislike with all of them. The wealthy, spendthrift ones squander fortunes in Venice or Monte Carlo: fabulous, ageless women whose birthdays and incomes and origins nobody knows, putting charms on roulette wheels for the dubious pleasure of seeing the same number come up more often than it ought. There they sit, puffing smoke from long cigarette-holders, raking in the chips, and looking bored. Others spend the hours of darkness hanging their apartments in Paris or New York with Gothic tapestries, hitherto unrecorded, that drive the art dealers demented—gorgeous tapestries kept hidden away in massive chests beneath deserted abbeys and castles since their own *belle époque* in the Middle Ages. Some stick to their original line of country, agitating tables at seances or organizing the excitement in haunted houses; some perform kind deeds, but in a capricious and uncertain manner that frequently goes wrong. And then there are the amorous fairies, who never give up. They were to be seen fluttering through the Val sans Retour in the forest of Brocéliande, where Morgan la Fée concealed the handsome knight Guyomar and many lost lovers besides, or over the Isle of Avallon where the young knight Lanval lived happily with a fairy who had stolen him away. Now wrinkled with age, the amorous ones contrive to lure young men on the make who, immaculately tailored and bedecked with baubles from Cartier, escort them through the vestibules of international hotels. Yet other fairies, more studious and respectable, devote themselves to science, whirring and breathing above tired inventors and inspiring original ideas— though lately the unimaginable numbers, the formulae and the electronics, tend to overwhelm them. The scarcely comprehensible discoveries multiply around them and shake a world that is not theirs any more, that slips through their immaterial fingers. And so it goes on—all sorts and conditions of fairies, whispering together, purring to themselves, unnoticed on the impercipient earth. And I am one of them.

There are angels, too. You may be sure that angels as well as fairies exist, as they did in the Middle Ages. Angel and fairy—they *were* the Middle Ages ... When I myself was the young Countess of Lusignan ... fairies and angels had regular encounters, for some of our duties were similar and we often used the same routes. You ran across angels in the most unlikely places—forest crossroads, convent kitchens. They were tall and willowy, rather shy, holding up their bright robes and raising tenuous fingers in blessing; going with a basket of sweet cakes to a hermit, perhaps, or to receive the prayers of a pious duchess, to catch them as they fell from her lips like fragrant incense. We were as busy as they were, and of the same essence, but etiquette demanded that neither side acknowledge the other or admit the relationship when we met. Yet they could be so good-looking, could remind us so much of the pages and noble youths who were our protégés, that we could not always suppress a smile of appreciation. Then they would bow very slightly—the merest shadow of a bow—and pass on, mild and straight-faced as before. However, as I said, everything is different now. Angels, though they are still around, are different too; even we, who understood them and in some ways resembled them, can no longer recognize them ...

My name is Melusine, which should tell you all you need to know. But alas, at present it may not be enough. Indeed, what is enough these days, when students have to absorb so much abstruse and futile information that they have no time left for the fundamentals?

MANUEL MUJICA LAINEZ, *The Wandering Unicorn*, 1965; tr. Mary Fitton

'Are you kidnapping me? I'm afraid there's no money for my ransom.' Although she experienced a normal spasm of laughter it came out as a squawk. 'You should try Barbara Cartland!'

'She does not write about fairies.'

Looking at him made her head swim, but Elvira forced herself. 'What's that got to do with it?'

'Everything. There is great exception to the image you give us. Although you have no public to speak of, you inculcate a ridiculous and obnoxious idea in immature minds. They receive it, retain it without question, and pass it on to the next generation. There is no surer way of perpetuating a lie than by telling it to children . . . For thirty years you have made us a laughing stock.' He held up his hand like a traffic policeman as she opened her mouth. 'I am aware that Andersen and the Brothers Grimm began it, and the mawkish element was introduced by Mrs Herbert Strang. But you, you have not merely perpetuated it, you have brought it to the peak of banality and made us risible and totally negligible. We will not wear this image in the eyes of the human race.'

'Who? What?' cried Elvira wildly. 'Who is *we*?'

'The little people.'

'Little?'

'This,' he said, splaying his fingers across his chest, 'is an adaptation. For the sake of convenience.'

'Whose convenience?'

'We are none of us more than four inches tall . . . Had I retained my natural size I should have been obliged to shout. Tiresome.' . . .

Elvira, who no longer cared what impression she gave, was about to lean against the desk for support when she realized that the surface was occupied, every inch. Tiny figures stood in ranks, watching her. She thought they were nude, then she saw that they wore unigarments like children's sleeping-suits with feet, the colour of plasma. She retreated against the bookshelves. 'Are they—'

'They are we. Is that grammatically correct?'

'I think it ought to be "us"—I don't know—Oh God!'

'That,' said the man at the desk—was he man or manifestation?—'is the original fairy story. The first cognizant act of mankind was to find a culpable creator. Someone to blame. An exerter of undue influence, ergo, man could then claim total exoneration from frailty, mismanagement, lunacy and sin. That is the theme of all fairy stories.'

Elvira said bitterly, 'You like to talk, don't you!'

'I am here to talk, you will do well to listen. At this moment you are being better informed than your philosophers and scientists. You are in a position to confirm the fears of the fearful and the dreams of the dreamers.'

'I am?'

'You are looking at what you call the secret of the universe.'

Elvira said wildly, '*You*?'

'Us.' Again there came the sharp effervescence from the waiting multitude. 'We have taken over the universe. Never mind from whom, though in view of your egomania I had better say that it was not from you, because you do not possess even your own planet. Mankind is merely an element in an everlasting state of flux. There have been, and will continue to be, other takeovers, and the life expectancy of the human race is too minimal for consideration. Suffice it to say that we need this planet for our own purpose . . . Time has no significance for us, but it may mean something to you if we say that we have been waiting since the first viable conglomeration of atoms and molecules resulted in the first living entity.'

A. L. BARKER, from 'The Little People', 1981

Before Printing, Old-wives Tales were ingeniose: and since Printing came in fashion, till a little before the Civil-warres, the ordinary sort of People were not taught to reade: now-a-dayes Bookes are common, and most of the poor people understand letters: and the many good Bookes, and variety of Turnes of Affaires, have put all the old Fables out of dores: and the divine art of Printing and Gunpowder have frighted away Robin-good-fellow and the Fayries.

AUBREY, *Remaines of Gentilisme and Judaisme*

Anno 1670, not far from Cyrencester, was an Apparition: Being demanded, whether a good Spirit, or a bad? returned no answer, but disappeared with a curious Perfume and most melodious Twang. Mr W. Lilley believes it was a Fairie.

AUBREY, *Miscellanies*

This medley of myth and realism must have forged a strangely dual mind in the race that found itself oscillating so gently between both. Possibly the greatest degree of objectivity that the native mind can have reached when listening to these half-credible, half-incredible wonders—which, as with the folk of today or yesterday, was not just something adverted to occasionally and briefly but something impinging on them at every hour of their lives—was that of the old West Cork woman who was recently asked, 'Do you really believe in the fairies?' and who replied, 'I do not, but they're there!'

SEAN O'FAOLAIN, *The Irish*, 1947

Some people think that there are no fairies. Cousin Cramchild tells little folks so in his Conversations. Well, perhaps there are none—in Boston, U.S., where he was raised. There are only a clumsy lot of spirits there, who can't make people hear without thumping on the table: but they get their living thereby, and I suppose that is all they want. And Aunt Agitate, in her Arguments on political economy, says there are none. Well, perhaps there are none—in her political economy. But it is a wide world, my little man—and thank Heaven for it, for else, between crinolines and theories, some of us would get squashed— and plenty of room in it for fairies, without people seeing them; unless, of course, they look in the right place. The most wonderful and the strongest things in the world, you know, are just the things which no one can see. There is life in you; and it is the life in you which makes you grow, and move, and think: and yet you can't see it.

But remember always, as I told you at first, that this is all a fairy tale, and only fun and pretence: and, therefore, you are not to believe a word of it, even if it is true.

CHARLES KINGSLEY, *The Water-Babies*, 1863

MIRACLES AND PROGNOSTICATIONS

Nᴏᴛ unlike the status of Satan, miracles are in the grip of a double bind. They are undoubtedly popular, yet also more than a trifle vulgar (Donne declared in one of his sermons that in every miracle there is 'a silent chiding . . . a tacit reprehension' of those who need them); they reinforce faith and win converts, but they come close to encroaching on our freedom of will and the requirement that we face the consequences of our actions. And why, if one person is saved by a miracle, are untold thousands left to perish? Again, mysterious motives, mysterious restrictions, mysterious laws . . . Even so, to use Hume's terms, it ought to be possible to keep a balance between common sense and the passion of wonder. 'Miracles don't happen,' we say, but we still hope one will. If it does, though, it is no longer a miracle, just good luck, if not good judgement.

In a chapter in *The Unknown Guest* on precognition Maeterlinck speaks of a Dr Alphonse Teste, an expert on hypnotism, putting to sleep a lady who then announced that she was pregnant, and that at a particular hour four days later, as a result of a fright, she would have a fall and miscarry, and suffer three days' loss of reason before recovering. On awaking she had no memory of what she had said. Four days later she was hypnotized again, and she repeated the same words. As the designated hour drew near, every possible precaution was taken against harm. When the lady expressed a wish to leave the room, the doctor told her she must not, in the interest of her health. Her health, she retorted, was a good reason why she should be allowed to withdraw briefly. Her husband insisted on accompanying her. As the two were leaving, the wife a step ahead of the husband, the doctor heard a shriek and the sound of a body falling. At the moment the lady opened the door, a rat had rushed at her. Thereafter events took the course she had related in her trance.

Conceivably, Maeterlinck observes, the lady created her fright and her fall by self-suggestion; and unfortunately she alone had seen the rat, which therefore could also be the very coinage of her brain.

As regards prophetic dreams, balance requires that, side by side with Clement Attlee's experience, we place that of H. J. Eysenck, who has related how, the night before the Grand National, he had a dream in which he identified the winner clearly. The following day he kept a close eye on that particular horse. 'She fell at the first hurdle!'

~

Lafeu. They say miracles are past; and we have our philosophical persons, to make modern and familiar, things supernatural and causeless. Hence is it that we make trifles of terrors, ensconcing ourselves into seeming knowledge, when we should submit ourselves to an unknown fear.

Parolles. Why, 'tis the rarest argument of wonder that hath shot out in our latter times.

SHAKESPEARE, *All's Well that Ends Well, c.*1603

The same night also I [Tobit] returned from the burial, and slept by the wall of my courtyard, being polluted, and my face was uncovered:

And I knew not that there were sparrows in the wall, and mine eyes being open, the sparrows muted warm dung into mine eyes, and a whiteness came in mine eyes; and I went to the physicians, but they helped me not.

It came to pass the same day, that in Ecbatane a city of Media Sara the daughter of Raguel was also reproached by her father's maids;

Because that she had been married to seven husbands, whom Asmodeus the evil spirit had killed, before they had lain with her. Dost thou not know, said they, that thou hast strangled thine husbands? thou hast had already seven husbands, neither wast thou named after any of them . . .

When she heard these things, she was very sorrowful, so that she thought to have strangled herself; and she said, I am the only daughter of my father, and if I do this, it shall be a reproach unto him, and I shall bring his old age with sorrow unto the grave.

And now I signify this to thee, that I committed ten talents to Gabael the son of Gabrias at Rages in Media . . .

Tobias then answered and said, Father, I will do all things which thou hast commanded me:

But how can I receive the money, seeing I know him not?

Then he gave him the handwriting, and said unto him, Seek thee a man which may go with thee, whiles I yet live, and I will give him wages: and go and receive the money.

Therefore when he went to seek a man, he found Raphael that was an angel.

But he knew not; and he said unto him, Canst thou go with me to Rages? and knowest thou those places well?

To whom the angel said, I will go with thee, and I know the way well: for I have lodged with our brother Gabael . . .

And as they went on their journey, they came in the evening to the river Tigris, and they lodged there.

And when the young man went down to wash himself, a fish leaped out of the river, and would have devoured him.

Then the angel said unto him, Take the fish. And the young man laid hold of the fish, and drew it to land.

To whom the angel said, Open the fish, and take the heart and the liver and the gall, and put them up safely.

So the young man did as the angel commanded him; and when they had roasted the fish, they did eat it: then they both went on their way, till they drew near to Ecbatane.

Then the young man said to the angel, Brother Azarias, to what use is the heart and the liver and the gall of the fish?

And he said unto him, Touching the heart and the liver, if a devil or an evil spirit trouble any, we must make a smoke thereof before the man or the woman, and the party shall be no more vexed.

As for the gall, it is good to anoint a man that hath whiteness in his eyes, and he shall be healed.

And when they were come near to Rages,

The angel said to the young man, Brother, today we shall lodge with Raguel, who is thy cousin; he also hath one only daughter, named Sara; I will speak for her, that she may be given thee for a wife.

For to thee doth the right of her appertain, seeing thou only art of her kindred.

And the maid is fair and wise: now therefore hear me, and I will speak to her father; and when we return from Rages we will celebrate the marriage.

And when they had supped, they brought Tobias unto her.

And as he went, he remembered the words of Raphael, and took the ashes of the perfumes, and put the heart and the liver of the fish thereupon, and made a smoke therewith.

The which smell when the evil spirit had smelled, he fled into the utmost parts of Egypt, and the angel bound him.

And after that they were both shut in together, Tobias rose out of the bed, and said, Sister, arise, and let us pray that God would have pity on us . . .

And now, O Lord, I take not this my sister for lust, but uprightly: therefore mercifully ordain that we may become aged together.

And she said with him, Amen.

After these things Tobias went his way, praising God that he had given him a prosperous journey . . .

Then Raphael said to Tobias, Thou knowest, brother, how thou didst leave thy father:

Let us haste before thy wife, and prepare the house.

And take in thine hand the gall of the fish. So they went their way, and the dog went after them . . .

Then, said Raphael, I know, Tobias, that thy father will open his eyes.

Therefore anoint thou his eyes with the gall, and being pricked therewith, he shall rub, and the whiteness shall fall away, and he shall see thee.

Then Anna ran forth, and fell upon the neck of her son, and said unto him, Seeing I have seen thee, my son, from henceforth I am content to die. And they wept both.

Tobit also went forth toward the door, and stumbled: but his son ran unto him,

And took hold of his father: and he strake of the gall on his father's eyes, saying, Be of good hope, my father.

And when his eyes began to smart, he rubbed them;

And the whiteness pilled away from the corners of his eyes: and when he saw his son, he fell upon his neck.

And he wept, and said, Blessed art thou, O God, and blessed is thy name for ever; and blessed are all thine holy angels:

For thou hast scourged, and hast taken pity on me: for, behold, I see my son Tobias.

Tobit (Apocrypha), from chapters 2–11

Joseph was an old man,
    And an old man was he,
When he wedded Mary
    In the land of Galilee.

Joseph and Mary walked
    Through an orchard good,

Where was cherries and berries
So red as any blood.

Joseph and Mary walked
Through an orchard green,
Where was berries and cherries
As thick as might be seen.

O then bespoke Mary
So meek and so mild:
Pluck me one cherry, Joseph,
For I am with child.

O then bespoke Joseph
With words most unkind:
Let him pluck thee a cherry
That brought thee with child.

O then bespoke the Babe
Within his Mother's womb:
Bow down then the tallest tree
For my Mother to have some.

Then bowed down the highest tree
Unto his Mother's hand;
Then she cried, See, Joseph,
I have cherries at command.

O then bespoke Joseph:
I have done Mary wrong;
But cheer up, my dearest,
And be not cast down.

Then Mary plucked a cherry
As red as the blood;
Then Mary went home
With her heavy load.

Then Mary took her Babe
And sat him on her knee,
Saying, My dear Son, tell me
What this world will be.

O I shall be as dead, Mother,
As the stones in the wall;
O the stones in the streets, Mother,
Shall mourn for me all.

Upon Easter-day, Mother,
  My uprising shall be;
O the sun and the moon, Mother,
  Shall both rise with me.

ANON., 'The Cherry-Tree Carol'

And the third day there was a marriage in Cana of Galilee; and the mother of Jesus was there:

And both Jesus was called, and his disciples, to the marriage.

And when they wanted wine, the mother of Jesus saith unto him, They have no wine.

Jesus saith unto her, Woman, what have I to do with thee? mine hour is not yet come.

His mother saith unto the servants, Whatsoever he saith unto you, do it.

And there were set there six water-pots of stone, after the manner of purifying of the Jews, containing two or three firkins apiece.

Jesus saith unto them, Fill the water-pots with water. And they filled them up to the brim.

And he saith unto them, Draw out now, and bear unto the governor of the feast. And they bare it.

When the ruler of the feast had tasted the water that was made wine, and knew not whence it was (but the servants which drew the water knew), the governor of the feast called the bridegroom,

And saith unto him, Every man at the beginning doth set forth good wine; and when men have well drunk, then that which is worse: but thou hast kept the good wine until now.

This beginning of miracles did Jesus in Cana of Galilee, and manifested forth his glory; and his disciples believed on him.

John 2

As I in hoary Winter's night stood shiveringe in the snowe,
Surpris'd I was with sodayne heat, which made my hart to glowe;
And lifting upp a fearefull eye to vewe what fire was nere,
A pretty Babe all burninge bright, did in the ayre appeare,
Who scorchèd with excessive heate, such floodes of teares did shedd,

As though His floodes should quench His flames which with His teares
   were fedd;
Alas! quoth He, but newly borne, in fiery heates I frye,
Yet none approch to warme their hartes or feele my fire but I!
My faultles brest the fornace is, the fuell woundinge thornes,
Love is the fire, and sighes the smoke, the ashes shame and scornes;
The fuell Justice layeth on, and Mercy blowes the coales,
The metall in this fornace wrought are men's defilèd soules,
For which, as nowe on fire I am, to worke them to their good,
So will I melt into a bath to washe them in My bloode:
With this He vanisht out of sight, and swiftly shroncke awaye,
And straight I callèd unto mynde that it was Christmas-daye.

                 St Robert Southwell, 'The Burning Babe', 1595

A certain Syriarch, Alexander by name, saw Thecla and was enamoured of her
. . . as he was of great power, he himself embraced her in the highway: and she
endured it not . . . and cried out bitterly, saying: Force not the stranger, force
not the handmaid of God . . . And she caught at Alexander and rent his cloak
and took the wreath from his head and made him a mocking-stock.

But he alike loving her and being ashamed of what had befallen him, brought
her before the governor; and when she confessed that she had done this, he
condemned her to the beasts . . .

Thecla . . . was stripped and a girdle put upon her, and was cast into the
stadium: and lions and bears were set against her. And a fierce lioness running
to her lay down at her feet, and the press of women cried aloud. And a bear ran
upon her; but the lioness ran and met him, and tore the bear in sunder. And
again a lion, trained against men, which was Alexander's, ran upon her, and
the lioness wrestled with him and was slain along with him. And the women
bewailed yet more, seeing that the lioness also that succoured her was dead.

Then did they put in many beasts, while she stood and stretched out her
hands and prayed. And when she had ended her prayer, she turned and saw a
great tank of water, and said: Now is it time that I should wash myself. And
she cast herself in, saying: In the name of Jesus Christ do I baptize myself on
the last day. And all the women seeing it and all the people wept, saying: Cast
not thyself into the water: so that even the governor wept that so great beauty
should be devoured by seals. So, then, she cast herself into the water in the
name of Jesus Christ; and the seals, seeing the light of a flash of fire, floated

dead on the top of the water. And there was about her a cloud of fire, so that neither did the beasts touch her, nor was she seen to be naked.

Now the women, when other more fearful beasts were put in, shrieked aloud, and some cast leaves, and others nard, others cassia, and some balsam, so that there was a multitude of odours; and all the beasts that were struck thereby were held as it were in sleep and touched her not; so that Alexander said to the governor: I have some bulls exceeding fearful, let us bind the criminal to them. And the governor, frowning, allowed it, saying: Do that thou wilt. And they bound her by the feet between the bulls, and put hot irons under their bellies that they might be the more enraged and kill her. They then leaped forward; but the flame that burned about her, burned through the ropes, and she was as one not bound.

The Acts of Paul, 2nd century, Apocryphal New Testament; tr. M. R. James

After they had put up in the inn and rested a little space they went to the marriage [of the daughter of the king of Andrapolis] . . . And as they dined and drank, the apostle tasted nothing; so they that were about him said unto him: Wherefore art thou come here, neither eating nor drinking? but he answered them, saying: I am come here for somewhat greater than the food or the drink, and that I may fulfil the king's will. For the heralds proclaim the king's message, and whoso hearkeneth not to the heralds shall be subject to the king's judgement . . .

Now the flute-girl, holding her flute in her hand, went about to them all and played, but when she came to the place where the apostle was, she stood over him and played at his head for a long space: now this flute-girl was by race an Hebrew.

And as the apostle continued looking on the ground, one of the cup-bearers stretched forth his hand and gave him a buffet; and the apostle lifted up his eyes and looked upon him that smote him and said: My God will forgive thee in the life to come this iniquity, but in this world thou shalt show forth his wonders, and even now shall I behold this hand that hath smitten me dragged by dogs . . .

But the cup-bearer that had buffeted him went down to the well to draw water; and there chanced to be a lion there, and it slew him and left him lying in that place, having torn his limbs in pieces, and forthwith dogs seized his members, and among them one black dog holding his right hand in his mouth bare it into the place of the banquet.

And all when they saw it were amazed and inquired which of them it was that was missing. And when it became manifest that it was the hand of the cup-bearer which had smitten the apostle, the flute-girl brake her flute and cast it away and went and sat down at the apostle's feet, saying: This is either a god or an apostle of God, for I heard him say in the Hebrew tongue: 'I shall now see the hand that hath smitten me dragged by dogs', which thing ye also have now beheld; for as he said, so hath it come about. And some believed her, and some not.

> The Acts of Thomas, 3rd century, Apocryphal New Testament

The representation of St Christopher, which so frequently adorned the walls of English village churches, was said to offer a day's preservation from illness or death to all those who looked upon it. St Wilgerfort, better known as St Uncumber, whose statue stood in St Paul's, could eliminate the husbands of those discontented wives who chose to offer her a peck of oats. The large mounted wooden figure of Derfel Gadarn at Llandderfel, near Bala, protected men and cattle, rescued souls from Purgatory, and inflicted disease upon his enemies: Henry VIII's visitors found five or six hundred worshippers at the shrine on the day they went there to pull it down. Saints indeed were believed to have the power to bestow diseases as well as to relieve them. 'We worship saints for fear,' wrote William Tyndale in the early sixteenth century, 'lest they should be displeased and angry with us, and plague or hurt us; as who is not afraid of St Laurence? Who dare deny St Anthony a fleece of wool for fear of his terrible fire, or lest he send the pox among our sheep?'

> THOMAS, *Religion and the Decline of Magic*

Some have thought that it was on account of his very early abstinence [fasting] that he was chosen patron of schoolboys; but a much better reason is afforded to us by a writer in the Gent.'s Magazine for April, 1777, who mentions having in his possession an Italian Life of St Nicholas, 1645, from which he translates the following story, which fully explains the occasion of boys addressing themselves to St Nicholas's patronage:—'The fame of St Nicholas's virtues was so great, that an Asiatic gentleman, on sending his two sons to Athens for education, ordered them to call on the bishop for his benediction, but they, getting to Myra late in the day, thought proper to defer their visit till the morrow, and took up their lodgings at an inn, where the landlord, to secure their baggage and effects to himself, murdered them in their sleep, and then cut them into pieces, salting them, and putting them into a pickling tub, with some pork which was there already, meaning to sell the whole as such. The bishop, however, having had a vision of this impious transaction, immediately resorted to the inn, and, calling the host to him, reproached him for his horrid villainy. The man, perceiving that he was discovered, confessed his crime, and entreated the bishop to intercede on his behalf to the Almighty for his pardon; who, being moved with compassion at his contrite behaviour, confession, and thorough repentance, besought Almighty God not only to pardon the murderer, but also, for the glory of his name, to restore life to the poor innocents who had been so inhumanly put to death. The saint had hardly finished his prayer, when the mangled and detached portions of the two youths were, by divine power, reunited, and perceiving themselves alive, threw themselves at the feet of the holy man to kiss and embrace them. But the bishop, not suffering their humiliation, raised them up, exhorting them to return thanks to God alone for this mark of his mercy, and gave them good advice for the future conduct of their lives; and then giving them his blessing, he sent them with great joy to prosecute their studies at Athens.' And adds: 'This, I suppose, sufficiently explains the naked children and tub', the well-known emblems of St Nicholas.

BRAND, *Observations on Popular Antiquities*

We spent three days at Madeira, taking on supplies, during which time I took the opportunity to make an excursion to the Palheiro with Titus Oates and Birdie Bowers . . . From the Palheiro we rode across to the Curral dos Romeiros to look at the Mount Church associated with so many miracles. Birdie was particularly taken with the one concerning the Virgin. The island being caught in the grip of famine, the inhabitants climbed in procession to the church and prayed to the statue of the Madonna for deliverance. Next day a ship loaded with grain came into the harbour, and the statue of the Madonna was found to be dripping with moisture. Some even claimed to have seen the Virgin swimming ahead of the ship, towing her in with the cable between her teeth!

BERYL BAINBRIDGE, *The Birthday Boys*, 1991; the speaker is Dr Edward Wilson, a member of Captain Scott's Antarctic expedition of 1910–12

There was a man, which had great devotion to S. Augustin, gave great good to a monk that kept the body of S. Augustin, for to have a finger of the glorious saint. And this monk took this money and delivered to him the finger of another dead man, wrapped in silk, and feigned that it was the finger of the glorious S. Augustin. And the good man received it much honourably and in great reverence, and honoured it every day devoutly and touched withal his eyes and his mouth, and oft embraced it against his breast. And God by his mercy, that beholdeth all things, and the faith of this man, gave to him for that finger the very proper finger of S. Augustin, and when he came into his country, there were many miracles showed thereby. The renown and fame thereof came to Pavia of this finger, and the monk aforesaid affirmed always that it was the finger of another dead man. The sepulchre was opened for to know the truth, and it was found that there lacked one of the fingers of the glorious saint. And when the abbot had knowledge of this thing, he put out the monk of that office and tormented and punished him sore.

> JACOBUS DE VORAGINE (1230–98), *The Golden Legend*; tr. William Caxton, ed. George V. O'Neill

Far be it from us to think God's power insufficient to re-collect and unite every atom of the body, were it burnt, or torn by beasts, or fallen to dust, or dissolved into moisture, or exhaled into air. God forbid that any corner of nature (though it may be unknown to us) should lie hid from the eye and power of the Almighty . . . And now may we answer the doubt that seems most difficult: that is, whose flesh shall that man's be at the resurrection, which another man eats? Ancient stories, and late experience, have lamentably informed us, that this has often come to pass, that one man has eaten another: in which case none will say that all the flesh went quite through the body, and none was turned into nutriment: the meagre places becoming by this only meat more full and fleshy, do prove the contrary. Now then my premises shall serve to resolve this ambiguity.

The flesh of the famished man that hunger consumed, is exhaled into air, and thence (as we said before) the Creator can fetch it again. This flesh therefore of the man that was eaten, shall return to the first owner, of whom the famished man does but as it were borrow it, and so must repay it again. And that of his own which famine dried up into air, shall be re-collected, and restored into some convenient place of his body, which were it so consumed that no part thereof remained in nature, yet God could fetch it again in an instant, and when He would Himself. But seeing that 'not an hair of your head shall perish', it were absurd to imagine that famine should have the power to deprive us of so much of our flesh.

These things being duly considered, this is the sum of all, that in the resurrection every man shall arise with the same body that he had, or would have had in his fullest growth, in all comeliness, and without deformity of any the least member.

St Augustine, *The City of God*, 413–26; tr. J.H.

Of Maria Domenica Lazzari [a peasant girl of Capriana], who was born March 16th, 1815 . . . Mr Allies, then a clergyman of the Church of England, wrote the following account: 'In August 1833, she had an illness, not in the first instance of an extraordinary nature; but it took the form of an intermittent fever, confining her completely to her bed, and finally contracting the nerves of her hands and feet so as to cripple them. On the 10th of January, 1834, she received on her hands, feet, and left side, the marks of our Lord's Five Wounds . . . Three weeks afterwards, her family found her in the morning covering her face in a state of great delight—a sort of trance. On removing the handkerchief, letters were found on it marked in blood, and Domenica's brow had a complete impression of the crown of thorns, in a line of small punctures about a quarter of an inch apart, from which the blood was flowing freshly. They asked her who had torn her so. She replied, "A very fair lady had come in the night and adorned her." . . . From the time that she first received the stigmata to the present time [1847], the wounds have bled every Friday, with a loss of from one to two ounces of blood, beginning early in the morning, and on Friday only. The above information we received from Signor Yoris, a surgeon of Cavalese, the chief village of the district in which Capriana lies.'

Revd Frederick George Lee, *The Other World*, 1875

Many years ago there was a very religious and holy man, one of the monks of a convent, and he was one day kneeling at his prayers in the garden of his monastery, when he heard a little bird singing in one of the rose-trees of the garden, and there never was anything that he had heard in the world so sweet as the song of that little bird . . .

And the little bird, after singing for some time longer on the rose-tree, flew away to a grove at some distance from the monastery, and the holy man followed it to listen to its singing, for he felt as if he would never be tired of listening to the sweet song it was singing out of its throat.

And the little bird after that went away to another distant tree, and sung there for a while, and then to another tree, and so on in the same manner, but ever further and further away from the monastery, and the holy man still following it farther, and farther, and farther, still listening delighted to its enchanting song.

But at last he was obliged to give up, as it was growing late in the day, and he returned to the convent; and as he approached it in the evening, the sun was setting in the west with all the most heavenly colours that were ever seen in the world, and when he came into the convent, it was nightfall.

And he was quite surprised at everything he saw, for they were all strange faces about him in the monastery that he had never seen before, and the very place itself, and everything about it, seemed to be strangely altered; and, altogether, it seemed entirely different from what it was when he had left in the morning; and the garden was not like the garden where he had been kneeling at his devotion when he first heard the singing of the little bird.

And while he was wondering at all he saw, one of the monks of the convent came up to him, and the holy man questioned him, 'Brother, what is the cause of all these strange changes that have taken place here since the morning?'

And the monk that he spoke to seemed to wonder greatly at his question, and asked him what he meant by the change since morning? for, sure, there was no change; that all was just as before. And then he said, 'Brother, why do you ask these strange questions, and what is your name? for you wear the habit of our order, though we have never seen you before.'

So upon this the holy man told his name, and said that he had been at mass in the chapel in the morning before he had wandered away from the garden listening to the song of a little bird that was singing among the rose-trees, near where he was kneeling at his prayers.

And the brother, while he was speaking, gazed at him very earnestly, and then told him that there was in the convent a tradition of a brother of his name, who had left it two hundred years before, but that what was become of him was never known.

And while he was speaking, the holy man said, 'My hour of death is come; blessed be the name of the Lord for all his mercies to me, through the merits of his only-begotten Son.'

And he kneeled down that very moment, and said, 'Brother, take my confession, for my soul is departing.'

And he made his confession, and received his absolution, and was anointed, and before midnight he died.

The little bird, you see, was an angel, one of the cherubims or seraphims;

and that was the way the Almighty was pleased in His mercy to take to Himself the soul of that holy man.

> THOMAS CROFTON CROKER, 'The Story of the Little Bird', 1827. Croker said that he wrote this word for word as he heard it from an old Irish woman at a holy well

One day [in 1936, at Rugby School] a sixteen-year-old Jewish boy was sitting alone in his study, feeling rather melancholy, thinking of nothing. Suddenly he saw a distant figure in white, whom he instinctively knew to be Jesus, beckoning towards him. The figure said, 'Follow me.' He went to bed but he could not sleep. John Hoskyns, another school friend who was later ordained, writes: 'He woke me up in my dormitory and said, "I have seen the Lord!" I told him to go back to bed and go to sleep.'

But Montefiore could not sleep. What he knew at the time was that: 'In the morning I was a Jew and by the evening I had become a Christian as well . . .' . . .

Here was someone who had never read the New Testament nor taken part in Christian worship yet who was granted a vision of the person of Jesus.

> JOHN S. PEART-BINNS, *Bishop Hugh Montefiore*, 1990

The revival of a new mythology in the world of Hasidism . . . draws not the least part of its strength from its connection between the magical and the mystical faculties of its heroes. When all is said and done it is this myth which represents the greatest creative expression of Hasidism. In the place of the theoretical disquisition, or at least side by side with it, you get the Hasidic tale . . . And so perhaps I may also be permitted to close these lectures by telling you a story of which the subject, if you like, is the very history of Hasidism itself. And here it is, as I have heard it told by that great Hebrew novelist and storyteller, S. Y. Agnon:

When the Baal Shem had a difficult task before him, he would go to a certain place in the woods, light a fire and meditate in prayer—and what he had set out to perform was done. When a generation later the 'Maggid' of Meseritz was faced with the same task he would go to the same place in the woods and say: We can no longer light the fire, but we can still speak the prayers—and what he wanted done became reality. Again a generation later Rabbi Moshe Leib of Sassov had to perform this task. And he too went into the woods and said: We can no longer light a fire, nor do we know the secret meditations belonging to the prayers, but we do know the place in the woods to which it all belongs—and that must be sufficient; and sufficient it was. But when another generation had passed and Rabbi Israel of Rishin was called upon to perform the task, he sat down on his golden chair in his castle and said: We cannot light the fire, we cannot speak the prayers, we do not know the place, but we can tell the story of how it was done. And, the storyteller adds, the story which he told had the same effect as the actions of the other three.

GERSHOM G. SCHOLEM, *Major Trends in Jewish Mysticism*, 1941

Jabir relates: When the moat was being dug I perceived the signs of hunger on the Holy Prophet: so I returned to my wife and said to her: Have you anything in the house? I have perceived the signs of severe hunger on the Holy Prophet. She brought out a leather bag in which there was a measure of barley and we had a home-reared lamb. I slaughtered the lamb and she prepared the flour for baking. I then cut up the meat and put it in the cooking pot. Then I turned to go to the Holy Prophet and my wife said to me: Do not humiliate me in the eyes of the Holy Prophet and those who are with him. When I came to him I said to him in a low tone: Messenger of Allah, we have slaughtered a small lamb and have ground a measure of barley. Please come with a few people. The Holy Prophet thereupon announced in a loud tone: O ye of the moat, Jabir has prepared an entertainment for you, so come along all of you; and addressing me he said: Do not take the pot off the fire, nor bake the dough till I arrive. So I came home and the Holy Prophet came leading the people. My wife said: It will all rebound on you. I said: I have only done what you told me. She brought out the dough and the Holy Prophet spat into it and blessed it, and then advanced towards the cooking pot and spat into it and blessed it. Then he said: Summon the woman who bakes, and let her bake along with you, and let her ladle out from the cooking pot, but do not take it off the fire. There were altogether a thousand of them. Verily, all of them ate till they left the food and went off; while our pot still bubbled as before and the dough was being baked as before.

IMAM NAWAWI, *Gardens of the Righteous*, 13th century; tr. Muhammad Zafrulla Khan

The curious phenomenon of God's name appearing in Arabic inside aubergines has spread from Nottingham to Leicester, where three cases have been reported by devout Muslims in the past week. As many as 5,000 pilgrims from all over the Midlands are reported to have visited the remarkable vegetables.

Tasleem Moulvi, of Kingnewton Street, Leicester, told the *Independent* yesterday that her mother found two significant aubergines on Friday night when she sliced them open after visiting another one, exposed in Bakewell Street. One, sliced twice, shows the Arabic characters for Allah repeated three times; the other, she said, appeared to contain a verse from the Koran, though this has not yet been deciphered.

'It's quite clear,' she said. 'You don't even have to have a magnifier. Everyone who has been round to see it and pay their respects has said it's a message that it's going to be the end of the world or whatever. It is a message to tell all the Muslims, and all the other faiths, that this is the true faith. No other religions have had this happen to them. A human being could have written the name in a frame. To have this written in a fruit or vegetable is a miracle.' . . .

Manzoor Moghal, vice-chairman of the Leicester County Council Race Relations Board, said: 'As far as Muslims are concerned, they can find Allah in all the objects on this earth, because Allah is everywhere. The fact that certain configurations can appear to read as the word Allah should not surprise anyone because Allah's ways are very mysterious.'

ANDREW BROWN, from 'Aubergines reveal true faith to Muslim pilgrims', *The Independent*, 28 March 1990

The two foundations, one interior, the other exterior: grace, miracles; both of them supernatural.

Miracles and truth are necessary, in order to convince the whole man, in body and in soul.

Miracles prove the power God has over our hearts, through the power he exercises over our bodies.

Miracles sort out doctrine, and doctrine sorts out miracles.

There are false miracles and real ones. A sign is needed to distinguish between them; otherwise they would be useless. Now, they are not useless, on the contrary they are fundamental. Hence, the rule that God gives us must be such that it does not destroy the proof which real miracles give of the truth, which is their prime end.

Rule: we must judge of doctrine by miracles, miracles we must judge of by doctrine. Both statements are true, but there is no contradiction: for we have to consider the particular occasion.

BLAISE PASCAL (1623–62), *Pensées*

For our endeavours are not only to combat with doubts, but always to dispute with the Devil. The villany of that Spirit takes a hint of Infidelity from our Studies, and, by demonstrating a naturality in one way, makes us mistrust a miracle in another . . . And thus would he inveagle my belief to think that the combustion of Sodom might be natural, and that there was an Asphaltick and Bituminous nature in that Lake before the Fire of Gomorrah. I know that *Manna* is now plentifully gathered in Calabria; and Josephus tells me, in his days it was as plentiful in Arabia; the Devil therefore made the *quaere, Where was then the miracle in the days of Moses? the Israelites saw but that in his time, the Natives of those Countries behold in ours.* Thus the Devil played at Chess with me, and yielding a Pawn, thought to gain a Queen of me, taking advantage of my honest endeavours; and whilst I laboured to raise the structure of my Reason, he strived to undermine the edifice of my Faith.

That there was a Deluge once, seems not to me so great a Miracle, as that there is not one always.

BROWNE, *Religio Medici*

The passion of *surprise* and *wonder*, arising from miracles, being an agreeable emotion, gives a sensible tendency towards the belief of those events, from which it is derived. And this goes so far, that even those who cannot enjoy this pleasure immediately, nor can believe those miraculous events, of which they are informed, yet love to partake of the satisfaction at second-hand or by rebound, and place a pride and delight in exciting the admiration of others.

With what greediness are the miraculous accounts of travellers received, their descriptions of sea and land monsters, their relations of wonderful adventures, strange men, and uncouth manners? But if the spirit of religion join itself to the love of wonder, there is an end of common sense; and human testimony, in these circumstances, loses all pretensions to authority . . .

The many instances of forged miracles, and prophecies, and supernatural events, which, in all ages, have either been detected by contrary evidence, or which detect themselves by their absurdity, prove sufficiently the strong propensity of mankind to the extraordinary and the marvellous, and ought reasonably to beget a suspicion against all relations of this kind.

DAVID HUME, 'Of Miracles', *An Enquiry Concerning Human Understanding*, 1748

Miracles do more to unsettle faith in the existing order than to settle it in any other; similarly, missionaries are more valuable as underminers of old faiths than as propagators of new. Miracles are not impossible; nothing is impossible till we have got an incontrovertible first premise. The question is not 'Are the Christian miracles possible?' but 'Are they convenient? Do they fit comfortably with our other ideas?'

BUTLER, *Notebooks*

The nineteenth-century Indian mystic Ramakrishna used to tell his disciples of the man who had spent years acquiring the power of walking on the water. Crossing a river on foot, the man went proudly to his guru, only to be told: 'My poor boy, what you have accomplished after fourteen years' arduous labour, ordinary men do by paying a penny to the boatman.'

MICHAEL EDWARDES, *The Dark Side of History*, 1978; drawn from F. Max-Müller: *Ramakrishna: His Life and Work*

The miracle according to Simone Weil: not a violation of laws but accordance with laws unknown to us. Thinking along the same lines I can believe that the Holy Virgin appeared at Fatima and Lourdes, but it is much more difficult to believe in God's rule over this world.

CZESLAW MILOSZ, *Unattainable Earth*, 1986; tr. the author and Robert Hass

Here open'd Hell, all Hell I here implor'd,
And from the scabbard drew the shining sword;
And trenching the black earth on ev'ry side,
A cavern form'd, a cubit long and wide.
New wine, with honey-temper'd milk, we bring,
Then living waters from the crystal spring;
O'er these was strow'd the consecrated flour,
And on the surface shone the holy store . . .
     Thus solemn rites and holy vows we paid
To all the Phantom nations of the dead.

Then died the sheep; a purple torrent flow'd,
And all the cavern smok'd with streaming blood.
When lo! appear'd along the dusky coasts,
Thin, airy shoals of visionary ghosts;
Fair, pensive youths, and soft-enamour'd maids,
And wither'd Elders, pale and wrinkled shades:
Ghastly with wounds the forms of warriors slain
Stalk'd with majestic port, a martial train:
These, and a thousand more swarm'd o'er the ground,
And all the dire assembly shriek'd around.
Astonish'd at the sight, aghast I stood,
And a cold fear ran shivering thro' my blood;
Straight I command the sacrifice to haste,
Straight the flay'd victims to the flames are cast,
And mutter'd vows, and mystic song apply'd
To grisly *Pluto*, and his gloomy bride.
   Now swift I wav'd my falchion o'er the blood;
Back started the pale throngs, and trembling stood.
Round the black trench the gore untasted flows,
'Till awful, from the shades *Tiresias* rose.

When lo! the mighty *Theban* I behold;
To guide his steps he bore a staff of gold;
Awful he trod! majestic was his look,
And from his holy lips these accents broke:
   Why, mortal, wandrest thou from cheerful day,
To tread the downward, melancholy way?
What angry Gods to these dark regions led
Thee yet alive, companion of the dead?
But sheathe thy poniard, while my tongue relates
Heav'n's steadfast purpose, and thy future fates.
   While yet he spoke, the Prophet I obey'd,
And in the scabbard plung'd the glitt'ring blade:
Eager he quaff'd the gore, and then exprest
Dark things to come, the counsels of his breast:
   Weary of light, *Ulysses* here explores
A prosp'rous voyage to his native shores;
But know—by me unerring Fates disclose
New trains of dangers, and new scenes of woes:
I see! I see, thy bark by *Neptune* tost,

For injur'd *Cyclops*, and his eyeball lost!
Yet to thy woes the Gods decree an end,
If heav'n thou please; and how to please attend!
Where on *Trinacrian* rocks the Ocean roars,
Graze num'rous herds along the verdant shores;
Tho' hunger press, yet fly the dang'rous prey,
The herds are sacred to the God of day . . .
Rob not the God, and so propitious gales
Attend thy voyage, and impel thy sails:
But if his herds ye seize, beneath the waves
I see thy friends o'erwhelm'd in liquid graves!
The direful wreck *Ulysses* scarce survives!
Ulysses at his country scarce arrives!
Strangers thy guides! nor there thy labours end,
New foes arise, domestic ills attend!
There foul adult'rers to thy bride resort,
And lordly gluttons riot in thy court.
But vengeance hastes amain! . . .

> HOMER (?8th century BC), *Odyssey*; tr. Alexander Pope. Ulysses consults the shade of the prophet Tiresias

Pythagoras possessed the faculty which by us is termed second sight and was known then as divination. Being with his disciples one day on the seashore, a vessel appeared on the horizon. 'Master,' said one of the companions, 'would it mean wealth if they gave me the cargo carried by that ship?' 'To you it would be more than useless,' Pythagoras answered. 'In such case I would keep it for my heirs.' 'Would you wish to bequeath them two corpses?' The vessel came into port and proved to be bearing the body of a man who desired to be buried in his own country.

> LÉVI, *The History of Magic*

Nero wasn't worried at all when he heard
what the Delphic Oracle had to say:
'Beware the age of seventy-three.'
Plenty of time to enjoy himself.

He's thirty. The deadline
the god has given him is quite enough
to cope with future dangers.

Now, a little tired, he'll return to Rome—
but wonderfully tired from that journey
devoted entirely to pleasure:
theatres, garden-parties, stadiums . . .
evenings in the cities of Achaia . . .
and, above all, the delight of naked bodies . . .

So much for Nero. And in Spain Galba
secretly musters and drills his army—
Galba, now in his seventy-third year.

C. P. CAVAFY, 'Nero's Deadline', written 1915; tr. Edmund Keeley and Philip
Sherrard. In AD 68 Galba replaced Nero, and Nero committed suicide

Here is a strange story that the Duc d'Orléans told me one day [May 1706] in
a *tête-à-tête* at Marly, he having just run down from Paris before he started for
Italy; and it may be observed that all the events predicted came to pass, though
none of them could have been foreseen at the time. His interest in every kind
of art and science was very great, and in spite of his keen intellect, he was all
his life subject to a weakness which had been introduced (with other things)
from Italy by Catherine de Medici, and had reigned supreme over the courts
of her children. He had exercised every known method of inducing the devil
to appear to him in person, though, as he has himself told me, without the
smallest success. He had spent much time in investigating matters that touched
on the supernatural, and dealt with the future.

Now La Sery (his mistress) had in her house a little girl of eight or nine
years of age, who had never resided elsewhere since her birth. She was to all
appearances a very ordinary child, and from the way in which she had been
brought up, was more than commonly ignorant and simple. One day, during
the visit of M. d'Orléans, La Sery produced for his edification one of the
charlatans with whom the duke had long been familiar, who pretended that by
means of a glass of water he could see the answer to any question that might
be put. For this purpose it was necessary to have as a go-between some one
both young and innocent, to gaze into the water, and this little girl was at once
sent for. They amused themselves by asking what was happening in certain

distant places; and after the man had murmured some words over the water, the child looked in and always managed to see the vision required of her.

M. le duc d'Orléans had so often been duped in matters of this kind that he determined to put the water-gazer to a severe test . . . he resolved to put to her a more important question, namely, as to the scene that would occur at the death of the king [Louis XIV, in 1715]. The child had never seen any one who was about the court, and had never even heard of Versailles, but she described exactly and at great length the king's bedroom at Versailles and all the furniture which was in fact there at the date of his death. She gave every detail as to the bed, and cried out on recognizing, in the arms of Madame de Ventadour, a little child decorated with an order whom she had seen at the house of Mademoiselle la Sery; and again at the sight of M. le duc d'Orléans. From her account, Madame de Maintenon, Fagon with his odd face, Madame la duchesse d'Orléans, Madame la Duchesse, Madame la princesse de Conti, besides other princes and nobles, and even the valets and servants were all present at the king's deathbed. Then she paused, and M. le duc d'Orléans, surprised that she had never mentioned Monseigneur, Monsieur le duc de Bourgogne, Madame la duchesse de Bourgogne, nor M. le duc de Berry, inquired if she did not see such and such people answering to their description. She persisted that she did not, and went over the others for the second time. This astonished M. le duc d'Orléans deeply, as well as myself, and we were at a loss to explain it, but the event proved that the child was perfectly right. This *séance* took place in 1706. These four members of the royal family were then full of health and strength; and they all died before the king . . . But of course this fact was unknown till eight years after.

Duc de Saint-Simon, *Memoirs*; tr. Andrew Lang

Old William Halliday told me he had heard from the old people of Allington and especially from the Taverners, when he was young, strange tales of ancient times and how the world was once full of 'witches, weasels (wizards) and wolves'. Also how there was once a Prophet named Saxon, who was born a peasant boy and used to drive plough oxen. One day the carter gave him some orders about one of the oxen. Upon which the boy broke into prophecy and predicted that that ox would not belong to his master another day, for that someone would take the beast from him. Which came to pass. This boy Saxon also prophesied his own death by famine which came to pass thus. A gentleman took the lad into his house, and not wishing him to communicate with the servants kept him locked up in a room by himself. But being suddenly called away on business he went off with the key of the room in his pocket and forgot all about the young prophet for some days. When he remembered Saxon he came back in all haste. But it was too late. The boy had died of hunger.

REVD FRANCIS KILVERT, *Diary*, 4 March 1875

A former curate of mine, F. Howson, is spending this week with us. Last year he was one of the curates at All Saints', Margaret Street, and is now with Chadwick at St Michael's, Wakefield. Yesterday he told us this story, for the truth of which he vouches.

Some time ago, before there was telegraphic communication with India, a lady was sitting one spring day in her garden in the Isle of Wight, when she saw a duel in the air between two rooks, one of which fell bleeding at her feet, so that her white gown was sprinkled with blood. She got up in great alarm, declaring that she was certain she would shortly hear bad news of her only son, who was in India. She forthwith retired to her room, where she wrote on the window shutter the date, day and hour of her experience. The days passed, the poor woman awaiting in great anxiety the arrival of the Indian mail. When at last it came, it brought her a letter announcing that her son had been killed in a duel. When dates and times were compared, it was found that he had met his death on the very day and at the very hour when his mother had witnessed the duel between the rooks.

'The Fighting Rooks . . .', in *Further Stories from Lord Halifax's Ghost Book*, 1937. The story was sent to Lord Halifax in 1880 by his uncle, the Revd Francis R. Gray

One night several years ago I had a very vivid dream, so vivid that not only did I wake up, but I remembered every detail the following morning.

I was at a dog meeting, and suddenly I knew that I held in my hand the winner and second of the Grand National. The ticket had a diagonal stripe across it, with a number in each segment. Perhaps I should mention that I don't bet on horses, except very rarely, and I don't go to the dogs! This dream took place about a week before the National, and I told everyone in the office that I had dreamt of backing both the winner and second horse.

On Grand National Day itself I was very busy, and it was only by chance that I heard someone call out and ask if anyone else wanted to place a bet on the race. I said I did, and was asked which horse I wanted to back. In reply, I gave the two numbers I'd dreamt . . . Someone fetched a paper and looked up the names of the horses running under the numbers I had given. I placed a modest bet on them.

They came in first and second. That was the year when the form was upset, because several of the fancied horses fell soon after the start.

How did I dream these winners? If I had dreamt the names of the horses, it could have been put down to my subconsciously having heard or read about them. But I didn't. I dreamt the numbers under which they would be running—well before these numbers had even been allocated!

ATTLEE, CLEMENT, EARL, in '*I Saw a Ghost . . .*', ed. Ben Noakes, 1986

Although they lived in style, they felt always an anxiety in the house. There was never enough money. The mother had a small income, and the father had a small income, but not nearly enough for the social position which they had to keep up . . . There was always the grinding sense of the shortage of money, though the style was always kept up . . .

And so the house came to be haunted by the unspoken phrase: *There must be more money! There must be more money!* The children could hear it all the time, though nobody said it aloud. They heard it at Christmas, when the expensive and splendid toys filled the nursery. Behind the shining modern rocking-horse, behind the smart doll's-house, a voice would start whispering: 'There *must* be more money! There *must* be more money!' And the children would stop playing, to listen for moment. They would look into each other's eyes, to see if they had all heard. And each one saw in the eyes of the other two that they too had heard. 'There *must* be more money! There *must* be more money!'

It came whispering from the springs of the still-swaying rocking-horse, and even the horse, bending his wooden, champing head, heard it. The big doll, sitting so pink and smirking in her new pram, could hear it quite plainly, and seemed to be smirking all the more self-consciously because of it. The foolish puppy, too, that took the place of the teddy-bear, he was looking so extraordinarily foolish for no other reason but that he heard the secret whisper all over the house: 'There *must* be more money!'

The boy . . . went off by himself, vaguely, in a childish way, seeking for the clue to 'luck'. Absorbed, taking no heed of other people, he went about with a sort of stealth, seeking inwardly for luck. He wanted luck, he wanted it, he wanted it. When the two girls were playing dolls in the nursery, he would sit on his big rocking-horse, charging madly into space, with a frenzy that made the little girls peer at him uneasily. Wildly the horse careered, the waving dark hair of the boy tossed, his eyes had a strange glare in them. The little girls dared not speak to him.

When he had ridden to the end of his mad little journey, he climbed down and stood in front of his rocking-horse, staring fixedly into its lowered face. Its red mouth was slightly open, its big eye was wide and glassy-bright.

'Now!' he would silently command the snorting steed. 'Now, take me to where there is luck! Now take me!'

And he would slash the horse on the neck with the little whip he had asked Uncle Oscar for. He *knew* the horse could take him to where there was luck, if only he forced it. So he would mount again, and start on his furious ride, hoping at last to get there. He knew he could get there.

Then, because of the strange anxiety at her heart, she stole upstairs to her son's room. Noiselessly she went along the upper corridor. Was there a faint noise? What was it?

She stood, with arrested muscles, outside his door, listening. There was a strange, heavy, and yet not loud noise. Her heart stood still. It was a soundless noise, yet rushing and powerful. Something huge, in violent, hushed motion. What was it? What in God's name was it? She ought to know. She felt that she knew the noise. She knew what it was.

Yet she could not place it. She couldn't say what it was. And on and on it went, like a madness.

Softly, frozen with anxiety and fear, she turned the door-handle.

The room was dark. Yet in the space near the window, she heard and saw something plunging to and fro. She gazed in fear and amazement.

Then suddenly she switched on the light, and saw her son, in his green pyjamas, madly surging on the rocking-horse. The blaze of light suddenly lit him up, as he urged the wooden horse, and lit her up, as she stood, blonde, in her dress of pale green and crystal, in the doorway.

'Paul!' she cried. 'Whatever are you doing?'

'It's Malabar!' he screamed, in a powerful, strange voice. 'It's Malabar!'

His eyes blazed at her for one strange and senseless second, as he ceased urging his wooden horse. Then he fell with a crash to the ground, and she, all her tormented motherhood flooding upon her, rushed to gather him up.

But he was unconscious, and unconscious he remained, with some brain-fever. He talked and tossed, and his mother sat stonily by his side.

'Malabar! It's Malabar! Bassett, Bassett, I *know*! It's Malabar!'

So the child cried, trying to get up and urge the rocking-horse that gave him his inspiration.

'What does he mean by Malabar?' asked the heart-frozen mother . . . 'What does he mean by Malabar?' she asked her brother Oscar.

'It's one of the horses running for the Derby,' was the answer.

And, in spite of himself, Oscar Cresswell spoke to Bassett, and himself put a thousand on Malabar: at fourteen to one.

The third day of the illness was critical: they were waiting for a change. The boy, with his rather long, curly hair, was tossing ceaselessly on the pillow. He neither slept nor regained consciousness, and his eyes were like blue stones. His mother sat, feeling her heart had gone, turned actually into a stone . . .

The gardener, a shortish fellow with a little brown moustache, and sharp little brown eyes, tiptoed into the room, touched his imaginary cap to Paul's mother, and stole to the bedside, staring with glittering, smallish eyes at the tossing, dying child.

'Master Paul!' he whispered. 'Master Paul! Malabar came in first all right, a clean win. I did as you told me. You've made over seventy thousand pounds, you have; you've got over eighty thousand. Malabar came in all right, Master Paul.'

'Malabar! Malabar! Did I say Malabar, mother? Did I say Malabar? Do you think I'm lucky, mother? I knew Malabar, didn't I? Over eighty thousand pounds! I call that lucky, don't you, mother? Over eighty thousand pounds! I knew, didn't I know I knew? Malabar came in all right. If I ride my horse till I'm sure, then I tell you, Bassett, you can go as high as you like. Did you go for all you were worth, Bassett?'

'I went a thousand on it, Master Paul.'

'I never told you, mother, that if I can ride my horse, and *get there*, then I'm absolutely sure—oh, absolutely! Mother, did I ever tell you? I *am* lucky!'

'No, you never did,' said the mother.

But the boy died in the night.

And even as he lay dead, his mother heard her brother's voice saying to her: 'My God, Hester, you're eighty-odd thousand to the good, and a poor devil of a son to the bad. But, poor devil, poor devil, he's best gone out of a life where he rides his rocking-horse to find a winner.'

LAWRENCE, from 'The Rocking-Horse Winner', 1926

In the autumn of 1955 I went to Los Angeles to make my first Hollywood film . . . I arrived, tired and crumpled, after a sixteen-hour flight from Copenhagen. Thelma Moss, who had written the film script of *Father Brown* (*The Detective* in the USA), had said she wished to take me out to dinner my first night in town. We arrived at three restaurants of repute at each of which we were refused admission because she was wearing slacks (ah, far-off days), and finally settled for a delightful little Italian bistro, where she was confident of a welcome. When we got there—Los Angeles is an endless city to drive through—there was no table available. As we walked disconsolately away I said, 'I don't care where we eat or what. Just something, somewhere.' I became aware of running, sneakered feet behind us and turned to face a fair young man in sweat-shirt and blue-jeans. 'You want a table?' he asked. 'Join me. My name is James Dean.' We followed him gratefully, but on the way back to the restaurant he turned into a car-park, saying, 'I'd like to show you something.' Among the other cars there was what looked like a large, shiny, silver parcel wrapped in cellophane and tied with ribbon. 'It's just been delivered,' he said, with bursting pride. 'I haven't even driven it yet.' The sports-car looked sinister to me, although it had a large bunch of red carnations resting on the bonnet. 'How fast is it?' I asked. 'She'll do a hundred and fifty,' he replied. Exhausted, hungry, feeling a little ill-tempered in spite of Dean's kindness, I heard myself saying in a voice I could hardly recognize as my own, 'Please, never get in it.' I looked at my watch. 'It is now ten o'clock, Friday the 23rd of September, 1955. If you get in that car you will be found dead in it by this time next week.' He laughed. 'Oh, shucks! Don't be so mean!' I apologized for what I had said, explaining it was lack of sleep and food. Thelma Moss and I joined him at his table and he proved an agreeable, generous host ... We parted an hour later, full of smiles. No further reference was made to the wrapped-up car. Thelma was relieved by the outcome of the evening and rather impressed. In my heart I was uneasy—with myself. At four o'clock in the afternoon of the following Friday James Dean was dead, killed while driving the car.

ALEC GUINNESS, *Blessings in Disguise*, 1985

Gloucester. These late eclipses in the sun and moon portend no good to us: though the wisdom of Nature can reason it thus and thus, yet Nature finds itself scourg'd by the sequent effects. Love cools, friendship falls off, brothers divide: in cities, mutinies; in countries, discord; in palaces, treason; and the bond crack'd 'twixt son and father ... We have seen the best of our time: machinations, hollowness, treachery, and all ruinous disorders follow us disquietly to our graves ...   [*Exit*]

Edmund. This is the excellent foppery of the world, that, when we are sick in fortune, often the surfeits of our own behaviour, we make guilty of our disasters the sun, the moon, and stars; as if we were villains on necessity, fools by heavenly compulsion, knaves, thieves, and treachers by spherical predominance, drunkards, liars, and adulterers by an enforc'd obedience of planetary influence; and all that we are evil in, by a divine thrusting on. An admirable evasion of whoremaster man, to lay his goatish disposition to the charge of a star! My father compounded with my mother under the dragon's tail, and my nativity was under Ursa Major; so that it follows I am rough and lecherous. Fut! I should have been that I am had the maidenliest star in the firmament twinkled on my bastardizing.

SHAKESPEARE, *King Lear*, 1604–5

I mean not to speak of Divine Prophecies, nor of heathen Oracles, nor of natural Predictions; but only of Prophecies that have been of certain memory, and from hidden causes . . .

Seneca the tragedian hath these verses:

Venient annis saecula seris . . .

(After many years the time shall come when Oceanus loosens the bounds, and a vast continent shall appear, and Tiphys [the helmsman] shall disclose new worlds, and Thule no longer be furthermost on the earth)—

a Prophecy of the discovery of America. The daughter of Polycrates dreamed that Jupiter bathed her father, and Apollo anointed him; and it came to pass that he was crucified in an open place, where the sun made his body run with sweat, and the rain washed it. Philip of Macedon dreamed he sealed up his wife's belly; whereby he did expound it, that his wife should be barren; but Aristander the soothsayer told him his wife was with child, because men do not use to seal vessels that are empty . . .

When I was in France, I heard from one Dr Pena, that the queen mother [Catherine de' Medici], who was given to curious arts, caused the king [Henri II] her husband's nativity to be calculated under a false name; and the astrologer gave a judgement, that he should be killed in a duel; at which the queen laughed, thinking her husband to be above challenges and duels; but he was slain upon a course at tilt, the splinters of the staff of Montgomery going in at his beaver. The trivial [well-known] Prophecy which I heard when I was a child, and Queen Elizabeth was in the flower of her years, was:

When hempe is spunne
England's done—

whereby it was generally conceived, that after the princes had reigned which had the principal letters of that word *hempe* (which were *Henry, Edward, Mary, Philip, and Elizabeth*), England should come to utter confusion; which, thanks be to God, is verified only in the change of the name; for that the king's style is now no more '*of England*', but '*of Britain*' . . .

There are numbers of the like kind; especially if you include dreams, and predictions of astrology: but I have set down these few only of certain credit, for example.

My judgement is, that they ought all to be despised, and ought to serve but for winter talk by the fireside: though when I say despised, I mean it as for belief; for otherwise, the spreading or publishing of them is in no sort to be despised, for they have done much mischief; and I see many severe laws made to suppress them.

> FRANCIS BACON, VISCOUNT OF ST ALBANS, from 'Of Prophecies', 1625. Several Acts had been passed against 'fond and fantastical prophecies', on the grounds that they led to public uneasiness and turbulence

                    Earnest I look'd
Into the depth, that open'd to my view,
Moisten'd with tears of anguish, and beheld
A tribe, that came along the hollow vale,
In silence weeping: such their step as walk
Quires, chanting solemn litanies on earth.
   As on them more direct mine eye descends,
Each wondrously seem'd to be reversed
At the neck-bone, so that the countenance
Was from the reins averted; and because
None might before him look, they were compell'd
To advance with backward gait. Thus one perhaps
Hath been by force of palsy clean transposed,
But I ne'er saw it nor believe it so.
   Now, reader! think within thyself, so God
Fruit of thy reading give thee! how I long
Could keep my visage dry, when I beheld
Near me our form distorted in such guise,
That on the hinder parts fallen from the face
The tears down-streaming roll'd. Against a rock
I leant and wept, so that my guide exclaim'd:

'What, and art thou, too, witless as the rest?
Here pity most doth show herself alive,
When she is dead. What guilt exceedeth his,
Who with Heaven's judgement in his passion strives? . . .
                    Lo! how he makes
The breast his shoulders; and who once too far
Before him wish'd to see, now backward looks,
And treads reverse his path.'

DANTE (1265–1321), *Inferno*; tr. Henry Cary: the punishment of those who presumed to foretell the future

I am very much ready to part with any Errors, upon an assured Conviction they are such; yet, I shall not, can not, wholly Renounce, or bid Good Night to Astrology: Lest in so doing I should Espouse a far greater Error, than any I am willing to part with. For Astrology is the language of the Heavens; and the Royal Psalmist says, The HEAVENS declare the GLORY of GOD. Howbeit, for my Great Creator's Honour, the Welfare of the Church and Nation, and Benefit of true Philosophy, I wish this Noble Art were well corrected.

JOHN GADBURY, *A Diary Astronomical and Astrological*, 1703

ART AND INTELLECT

T HE Daemon referred to by Socrates onwards is a masculine counterpart of the fickle Muse, whose inspiring breath bloweth where it listeth and none can tell where it comes from or where it goes. Goethe conceives of the daemon in more sweeping terms, as manifest in those men who draw the masses after them by some power having nothing to do with moral or intellectual stature or goodness of heart.

'Tho' I call them Mine,' Blake remarked of his designs, 'I know that they are not mine.' It is no great wonder that inspiration should on occasion assume a diabolic face. In the vicinity of the final passage in this section, Leverkühn's mysterious visitor confirms the traditional bargain, granting the composer twenty-four years of creativity, 'towering flights and illuminations, experiences of upliftings and unfetterings, of freedom, facility, feeling of power and tri-umph', together with the 'honourable' pains and sickness which he compares to the knife-pains suffered by Hans Andersen's little sea-maid when, in the hope of gaining an immortal soul, she exchanged her fish-tail for human legs. (A recent novel by Isaac Asimov and Robert Silverberg features a robot who longs for 'humanity', a modern substitute for 'soul', and achieves it only by embracing pain, decay, and death.) As Leverkühn sinks into his final madness he babbles of art grown impossible without the devil's help and fires of hell under the cauldron. His story is on one level an allegory of the rise and fall of the Third Reich.

At the other end of the scale, in his foreword to *Unfinished Symphonies* the Right Revd Mervyn Stockwood, at the time Bishop of Southwark, said that when he was asked why the deceased composers should have chosen Rosemary Brown as their go-between rather than some famous living musician, he answered: 'Perhaps it is another example of the Biblical method whereby Truth is revealed through the humble and unpretentious. The heroes in the Old and New Testament were distinguished by their integrity, not by their birth or their possessions.'

Henry James's 'The Real Right Thing' is a warning to biographers that their subjects won't necessarily be grateful for being 'served up' to the world. Thus Kipling's 'Appeal': 'And for the little, little, span The dead are borne in mind, Seek not to question other than The books I leave behind.' There is a fine story by Walter de la Mare, 'The Revenant', published in 1936, in which a Professor Monk, having delivered a lecture on Poe, is afterwards accosted by the shade of his subject, who reads him a rather superior lecture. The Professor's better nature, the shade grants, gave him his title, 'The Writings of Edgar Allan Poe', but his worse nature led him to 'the easier, the more popular, the charnel-house treatment', dwelling censoriously on Poe's life in as far as he could know it. The revenant concludes by quoting from the ballad, 'The Wife of Usher's Well': 'The cock he hadna craw'd but once . . . Brother, we must awa'.'

~

Friends, who would have acquitted me, I would like also to talk with you about this thing which has happened, while the magistrates are busy, and before I go to the place at which I must die . . . O my judges—for you I may truly call judges—I should like to tell you of a wonderful circumstance. Hitherto the familiar oracle within me has constantly been in the habit of opposing me even about trifles, if I was going to make a slip or error in any matter; and now as you see there has come upon me that which may be thought, and is generally believed to be, the last and worst evil. But the oracle made no sign of opposition, either as I was leaving my house and going out in the morning, or when I was going up into this court, or while I was speaking, at anything which I was going to say; and yet I have often been stopped in the middle of a speech, but now in nothing I either said or did touching this matter has the oracle opposed me. What do I take to be the explanation of this? I will tell you. I regard this as a great proof that what has happened to me is a good, and that those of us who think that death is an evil are in error. For the customary sign would surely have opposed me had I been going to evil and not to good.

PLATO (?429–347 BC), *Apology*; tr. Benjamin Jowett

After the defeat of the Athenian army commanded by Laches, Socrates fled
together with others, including the General Laches. Arriving at a spot where
several roads met, Socrates refused to take the road followed by the other
fugitives, because, he explained, his genius (daemon) drew him away from it.
All those who took that road were either killed or captured by the enemy.

MARCUS TULLIUS CICERO, drawn from *De Divinatione*, 44 BC

Xenophon testified that Socrates obtained from the voice and imparted to his
intimates many foreshadowings of perils which awaited them, and was never
convicted of error. Plato relates that Timarchus, a noble Athenian, being at
a feast in company with Socrates, and rising to depart, was peremptorily bidden by the latter to reseat himself. 'For,' said he, 'the spirit has just given me
the accustomed sign that some danger menaces you.' Some little time after
Timarchus offered again to be gone, and was again stayed by Socrates, who
had heard the warning repeated. Taking advantage, at length, of a moment
when the philosopher was absorbed in earnest discourse, Timarchus stole off
unobserved, and a few minutes afterwards committed a murder, for which
being carried to execution, his last words were, 'that he had come to that
untimely end by not obeying the spirit of Socrates'.

DANIEL DUNGLAS HOME, *Lights and Shadows of Spiritualism*, 1877

The Daemon of Socrates was peradventure a certaine impulsion or will, which
without the advice of his discourse presented it selfe unto him. In a minde so
well purified, and by continuall exercise of wisedome and vertue so well prepared, as his was, it is likely, his inclinations (though rash and inconsiderate)
were ever of great moment, and worthie to be followed. Every man feeleth in
himselfe some image of such agitations, of a prompt, vehement and casuall
opinion . . . I have had some, equally weake in reason, and violent in perswa-
sion and disswasion (which was more ordinarie to Socrates), by which I have
so happily and so profitably suffred my selfe to be transported, as they might
perhaps be thought to containe some matter of divine inspiration.

MICHEL DE MONTAIGNE, from 'Of Prognostications', *Essays*, 1580; tr. John
Florio

He [the young Goethe] thought he could detect in nature—both animate and inanimate, with soul or without soul—something which manifests itself only in contradictions, and which, therefore, could not be comprehended under any idea, still less under one word. It was not godlike, for it seemed unreasonable; not human, for it had no understanding; nor devilish, for it was beneficent; nor angelic, for it often betrayed a malicious pleasure. It resembled chance, for it evolved no consequences; it was like Providence, for it hinted at connection. All that limits us it seemed to penetrate; it seemed to sport at will with the necessary elements of our existence; it contracted time and expanded space. In the impossible alone did it appear to find pleasure, while it rejected the possible with contempt.

To this principle, which seemed to come in between all other principles to separate them, and yet to link them together, I gave the name of Demonic, after the example of the ancients and of those who, at any rate, had perceptions of the same kind. I sought to screen myself from this fearful principle, by taking refuge, according to my usual habits, in an imaginary creation . . .

Although this Demonical element can manifest itself in all corporeal and incorporeal things, and even expresses itself most distinctly in animals, yet, with man, especially does it stand in a most wonderful connection, forming in him a power which, if it be not opposed to the moral order of the world, nevertheless does often so cross it that one may be regarded as the warp, and the other as the woof . . .

But the most fearful manifestation of the Demonical, is when it is seen predominating in some individual character. During my life I have observed several instances of this, either more closely or remotely. Such persons are not always the most eminent men, either morally or intellectually, and it is seldom that they recommend themselves to our affections by goodness of heart; a tremendous energy seems to be seated in them, and they exercise a wonderful power over all creatures, and even over the elements; and, indeed, who shall say how much farther such influence may extend? All the moral powers combined are of no avail against them; in vain does the more enlightened portion of mankind attempt to throw suspicion upon them as deceived if not deceivers— the mass is still drawn on by them. Seldom if ever do the great men of an age find their equals among their cotemporaries, and they are to be overcome by nothing but by the universe itself; and it is from observation of this fact that the strange, but most striking, proverb must have risen: *Nemo contra Deum nisi Deus ipse*, No one opposes God save God himself.

From these lofty reflections I return to the littleness of my own life, for which strange events, clothed at least with a demonical appearance, were in store.

GOETHE, *Poetry and Truth*, 1809–31; tr. John Oxenford

After it had been revealed to me that an unseen Hand was guiding my steps along this rough path I no longer felt alone. I kept strict watch over my actions and my words, though in this I sometimes failed. But as soon as I sinned I was instantly caught, and the punishment administered was so punctual and so exactly suited to the crime that it left no room for doubts about the intervention of a Power who chastised in order to reform.

I felt that I was personally acquainted with this unknown Power. I talked to him, I thanked him, I asked his advice. Sometimes I imagined him to be my servant, the counterpart of Socrates's daimon, and the consciousness that I could count on his assistance restored to me an energy and a feeling of confidence that spurred me on to exertions of which I had not thought myself capable.

STRINDBERG, *Inferno*

Let us now consider the Personal Daemon of Aristotle [*sic*] and others, of whom it has been truthfully written, though not published:

> This is the doom of the Makers—their Daemon lives in their pen.
> If he be absent or sleeping, they are even as other men.
> But if he be utterly present, and they swerve not from his behest,
> The word that he gives shall continue, whether in earnest or jest.

Most men, and some most unlikely, keep him under an alias which varies with their literary or scientific attainments. Mine came to me early, when I sat bewildered among other notions, and said: 'Take this and no other.' I obeyed, and was rewarded . . .

My Daemon was with me in the *Jungle Books*, *Kim*, and both Puck books, and good care I took to walk delicately, less he should withdraw. I know that he did not, because when those books were finished they said so themselves with, almost, the water-hammer click of a tap turned off. One of the clauses in our contract was that I should never follow up 'a success', for by this sin fell Napoleon and a few others. *Note here*. When your Daemon is in charge, do not try to think consciously. Drift, wait, and obey.

KIPLING, *Something of Myself*, 1937

Certaine Players at Exeter, acting upon the stage the tragical storie of Dr. Faustus the Conjurer; as a certain number of Devels kept everie one his circle there, and as Faustus was busie in his magicall invocations, on a sudden they were all dasht, every one harkning other in the eare, for they were all perswaded, there was one devell too many amongst them; and so after a little pause desired the people to pardon them, they could go no further with this matter; the people also understanding the thing as it was, every man hastened to be first out of dores. The players (as I heard it) contrarye to their custome spending the night in reading and in prayer got them out of the town the next morning.

'J.G.R.', MS note, n.d.; quoted by E. K. Chambers: *The Elizabethan Stage*

'Ah yes, my dear young sir! You wish to play the part of the Devil. But you were very mediocre in the first act, and truly you will give a much too low opinion of me to the good people of Vienna. Will you perhaps permit me to stand in for you this evening? And in case you should get in my way, I shall despatch you to the second level of the Underworld.'

Heinrich had now fully recognized the Angel of Darkness. He knew that he was lost. His hand moved automatically to the little cross Katey had given him, which never left his neck, and he struggled to call for aid and whisper the prayer of exorcism. But terror had seized him too powerfully by the throat, and nothing came out, save a feeble gurgling sound. The Devil placed his taloned hands on Heinrich's shoulders, and with a single thrust rammed him down through the floorboards. Then, calmly taking his cue, he walked onto the stage like a consummate actor.

At first the audience were taken aback by the caustic, venomous style of acting and incisive delivery. It was truly diabolic.

'Heinrich's really laying it on tonight,' people exclaimed on every side.

But the thing that had a real impact was the harsh, sneering laughter, like the shrieking of a saw. It was the laughter of a damned soul blaspheming the joys of Paradise. No actor before had ever achieved such a force of sarcasm or such a depth of villainy. The audience laughed, but they trembled as well, while the whole theatre seemed to shudder with emotion. Phosphorescent sparks began to leap from the fingertips of the formidable actor, suggestions of flame flickered around his feet, the chandeliers grew dim, and the footlights gave out a red and greenish glow. An indescribable stench of sulphur spread through the theatre. The audience seemed to become delirious, thunders of frenzied applause burst upon every speech by the superb Mephistopheles. Frequently he improvised his own verse lines in place of the poet's text, producing unfailingly brilliant substitutions that were greeted with transports of delight.

Katey, to whom Heinrich had sent a box ticket, was in a state of extraordinary alarm. She could not recognize her own dear Heinrich, and she felt a terrible presentiment of evil, aided by that lover's instinct which is the second-sight of the heart.

The performance ended in an unbelievable storm of applause. The curtain fell, and the audience called for Mephistopheles to take another bow amidst a roar of acclaim. He was sought for without success behind the scenes. Finally a stagehand came to tell the producer that Monsieur Heinrich had just been found on the second level below-stage. No doubt he had stumbled through a trap-door.

Heinrich was unconscious. He was carried home, and when he was being undressed it was remarked with surprise that he had deep incisions upon his shoulders, as if a tiger had tried to crush him between its paws.

Perhaps it was Katey's little cross that had saved him from death. Overcome by its power, perhaps the Devil may have had to content himself with hurling him down as far as the cellarage of the theatre . . .

The theatre-goers of Vienna still talk with admiration of that marvellous evening's performance, and puzzle over Heinrich's strange behaviour in retiring so precipitately from the theatre after his triumphant début.

THÉOPHILE GAUTIER, from 'The Actor', 1841; tr. Richard Holmes

Two old friends of mine, Frances Doble and Anton (Pat) Dolin, co-starred in *Ballerina* [a play adapted by Rodney Ackland from her book of the same name] . . .

Once, at a dress rehearsal at the Scala Theatre, something happened that made a profound impression upon my mind. If I had been the only person to see what I saw, I should be willing to dismiss the whole matter as an illusion. But I was not alone; Pat was with me, and saw it, too; Charles Landstone, our level-headed business manager, was another witness, so was Hank [Henry Sullivan, who wrote the score], so was Hank's manager, Ralph Glover.

It was about three o'clock in the morning, and the auditorium was dark and empty. The five of us sat together in the dress circle, watching the final rehearsal of the 'Snowbird' Ballet. Pat had purposely put on his understudy, Freddy Franklin, because he wanted to watch, in complete concentration, Frances's efforts as a dancer.

I have explained before that watching Pavlova from the side of the stage had inspired me to write *Ballerina*. Had I not watched Pavlova so closely that day at Golders Green, the book would never have been written . . .

The stage revolved to show a woodland glade, with nymphs in white tarlatan grouped in a traditional entrance. Previously, we had seen 'Varsovina' haggard and dejected in her dressing-room, wrapped, shivering, in her shabby grey dressing-gown. Now, as we watched, a slight figure walked on to the stage. A figure snow-white in a fluffy *tutu*, its head bound with swans' plumage. The figure paused, crossing itself. It seemed to me that Frances had grown much smaller.

Then, as it glided into the spotlight, I caught my breath.

For the figure was not that of Frances. It had assumed the form of Anna Pavlova.

Pat gripped my hand until I thought he would break it. I looked at him; he was ice-pale, and there was sweat on his face.

He muttered:

'This is uncanny . . . it's awful . . . what have we done? Oh, God—why did we ever bring up the past?'

The white form on the stage stood effortlessly upon one '*pointe*'; it pirouetted three times—a thing Frances could not do—and drifted like swansdown into 'Borek's' arms, as the curtain fell. I looked again at my companions. They were white and dazed.

Somebody mumbled:

'We're all very tired . . . don't let's imagine things . . .'

Somebody else said:

'We can't *all* have seen—what we saw . . .'

Pat and I ran to the pass-door.

We were afraid.

Frances stood there on the stage, and said to Pat in a perplexed, mechanical voice:

'Pat, I'm sorry . . . let's take it again.'

'Take it again? Why?'

'I couldn't dance. I must be awfully tired. My mind suddenly seemed to go blank. Will someone get me a glass of water?'

Pat gave me a warning look, and we said nothing at the time.

Later he affirmed:

'We can't deny it. For a moment that particular spirit from the past took possession of Frances's mind and body.'

ELEANOR SMITH, *Life's a Circus*, 1939

It is easy to understand that mental work, when it is the result of a cerebral impulse given during the evening and completing itself during sleep, may produce dreams which will be to some extent the *reflected expression* of the problem on which the sleeper was engaged, or the preoccupation which possessed him . . .

One celebrated dream is often referred to in this connection. It is one in which a scene of the most curious and fantastic character accompanied the unconscious intellectual labour of the dreamer, who was no other than Tartini. This celebrated composer went to sleep after having tried in vain to conclude a sonata; his preoccupation followed him into his sleep. In his dream he thought that he began his work over again, and that he was in despair at composing with so little inspiration and success; at that moment the devil suddenly appeared to him and offered to finish the sonata for him in exchange for his soul. Tartini, entirely overmastered by the apparition, accepted the devil's terms, and then distinctly heard the latter execute the longed-for sonata on the violin, with an inexpressible charm of execution. He awoke, and in a transport of joy he ran to his desk and wrote from memory the part which he really believed he had heard.

FLAMMARION, *The Unknown*

Such an accent, the accent of Vinteuil, is separated from the accents of other composers by a difference far greater than that which we perceive between the voices of two people, even between the bellowings and the squeals of two animal species; by the real difference that exists between the thought of this or that other composer and the eternal investigations of Vinteuil, the question that he put to himself in so many forms, his habitual speculation, but as free from analytical forms of reasoning as if it were being carried out in the world of the angels, so that we can gauge its depth, but no more translate it into human speech than can disembodied spirits when, evoked by a medium, they are questioned by him about the secrets of death. And even when I bore in mind that acquired originality which had struck me that afternoon, that kinship, too, which musicologists might discover between composers, it is indeed a unique accent, an unmistakable voice, to which in spite of themselves those great singers that original composers are rise and return, and which is a proof of the irreducibly individual existence of the soul.

MARCEL PROUST, *In Search of Lost Time: The Captive*, 1923; tr. C. K. Scott Moncrieff and Terence Kilmartin

The first time I saw Franz Liszt, I was about seven years old, and already accustomed to seeing the spirits of the so-called dead.

I was in the top bedroom in the big, old house in London where I still live. That particular morning I remember I had woken early, and was lying there enjoying the warmth of the bed, and waiting to hear my mother's voice call when it was time to get up . . .

It was in this almost primitively simple room that Liszt first appeared to me. I was not in the least scared when I saw him standing at my bedside. I had been accustomed to seeing discarnate beings—or spirits as most people call them—since I was a tiny child, so there was nothing frightening about the vision. In fact, I don't think I was even surprised. You take a lot in your stride when you are a child.

He came on that first occasion as a very old man. His long hair was very white and he was wearing what I took to be a long black dress. At seven I didn't know what a cassock was. But I remember thinking it funny that a man should be wearing something like that, though his visit was so brief that I hardly had time to wonder about any of it before he was gone.

For some reason he never said who he was that morning. I suppose he knew I would eventually see a picture of him somewhere and would recognize him. There is, after all, no mistaking Liszt for anyone else, especially when he was an elderly man with long white hair and wearing the sombre robes.

All he said that morning, speaking slowly because I was a child, was that when he had been in this world he had been a composer and pianist.

He then said: 'When you grow up I will come back and give you music.' . . .

Today Liszt is the organizer and leader of a group of famous composers who visit me at my home and give me their new compositions. There are twelve at present in the group—Liszt, Chopin, Schubert, Beethoven, Bach, Brahms, Schumann, Debussy, Grieg, Berlioz, Rachmaninov and Monteverdi. I have placed them in the order in which they communicated. Others, such as Albert Schweitzer, appear briefly and give me a little music then don't seem to return. Mozart, for example, has been just three times. But after six years of work I have today, in drawers and cupboards all over my big rambling house, some 400 pieces of music—songs, piano pieces, some incomplete string quartets, the beginning of an opera as well as partly completed concertos and symphonies . . .

Some of it is beginning to be heard in public, and in May 1970, just a little more than six years after Liszt communicated with me again, there was launched a long-playing record of eight different composers' 'other side' music. The composers themselves were naturally pleased with this break-through.

One day after they had been together at my home several times, I could hear them talking to each other in English while I jotted down a few bars of music.

Chopin said, with his very strong accent: 'She seems very nice, your English girl.'

Liszt said carelessly: 'Yes, she is quite nice. But she is rather stupid.'

I think Liszt had realized that I could hear what they were saying and he had said that deliberately to tease me. So I kept quiet but I also thought: 'Perhaps he is right. I probably do seem rather stupid to them.'

It was some days later when they were with me on a different occasion and Liszt was giving me something rather complicated to take down. Funnily enough, the notes were coming quite clearly and easily and I was getting on rather well with the piece.

Suddenly Chopin said: 'Your English girl—she is not so stupid.' And Liszt laughed—rather as if he were pleased.

Some time ago I was very thrilled to get an invitation to visit Leonard Bernstein. He wanted to see some of my music and asked questions about the way I received it. He said to me: 'Chopin used to be a very sexy man. Is he still?'

I said: 'I don't think so. I've never noticed. But in any case he would not be like that now. Sex is a physical aspect of life which would hardly manifest itself in a non-physical being.'

ROSEMARY BROWN, *Unfinished Symphonies: Voices from the Beyond*, 1971

All his life long he [Victor Hugo] had been obsessed by vague visions of such intensity that they had almost the quality of hallucinations . . . He maintained that all thinkers have, at some time or another, seen 'nameless things' in the darkness of the night. He heard nocturnal rappings on the walls of his room . . . For him, the supernatural was natural. Furthermore, he believed in the immortality of souls, in their successive migrations, in a continuous ladder leading from the inanimate to God, from matter to the ideal. Why not, therefore, admit the possibility of immaterial beings seeking to communicate? Last of all, his surroundings and the circumstances of his life were favourable to strange experiences: the mental topsyturvydom of exile; the ever-present shade of Léopoldine [his eldest daughter, drowned in a boating accident]; local legends. Marine Terrace was reputed to have a ghost—*The White Lady*.

The first occasion on which Delphine de Girardin dined with the family she asked whether they indulged in table-turning, and suggested a seance. Hugo refused to take part . . . For five days there were no results, and those present began to treat the whole thing as a joke. Delphine de Girardin, nettled by their failure, said: 'The spirits are not like cab-horses, obedient to the whim of those who hire them. They are free, and come only when they feel inclined.' Besides, the master of the house was deliberately absenting himself from the seances. Finally, just to please his guests, Hugo consented to participate. At once, the table made a cracking sound, quivered, and began to move. 'Is there anybody present?' asked Madame de Girardin. A single rap: *Yes.* 'Who is it?' *Léopoldine.* Everybody was much upset . . . The whole night passed in addressing questions to the dear, ghostly presence . . .

After that, for more than a year, life at Marine Terrace passed in a swarm of spirits. Madame Hugo found no difficulty in believing. 'For a long time,' she said, 'I have held communion with my dead. The table has come to tell me that I was not suffering from illusions.' In addition to the members of the family, several from among the political exiles attended the seances: General le Flô, Hennet de Kesler, Teleki, the Hungarian. Many were the spirits who answered the call: Molière, Shakespeare, Anacreon, Dante, Racine, Marat, Charlotte Corday, Latude, Mahomet, Jesus Christ, Plato, Isaiah; animals, too: the dove of the Ark, Balaam's ass; nameless visitors: the Ghost of the Sepulchre, the White Lady; as well as abstractions: the Novel, the Drama, Criticism, the Idea. Phantoms, these, suited to literary folk. Many spoke in verse and, strangely enough, in verse which might have been written by Victor Hugo. Meanwhile, Marine Terrace became the centre of an increasing number of odd occurrences. The White Lady announced that she would appear in front of the house at three o'clock in the morning. No one dared to go downstairs, but at three o'clock the door-bell rang. Who could have been responsible, if not the ghost? Charles and François-Victor [Hugo's sons], coming home one evening, saw the drawing-room lit up. The room, as it happened, was empty and contained no means of illumination. Strange and piercing cries were heard . . . That the visitants possessed considerable talents there could be no doubt. They also, on occasion, showed a high degree of intelligence. But talents and intelligence were invariably typical of Victor Hugo.

ANDRÉ MAUROIS, *Victor Hugo*, 1954; tr. Gerard Hopkins. Marine Terrace was the house in Jersey occupied by the Hugo family in exile in 1853

Victor Hugo was converted [to spiritualism] by Mme Emile de Girardin in Jersey, September 6, 1853. At the first seance [Auguste] Vacquerie asked, What word am I thinking of? The table answered, You mean 'suffering'. The word in Vacquerie's mind was 'love'. The answer was ingenious and unexpected. In later seances Victor Hugo was not at the table: Charles Hugo was

the medium. He knew no English. An Englishman came in and called Lord
Byron, who replied in English:

> Vex not the bard, his lyre is broken,
> His last song sung, his last word spoken.

Strange apocalyptic answers are attributed to Ezekiel and—to the lion of
Androcles!

CHARLES RICHET, Thirty Years of Psychical Research, 1922; tr. Stanley De Brath

Let me illustrate what I mean from an experiment which Paracelsus describes
as not difficult, and which the author of the *Curiosities* of Literature cites as
credible: A flower perishes; you burn it. Whatever were the elements of that
flower while it lived are gone, dispersed, you know not whither; you can never
discover nor re-collect them. But you can, by chemistry, out of the burnt dust
of that flower, raise a spectrum of the flower, just as it seemed in life. It may
be the same with the human being. The soul has as much escaped you as the
essence or elements of the flower. Still you may make a spectrum of it. And
this phantom, though in the popular superstition it is held to be the soul of the
departed, must not be confounded with the true soul; it is but the eidolon of
the dead form. Hence, like the best-attested stories of ghosts or spirits, the
thing that most strikes us is the absence of what we hold to be soul—that is,
of superior emancipated intelligence. They come for little or no object . . . These
American spirit-seers have published volumes of communications in prose and
verse, which they assert to be given in the names of the most illustrious dead—
Shakespeare, Bacon—heaven knows whom. These communications, taking
the best, are certainly not a whit of higher order than would be communications from living persons of fair talent and education; they are wondrously
inferior to what Bacon, Shakespeare, and Plato said and wrote when on earth.
Nor, what is more notable, do they ever contain an idea that was not on the
earth before. Wonderful, therefore, as such phenomena may be (granting them
to be truthful), I see much that philosophy may question, nothing that it is
incumbent on philosophy to deny—namely, nothing supernatural.

BULWER-LYTTON, from 'The Haunted and the Haunters'

Martin [Violet Martin, 'Martin Ross']. My dear, I am feeling so happy today.
  You are nearer. I wonder why that is. (I [Edith Somerville] said that possi-.
  bly I was beginning to realize better that it was she.)

Martin. I know you must be convinced.

Edith. How did you know that you could communicate with us? We were trying to find out about Colonel Isherwood.

Martin. I had so often watched and I knew that sooner or later Jem would help. Of course, Edith, I wished to speak to you. In fact I have spoken, but you cannot hear my voice.

Edith. Shall I ever hear it?

Martin. I cannot say. I suppose you might develop what is called clair audience . . .

Edith. Have you met other of our dogs?

Martin. Several.

Edith. How did you find Candy [a fox terrier]?

Martin. It just happened.

Edith. Did she know you?

Martin. At once.

Edith then proceeds to ask questions about the other deceased dogs and is assured that Martin is looking after them all . . . Martin refers vaguely to the tasks which have been allotted to her, but when pressed to state who is instructing her in her new duties, replies that she is not permitted to be more specific.

There is, however, one point on which she is emphatic. Edith must not give up her writing. She has not written a line for over a year. No doubt she has hardly been in the mood for the humorous vein for which their stories in the past have been admired. But she should not give up. Edith replied that she could not write without her.

Martin. I cannot help thinking that I may be allowed to help.

Edith. I shouldn't know which were my own thoughts and which yours.

Martin. That would not matter.

Edith. I don't feel any desire to write.

Martin. Not now, but perhaps you may.

Edith. I don't feel like being amusing.

Martin. Yes, I know that, my dear, only too well.

Edith. Shall I try and collect your writings and add an account of you?

Martin replied that she would like that, but warns her to tell nobody at present that they are collaborating . . . 'I do not believe that they would understand.' . . .

Though this is the last full account of a seance with Martin, the papers show that from this date Edith continued to consult, as she now firmly believed, her former collaborator and considered that the fifteen books which she subsequently wrote between 1915 and her death in 1949 were their joint work. As no full account of such collaboratory seances is extant it is not possible to be clear how such a collaboration could have operated. It is true that at times Edith seems to have been able to get the automatic pencil moving without the assistance of Jem Barlow or any other medium, but how the question and answer went in so difficult and technical a matter as writing a book is hard to conceive. Nevertheless, Edith was satisfied that such a collaboration was taking place.

> MAURICE COLLIS, *Somerville and Ross*, 1968. These sessions of automatic writing, through the agency of Jem Barlow, a medium living nearby, took place on 20 and 21 June 1916, and were transcribed by Edith Somerville. Martin Ross had died on 21 December 1915

On the first day of December 1741 I departed this life at my lodgings in Cheapside. My body had been some time dead before I was at liberty to quit it, lest it should by any accident return to life: this is an injunction imposed on all souls by the eternal law of fate, to prevent the inconveniences which would follow. As soon as the destined period was expired (being no longer than till the body is become perfectly cold and stiff) I began to move; but found myself under a difficulty of making my escape, for the mouth or door was shut, so that it was impossible for me to go out at it; and the windows, vulgarly called the eyes, were so closely pulled down by the fingers of a nurse, that I could by no means open them. At last I perceived a beam of light glimmering at the top of the house (for such I may call the body I had been inclosed in), whither ascending, I gently let myself down through a kind of chimney, and issued out at the nostrils.

No prisoner discharged from a long confinement ever tasted the sweets of liberty with a more exquisite relish than I enjoyed in this delivery from a dungeon wherein I had been detained upwards of forty years . . .

As the window was wide open, I sallied forth into the open air: but, to my great astonishment, found myself unable to fly, which I had always during my habitation in the body conceived of spirits; however, I came so lightly to the ground that I did not hurt myself; and, though I had not the gift of flying (owing probably to my having neither feathers nor wings), I was capable of hopping such a prodigious way at once, that it served my turn almost as well.

I had not hopped far before I perceived a tall young gentleman in a silk waistcoat, with a wing on his left heel, a garland on his head, and a caduceus in his right hand. I thought I had seen this person before, but had not time to recollect where, when he called out to me and asked me how long I had been departed. I answered I was just come forth. 'You must not stay here,' replied he, 'unless you had been murdered: in which case, indeed, you might have been suffered to walk some time; but if you died a natural death you must set out for the other world immediately.' I desired to know the way. 'O,' cried the gentleman, 'I will show you to the inn whence the stage proceeds; for I am the porter. Perhaps you never heard of me—my name is Mercury.' 'Sure, sir,' said I, 'I have seen you at the playhouse.'

We pursued our way through a delicious grove of orange-trees, where I saw infinite numbers of spirits, every one of whom I knew, and was known by them (for spirits here know one another by intuition) . . .

I then observed Shakespeare standing between Betterton and Booth, and deciding a difference between those two great actors concerning the placing an accent in one of his lines: this was disputed on both sides with a warmth which surprised me in Elysium, till I discovered by intuition that every soul retained its principal characteristic, being, indeed, its very essence. The line was that celebrated one in *Othello*—

> *Put out the light, and then put out the light,*

according to Betterton. Mr Booth contended to have it thus—

> *Put out the light, and then put out THE light.*

I could not help offering my conjecture on this occasion, and suggested it might perhaps be—

> *Put out the light, and then put out THY light.*

Another hinted a reading very sophisticated in my opinion—

> *Put out the light, and then put out THEE, light,*

making light to be the vocative case. Another would have altered the last word, and read—

> *Put out thy light, and then put out thy sight.*

But Betterton said, if the text was to be disturbed, he saw no reason why a word might not be changed as well as a letter, and, instead of 'put out thy light', you may read 'put out thy eyes'. At last it was agreed on all sides to refer the matter to the decision of Shakespeare himself, who delivered his sentiments as follows: 'Faith, gentlemen, it is so long since I wrote the line, I have forgotten my meaning. This I know, could I have dreamt so much nonsense would have been talked and writ about it, I would have blotted it out of my works; for I am sure, if any of these be my meaning, it doth me very little honour.'

HENRY FIELDING, *A Journey from This World to the Next*, 1743

On Saturday night as I was sitting by myself all alone I heard a creaking sound, something like the noise which a crazy chair would make, if pressed by the tremendous weight of Mrs Barlow's extremities. I cast my eyes around—and what should I behold, but a *Ghost* rising out of the floor! A deadly paleness instantly overspread my body, which retained no other symptom of Life, but its violent trembling: my hair (as is usual in frights of this nature) stood upright by many degrees stiffer than the Oaks of the Mountains, yea, stiffer than Mr ——; yet was it rendered *oily* by the profuse perspiration, that burst from every pore. The Spirit advanced with a book in his hand, and having first dissipated my terrors, said as follows: I am the Ghost of Gray—there lives a young Lady (then he mentioned *your* name) of whose judgment I entertain so high an opinion, that *her* approbation of my Works would make the turf lie lighter on me: present her with this book—and transmit it to her as soon as possible—adding my Love to her. And as for you, O Young Man (*now* he addressed himself to me) write no more verses—in the first place, your poetry is vile stuff; and secondly (here he sighed almost to bursting) all Poets go to —ll, we are so intolerably addicted to the Vice of Lying!—He vanished— and convinced me of the truth of his last dismal account by the sulphureous stink, which he left behind him.

COLERIDGE, from letter to Mary Evans, 13 February 1792

'Well,' says he, smiling, 'The devil shall never want a friend at court, so long as there is a poet within the walls. And indeed the poets do us many a good turn, both by pimping and otherwise . . .' I asked him what store of poets they had there. 'Prodigious numbers,' says the devil, 'So many that we have been forced to make more room for them; nor is there anything in nature so pleasant as a poet in the first year of his probation; he comes laden with letters of recommendation to our superiors, and enquires very gravely for Cerebus, Rhadamanthus, and Aeacus.'

'Well,' said I, 'But in what manner are they punished?'

'Their punishments,' replied the devil, 'are many, and suited to the trade they drive. Some are condemned to listen to praise of other men's works. We have some that are in for a thousand years and yet still poring upon some old stanza they have made on their mistress. Some again are beating their fore-heads with the palms of their hands; and even boring their very noses with hot irons, in rage that they cannot come to a decision whether they shall say face or visage, or whether they shall write jail or gaol. Others are biting their nails to the quick and are at their wits' end to find a rhyme for some odd word; and doze up and down in a brown study, till they drop into some hole at last, and give us trouble enough to get them out again . . . Things are admirably ordered in hell, and there is a place reserved for all.'

Francisco de Quevedo y Villegas, *The Visions*, 1627; tr. Sir Roger L'Estrange

. . . Japanese literature seems to welcome some kind of unnatural death in a poet—whether by another's hand, or in some calamity, or even, taking its wider meaning, simply in unfortunate circumstances—as a final accolade set upon his life and work. If the death of a literary figure is particularly striking, its tragic nature will bestow on his work a preposterously high value, and his fame becomes eternal. Minamoto Sanetomo's assassination at Tsurugaoka Hachiman Shrine, and Kobayashi Takiji's death by torture at the Tsukiji police station, have wrapped their names in a good deal of additional glory by reason of the existence of this tradition. Thus it is that a form of spiritualism, a belief in the powers of the souls of the dead, has had a profound effect on literary appreciation, since this honouring of their names is really a placating of their tortured souls . . .

To find the first example of a poet meeting an untimely death we probably have to go back to the fourth century and Prince Yamato Takeru, who pronounced an inappropriate spell when he encountered a sacred white boar in the foothills of a mountain. His health was impaired by a hailstorm during the subsequent climb, which led eventually to his death, though not before he'd composed a poem bewailing his fate . . . That the soul of a great departed poet was something not merely to be admired but also solemnly placated can be seen in the case of the early Heian poet, Sugawara Michizane, who not only died in exile while gazing in a melancholy manner at the moon, but sadly failed to achieve his proposed visit to China, something as important for a famous writer of Chinese poetry as the death in exile itself. After his unappeased spirit had plagued the capital with thunderstorms and other misfortunes, shrines were set up all over the country, dedicated to Tenjinsama (the heavenly person) as he was dubbed, it being his new fate to become the god of learning.

Saiichi Maruya, from 'Rain in the Wind', 1975; tr. Dennis Keene

The psychic faculty that had made me foresee the assassination of Kennedy had been a long time sleeping, but it awoke when I was asked to read some of

Keats's poems at the house on the Spanish Steps where he died. Reciting the odes, I became aware of a kind of astral wind, a malevolent chill, of a soul chained to the place where the body died, of a silent malignant laughter that mocked not my reading but the poems themselves. Later, making a television film on Rome for Canada, I recited the last sonnet—'When I have fears that I may cease to be'—on the steps outside the Keats house. It was high summer, and the sky was cloudless, but within the space of fourteen lines of iambic pentameters a storm arose, the rain teemed, I and the television team were drenched, and the final couplet was drowned by thunder. The camera caught all this. I am not imputing a demonic vindictiveness to the soul of John Keats. It seemed to me rather that a fierce creative energy, forbidden its total fulfilment by a premature physical death, frustrated into destructiveness, was hovering around the house where he died.

ANTHONY BURGESS, *You've Had Your Time*, 1990

The night that I passed at Goslar a strange thing happened to me. At this very day I cannot look back on it without terror. I am not nervous by nature, and God knows that I never experienced any special sinking at the heart, when, for instance, a naked rapier was trying to make acquaintance with my nose, or when I had lost my way at night in an ill-reputed forest, or when at a concert a gaping lieutenant threatened to swallow me; but of spirits I am nearly as much afraid as the 'Austrian Observer'. What is fear? Is it a process of reason or a matter of temperament? This question was a standing subject of dispute between Dr Saul Ascher [Berlin bookseller and philosopher] and myself whenever we chanced to meet in Berlin at the Café Royal, where for some time I regularly dined. The doctor always asserted that we fear anything because we know it to be fearful by a process of reasoning. Reason alone is a motive force, not temperament. All the while that I was making a good dinner, he went on demonstrating the pre-eminence of reason. As his demonstration was drawing to a close, he used to look at his watch, and invariably ended off with 'Reason is the highest principle.' Reason! Even now, whenever I hear the word, I see before me Dr Saul Ascher with his abstractions of legs, his close-fitting coat of transcendental grey, and his angular frozen face which might have served for a diagram in a treatise on geometry. He was well over fifty, and so thin that he looked like an incarnate and personified straight line. In his endeavour after positive fact, the poor man had philosophized away all the brightness of life, all sunbeams, all beliefs and all flowers, and nothing was left him but the cold fact of the grave. Against the Apollo Belvedere and Christianity he had a special grudge. He actually wrote a pamphlet against Christianity, proving its irrationality and untenability. There are numerous other works of his, in all of which the admirable nature of reason is extolled. In so far as these expressed the poor doctor's most serious convictions (of which there can be no doubt), he deserved all respect. But the best joke of it all was to see his solemn puzzled look when he failed to understand what every child understands just because it is a child. Sometimes, too, I visited the Doctor of Reason at his own house, where I used to find him with pretty girls, for reason does not forbid sensibility. One day, when I was going to pay him a visit, his servant, who opened the door, told me, 'The Doctor has just died.' I felt no more concern than if he had told me 'The Doctor is out.'

But to return to Goslar. 'The highest principle is reason,' I repeated to myself to calm my nerves, as I got into bed. It was, however, no good. I had just been reading in Varnhagen von Ense's 'German Tales', which I had taken with me from Klausthal, the terrible story of the son on the point of being murdered by his own father, who is warned in the night by the ghost of his mother. The story is told so graphically that a cold shiver ran through me as I read it; and generally ghost stories affect one's nerves more when read on a journey, especially if at night in a town, in a house, in a room where one has never been before. You cannot help thinking of the horrors that may have been perpetrated on the very spot where you are now lying. Moreover, at this moment, the moon made a ghost-like twilight in my chamber; all sorts of shadows began moving on the wall without visible cause; and, as I sat up in bed to look, I beheld——

There is nothing more uncanny than casually to see your own face in the glass by moonlight. At the same instant a ponderous sleepy clock struck, so solemnly and slowly that by the time the twelfth stroke was finished I made sure that twelve full hours must have passed, and it was bound to begin striking twelve over again. Between the last stroke and the last but one, another clock struck, fast and almost shrewishly shrill, as if angry with the slowness of its gossip. When both iron tongues had stopped and the whole house was still as death, I suddenly seemed to hear a shuffling and hobbling in the passage outside my room, like the uncertain steps of an old man. At last my door opened and there entered slowly the late Dr Saul Ascher. My blood ran cold, I shivered like an aspen leaf, and hardly dared look at the ghost. He had the same appearance as of old, the same coat of transcendental grey, the same abstract legs, the same mathematical face—only it was a shade yellower—and the mouth that used to make two angles of $22\frac{1}{2}$ degrees was pinched, and his eye-balls had a larger radius. Tottering, and supporting himself, as his wont was, on his malacca cane, he approached me, and addressing me in his familiar drawling tones, 'Fear not,' he said, 'do not imagine that I am a ghost. It is an illusion of your imagination if you take me for a ghost. What is a ghost? I will trouble you to define a ghost, and deduce by logical reasoning the possibility of a ghost. What reasonable connection can there be between such an appearance and reason. Reason I say,'—and hereupon the ghost proceeded to an analysis of reason, quoted Kant's 'Critique of Pure Reason', Part II, Sect. 1, Book II, Par. 3, 'On the distinction of Phænomena and Noumena', constructed next a hypothetical ghost creed, piled syllogism on syllogism, and ended by drawing the logical conclusion that there is no such thing as a ghost. All the time cold sweat ran down my back, my teeth chattered like castanets, in my agony I nodded unqualified assent to each proposition by which the ghostly doctor proved the absurdity of all fear of ghosts, growing so eagerly excited in his demonstration, that once in his excitement, instead of his gold watch, he pulled out of his fob a handful of worms, and noticing his mistake nervously thrust them back with comic haste. 'Reason is the highest——': the clock struck one, and the ghost vanished.

> HEINRICH HEINE, from 'A Tour in the Harz', *Travel Pictures*, 1826; tr. Francis Storr. *Austrian Observer*: 'government newspaper in Vienna, strongly reactionary and hence afraid of the "ghosts" of the French Revolution' (Ritchie Robertson, *Heinrich Heine: Selected Prose*)

She was a maiden of rarest beauty, and not more lovely than full of glee. And evil was the hour when she saw, and loved, and wedded the painter. He, passionate, studious, austere, and having already a bride in his Art: she . . . all light and smiles, and frolicsome as the young fawn; loving and cherishing all things; hating only the Art which was her rival; dreading only the palette and brushes and other untoward instruments which deprived her of the countenance of her lover. It was thus a terrible thing for this lady to hear the painter speak of his desire to portray even his young bride. But she was humble and obedient, and sat meekly for many weeks in the dark high turret-chamber where the light dripped upon the pale canvas only from overhead. But he, the painter, took glory in his work, which went on from hour to hour, and from day to day. And he was a passionate, and wild, and moody man, who became lost in reveries; so that he *would* not see that the light which fell so ghastly in that lone turret withered the health and the spirits of his bride, who pined visibly to all but him. Yet she smiled on and still on, uncomplainingly, because she saw that the painter (who had high renown) took a fervid and burning pleasure in his task, and wrought day and night to depict her who so loved him, yet who grew daily more dispirited and weak. And in sooth some who beheld the portrait spoke of its resemblance in low words, as of a mighty marvel, and a proof not less of the power of the painter than of his deep love for her whom he depicted so surpassingly well. But at length, as the labour drew nearer to its conclusion, there were admitted none into the turret; for the painter had grown wild with the ardour of his work, and turned his eyes from the canvas rarely, even to regard the countenance of his wife. And he *would* not see that the tints which he spread upon the canvas were drawn from the cheeks of her who sat beside him. And when many weeks had passed, and but little remained to do, save one brush upon the mouth and one tint upon the eye, the spirit of the lady again flickered up as the flame within the socket of the lamp. And then the brush was given, and then the tint was placed; and, for one moment, the painter stood entranced before the work which he had wrought; but in the next, while he yet gazed, he grew tremulous and very pallid, and aghast, and crying with a loud voice, 'This is indeed *Life* itself!', turned suddenly to regard his beloved:—*She was dead*!

EDGAR ALLAN POE, from 'The Oval Portrait', 1845

In the past, when he was younger and more inclined to see things as black or white, he had let himself go once or twice. He did not remember his old books very well but there was a character in one, 'The Outcast', into whom he had really got his knife. He had written about him with extreme vindictiveness, just as if he was a real person whom he was trying to show up. He had experienced a curious pleasure in attributing every kind of wickedness to this man. He never gave him the benefit of the doubt. He had never felt a twinge of pity for him, even when he paid the penalty for his misdeeds on the gallows. He had so worked himself up that the idea of this dark creature, creeping about brimful of malevolence, had almost frightened him.

'No room's private when the street door's once passed,' he said. 'Had you forgotten I was a policeman?'

'Was?' said Walter, edging away from him. 'You *are* a policeman.'

'I have been other things as well,' the policeman said. 'Thief, pimp, black-mailer, not to mention murderer. *You* should know.' . . .

'I don't know what you mean,' he said. 'Why do you speak like that? I've never done you any harm. I've never set eyes on you before.'

'Oh, haven't you?' the man said. 'But you've thought about me and'—his voice rose—'and you've written about me. You got some fun out of me, didn't

you? Now I'm going to get some fun out of you. You made me just as nasty
as you could. Wasn't that doing me harm? You didn't think what it would feel
like to be me, did you? You didn't put yourself in my place, did you? You
hadn't any pity for me, had you? Well, I'm not going to have any pity for you.'

'But I tell you,' cried Walter, clutching the table's edge. 'I don't know you!'

'And now you say you don't know me! You did all that to me and then
forgot me!' His voice became a whine, charged with self-pity. 'You forgot
William Stainsforth.'

'William Stainsforth!'

'Yes. I was your scapegoat, wasn't I? You unloaded all your self-dislike on
me. You felt pretty good while you were writing about me. You thought, what
a noble, upright fellow you were, writing about this rotter. Now, as one W.S.
to another, what shall I do, if I behave in character?'

'I . . . I don't know,' muttered Walter.

'You don't know?' Stainsforth sneered. 'You ought to know, you fathered
me. What would William Stainsforth do if he met his old dad in a quiet place,
his kind old dad who made him swing?'

Walter could only stare at him.

'You know what he'd do as well as I,' said Stainsforth. Then his face
changed and he said abruptly, 'No, you don't, because you never really understood me. I'm not so black as you painted me.' He paused, and a flicker of hope
started in Walter's breast. 'You never gave me a chance, did you? Well, I'm
going to give you one. That shows you never understood me, doesn't it?'

Walter nodded.

'And there's another thing you have forgotten.'

'What is that?'

'I was a kid once,' the ex-policeman said.

Walter said nothing.

'You admit that?' said William Stainsforth grimly. 'Well, if you can tell me
of one virtue you ever credited me with—just one kind thought—just one
redeeming feature—'

'Yes?' said Walter, trembling.

'Well, then I'll let you off.'

'And if I can't?' whispered Walter.

'Well, then, that's just too bad. We'll have to come to grips and you know
what that means. You took off one of my arms but I've still got the other.
"Stainsforth of the iron hand" you called me.'

Walter began to pant.

'I'll give you two minutes to remember,' Stainsforth said. They both looked
at the clock. At first the stealthy movement of the hand paralysed Walter's

thought. He stared at William Stainsforth's face, his cruel, crafty face, which seemed to be always in shadow, as if it was something the light could not touch. Desperately he searched his memory for the one fact that would save him; but his memory, clenched like a fist, would give up nothing. 'I must invent something,' he thought, and suddenly his mind relaxed and he saw, printed on it like a photograph, the last page of the book. Then, with the speed and magic of a dream, each page appeared before him in perfect clarity until the first was reached, and he realized with overwhelming force that what he looked for was not there. In all that evil there was not one hint of good. And he felt, compulsively and with a kind of exaltation, that unless he testified to this the cause of goodness everywhere would be betrayed.

'There's nothing to be said for you!' he shouted. 'And you know it! Of all your dirty tricks this is the dirtiest! You want me to whitewash you, do you? . . . How dare you ask me for a character? I've given you one already! God forbid that I should ever say a good word for you! I'd rather die!'

Stainsforth's one arm shot out. 'Then die!' he said.

The police found Walter Streeter slumped across the dining-table. His body was still warm, but he was dead. It was easy to tell how he died; for it was not his hand that his visitor had shaken, but his throat.

L. P. HARTLEY, from 'W.S.', 1954

'Twas at the solemn hour of night,
    When men and spirits meet,
That Johnson, huge majestic sprite,
    Repaired to Boswell's feet.

His face was like the full-orbed moon
    Wrapped in a threatening cloud,
That bodes the tempest bursting soon,
    And winds that bluster loud.

Terrific was his angry look,
    His pendent eyebrows frowned;
Thrice in his hand he waved a book,
    Then dashed it to the ground.

'Behold,' he cried, 'perfidious man,
    This object of my rage:

Bethink thee of the sordid plan
　　That formed this venal page.

'Was it to make this base record
　　That you my friendship sought;
Thus to retain each vagrant word,
　　Each undigested thought?

'Dar'st thou pretend that, meaning praise,
　　Thou seek'st to raise my name,
When all thy babbling pen betrays
　　But gives me churlish fame?

'Do readers in these annals trace
　　The man that's wise and good?
No!—rather one of savage race,
　　Illiberal, fierce and rude.

'A traveller, whose discontent
　　No kindness can appease;
Who finds for spleen perpetual vent
　　In all he hears and sees.

'One whose ingratitude displays
　　The most ungracious guest;
Who hospitality repays
　　With bitter, biting jest.

'Ah! would, as o'er the hills we sped,
　　And climbed the sterile rocks,
Some vengeful stone had struck thee dead,
　　Or steeple, spared by Knox!

'Thy adulation now I see,
　　And all its schemes unfold:
Thy avarice, Boswell, cherished me
　　To turn me into gold.

'So keepers guard the beasts they show,
　　And for their wants provide;
Attend their steps where'er they go,
　　And travel by their side.

'O! were it not that, deep and low,
　　Beyond thy reach I'm laid,
Rapacious Boswell had ere now
　　Johnson a mummy made.'

He ceased, and stalked from Boswell's sight
    With fierce indignant mien,
Scornful as Ajax' sullen sprite
    By sage Ulysses seen.

Dead paleness Boswell's cheek o'erspread,
    His limbs with horror shook;
With trembling haste he left his bed,
    And burnt his fatal book.

And thrice he called on Johnson's name,
    Forgiveness to implore!
Then thrice repeated—'injured fame!'
    And word—wrote never more.

ELIZABETH MOODY, 'Dr Johnson's Ghost', 1786; the 'fatal book' is Boswell's
Journal of a Tour to the Hebrides, which appeared after Johnson's death

When, after the death of Ashton Doyne—but three months after—George
Withermore was approached, as the phrase is, on the subject of a 'volume', the
communication came straight from his publishers, who had been, and indeed
much more, Doyne's own; but he was not surprised to learn, on the occurrence
of the interview they next suggested, that a certain pressure as to the early
issue of a Life had been brought to bear upon them by their late client's
widow. Doyne's relations with his wife had been, to Withermore's knowledge,
a very special chapter—which would present itself, by the way, as a delicate
one for the biographer; but a sense of what she had lost, and even of what she
had lacked, had betrayed itself, on the poor woman's part, for the first days of
her bereavement, sufficiently to prepare an observer at all initiated for some
attitude of reparation, some espousal even exaggerated of the interests of a
distinguished name . . .

These materials—diaries, letters, memoranda, notes, documents of many
sorts—were her property, and wholly in her control, no conditions at all
attaching to any portion of her heritage; so that she was free at present to
do as she like—free, in particular, to do nothing. What Doyne would have
arranged had he had time to arrange could be but supposition and guess.

'My thought went straight to *you*, as his own would have done,' she had said
almost as soon as she rose before him there in her large array of mourning—
with her big black eyes, her big black wig, her big black fan and gloves, her

general gaunt, ugly, tragic, but striking and, as might have been thought from a certain point of view, 'elegant' presence. 'You're the one he liked most; oh, *much!*'—and it had been quite enough to turn Withermore's head. It little mattered that he could afterward wonder if she had known Doyne enough, when it came to that, to be sure. He would have said for himself indeed that her testimony on such a point could scarcely count. Still, there was no smoke without fire; she knew at least what she meant, and he wasn't a person she could have an interest in flattering. They went up together, without delay, to the great man's vacant study, which was at the back of the house and looked over the large green garden—a beautiful and inspiring scene, to poor Withermore's view—common to the expensive row.

'You can perfectly work here, you know,' said Mrs Doyne; 'you shall have the place quite to yourself—I'll give it all up to you; so that in the evenings, in particular, don't you see? for quiet and privacy, it will be perfection.'

Perfection indeed, the young man felt as he looked about—having explained that, as his actual occupation was an evening paper and his earlier hours, for a long time yet, regularly taken up, he would have to come always at night. The place was full of their lost friend; everything in it had belonged to him; everything they touched had been part of his life. It was for the moment too much for Withermore—too great an honour and even too great a care; memories still recent came back to him, and, while his heart beat faster and his eyes filled with tears, the pressure of his loyalty seemed almost more than he could carry.

How did he know, without more thought, he might begin to ask himself, that the book was, on the whole, to be desired? What warrant had he ever received from Ashton Doyne himself for so direct and, as it were, so familiar an approach? Great was the art of biography, but there were lives and lives, there were subjects and subjects. He confusedly recalled, so far as that went, old words dropped by Doyne over contemporary compilations, suggestions of how he himself discriminated as to other heroes and other panoramas. He even remembered how his friend, at moments, would have seemed to show himself as holding that the 'literary' career might—save in the case of a Johnson and a Scott, with a Boswell and a Lockhart to help—best content itself to be represented. The artist was what he *did*—he was nothing else. Yet how, on the other hand, wasn't *he*, George Withermore, poor devil, to have jumped at the chance of spending his winter in an intimacy so rich? It had been simply dazzling—that was the fact. It hadn't been the 'terms', from the publishers—though these were, as they said at the office, all right; it had been Doyne himself, his company and contact and presence—it had been just what it was turning out, the possibility of an intercourse closer than that of life. Strange that death, of the two things, should have the fewer mysteries and secrets! The first night our young man was alone in the room it seemed to him that his master and he were really for the first time together.

There were moments, for instance, when, as he bent over his papers, the light breath of his dead host was as distinctly in his hair as his own elbows were on the table before him. There were moments when, had he been able to look up, the other side of the table would have shown him this companion as vividly as the shaded lamplight showed him his page. That he couldn't at such a juncture look up was his own affair, for the situation was ruled—that was but natural—by deep delicacies and fine timidities, the dread of too sudden or too rude an advance. What was intensely in the air was that if Doyne *was* there it wasn't nearly so much for himself as for the young priest of his altar. He hovered and lingered, he came and went, he might almost have been, among the books and the papers, a hushed, discreet librarian, doing the particular things, rendering the quiet aid, liked by men of letters.

Withermore himself, meanwhile, came and went, changed his place, wandered on quests either definite or vague; and more than once, when, taking a book down from a shelf and finding in it marks of Doyne's pencil, he got drawn on and lost, he had heard documents on the table behind him gently shifted and stirred, had literally, on his return, found some letter he had mislaid pushed again into view, some wilderness cleared by the opening of an old journal at the very date he wanted. How should he have gone so, on occasion, to the special box or drawer, out of fifty receptacles, that would help him, had not his mystic assistant happened, in fine prevision, to tilt its lid, or pull it half open, in just the manner that would catch his eye?—in spite, after all, of the fact of lapses and intervals in which, *could* one have really looked, one would have seen somebody standing before the fire a trifle detached and over-erect—somebody fixing one the least bit harder than in life.

That this auspicious relation had in fact existed, had continued, for two or three weeks, was sufficiently proved by the dawn of the distress with which our young man found himself aware of having, for some reason, from the close of a certain day, begun to miss it. The sign of that was an abrupt, surprised sense—on the occasion of his mislaying a marvellous unpublished page which, hunt where he would, remained stupidly, irrecoverably lost—that his protected state was, after all, exposed to some confusion and even to some depression. If, for the joy of the business, Doyne and he had, from the start, been together, the situation had, within a few days of his first new suspicion of it, suffered the odd change of their ceasing to be so . . .

'I can't make it out—I'm at sea. Do what I will, I feel I'm wrong.'

She covered him a moment with her pompous pain. 'How do you feel it?'

'Why, by things that happen. The strangest things. I can't describe them—and you wouldn't believe them.'

'Oh yes, I would!' Mrs Doyne murmured.

'Well, he intervenes.' Withermore tried to explain. 'However I turn, I find him.'

She earnestly followed. ' "Find" him?'

'I meet him. He seems to rise there before me.'

Mrs Doyne, staring, waited a little. 'Do you mean you see him?'

'I feel as if at any moment I may. I'm baffled. I'm checked.' Then he added: 'I'm afraid.'

'Of *him*?' asked Mrs Doyne.

He thought. 'Well—of what I'm doing.'

'Then what, that's so awful, *are* you doing?'

'What you proposed to me. Going into his life.'

She showed, in her gravity, a new alarm. 'And don't you *like* that?'

'Doesn't *he*? That's the question. We lay him bare. We serve him up. What is it called? We give him to the world.'

Poor Mrs Doyne, as if on a menace to her hard atonement, glared at this for an instant in deeper gloom. 'And why shouldn't we?'

'Because we don't know. There are natures, there are lives, that shrink. He mayn't wish it,' said Withermore. 'We never asked him.'

'How *could* we?'

He was silent a little. 'Well, we ask him now. That's after all, what our start has, so far, represented. We've put it to him.'

'Then—if he has been with us—we've had his answer.'

Withermore spoke now as if he knew what to believe. 'He hasn't been "with" us—he has been against us.'

'Then why did you think——'

'What I *did* think, at first—that what he wishes to make us feel is his sympathy? Because, in my original simplicity, I was mistaken. I was—I don't know what to call it—so excited and charmed that I didn't understand. But I understand at last. He only wanted to communicate. He strains forward out of his darkness; he reaches toward us out of his mystery; he makes us dim signs out of his horror.'

' "Horror"?' Mrs Doyne gasped with her fan up to her mouth.

'At what we're doing.' He could by this time piece it all together. 'I see now that at first——'

'Well, what?'

'One had simply to feel he was there, and therefore not indifferent. And the beauty of that misled me. But he's there as a protest.'

'Against *my* Life?' Mrs Doyne wailed.

'Against *any* Life. He's there to *save* his Life. He's there to be let alone.'

'I give up.'

'Then you've seen him?'

'On the threshold—guarding it.'

'Guarding it?' She glowed over her fan. 'Distinct?'

'Immense. But dim. Dark. Dreadful,' said poor George Withermore.

She continued to wonder. 'You didn't go in?'

The young man turned away. 'He forbids!'

'You say *I* needn't,' she went on after a moment. 'Well then, need I?'

'See him?' George Withermore asked.

She waited an instant. 'Give up.'

'You must decide.' For himself he could at last but sink to the sofa with his bent face in his hands. He wasn't quite to know afterwards how long he had sat so; it was enough that what he did next know was that he was alone among her favourite objects. Just as he gained his feet, however, with this sense and that of the door standing open to the hall, he found himself afresh confronted, in the light, the warmth, the rosy space, with her big black perfumed presence. He saw at a glance, as she offered him a huger, bleaker stare over the mask of her fan, that she had been above; and so it was that, for the last time, they faced together their strange question. 'You've seen him?' Withermore asked.

He was to infer later on from the extraordinary way she closed her eyes, and, as if to steady herself, held them tight and long, in silence, that beside the unutterable vision of Ashton Doyne's wife his own might rank as an escape. He knew before she spoke that all was over. 'I give up.'

HENRY JAMES, from 'The Real Right Thing', 1899

He sensed from Tyrrel's manner and appearance that something was coming. The Old Man's eyes were brighter, his clipped speech was quicker and he seemed, for a while, younger.

Eventually, he said to Edward: 'All my books have been taken from one text, you know, from one great manuscript that contains them.'

'You mean you'd written them before?'

'No, but they pre-exist.'

'A writer's notebook?'

The glitter in the Old Man's eyes was subdued. 'Not a notebook but a text, a blueprint, a sort of literary genetic code . . . It is very old. I have never told anyone else about it.'

'It's nothing to be ashamed of.'

'Would you like to see it?'

'Well—yes.' Edward felt uneasy, as if there was something sinister in progress. Yet when he looked at the frail, stooping old man he felt ashamed of himself.

'It doesn't hurt,' said Tyrrel, perhaps sensing Edward's reactions, 'so long as you go along with it.'

He got slowly to his feet and shuffled over to his desk drawer. At that moment he no longer looked younger but seemed every day of his eighty-five years . . . He opened the drawer an inch at a time. Then, moving as in slow motion, he reached in with both hands and withdrew the manuscript. It was not as bulky as Edward had thought and it was bound in yellowing string. The edges were tattered and the paper looked old and unusually thick. If what Tyrrel had said was true, he had taken over twenty books from it. It did not look big enough.

Tyrrel held the manuscript close to his chest, breathing heavily.

'Come here,' he said. His voice was again gruff and though he faced Edward across the desk he did not look up.

Edward approached. There were drops—tears or sweat—on Tyrrel's cheeks . . .

'Take it,' he whispered. His big hands shook, and Edward was sure now that it was sweat running down his cheeks. He prodded Edward with the manuscript. 'You must take it.' . . .

Tyrrel spoke again. The words sounded like, 'It is for you,' or, 'It is meant for you.' Edward couldn't be sure because the voice was less than a whisper. They were the last words Tyrrel spoke.

Certainly, that night I took the book for signing all appeared as usual. We talked over coffee and I gave him the book. He had met the friend it was for and so said he would add an inscription of his own.

I sat in the tubular-framed chair and Edward sat at his desk, his swivel chair turned side-on and his pen above the open book. He had paused while thinking what to say and my eye wandered round the white walls and the shelves of shiny books. I never could get used to the room being so antiseptic, so lacking in human warmth. I heard the scratching of pen on paper and looked back at Edward. His pen was motionless an inch or two above the open page yet the scratching continued. I looked around the room for some other source of noise but it was impossible to believe it was anything else. It had the rhythm of someone writing rapidly and regularly; I could tell long and short words and punctuation marks. The paper sounded coarse and the nib cruder than a modern one, like the sort you used to have to dip in the ink, or like a quill. The silence that always inhabited the room served to emphasize the thin, unremitting scratching . . .

'What's that noise?' I asked Edward.

He started as if someone had slapped his face and for a moment seemed not to know where the question had come from. 'What noise?'

My impulse was to apologize but I felt suddenly guilty and I wanted to justify myself. 'That scratching. I could hear someone writing and I thought it was you but you weren't moving.'

He stared at me. 'You heard it?'

'Yes. Pen on paper. I'm sure that's what it was.'

'How long for?'

'The last minute or two. Since you've been thinking what to write.'

'Can you hear it now?'

'No.'

He looked down. 'It only happens when I'm thinking.' He quickly wrote an inscription in the book and handed it back.

The scratching, the writing sound, did not begin until he was back in London. At first he thought it was something to do with his room, expansion in the heating pipes or even mice in the ceiling, but then he noticed that it occurred only when he was writing or thinking about writing. Even then he still sought an everyday explanation but the rhythm and the sound of page after page being filled by an unfaltering pen ruled out everything normal. Whenever he sat down to write he would wait, pen in hand, for the sounds to start, and his own thoughts were strangled at birth . . .

The manuscript still baffled him whenever he looked at it—which he did often though never for long because of the sickening properties of the gibberish . . . Now, when he looked at the manuscript or heard the noise, his head filled with words, scenes, characters, voices and echoes in such profusion that he felt he couldn't contain them. All he could do was to siphon them off through his own pen, writing automatically with hardly a shaping thought of his own. That is how he started the fashion for so-called fictive realism which made him so famous and rich. He had only to sit and wait for the sounds or turn the pages of the gibberish for it all to rush into his head like water from a sluice, and then he had simply to open his pen. As he went on the process became ever easier and he became immensely prolific and successful, as we know; but his own thoughts and his own imagination perished . . .

By the end he could write only about himself and as that entity became possessed and consumed, so he became ever more fantastical. The reality of evil is that it is the opposite of real.

ALAN JUDD, The Devil's Own Work, 1991

Know, then, we pledge you the success of that which with our help you will accomplish. You will lead the way, you will strike up the march of the future, the lads will swear by your name, who thanks to your madness will no longer need to be mad. On your madness they will feed in health, and in them you will become healthy. Do you understand? Not only will you break through the paralysing difficulties of the time—you will break through time itself, by which I mean the cultural epoch and its cult, and dare to be barbaric, twice barbaric indeed, because of coming after the humane, after all possible root-treatment and bourgeois raffinement. Believe me, barbarism even has more grasp of theology than has a culture fallen away from cult, which even in the religious has seen only culture, only the humane, never excess, paradox, the mystic passion, the utterly unbourgeois ordeal. But I hope you do not marvel that 'the Great Adversary' speaks to you of religion. Gog's nails! Who else, I should like to know, is to speak of it today? Surely not the liberal theologian! After all I am by now its sole custodian! In whom will you recognize theological existence if not in me? And who can lead a theological existence without me? The religious is certainly my line: as certainly as it is not the line of bourgeois culture. Since culture fell away from the cult and made a cult of itself, it has become nothing else than a falling away; and all the world after a mere five hundred years is as sick and tired of it as though, *salva venia*, they had ladled it in with cooking-spoons.

THOMAS MANN, Doctor Faustus, 1947; tr. H. T. Lowe-Porter

Dreams, Coincidences, Telepathy

Two famous cases are given below, the Chaffin will and the appearance of Mrs Wilmot to her husband while he was far away at sea. The Aberfan reports are the more heart-rending through the mixture in them of the homely and the uncanny, the trivial and the tragic. As for the affair of MM. Deschamps and de Fortgibu and the exotic plum pudding, while it has no supernatural properties, it consists in a sequence of coincidences so improbable as barely to be considered natural.

One of Flammarion's correspondents related of his great-aunt, Mme de Thiriet, that four or five hours before her death, in Nancy, in April 1807, she seemed to be thinking deeply. When asked whether she felt worse, she answered, 'No, my dear, but I have just sent for Midon to attend to my burial.' Midon had once been the lady's servant, and lived in Eulmont, a village some five miles away. The attendant at the bedside supposed that the dying woman was dreaming, but two hours later she saw Midon arrive, carrying her mourning clothes in her arms, and saying that she had heard Madame calling her to come and see her die and to perform the last offices for her.

In 'The Transcendent Function', an essay written in 1916, Jung mentions an acquaintance who told him of a dream in which he stepped out into space from the top of a mountain. Jung explained 'something of the influence of the unconscious', and warned him against dangerous mountaineering expeditions. The other, who was a keen climber, laughed. A few months later, while climbing a mountain, he actually did step off into space, and was killed. Such accidents are not uncommon, and the risk must surely have been long present to his conscious mind. Jung has also told of a patient who dreamt that someone had given her a costly piece of jewellery, a golden scarab. On the following day, as she was relating her dream, a scarabaeid, a gold-green beetle, flew into the consulting room. 'Here is your scarab,' Jung said, handing it to her. Hitherto she had preserved 'a highly polished Cartesian rationalism', but this incident 'broke the ice of her intellectual resistance', and the treatment took a turn for the better.

The literature of dreams, precognitive, premonitory, or revelatory, is a vast one. For a handy survey, the reader may care to consult Brian Inglis's *The Power of Dreams*, 1987, while *The Oxford Book of Dreams*, edited by Stephen Brook, 1983, is a more general round-up of dreams in life and in literature.

~

Some Dreams I confess may admit of easie and feminine Exposition: he who dreamed that he could not see his right Shoulder, might easily fear to lose the sight of his right Eye; he that before a Journey dreamed that his Feet were cut off, had a plain warning not to undertake his intended Journey. But why to dream of Lettuce should presage some ensuing disease, why to eat Figs should signify foolish Talk, why to eat Eggs great Trouble, and to dream of Blindness should be so highly commended, according to the oneirocritical Verses of Astrampsychus and Nicephorus, I shall leave unto your Divination.

SIR THOMAS BROWNE, *A Letter to a Friend*, published posthumously, 1690

A dreame is nothing els but a bubling scum or froath of the fancie, which the day hath left undigested; or an after feast made of the fragments of idle imaginations . . . Divers have written diversly of their causes, but the best reason among them all that I could ever picke out, was this, that as an arrow which is shot out of a bow, is sent forth manie times with such force, that it flyeth farre beyond the marke wherat it was aymed; so our thoughts intensively fixt all the day time upon a marke wee are to hit, are now and then over-drawne with such force, that they flye beyonde the marke of the day into the confines of the night. There is no man put to any torment, but quaketh & trembleth a great while after the executioner hath withdrawne his hand from him. In the daye time wee torment our thoughts and imaginations with sundry cares and devices; all the night time they quake and tremble after the terror of their late suffering, and still continue thinking of the perplexities they have endured. To nothing more aptly can I compare the working of our braines after we have unyoakt and gone to bed, than to the glimmering and dazeling of a mans eyes when hee comes newly out of the bright Sunne into darke shadow.

NASHE, *The Terrors of the Night*

In the ages of rude primeval culture, man believed that in dreams he was coming to know a *second real world*; here is the source of all metaphysics. Without dreams one would have found no cause to split the world. The division into soul and body is also connected with the oldest conception of the dream, and similarly the postulation of a life of the soul, thus the origin of all belief in spirits, and probably of belief in gods too. 'The dead live on, *because* they appear to the living in dreams': thus man used to reason, throughout thousands of years.

FRIEDRICH NIETZSCHE, *Human, All Too Human*, 1878

As two certain Arcadians, intimate Companions, were travelling together, it so happened, that, as they came to Megara, one of them went to an Inn and the other to a Friend's House. Both had Supped at their respective places and were gone to Bed; when lo! He, that was at his Friend's House, Dreamt, that his Companion came to him and begg'd him for Heaven's Sake to assist him, for that the Inn Keeper had contrived a way to murder him: Frightened at first out of his Sleep he rose up, but soon afterward coming a little better to himself, he thought, upon recollection, there was no heed to be given to a Vision, and went very quietly to Bed again. But as soon as he was got into his second Sleep, the same Vision repeated the Visit, but the form of his Petition was quite altered. He beseeched him, that, since he had not come to his assistance, while he was among the Living, he would not suffer his Death however, to go unrevenged. Told him that as soon as he was murdered he was toss'd by the Innkeeper into a Waggon, and had a little Straw thrown over his Corpse. He intreated him to be ready very early at the Door before the Waggon was to go out of Town. This Dream truly disturb'd him it seems very much, and made him get up very early: He nicked the time, and met the Waggoner just at the very Door, and asked him what he had in his Cart. The Fellow run away frightened and confounded. The dead Body was pulled out of it, and the whole matter, coming plainly to light, the Innkeeper suffered for the Crime. What is there that one can call more Divine than a Dream like this?

CICERO, *De Divinatione*; tr. John Aubrey

 Caesar. Calphurnia here, my wife, stays me at home.
  She dreamt tonight she saw my statue,
  Which, like a fountain with an hundred spouts,
  Did run pure blood; and many lusty Romans
  Came smiling, and did bathe their hands in it.
  And these does she apply for warnings and portents
  And evils imminent; and on her knee
  Hath begg'd that I will stay at home today.
 Decius. This dream is all amiss interpreted;
  It was a vision fair and fortunate:
  Your statue spouting blood in many pipes,
  In which so many smiling Romans bath'd,
  Signifies that from you great Rome shall suck
  Reviving blood, and that great men shall press
  For tinctures, stains, relics, and cognizance.
  This by Calphurnia's dream is signified.
 Caesar. And this way have you well expounded it.

SHAKESPEARE, *Julius Caesar*; Decius was one of the conspirators who stabbed
Caesar to death in the Senate House

On the night before his assassination, Caligula dreamt that he was standing
beside Jupiter's throne in the heavens. The God kicked him with the big toe
of his right foot, and sent him plummeting down to earth.

SUETONIUS (*c.*70–*c.*140), *Lives of the Caesars*

From the *Various History* of Aelian [Claudius Aelianus]: The Peripateticks
assert, that the Soul in the Day-time is inslaved and involved in the Body, so
that she cannot behold Truth; but in the Night, being freed from this servitude, and gathered together, as it were, in a round about the Parts that are in
the Breast, she is more Prophetick, whence proceed Dreams.

When Sir Christopher Wren was at Paris about 1671, he was Ill and Feverish,
made but little Water, had a pain in his Reins. He sent for a Physitian, who
advis'd him to be let Blood, thinking he had a Pleurisy: But Bleeding much
disagreeing with his Constitution, he would defer it a Day longer: That Night
he dreamt, that he was in a place where Palm-Trees grew (suppose Egypt), and

that a woman in a Romantick Habit, reach'd him Dates. The next Day he sent for Dates, which Cured him of the pain in his Reins.

AUBREY, *Miscellanies*

It chanced at Carthage that the rhetorician Eulogius, who had been my disciple in that art, being (as he himself, after our return to Africa, told us the story) in course of lecturing to his disciples on Cicero's rhetorical books, as he looked over the portion of reading which he was to deliver on the following day, fell upon a certain passage, and not being able to understand it, was scarce able to sleep for the trouble of his mind: in which night, as he dreamed, I expounded to him that which he did not understand; nay, not I, but my likeness, while I was unconscious of the thing, and far away beyond sea, it might be doing, or it might be dreaming, some other thing, and not in the least caring for his cares. In what way these things come about, I know not; but in what way soever they come, why do we not believe it comes in the same way for a person in a dream to see a dead man, as it comes that he sees a living man? both no doubt, neither knowing nor caring who, or where, or when, dreams of their images.

ST AUGUSTINE, from 'On Care to be had for the Dead', *Retractions*, 427; tr. Revd H. Browne

There lived once in Baghdad a wealthy man and made of money, who lost all his substance and became so destitute that he could earn his living only by hard labour. One night, he lay down to sleep, dejected and heavy hearted, and saw in a dream a Speaker, who said to him, 'Verily thy fortune is in Cairo; go thither and seek it.' So he set out for Cairo; but when he arrived there, evening overtook him and he lay down to sleep in a mosque.

Presently, by decree of Allah Almighty, a band of bandits entered the mosque and made their way thence into an adjoining house; but the owners, being aroused by the noise of the thieves, awoke and cried out; whereupon the Chief of Police came to their aid with his officers. The robbers made off; but the Wali entered the mosque and, finding the man from Baghdad asleep there, laid hold of him and beat him with palm rods so grievous a beating that he was wellnigh dead. Then they cast him into jail, where he abode three days; after which the Chief of Police sent for him and asked him, 'Whence art thou?';

and he answered, 'From Baghdad.' Quoth the Wali, 'And what brought thee to Cairo?'; and quoth the Baghdadi, 'I saw in a dream one who said to me, "Thy fortune is in Cairo; go thither to it." But when I came to Cairo the fortune which he promised me proved to be the palm rods thou so generously gavest me.'

The Wali laughed till he showed his wisdom-teeth and said, 'O man of little wit, thrice have I seen in a dream one who said to me, "There is in Baghdad a house in such a district and of such a fashion and its courtyard is laid out garden-wise, at the lower end whereof is a jetting fountain and under the same a great sum of money lieth buried. Go thither and take it." Yet I went not; but thou, of the briefness of thy wit, hast journeyed from place to place, on the faith of a dream, which was but an idle galimatias of sleep.' Then he gave him money, saying, 'Help thee back herewith to thine own country'; and he took the money and set out upon his homewards march. Now the house the Wali had described was the man's own house in Baghdad; so the wayfarer returned thither and, digging underneath the fountain in his garden, discovered a great treasure. And thus Allah gave him abundant fortune; and a marvellous co-incidence occurred.

'The Ruined Man Who Became Rich Again Through A Dream', *The Thousand Nights and a Night*; tr. Sir Richard Burton

Once upon a time in the province of Shinano there were two good friends who liked to hunt together in the forest. One day, after they had taken their midday meal, one of them fell asleep. Before long, a horse-fly came out of his nose, flew off, and then returned a little later. The other watched all this. When the man woke up, he told his friend that he had dreamt he was a horse-fly, and that he flew to the house of a rich landowner on the island of Sado, a good fifty leagues distant, where he settled on a beautiful camellia tree in the garden. Beneath the tree, as the horse-fly knew, there was buried treasure. Having changed back into a man, the dreamer dug away and found hundreds of gold coins.

His friend, who had listened carefully, offered him a hundred copper coins in exchange for the dream, and he agreed readily. Then the man who had bought the dream travelled to the island of Sado and entered the rich landowner's service. One moonlit night, when the rest of the household were sleeping, he dug a hole under the camellia tree, gathered up all the gold coins lying there, and returned home a wealthy man.

Japanese tale

Mrs A., a mother, whose son was in India, dreamed this dream thus given in her own words:—

'I dreamed that I saw David, my son, on a boat of a strange shape. I appeared to be standing in the boat with him at the foot of a ladder, which led to an upper deck. My son looked extremely pale and worn, his eyes being very heavy. I said to him, "Oh, darling, are you not sorry you went away?" He looked earnestly at me and replied, "Mother, I have nowhere to sleep."

I awoke, anxious and uneasy, and wrote down the dream and date in a diary. My friends shared with me the anxiety I felt for news of him.

A letter arrived in due course, stating that on his voyage up an Indian river, a storm nearly swamped the boat. "I send you a rough sketch," he wrote, "of the boat, different to any you have seen. A ladder leads to the upper deck. My bed in the cabin was soaked, the boat nearly wrecked. I wrapped myself in blankets, and sat on the upper deck, thinking much of you all. *I had nowhere to sleep.*" '

The mother had, before this letter came, written her dream to her son.

'In due time another letter came from him: "I shall never laugh at you for being superstitious again, dear mother. The storm occurred at the exact date of your dream." '

The same lady dreamed very vividly, early on a certain Sunday morning, that she saw her same son David, still in India. His forehead was sorely bruised, his eyes were so heavy that they seemed half closed, but gazing at her with a most loving, but sad, expression.

She rose, and went to early Holy Communion, earnestly praying for him and his temporal and spiritual welfare . . .

On the Wednesday after her dream, however, a telegram came, saying that David had been drowned on the very Sunday of her dream.

FREDERICK GEORGE LEE, *Glimpses in the Twilight,* 1885

A long time ago, a gentleman who may be called A. lost a child by death. He had been very fond and proud of the boy, who was seven or eight years old, I think, when he died. Indeed, between the two there had always been a strong sympathy, and when the child was taken the father was plunged into the deepest grief. Like many another in the same situation, his thoughts by day and night were tortured by the question, 'But yet is he still in existence? Is there a place in this vast universe where I may think of him as living—no matter how infinite the distance, or even if we are parted not only now but for ever and ever?' . . .

And to this great trouble was added another, which took the shape of a deep and surprising disappointment. At first, one of the poor man's very few comforts was that the boy would haunt his dreams, and that they would be together many a time that way. But it is not invariably true that what you think of most you dream of most; and for all his hoping and praying the father never once dreamt of his son. He never had any such dream for a whole year; by which time, I dare say, the praying had been given up and the hope exhausted. But then, on the morning of the anniversary of the child's death, and at the very hour at which he died, the father woke from a wonderful dream, so intimately and touchingly responsive to the whole year's grief that it cannot be thrown into the glare of print. It is only mentioned, together with the fact that after another twelve months of blank and empty nights another dream of the same character occurred at the same hour, in order to give its own setting to the third dream.

The morning had again come round. A. dreamed that he had awakened about dawn, and, thinking of nothing but the hour to rise, had drawn his watch from under his pillow. In doing so he saw that it had been completely shattered. But how could it have been broken so violently, lying where it had been snugly placed a few hours before? A reasonable but an injurious conjecture occurred to him: at some time in the night the watch had been taken from beneath his pillow by his wife, who had allowed it to fall. Satisfied that there could be no other explanation, he was about to drop asleep again, to get rid of ill humour at the accident (this is all in the dream, be it understood), when the door opened and in came a foreman of works to whom A. gave instructions every day, and between whom and himself there was a great liking. It seemed as if the man had come for the usual draft of work to be done, and it did not strike A. as anything out of the way that he should be visited in his bedroom for it. But he *was* struck by the mysterious look of inquiry on the man's face. The next moment he connected this look with the broken watch, and drew it out again; the glass gone, the hands swept from the dial, but seeming less like his own watch now. What was the meaning of it? While A. was asking himself the question in a sort of expectant trepidation, the foreman of works said, 'Put it to your ear, sir,' meaning, of course, the broken watch. This A. did; and as he listened to the even beat within, the other said, 'Sir, we know how much you are troubled, and this is our way of showing you that though every sign of life is destroyed, life may still be going on.' Whereupon A. woke all of a tremble, heard the tranquil tick-ticking of his watch under his pillow, and when he could compose himself to take it forth, saw that the hands stood at within five or eight minutes of the time when his boy died on the same day in the calendar . . .

The fourth dream occurred a quarter of a century after the third, which was the watch dream. Not once in the interval had A. dreamed of his son. On this last occasion the vision was as clear and as impressive as the others, and full of meaning expressed darkly in a noble dramatic form. Of course, such visitations must needs be disturbing; and as A. sat in after-dinner idleness with one of his kinsfolk next evening, the dream recurred to him and he became lost in thought about it. By and by his absorption must have been manifest; for his kinswoman asked what he was thinking of. She was answered, of a wonderful dream, and of whom; upon which she said, 'Why, don't you know what day it is?'—Again the anniversary dream, after twenty-five years of interruption and although he had forgotten the day! And since he had forgotten the day, whose memory was it that inspired the dream, or what magic of imagination framed it so wittingly for that morning of all mornings of the year?

FREDERICK GREENWOOD, *Imagination in Dreams*, 1894

Mr D., owner of an 'old mechanical business' in Glasgow, stated that some thirty-five years earlier he had taken a 'delicate-looking boy', Robert Mackenzie, into his employ. He had been very kind to the boy, and the boy was obviously grateful: 'I seemed to be the polar star of his existence.' Years later, when Mr D. had opened a branch in London and moved there himself, his employees had their annual ball in Glasgow, on a Friday night. On the following Tuesday morning, Mr D. dreamt that he was engaged in business with an unknown gentleman, when Robert Mackenzie broke in on them. Mr D. spoke sharply to him regarding this lack of manners. When the other person left, Mackenzie insisted that he must speak to him at once, saying that he wished to tell him that he had not done the thing of which he was accused, and he wanted Mr D.'s forgiveness. 'How can I forgive you if you do not tell me what you are accused of?' said Mr D. To which, in his Scottish dialect, Mackenzie replied: 'Ye'll sune ken.' Later in the day a letter came from the manager in Glasgow announcing that on the Saturday night after the workmen's ball Mackenzie had committed suicide. The following post brought another letter, to the effect that the death was accidental: Mackenzie had drunk from a bottle of aqua fortis, used for staining the wood of birdcages, a hobby of his, in mistake for whisky.

Drawn from Sir Ernest Bennett: *Apparitions and Haunted Houses*

In 1905 a North Carolina farmer, James L. Chaffin, made a will leaving his property to his third son, Marshall, with no provision for his wife or the three other sons. It appears that, unknown to anyone else, Chaffin made a new will, unattested, in 1919, whereby the property was to be divided equally among his four sons, who were enjoined to look after their mother. These second thoughts resulted from a reading of Chapter 27 of Genesis, the story of Isaac and his sons, Esau and Jacob. Chaffin died in 1921, and Marshall took possession of the entire property. James, the second son, gave an account of subsequent events, as follows.

'I think it was in June of 1925 that I began to have very vivid dreams that my father appeared to me at my bedside but made no verbal communications. Some time later, I think it was the latter part of June, 1925, he appeared at my bedside again, dressed as I had often seen him dressed in life, wearing a black overcoat which I knew to be his own coat. This time my father's spirit spoke to me, he took hold of his overcoat and pulled it back and said, "You will find my will in my overcoat pocket", and then disappeared. The next morning I arose fully convinced that my father's spirit had visited me for the purpose of explaining some mistake. I went to mother's and sought for the overcoat but found that it was gone. Mother stated that she had given the overcoat to my brother John who lives in Yadkin County about twenty miles north-west of my home. I think it was on the 6th of July I went to my brother's home in Yadkin County and found the coat. On examination of the inside pocket I found that the lining had been sewed together. I immediately cut the stitches and found a little roll of paper tied with a string which was in my father's handwriting and contained only the following words: "Read the 27th chapter of Genesis in my daddie's old Bible".

At this point I was so convinced that the mystery was to be cleared up I was unwilling to go to mother's home to examine the old Bible without the presence of a witness and I induced a neighbour, Mr Thos. Blackwelder, to accompany me, also my daughter and Mr Blackwelder's daughter were present. Arriving at mother's home we had a considerable search before we found the old Bible. At last we did find it in the top bureau drawer in an upstairs room. The book was so dilapidated that when we took it out it fell into three pieces. Mr Blackwelder picked up the portion containing the Book of Genesis and turned the leaves until he came to the 27th chapter and there we found two leaves folded together, the left hand page folded to the right and the right hand page folded to the left forming a pocket and in this pocket Mr Blackwelder found the will which has [since] been probated.

During the month of December, 1925, my father again appeared to me about a week before the trial of the case of Chaffin vs. Chaffin and said "Where is my old will", and showed considerable temper. I believed from this that I would win the lawsuit, as I did.'

Then came a dream which somewhat simplified matters. For it ruled out definitely: insanity, clairvoyance, astral-wandering, spirit-messages, and telepathy. But it left me face to face with something much more staggering than any of these.

In 1904 . . . I was staying at the Hotel Scholastika, on the borders of the Aachensee, in Austria. I dreamed one night that I was walking down a sort of pathway between two fields, separated from the latter by high iron railings, eight or nine feet high, on each side of the path. My attention was suddenly attracted to a horse in the field on my *left*. It had apparently gone mad, and was tearing about, kicking and plunging in a most frenzied fashion. I cast a hasty glance backwards and forwards along the railings to see if there were any openings by which the animal could get out. Satisfied that there was none, I continued on my way. A few moments later I heard hoofs thundering behind me. Glancing back I saw, to my dismay, that the brute *had* somehow got out after all, and was coming full tilt after me down the pathway. It was a full-fledged nightmare—and I ran like a hare. Ahead of me the path ended at the foot of a flight of wooden steps rising upward. I was striving frantically to reach these when I awoke.

Next day I went fishing with my brother down the little river which runs out of the Aachensee. It was wet-fly work, and I was industriously flogging the water when my brother called out: 'Look at that horse!' Glancing across the river, I saw the scene of my dream. *But, though right in essentials, it was absolutely unlike in minor details.* The two fields with the fenced-off pathway running between them were there. The horse was there, behaving just as it had done in the dream. The wooden steps at the end of the pathway were there (they led up to a bridge crossing the river). But the fences were wooden and small—not more than four or five feet high—and the fields were ordinary small fields, whereas those in the dream had been park-like expanses. Moreover, the horse was a small beast, and not the rampaging great monster of the dream—though its behaviour was equally alarming. Finally, it was in the wrong field, the field which would have been on my *right*, had I been walking, as in the dream, down the path towards the bridge. I began to tell my brother about the dream, but broke off because the beast was behaving so very oddly that I wanted to make sure that it could not escape. As in the dream, I ran my eye critically along the railings. As in the dream, I could see no gap, or even gate, in them anywhere. Satisfied, I said, 'At any rate, *this* horse cannot get out', and recommenced fishing. But my brother interrupted me by calling, 'Look out!' Glancing up again, I saw that there was no dodging fate. The beast *had*, inexplicably, just as in the dream, got out (probably it had jumped the fence), and, just as in the dream, it was thundering down the path towards the wooden steps. It swerved past these and plunged into the river, coming straight towards us. We both picked up stones, ran thirty yards or so back from the bank, and faced about. The end was tame, for, on emerging from the water on our side, the animal merely looked at us, snorted, and galloped off down a road.

J. W. DUNNE, *An Experiment with Time*, 1927

Our house on Terrace Avenue [New York] was burglarized twice that year. The first robbery occurred while we were away over the weekend . . . All my gold cuff-links were gone, as well as a watch I particularly treasured, left me by Aunt Adelaide. Mother spent the evening pondering the fact that several drawers full of dinner silver were open, yet nothing was missing. 'Now, something obviously scared them away,' she kept saying. 'But what could it have been?'

Then one night I had a dream, and I dreamed that I was standing downstairs in the dining-room, looking toward the windows. I went over and pulled back the first curtains, and the second curtains, and saw that one of the windows had been broken and was open and the screen outside cut and unhooked. I stared, seeing the picture with an abnormal clarity and at the same time with a feeling of foreboding. (It comes at the moment when a dream ceases to be a neutral experience and declares itself a nightmare.) I realized that someone had seen me discover the broken window and very likely was watching me even as I stood there. I could go one of two ways in order to escape . . . But even as I looked at the curtains, I saw part of a hand slip between them. Then the lights went out, I was being strangled, and that awakened me.

The next morning early I was in a great hurry to get downstairs. The memory of the dream was so vivid and unpleasant in my head that I wanted to erase it by seeing the reality of the intact window and window screen. The trouble was that when I pulled back the curtains and looked at the window, the glass was broken and the screening cut, both just as I had seen them and in precisely the same places. It was a jolt, because I did not 'believe in' such phenomena. Still, I could not deny that I had had the dream . . . Naturally I ran upstairs and told my parents about it, but they were far more interested in the fact that the house had been broken into than in the manner of my discovering it. For me it was an unsettling experience and one that temporarily shook my stubborn faith in a rationally motivated cosmos. The only thing was to ignore it, which I managed more or less successfully to do.

> PAUL BOWLES, *Without Stopping: An Autobiography*, 1972; the incident happened *c*.1921, when the author was 12 years old

At 9.15 a.m. on 21 October 1966 a huge slag-heap collapsed on the Welsh mining village of Aberfan. A junior school lay in the path of the avalanche: 144 people died, 116 of them children. In response to a newspaper appeal, Dr J. C. Barker, a consultant psychiatrist at a Shrewsbury hospital and a member of the Society for Psychical Research, received 76 letters from people claiming to have had precognition of the disaster; in 22 cases confirmation was obtained from witnesses. The first passage printed below is an account compiled by a local minister, the Revd Glannant Jones, and signed as correct by the parents of the child, Eryl Mai Jones, aged 10. The succeeding letter, dated 19 December 1966, came from Mrs Mary Hennessy of Barnstaple, North Devon, and the verifying letter was written by her daughter-in-law, Mrs Peggy Hennessy, also of Barnstaple.

She was an attractive dependable child, not given to imagination. A fortnight before the disaster she said to her mother, who at the time was putting some money aside for her, 'Mummy, I'm not afraid to die.' Her mother replied, 'Why do you talk of dying, and you so young; do you want a lollipop?' 'No,' she said, 'but I shall be with Peter and June' (schoolmates). The day before the disaster she said to her mother, 'Mummy, let me tell you about my dream last night.' Her mother answered gently, 'Darling, I've no time now. Tell me again later.' The child replied, 'No, Mummy, you must listen. I dreamt I went to school and there was no school there. Something black had come down all over it.' Her mother answered, 'You mustn't have chips for supper for a bit.' The next day off to school went her daughter as happy as ever. In the communal grave she was buried with Peter on one side and June on the other. (This last point may not, however, be significant, since the order of burial was apparently influenced by parents' requests.)

The night before the Aberfan disaster I dreamt of a lot of children in two rooms. After a while some of the children joined some others in an oblong-shaped room and were in different little groups. At the end of the room there were long pieces of wood, or wooden bars. The children were trying to get over the top or through the bars. I tried to warn someone by calling out, but before I could do so one little child just slipped out of sight. I myself was not in either of the rooms, but was watching from the passageway or corridor. The next thing in my dream was hundreds of people all running to the same place. The looks on the people's faces were terrible. Some were crying and others were holding handkerchiefs to their faces. It frightened me so much that it woke me up.

I wanted to get out of bed and telephone my son and his wife and ask them to take special care of my two little granddaughters. When I did get up it was 6.45 a.m. I told my brother-in-law that I had this terrible dream and that I was going to telephone my son and daughter-in-law, but he said it was too early. I therefore waited until 8.45 a.m. and telephoned, telling them about my dream and that I was very worried as the dream was about children. I told them it wasn't our two little girls in the dream as they looked more like schoolchildren.

The dream upset me very much all the next day. I did not hear about the Aberfan disaster until 5.15 p.m.

I confirm that on the morning of the Aberfan disaster, Mrs Mary Hennessy (my mother-in-law) telephoned me before 9 a.m. She asked me to take special care of our two small daughters. She said she had had a frightening dream about children running about screaming and some were falling. One fell out of sight. She said she felt she had to warn us about our children, although she thought it was more likely to have been at school, because it was a lot of children all together in a long room.

> These letters and others of a similar nature are given in Andrew MacKenzie: *Frontiers of the Unknown*, 1968

On Thursday, the 7th of November, 1850, at the moment when the coalminers at Belfast were about to begin their work, the wife of one of them advised him to examine carefully the ropes of the basket, or cage, in which he was about to descend to the depths of the pit.

'I dreamed,' she said, 'that they cut it during the night.'

The miner did not, at first, attach great importance to this advice; nevertheless, he communicated it to his comrades. They unrolled the descending cable, and there, to the great surprise of all, they found it hacked in several places. Some moments later the workmen would have gotten into the basket, from which they would inevitably have been thrown; and if the *Newcastle Journal* is to be believed, they owed their safety to this dream.

> FLAMMARION, *The Unknown*, quoting 'my lamented friend, Dr Macario'

'Constantius . . . Have you ever seen the dead?'

No answer was obvious. Dead bodies he had often seen; he had killed people. The slashed and gouged, the skewered, the dried, ripped throat and oozing stump, the stare when all light had gone, the mess of brains on a fallen shield. But these she did not mean.

'Like most of us, Clodia, I never really know. Sometimes the dead are thought to be standing amongst us, obstructing, helping, or merely weak and wretched. I know little of dreams, though the dead fill them. They may be messengers, or bits of other people's thoughts that have somehow got lost, or spirits trapped because none cared to attend them in death. Outside Palmyra is a city kept for the dead alone. It has tombs like small temples, houses, squares, parks. Many cells are underground or hollowed out of great rocks. Paintings too, scorched by the sun.'

Constantius had never succeeded in answering Clodia's questions about dreams. Years ago, Bran dreamed regularly of a snake which, with each dream, had crept nearer him, he himself being inextricably bound, heavy as iron, unable to move. Finally, with the snake almost upon him, Bran dared not sleep but, waiting until noon, searched the woods, found an identical snake and killed it, whereupon the dreams ceased.

PETER VANSITTART, *The Wall*, 1990

I have come across many cases of dreams which 'speak the truth' about something which at first sight seems to have been communicated to the brain by paranormal means, and they often give the dreamer feelings of distinct discomfort and unease. My first experience of this, as far as I remember, occurred at school when the headmistress announced one day that Miss R. had left to nurse her mother, who had suddenly been taken ill. That night I dreamed that Miss R. and the school gardener were getting married. I told the other girls next morning and we all giggled at the thought of our rather uptight Miss R. marrying our rather handsome young gardener. However, when he was not to be seen for several weeks afterwards, we made enquiries and discovered that my dream had indeed 'spoken the truth'. We were all frightfully impressed, and I received requests to dream examination questions, my friends' futures, and so on. The results were usually disappointing, but had I persevered I might well have become a prophetess instead of a psychologist!

However, when I came to reconsider the experience later, I recalled that I had in fact once or twice noticed Miss R. walking with the gardener in the grounds, and several days before her departure some of the girls had remarked that the gardener seemed to be missing. I also recalled hearing Miss R. humming beneath her breath, 'If you're in love the whole world sings a melody . . .' as she passed me in the corridor the day before she left . . . and somewhere at the back of my mind I had run over a possible solution in terms of a romance with the gardener. My sleeping mind then picked this up in its nightly turnover of the day's material and presented it in terms of a picture story.

ANN FARADAY, *Dream Power*, 1972

During the night of Sunday the 27th of December 1992 I dreamt that I went into my local library, in Southfields, London SW18, and observed to my astonishment that the staff were sitting companionably at a table in the very middle and smoking. Smoking in a public library? Then I saw they were eating and drinking as well, and showing signs of merriment. Clearly they weren't going to help me locate whatever it was I wanted, and in any case I had forgotten what it was. So I would have to ramble round the shelves from one end to the other, hoping to find out. I began to do so . . .

The next morning I was setting out for the library, where a volume I needed urgently for *The Oxford Book of the Supernatural* was waiting to be collected, when I remembered my dream. And then it struck me that Monday the 28th was a public holiday, replacing Boxing Day which had come on the Saturday. No doubt the library staff would be away, enjoying themselves, eating and drinking, just possibly smoking.

A mild, even drab, example of a premonitory dream. But it saved me a fruitless journey.

THE EDITOR

What is the explanation of the fact that frequently (in nine cases out of ten) after meeting some person in the street who has recalled another to me by some vague resemblance, I find myself a moment after, or at any rate in the course of the day, in the presence of that very person who was recalled to my mind, although nothing brings that person to see me?

Letter from J. Renier, in Flammarion: *The Unknown*

One, two, three, four, five. There were five of them.

Five couriers, sitting on a bench outside the convent on the summit of the Great St Bernard in Switzerland, looking at the remote heights, stained by the setting sun, as if a mighty quantity of red wine had been broached upon the mountain top, and had not yet had time to sink into the snow . . .

'My God!' said the Swiss courier, speaking in French, which I do not hold (as some authors appear to do) to be such an all-sufficient excuse for a naughty word, that I have only to write it in that language to make it innocent; 'if you talk of ghosts—'

'But I *don't* talk of ghosts,' said the German.

'Of what then?' asked the Swiss.

'If I knew of what then,' said the German, 'I should probably know a great deal more.'

It was a good answer, I thought, and it made me curious. So, I moved my position to that corner of my bench which was nearest to them, and leaning my back against the convent wall, heard perfectly, without appearing to attend.

'Thunder and lightning!' said the German, warming, 'when a certain man is coming to see you, unexpectedly; and, without his own knowledge, sends some invisible messenger, to put the idea of him into your head all day, what do you call that? When you walk along a crowded street—at Frankfurt, Milan, London, Paris—and think that a passing stranger is like your friend Heinrich, and then that another passing stranger is like your friend Heinrich, and so begin to have a strange foreknowledge that presently you'll meet your friend Heinrich—which you do, though you believed him at Trieste—what do you call *that*?'

'It's not uncommon, either,' murmured the Swiss and the other three.

'Uncommon!' said the German. 'It's as common as cherries in the Black Forest. It's as common as macaroni at Naples. And Naples reminds me! When the old Marchesa Senzanima shrieks at a card-party on the Chiaja—as I heard and saw her, for it happened in a Bavarian family of mine, and I was overlooking the service that evening—I say, when the old Marchesa starts up at the card-table, white through her rouge, and cries, "My sister in Spain is dead! I felt her cold touch on my back!"—and when that sister *is* dead at the moment—what do you call that?'

'Or when the blood of San Gennaro liquefies at the request of the clergy—as all the world knows that it does regularly once a year, in my native city,' said the Neapolitan courier after a pause, with a comical look, 'what do you call that?'

'*That*!' cried the German. 'Well, I think I know a name for that.'

'Miracle?' said the Neapolitan, with the same sly face.

The German merely smoked and laughed; and they all smoked and laughed.

DICKENS, from 'To be Read at Dusk', 1852

Émile Deschamps [1791–1871], a distinguished poet . . . tells of a curious series of fortuitous coincidences as follows:

In his childhood, being at a boarding-school at Orleans, he chanced to find himself on a certain day at table with a M. de Fortgibu, an émigré recently returned from England, who made him taste a plum pudding, a dish almost unknown at that time in France.

The remembrance of that feast had by degrees faded from his memory, when, ten years later, passing by a restaurant on the Boulevard Poissonière, he perceived inside it a plum pudding of most excellent appearance.

He went in and asked for a slice of it, but was informed that the whole had been ordered by another customer. 'M. de Fortgibu,' cried the *dame du comptoir*, seeing that Deschamps looked disappointed, 'would you have the goodness to share your plum pudding with this gentleman?'

Deschamps had some difficulty in recognizing M. de Fortgibu in an elderly man, with powdered hair, dressed in a colonel's uniform, who was taking his dinner at one of the tables.

The officer said it would give him pleasure to offer part of his pudding to the gentleman.

Long years had passed since Deschamps had even thought of plum pudding, or of M. de Fortgibu.

One day he was invited to dinner where there was to be a real English plum pudding. He accepted the invitation, but told the lady of the house, as a joke, that he knew M. de Fortgibu would be of the party, and he caused much amusement by giving the reason.

The day came, and he went to the house. Ten guests occupied the ten places at table, and a magnificent plum pudding was served. They were beginning to laugh at Deschamps about his M. de Fortgibu, when the door opened and a servant announced:

'M. de Fortgibu.'

An old man entered, walking feebly, with the help of a servant. He went slowly round the table, as if looking for somebody, and he seemed greatly disconcerted. Was it a vision? or was it a joke?

It was the time of the Carnival, and Deschamps was sure it was a trick. But as the old man approached him he was forced to recognize M. de Fortgibu in person.

'My hair stood up on my head,' he said. 'Don Juan, in the *chef d'œuvre* of Mozart, was not more terrified by his guest of stone.'

All was soon explained. M. de Fortgibu had been asked to dinner by a friend who lived in the same house, but had mistaken the door of his apartment.

FLAMMARION, *The Unknown*

I have always been sceptical of unworldly coincidences. So when a friend of mine, the novelist William Gerhardie, died in the summer of 1977 having said that if there was another life he would come back and pull the leg of his disbelieving fellow-novelist Olivia Manning—who fell and broke her leg at the scattering of Gerhardie's ashes in Regent's Park—I dismissed this as a joke in rather painful taste.

A little later I edited, with Robert Skidelsky, Gerhardie's posthumous work *God's Fifth Column*. This book uses as its motif Mozart's Concertante Sinfonie for violin and viola to represent the influence of the imagination versus the will. The publishers sent me an early copy which arrived on a Saturday morning. I unpacked it, opened its pages, and turned to the end where Gerhardie describes the feelings aroused in him by the concluding bars of the second movement of the Andante. As I read it, these very bars of music were played on the radio exactly as he described them. The emotional force of that coincidence, as if William were signalling his approval of our work, has seriously dented my scepticism.

MICHAEL HOLROYD, in '*I Saw a Ghost . . .*'

Earlier this year, the authorities in charge of the national lottery of the Philippines took action to counter widespread rumours that the drawing of the lottery was rigged. They invited the retired and much respected General Alfredo Lim to perform the draw live on national television. Each step of the process was open to scrutiny by the cameras, and the result proved beyond doubt that the draw was fair. Out of the giant urn the general drew a ticket bearing the name of General Alfredo Lim.

PAUL SEABRIGHT, from 'Is life a lottery?', *The Times Literary Supplement*, 1990

The idea of the Trickster, the archetypal destroyer of men's fortunes and souls, is present in many ancient cultures. Often indistinguishable from the Devil, he amuses himself by changing shape and form and toying with human fate. Charles Fort [1874–1932, 'father of anomalistics'] wrote: 'We are being played with', and suggested that the controller of the revels was a cruel, bored child, a Cosmic Joker who uses us as pawns in his game. Certainly many examples of fate or synchronicity seem to attest to the malign influence of some organizing intelligence.

The lives and violent deaths of Presidents Lincoln and Kennedy have been found to show no fewer than seventeen marked synchronicities:

1. Lincoln was elected president in 1860 and Kennedy in 1960.
2. Both men were involved in civil rights.
3. Both were assassinated on a Friday and in the presence of their wives.
4. Both were shot in the head, from behind.
5. Both their successors were called Johnson, were Southern Democrats and in the Senate.
6. Andrew Johnson was born in 1808 and Lyndon B. Johnson in 1908.
7. The assassins, John Wilkes Booth and Lee Harvey Oswald, were born in 1839 and 1939 respectively.
8. Booth and Oswald were both Southerners favouring unpopular ideas.
9. Lincoln was killed in Ford's Theater, Kennedy in a Ford automobile.
10. Both Presidents had a son die while they were in the White House.
11. Lincoln's secretary, whose first name was John, advised him not to go to the theatre. Kennedy's secretary, whose name was Lincoln, advised against the trip to Dallas.
12. Booth shot Lincoln in a theatre and ran to a warehouse. Oswald shot Kennedy from a warehouse and ran to a theatre.
13. The names Lincoln and Kennedy each contain seven letters.
14. The names John Wilkes Booth and Lee Harvey Oswald each contain fifteen letters.
15. Both assassins were killed before coming to trial.
16. The names Andrew Johnson and Lyndon Johnson each contain thirteen letters.
17. The first public proposal that Lincoln be a Presidential candidate endorsed a John Kennedy as his running mate.

Academic discussion of synchronicity inevitably includes the theory that apparent links are imposed on a random universe by the observer, oneself. But when the hand of fate deals the cards it is difficult to escape the notion of divine retribution, or the malign influence of the Cosmic Joker.

LYNN PICKNETT, *The Encyclopaedia of the Paranormal*, 1990

There are few persons, even among the calmest thinkers, who have not occasionally been startled into a vague yet thrilling half-credence in the supernatural, by *coincidences* of so seemingly marvellous a character that, as *mere* coincidences, the intellect has been unable to receive them. Such sentiments—for the half-credences of which I speak have never the full force of *thought*—such sentiments are seldom thoroughly stifled unless by reference to the doctrine of chance, or, as it is technically termed, the Calculus of Probabilities. Now this Calculus is, in its essence, purely mathematical; and thus we have the anomaly of the most rigidly exact in science applied to the shadow and spirituality of the most intangible in speculation.

It will be understood that I speak of coincidences and *no more*. What I have said above upon this topic must suffice. In my own heart there dwells no faith in preter-nature. That Nature and its God are two, no man who thinks will deny. That the latter, creating the former, can, at will, control or modify it, is also unquestionable. I say 'at will'; for the question is of will, and not, as the insanity of logic has assumed, of power. It is not that the Deity *cannot* modify his laws, but that we insult him in imagining a possible necessity for modification. In their origin these laws were fashioned to embrace all contingencies which *could* lie in the Future. With God all is *Now*.

POE, from 'The Mystery of Marie Roget', 1842

Suddenly I was conscious that my father was in the room, but not alone: there were two persons with him. Strange! I had heard no footstep, I had not seen the door open; but I saw my father, and at his right hand our neighbour Mrs Filmore, whom I remembered very well, though I had not seen her for five years. She was a commonplace middle-aged woman, in silk and cashmere; but the lady on the left of my father was no more than twenty, a tall, slim, willowy figure, with luxuriant blond hair, arranged in cunning braids and folds that looked almost too massive for the slight figure and the small-featured, thin-lipped face they crowned. But the face had not a girlish expression: the features were sharp, the pale grey eyes at once acute, restless, and sarcastic . . .

'Well, Latimer, you thought me long,' my father said . . .

But while the last word was in my ears, the whole group vanished, and there was nothing between me and the Chinese painted folding-screen that stood before the door. I was cold and trembling; I could only totter forward and throw myself on the sofa. This strange new power had manifested itself again . . . But *was* it a power? Might it not rather be a disease—a sort of intermittent delirium, concentrating my energy of brain into moments of unhealthy activity, and leaving my saner hours all the more barren? I felt a dizzy sense of unreality in what my eye rested on; I grasped the bell convulsively, like one trying to free himself from nightmare, and rang it twice. Pierre came with a look of alarm in his face.

'Monsieur ne se trouve pas bien?' he said, anxiously.

'I'm tired of waiting, Pierre,' I said, as distinctly and emphatically as I could, like a man determined to be sober in spite of wine; 'I'm afraid something has happened to my father—he's usually so punctual. Run to the Hôtel des Bergues and see if he is there.'

Pierre left the room at once, with a soothing 'Bien, Monsieur'; and I felt the better for this scene of simple, waking prose. Seeking to calm myself still further, I went into my bedroom, adjoining the salon, and opened a case of eau-de-Cologne; took out a bottle; went through the process of taking out the cork very neatly, and then rubbed the reviving spirit over my hands and forehead, and under my nostrils, drawing a new delight from the scent because I had procured it by slow details of labour, and by no strange sudden madness. Already I had begun to taste something of the horror that belongs to the lot of a human being whose nature is not adjusted to simple human conditions.

Still enjoying the scent, I returned to the salon, but it was not unoccupied, as it had been before I left it. In front of the Chinese folding-screen there was my father, with Mrs Filmore on his right hand, and on his left—the slim blond-haired girl, with the keen face and the keen eyes fixed on me in half-smiling curiosity.

'Well, Latimer, you thought me long,' my father said . . .

I heard no more, felt no more, till I became conscious that I was lying with my head low on the sofa, Pierre and my father by my side.

Shortly after this last occurrence—I think the very next day—I began to be aware of a phase in my abnormal sensibility, to which, from the languid and slight nature of my intercourse with others since my illness, I had not been alive before. This was the obtrusion on my mind of the mental process going forward in first one person, and then another, with whom I happened to be in contact: the vagrant, frivolous ideas and emotions of some uninteresting acquaintance—Mrs Filmore, for example—would force themselves on my consciousness like an importunate, ill-played musical instrument, or the loud activity of an imprisoned insect. But this unpleasant sensibility was fitful, and left me moments of rest, when the souls of my companions were once more shut out from me, and I felt a relief such as silence brings to wearied nerves. I might have believed this importunate insight to be merely a diseased activity of the imagination, but that my prevision of incalculable words and actions proved it to have a fixed relation to the mental process in other minds. But this superadded consciousness, wearying and annoying enough when it urged on me the trivial experience of indifferent people, became an intense pain and grief when it seemed to be opening to me the souls of those who were in a close relation to me—when the rational talk, the graceful attentions, the wittily-turned phrases, and the kindly deeds, which used to make the web of their characters, were seen as if thrust asunder by a microscopic vision, that showed all the intermediate frivolities, all the suppressed egoism, all the struggling chaos of puerilities, meanness, vague capricious memories, and indolent makeshift thoughts, from which human words and deeds emerge like leaflets covering a fermenting heap.

GEORGE ELIOT, *The Lifted Veil*, written 1859

On October 3rd, 1863, I sailed from Liverpool to New York, on the steamer *City of Limerick*, of the Inman line, Captain Jones commanding. On the evening of the second day out, soon after leaving Kinsale Head, a severe storm began, which lasted for nine days. During this time we saw neither sun nor stars nor any vessel; the bulwarks on the weather bow were carried away, one of the anchors broke loose from its lashings, and several stout storm sails were carried away, and the booms broken.

Upon the night following the eighth day of the storm the tempest moderated a little, and for the first time since leaving port I enjoyed refreshing sleep. Toward morning I dreamed that I saw my wife, whom I had left in the United States, come to the door of my stateroom, clad in her nightdress. At the door she seemed to discover that I was not the only occupant of the room, hesitated a little, then advanced to my side, stooped down and kissed me, and after gently caressing me for a few moments, quietly withdrew.

Upon waking I was surprised to see my fellow passenger, whose berth was above mine, but not directly over it—owing to the fact that our room was at the stern of the vessel—leaning upon his elbow, and looking fixedly at me. 'You're a pretty fellow,' said he at length, 'to have a lady come and visit you in this way.' I pressed him for an explanation, which he at first declined to give, but at length related what he had seen while wide awake, lying in his berth. It exactly corresponded with my dream.

This gentleman's name was William J. Tait, and he had been my room-mate in the passage out, in the preceding July, on the Cunard steamer *Olympus*; a native of England . . . He was at this time perhaps fifty years of age—by no means in the habit of practical joking, but a sedate and very religious man, whose testimony upon any subject could be taken unhesitatingly . . .

The day after landing I went by rail to Watertown, Conn., where my children and my wife had been for some time, visiting her parents. Almost her first question, when we were alone together, was, 'Did you receive a visit from me a week ago Tuesday?' 'A visit from you?' said I, 'We were more than a thousand miles at sea.' 'I know it,' she replied, 'but it seemed to me that I visited you.' 'It would be impossible,' said I, 'Tell me what makes you think so.'

My wife then told me that on account of the severity of the weather and the reported loss of the *Africa*, which sailed for Boston on the same day that we left Liverpool for New York, and had gone ashore at Cape Race, she had been extremely anxious about me. On the night previous, the same night when, as mentioned above, the storm had just begun to abate, she had lain awake for a long time thinking of me, and about four o'clock in the morning it seemed to her that she went out to seek me. Crossing the wide and stormy sea, she came at length to a low, black steamship, whose side she went up, and then descending into the cabin, passed through it to the stern until she came to my stateroom. 'Tell me,' said she, 'do they ever have staterooms like the one I saw, where the upper berth extends further back than the under one? A man was in the upper berth, looking right at me, and for a moment I was afraid to go in, but soon I went up to the side of your berth, bent down and kissed you, and embraced you, and then went away.'

The description given by my wife of the steamship was correct in all particulars, though she had never seen it.

> S. R. WILMOT, from *Proceedings* of the Society for Psychical Research, Vol. 7, 1891–2. The account was confirmed by Wilmot's sister, who was with him on the voyage; his fellow passenger, Mr Tait, had asked her whether she was the lady who came to the stateroom, and when she expressed astonishment, 'he said he saw *some* woman, in white, who went up to my brother'

The protocol indicates first the name of the agent; then the subject which [Gilbert] Murray was to guess as it was written down; then Murray's words on being called back to the drawing-room:

COUNTESS OF CARLISLE (agent): 'The Crimean soldiers after their return receiving their medals from Queen Victoria at the Horse Guards.'

PROFESSOR MURRAY: 'Is it the King giving VCs and things to people? Yes, I think it's an investiture of some sort.'

COUNTESS OF CARLISLE: 'Thinking of the *Lusitania*.'

PROFESSOR MURRAY: 'I have got this violently. I have got an awful impression of naval disaster. I should think it was the torpedoing of the *Lusitania*.'

MURRAY'S DAUGHTER, ROSALIND: 'I think of dancing with the Head of the Dutch Foreign Office at a *café chantant* at The Hague.'

PROFESSOR MURRAY: 'A faint impression of your journey abroad. I should say something official; sort of official soirée or dancing or something. Feel as if it was in Holland.'

Sometimes the experiments classified as failures are as revealing as the successes:

MARGARET DAVIS: 'Medici Chapel and tombs; sudden chill; absolute stillness. Marble figures who seem to have been there all night.'

PROFESSOR MURRAY: 'I wonder if this is right. I have got a feeling of a scene in my *Nefrekepta*, where the man goes in, passage after passage, to an inner chamber where Nefrekepta is lying dead with the shadows of his wife and child sitting beside him. But I think it's Indian.'

Murray comments: 'My poem was translated from an Egyptian story; I suppose I felt the subject was not Egyptian.'

Earlier in his address [to the Society for Psychical Research, 1952] he wrote:

Of course, the personal impression of the percipient himself is by no means conclusive evidence, but I do feel there is one almost universal quality in these guesses of mine which does suit telepathy and does not suit any other explanation. They always begin with a vague emotional quality or atmosphere . . . Even in the failures this feeling of atmosphere often gets through. That is, it was not so much an act of cognition, or a piece of information, that was transferred to me, but rather a feeling or an emotion; and it is notable that I never had any success in guessing mere cards or numbers, or any subject that was not in some way interesting or amusing.

> KOESTLER, *The Roots of Coincidence*. Gilbert Murray and a circle of friends played 'thought-transference' over many years as a kind of parlour game: he went to another part of the house, while the others remained in the drawing-room, where they chose subjects and wrote them down; then he returned and his 'guesses' were written down

During the first three weeks of solitary confinement [in Seville], before I was allowed books from the prison library, my only intellectual nourishment had been the remembrance of books read in the past. In the course of these memory exercises, a certain passage from *Buddenbrooks* came back to me and gave me great spiritual comfort—so much so, that at times when I felt particularly dejected, I would have recourse to that scene as if it were a pain-soothing pill. The content of the passage, as I remembered it, was this. Consul Thomas Buddenbrook, though only in his late forties, knows that he is about to die. He was never given to religious or metaphysical speculation, but now he falls under the spell of a book which for years has stood unread in his library, and in which he finds explained that death is nothing final, merely a transition to another, impersonal form of existence in the All-One. '. . . He felt that his whole being had been unaccountably expanded and . . . there clung to his senses a profound intoxication, a strange, sweet, vague allurement . . . He was no longer prevented from grasping eternity . . .' The book to which Consul Buddenbrook owes his revelation is Schopenhauer's essay *On Death, and its Relation to the Indestructibility of our Essential Selves.*

The day after I was set free, I wrote Thomas Mann a letter (I knew that he lived in Zurich-Küsnacht), in which I explained to him what I have just explained, and thanked him for the spiritual comfort that I had derived from his work. The title of Schopenhauer's essay was expressly mentioned in my letter, which was dated from the Rock Hotel, Gibraltar, May 16 or 17, 1937.

Thomas Mann's answer reached me a few days later in London. It was a handwritten letter which I lost, together with all my files, on my flight from France in 1940. I cannot, of course, remember its actual text, only its content which, for the sake of simplicity, I shall paraphrase in direct speech:

Dear Sir,
  Your letter arrived on May . . . On the afternoon of that day I was sitting in my garden in Küsnacht. I had read Schopenhauer's essay in 1897 or 98, while I was writing *Buddenbrooks*, and had never read it again as I did not want to weaken its original strong impact on me. On that afternoon, however, I felt a sudden impulse to re-read the essay after nearly forty years. I went indoors to my library to fetch the volume. At that moment the postman rang and brought me your letter . . .

                                        KOESTLER, *The Invisible Writing*, 1954

. . . Stirring letter from the journalist Koestler writing from Gibraltar. Sentenced to death and only saved at the last moment, he claims he was able to endure the ordeal with the help of my writings, specially the Schopenhauer chapter in *Buddenbrooks*. When his letter arrived I was reading that very chapter in Schopenhauer, 'Concerning Death', which I had not looked at for thirty-five years. Life's strange games. 'In the past I would not have believed that art could have so strong an influence on life.' Nor would I have, in the past.

                    MANN, *Diaries 1918–1939*, entry dated 22 May 1937; tr. Richard and Clara
                    Winston

From CIA agents stationed behind the Iron Curtain came reports that the Russians were able to influence telepathically the behaviour of people, alter their emotions or health, and even kill at long distance by using only psychic powers.

A US Defense Intelligence Agency report stated, 'Other Soviet tests included inducing the subject with anxiety associated with suffocation and the sensation of a dizzying blow to the head. Some Western followers of psychic phenomena research are concerned, for example, with the detrimental effects of subliminal perception techniques being targeted against the US or Allied personnel in nuclear missile sites. The subliminal message could be carried by television signals or by telepathic means.' There were other fears that our national leaders might be targeted for telepathic mind control.

In 1973, for instance, the CIA carried out tests of 'astral projection', or 'out-of-the-body experiences', with two noted US psychics, Ingo Swann and Pat Price. The experiments, conducted by physicists Harold E. Puthoff and Russell Targ at the Stanford Research Institute in California, produced amazing results. In controlled tests, the psychics projected their minds over long distances, apparently accurately describing supersecret military installations and even the contents of confidential files in these bases. During one experiment, Price described in minute detail a Soviet installation hidden in the Ural Mountains. CIA agents in Russia confirmed his description. The two psychics 'spied' on China and once again 'ground truth' agents—CIA contacts in the People's Republic—were able to confirm their accuracy. United States government officers were astounded. When he saw the results of the tests, a security officer exclaimed, 'Hell, there's no security left!'

HENRY GRIS and WILLIAM DICK, *The New Soviet Psychic Discoveries*, 1978

All this she told with some confusion and
    Dismay, the usual consequence of dreams
Of the unpleasant kind, with none at hand
    To expound their vain and visionary gleams.
I've known some odd ones which seem'd really plann'd
    Prophetically, or that which one deems
A 'strange coincidence', to use a phrase
By which such things are settled now-a-days.

BYRON, *Don Juan*, 1819–24

Sex and the Supernatural

Since the supernatural is continually intersecting with the natural, it is no cause for surprise that sex should rear its head in these surroundings as well.

As Chaucer insinuates and Reginald Scot alleges, incubi and succubi could furnish a serviceable alibi in time of need. At the opposite end of the spectrum, King James, having swallowed one camel, strains at another: the notion that there could possibly be offspring of the intercourse between humans and evil spirits is nothing but an old wives' tale. (Hoffmann's elemental spirits, on the contrary, are usefully fertile.) Any such appearance, the authors of the *Malleus Maleficarum* assert, after a side-swipe at female vanity (here too a woman's hair is the devil's snare), and with their habitual air of authority and judiciousness, is due solely to wind in the belly. This diagnosis they would have seen confirmed early in the nineteenth century by Joanna Southcott, who mistakenly believed herself to be the woman in Revelation 'clothed with the sun, and the moon under her feet', and pregnant with the second Messiah.

The story told by Sprenger and Krämer of the young man of Ratisbon and the 'astute' woman demonstrates how fanatics, when they enjoy power, are never afraid of provoking irreverent titters. Prurience is plainly in evidence in Burton's weird reference to the 'Japanese' idol, as is voyeuristic lip-smacking in the excerpt from *The Monk*. But we are in no position to wax self-righteous on that score.

When it comes to the conjugation of ghosts, the Chinese order matters more poetically, although Edith Nesbit's is a touching tale, and Buzzati's, if less innocent, a satisfying one, while Apollinaire's time-travel machine holds out the prospect of loving above one's station.

Philomathes. . . . I would knowe in two thinges your opinion herein: First if suche a thing can be: and next if it be: whether there be a difference of sexes amongst these spirites or not.

Epistemon. That abhominable kinde of the Devils abusing of men or women, was called of old, *Incubi* and *Succubi*, according to the difference of the sexes that they conversed with. By two meanes this great kinde of abuse might possibly be performed: The one, when the Devill onelie as a spirite, and stealing out the sperme of a dead bodie, abuses them that way, they not graithlie seeing anie shape or feeling anie thing, but that which he so convayes in that part: As we reade of a Monasterie of Nunnes which were burnt for their being that way abused. The other meane is when he borrowes a dead bodie and so visiblie, and as it seemes unto them naturallie as a man converses with them. But it is to be noted, that in whatsoever way he useth it, that sperme seemes intollerably cold to the person abused. For if he steale out the nature of a quick person, it cannot be so quicklie carryed, but it will both tine [lose] the strength and heate by the way, which it could never have had for lacke of agitation, which in the time of procreation is the procurer & wakener up of these two natural qualities. And if he occupying the dead bodie as his lodging expell the same out thereof in the dewe time, it must likewise be colde by the participation with the qualities of the dead bodie whereout of it comes . . .

Philomathes. How is it then that they say sundrie monsters have bene gotten by that way.

Epistemon. These tales are nothing but *Aniles fabulae* [old wives' tales]. For that they have no nature of their owne, I have shewed you alreadie . . . Indeede, it is possible to the craft of the Devill to make a womans bellie to swel after he hath that way abused her, which he may do, either by steiring up her own humor, or by herbes, as we see beggars daily doe. And when the time of her delivery should come to make her thole great doloures, like unto that naturall course, and then subtillie to slippe in the Mid-wives handes, stockes, stones, or some monstrous barne brought from some other place, but this is more reported and gessed at by others, nor beleeved by me.

Philomathes. But what is the cause that this kinde of abuse is thought to be most common in such wild partes of the worlde, as *Lap-land*, and *Fin-land*, or in our North Iles of *Orknay* and *Schet-land*.

Epistemon. Because where the Devill findes greatest ignorance and barbaritie, there assayles he grosseliest, as I gave you the reason wherefore there was moe Witches of women kinde nor men.

> JAMES I, *Daemonologie*. The author concludes his preface thus: 'And so wishing my pains in this Treatise (beloved Reader) to be effectuall, in arming al them that reades the same, against these above mentioned erroures . . . I bid thee hartely fare-well'

William of Paris notes also that Incubi seem chiefly to molest women and girls with beautiful hair; either because they devote themselves too much to the care and adornment of their hair, or because they are wont to try to excite men by means of their hair, or because they are boastfully vain about it, or because God in His goodness permits this so that women may be afraid to entice men by the very means by which the devils wish them to entice men.

At times also women think they have been made pregnant by an Incubus, and their bellies grow to an enormous size; but when the time of parturition comes, their swelling is relieved by no more than the expulsion of a great quantity of wind. For by taking ants' eggs in drink, or the seeds of spurge or of the black pine, an incredible amount of wind and flatulence is generated in the human stomach. And it is very easy for the devil to cause these and even greater disorders in the stomach. This has been set down in order that too easy credence should not be given to women, but only to those whom experience has shown to be trustworthy, and to those who, by sleeping in their beds or near by them, know for a fact that such things as we have spoken of are true.

Sprenger and Krämer, Malleus Maleficarum

There were giants in the earth in those days; and also after that, when the sons of God came in unto the daughters of men, and they bare children to them, the same became mighty men which were of old, men of renown.

Genesis 6

Though many be against it, yet I, for my part, will subscribe to Lactantius, *lib*. 14, *cap*. 15, 'God sent angels to the tuition of men; but whilst they lived amongst us, that mischievous all-commander of the earth, and hot in lust, enticed them by little and little to this vice, and defiled them with the company of women'; and to Anaxagoras, *de Resurrect*., 'Many of those spiritual bodies, overcome by the love of maids, and lust, failed, of whom those were born we call giants.' . . . At Japan in the East Indies, at this present (if we may believe the relation of travellers) there is an idol called Teuchedy, to whom one of the fairest virgins in the country is monthly brought, and left in a private room, in the *fotoqui*, or church, where she sits alone to be deflowered. At certain times the Teuchedy (which is thought to be the devil) appears to her, and knoweth her carnally. Every month a fair virgin is taken in; but what becomes of the old, no man can tell.

Burton, The Anatomy of Melancholy

The *Concubitus* of the Devils with Witches (Males and Females) hath so full Testimonies, as is not to be denied . . . Near *Witeberg*, a Merchant's Wife, that pass'd for an honest Woman, was used to admit one peculiar Concubine: And once, her Husband being from home, her Lover came to her in the Night; and having pleased his Lust, in the Morning he arose, and sate on the top of the Door, in the shape of a Magpye, and said to her this Farewell: *Hitherto this hath been thy Sweetheart*, and vanished with the Words.

RICHARD BAXTER, *The Certainty of the Worlds of Spirits*, 1691

The injury to reputation is shown in the history of the Blessed Jerome, that the devil transformed himself into the appearance of S. Silvanus, Bishop of Nazareth, a friend of S. Jerome. And this devil approached a noble woman by night in her bed and began first to provoke and entice her with lewd words, and then invited her to perform the sinful act. And when she called out, the devil in the form of the saintly Bishop hid under the woman's bed, and being sought for and found there, he in lickerish language declared lyingly that he was the Bishop Sylvanus. On the morrow therefore, when the devil had disappeared, the holy man was scandalously defamed; but his good name was cleared when the devil confessed at the tomb of S. Jerome that he had done this in an assumed body.

SPRENGER and KRÄMER, *Malleus Maleficarum*

Of bishop Sylvanus his lecherie opened and covered againe . . . You shall read in the legend, how in the night time *Incubus* came to a ladies bed side, and made hot loove unto hir: whereat she being offended, cried out so lowd, that companie came and found him under hir bed in the likenesse of the holie bishop *Sylvanus*, which holie man was much defamed therebie, untill at the length this infamie was purged by the confession of a divell made at *S. Jeroms* toombe. Oh excellent peece of witchcraft or cousening wrought by *Sylvanus*!

SCOT, *The Discoverie of Witchcraft*

In th'olde dayes of the Kyng Arthour,
Of which that Britons speken greet honour,
Al was this land fulfild of fayerye.
The elf-queene, with hir joly compaignye,

Daunced ful ofte in many a grene mede;
This was the olde opinion, as I rede,
I speke of manye hundred yeres ago;
But now kan no man se none elves mo.
For now the grete charitee and prayeres
Of lymytours and othere holy freres,   *friars licensed to beg*
That serchen every lond and every streem,   *within certain limits*
As thikke as motes in the sonne-beem,
Blessynge halles, chambres, kichenes, boures,   *bed-chambers*
Citees, burghes, castels, hye toures,
Thropes, bernes, shipnes, dayeryes,   *thorps, barns, stables,*
This maketh that ther been no fayeryes.   *dairies*
For ther as wont to walken was an elf,
Ther walketh now the lymytour hymself
In undermeles and in morwenynges,   *afternoons; mornings*
And seyth his matyns and his holy thynges
As he gooth in his lymytacioun.
Wommen may go saufly up and doun
In every bussh or under every tree;
Ther is noon oother incubus but he . . .

GEOFFREY CHAUCER, from 'The Tale of the Wyf of Bathe', *The Canterbury Tales*, *c*.1387–1400

Of *Merlin* and his skill what Region doth not heare?
The world shall still be full of *Merlin* everie where.
A thousand lingering yeeres his prophecies have runne,
And scarcely shall have end till Time it selfe be done:
Who of a *British nymph* was gotten, whilst she plaid
With a seducing Spirit, which wonne the goodlie maid;
(As all *Demetia* through, there was not found her peere)
Who, be'ing so much renown'd for beautie farre and neere,
Great Lords her liking sought, and still in vaine they prov'd:
That Spirit (to her unknowne) this Virgin onelie lov'd;
Which taking humane shape, of such perfection seemd,
As (all her Suters scorn'd) shee onelie him esteem'd.
Who, fayning for her sake that he was come from farre,
And richlie could endow (a lustie Batcheler)

On her that Prophet got, which from his Mothers wombe
Of things to come fore-told untill the generall Doome.

MICHAEL DRAYTON, *Poly-Olbion*, 1612

Philostratus, in his fourth book *de vita Apollonii*, hath a memorable instance
in this kind, which I may not omit, of one Menippus Lycius, a young man
twenty-five years of age, that going between Cenchreas and Corinth, met such
a phantasm in the habit of a fair gentlewoman, which, taking him by the hand,
carried him home to her house in the suburbs of Corinth, and told him she was
a Phoenician by birth, and if he would tarry with her, 'he should hear her sing
and play, and drink such wine as never any drank, and no man should molest
him; but she being fair and lovely would live and die with him, that was fair
and lovely to behold.' The young man, a philosopher, otherwise staid and
discreet, able to moderate his passions, though not this of love, tarried with her
awhile to his great content, and at last married her, to whose wedding, amongst
other guests, came Apollonius [of Tyana], who, by some probable conjectures,
found her out to be a serpent, a lamia, and that all her furniture was like
Tantalus' gold described by Homer, no substance, but mere illusions. When
she saw herself descried, she wept, and desired Apollonius to be silent, but he
would not be moved, and thereupon she, plate, house, and all that was in it,
vanished in an instant: 'many thousands took notice of this fact, for it was done
in the midst of Greece.'

One more I will relate out of Florilegus, *ad annum* 1058, an honest historian of
our nation, because he telleth it so confidently, as a thing in those days talked
of all over Europe. A young gentleman of Rome, the same day that he was
married, after dinner with the bride and his friends went a-walking into the
fields, and towards evening to the tennis-court to recreate himself; whilst he
played, he put his ring upon the finger of Venus' statua, which was thereby,
made in brass; after he had sufficiently played, and now made an end of his
sport, he came to fetch his ring, but Venus had bowed her finger in, and he
could not get it off; whereupon, loath to make his company tarry, at the
present there left it, intending to fetch it the next day or at some more
convenient time, went thence to supper, and so to bed. In the night, when he
should come to perform those nuptial rites, Venus steps between him and his
wife (unseen or felt of her), and told her that she was his wife, that he had
betrothed himself unto her by that ring which he put upon her finger: she

troubled him for some following nights. He, not knowing how to help himself, made his moan to one Palumbus, a learned magician in those days, who gave him a letter, and bid him at such a time of the night, in such a cross-way, at the town's end, where old Saturn would pass by with his associates in procession, as commonly he did, deliver that script with his own hands to Saturn himself; the young man, of a bold spirit, accordingly did it; and when the old fiend had read it, he called Venus to him, who rode before him, and commanded her to deliver his ring, which forthwith she did, and so the gentleman was freed.

BURTON, *The Anatomy of Melancholy*

I went down into the garden and soon found myself in front of an admirable statue.

It was indeed a Venus, and one of extraordinary beauty. The upper part of her body was bare, just as the ancients usually depicted their great deities; her right hand, raised to the level of her breast, was turned palm inwards, the thumb and two first fingers extended, while the other two were slightly curved. The other hand was near the hips, and held up the drapery which covered the lower part of the body . . .

As for the face, I should never be able to express its strange character . . . It was not at all the calm and austere beauty of the Greek sculptors, whose rule was to give a majestic immobility to every feature. Here, on the contrary, I noticed with astonishment that the artist had deliberately set out to express ill-nature raised to the level of wickedness. Every feature was slightly contracted: the eyes were rather slanted, the mouth turned up at the corners, and the nostrils somewhat distended. Disdain, irony, cruelty, could be distinguished in that face which was, notwithstanding, of incredible beauty.

Contrary to general expectation, Monsieur Alphonse missed the first ball; true, it grazed the ground, hit with astonishing force by one of the players from Aragon, who seemed to be the leader of the Spaniards . . .

Monsieur Alphonse threw his racquet on the ground in a rage.

'It's this damned ring,' he exclaimed, 'which is too tight on my finger and made me miss a sure thing.'

With some difficulty he took off his diamond ring, and I went over to him to take it, but he forestalled me, ran to the Venus, slipped the ring on her third finger, and resumed his position at the head of his fellow villagers.

He was pale, but calm and determined. From then on he made no more mistakes, and the Spaniards were soundly beaten . . .

Monsieur Alphonse drew me aside into the recess of a window, and, turning his eyes away, said to me:

'You will laugh at me . . . but I don't know what is the matter with me . . . I am bewitched, dammit!' . . .

His voice was broken, and I thought he was quite drunk.

'You know my ring?' he continued, after a pause.

'Yes. Has it been taken?'

'No.'

'In that case you have it?'

'No—I—I could not get it off the finger of that confounded Venus.'

'Nonsense! You didn't pull hard enough.'

'Yes, I did . . . But the Venus . . . has clenched her finger.'

He looked at me fixedly with a haggard expression, leaning against the window-latch to keep himself from falling.

'What a ridiculous tale!' I said. 'You pushed the ring too far. Tomorrow you must use pincers, only be careful not to injure the statue.'

'No, I tell you. The Venus's finger has contracted and bent up; she has closed her hand, do you hear? . . . She's my wife, apparently, because I gave her my ring . . . She won't give it back.'

I dressed rapidly and went into the corridor. Cries and wails were coming from the opposite end, and one piercing cry sounded above all the others: 'My son! My son!' Obviously some accident had happened to Monsieur Alphonse. I ran to the bridal-chamber; it was full of people. The first sight which met my eyes was the young man, half dressed, stretched across the bed, the wood of which was broken . . . On a couch at the other end of the room, the bride was in the grip of terrible convulsions. She was uttering inarticulate cries, and two strapping servants were having the greatest difficulty in holding her down.

'Good God!' I exclaimed. 'What has happened?'

I went to the bedside and raised the body of the unfortunate young man; he was already cold and stiff. His clenched teeth and blackened face denoted the most frightful pain. It was obvious that his death had been violent and his agony terrible. There was, however, no trace of blood on his clothes. I opened his shirt and found a livid mark on his breast which extended down his sides and over his back. It was as if he had been crushed in a band of iron. My foot stepped on something hard which was lying on the rug; I bent down and saw the diamond ring.

'Have you learnt anything from Madame Alphonse?' I asked the magistrate, when my statement had been taken down and signed.

'That unfortunate young lady has gone mad,' he said, with a sad smile. 'Mad, completely mad. This is what she told me: She had been in bed, she said, for a few minutes with the curtains drawn, when the bedroom door opened and someone came in. Madame Alphonse was lying on the inside of the bed, with her face turned to the wall. She did not stir, convinced that it was her husband. A moment later the bed creaked as though it were burdened with an enormous weight. She was terribly frightened, but did not dare to turn round. Five minutes, or perhaps ten—she could not tell how long—passed. Then she made an involuntary movement, or else the other person in the bed made one, and she felt the touch of something as cold as ice—those are her very words. She pressed herself to the wall, trembling in every limb. Shortly after, the door opened again, and someone entered, who said: "Good evening, my little wife", and a little later the curtains were drawn. She heard a stifled cry. The person who was in bed beside her sat up, and seemed to stretch out both arms in front. Then she turned her head . . . and saw, so she says, her husband on his knees by the bed, with his head on a level with the pillow, in the arms of a sort of greenish giant who was embracing him with all its might. She said—and she repeated it to me over and over again, poor woman!—she said that she recognized . . . can you guess? The bronze Venus . . . Since it was found here, everybody has been dreaming about it. But to go on with the story of the poor mad girl, she lost consciousness at this sight, and probably she had lost her reason a little earlier. She cannot say how long she remained in a faint. When she came to, she saw the phantom again—or the statue, as she persists in calling it—motionless, its legs and the lower half of its body on the bed, the bust and arms stretched out before it, and in its arms her lifeless husband. A cock crew, and then the statue got out of the bed, dropped the dead body, and went out. Madame Alphonse tugged at the bell, and you know the rest.'

PROSPER MÉRIMÉE, from 'The Venus of Ille', 1837; tr. Jean Kimber

I will, said Friar John, show thee a way, and teach thee an expedient, by means whereof thy wife shall never make thee a cuckold without thy knowledge and thine own consent . . . Take Hans Carvel's ring upon thy finger, who was the King of Melinda's chief jeweller. Besides that this Hans Carvel had the reputation of being very skilful and expert in the lapidary's profession, he was a studious, learned, and ingenious man, a scientific person, full of knowledge, a great philosopher, of sound judgement . . . and of a jovial humour, a boon companion, and a merry blade, if ever there was any in the world. He was somewhat gorbellied, had a little shake in his head, and was in effect unwieldy of his body. In his old age he took to wife the bailiff of Concordat's daughter, young, fair, jolly, gallant, spruce, frisk, brisk, neat, feat, smirk, smug, compt, quaint, gay, fine, trixy, trim, decent, proper, graceful, handsome, beautiful, comely, and kind—a little too much—to her neighbours and acquaintance.

Hereupon it fell out, after the expiring of a scantling of weeks, that Master Carvel became as jealous as a tiger, and entered into a very profound suspicion that his new-married gixy did keep a buttock-stirring with others. To prevent which inconveniency, he did tell her many tragical stories of the total ruin of several kingdoms by adultery; did read unto her the legend of chaste wives; then made some lectures to her in the praise of the choice virtue of pudicity, and did present her with a book in commendation of conjugal fidelity, wherein the wickedness of all licentious women was odiously detested; and withal he gave her a chain enriched with pure oriental sapphires. Notwithstanding all this, he found her always more and more inclined to the reception of her neighbour copes-mates, so that day by day his jealousy increased. In sequel whereof, one night as he was lying by her, whilst in his sleep the rambling fancies of the lecherous deportments of his wife did take up the cellules of his brain, he dreamt that he encountered with the devil, to whom he had discovered to the full the buzzing of his head, and suspicion that his wife did tread her shoe awry. The devil, he thought, in this perplexity, did for his comfort give him a ring, and therewithal did kindly put it on his middle finger, saying, Hans Carvel, I give thee this ring—whilst thou carriest it upon that finger, thy wife shall never carnally be known by any other than thyself, without thy special knowledge and consent. Grammercy, quoth Hans Carvel, my Lord Devil, I renounce Mahomet, if ever it shall come off my finger. The devil vanished, as is his custom, and then Hans Carvel, full of joy awaking, found that his middle finger was as far as it could reach within the what-do-you-call-it of his wife. I did forget to tell thee, how his wife, as soon as she had felt the finger there, said, in recoiling her buttocks, Off, yes, nay, tut, pish, tush, aye, lord, that is not the thing which should be put up in that place. With this Hans Carvel thought that some pilfering fellow was about to take the ring from him. Is not this an infallible and sovereign antidote?

FRANÇOIS RABELAIS, *Pantagruel*, 1532; tr. Sir Thomas Urquhart

The Spectre, fiercely staring, thus reply'd:
  'Know, *Theodore*, thy Ancestry I claim,
And *Guido Cavalcanti* was my Name.
One common Sire our Fathers did beget,
My Name and Story some remember yet:

Thee, then a Boy, within my Arms I laid,
When for my Sins I lov'd this haughty Maid . . .
What did I not her stubborn Heart to gain?
But all my Vows were answer'd with Disdain;
She scorn'd my Sorrows, and despis'd my Pain.
Long time I dragg'd my Days in fruitless Care,
Then loathing Life, and plung'd in deep Despair,
To finish my unhappy Life, I fell
On this sharp Sword, and now am damn'd in Hell.
   Short was her Joy; for soon th'insulting Maid
By Heav'n's Decree in the cold Grave was laid,
And as in unrepenting Sin she dy'd,
Doom'd to the same bad Place, is punish'd for her Pride;
Because she deem'd I well deserv'd to die,
And made a Merit of her Cruelty.
There, then, we met; both try'd, and both were cast,
And this irrevocable Sentence pass'd;
That she whom I so long pursu'd in vain,
Should suffer from my Hands a ling'ring Pain:
Renew'd to Life, that she might daily die,
I daily doom'd to follow, she to fly;
No more a Lover but a mortal Foe,
I seek her Life (for Love is none below):
As often as my Dogs with better speed
Arrest her Flight, is she to Death decreed:
Then with this fatal Sword on which I dy'd,
I pierce her open'd Back or tender Side,
And tear that harden'd Heart from out her Breast,
Which, with her Entrails, makes my hungry Hounds a Feast.
Nor lies she long, but as her Fates ordain,
Springs up to Life, and fresh to second Pain,
Is sav'd Today, Tomorrow to be slain.'
   This, vers'd in Death, th'infernal Knight relates,
And then for Proof fulfill'd their common Fates;
Her Heart and Bowels through her Back he drew,
And fed the Hounds that help'd him to pursue.
Stern look'd the Fiend, as frustrate of his Will,
Not half suffic'd, and greedy yet to kill.
And now the Soul expiring through the Wound,
Had left the Body breathless on the Ground,

When thus the grisly Spectre spoke again:
  'Behold the Fruit of ill-rewarded Pain:
As many Months as I sustain'd her Hate,
So many Years is she condemn'd by Fate
To daily Death; and ev'ry several Place,
Conscious of her Disdain, and my Disgrace,
Must witness her just Punishment; and be
A Scene of Triumph and Revenge to me.
As in this Grove I took my last Farewel,
As on this very spot of Earth I fell,
As *Friday* saw me die, so she my Prey
Becomes ev'n here, on this revolving Day.'
  Thus while he spoke, the Virgin from the Ground
Upstarted fresh, already clos'd the Wound,
And unconcern'd for all she felt before,
Precipitates her Flight along the Shore:
The Hell-hounds, as ungorg'd with Flesh and Blood
Pursue their Prey, and seek their wonted Food:
The Fiend remounts his Courser, mends his Pace,
And all the Vision vanish'd from the Place.

      DRYDEN, from 'Theodore and Honoria', 1700; from a tale of Boccaccio

    'O what can ail thee, knight-at-arms,
      Alone and palely loitering?
    The sedge is wither'd from the lake,
      And no birds sing.

    O what can ail thee, knight-at-arms,
      So haggard and so woe-begone?
    The squirrel's granary is full,
      And the harvest's done.

    I see a lily on thy brow
      With anguish moist and fever dew;
    And on thy cheek a fading rose
      Fast withereth too.'

    'I met a lady in the meads,
      Full beautiful—a faery's child,
    Her hair was long, her foot was light,
      And her eyes were wild.

I made a garland for her head,
    And bracelets too, and fragrant zone;
She look'd at me as she did love,
    And made sweet moan.

I set her on my pacing steed
    And nothing else saw all day long,
For sideways would she lean, and sing
    A faery's song.

She found me roots of relish sweet,
    And honey wild and manna dew,
And sure in language strange she said,
    "I love thee true."

She took me to her elfin grot,
    And there she wept and sigh'd full sore,
And there I shut her wild wild eyes
    With kisses four.

And there she lullèd me asleep,
    And there I dream'd—Ah! woe betide!
The latest dream I ever dream'd
    On the cold hill side.

I saw pale kings and princes too,
    Pale warriors, death-pale were they all;
Who cried—"La belle Dame sans Merci
    Hath thee in thrall!"

I saw their starv'd lips in the gloom
    With horrid warning gapèd wide,
And I awoke and found me here
    On the cold hill side.

And this is why I sojourn here
    Alone and palely loitering,
Though the sedge is wither'd from the lake,
    And no birds sing.'

                              KEATS, 'La Belle Dame sans Merci', 1820

In this grave age, when comedies are few,
We crave your patronage for one that's new...

If cruel men are still averse to spare
These scenes, they fly for refuge to the fair.
Though with a ghost our comedy be heighten'd,
Ladies, upon our word, you shan't be frighten'd;
O, 'tis a ghost that scorns to be uncivil,
A well-spread, lusty, jointure-hunting devil;
An am'rous ghost, that's faithful, fond, and true,
Made up of flesh and blood—as much as you.
Then ev'ry evening come in flocks, undaunted,
We never think this house is too much haunted.

JOSEPH ADDISON, from the Prologue, *The Drummer, or the Haunted House*, 1715;
see pp. 54–5

The celebrated ascetic philosopher, Shri Sankarācharya, challenged a rival philosopher, Mandana, to a disputation, it being agreed that the loser should become his opponent's disciple and adopt his way of life. If Sankara won, Mandana would have to renounce his wife and home and become a mendicant, while if Mandana won, Sankara would have to doff the orange robe and marry.

Sankara was about to claim victory when Mandana's wife, Bharati, reminded him that according to the sacred books husband and wife were one, and hence he had defeated only half of his opponent. Sankara admitted the doctrinal justice of this, and proceeded to engage Bharati in argument.

Knowing her limits, and guessing Sankara's, Bharati turned the controversy to questions concerning the art of sensual love, a science embraced by the Indian scriptures. Sankara pointed out that, as a lifelong celibate, he knew nothing about such matters, but reckoned that in a month's time he could acquire the necessary knowledge to pursue the subject. Bharati acquiesced, and the debate was adjourned.

It so happened that a rajah named Amaruka died at that time. Sankara therefore left his own body in the care of his disciples and translated his 'subtle self' into the body of the prince, who thus apparently revived while on the way to the funeral pyre.

Amaruka's wives and concubines were overjoyed to discover that the elderly prince, who had previously neglected them, was now a new man. And the palace councillors observed that their lord's intelligence had improved amazingly. It struck them that some powerful spirit had taken over Amaruka's body, and in order to keep it there, they would need to find the spirit's abandoned body and burn it.

Sankara was so engrossed in his new life and studies that he had quite forgotten his ascetic past. Hearing of the search for his body, his disciples rushed to the palace and sang a religious song composed by their guru. Whereupon Sankara remembered himself and swiftly re-entered his body, by this time discovered and already placed on a pyre.

The disputation was resumed, and Sankara astonished Bharati by his intimate knowledge of the subject in question. She was forced to admit defeat.

Indian legend, drawn from Alexandra David-Neel: *With Mystics and Magicians in Tibet*

The *baloma* [main form of a dead man's spirit] leaves the body immediately after death has occurred, and goes to Tuma [small island some ten miles northwest of the Trobriands] . . . The spirit enters the village in which he will dwell henceforth. He always finds some of his relatives, and these may stay with him till a house is found or built for him. The natives imagine this exactly as happens in this world when a man has to move to another village—a by no means rare event in the Trobriands. For a time the stranger is very sad, and weeps. There are, however, decided attempts on the part of the other *baloma*, especially those of the opposite sex, to make him comfortable in his new existence, and to induce him to form new ties and attachments and forget the old ones. My informants (who were all men) were unanimous in declaring that a man coming to Tuma is simply pestered by the advances of the fair, and, in this world, bashful, sex. At first the spirit wants to weep for those left behind; his relative *baloma* protect him, saying, 'Wait, let him have a spell; let him cry.' If he has been happily married, and has left a widow for whom he cares, he naturally wants to be left for a somewhat longer time to his grief. All in vain! It seems (this is again the male opinion only) that there are many more women in the other world than men, and that they are very impatient of any prolonged mourning. If they cannot succeed otherwise, they try magic, the all-powerful means of gaining another person's affection. The spirit women on Tuma are not less expert than the living women in Kiriwina. The stranger's grief is very soon overcome, and he accepts the offering called *nabuoda'u*—a basket filled with *bu'a* (betel nut), *mo'i* (betel pepper), and scented herbs. This is offered to him with the words '*Kam paku*', and if accepted, the two belong to each other. A man may wait for his widow to join him in Tuma, but my informants did not seem inclined to think that many would do this.

BRONISLAW MALINOWSKI, from 'Baloma: The Spirits of the Dead in the Trobriand Islands', *Journal* of the Royal Anthropological Institute of Great Britain and Ireland, Vol. XLVI, 1916

Tellus. Dipsas, whom as many honour for age as wonder at for cunning, listen in a few words to my tale, and answere in one word to the purpose, for that neither my burning desire can afforde long speech, nor the short time I have to stay manie delayes. Is it possible by hearbes, stones, spels, incantation, enchauntment, exorcismes, fire, mettals, plannets, or any practise, to plant affection where it is not, and to supplant it where it is?

Dipsas. Faire Ladie, you may imagin that these horie haires are not void of experience, nor the great name that goeth of my cunning to bee without cause. I can darken the Sunne by my skil, and remove the Moone out of her course; I can restore youth to the aged, and make hills without bottoms; there is nothing that I can not doe, but that onely which you would have me doe; and therein I differ from the Gods, that I am not able to rule harts; for were it in my power to place affection by appointment, I would make such evill appetites, such inordinate lusts, such cursed desires, as all the worlde should be filled both with supersticious hates, and extreame love . . . This I can,—breede slacknes in love, though never roote it out.

JOHN LYLY, Endimion, 1591; Dipsas: 'an old Enchantress'

Few people in love are patient. If you desire a person passionately, you can, if you can summon up enough intensity of concentration, bring that person to you in a state of sexual hunger. It would, however, be wise to think at least twice about using this spell . . . There are two versions, one for a woman to attract a man, and one for a man to attract a woman. First, the woman's spell:

> This I lay upon you:
> when we meet
> put your mouth to my mouth,
> and, furthermore,
> this I lay upon you:
> when we meet
> put your breast to my breasts,
> and, furthermore,
> this I lay upon you:
> when we meet
> offer your swelling manhood
> up to me.

The second version runs:

> This I lay upon you:
> when we meet
> put your mouth to my mouth,
> and, furthermore,

> this I lay upon you:
> when we meet
> put your breasts to my breast,
> and, furthermore,
> this I lay upon you:
> when we meet
> open your thighs
> and call me into you.
>
> SKELTON, *The Practice of Witchcraft Today*

Enter the churchyard at midnight, carrying a *twca*, which is a sort of knife made out of an old razor, with a handle of sheep or goat-horn, and encircle the church edifice seven times, holding the *twca* at arm's length, and saying, 'Dyma'r twca, p'le mae'r wain?' (Here's the *twca*—where's the sheath?).

> WILLIAM WIRT SIKES, *British Goblins: Welsh Folk-Lore, Fairy Mythology, Legends and Traditions*, 1880. A mode of divination: the man will marry the first woman he meets thereafter

'Oh! cease, Matilda! . . . I will not follow you to the Sepulchre, or accept the services of your infernal Agents. Antonia shall be mine, but mine by human means.'

'Then yours she never will be! You are banished her presence; her mother has opened her eyes to your designs, and she is now upon her guard against them. Nay more, she loves another. A Youth of distinguished merit possesses her heart, and unless you interfere, a few days will make her his Bride. This intelligence was brought me by my invisible Servants, to whom I had recourse on first perceiving your indifference . . . Though you shunned my presence, all your proceedings were known to me: nay, I was constantly with you in some degree, thanks to this precious gift!'

With these words she drew from beneath her habit a mirror of polished steel, the borders of which were marked with various strange and unknown characters.

'Amidst all my sorrows, amidst all my regrets for your coldness, I was sustained from despair by the virtues of this Talisman. On pronouncing certain words the Person appears in it, on whom the Observer's thoughts are bent: thus though *I* was exiled from *your* sight, you, Ambrosio, were ever present to mine.'

The Friar's curiosity was excited strongly.

'What you relate is incredible! Matilda, are you not amusing yourself with my credulity?'

'Be your own eyes the Judge.'

She put the mirror into his hand. Curiosity induced him to take it, and Love, to wish that Antonia might appear. Matilda pronounced the magic words. Immediately, a thick smoke rose from the characters traced upon the borders, and spread itself over the surface. It dispersed again gradually. A confused mixture of colours and images presented themselves to the Friar's eyes, which at length arranging themselves in their proper places, he beheld in miniature Antonia's lovely form.

The scene was a small closet belonging to her apartment. She was undressing to bathe herself. The long tresses of her hair were already bound up. The amorous Monk had full opportunity to observe the voluptuous contours and admirable symmetry of her person. She threw off her last garment, and advancing to the Bath prepared for her, she put her foot into the water. It struck cold, and she drew it back again. Though unconscious of being observed, an in-bred sense of modesty induced her to veil her charms; and she stood hesitating upon the brink, in the attitude of the Venus de Medicis. At this moment a tame Linnet flew towards her, nestled its head between her breasts, and nibbled them in wanton play. The smiling Antonia strove in vain to shake off the Bird, and at length raised her hands to drive it from its delightful harbour. Ambrosio could bear no more: his desires were worked up to phrenzy.

'I yield!' he cried, dashing the mirror upon the ground: 'Matilda, I follow you! Do with me what you will!'

M. G. LEWIS, The Monk, 1796; see pp. 395–6, 535

In the town of Ratisbon a certain young man who had an intrigue with a girl, wishing to leave her, lost his member; that is to say, some glamour was cast over it so that he could see or touch nothing but his smooth body. In his worry over this he went to a tavern to drink wine; and after he had sat there for a while he got into conversation with another woman who was there, and told her the cause of his sadness, explaining everything, and demonstrating in his body that it was so. The woman was astute, and asked whether he suspected anyone; and when he named such a one, unfolding the whole matter, she said: 'If persuasion is not enough, you must use some violence, to induce her to restore to you your health.' So in the evening the young man watched the way by which the witch was in the habit of going, and finding her, prayed her to restore to him the health of his body. And when she maintained that she was innocent and knew nothing about it, he fell upon her, and winding a towel tightly round her neck, choked her, saying: 'Unless you give me back my health, you shall die at my hands.' Then she, being unable to cry out, and with her face already swelling and growing black, said: 'Let me go, and I will heal you.' The young man then relaxed the pressure of the towel, and the witch touched him with her hand between the thighs, saying: 'Now you have what you desire.' And the young man, as he afterwards said, plainly felt, before he had verified it by looking or touching, that his member had been restored to him by the mere touch of the witch.

SPRENGER and KRÄMER, *Malleus Maleficarum*

Helen Fraser, of the same [Aberdeen] 'coven', was a most dangerous witch. She had the power to make men transfer their affections, no matter how good and wholesome the wife deserted:—and she never spared her power. By her charms she caused Andrew Tullideff to leave off loving his lawful wife and take to Margaret Neilson instead: so that 'he could never be reconceillit with his wife, or remove his affection frae the said harlot'; and she made Robert Merchant fall away from the duty owing to his wife, Christian White, and transfer himself and his love to a certain widow, Isobel Bruce, for whom he once went to sow corn, and fell so madly in love that he could never quit the house or the widow's side again; 'whilk thing the country supposed to be brought about by the unlawful travelling of the said Helen'; and was further *testified by Robert himself*, says Chambers significantly. Helen Fraser was therefore burnt; and it is to be hoped that the men returned to their lawful mates.

LYNN LINTON, *Witch Stories*. Robert Chambers's *Domestic Annals of Scotland*, referred to here, was published 1859–61

A fair witch crept to a young man's side,
And he kiss'd her and took her for his bride.

But a Shape came in at the dead of night,
And fill'd the room with snowy light.

And he saw how in his arms there lay
A thing more frightful than mouth may say.

And he rose in haste, and follow'd the Shape
Till morning crown'd an eastern cape.

And he girded himself, and follow'd still
When sunset sainted the western hill.

But, mocking and thwarting, clung to his side,
Weary day!—the foul Witch-Bride.

WILLIAM ALLINGHAM, 'The Witch-Bride', 1850

When by thy scorn, O murd'ress, I am dead,
    And that thou thinkst thee free
From all solicitatiòn from me,
Then shall my ghost come to thy bed,
And thee, feign'd vestal, in worse arms shall see;
Then thy sick taper will begin to wink,
And he, whose thou art then, being tir'd before,
Will, if thou stir, or pinch to wake him, think
    Thou call'st for more,
And in false sleep will from thee shrink;
And then, poor aspen wretch, neglected thou
Bath'd in a cold quicksilver sweat wilt lie,
    A verier ghost than I:
What I will say, I will not tell thee now,
Lest that preserve thee; and since my love is spent,
I had rather thou shouldst painfully repent,
Than by my threat'nings rest still innocent.

JOHN DONNE (1572–1631), 'The Apparition'

My window, framed in pear-tree bloom,
    White-curtained shone, and softly lighted:
So, by the pear-tree, to my room
    Your ghost last night climbed uninvited.

Your solid self, long leagues away,
    Deep in dull books, had hardly missed me;
And yet you found this Romeo's way,
    And through the blossom climbed and kissed me.

I watched the still and dewy lawn,
  The pear-tree boughs hung white above you;
I listened to you till the dawn,
  And half forgot I did not love you.

Oh, dear! what pretty things you said,
  What pearls of song you threaded for me!
I did not—till your ghost had fled—
  Remember how you always bore me!

E. NESBIT, 'Villeggiatura', 1895

I also felt invisible presences in another aunt's house in Norfolk—melancholy frightening presences—but again, not until I was grown-up did I learn that to her they were not invisible, but she often saw them and took them in her stride. Years later I was told—too late to check it with her—that soon after her marriage she was lunching the other side of the county and saw a portrait of a man in seventeenth-century clothes.

'Why,' she exclaimed, surprised into an indiscretion, 'that's the man who is always trying to stop me going upstairs at home.'

'That,' said her host, 'was Oliver Cromwell as a young man. As it happens when he was young he was involved in an unfortunate love affair with a girl who lived in your house.'

ROSALIND HEYWOOD, *The Infinite Hive*, 1964

And at the very core of the deep night the ghost came to me, at the heart of the ocean of oblivion, which is also the heart of life. Beyond hearing, or even knowledge of contact, I met her and knew her. How I know it I don't know. Yet I know it with eyeless, wingless knowledge.

For man in the body is formed through countless ages, and at the centre is the speck, or spark, upon which all his formation has taken place. It is even not himself, deep beyond his many depths. Deep from him calls to deep. And according as deep answers deep, man glistens and surpasses himself.

Beyond all the pearly mufflings of consciousness, of age upon age of consciousness, deep calls yet to deep, and sometimes is answered . . . And sometimes the other deep is a woman, as it was with me, when my ghost came.

Women were not unknown to me. But never before had woman come, in the depths of night, to answer my deep with her deep. As the ghost came, came as a ghost of silence, still in the depth of sleep.

I know she came. I know she came even as a woman, to my man. But the knowledge is darkly naked as the event. I only know, it was so. In the deep of sleep a call was called from the deeps of me, and answered in the deeps, by a woman among women. Breasts or thighs or face, I remember not a touch, no, nor a movement of my own. It is all complete in the profundity of darkness. Yet I know it was so.

I awoke towards dawn, from far, far away. I was vaguely conscious of drawing nearer and nearer, as the sun must have been drawing towards the horizon, from the complete beyond. Till at last the faint pallor of mental consciousness coloured my waking.

And then I was aware of a pervading scent, as of plum-blossom, and a sense of extraordinary silkiness—though where, and in what contact, I could not say. It was as the first blemish of dawn.

And even with so slight a conscious registering, *it* seemed to disappear. Like a whale that has sounded to the bottomless seas. That knowledge of *it*, which was the mating of the ghost and me, disappeared from me, in its rich weight of certainty, as the scent of the plum-blossom moved down the lanes of my consciousness, and my limbs stirred in a silkiness for which I have no comparison.

As I became aware, I also became uncertain. I wanted to be certain of *it*, to have definite evidence. And as I sought for evidence, *it* disappeared, my perfect knowledge was gone. I no longer knew in full . . .

I shall never know. I shall never know if it was a ghost, some sweet spirit from the innermost of the ever-deepening cosmos; or a woman, a very woman, as the silkiness of my limbs seems to attest; or a dream, a hallucination!

LAWRENCE, from 'Glad Ghosts', 1926

The lad came to the door at night,
    When lovers crown their vows,
And whistled soft and out of sight
    In shadow of the boughs.

'I shall not vex you with my face
    Henceforth, my love, for aye;
So take me in your arms a space
    Before the east is grey.

'When I from hence away am past
    I shall not find a bride,

And you shall be the first and last
    I ever lay beside.'

She heard and went and knew not why;
    Her heart to his she laid;
Light was the air beneath the sky
    But dark under the shade.

'Oh do you breathe, lad, that your breast
    Seems not to rise and fall,
And here upon my bosom prest
    There beats no heart at all?'

'Oh loud, my girl, it once would knock,
    You should have felt it then;
But since for you I stopped the clock
    It never goes again.'

'Oh lad, what is it, lad, that drips
    Wet from your neck on mine?
What is it falling on my lips,
    My lad, that tastes of brine?'

'Oh like enough 'tis blood, my dear,
    For when the knife has slit
The throat across from ear to ear
    'Twill bleed because of it.'

Under the stars the air was light,
    But dark below the boughs,
The still air of the speechless night,
    When lovers crown their vows.

        A. E. HOUSMAN, 'The True Lover', 1896

The wind doth blow today, my love,
    And a few small drops of rain;
I never had but one true-love,
    In cold grave she was lain.

I'll do as much for my true-love
    As any young man may:

I'll sit and mourn all at her grave
  For a twelvemonth and a day.

The twelvemonth and a day being up
  The dead began to speak:
Oh who sits weeping on my grave
  And will not let me sleep?—

'Tis I, my love, sits on your grave
  And will not let you sleep;
For I crave one kiss of your clay-cold lips
  And that is all I seek.—

You crave one kiss of my clay-cold lips,
  But my breath smells earthy strong;
If you have one kiss of my clay-cold lips
  Your time will not be long.

'Tis down in yon garden green,
  Love, where we used to walk,
The finest flower that ere was seen
  Is withered to a stalk.

The stalk is withered dry, my love,
  So will our hearts decay;
So make yourself content, my love,
  Till God calls you away.

                              ANON., 'The Unquiet Grave'

'Learn, my charming child, blessed as you are with absence of knowledge, that the depths of the earth, and the air, water, and fire are filled with spiritual beings of higher and yet of more restricted nature than mankind. It seems unnecessary, my little unwise one, to explain to you the peculiar nature and characteristics of the gnomes, the salamanders, sylphs and undines; you would not be able to understand them. To give you some slight idea of the danger which you may be undergoing, it is sufficient that I should tell you that these spirits are always striving eagerly to enter into unions with human beings; and as they are well aware that human beings are strongly adverse to those unions, they employ all manner of subtle and crafty artifices to delude those they have fixed their affections upon. Often it is a twig, a flower, a glass of water, a fire-steel, or something else, in appearance of no importance, which they employ as a means of carrying out their intent. It is true that unions of this sort often turn out exceedingly happy, as in the case of two priests, mentioned by Prince della Mirandola, who spent forty years of the happiest possible wedlock with a spirit of this description. It is true, moreover, that the most renowned sages have been the offspring of such unions between human beings and elementary spirits. Thus, the great Zoroaster was a son of the salamander Oromasis; the great Apollonius, the sage Merlin, the valiant Count of Cleve, and the great cabbalist, Ben-Syra, were the glorious fruits of marriages of this description, and according to Paracelsus the beautiful Melusina was no other than a sylph. But yet the peril of such a union is much too great, for not only do the elemental spirits require of those on whom they confer their favours that the clearest light of the profoundest wisdom shall have arisen and shall shine upon them, but besides this they are extraordinarily touchy and sensitive, and re-venge offences with extreme severity. Thus, it once happened that a sylph who was in union with a philosopher, on an occasion when he was talking with friends about a pretty woman—and perhaps rather too warmly—suddenly allowed her white beautifully formed leg to become visible in the air, as if to convince the friends of her beauty, and then killed the poor philosopher on the spot. But ah! why should I refer to others? Why don't I speak of myself? I am aware that for the last twelve years I have been beloved by a sylph, but she is timorous and coy, and I am tortured by the thought of the danger of fettering her to me more closely by cabbalistic processes, inasmuch as I am still much too dependent on earthly necessities, and consequently lack the necessary degree of wisdom. Every morning I make up my mind to fast, and I succeed in letting breakfast pass without touching any food; but when midday comes, oh! Anna, my daughter Anna, you know well that I cannot stop eating.'

These latter words Herr Dapsul uttered almost in a howl, while bitter tears rolled down his lean chop-fallen cheeks. He then went on more calmly:

'But I take the greatest of pains to behave towards the elemental spirit who is thus favourably disposed towards me with the utmost refinement of manners, the most exquisite *galanterie*. I never venture to smoke a pipe of tobacco without employing the proper cabbalistic precautions, for I cannot tell whether or not my tender air-spirit may like the brand of the tobacco, and so be annoyed at the defilement of her element. For this reason those who smoke Hunter's mix or Flower of Saxony can never become wise or win the love of a sylph. And I take the same precautions when I cut a hazel twig, pluck a flower, eat a fruit, or strike fire, all my efforts being directed to avoid giving offence to any elementary spirit.'

E. T. A. HOFFMANN, from 'The King's Betrothed', 1821; tr. Major Alexander Ewing

Fu-ch'ai, King of the land of Wu, had a little daughter who was called Purple Jade. She was eighteen years old and of perfect beauty. At her father's court there dwelt also a youth by the name of Han Chung, who was a year older than she was and who for his profession had learned the Taoist doctrines. Now the girl fell in love with him, and before long secret love letters were passing to and fro and finally she promised the youth that she would be his wife.

But one day Chung had to prepare for his departure, for he wanted to go to the east to complete his education in the lands of Ch'i and Lu. So he sent a messenger to the girl's parents and asked for their daughter's hand in marriage. The King was merely irritated and rejected the request. But when the youth departed alone, Purple Jade's heart broke for love. Her corpse was carried out in front of the palace and buried with all due pomp. Three years passed before Han Chung returned home to the land of Wu and asked the King and Queen about their daughter. They answered: 'Because we were so terribly angry, and did not comply with your wishes, she died from the pangs of love. Her body is already buried.'

When the youth heard this, the tears burst from his eyes and pain gnawed at his vitals. He bought a sacrificial animal and bales of silk and went out to the grave, to offer them to the dead person. When he arrived at that place Purple Jade's soul rose up out of the vault and became visible to the young man. With tears in her eyes, she approached him and sobbed: 'After you left me that time, I realized that I was going to have to renounce my life's dearest wish, for I loved you, a mere retainer of my royal parents, and I could not imagine that fate would ever bring us together again after this separation. What else could I do but die?' . . .

She broke out again in loud weeping and asked Chung to accompany her back into her funeral vault. But the young man hesitated and said: 'Life and death go separate ways. I am afraid to heap up yet more guilt upon myself, and so I dare not meet your wishes.' But Purple Jade replied: 'I know only too well that life and death go separate ways. But if we part at this hour we shall never in all eternity meet again. Are you perhaps afraid that I am some evil spirit and want to do you harm? Truly, I want only the best for you. How can you fail to trust me?'

Chung was touched by her words and followed her back into the funeral vault. Purple Jade gave him wine to drink and pleaded with him to stay with her three days and three nights. In this time they celebrated their nuptials in exact accordance with ritual custom. As the hour of their separation drew near, she gave him as a farewell present a gleaming pearl an inch across and said: 'My name is forgotten among the living, my wishes were not fulfilled—what else can I say to you? Think of me from time to time with love. And if you should go again sometime to my father's palace, continue to honour him as a great king.'

When Chung left the tomb he went at once to the King and informed him in person of what he had experienced with Purple Jade. However, the King did not believe his words and shouted in the greatest fury: 'My little daughter is dead, and now you come along with some lying tale, to smear her departed spirit with filth! You have nothing else in your head but breaking open graves and looting valuables and then inventing ghost stories as an excuse.'

And he had him arrested on the spot by the guards.

Chung, however, managed to escape from the prison. He rushed to Purple Jade's tomb and told her what had happened. Then she said: 'Do not worry. I will myself go to my royal father and tell him the truth.'

And indeed some days later, just as the King was busy dressing, Purple Jade's spirit appeared before him. Terrified and shocked, his feelings alternated between joy and uneasiness.

'For what reason have you wakened to life again?' he asked.

Thereupon the girl bent her knee and said: 'Once, my royal father, a young and learned man came to you and begged you passionately for your daughter's hand. After I had left this world he returned from afar. At my tomb, where he offered up a sacrifice and prayed, we met again, because our love had been pure unto death. It was there I gave him the pearl as a present. He never broke open my grave. I should not like you to stain your royal office with murder.'

In an adjoining room the women heard the conversation. But when they hurried out and tried to seize the apparition, it faded away as light as smoke.

CHAO YEH (attrib.), from 'Princess Purple Jade', *c*.40; tr. Christopher Levenson

Dialogue between a female fox spirit and a female ghost over a young man's sick-bed

Lien-hsiang: I have heard that the female ghost selfishly hastens a man's death, so that, after his decease, she may the more readily cohabit with him. Is this true?

Li: Not so! There is no pleasure when two ghosts conjugate. If indeed there were pleasure, there is certainly no lack of young male ghosts in the nether world.

Lien-hsiang: The silly girl! If a man indulged in love with a woman night after night, he would soon be enfeebled; how much more so with a ghost!

Li: But equally an amorous fox can be the cause of a man's death. What art is it that you alone possess in being capable of preserving his health?

Lien-hsiang: You are thinking of creatures that sap the vitality of men to invigorate their own constitution. I am not one of those. For there *are* foxes that do no harm to the men with whom they come into contact, but there are *no* ghosts that do no harm to the men with whom they unite, on account of their spectral coldness.

P'U SUNG-LING (1640–1715), from 'Lien-hsiang'; tr. H. C. Chang

A ghost, that loved a lady fair,
Ever in the starry air
  Of midnight at her pillow stood;
And, with a sweetness skies above
The luring words of human love,
  Her soul the phantom wooed.
Sweet and sweet is their poisoned note,
The little snakes of silver throat,
In mossy skulls that nest and lie,
Ever singing 'die, oh! die'.

Young soul, put off your flesh, and come
With me into the quiet tomb,
  Our bed is lovely, dark, and sweet;
The earth will swing us, as she goes,
Beneath our coverlid of snows,
  And the warm leaden sheet.
Dear and dear is their poisoned note,
The little snakes of silver throat,
In mossy skulls that nest and lie,
Ever singing 'die, oh! die'.

THOMAS LOVELL BEDDOES (1803–49), 'The Phantom-Wooer'

Amid all this pressure and confusion I could not fail to see Frederica once more. Those were painful days, the memory of which has not remained with me. When I reached her my hand from my horse, the tears stood in her eyes, and I felt very uneasy. I now rode along the footpath towards Drusenheim, and here one of the most singular forebodings took possession of me. I saw, not with the eyes of the body, but with those of the mind, my own figure coming towards me, on horseback, and on the same road, attired in a dress which I had never worn;—it was pike-grey (*hecht-grau*) with somewhat of gold. As soon as I shook myself out of this dream, the figure had entirely disappeared. It is strange, however, that eight years afterwards, I found myself on the very road, to pay one more visit to Frederica, in the dress of which I had dreamed, and which I wore, not from choice, but by accident. However it may be with matters of this kind generally, this strange illusion in some measure calmed me at the moment of parting . . . I found myself on a peaceful and quiet journey, pretty well recovered.

GOETHE, Poetry and Truth

All the house was still; for I believe all, except St John and myself, were now retired to rest. The one candle was dying out; the room was full of moonlight. My heart beat fast and thick: I heard its throb. Suddenly it stood still to an inexpressible feeling that thrilled it through, and passed at once to my head and extremities. The feeling was not like an electric shock: but it was quite as sharp, as strange, as startling: it acted on my senses as if their utmost activity hitherto had been but torpor, from which they were now summoned, and forced to wake. They rose expectant: eye and ear waited, while the flesh quivered on my bones.

'What have you heard? What do you see?' asked St John. I saw nothing: but I heard a voice somewhere cry:—

'Jane! Jane! Jane!' nothing more.

'O God! what is it?' I gasped.

I might have said, 'Where is it?' for it did not seem in the room—nor in the house—nor in the garden: it did not come out of the air—nor from under the earth—nor from overhead. I had heard it—where, or whence, for ever impossible to know! And it was the voice of a human being—a known, loved, well-remembered voice—that of Edward Fairfax Rochester; and it spoke in pain and woe, wildly, eerily, urgently.

'I am coming!' I cried. 'Wait for me! Oh, I will come!' I flew to the door, and looked into the passage: it was dark. I ran out into the garden: it was void.

'Where are you?' I exclaimed.

The hills beyond Marsh Glen sent the answer faintly back—'Where are you?' I listened. The wind sighed low in the firs: all was moorland loneliness and midnight hush.

'Down, superstition!' I commented, as that spectre rose up black by the black yew at the gate. 'This is not thy deception, nor thy witchcraft: it is the work of Nature. She was roused, and did—no miracle—but her best.'

CHARLOTTE BRONTË, Jane Eyre, 1847

'You know I was wild after she died; and eternally, from dawn to dawn, praying her to return to me her spirit! I have a strong faith in ghosts: I have a conviction that they can, and do, exist among us! The day she was buried there came a fall of snow. In the evening I went to the churchyard. It blew as bleak as winter—all round was solitary. I didn't fear that her fool of a husband would wander up the den so late; and no one else had business to bring them there. Being alone, and conscious two yards of loose earth was the sole barrier between us, I said to myself—"I'll have her in my arms again! If she be cold, I'll think it is this north wind that chills *me*; and if she be motionless, it is sleep." I got a spade from the tool-house, and began to delve with all my might—it scraped the coffin; I fell to work with my hands; the wood commenced cracking about the screws; I was on the point of attaining my object, when it seemed that I heard a sigh from some one above, close at the edge of the grave, and bending down. "If I can only get this off," I muttered, "I wish they may shovel in the earth over us both!" and I wrenched at it more desperately still. There was another sigh, close at my ear. I appeared to feel the warm breath of it displacing the sleet-laden wind. I knew no living thing in flesh and blood was by; but, as certainly as you perceive the approach to some substantial body in the dark, though it cannot be discerned, so certainly I felt that Cathy was there: not under me, but on the earth. A sudden sense of relief flowed from my heart through every limb. I relinquished my labour of agony, and turned consoled at once: unspeakably consoled. Her presence was with me: it remained while I refilled the grave, and led me home. You may laugh, if you will; but I was sure I should see her there . . . I looked round impatiently—I felt her by me—I could *almost* see her, and yet I *could not*! I ought to have sweat blood then, from the anguish of my yearning—from the fervour of my supplications to have but one glimpse! I had not one. She showed herself, as she often was in life, a devil to me! And, since then, sometimes more and sometimes less, I've been the sport of that intolerable torture! . . . It was a strange way of killing, not by inches, but by fractions and hair-breadths, to beguile me with the spectre of a hope, through eighteen years!'

We buried him, to the scandal of the whole neighbourhood, as he wished . . . The six men departed when they had let the coffin down into the grave: we stayed to see it covered . . . at present it is as smooth and verdant as its companion moulds—and I hope its tenant sleeps as soundly. But the country folk, if you ask them, would swear on the Bible that he *walks*: there are those who speak to having met him near the church, and on the moor, and even in this house. Idle tales, you'll say, and so say I. Yet that old man by the kitchen fire affirms he has seen two on 'em, looking out of his chamber window, on every rainy night since his death: and an odd thing happened to me about a month ago. I was going to the Grange one evening—a dark evening, threatening thunder—and, just at the turn of the Heights, I encountered a little boy with a sheep and two lambs before him; he was crying terribly; and I supposed the lambs were skittish, and would not be guided.

'What's the matter, my little man?' I asked.

'There's Heathcliff and a woman, yonder, under t' nab,' he blubbered, 'un I darnut pass 'em.'

I saw nothing; but neither the sheep nor he would go on; so I bid him take the road lower down.

EMILY BRONTË, *Wuthering Heights*, 1847

'No, my dear,' my Uncle Abraham answered me, 'no—nothing romantic ever happened to me—unless—but no, that wasn't romantic either—'

I was. To me, I being eighteen, romance was the world. My Uncle Abraham was old and lame. I followed the gaze of his faded eyes, and my own rested on a miniature that hung at his elbow-chair's right hand, a portrait of a woman, whose loveliness even the miniature-painter's art had been powerless to disguise—a woman with large eyes that shone, and face of that alluring oval which one hardly sees nowadays.

I rose to look at it. I had looked at it a hundred times. Often enough in my baby days I had asked, 'Who's that, uncle?' and always the answer was the same: 'A lady who died long ago, my dear.'

As I looked again at the picture, I asked, 'Was she like this?'

'Who?'

'Your—your romance!'

Uncle Abraham looked hard at me. 'Yes,' he said at last. 'Very—very like.'

I sat down on the floor by him. 'Won't you tell me about her?'

'There's nothing to tell,' he said. 'I think it was fancy mostly, and folly; but it's the realest thing in my life, my dear.'

A long pause. I kept silent. You should always give people time, especially old people.

'I remember,' he said in the dreamy tone always promising so well to the ear that loves a story—'I remember, when I was a young man, I was very lonely indeed. I never had a sweetheart. I was always lame, my dear, from quite a boy; and the girls used to laugh at me.'

Silence again. Presently he went on—

'And so I got into the way of mooning off by myself in lonely places, and one of my favourite walks was up through our churchyard, which was set on a hill in the middle of the marsh country. I liked that because I never met anyone there. It's all over, years ago. I was a silly lad; but I couldn't bear of a summer evening to hear a rustle and a whisper from the other side of the hedge, or maybe a kiss, as I went by.

Well, I used to go and sit all by myself in the churchyard, which was always sweet with the thyme and quite light (on account of its being so high) long after the marshes were dark. I used to watch the bats flitting about in the red light, and wonder why God didn't make everyone's legs straight and strong, and wicked follies like that. But by the time the light was gone I had always worked it off, so to speak, and could go home quietly, and say my prayers without bitterness.

Well, one hot night in August, when I had watched the sunset fade and the crescent moon grow golden, I was just stepping over the low stone wall of the churchyard when I heard a rustle behind me. I turned round, expecting it to be a rabbit or a bird. It was a woman.'

He looked at the portrait. So did I.

'Yes,' he said, 'that was her very face. I was a bit scared and said something— I don't know what—she laughed and said, did I think she was a ghost? and I answered back; and I stayed talking to her over the graveyard wall till 'twas quite dark, and the glow-worms were out in the wet grass all along the way home.

Next night, I saw her again; and the next, and the next. Always at twilight-time; and if I passed any lovers leaning on the stiles in the marshes it was nothing to me now.'

Again my uncle paused. 'It was very long ago,' he said shyly, 'and I'm an old man; but I know what youth means, and happiness, though I was always lame, and the girls used to laugh at me. I don't know how long it went on—you don't measure time in dreams—but at last your grandfather said I looked as if I had one foot in the grave, and he would be sending me to stay with our kin at Bath, and take the waters. I had to go. I could not tell my father why I would rather die than go.'

'What was her name, Uncle?' I asked.

'She never would tell me her name, and why should she? I had names enough in my heart to call her by. Marriage? My dear, even then I knew marriage was not for me. But I met her night after night, always in our churchyard where the yew-trees were, and the old crooked gravestones so thick in the grass. It was there we always met and always parted. The last time was the night before I went away. She was very sad, and dearer than life itself.

And she said, "If you come back before the new moon, I shall meet you here just as usual. But if the new moon shines on this grave and you are not here— you will never see me again any more."

She laid her hand on the tomb against which we had been leaning. It was an old, lichened, weather-worn stone, and its inscription was just "SUSANNAH KINGSNORTH, *Ob.* 1723".

"I shall be here," I said.

"I mean it," she said, very seriously and slowly, "it is no fancy. You will be here when the new moon shines?"

I promised, and after a while we parted.

I had been with my kinsfolk at Bath for nearly a month. I was to go home on the next day when, turning over a case in the parlour, I came upon that miniature. I could not speak for a minute. At last I said, with dry tongue, and heart beating to the tune of heaven and hell: "Who is this?"

"That?" said my aunt. "Oh! She was betrothed to one of our family years ago, but she died before the wedding. They say she was a bit of a witch. A handsome one, wasn't she?"

I looked again at the face, the lips, the eyes of my dear lovely love, whom I was to meet tomorrow night when the new moon shone on that tomb in our churchyard.

"Did you say she was dead?" I asked, and I hardly knew my own voice.

"Years and years ago! Her name's on the back, and the date—"

I took the portrait out from its case—I remember just the colour of its faded, red-velvet bed, and read on the back—"Susannah Kingsnorth, *Ob.* 1723".... That was in 1823.' My uncle stopped short.

'What happened?' I asked breathlessly.

'I believe I had a fit,' my uncle answered slowly; 'at any rate, I was very ill.'

'And you missed the new moon on the grave?'

'I missed the new moon on the grave.'

'And you never saw her again?'

'I never saw her again—'

'But, Uncle, do you really believe? Can the dead—was she—did you—'

My uncle took out his pipe and filled it.

'It's a long time ago,' he said, 'a many, many years. Old man's tales, my dear! Old man's tales. Don't you take any notice of them.'

He lighted the pipe, and puffed silently a moment or two before he said: 'But I know what youth means, and love and happiness, though I was always lame, and the girls used to laugh at me.'

E. NESBIT, 'Uncle Abraham's Romance', 1893

... I will relate an instance taken from psychoanalytical experience; if it does not rest upon mere coincidence, it furnishes a beautiful confirmation of our theory of the uncanny. It often happens that male patients declare that they feel there is something uncanny about the female genital organs. This *unheimlich* [uncanny] place, however, is the entrance to the former *heim* [home] of all human beings, to the place where everyone dwelt once upon a time and in the beginning. There is a humorous saying: 'Love is home-sickness'; and whenever a man dreams of a place or a country and says to himself, still in the dream, 'this place is familiar to me, I have been there before', we may interpret the place as being his mother's genitals or her body. In this case, too, the *unheimlich* is what was once *heimisch*, home-like, familiar; the prefix 'un' is the token of repression.

Sigmund Freud, from 'The "Uncanny" ', 1919; tr. Alix Strachey

May 10th 1908

This telepathic state of affairs (marriage, which has also been a fact) began before our engagement, when Harriet [Bosse], in a manner which I cannot explain, sought me at night. I was awakened, even as I slept, and experienced the illusion that she lay beside me, that I held her in my arms and possessed her and had possessed her before I proposed. But then I did not think of it (when I proposed that is). Since then it has manifested itself every time we have been parted. Distance does not exist for us. She has sought me from Paris and Vienna, and we have come together as man and wife. It can never cease!

Drank wine in the evening; it gave me courage and the life I am living seemed to me unworthy. I determined to break out of it, even felt that I was on the way to freeing myself. Fell asleep! Slept until 3.30 when she woke me though she did not receive me until about 5, and then briefly and ardently. After that she would not have me. Beforehand she had played with me and kissed me too, submissively, in the way she did just once before, but not quite the same.

May 11th

NB! Harriet and I got engaged on March 5th, 1901; but before that time I had possessed her at *night*, telepathically, from January 13th, 9 times in all; Jan. 13th and 26th, Feb. 12th, 18th, 20th, 21st, 22nd, 25th, and 27th. During that time she came to visit me in the daytime, looking just as innocent as before and behaving as if nothing had happened. It is very strange. Does she know nothing about her nocturnal adventures and her visits to me?

Strindberg, *From an Occult Diary*; tr. Mary Sandbach

Therein was writ, how often thundring *Jove*
　　Had felt the point of his hart-piercing dart,
　　And leaving heavens kingdome, here did rove
　　In straunge disguize, to slake his scalding smart . . .

Then was he turned into a snowy Swan,
　　To win faire *Leda* to his lovely trade:
　　O wondrous skill, and sweet wit of the man,
　　That her in daffadillies sleeping made,
　　From scorching heat her daintie limbes to shade:
　　Whiles the proud Bird ruffing his fethers wyde,
　　And brushing his faire brest, did her invade;
　　She slept, yet twixt her eyelids closely spyde,
How towards her he rusht, and smiled at his pryde.

EDMUND SPENSER, *The Faerie Queene*, 1590; the tapestries in the House of
Busyrane, showing 'all *Cupids* warres . . . Gainst all the Gods, to make his
empire great'

'The boxes,' I told myself, 'are cemeteries where these necrophiles dig up
amorous corpses.'

The idea carried me away. I found myself in sympathy with these debauchees
and, reaching out, I seized the box near the door without anyone noticing. I
opened it and started it up, as I had seen the others do, girded my loins, and
immediately there materialized before my ravished eyes a naked body which
was smiling up at me voluptuously . . .

These machines must have been set up at great expense, because patience
alone, on the part of the inventor, could have brought him to meet these
voluptuous characters at the height of their passion, and much probing must
have been necessary, and many cylinders must have met with only unimportant people doing anything but making love.

I would guess that an elaborate study of history, especially chronology, must
have been indispensable to the builders. They aimed their machine at the spot
where they knew that at a certain date a certain woman had lain down, and,
setting the machine in motion, had it reach the precise moment when they
could encounter the subject in the proper attitude.

Machines more powerful and built for an end more in keeping with current
morals could serve to reconstruct historic scenes . . . One of these explorers
would try, roll by roll, to reconstruct the life of Napoleon. Newspapers would
publish articles such as: 'Mr X . . . , the time explorer, has just, through a

lucky accident, discovered the poet Villon, of whose life so little is known still, and cylinder by cylinder, he is following him step by step.'

But let us not anticipate. All this is still in the realm of utopia, whereas the body I held in my arms seemed so pleasurable to me that I made liberal use of it without its suspecting a thing.

It was a dark and voluptuous woman with white skin and so many delicate dark blue veins that she appeared to be blue, that wonderful navy blue out of which the foam condensed into what was the divine body of Aphrodite. And with her arms out in front of her, breast-high, she seemed to be pushing something back—I imagined it to be the white and flexible body of the swan which will never sing and that she was Leda, mother of the Dioscuri. Soon she disappeared when the machine stopped and then I tiptoed away, overwhelmed by my good fortune.

Back in the corridor, the silly graffiti and the famous names filled me with disgust, but so proud was I of being henceforth linked to the horrible house of the Tyndarides that I was unable to refrain from writing in pencil:

I HAVE CUCKOLDED THE SWAN.

GUILLAUME APOLLINAIRE, from 'The Moon King', 1916; tr. Ron Padgett

One night, while caressing the back of his young wife, Lucina, Count Giorgio Venanzi feels something like a small scab on her left shoulder blade. Before long two wings have formed, much to Giorgio's horror. He consults Don Francesco, an old priest, virtually the family chaplain.

'Let us reason calmly, my son,' said Don Francesco to Giorgio. 'Your very young wife, who I agree is an admirable creature from any point of view, has grown two wings. We—you, your mother, and I—have verified that with these wings Lucina is capable of flying, a sign that they are not the result of a demonic intervention. On this point, I assure you, all the church fathers are in agreement; I purposely went to reread them. Hence the wings are a divine investiture, if we don't wish to call them a miracle. Let me also add that today, from a strictly theological point of view, Lucina would have to be considered an angel.'

'But if I am not mistaken, angels have never had a sex.'

'I agree with you, my son. Yet I am persuaded that your wife would never have grown these wings if the Almighty had not designed her for an important mission.'

'What mission?'

'Inscrutable are the decisions of the Omniscient. However, I don't believe you have the right to keep this poor creature shut away as if she had become a leper.'

'What do you expect me to do, Don Francesco? Should I exhibit her to the world? Can you imagine the uproar it would cause? The gross headlines in the newspapers, the siege of the curious, the interviews, the pilgrimages, every kind of annoyance. Heaven help me! I guarantee that someone would offer her a movie contract. And all this here at Casa Venanzi! The scandal! No, she shouldn't be seen, a thousand times no!'

'And who is to say that even this publicity is not part of the divine plan? That precisely the knowledge of the prodigy cannot have incalculable effects on consciences? Like a sort of new messiah, of the female sex . . .'

'I beg you, Don Francesco, enough! It seems mad to me. What have I done to merit such a disgrace?'

Docile by temperament, even rather listless, Lucina had adjusted to the harsh imprisonment that Giorgio had inflicted on her. All the same, the exasperation rose within her day after day. She was less than twenty years old, and she had to remain chained in her house without being able to see a friend, without having any dealings with anyone . . . Moreover, it tortured her that she couldn't stretch those stupendous wings, vibrant with youth and health . . .

Well, on one grey afternoon near the middle of October, the fog had fallen over the town, paralysing traffic. Dressed in double-knit wool tights and wrapped in a cape, Lucina avoided the servants' rooms and slipped into the garden. She looked around. She seemed to be in a dream world with the dense mist; absolutely no one could see her. She threw off the cape which she hid at the base of a tree. Then she went out into the open, beat her dear wings, and flew away over the roofs . . .

In her slightly frivolous innocence, the young contessa didn't ask herself why it was that she in particular, the only person in the world, had grown wings. It had happened, and that was it. The suspicion that she was elected for divine missions didn't even cross her mind. She knew only that she felt fine, sure of herself, endowed with a superhuman power which carried her, during these flights, to a blissful delirium.

As often happens, growing accustomed to impunity winds up dulling prudence. One afternoon, after leaving a high smoky layer of fog which hermetically sealed off the countryside and basking for a while in the pleasant autumnal sun, she grew curious to explore the underlying zone. She plunged headlong in the cool shadow of the mist and didn't stop until she was a few metres from the ground.

Exactly beneath her a young man with a rifle was about to reach what was probably a small hunting lodge on one of his many preserves. Having heard the beating of the huge wings, the hunter suddenly spun around and instinctively pointed his shotgun.

Lucina perceived the danger. Instead of rising again—she would never have made it in time—she risked revealing her secret and shouted in a loud voice, 'Wait, don't shoot!' Before the man could recover from the shock, she touched down a short distance in front of him.

The hunter was Massimo Lauretta, one of the most brilliant young men of the small provincial community. Born into a rich and honourable family, he was a recent graduate from the university, an expert skier and racing car driver, and the best friend of the Count and Contessa Venanzi. Notwithstanding his usual self-possession, he was so bewildered that he let his gun fall and knelt with joined hands, reciting out loud:

'Hail Mary, full of grace . . .'

Lucina burst out laughing. 'What are you doing, silly? Don't you see it's Lucina Venanzi?'

The man stood up, staggering: 'You? What happened? How did you get . . .'

'Don't waste time, Massimo . . . It's freezing out here . . .'

'Let's go inside,' said the young man, pointing to the cabin. 'There should be a fire lit.' . . .

They stood a little while watching one another, puzzled. Then Lucina said: 'I'm cold, I told you. At least hold me.'

Although the young man was still trembling, he didn't need to be told twice.

When Giorgio returned home that evening, he found his wife sitting in the parlour, sewing. Without any trace of the wings.

'Lucina!' he shouted. 'Sweetheart! How did it happen?'

'What?' she said, without getting excited.

'Your wings! What happened to them?'

'My wings? Have you gone mad?'

Violently shocked, he stood there speechless. 'But . . . I don't understand . . . I must've had a bad dream.'

No one knew anything about the miracle, or ugly incident, except for Giorgio, his mother, Don Francesco, and the young Massimo, who was too much of a gentleman to mention it to anyone. Yet even among those who knew about it, any talk of the matter was considered taboo.

Only Don Francesco, finding himself alone with Lucina some months later, said to her with a smile, 'God really loves you, Lucina. You will not deny that as an angel you had the most extraordinary luck.'

'What luck?'

'You were able to meet the Devil at the right moment.'

DINO BUZZATI, from 'The Count's Wife', 1971; tr. Lawrence Venuti

When Sir George Joy, then Honorary Secretary of the Society for Psychical Research, invited me to address my fellow members on whatever aspect of psychical research that I liked, I decided on Sex and Psychic Phenomena. The SPR Council were not happy with the title and preferred The Erotic Element in Spontaneous Psychic Phenomena, and so under that heading I began my lecture: 'This evening my subject is Sex and Psychic Phenomena . . .' The lecture was a very frank one, and I talked about sexual stimulation and psychic activity; the fact that some physical mediums, including Rudi Schneider, achieved a sexual climax during their seances; that telepathic experiments using sexual symbols produce significantly better results: the correlation between adolescence and poltergeist phenomena which often ceases overnight when the subject has her first menses; that paranormal movements of objects and other disturbances sometimes occur at the height of sexual excitement; the signifi-cance of masturbation and poltergeist activity; the physical make-up of the female genital organs and the occurrence of minute spontaneous rhythmic contractions that may contribute (in a few individuals of child-bearing age who practise mediumship) to produce a unique type of energy; and I discussed several case histories that involved advanced sexual techniques . . .

Subsequently I gave a similar lecture at Sussex University, and was reminded of the occasion when Geraldine Cummins gave a lecture at Sussex. One of her best-known books was *The Road to Immortality*, and the printed notice for her talk stated: 'Speaker, Miss Geraldine Cummins, writer of *The Road to Immorality*, fifteen years experience.' She arrived to find the hall packed and many people standing. 'Never before or since have I been welcomed at a lecture with such enthusiasm and warm applause,' she told me!

PETER UNDERWOOD, President of the Ghost Club, *No Common Task: The Autobiography of a Ghost-hunter*, 1983

In such white robes heav'n's angels used to be
Receiv'd by men; thou angel bringst with thee
A heaven like Mahomet's paradise; and though

Ill spirits walk in white, we easily know
By this these angels from an evil sprite:
Those set our hairs, but these our flesh upright.

DONNE, from 'To his Mistress Going to Bed'

ANIMAL SPIRITS

CHRISTINA HOLE hints at the ambivalence in our attitude to animals. We may love them, but if it shows too much, we shall be charged with deficiency of good will towards our fellow humans, if not with positive ill will. Flaubert's fanatical hunter became a saint not through any change of heart towards animals, but by virtue of embracing a leper. In the past the association between a cat and a childless, friendless old woman spelt danger for both of them. Cats are particularly suspect because of the combination in them of insidious persuasiveness and manifest hauteur, two qualities ascribed to the devil.

Accounts of the seemingly paranormal faculties of pets are rife. In the first year of the Great War, one report has it, an Irish terrier travelled from the north of England to the south, crossed the Channel, and then made its way through the French countryside to its master, in a trench on the front line near Armentières. And a writer in *New Scientist* in 1968 speaks of a 'gifted ten per cent' of dogs who, having been settled for a week or two in boarding kennels, 'become wildly excited at almost the exact moment when their owners begin the return journey from their holiday', no matter how far away the owners had travelled.

Desmond Morris has unkindly suggested, apropos of the phenomenon of 'psychic trailing', that the cats—or it might be dogs—famous for having turned up at their owners' new house, maybe hundreds of miles away, and sometimes after a lapse of several years, are very probably foreign strays on the lookout for accommodation. There are those who will consider this theory a sad case of superstitious rationalism.

Miss Murray tells us that domestic familiars were used only for magic and were peculiar to England. They flourished particularly in the Eastern Counties. Whether this national peculiarity was due to the English fondness for keeping pets, which even witches shared, or to some other cause, is not clear, but certainly the possession of any animal was a danger to a suspected witch, especially if he or she was known to treat it with affection.

CHRISTINA HOLE, *Witchcraft in England*

The sheykh Khaleel El-Medábighee, one of the most celebrated of the 'Ulamà of Egypt, and author of several works on various sciences, who died, at a very advanced age, during the period of my first visit to this country, used to relate the following anecdote:—He had, he said, a favourite black cat, which always slept at the foot of his mosquito-curtain. Once, at midnight, he heard a knocking at the door of his house; and his cat went, and opened the hanging shutter of his window, and called, 'Who is there?' A voice replied, 'I am such a one' (mentioning a strange name) 'the ginnee: open the door.' 'The lock,' said the sheykh's cat, 'has had the name [of God] pronounced upon it.' 'Then throw me down,' said the other, 'two cakes of bread.' 'The bread-basket,' answered the cat at the window, 'has had the name pronounced upon it.' 'Well,' said the stranger, 'at least give me a draught of water.' But he was answered that the water-jar had been secured in the same manner; and asked what he was to do, seeing that he was likely to die of hunger and thirst: the sheykh's cat told him to go to the door of the next house; and went there also himself, and opened the door, and soon after returned. Next morning, the sheykh deviated from a habit which he had constantly observed: he gave, to the cat, half of the fateereh [thin buttered pastry] upon which he breakfasted, instead of a little morsel, which he was wont to give; and afterwards said, 'O my cat, thou knowest that I am a poor man: bring me, then, a little gold': upon which words, the cat immediately disappeared, and he saw it no more.

LANE, *The Manners . . . of the Modern Egyptians*

A gentleman on a visit to a friend who lived on the skirts of an extensive forest in the east of Germany lost his way. He wandered for some hours among the trees, when he saw a light at a distance. On approaching it, he was surprised to observe, that it proceeded from the interior of a ruined monastery. Before he knocked he thought it prudent to look through the window. He saw a multitude of cats assembled round a small grave, four of whom were letting down a coffin with a crown upon it. The gentleman, startled at this unusual sight, and imagining that he had arrived among the retreats of fiends or witches, mounted his horse and rode away with the utmost precipitation. He arrived at his friend's house at a late hour, who had sate up for him. On his arrival his friend questioned as to the cause of the traces of trouble visible in his face. He began to recount his adventures, after much difficulty, knowing that it was scarcely possible that his friends should give faith to his relation. No sooner had he mentioned the coffin with a crown upon it, than his friend's cat, who seemed to have been lying asleep before the fire, leaped up, saying— 'Then I am the King of the Cats!' and scrambled up the chimney, and was seen no more.

> SHELLEY, from 'Journal', Geneva, 18 August 1816; a tale related by M. G. ('Monk') Lewis

A few weeks previously, we had lost our dear cat, Dina, under the wheels of a car . . . and her loss upset me dreadfully. She was part of the family, but I decided that I would again open my door to another feline creature, and we purchased two adorable Brown Burmese which we named Aquarius and Scorpio.

Dina's original basket was in use again—and it was placed, as always, just by the radiator in the lounge. At that particular time, my sister and brother-in-law were visiting us, and it must have been around the 10 p.m. mark when suddenly Aquarius' and Scorpio's hackles were raised several inches! They appeared to be staring at the basket. Their backs were arched—they were spitting, and I immediately thought that each had offended the other in some way. They went on for some four or five minutes . . .

Given the evening's performance, I said to my husband, after our guests had left, that I hoped our pets would not offend each other too often. He replied quietly that he had seen Dina sitting in her basket quite happily, gazing round the room and finally staring at him, at which point she faded out as noiselessly as she had come. I asked why on earth he hadn't said anything at the time, to which he replied that it would only have upset me—which was true.

> PAULE V. HAMPSO, *The Cat-Lover's Journal*, 1974–5

For I will consider my Cat Jeoffrey.
For he is the servant of the Living God, duly and daily serving him.

For at the first glance of the glory of God in the East he worships
  in his way.
For this is done by wreathing his body seven times round with elegant
  quickness . . .
For when his day's work is done his business more properly begins.
For he keeps the Lord's watch in the night against the adversary.
For he counteracts the powers of darkness by his electrical skin and
  glaring eyes.
For he counteracts the Devil, who is death, by brisking about the life.

> CHRISTOPHER SMART, *Jubilate Agno*, written between 1758 and 1763

Lady Howard (of Fitzford, Tavistock).—Said (not truthfully) to have murdered four husbands. Every night she runs from the still existing, though
restored, gatehouse to Okehampton Castle, where she picks a blade of grass
and returns with it, till the castle mound is bare, when the world will end. She
does this either (1) in the form of a hound or (2) riding in a coach of bones,
preceded by a black hound with one eye in the middle of its forehead.

Sir William de Tracy.—(1) Haunts Woolacombe Sands and Braunton Burrows,
spinning ropes of sand. When nearly complete, a black dog appears with a ball
of fire in his mouth and breaks the cord, so that the penance (for the murder
of St Thomas à Becket) is recommenced. (2) Many years ago a ferryman of
Appledore heard someone hailing from Braunton and rowed across. There was
only a black dog there, which jumped into the boat. The man rowed back, but
as he neared Appledore the dog swamped the boat, swam ashore, and vanished
over Northam Burrows.

> THEO BROWN, from 'The Black Dog in Devon', *Transactions* of the Devonshire
> Association, Vol. 91, 1959

A naval officer visited a friend in the country. Several men were sitting round
the smoking-room fire when he arrived, and a fox-terrier was with them.
Presently the heavy, shambling footsteps of an old dog, and the metallic
shaking sound of his collar, were heard coming upstairs.
  'Here's old Peter!' said the visitor.
  '*Peter's dead!*' whispered his owner.
  The sounds passed through the closed door, heard by all; they pattered into
the room; the fox-terrier bristled up, growled, and pursued a viewless object

across the carpet; from the hearth-rug sounded a shake, a jingle of a collar, and the settling weight of a body collapsing into repose.

> From a letter sent by Lieutenant —— of HMS gunboat ——; in Andrew Lang: *The Book of Dreams and Ghosts*, 1897

One of the best examples I have come across of the entry of the animal mind into telepathic phenomena is that of Mr Rider Haggard's dog.

One night Mr Rider Haggard had what at first he took to be a nightmare. 'I was awakened,' he says, 'by my wife's voice calling to me from her own bed upon the other side of the room. As I awoke, the nightmare itself, which had been long and vivid, faded from my brain. All I could remember of it was a sense of awful oppression and of desperate and terrified struggle for life such as the act of drowning would probably involve. But between the time when I heard my wife's voice and the time that my consciousness answered to it, or so it seemed to me, I had another dream. I dreamed that a black retriever dog, a most amiable and intelligent beast named Bob . . . was lying on its side among brushwood, or rough growth of some sort, by water. My own personality in some mysterious way seemed to me to be arising from the body of the dog, which I knew quite surely to be Bob and no other, so much so that my head was against his head, which was lifted up at an unnatural angle. In my vision the dog was trying to speak to me in words, and, failing, transmitted to my mind in an undefined fashion the knowledge that it was dying. Then everything vanished, and I woke to hear my wife asking me why on earth I was making those horrible and weird noises. I replied that I had had a nightmare about a fearful struggle, and that I had dreamed that old Bob was in a dreadful way, and was trying to talk to me and to tell me about it.'

Railway men found the dog's collar on an openwork bridge over some water, and it appeared that the dog had been struck by a passing train in the night and thrown down into the water below. Its body was found three days later.

T<small>YRRELL</small>, Apparitions

Another case concerned Josef Becker, who went for a stroll with his Alsatian, Strulli, and looked in at a local inn in Saar Louis. The dog became agitated, doing everything possible to attract attention, running round in circles, howling at his master, tugging at his clothes and trying to drag him from his seat. Strulli was such a nuisance that Becker, intent on his drink and convivial company, put the dog outside and shut the door.

Somehow the dog got into the inn by another entrance and began to tug frantically at Becker's clothes. Tired of this losing battle and seeing that he would never enjoy his drink in peace, Becker left the inn at two minutes to five. Two minutes later, to the deafening crash of timber, bricks and plaster, the inn collapsed on its occupants, killing nine people and injuring over twenty others.

Builders excavating next door had damaged the inn's foundations. Nobody suspected it, but the dog knew something was wrong.

DENNIS BARDENS, *Psychic Animals*, 1987

Littlecote, as everyone knows, is haunted by the spirits of the notorious 'Wild Will Darrell' and the horse he invariably rode, and which eventually broke his neck.

But there are many Wild Darrells; all Europe is overrun by them. They nightly tear, on their phantom horses, over the German and Norwegian forests and moorlands that echo and re-echo with their hoarse shouts and the mournful baying of their grisly hounds . . .

According to various authorities on the subject, this spectral chase goes by different names. In Thuringia and elsewhere, it is 'Hakelnberg' or 'Hackelnbarend'—the story being that Hakelnberg, a German knight, who had devoted his whole life to the chase, on his deathbed had told the officiating priest that he cared not a jot for heaven, but only for hunting; the priest losing patience and exclaiming, 'Then hunt till Doomsday.'

ELLIOTT O'DONNELL, *Animal Ghosts*, 1913. According to other sources the name 'Hackelnbarend', met in different forms, is an old word meaning 'mantle-wearer'

Baring-Gould . . . accepts the spectral coach as the descendant of *Herla's Hell-Wain* and the Wagon of *Ankon*. He gives Lady Howard's death coach as the West Country example, and quotes a folk-poem about it from the many which he had collected.

The coach is all black, with a headless coachman, black horses, and a black hound running before. Riding in this, Lady Howard drives round the countryside, picking up those who are destined for death.

'Now pray step in!' my lady saith,
  'Now pray step in and ride!'
'I thank thee, I had rather walk
  Than gather to thy side.'

The wheels go round without a sound
   Of tramp or turn of wheels,
As cloud at night, in pale moonlight,
   Along the carriage steals.

I'd rather walk a hundred miles
   And run by night and day,
Than have that carriage halt for me,
   And hear my lady say—
'Now pray step in and make no din,
   Step in with me to ride:
There's room I trow by me for you,
   And all the world beside.'

K. M. BRIGGS, from 'Tradition and Invention in Ghost Stories', 1980. The legend concerns Lady Howard (1596–1671) of Tavistock, West Devon: see p. 397

[Karl] Krall, who is a little nervous, makes no secret of his uneasiness. His horses are fickle animals, uncertain, capricious and extremely sensitive. A trifle disturbs them, confuses them, puts them off. At such times, threats, prayers and even the irresistible charm of carrots and good rye bread are useless. They obstinately refuse to do any work and they answer at random. Everything depends on a whim, the state of the weather, the morning meal or the impression which the visitor makes on them. Still, Krall seems to know, by certain imperceptible signs, that this is not going to be a bad day. Muhamed quivers with excitement, snorts loudly through his nostrils, utters a series of indistinct little whinnyings: excellent symptoms, it appears. I take my seat on the corn bin. The master, standing beside the blackboard, chalk in hand, introduces me to Muhamed in due form, as to a human being:

'Muhamed, attention! This is your uncle'—pointing to me—'who has come all the way to honour you with a visit. Mind you don't disappoint him. His name is Maeterlinck.' Krall pronounces the first syllable German-fashion: *Mah*. 'You understand: Maeterlinck. Now show him that you know your letters and that you can spell a name correctly, like a clever boy. Go ahead, we're listening.'

Muhamed gives a short neigh and, on the small, movable board at his feet, strikes first with his right hoof and then with his left the number of blows which correspond with the letter M in the conventional alphabet used by the horses. Then, one after the other, without stopping or hesitating, he marks the letters A D R L I N S H, representing the unexpected aspect which my humble name assumes in the equine mind and phonetics. His attention is called to the fact that there is a mistake. He readily agrees and replaces the S H by a G and then the G by a K. They insist that he must put a T instead of the D; but Muhamed, content with his work, shakes his head to say no and refuses to make any further corrections.

> MAURICE MAETERLINCK, from 'The Elberfeld Horses', *The Unknown Guest*, 1914; tr. Alexander Teixeira de Mattos

Maeterlinck wittily describes how he named a chance number for Muhamed to give its square root, but the horse did not reply, the number having no exact square root; a fact that vastly astonished M. Maeterlinck.

But there is more yet. The Elberfeld horses, by choosing cards with letters on them, could carry on conversations . . . Their conversations are curious, as one may well imagine. One day Muhamed denounced the groom for having struck Hänschen [a pony]. Sometimes they say they are tired and will not answer. They knew one person present to be a lady because 'she had long hair' . . .

The solution reached is often too quick even for a good arithmetician. Mr Krall wrote on the blackboard $\sqrt[3]{91125}$, the number given him by M. Assagioli, and in a few seconds Muhamed gave the correct answer.

> RICHET, *Thirty Years of Psychical Research*

And Balaam rose up in the morning, and saddled his ass, and went with the princes of Moab.

And God's anger was kindled because he went: and the angel of the Lord stood in the way for an adversary against him. Now he was riding upon his ass, and his two servants were with him.

And the ass saw the angel of the Lord standing in the way, and his sword drawn in his hand: and the ass turned aside out of the way, and went into the field: and Balaam smote the ass, to turn her into the way.

But the angel of the Lord stood in a path of the vineyards, a wall being on this side, and a wall on that side.

And when the ass saw the angel of the Lord, she thrust herself unto the wall, and crushed Balaam's foot against the wall: and he smote her again.

And the angel of the Lord went further, and stood in a narrow place, where was no way to turn either to the right hand or to the left.

And when the ass saw the angel of the Lord, she fell down under Balaam: and Balaam's anger was kindled, and he smote the ass with a staff.

And the Lord opened the mouth of the ass, and she said unto Balaam, What have I done unto thee, that thou hast smitten me these three times?

And Balaam said unto the ass, Because thou hast mocked me: I would there were a sword in my hand, for now would I kill thee.

And the ass said unto Balaam, Am not I thine ass, upon which thou hast ridden ever since I was thine unto this day? was I ever wont to do so unto thee? And he said, Nay.

Then the Lord opened the eyes of Balaam, and he saw the angel of the Lord standing in the way, and his sword drawn in his hand: and he bowed down his head, and fell flat on his face.

And the angel of the Lord said unto him, Wherefore hast thou smitten thine ass these three times? behold, I went out to withstand thee, because thy way is perverse before me:

And the ass saw me, and turned from me these three times: unless she had turned from me, surely now also I had slain thee, and saved her alive.

Numbers 22

To the savage, therefore, who regards all living creatures as practically on a footing of equality with man, the act of killing and eating an animal must wear a very different aspect from that which the same act presents to us who regard the intelligence of animals as far inferior to our own and deny them the possession of immortal souls . . .

When a party of Koriaks have killed a bear or a wolf, they skin the beast and dress one of themselves in the skin. Then they dance round the skin-clad man, saying that it was not they who killed the animal, but some one else, generally a Russian. When they kill a fox they skin it, wrap the body in grass, and bid him tell his companions how hospitably he has been received, and how he has received a new cloak instead of his old one. The Finns used to try to persuade a slain bear that he had not been killed by them, but had fallen from a tree, etc. When the Lapps had succeeded in killing a bear with impunity, they thanked him for not hurting them and for not breaking the clubs and spears which had given him his death wounds; and they prayed that he would not visit his death upon them by sending storms or in any other way. His flesh then furnished a feast.

FRAZER, *The Golden Bough*

Among the latest Soviet propaganda is the utilization of fantastic legends about Lenin. In Siberia, among the aborigines, the story runs that Lenin was originally a bear, for the bear is the Siberian totem. 'The bear Lenin lived for a long time in the virgin forest. There came a Russian general to the forest and tried to trap the bear. He placed a barrel of vodka in the forest, and Lenin having drunk it became intoxicated. Thus he fell into the hands of the Russian general who compelled him to wander about all over the world and to dance for him. Finally he escaped, became a man, and now he is revenging himself on all generals.'

> SUMMERS, *The Werewolf*; the author gives as authority an article in *Anglo-Russian News*, 18 January 1929

A woman staying with the bereaved family asked the widow, 'Have the bees been told?' The reply being 'No', she at once took some spice cake and some sugar in a dish [for the bees], then, rattling a bunch of small keys (I suppose to attract the attention of the indwellers), she repeated this formula: 'Honey bees! honey bees! hear what I say! Your master, J.A., has passed away. But his wife now begs you will freely stay, And still gather honey for many a day. Bonny bees, bonny bees, hear what I say!'

> *Stamford Mercury*, 15 April 1870

It faded on the crowing of the cock.
Some say that ever 'gainst that season comes
Wherein our Saviour's birth is celebrated,
The bird of dawning singeth all night long;
And then, they say, no spirit can walk abroad;
The nights are wholesome; then no planets strike,
No fairy takes, nor witch hath power to charm,
So hallow'd and so gracious is the time.

> SHAKESPEARE, *Hamlet*

From the standpoint of magical folklore, the cock is a bird of much interest and many virtues. It is endowed with the remarkable power of putting to flight the infernal hosts, and as according to Peter Delancre [early 17th century] in his *Tableau de l'inconstance des Démons*, the devil, who is the lion of hell, will vanish the moment that he hears the voice of this domestic fowl, it is popularly supposed that the natural lion, who is the king of beasts, can be subdued and put to flight thereby. The entire fantasmagoria of the Black Sabbath disappears when the cock crows, and to prevent him from sounding his clarion during the night hours, and routing the whole assembly, the sorcerer, instructed by the devil, anointed his head with olive oil, and twined a collar of vine leaves about his neck. But while his voice was inimical to the midnight mysteries of the wizard world, his flesh was supposed to be possessed of valuable virtues in sorcery, and, in particular, an ancient and venerable method of divination was practised by the instrumentality of this bird of the gods and of Aesculapius.

WAITE, *The Occult Sciences*

'The very birds are in being,' said a sacristan. 'What!' answered I, 'the individual crows who attended St Vincent?'—'Not exactly,' was the reply (in a whisper, intended for my private ear), 'but their immediate descendants.'—'Mighty well; this very evening, please God, I will pay my respects to them . . .'

At length . . . we set forth on the wings of holiness, to pay our devoirs to the holy crows. A certain sum having been allotted time immemorial for the maintenance of two birds of this species, we found them very comfortably established in a recess of a cloister adjoining the cathedral, well fed and certainly most devoutly venerated.

The origin of this singular custom dates as high as the days of St Vincent, who was martyrized near the Cape which bears his name, and whose mangled body was conveyed to Lisbon in a boat, attended by crows. These disinterested birds, after seeing it decently interred, pursued his murderers with dreadful screams and tore their eyes out . . .

It was growing late when we arrived, and their feathered sanctities were gone quietly to roost: but the sacristans in waiting, the moment they saw us approach, officiously roused them. Oh, how plump and sleek and glossy they are! My admiration of their size, their plumage, and their deep-toned croakings carried me, I fear, beyond the bounds of saintly decorum. I was just stretching out my hand to stroke their feathers, when the missionary checked me with a solemn forbidding look. The rest of the company, aware of the proper ceremonial, kept a respectful distance, whilst the sacristan and a toothless priest, almost bent double with age, communicated a long string of miraculous anecdotes concerning the present holy crows, their immediate predecessors, and other holy crows in the old time before them.

To all these super-marvellous narrations, the missionary appeared to listen with implicit faith, and never opened his lips during the time we remained in the cloister, except to enforce our veneration, and exclaim with pious composure, 'Honrado corvo'.

BECKFORD, *Dreams, Waking Thoughts, and Incidents*, 1783, rev. 1834; recording a visit to Lisbon in 1787

There were three Ravens sat on a tree,
They were as blacke as they might be.

The one of them said to his make,   *mate*
Where shall we our breakefast take?

Downe in yonder greene field
There lies a Knight slain under his shield.

His Hounds they lie downe at his feete,
So well they can their Master keepe.

His Hawkes they flie so eagerly
There's no fowle dare him come nie.

Downe there comes a fallow Doe
As great with yong as she might goe.

She lift up his bloudy hed
And kist his wounds that were so red.

She got him up upon her backe
And carried him to earthen lake.

She buried him before the prime,   *sunrise*
She was dead her selfe ere even-song time.

God send every gentleman
Such hawkes, such hounds, and such a Leman.   *lover*

ANON., 'The Three Ravens'

The beetle is not killed by the people for the following reason: they have a tradition that one day the chief priests sent messengers in every direction to look for the Lord Jesus, and they came to a field where a man was reaping, and asked him—

'Did Jesus of Nazareth pass this way?'

'No,' said the man, 'I have not seen him.'

'But I know better,' said a little clock [dung beetle] running up, 'for He was here today and rested, and has not long gone away.'

'That is false,' said a great big black beetle, coming forward; 'He has not passed since yesterday, and you will never find Him on this road; try another.'

So the people kill the clock because he tried to betray Christ; but they spare the beetle and will not touch him, because he saved the Lord on that day.

LADY WILDE, *Ancient Legends . . . of Ireland*

While snoozing one afternoon, a child dreamt he had become a wasp. A wasp flew out of the child's nose, and his mother swatted it. It fell to the ground dead. And the child died too. This is why you should never kill wasps if people are sleeping nearby.

Japanese tale

Conradin was ten years old, and the doctor had pronounced his professional opinion that the boy would not live another five years. The doctor was silky and effete, and counted for little, but his opinion was endorsed by Mrs De Ropp, who counted for nearly everything. Mrs De Ropp was Conradin's cousin and guardian, and in his eyes she represented those three-fifths of the world that are necessary and disagreeable and real; the other two-fifths, in perpetual antagonism to the foregoing, were summed up in himself and his imagination . . . Without his imagination, which was rampant under the spur of loneliness, he would have succumbed long ago.

Mrs De Ropp would never, in her honestest moments, have confessed to herself that she disliked Conradin, though she might have been dimly aware that thwarting him 'for his good' was a duty which she did not find particularly irksome. Conradin hated her with a desperate sincerity which he was perfectly able to mask . . .

In the dull, cheerless garden, overlooked by so many windows that were ready to open with a message not to do this or that, or a reminder that medicines were due, he found little attraction . . . In a forgotten corner, however, almost hidden behind a dismal shrubbery, was a disused tool-shed of respectable proportions, and within its walls Conradin found a haven, something that took on the varying aspects of a playroom and a cathedral. He had peopled it with a legion of familiar phantoms, evoked partly from fragments of history and partly from his own brain, but it also boasted two inmates of flesh and blood. In one corner lived a ragged-plumaged Houdan hen, on which the boy lavished an affection that had scarcely another outlet. Further back in the gloom stood a large hutch, divided into two compartments, one of which was fronted with close iron bars. This was the abode of a large polecat-ferret, which a friendly butcher-boy had once smuggled, cage and all, into its present quarters, in exchange for a long-secreted hoard of small silver. Conradin was dreadfully afraid of the lithe, sharp-fanged beast, but it was his most treasured possession. Its very presence in the tool-shed was a secret and fearful joy, to be kept scrupulously from the knowledge of the Woman, as he privately dubbed his cousin. And one day, out of Heaven knows what material, he spun the beast a wonderful name, and from that moment it grew into a god and a religion . . . Every Thursday, in the dim and musty silence of the tool-shed, he worshipped with mystic and elaborate ceremonial before the wooden hutch where dwelt Sredni Vashtar, the great ferret. Red flowers in their season and scarlet berries in the winter-time were offered at his shrine, for he was a god who laid some special stress on the fierce impatient side of things, as opposed to the Woman's religion, which, as far as Conradin could observe, went to great lengths in the contrary direction.

After a while Conradin's absorption in the tool-shed began to attract the notice of his guardian. 'It is not good for him to be pottering down there in all weathers,' she promptly decided, and at breakfast one morning she announced that the Houdan hen had been sold and taken away overnight. With her short-sighted eyes she peered at Conradin, waiting for an outbreak of rage and sorrow, which she was ready to rebuke with a flow of excellent precepts and reasoning. But Conradin said nothing: there was nothing to be said . . .

In the shed that evening there was an innovation in the worship of the hutch-god. Conradin had been wont to chant his praises, tonight he asked a boon.

'Do one thing for me, Sredni Vashtar.'

The thing was not specified. As Sredni Vashtar was a god he must be supposed to know. And choking back a sob as he looked at that other empty corner, Conradin went back to the world he so hated.

And every night, in the welcome darkness of his bedroom, and every evening in the dusk of the tool-shed, Conradin's bitter litany went up: 'Do one thing for me, Sredni Vashtar.'

Mrs De Ropp noticed that the visits to the shed did not cease, and one day she made a further journey of inspection.

'What are you keeping in that locked hutch?' she asked. 'I believe it's guinea-pigs. I'll have them all cleared away.'

Conradin shut his lips tight, but the Woman ransacked his bedroom till she found the carefully hidden key, and forthwith marched down to the shed to complete her discovery. It was a cold afternoon, and Conradin had been bidden to keep to the house. From the furthest window of the dining-room the door of the shed could just be seen beyond the corner of the shrubbery, and there Conradin stationed himself. He saw the Woman enter, and then he imagined her opening the door of the sacred hutch and peering down with her short-sighted eyes into the thick straw bed where his god lay hidden. Perhaps she would prod at the straw in her clumsy impatience. And Conradin fervently breathed his prayer for the last time. But he knew as he prayed that he did not believe. He knew that the Woman would come out presently with that pursed smile he loathed so well on her face, and that in an hour or two the gardener would carry away his wonderful god, a god no longer, but a simple brown ferret in a hutch. And he knew that the Woman would triumph always as she triumphed now, and that he would grow ever more sickly under her pestering and domineering and superior wisdom, till one day nothing would matter much more with him, and the doctor would be proved right. And in the sting and misery of his defeat, he began to chant loudly and defiantly the hymn of his threatened idol:

> Sredni Vashtar went forth,
> His thoughts were red thoughts and his teeth were white.
> His enemies called for peace, but he brought them death.
> Sredni Vashtar the Beautiful.

And then of a sudden he stopped his chanting and drew closer to the window-pane. The door of the shed still stood ajar as it had been left, and the minutes were slipping by. They were long minutes, but they slipped by nevertheless. He watched the starlings running and flying in little parties across the lawn; he counted them over and over again, with one eye always on that swinging door. A sour-faced maid came in to lay the table for tea, and still Conradin stood and waited and watched. Hope had crept by inches into his heart, and now a look of triumph began to blaze in his eyes that had only known the wistful patience of defeat. Under his breath, with a furtive exultation, he began once again the paean of victory and devastation. And presently his eyes were rewarded; out through that doorway came a long, low, yellow-and-brown beast, with eyes a-blink at the waning daylight, and dark wet stains around the fur of jaws and throat. Conradin dropped on his knees. The great polecat-ferret made its way down to a small brook at the foot of the garden, drank for a moment, then crossed a little plank bridge and was lost to sight in the bushes. Such was the passing of Sredni Vashtar.

SAKI, from 'Sredni Vashtar', 1911

As a child Julian killed a mouse which angered him by creeping out of the church wall during Mass. Then he killed small birds in the garden. Before long his father taught him the art of hunting.

He killed bears with the knife, bulls with the axe, boars with the spear. Once, armed with nothing more than a stick, he even fought wolves who were gnawing at bodies under a gibbet.

One winter morning he left home before dawn, fully equipped, his crossbow on his shoulder and a bundle of arrows hanging from his saddle. His Danish jennet, followed by two bassets, moving at a steady pace, made the earth ring under their steps . . . He caught sight of rabbits hopping about in front of their burrows. The bassets at once rushed on them, darting this way and that, quickly breaking their backs.

Soon he entered a wood. At the end of a branch a grouse, numb with cold, was asleep, its head under its wing. With a stroke of his sword, Julian sliced off its legs, and went on his way without picking it up . . .

Cranes, flying very low, passed over his head from time to time. Julian brought them down with his whip, not missing one . . . Then he pressed on along an avenue of tall trees, whose tops formed a triumphal arch, at the entrance to the forest. A roe leapt out of a thicket; a buck appeared in a clearing; a badger came out of a hole; a peacock spread its tail. And when he had killed them all, other deer, other badgers, other peacocks presented themselves, and blackbirds, jays, skunks, foxes, hedgehogs, lynxes, an infinitude of beasts, increasing with every step he took. They turned around him, trembling, gazing at him with gentle, pleading eyes. But Julian never tired of killing. Bending his crossbow, drawing his sword, pointing his knife, he thought of nothing, he remembered nothing. He had been hunting in some uncertain country, for an indeterminate time, and by the sole fact of his existence everything was done with the effortlessness experienced in dreams.

An extraordinary sight arrested him. A glen, shaped like a circus, was crowded with stags; they pressed against one another, warming themselves with their breath, which steamed in the mist. For a few moments the thought of such carnage suffocated him with pleasure. Then he dismounted, turned up his sleeves, and took aim . . . The edge of the glen was too high for the stags to cross. They were leaping in the enclosure, trying to escape. Julian shot, and the arrows fell like shafts of rain in a storm . . .

At last they died, lying in the sand, nostrils oozing, entrails hanging out, the quivering of their bellies weakening little by little. Then all was still.

Night was falling, and behind the wood, between the branches, the sky was red as a pool of blood. Julian leant against a tree, contemplating with gaping eyes the enormity of the massacre, unable to understand how he could have committed it.

On the other side of the glen, on the edge of the forest, he caught sight of a stag, a hind and her fawn. The stag was black, and monstrous in size, bearing sixteen antlers and a white beard. The hind, the colour of dead leaves, was grazing, while the spotted fawn suckled her as she moved.

Once again the crossbow hummed, and the fawn died. Its mother, her eyes turned towards the sky, cried out with a deep, heart-rending, human voice. Incensed, Julian felled her with one arrow full in the breast.

The great stag had seen him, and it leapt towards him. Julian shot his last arrow, which struck it in the forehead and remained there. The stag seemed not to have felt anything; stepping over the dead, it kept coming forward, as if to spring on Julian and rip him open. Julian backed away in inexpressible fear. The prodigious creature halted, and with flaming eyes, as solemn as a patriarch, as a judge passing sentence, repeated three times, while a bell was ringing in the distance: 'Accursed! Accursed! Accursed! One day, barbarous heart, you will murder your father and your mother!'

It bent down on its knees, gently closed its eyelids, and died.

Julian renounced hunting. He joined a band of adventurers, travelled far and wide, eventually married the beautiful daughter of an emperor whom he had saved from his enemies, and became a wise and powerful prince. But he suffered from bad dreams, and one day, to distract him from his melancholy, his wife encouraged him to go out hunting again. In the meanwhile his parents journeyed to Julian's palace, and were received hospitably by his wife, who gave them her bedroom.

In a ravine he met a furious bull, pawing the sand with its feet, lowering its horns. He thrust his spear into the animal's dewlap; the spear shattered as if the bull were made of bronze. Julian closed his eyes and waited for death. When he opened them, the bull had disappeared . . .

There was a monstrous jackdaw in the foliage, staring at him; and here and there, between the branches, flashed points of light, as though the sky were showering the forest with its stars. They were the eyes of animals, wild cats, squirrels, owls, parrots, monkeys.

Julian launched his arrows at them, and the shafts alighted on the leaves like white butterflies. He threw stones at them, and the stones fell without hitting anything. He cursed himself, eager to fight, choking with rage.

Then all the animals he had hunted came back, gathering in a narrow circle around him. Some sat on their haunches, others raised themselves to their full height. He stood in the middle, frozen with terror, unable to make the slightest movement. At last, by a supreme effort of will, he took a step. The animals perched on the trees opened their wings; those on the ground stirred their limbs; they all followed him. The hyenas walked in front of him, the wolf and the boar behind. On his right the bull was tossing its head; on his left the snake writhed in the grass; the panther reared its back and advanced with velvety steps. He slowed down as much as he could, in order not to anger them; and he saw, coming out of the deep bushes, hedgehogs, foxes, adders, jackals, bears.

Julian began to run. And they ran. The snake hissed, the stinking animals slobbered, the boar rubbed against his heels with its tusks, the wolf against the palms of his hands with the hairs of its muzzle. The monkeys, making faces, pinched him; the weasel rolled over his feet. With a blow of its paw, a bear sent his cap flying, and the panther contemptuously let fall an arrow it was carrying in its mouth.

Irony showed through their sly bearing. While watching him from the corner of their eyes, they seemed to be meditating a plan of revenge; and, deafened by the buzzing of the insects, beaten by the tails of birds, suffocated by the breath of the animals, he walked, arms outstretched, eyes closed like a blind man, lacking even the strength to cry for mercy.

A cock's crowing rang through the air; others responded. It was day, and above the orange trees he recognized the roof of his palace.

Then, at the side of a field, he saw, three steps away, red partridges fluttering in the stubble. He unfastened his cloak, and threw it over them like a net. When he lifted it, he found only one there, long dead, rotten.

Returning home, Julian went to his wife's shuttered bedroom. As he bent down to kiss her, he saw a bearded man lying beside her. In a mad fury he seized a dagger and stabbed them to death. They were his mother and his father. Thereafter Julian became a hermit and ferryman. One day he rows a leper across the river, and brings him to his hut. 'I am hungry!' the leper says. Julian gives him bread. 'I am thirsty!' And he gives him wine. 'I am cold!' the leper says, telling Julian to undress so that he may warm himself against his body. Julian clasps him, chest to chest, mouth to mouth. The leper's eyes turn into stars, his hair into the rays of the sun, his breath into the scent of roses. Joy floods Julian's soul. It is Christ holding him, bearing him up into the sky.

GUSTAVE FLAUBERT, from 'The Legend of St Julian the Hospitaller', 1877

Within the streams, Pausanias saith,
  That down Cocytus valley flow,
Girdling the grey domain of Death,
  The spectral fishes come and go;
The ghosts of trout flit to and fro.
  Persephone, fulfil my wish,
And grant that in the shades below
  My ghost may land the ghosts of fish.

ANDREW LANG, 'The Last Chance', 1888

Near-Death Experiences, Spontaneous Combustion, Immortality

RECENT years have seen numerous books, packed with testimonies, on near-death and out-of-the-body experiences. Commonly the soul or spirit or 'other self' has left the body, viewing it, and perhaps other people, dispassionately from above, and often a bright light, as if at the end of a tunnel, plays a prominent part.

When the instalment of *Bleak House* describing Krook's death came out in December 1852, G. H. Lewes published an article accusing Dickens of perpetuating 'a vulgar error' by making out that spontaneous combustion was a scientific reality. Stung by this attack from a friend, Dickens inserted in the next month's part sarcastic remarks on sceptical wiseacres and adduced documents (of some antiquity and remoteness) to support the hypothesis; for which see the second extract printed here.

The early assumption, not unnatural but not always strictly applicable, had it that this sensational end befell heavy drinkers of alcohol. In the work cited later Jenny Randles and Peter Hough discuss another possible and more esoteric solution to the mystery, in a chapter concerning the reservoir of energy known in Hindu tradition as *kundalini* ('the fiery serpent within'), located at the base of the spine, and the burning heat said to be attendant on its awakening or release (and, in cases of combustion, out of spiritual control). Disrespectful allusions to *kundalini* occur in the passage from Umberto Eco on p. 529 and ('orangefiery and scarlet rays emanating from the sacral region') in James Joyce's parody on p. 462.

A half-brother of George Sand often referred to the time 'when I was a dog . . .' Mrs Besant's bracing endorsement of reincarnation will have its adherents—you don't rely on charity, you pay your own way upwards—but outside the framework of Buddhism and Hinduism it seems a questionably attractive future or sequence of futures, and a doctrine that poses problems all round. Rumour has it that at theosophical meetings a certain cat, which on high authority would be a person of consequence in its next incarnation, was always offered the best seat; when it wandered into a lady's bedroom, she felt dreadfully awkward about undressing in its presence.

Yet in spite of Pascal's eloquent questioning as to which was the harder, that one should be born or that one should be reborn, that what has never been should be or that what has already existed once should exist again, or for all our determination to put such thoughts aside and let immortality look after itself ('Existence is duty,' said Faust, speaking for Goethe, 'though it last but a moment'), there can be few of us who have not at some time echoed, incredulously, Belial's chilling question in *Paradise Lost*:

> For who would lose,
> Though full of pain, this intellectual being,
> Those thoughts that wander through eternity,
> To perish rather, swallowed up and lost
> In the wide womb of uncreated Night,
> Devoid of sense and motion?

～

Death-trance is the image of death. The heart does not act; the breathing is suspended; the body is motionless; not the slightest sign of sensibility or consciousness can be detected . . . So the only means of knowing whether life be still present is to wait the event . . .

Henry Engelbrecht, as we learn in a pamphlet published by him in 1639, after an ascetic life, during which he had experienced sensorial illusions, fell into the deepest form of trance, which he thus describes: In the year 1623, exhausted by intense mental excitement of a religious kind, and by abstinence from food, after hearing a sermon which strongly affected him, he felt as if he could combat no longer; so he gave in and took to his bed. There he lay a week, without tasting anything but the bread and wine of the sacrament. On the eighth day, he thought he fell into the death-struggle. Death seemed to invade him from below upwards. His body became to his feelings rigid; his hands and feet insensible; his tongue and lips incapable of motion; gradually his sight failed him. But he still heard the laments and consultations of those around him.

This gradual demise lasted from midday till eleven at night, when he heard the watchmen. Then he wholly lost sensibility to outward impressions. But an elaborate vision of immense detail began; the theme of which was, that he was first carried down to hell, and looked into the place of torment; from whence, after a time, quicker than an arrow he was borne to Paradise. In these abodes of suffering and happiness, he saw and heard and smelt things unspeakable. These scenes, though long in apprehension, were short in time; for he came enough to himself, by twelve o'clock, again to hear the watchmen. It took him another twelve hours to come round entirely. His hearing was first restored; then his sight; feeling and power of motion followed; as soon as he could move his limbs, he rose. He felt himself stronger than before the trance.

HERBERT MAYO, *On the Truths Contained in Popular Superstitions*, 1851

The late Mr J. Holloway, of the Bank of England, brother to the engraver of that name, related of himself that, being one night in bed, and unable to sleep, he had fixed his eyes and thoughts with uncommon intensity on a beautiful star that was shining in at the window, when he suddenly found his spirit released from his body and soaring into space. But instantly seized with anxiety for the anguish of his wife, if she discovered his body apparently dead beside her, he returned, and re-entered it with difficulty. He described that returning as a returning from light into *darkness*, and that whilst the spirit was free, he was alternately in the light or the dark, accordingly as his thoughts were with his wife or with the star.

BARING-GOULD, *The Book of Werewolves*

Dr A. S. Wiltse, of Skiddy, Kansas, lay ill with typhoid and subnormal temperature and pulse, felt himself to be dying, and said goodbye to his family and friends. He managed to straighten his legs, arrange his arms over his breast, and sank into utter unconsciousness. Dr S. H. Raynes, the only physician present, said that he passed four hours without pulse or perceptible heart-beat. He was thought to be dead, and the church bell was tolled. The doctor, however, thought he could perceive occasionally a very slight gasp; he thrust a needle into the flesh but got no response. The percipient, however, says that at last he again came into a state of conscious existence and found he was still in the body, 'but the body and I no longer had any interests in common'. He seemed to be getting out of his body, rocking to and fro and breaking connection with the body's tissues. He seemed to feel and hear the snapping of innumerable small cords and then, he says, 'I began slowly to retreat from the feet, towards the head, as a rubber cord shortens.' Presently he felt he was in the head and then emerging through the sutures of the skull. 'I recollect distinctly,' he continues, 'how I appeared to myself something like a jellyfish as regards colour and form. As I emerged I saw two ladies sitting at my head. I measured the distances between the head of my cot and the knees of the lady opposite the head and concluded there was room for me to stand, but felt considerable embarrassment as I reflected that I was about to emerge naked before her . . . As I emerged from the head I floated up and down and laterally like a soap-bubble attached to the bowl of a pipe until I at last broke loose from the body and fell lightly to the floor, where I slowly rose and expanded into the full stature of a man. I seemed to be translucent, of a bluish cast and perfectly naked.' The percipient fled towards the door, but when he got there, found himself suddenly clothed, and his elbow came into contact with one of two men standing in the doorway (they were actually there) and to his surprise went through him without encountering any resistance. He tried to attract the attention of his friends but without success, so he walked out of the door and into the street. He says, 'I never saw that street more distinctly than I saw it then. I took note of the redness of the soil and of the washes the rain had made.' (There had been heavy rains and there were marked rain-washes.) He then noticed that he was attached by means of a small cord, like a spider's web, to his body in the house, the cord coming from his shoulders. He then seemed to be propelled, as if by a pair of hands, and found himself on a roadway, while below him was a scene of mountain and forest which looked very like the local scenery. After various experiences he came to rocks blocking the road which he tried to climb round. But at that moment a black cloud descended on him; and he opened his eyes to find himself back in his sick-bed.

Drawn from *Proceedings* of the Society for Psychical Research, Vol. 8, 1892

A woman patient, whose reliability and truthfulness I have no reason to doubt, told me that her first birth was very difficult. After thirty hours of fruitless labour the doctor considered that a forceps delivery was indicated. This was carried out under light narcosis. She was badly torn and suffered great loss of blood. When the doctor, her mother, and her husband had gone, and everything was cleared up, the nurse wanted to eat, and the patient saw her turn round at the door and ask, 'Do you want anything before I go to supper?' She tried to answer, but couldn't. She had the feeling that she was sinking through the bed into a bottomless void. She saw the nurse hurry to the bedside and seize her hand in order to take her pulse. From the way she moved her fingers to and fro the patient thought it must be almost imperceptible. Yet she herself felt quite all right, and was slightly amused at the nurse's alarm. She was not in the least frightened. That was the last she could remember for a long time. The next thing she was aware of was that, without feeling her body and its position, she was *looking down* from a point in the ceiling and could see everything going on in the room below her: she saw herself lying in the bed, deadly pale, with closed eyes. Beside her stood the nurse. The doctor paced up and down the room excitedly, and it seemed to her that he had lost his head and didn't know what to do. Her relatives crowded to the door. Her mother and her husband came in and looked at her with frightened faces. She told herself it was too stupid of them to think she was going to die, for she would certainly come round again. All this time she knew that behind her was a glorious, park-like landscape shining in the brightest colours, and in particular an emerald green meadow with short grass, which sloped gently upwards beyond a wrought-iron gate leading into the park. It was spring, and little gay flowers such as she had never seen before were scattered about in the grass. The whole demesne sparkled in the sunlight, and all the colours were of an indescribable splendour. The sloping meadow was flanked on both sides by dark green trees. It gave her the impression of a clearing in the forest, never yet trodden by the foot of man. 'I knew that this was the entrance to another world, and that if I turned round to gaze at the picture directly, I should feel tempted to go in at the gate, and thus step out of life.' She did not actually *see* this landscape, as her back was turned to it, but she *knew* it was there. She felt there was nothing to stop her from entering in through the gate. She only knew that she would turn back to her body and would not die. That was why she found the agitation of the doctor and the distress of her relatives stupid and out of place.

The next thing that happened was that she awoke from her coma and saw the nurse bending over her in bed. She was told that she had been unconscious for about half an hour. The next day, some fifteen hours later, when she felt a little stronger, she made a remark to the nurse about the incompetent and 'hysterical' behaviour of the doctor during her coma. The nurse energetically denied this criticism in the belief that the patient had been completely unconscious at the time and could therefore have known nothing of the scene. Only when she described in full detail what had happened during the coma was the nurse obliged to admit that the patient had perceived the events exactly as they happened in reality.

One might conjecture that this was simply a psychogenic twilight state in which a split-off part of consciousness still continued to function. The patient, however, had never been hysterical and had suffered a genuine heart collapse followed by syncope due to cerebral anaemia, as all the outward and evidently alarming symptoms indicated. She really was in a coma and ought to have had a complete psychic black-out and been altogether incapable of clear observation and sound judgement.

> Jung, from 'Synchronicity: An Acausal Connecting Principle', 1952; tr. R. F. C. Hull

The evangelist Dr Billy Graham has described how on the day his grandmother lay dying she apparently sat up in bed even though she had been too weak to do so earlier. She then claimed seeing her dead husband Ben, who had lost a leg and an eye in the Civil War, with the words: 'There is Ben, and he has both of his eyes and both of his legs!'

Among many other instances it has recently been reported that on the death of the Duke of Windsor on 22 May 1972 his last words, murmured very quietly, were: 'Mama . . . Mama . . . Mama . . . Mama.' Was he having his first encounter in decades with his deceased mother, Queen Mary, to whom in her lifetime he had caused such anguish as a result of his love for the American divorcee Wallis Simpson?

> IAN WILSON, *The After Death Experience*, 1987

There was a path leading up to the front door with masses of nasturtiums on either side. I thought, 'That's funny, my mum always wanted a prefab and she always loved nasturtiums.' . . . I could see my Uncle Alf inside; I never cared for him much in this life. They seemed to be getting ready for a visitor, as if they were expecting someone. I said, 'Can I come in?' It looked so nice and welcoming, but my mother said, 'No, you can't, it's not your time to stay.' I said, 'Please, Mum, it's so lovely here. I don't want to go back.' But she was very firm and would not allow me to cross the threshold.

I said, 'You seem to be expecting someone; if it's not me, then who are you expecting?' She said, 'We are getting ready for your Auntie Ethel. She is expected shortly.' I begged once again if she would let me come in, as it was so warm and sunny and I felt really happy and at peace there. I did not want to go back, but she would not allow me to come in. The next thing I remember is finding myself back in bed at the hospital. I had been unconscious for three days. The nurse said to me, 'You gave us a real scare, we all thought you were a goner.'

A day or two later my family were allowed to see me and they all looked very glum. I said, 'I don't know what you are all looking so glum for, I haven't died yet, you won't get rid of me so easily.' They said they had some bad news and didn't know if they should tell me as I had been so ill, nearly dying and all. So I said, 'You might as well tell me now that you've said that much.' And they said that since I had been in hospital my Auntie Ethel had unexpectedly died of a sudden heart attack. I thought, well I could have told them that, as I already knew.

> An elderly Cockney lady, of her near-death experience after a heart attack; in Margot Grey, *Return from Death*, 1985

From that moment on I became completely separated from my body and my machine.

My 'other self' stood in the centre of the road feeling no pain or concern. I watched my motor cycle fall over and my body tumbling towards me. I knew and was completely aware that it was my body . . . It is not difficult to recall the vivid impressions I had of the rear wheel still spinning and the engine ticking over . . . I saw the driver of the car which I had hit scramble out of his car on the near side and a car at a standstill immediately behind my disabled motor cycle . . .

I saw the other driver get out of his car and stop the motor-cycle engine and lift it upright as it blocked the way to my body whilst the first driver put his hand on my shoulder then under my armpit and lifted my body. As he did so I returned to my body.

> Informant in Celia Green: *Out-of-the-Body Experiences*, 1968, reporting his experience after an accident in which he suffered a blow to the head

In the reign of Cenred, who succeeded Ethelred [in 704], there was a layman in a military employment, no less acceptable to the king for his worldly industry than displeasing to him for his private neglect of himself. The king often admonished him to confess and amend, and to forsake his wicked courses, before he should lose all time for repentance and amendment by a sudden death. Though frequently warned, he despised the words of salvation, and promised he would do penance at some future time. In the meantime, falling sick, he was confined to his bed, and began to feel very severe pains. The king coming to him (for he loved the man), earnestly exhorted him, even then, before death, to repent of his offences. He answered, He would not then confess his sins, but would do it when he was recovered of his sickness, lest his companions should upbraid him of having done that for fear of death, which he had refused to do in health . . .

The distemper still increasing, when the king came again to visit and instruct him, he cried out with a lamentable voice, 'What will you have now? What are ye come for? For you can no longer do me any good.' The king answered, 'Do not talk so; behave yourself like a man in his right mind.'—'I am not mad,' replied he, 'but I have now all the guilt of my wicked conscience before my eyes.'—'What is the meaning of that?' rejoined the king. 'Not long since,' said he , 'there came into this room two most beautiful youths, and sat down by me, the one at my head, and the other at my feet. One of them produced a very small and most curious book, and gave it me to read; looking into it, I there found all the good actions I had ever done in my life written down, and they were very few and inconsiderable. They took back the book and said nothing to me. Then, on a sudden, appeared an army of wicked and deformed spirits, encompassing this house without, and filling it within. Then he, who, by the blackness of his dismal face, and his sitting above the rest, seemed to be the chief of them, taking out a book horrible to behold, of a prodigious size, and of almost insupportable weight, commanded one of his followers to bring it to me to read. Having read it, I found therein most plainly written in black characters, all the crimes I ever committed, not only in word and deed, but even in the least thought. He said to those men in white, who sat by me, 'Why do you sit here, since you most certainly know that this man is ours?' They answered, 'You are in the right; take and add him to the number of the damned.' This said, they immediately vanished, and two most wicked spirits rising, with knives in their hands, one of them struck me on the head, and the other on the foot. These strokes are now with great torture penetrating through my bowels to the inward parts of my body, and as soon as they meet I shall die, and the devils being ready to snatch me away, I shall be dragged into hell.'

Thus talked that wretch in despair, and dying soon after, he is now in vain suffering in eternal torments that penance which he refused to suffer during a short time, that he might obtain forgiveness . . . This story, as I learned it of the venerable Bishop Pehthelm, I have thought proper to relate in a plain manner, for the salvation of my hearers.

THE VENERABLE BEDE, *Ecclesiastical History of the English People*, 731; tr. John Stevens, rev. J. A. Giles

A strong empyreumatic, thick smoke ascended from the hatchway of the cabin, and, as it had now fallen calm, it mounted straight up the air in a dense column. I attempted to go in, but so soon as I encountered the smoke, I found that it was impossible; it would have suffocated me in half a minute. I did what most children would have done in such a situation of excitement and distress—I sat down and cried bitterly. In about ten minutes . . . I went to the hatchway, and although the smell was still overpowering, I found that I could bear it. I descended the little ladder of three steps, and called 'Mother!' but there was no answer. The lamp fixed against the after bulkhead, with a glass before it, was still alight, and I could see plainly to every corner of the cabin. Nothing was burning—not even the curtains to my mother's bed appeared to be singed . . . I ventured to draw back the curtains of the bed—my mother was not there! but there appeared to be a black mass in the centre of the bed. I put my hand fearfully upon it—it was a sort of unctuous, pitchy cinder. I screamed with horror—my little senses reeled—I staggered from the cabin and fell down on the deck in a state amounting almost to insanity: it was followed by a sort of stupor, which lasted for many hours.

As the reader may be in some doubt as to the occasion of my mother's death, I must inform him that she perished in that very peculiar and dreadful manner, which does sometimes, although rarely, occur to those who indulge in an immoderate use of spirituous liquors. Cases of this kind do indeed present themselves but once in a century, but the occurrence of them is too well authenticated. She perished from what is termed *spontaneous combustion*, an inflammation of the gases generated from the spirits absorbed into the system.

CAPTAIN FREDERICK MARRYAT, *Jacob Faithful*, 1834

'Have you got them?'

'Got them! No. The old man's not there.'

He has been so horribly frightened in the short interval, that his terror seizes the other, who makes a rush at him, and asks loudly, 'What's the matter?'

'I couldn't make him hear, and I softly opened the door and looked in. And the burning smell is there—and the soot is there, and the oil is there—and he is not there!'—Tony ends this with a groan.

Mr Guppy takes the light. They go down, more dead than alive, and holding one another, push open the door of the back shop. The cat has retreated close to it, and stands snarling—not at them; at something on the

ground, before the fire. There is a very little fire left in the grate, but there is
a smouldering suffocating vapour in the room, and a dark greasy coating on the
walls and ceiling. The chairs and table, and the bottle so rarely absent from the
table, all stand as usual. On one chair-back, hang the old man's hairy cap and
coat.

'Look!' whispers the lodger, pointing his friend's attention to these objects
with a trembling finger. 'I told you so. When I saw him last, he took his cap
off, took out the little bundle of old letters, hung his cap on the back of the
chair—his coat was there already, for he had pulled that off, before he went
to put the shutters up—and I left him turning the letters over in his hand,
standing just where that crumbled black thing is upon the floor.'

Is he hanging somewhere? They look up. No.

'See!' whispers Tony. 'At the foot of the same chair, there lies a dirty bit of
thin red cord that they tie up pens with. That went round the letters. He
undid it slowly, leering and laughing at me, before he began to turn them over,
and threw it there. I saw it fall.'

'What's the matter with the cat?' says Mr Guppy. 'Look at her!'

'Mad, I think. And no wonder in this evil place.'

They advance slowly, looking at all these things. The cat remains where
they found her, still snarling at the something on the ground, before the fire
and between the two chairs. What is it? Hold up the light.

Here is a small burnt patch of flooring; here is the tinder from a little bundle
of burnt paper, but not so light as usual, seeming to be steeped in something;
and here is—is it the cinder of a small charred and broken log of wood
sprinkled with white ashes, or is it coal? O Horror, he IS here! and this from
which we run away, striking out the light and overturning one another into the
street, is all that represents him . . .

Call the death by any name Your Highness will, attribute it to whom you
will, or say it might have been prevented how you will, it is the same death
eternally—inborn, inbred, engendered in the corrupted humours of the vi-
cious body itself, and that only—Spontaneous Combustion, and none other of
all the deaths that can be died.

Out of the court, and a long way out of it, there is considerable excitement too;
for men of science and philosophy come to look, and carriages set down
doctors at the corner who arrive with the same intent, and there is more
learned talk about inflammable gases and phosphuretted hydrogen than the
court has ever imagined. Some of these authorities (of course the wisest) hold
with indignation that the deceased had no business to die in the alleged manner; and being reminded by other authorities of a certain inquiry into the
evidence for such deaths, reprinted in the sixth volume of the Philosophical

Transactions; and also of a book not quite unknown, on English Medical Jurisprudence; and likewise of the Italian case of the Countess Cornelia Baudi as set forth in detail by one Bianchini, prebendary of Verona, who wrote a scholarly work or so, and was occasionally heard of in his time as having gleams of reason in him; and also of the testimony of Messrs Foderé and Mere, two pestilent Frenchmen who *would* investigate the subject; and further, of the corroborative testimony of Monsieur Le Cat, a rather celebrated French surgeon once upon a time, who had the unpoliteness to live in a house where such a case occurred, and even to write an account of it;—still they regard the late Mr Krook's obstinacy, in going out of the world by any such by-way, as wholly unjustifiable and personally offensive.

DICKENS, Bleak House, 1852–3

This afternoon I drove with Lord Stanhope in the long grassy glades of the park, the highest and prettiest of which gave a name to the place—Chevening, 'the Nook in the Hill' . . . and we came back by the Spottiswoodes'. It is a fine old place, intended as an imitation of the Villa Doria in Rome, and though in no wise like Villa Doria, it has a look of Italy in its groves of ilexes and its cypresses. Lady Frederick Campbell lived here. Her first husband was the Lord Ferrers who was hanged [for the murder of his steward], and some evidence which she gave was instrumental in bringing about his condemnation. Lord Ferrers cursed her, saying that her death would be even more painful than his; and so it was, for in 1807 she was burnt in one of the towers of the house, from spontaneous combustion it is said. Nothing was found of her but her thumb, she was so completely consumed, and ever since it is said that the ghost of Lady Frederick Campbell wanders in the grounds at night, brandishing her thumbless hand, and looking for her lost thumb.

> HARE, *The Story of My Life*. This Lord Ferrers is said to have been the last English nobleman to claim the privilege of being hanged with a silken cord; unfortunately the hangman could not lay his hands on one

Mrs Sara Ann Kirby, Mr John Henry Kirby and their daughters, Alice Ann Kirby, aged five, and Amy Kirby, aged four, lived in Sowerby Bridge, now in West Yorkshire. The family resided in Hargreaves Terrace on London Road, until the parents fell out and separated. When this happened . . . Alice Kirby went to live with her father and grandmother at no. 45 Wakefield Road.

Wakefield Road and London Road run parallel to one another, exactly a mile apart on opposite sides of the Calder Valley. The roads are linked by Fall Lane, which crosses a canal and the River Calder.

On Thursday 5 January 1899, Mrs Sara Kirby went outside Hargreaves Terrace to get some water from the well, twenty yards away. It was 11 a.m. Because it was raining heavily, the task took no more than two minutes. As she re-entered the house, she heard screams and found Amy ablaze. Mrs Kirby told the inquest: 'If she had had paraffin oil thrown over her she would not have burned faster.'

Another witness claimed that flames a yard high were coming from the child's head. It was stated that Amy was afraid of fire. Indeed there was no evidence of matches or charred paper. After it was all over, Mrs Kirby, in great distress, started down Fall Lane to communicate the tragedy to her husband. But the distress was compounded when, halfway across the valley, she was met by a messenger from her mother-in-law. The messenger was bringing terrible news. Sara's *other* daughter, Alice, had been discovered ablaze. The pair were reduced to hysterical tears as they each related an identical story.

Grandmother Susan Kirby had left young Alice in bed while she visited a neighbour. When she returned, she found the child 'enveloped in flames and almost burned to death'. There were no spent matches or burned paper, and the fire in the grate had not been disturbed. *The time was exactly 11 a.m.*

Both girls were taken away in the same horse-drawn ambulance to the Royal Halifax Infirmary. Alice died at 3 p.m. that day, and Amy just before midnight. In another of those strange name-related 'coincidences' seemingly endemic in SHC matters, the doctor who attended them both was called Dr Wellburn.

> JENNY RANDLES and PETER HOUGH, *Spontaneous Human Combustion*, 1992; based on an article in the *Halifax Evening Courier*, 13 April 1985, itself drawing on accounts published in the same paper in 1899

In 1966 a gas man, doing his meter-reading round in Coudersport, Pennsylvania, entered the house of a retired doctor, and was surprised to find a cone of ash on the floor, and light blue smoke hanging over it. Looking for the doctor, he eventually found what remained of him in the bathroom: a foot, still in its shoe. When the coroner arrived, he realized that the doctor's body (except for the foot) had turned to ash; beneath it was a small hole in the floor, through which the ash had dropped to form the cone seen by the gas man. Otherwise, apart from some slight charring, no damage had been done by the conflagration.

As Francis Hitching has commented in his *World Atlas of Mysteries* [1978], this left the coroner, as it leaves us, with certain unanswerable questions. The first guess was that the doctor, having inadvertently set his bathrobe alight, had rushed to the bathroom to dowse it. But the robe, lying in the bath, was barely singed. Even if it had begun to burn, how could that have incinerated the doctor? Why did the gas man smell, not burning flesh, but an odour which, he said, put him in mind of a new central heating system at work? Why was there no sign of the fire in the living-room—if that was where the robe had caught alight? 'And why was the paint on the bathtub, only inches away from the charred floor, blackened but not blistered?' Baffled, the coroner settled for a verdict of 'asphyxiation and 90 per cent burning of the body'.

BRIAN INGLIS, *The Hidden Power*, 1986

'You sit there, Father, and look so cool,' the bishop burst out . . . 'You look so cool, after telling me . . . that Mother Perpetua has burst into flames while on her parish visits—tell me, what did she say, she must have said something before they took her away, you do not have a nun, and a convent superior at that, just suddenly set on fire!' . . .

'She was in no condition for much conversation,' Father Angwin said. 'The stretcher-bearers said she mumbled something about a low blue flame, creeping towards her over the grass . . . They could make nothing of it.' . . .

'Oh dear, dear,' said the bishop again . . . 'It is a bad business, this, Angwin, it is a very bad business. It looks very bad, and it all comes back on me.'

'Do you think it was a diabolic manifestation?' Angwin asked.

'Tosh,' the bishop replied, with a flash of spirit.

Angwin gave him a warning look. 'Nuns have had their troubles in that line,' he said. 'Demons threw St Catherine of Siena into the fire many a time. They pulled her off her horse, and tipped her into a freezing river head first. Sister Mary Angelica, a nun from Évreux, was followed for two years by a devil in the form of a green scaly dog.' He paused, enjoying the effect he was making. 'A Mother Agnes, a Dominican, was attacked by the devil in the form of a pack of wolves. St Margaret Mary had her seat pulled from under her as she sat before the convent fire. Three other nuns testified in writing that they saw the holy person repeatedly and by supernatural forces dumped on her backside.'

'There must be some other explanation,' the bishop said pathetically.

'You mean a more modern explanation? A more relevant one? Some ecumenical kind of a reason why it occurred?'

'Do not torment me, Angwin,' the bishop wailed. 'I am a man sorely tried. I feel there must have been some chemical reaction that caused it.'

'The devil is a great chemist,' Angwin said.

'Of course there are cases of it, people bursting into flames, though I have never heard of it in a nun. There is a case of it in one of the novels of Dickens, is there not? And that fellow has written a study of it, what do you call him, the fellow with the deerstalker and the violin?'

'I think perhaps you mean Mr Arthur Conan Doyle,' Father Angwin said. 'I did not know you read such sensational stuff. More tea?'

'They call it spontaneous combustion,' the bishop said. He looked wild-eyed at the thought.

'Combustion, certainly,' Father Angwin agreed. Personally he doubted the spontaneity of it.

HILARY MANTEL, *Fludd*, 1989

❦

Let us start with a clear understanding of what is meant by Reincarnation. So far as the derivation of the word is concerned, any repeated entering into a physical, or fleshly, covering, might be included thereunder. It certainly implies the existence of something relatively permanent that enters into and inhabits successive somethings relatively impermanent. But the word tells us nothing of the nature of these relatively permanent and impermanent somethings, save that the impermanent habitations are of 'flesh'. Another word, often used as synonymous with Reincarnation, the word Metempsychosis, suggests the other side of the transaction; here the habitation is ignored, and the stress is laid on the transit of the Psyche, the relatively permanent. Putting the two together as descriptive of the whole idea, we should have the entry of a Psyche or 'soul' into successive 'bodies' of flesh; and though the word 'soul' is open to serious objections, from its looseness and its theological connotations, it may stand for the moment as representing in the minds of most people a form of existence which outlasts the physical frame with which it was connected during a life on earth . . .

Never, perhaps, has this doctrine, in its loftiest form, been put more clearly or more beautifully than in the famous encouragement of Arjuna by Krishna, given in the *Bhagavad-Gita*:

These bodies of the embodied One, who is eternal, indestructible and boundless, are known as finite . . . He who regardeth this as a slayer, and he who thinketh he is slain, both of them are ignorant. He slayeth not nor is he slain. He is not born, nor doth he die; nor having been, ceaseth he any more to be; unborn, perpetual, eternal and ancient, he is not slain when the body is slaughtered. Who knoweth him indestructible, unborn, undiminishing, how can that man slay, O Partha, or cause to be slain? As a man, casting off worn-out garments, taketh new ones, so the dweller in the body, casting off worn-out bodies, entereth into others that are new. Weapons cleave him not, nor fire burneth him, nor waters wet him, nor wind drieth him away. Indivisible he, incombustible he, and indeed neither to be wetted nor dried away; perpetual, all-pervasive, stable, immovable, ancient, unmanifest, unthinkable, immutable, he is called; therefore knowing him as such thou shouldst not grieve.

Thus step by step is brought about the evolution of man, character being moulded in personality after personality, gains and losses rigidly recorded in astral and mental forms, and these governing the succeeding physical manifestations. Every virtue is thus the outer sign and symbol of a step forward made, of repeated victories won over the lower nature, and the 'innate-quality', the mental or moral characteristic with which a child is born, is the indubitable proof of past struggle, of past triumphs, or of past failures. A distasteful doctrine enough to the morally or mentally slothful and cowardly, but a most cheering and heartening teaching for those who do not ask to be pensioners on any charity, human or divine, but are content to earn patiently and laboriously all they claim to own.

ANNIE BESANT, *Reincarnation*, 1893

A king was one day passing through the market-place of his city, when he observed a hunchbacked merryandrew, whose contortions and jokes kept the bystanders in a roar of laughter. Amused with the fellow, the king brought him to his palace. Shortly after, in the hearing of the clown, a necromancer taught the monarch the art of sending his soul into a body not his own.

Some little while after this, the monarch, anxious to put in practice his newly acquired knowledge, rode into the forest accompanied by his fool, who, he believed, had not heard, or at all events comprehended, the lesson. They came upon the corpse of a Brahmin lying in the depth of the jungle, where he had died of thirst. The king, leaving his horse, performed the requisite ceremony, and instantly his soul had migrated into the body of the Brahmin, and his own lay as dead upon the ground. At the same moment, however, the hunchback deserted his body, and possessed himself of that which had been the king's, and shouting farewell to the dismayed monarch, he rode back to the palace, where he was received with royal honours. But it was not long before the queen and one of the ministers discovered that a screw was somewhere loose, and when the quondam king, but now Brahmin, arrived and told his tale, a plot was laid for the recovery of his body. The queen asked her false husband whether it were possible to make her parrot talk, and he in a moment of uxorious weakness promised to make it speak. He laid his body aside, and sent his soul into the parrot. Immediately the true king jumped out of his Brahmin body and resumed that which was legitimately his own, and then proceeded, with the queen, to wring the neck of the parrot.

> BARING-GOULD, *The Book of Werewolves*; a tale from the *Pañcatantra*, *c*.6th century

There is in the Buddhist scriptures a very clear account of this process of conditionality. The Buddhist sage Nagasena explained it to the King Milinda in a set of famous answers to questions that the King posed him.

The King asked Nagasena: 'When someone is reborn, is he the same as the one who just died, or is he different?'

Nagasena replied: 'He is neither the same, nor different . . . Tell me, if a man were to light a lamp, could it provide light the whole night long?'

'Yes.'

'Is the flame then which burns in the first watch of the night the same as the one that burns in the second . . . or the last?'

'No.'

'Does that mean there is one lamp in the first watch of the night, another in the second, and another in the third?'

'No, it's because of that one lamp that the light shines all night.'

'Rebirth is much the same: one phenomenon arises and another stops, simultaneously. So the first act of consciousness in the new existence is neither the same as the last act of consciousness in the previous existence, nor is it different.' . . .

The King then asks: 'If there is no being that passes on from body to body, wouldn't we then be free of all the negative actions we had done in past lives?'

Nagasena gives this example: A man steals someone's mangoes. The mangoes he steals are not exactly the same mangoes that the other person had originally owned and planted, so how can he possibly deserve to be punished? The reason he does, Nagasena explains, is that the stolen mangoes only grew because of those that their owner had planted in the first place. In the same way, it is because of our actions in one life, pure or impure, that we are linked with another life, and we are not free from their results.

> SOGYAL RINPOCHE, *The Tibetan Book of Living and Dying*, 1992

One of the cases investigated by Ian Stevenson, a professor of psychiatry at the University of Virginia and a researcher into reincarnation, was that of Parmod Sharma, born in 1944, the son of a family living in Uttar Pradesh, in India. Stevenson wrote of the boy thus:

When he was about two and a half, he began to tell his mother not to cook because he had a wife in Moradabad who could cook. Later, between the age of three and four, he began to refer to a large soda and biscuit shop which he said he had in Moradabad. He asked to go to Moradabad. He said he was one of the 'Mohan Brothers'. He claimed to be well-to-do and to have had another shop in Saharanpur. He showed an extraordinary interest in biscuits and shops . . . He related how in the previous life he had become ill after eating too much curd and said he had 'died in a bathtub'.

Professor Stevenson visited India to interview the boy, and talked to the family, who declared that they had no previous knowledge of anyone named 'Mohan'. He then discovered that there was a biscuit shop in Moradabad known as 'The Mohan Brothers', who owned a second shop in Saharanpur. He also learnt that another brother, Parmanand, had died of a gastrointestinal illness.

The witnesses of the Mehra family stated that Parmanand tried a series of naturopathic bath treatments when he had appendicitis. He had some of these treatments during the days just before his death but did not actually die in a bathtub. In a letter dated 7 September 1949, Sri B. L. Sharma stated that Parmod had said he died of being 'wet with water' and that he (Sri B. L. Sharma) had learned (presumably from the Mehra family) that Parmanand had been given a bath immediately before his death.

> Drawn from Ian Stevenson: 'The Contribution of Apparitions to the Evidence for Survival', *Journal of the American Society for Psychical Research*, Number 76, 1982

When [Aunt] Rosemary was looking after Philip for his parents he suddenly said, 'When I was Andrew I saw Thomas Becket being assassinated.'

Rosemary was astounded because . . . she just couldn't believe she had heard the words 'Thomas Becket' and 'assassinated'. These words were totally outside the range of the three-year-old's vocabulary and the historical event was beyond the horizon of his knowledge. 'I could hardly speak I got such a shock,' says Rosemary. Philip told his aunt that when he was Andrew he was bigger than he is now because he was six years old and he could write.

Philip says, 'I wrote down everything I saw. I had lots of notebooks then but I think they got lost.' The child remembers that he had been taken to Canterbury for some reason from his home in Oxford, and it was during this visit to the city that the archbishop was murdered. He remembers seeing lots of people rushing about and he especially remembers that there were lots of soldiers in the city. He says, 'The soldiers had giant swords and big long shields with drawings on them and they wore funny masks on their faces. Some of them were on fancy horses and some were just standing about. They were very noisy and shouted a lot.'

Philip says that at the time of the murder he was actually in Canterbury Cathedral. 'Lots and lots of people were there,' he says. He remembers the clothes that the people wore: he describes them as 'long dresses'. He told his aunt, 'The men wore short dresses and the ladies wore long ones.'

It seems that although he had only been six years old at the time, the little boy was acutely aware that something terrible was taking place. He says, 'I knew it was a very bad thing and that's why I wrote it in my notebook. There was lots of noise and screams in church. It was very dark and I couldn't see very well. I was squashed with all the people. I couldn't see Thomas Becket because the big people were in front of me but I know that he was there and the soldiers murdered him then they ran out.' After that, Philip says, 'Everybody was pushing and screaming and frightened.'

When Philip described the scene to his Aunt Rosemary there was no doubt in her mind that her nephew's memories were real, and that he had lived before in the 12th century. 'No child of his age could have such knowledge of events which took place so long ago. We never discuss history or anything like that—we're just not that kind of family—and in any case we would never talk about a murder in front of a three-year-old child. As for Thomas Becket, I don't think any of us know anything about him. I just know that he existed once and that he was murdered but I've got no idea of how or why. In fact I know nothing at all about the man.'

Concerning Philip Harding, of Milton Keynes; in Peter and Mary Harrison: *Life Before Birth*, 1983

I feel that there is much to be said for the Celtic belief that the souls of those whom we have lost are held captive in some inferior being, in an animal, in a plant, in some inanimate object, and thus effectively lost to us until the day (which to many never comes) when we happen to pass by the tree or to obtain possession of the object which forms their prison. Then they start and tremble, they call us by our name, and as soon as we have recognized them the spell is broken. Delivered by us, they have overcome death and return to share our life.

PROUST, *Swann's Way*, 1913

Squats on a toad-stool under a tree
   A bodiless childfull of life in the gloom,
Crying with frog voice, 'What shall I be?
Poor unborn ghost, for my mother killed me
   Scarcely alive in her wicked womb.
What shall I be? shall I creep to the egg
   That's cracking asunder yonder by Nile,
     And with eighteen toes,
     And a snuff-taking nose,
   Make an Egyptian crocodile?
Sing, "Catch a mummy by the leg
     And crunch him with an upper jaw,
     Wagging tail and clenching claw;
     Take a billfull from my craw,
     Neighbour raven, caw, O caw,
     Grunt, my crocky, pretty maw!" '

BEDDOES, from Isbrand's 'Song', *Death's Jest-Book*, 1825 onwards; another character remarks, 'Would that Pythagoras had heard thee, boy!'

'Only the gods in heaven can enjoy the good fortune of a rain of flowers,' thought the hippie, observing him from the temple steps, where he had stationed himself since the previous evening. No need to explain who the hippie was, the whole basis of hippieness being the shedding of identity and all geographical associations. He might be from Berkeley or Outer Mongolia or anywhere. If you developed an intractable hirsuteness, you acquired a successful mask . . . In addition, if you draped yourself in a knee-length cotton dhoti and vest, and sat down with ease in the dust anywhere, your clothes acquired a spontaneous ochre tint worthy of a *sanyasi*. When you have acquired this degree of universality, it is not relevant to question who or what you are. You have to be taken as you are—a breathing entity, that's all. That was how the wayside cobbler viewed the hippie when he stepped up before him to get the straps of his sandals fixed.

He glanced up and reflected, 'With those matted locks falling on his nape, looks like God Shiva, only the cobra coiling around his neck missing.' In order to be on the safe side of one who looked so holy, he made a deep obeisance.

'Do you believe in God?' asked the hippie, a question that surprised the cobbler. How could a question of that nature ever arise? Probably he was being tested by this mysterious customer. Better be careful in answering him. The cobbler gestured towards the temple in front and threw up his arm in amazement. 'He just does not notice us sometimes. How could He? Must have so much to look after.' He brooded for a few minutes at a picture of God, whose attention was distracted hither and thither by a thousand clamouring petitioners praying in all directions. He added, 'Take the case of our big officer, our collector—can he be seen by everyone or will he be able to listen to everyone and answer their prayers? When a human officer is so difficult to reach, how much more a god? He has so much to think of . . .' He lifted his arms and swept them across the dome of heaven from horizon to horizon. It filled the hippie with a sense of immensity of God's programme and purpose, and the man added, 'And He can't sleep, either. Our pundit in this temple said in his lecture that gods do not wink their eyelids or sleep. How can they? In the winking of an eyelid, so many bad things might happen. The planets might leave their courses and bump into one another, the sky might pour down fire and brimstone or all the demons might be let loose and devour humanity. Oh, the cataclysm!' The hippie shuddered at the vision of disaster that'd overtake us within one eye-winking of God. The cobbler added, 'I ask God every day and keep asking every hour. But when He is a little free, He will hear me; till then, I have to bear it.'

'What, bear what?' asked the hippie, unable to contain his curiosity.

'This existence. I beg Him to take me away. But the time must come. It'll come . . . God punishes us in this life. In my last birth I must have been a moneylender squeezing the life out of the poor, or a shopkeeper cornering all the rice for profits—till I render all these accounts, God'll keep me here. I have only to be patient.'

'What do you want to be in your next birth?'

The cobbler got a sudden feeling again that he might be talking to a god or his agent. He brooded over the question for some time. 'I don't want birth in this world. Who knows, they may decide to send me to hell, but I don't want to go to hell.' He explained his vision of another world where a mighty accountant sat studying the debits and credits and drawing up a monumental balance sheet appropriate for each individual.

'What have you done?' asked the hippie.

A suspicion again in the cobbler's mind that he might be talking to a god. 'Now my limbs are weak, but in one's younger years, one might even set fire to an enemy's hut at night while his children are asleep. A quarrel could lead to such things. That man took away my money, threatened to molest my wife, and she lost an eye in the scuffle when I beat her up on suspicion . . .'

'I don't want to ask questions,' said the hippie, 'but I, too, set fire to villages and, flying over them, blasted people whom I didn't know or see.'

The cobbler looked up in surprise. 'When, where, where?'

The hippie said, 'In another incarnation; in another birth. Can you guess what may be in store for me next?'

The cobbler said, 'If you can wait till the priest of the temple comes . . . A wise man, he'll tell us.'

The hippie said, 'You were at least angry with the man whose hut you burned. I didn't even know whose huts I was destroying. I didn't even see them.' . . .

He gave the cobbler twenty-five paise, as agreed. He then took the silver figure from his bag and held it out to the cobbler. 'Here is something for you . . .'

The cobbler examined it and cried, 'Oh, this is Durga the goddess; she will protect you. Did you steal it?'

The hippie appreciated the question as indicating perfectly how he had ceased to look respectable. He replied, 'Perhaps the man who gave it to me stole it.'

'Keep it, it'll protect you,' said the cobbler, returning the silver figure. He reflected, after the hippie was gone, 'Even a god steals when he has a chance.'

R. K. NARAYAN, from 'God and the Cobbler', 1981

'However,' continued Goethe, 'I have had to endure not a little from Tiedge's *Urania*; for at one time nothing was sung and nothing was declaimed but this same *Urania*. Wherever you went, you found *Urania* on the table. *Urania* and immortality were the topics of every conversation. I would by no means dispense with the happiness of believing in a future existence, and indeed would say with Lorenzo de Medici that those are dead even for this life who hope for no other. But such incomprehensible matters lie too far off to be a theme of daily speculation. Let him who believes in immortality enjoy his happiness in silence, he has no reason to give himself airs about it. The occasion of Tiedge's *Urania* led me to observe that piety, like nobility, has its aristocracy. I met stupid women, who plumed themselves on believing, with Tiedge, in immortality; and I was forced to bear much dark examination on this point. They were vexed by my saying I should be well pleased if after the close of this life we were blessed with another, only I hoped I should hereafter meet none of those who had believed in it here. For how should I be tormented! The pious would throng around me, and say, "Were we not right? Did we not predict it? Has not it happened just as we said?" And so there would be ennui without end even in the other world.'

'This preoccupation with immortality,' he continued, 'is for people of rank, and especially ladies, who have nothing to do. But an able man, who has something regular to do here, and must toil and struggle and produce day by day, leaves the future world to itself, and is active and useful in this. Thoughts about immortality are also good for those who have not been very successful here; and I would wager that, if the good Tiedge had enjoyed a better lot, he would also have had better thoughts.'

GOETHE, *Conversations with Eckermann*, 25 February 1824; tr. John Oxenford.
Christoph August Tiedge's philosophical poem, *Urania*, was published in 1801

SPIRITUALISM

THE opening group of entries centres on Daniel Dunglas Home, the most celebrated medium of the nineteenth century. Brian Inglis has called 'Mr Sludge, "The Medium" ', a barely disguised satirical portrait of Home, the nastiest of Robert Browning's poems. It strikes me as an exceptionally lively one, and even fair-minded in that Mr Sludge, sly and ingenious, is allowed some shrewd arguments in his own favour; for instance, the analogy of the fake china egg placed under a hen to encourage it to lay real ones: 'I've told my lie, and seen truth follow.' Home may even have taken a tip from the poem, and scored a useful point by himself writing in sorrowful indignation about dishonest mediums and their faked manifestations.

Eusapia Palladino, albeit illiterate, showed astuteness too, in ascribing her occasional cheating to the pressure of expectation on the part of her audience. Reports of the tests she underwent in Paris between 1905 and 1908, conducted by eminent scientists including Pierre and Marie Curie, Jean Perrin, and Henri Bergson, all of them Nobel laureates, in which monitoring instruments were used to register any improper physical movements, tell of musical and telekinetic manifestations, of playful invisible hands untying the savants' cravats and pulling their hair, and of a stool advancing on Pierre Curie and making as if to crawl up his leg while a small table floated prettily over his shoulder.

Though the dealings of Doris Collins and Doris Stokes are apt to set on edge the teeth of those whom William James termed 'college-bred gentry', their slangy, down-to-earth homilies appear to have given comfort. Doris Stokes comes up with another reassurance, blunter than Tennyson's: those on the other side respect our privacy, she declares, they only come when invited. She wonders amusedly why people are so impressed by the accuracy of the spirit world where figures are concerned; when one of its inhabitants revealed that a woman in the audience had recently bought a new oven for £130 off the recommended price, they were all amazed, yet when the correct name was given of a relative's new baby, it was taken for granted. But then, one expects the other world to be interested in babies rather than the price paid for kitchen equipment.

After discoursing ruefully on incredulity, Camille Flammarion admits that credulity too seems to have no limits. He knew an officer who talked social philosophy with Jean Valjean, unaware that this person was fictitious, a creation of Victor Hugo's imagination, while 'a great lady of mature age, and very intelligent, who had been intimately associated with Lord Byron', was in the habit of calling up the dead poet every Saturday evening to consult him as to her investments. Pondering the strange uses to which spiritualism has been put, Flammarion mentions a woman, 'once very charming', who secured a marquis as her husband 'because she made a table say to the man that his first wife pointed her out as her successor'.

In Proust's *Time Regained* the narrator observes of a man now in old age but erstwhile a brilliant talker that one was astonished to see him so pale and dejected, passing infrequent remarks as dull and trivial as the answers elicited by a medium who is putting momentous and fascinating questions to the 'double' of a man who in his lifetime was celebrated for sagacious eloquence. Someone once wrote in the *Saturday Review*, more harshly: 'If this is the spirit-world, it is much better to be a respectable pig and accept annihilation, than to be cursed with such an immortality'; the comment was quoted 'with a certain sympathy' by William James when reviewing a book entitled *Planchette* in the *Boston Daily Advertiser*, 10 March 1869.

However, the writer of a letter in *The Times Saturday Review* of 16 January 1993 surmises that the 'lesser spirits' who are attracted to mediums find difficulty in communicating with their living relatives—we might note the suggestion on p. 520 here that the 'purer and nobler souls' may find intercourse 'painful or impossible'—and 'perhaps references to the trivia of everyday life are more convincing proof of survival than grand philosophical discourses'. In *The Occult* (1971) Colin Wilson quotes Dostoevsky, that God denied man certainty because it would negate his freedom, and conjectures that a more intimate knowledge of the next world might well be detrimental to us in this one. We need to be kept, if not exactly in suspense, then in uncertainty, on our toes.

Mr Home the medium

Mr and Mrs Rymer and their family were present at the seance [held at the Rymers' house in Ealing], which began by several of the ordinary manifestations. Mr Browning was requested to investigate everything as it occurred, and he availed himself freely of the invitation. Several times during the evening, he voluntarily and earnestly declared that anything like imposture was out of the question. Previously to the arrival of Mr and Mrs Browning, some of the children had been gathering flowers in the garden, and Miss Rymer and I had made a wreath of clematis . . . During the seance this wreath was raised from the table by supernatural power in the presence of us all, and whilst we were watching it, Mr Browning, who was seated at the opposite side of the table, left his place, and came and stood behind his wife, towards whom the wreath was being slowly carried, and upon whose head it was placed in full sight of us all, and whilst he was standing close behind her. He expressed no disbelief; as, indeed, it was impossible for any one to have any of what was passing under his eyes; whilst Mrs Browning was much moved, and she, not only then but ever since, expressed her entire belief and pleasure in what then occurred . . . All that was done in the presence of eight persons besides Mr and Mrs Browning, all of whom are still living, and are ready to testify to the truth of every word here written, if it should be gainsaid by Mr Browning.

> DANIEL DUNGLAS HOME, *Incidents in My Life*, 1872; the seance was held on 23 July 1855

> As for religion—why, I served it, sir!
> I'll stick to that! With my *phenomena*
> I laid the atheist sprawling on his back,
> Propped up Saint Paul, or, at least, Swedenborg!
> In fact, it's just the proper way to baulk
> These troublesome fellows—liars, one and all,
> Are not these sceptics? Well, to baffle them,
> No use in being squeamish: lie yourself!
> Erect your buttress just as wide o' of the line,
> Your side, as they build up the wall on theirs;
> Where both meet, midway in a point, is truth
> High overhead: so, take your room, pile bricks,
> Lie! . . .

Well, I add one use
To all the acknowledged uses, and declare
If I spy Charles's Wain at twelve tonight,
It warns me, 'Go, nor lose another day,
And have your hair cut, Sludge!' You laugh: and why?
Were such a sign too hard for God to give?
No: but Sludge seems too little for such grace:
Thank you, sir! So you think, so does not Sludge!
When you and good men gape at Providence,
Go into history and bid us mark
Not merely powder-plots prevented, crowns
Kept on kings' heads by miracle enough,
But private mercies—oh, you've told me, sir,
Of such interpositions! How yourself
Once, missing on a memorable day
Your handkerchief—just setting out, you know—
You must return to fetch it, lost the train,
And saved your precious self from what befell
The thirty-three whom Providence forgot.
You tell, and ask me what I think of this?
Well, sir, I think then, since you needs must know,
What matter had you and Boston city to boot
Sailed skyward, like burnt onion-peelings? Much
To you, no doubt: for me—undoubtedly
The cutting of my hair concerns me more,
Because, however sad the truth may seem,
Sludge is of all-importance to himself . . .
                    Was it likelier, now,
That this our one out of all worlds beside,
That what-d'you-call-'em millions, should be just
Precisely chosen to make Adam for,
And the rest o' the tale? Yet the tale's true, you know:
Such undeserving clod was graced so once;
Why not graced likewise undeserving Sludge?

                    Suppose
I blunder in my guess at the true sense
O' the knuckle-summons, nine times out of ten—
What if the tenth guess happen to be right?
If the tenth shovel-load of powdered quartz

Yield me the nugget? I gather, crush, sift all,
Pass o'er the failure, pounce on the success.

Why, which of those who say they disbelieve,
Your clever people, but has dreamed his dream,
Caught his coincidence, stumbled on his fact
He can't explain, (he'll tell you smilingly)
Which he's too much of a philosopher
To count as supernatural, indeed,
So calls a puzzle and problem, proud of it,
Bidding you still be on your guard, you know,
Because one fact don't make a system stand,
Nor prove this an occasional escape
Of spirit beneath the matter: that's the way!
Just so wild Indians picked up, piece by piece,
The fact in California, the fine gold
That underlay the gravel—hoarded these,
But never made a system stand, nor dug!
So wise men hold out in each hollowed palm
A handful of experience, sparkling fact
They can't explain; and since their rest of life
Is all explainable, what proof in this?
Whereas I take the fact, the grain of gold,
And fling away the dirty rest of life,
And add this grain to the grain each fool has found
O' the million other such philosophers—
Till I see gold, all gold and only gold,
Truth questionless though unexplainable,
And the miraculous proved the commonplace!

Don't let truth's lump rot stagnant for the lack
Of a timely helpful lie to leaven it!
Put a chalk-egg beneath the clucking hen,
She'll lay a real one, laudably deceived,
Daily for weeks to come. I've told my lie,
And seen truth follow, marvels none of mine.

ROBERT BROWNING, from 'Mr Sludge, "The Medium" ', 1864

She [Aunt Bell, Arabella Graham-Clarke] and you will both want to hear the
results of our seeing Hume [Home]—so I will tell you—on the condition though,

Spiritualism

that when you write to me you don't say a word on the subject—because it's a *tabooed* subject in this house—Robert and I taking completely different views, and he being a good deal irritated by any discussion of it . . .

We were touched by the invisible, heard the music and raps, saw the table moved, and had sight of the hands. Also, at the request of the medium, the spiritual hands took from the table a garland which lay there, and placed it upon my head. The particular hand which did this was of the largest human size, as white as snow, and very beautiful. It was as near to me as this hand I write with, and I saw it as distinctly . . .

I think that what chiefly went against the exhibition, in Robert's mind, was the trance at the conclusion during which the medium talked a great deal of much such twaddle as may be heard in any fifth-rate conventicle. But according to my theory (well thought-out and digested) this does not militate at all against the general facts. It's undeniable, and has been from first to last, that if these are spirits, many among them talk prodigious nonsense, or rather most ordinary commonplace.

For my own part I am confirmed in all my opinions. To me it was wonderful and conclusive.

ELIZABETH BARRETT BROWNING, from letter to her sister, Henrietta Barrett, 17 August 1855

Perhaps none of the thousand falsehoods circulated concerning Mr Home has been more persistently repeated than the assertion that he was found cheating by Mr Robert Browning. Mr Browning himself, in his unpoetic effusion, 'Mr Sludge, the Medium', appeared to lend a certain colour to the fable, or it would probably soon have died the death natural to slanders that have not a grain of fact in their composition. The press, on the appearance of 'Mr Sludge', insisted that he was meant for Home. Had this been an error, Mr Browning, as an honourable man, would of course have written to some leading English journal to correct it . . .

Would that Mr Browning had seized the hands he saw at Ealing, whose action, in placing a wreath on the brow of his wife and omitting to crown his own, may possibly have given him deep offence! Had the poet been a man of large and liberal nature, he would have forgiven the want of discernment the spirits showed—reflecting that, while all the world does homage to the genius of his wife, the larger half of it fails to comprehend his own . . .

Was Mr Browning annoyed that to him there came no crown? All the Rymer family thought so, at least. Yet the invisible wreath-bringers were probably only anticipating the verdict of posterity, both in their neglect of him and in crowning his gifted wife.

> Mme Dunglas Home, the medium's wife, *Daniel Dunglas Home: His Life and Mission*, 1888

Browning wrote a long poem—if such doggerel can be called poetry—to describe an exposure which had never taken place . . . Truly Mrs Browning was a better judge of character than her spouse, and Sir Galahad a better name than Sludge.

> Arthur Conan Doyle, *The History of Spiritualism*, 1926

Partially covering himself with the window curtains, but holding the glass with the brandy in it over his head, between us and the window so that we could see it, he was lifted off the floor about four or five feet. While in the air, we saw a bright light in the glass; presently he came down and showed us that the glass was empty, by turning it upside down upon our hands; then going to the window he held the glass up and we heard the liquid drop into it. He began talking about the brandy, and said, 'It is under certain circumstances a demon, a real devil, but, if properly used, it is most beneficial.' As he said this the light became visible in the glass, and he was again raised in the air. 'But,' he said, 'if improperly used, it becomes *so*' (the light disappeared) 'and drags you down, down, lower and lower', and as he spoke he sank gradually down till he touched the floor with the glass. He again raised the glass above his head, and the liquor fell over and through my fingers into the glass, dropping from the air above me.

> Viscount Adare, *Experiences in Spiritualism with Mr Daniel Dunglas Home*, 1870

For years I have seen with pain abuse after abuse attach itself to a cause in whose service my life has been passed, and with which such foulnesses have nothing in common. So wonderfully have these parasites increased and multiplied, that, like a pearl crusted with spots of dirt, the purity and beauty of the original seem at present almost hidden; and I cannot too strongly reiterate my conviction, that between spiritualism and the majority of the abuses by which it is disgraced there is just as little in common as between a precious stone and the mud which may happen to cling to it.

John Wilkes Booth is reported to have manifested to a certain American circle. The remorse that besets him can be sufficiently judged of from his communication. 'I and Lincoln,' he remarked, 'often have a cosy chat up here. We agree that it was just as well I shot him. You see, it was set down in the order of things for me to do it, and I don't see why I should be blamed for accomplishing my destiny. The world was all the better for it.'

The world is not much the better for such communications as these.

I have myself sat as spectator at a seance where the faces displayed were simply so many masks presented before an aperture. I called the attention of a credulous spiritualist beside me to the empty and eyeless sockets. His reply came promptly, and with a certain triumph:—'The dear spirits have not had time to materialize the eyes.' Is it surprising that cheats should be found to practise on folly like this?

HOME, *Lights and Shadows of Spiritualism*

I thank you for your communication to me about your experience with the *planchette*. You were right in supposing that I might feel some interest in anything at all that came from the pen of Samuel Taylor Coleridge. I must also feel, I shall tell you directly, considerable abhorrence at the thought of that bright spirit, having made his painful way out of our weary and oppressive earthly life, being constrained to heave mahogany tables, or float partially embodied, through firelit drawing-rooms, or turn his liberated Intelligence to the scrawling of such painful and inane nonsense as you have sent to me. Should he not now feed in peace on honeydew and drink the milk of Paradise?

I am not jesting, Madam. I have attended exhibitions of the kind of manifestations you allude to—*nihil humanum a me alienum puto*, I may say, as all of my profession should say—and I think the likeliest explanation is a combination of bald fraud and a kind of communal hysteria, a miasma or creeping mist of spiritual anxiety and febrile agitation, that plagues our polite society and titillates our tea-party talk. A speculative temperament might find the cause of this miasma in the increasing materialism of our society, and in the rigorous questioning—both natural and inevitable, given the present state of our intellectual Development—of our historical religious narratives. All is indeed uncertainty in that field, and the historian and the man of science alike make inroads on our simple faith . . .

Think what do you, Madam, in attempting to address them, the dear and terrible dead, *directly*. What wisdom in all this waste of time have they imparted? That Granny has left her new brooch in the grandfather clock, or that an ancient Aunt resents, from beyond the bourn, the imposition of an infant coffin upon her own in the family Vault. Or as your S.T.C. solemnly assures you, that there is 'eternal bliss for they who deserve such and a time of correction for they who do not' in the Beyond. (He who never misplaced a pronoun in seven languages.) It needs no ghost, Madam, come from the grave, to tell us this.

That there may be wandering spirits I grant you, earth-bubbles, exhalations, creatures of the air, who occasionally cross our usual currents of apprehension, proceeding on their own unseen errands. That agonized reminiscence of some kind in some mental form does inhere in some terrible places there is some evidence. There are indeed more things in heaven and earth than are dreamed of in our philosophy. But they will be found out I believe, not through rappings or tappings or palpable handlings or Mr Home floating round and round the chandelier with his arms stiffly upheld, nor yet through the scribblings of your *planchette*, but through long and patient contemplation of the intricate workings of dead minds and live organisms, through wisdom that looks before and after, through the microscope and the spectroscope and not through the interrogation of earth-obsessed spectres and revenants. I have known a good soul and a clear mind, quite unhinged by such meddling, and to no good end, indeed to a bad one.

A. S. BYATT, *Possession*, 1990; letter from the poet Randolph Henry Ash to Priscilla Penn Cropper, a spiritualist, 1860s or 1870s

Your experience with the *planchette* is amazing; but that the words which you found it to have written were dictated by the spirit of Charlotte Brontë is to me (whether rightly or not) so enormously improbable, that I could only accept it if every condition were laid bare, and every other explanation demonstrated to be impossible. If it were another spirit aping Charlotte Brontë—if here and there at rare spots and among people of a certain temperament, or even at many spots and among people of all temperaments, tricksy spirits are liable to rise as a sort of earth-bubbles and set furniture in movement, and tell things which we either know already or should be as well without knowing—I must frankly confess that I have but a feeble interest in these doings, feeling my life very short for the supreme and awful revelations of a more orderly and intelligible kind which I shall die with an imperfect knowledge of. If there were miserable spirits whom we could help—then I think we should pause and have patience with their trivial-mindedness; but otherwise I don't feel bound to study them more than I am bound to study the special follies of a particular phase of human society. Others, who feel differently, and are attracted towards this study, are making an experiment for us as to whether anything better than bewilderment can come of it. At present it seems to me that to rest any fundamental part of religion on such a basis is a melancholy misguidance of men's minds from the true sources of high and pure emotion.

> GEORGE ELIOT, from letter to Harriet Beecher Stowe, 24 June 1872. Mrs Stowe had had a 'weird and Brontëish' conversation with Charlotte Brontë, lasting over two hours, in which Charlotte 'spoke of her sister Emily, of whose character she gave a most striking analysis'

In the Salon Louis Quinze, at one of the Tuileries seances [in the presence of Napoleon III and the Empress Eugénie, 1857], the hand of a man appeared above the table, on which a sheet of paper and a pencil were lying, placed there that any communications received might be written down. The hand moved across the table, lifted the pencil, and wrote on the paper the single word, '*Napoleon*'. The writing was the autograph of the Emperor Napoleon I; the hand small and beautifully formed, as his is recorded to have been.

The Empress, moved by the sight of this hand, requested permission to kiss it; and it placed itself to her lips, then to the lips of the Emperor. The hand was distinctly seen; this seance, like all others at the Tuileries, being held in a good light.

> MME HOME, *Daniel Dunglas Home: His Life* . . .

The American Branch [of the Society for Psychical Research] had never fully paid its expenses; and although the Secretary's salary had always been very small [Richard] Hodgson had, after the first years, been reluctant to have any part of it charged to the mother country. The result had occasionally been pecuniary embarrassment on his part. During his last visit to England, this embarrassment had been extreme; but an American friend, divining it in the nick of time, rescued him by an impulsive and wholly unexpected remittance. To this remittance he replied by a letter which contained some banter and, among other things, cited the story of a starving couple who were overheard by an atheist who was passing the house, to pray aloud to God for food. The atheist climbed the roof and dropped some bread down the chimney, and heard them thank God for the miracle. He then went to the door and revealed himself as its author. The old woman replied to him: 'Well, the Lord sent it, even if the devil brought it.'

At this friend's sitting of January 30 [1906; Hodgson had died six weeks previously], R.H. suddenly says:

Do you remember a story I told you and how you laughed, about the man and woman praying?
(Oh, and the devil was in it. Of course I do.)
Yes, the devil, they told him it was the Lord who sent it if the devil brought it . . . About the food that was given to them . . . I want you to know who is speaking.

The sitter feels quite certain that no one but himself knew of the correspondence, and regards the incident as a good test of R.H.'s continued presence. Others will either favour this interpretation of it, or explain it by reading of the sitter's mind, or treat it as a chance coincidence, according to their several prepossessions. I myself feel morally certain that the waking Mrs Piper [L. E. Piper, Boston medium] was ignorant of the incident and of the correspondence. Hodgson was as likely to have informed *me*, as anyone, of the affair. He had given me at the time a vivid account of the trouble he had been in, but no hint of the quarter from which relief had come.

WILLIAM JAMES, *Proceedings* of the Society for Psychical Research, Vol. 23, 1909

In a case related by Professor Hyslop [*Proceedings* of the Society for Psychical Research, Vol. 14, 1898–9] we see the foreboding of the greatest misfortune that can befall a mother germinating, growing, sending out shoots, developing, like some gluttonous and deadly plant, to stop short on the verge of the last warning . . . It is the case of a woman who begins by experiencing a vague but powerful impression that a grievous 'burden' is going to fall upon her family. Next month, this premonitory feeling repeats itself very frequently, becomes more intense, and ends by concentrating itself upon the poor woman's little daughter. Each time that she is planning something for the child's future, she hears a voice saying:
'She'll never need it.'
A week before the catastrophe, a violent smell of fire fills the house. From that time the mother begins to be careful about matches, seeing that they are

in safe places and out of reach. She looks all over the house for them and feels a strong impulse to burn all matches of the kind easily lighted. About an hour before the fatal disaster, she reaches for a box to destroy it; but she says to herself that her eldest son is gone out, thinks that she may need the matches to light the gas stove, and decides to destroy them as soon as he comes back. She takes the child up to its crib for its morning sleep and, as she is putting it into the cradle, she hears the usual mysterious voice whisper in her ear:

'Turn the mattress.'

But, being in a great hurry, she simply says that she will turn the mattress after the child has taken its nap. She then goes downstairs to work. After a while, she hears the child cry and, hurrying up to the room, finds the crib and its bedding on fire and the child so badly burnt that it dies in three hours.

Does our unknown guest speak an unknown language and do the words which it speaks and which we think that we understand disclose its thought? Is every direct road pitilessly barred and is there nothing left to it but narrow, closed paths in which the best of what it had to reveal to us is lost? Is this the reason why it seeks those odd, childish, roundabout ways of automatic writing, cross-correspondence, symbolic premonition and all the rest? Yet, in the typical case which we have quoted, it seems to speak quite easily and plainly when it says to the mother:

'Turn the mattress.'

If it can utter this sentence, why should it find it difficult or impossible to add:

'You will find the matches there that will set fire to the curtains.'

What forbids it to do so and closes its mouth at the decisive moment? We relapse into the everlasting question: if it cannot complete the second sentence because it would be destroying in the womb the very event which it is foretelling, why does it utter the first?

MAETERLINCK, *The Unknown Guest*

Until 'Raymond', the son of Sir Oliver Lodge, purported to communicate through Mrs Leonard [Mrs Osborne Leonard, a well-known medium; see also p. 450], the spirits seldom condescended to give detailed accounts of their domestic life in the other world, but contented themselves with vague references to 'spiritual progress' and 'moral advancement'. But the ghost of Raymond Lodge told how the spirits live in houses made of bricks and surrounded by trees and flowers. They have bodies which appear to them as substantial as ours do to us. They see the sun as we do, and the earth on which they live is so real that when Raymond kneels down his clothes are muddied. Newcomers still unpurged of their gross desires demand 'whiskies' and cigars which are provided by the considerate chemists of the spirit world. Somehow these cigars are not very satisfying and there is no great demand for them. The clothes of the spirits are made apparently out of the 'smells' and emanations which arise from the terrestrial wardrobes . . . Yet there have been learned exponents of Spiritualism like the late Professor Hyslop who actually accepted these descriptions of a mundane afterlife. According to Hyslop's theory, the soul after death retains its power of creating mental images and these images will be based upon the memories of objects that it has known on earth.

S. G. SOAL, from 'Spiritualism', 1935

I don't seem to care much about Planchette, however I am mild and submit to be taken to Planchettes and Hume's and Dotens; (What was the name of the Boston preaching and poetizing woman?) I should like of all things to see a ghost, and if one would come and have it out with me on the square I think it would add vastly to my interest in life. Undoubtedly one would prefer half an hour with Washington or Hamilton to any amount of intercourse with even [Benjamin Franklin] Butler or Charles Sumner. But when tables rap, and boards write, and dead young women come and tickle my knee under a big table, I find the manifestation to be unworthy of the previous grand ceremony of death. Your visitor from above or below should be majestical, should stalk in all panoplied from head to foot—at least with a white sheet, and should not condescend to catechetical and alphabetical puzzles.

ANTHONY TROLLOPE, from letter to Kate Field, 3 June 1868. Kate Field was just publishing a book entitled *Planchette's Diary*; the allusions are to D. D. Home and Elizabeth Doten, a spiritualist poet

It is rather strange to be speaking, but I know you are there
Wanting to know, as if it were worth knowing.
Nor is it important that I died in combat
In a good cause or an indifferent one.
Such things, it may surprise you, are not regarded.
Something too much of this.

You are bound to be disappointed,
Wanting to know, are there any trees?
It is all different from what you suppose,
And the darkness is not darkness exactly,
But patience, silence, withdrawal, the sad knowledge
That it was almost impossible not to hurt anyone
Whether by action or inaction.
At the beginning of course there was a sense of loss,
Not of one's own life, but of what seemed
The easy, desirable lives one might have led.
Fame or wealth are hard to achieve,
And goodness even harder;
But the cost of all of them is a familiar deformity
Such as everyone suffers from:
An allergy to certain foods, nausea at the sight of blood,
A slight impediment of speech, shame at one's own body,
A fear of heights or claustrophobia.
What you learn has nothing whatever to do with joy,
Nor with sadness, either. You are mostly silent.
You come to a gentle indifference about being thought
Either a fool or someone with valuable secrets.
It may be that the ultimate wisdom
Lies in saying nothing.
I think I may already have said too much.

ANTHONY HECHT, 'A Voice at a Seance', 1977

Knock, knock, knock!
'Dear spirit! Is that really you, Napoleon?'
'Yes. What do you wish?'
'It would be so good of you if you'd go and find the Virgin Mary for us, for we want to ask her for some information about the apparitions of Lourdes.'
'All right, my friends. Wait a minute.'
Knock, knock, knock!
'Is this the Virgin Mary?'
'No, she's busy. But here's Messalina.'

FLAMMARION, *Death and Its Mystery*, 1922; tr. Latrobe Carroll. Illustrating false notions of *spiritisme*

Medium: I want to come to you, sir. Does the name Quentin Murgatroyd Bellamy mean anything to you?

Reluctant sitter: Well, perhaps.

Medium: He says that he was your stepfather by your mother's third marriage—and that her maiden name was Miranda Delgado.

Sitter (grudgingly): Mm! What else does this so-called entity say?

Medium (getting annoyed): He's telling me that your younger brother's name is Aloysius Lawrence, and that he was named after your maternal grandfather, who was a well-known amateur astronomer and an acknowledged authority on asteroids.

Sitter: Can he be more specific?

Medium (exasperated): Yes! He says that he was lost at sea on the *Titanic* and that he left you his collection of butterflies and rare sea shells. He also says you had a dog called Buonaparte, a cat named Hildegarde and a West African parakeet that could whistle 'Ave Maria'.

Sitter: In what key?

> MICHAEL BENTINE, *The Door Marked Summer*, 1981; an example of an uncooperative client

They always have the seances in the back parlour—a small, drab room looking out over the back garden. It was here, a couple of years ago, that Mrs Quigley talked to my Gran. Never has there been such a low-level conversation across the Great Divide.

'Are you all right, Maureen?'

'Oh yes. I'm fine.'

'Keeping well?'

'Oh yes. On the whole. Mustn't grumble. You?'

'We're fine. How are Stephen and Sarah?'

'Oh they're fine. They're all here and they're fine.'

It really was difficult to work out who was dead and who was alive. My favourite moment came when la Quigley, running out of more serious topics, asked my dear departed Gran, 'What are you all doing Over There?'

'Oh,' said Gran—'the usual things.'

The *usual things*, my friends! They are dead and they are still running their kids to piano lessons and worrying about whether to have the spare room decorated. What was the point in dying if that was all you got at the end of it?

> NIGEL WILLIAMS, *They Came from SW19*, 1992

December 28, 1925   *medium: Mrs Osborne Leonard*

Lady Barrett. Tell us what your life now is like. How is it different from ours?

Sir William Barrett. It is very different . . . Well, I do not eat and drink: I am fed from without: that is to say I do not absorb nourishment through the mouth but through the pores of my skin. I assume that we do that to some extent on earth: if not nourishment we absorb life-giving properties through the pores of the skin and the air we breathe.

I do live in a house—very like any house on earth—some of the rooms are like the rooms at home. My mind needed the rooms at home. We usually find ourselves in surroundings which become the habit or need of the mind during our latter years; we are not transplanted into entirely different surroundings. Nature never transplants except into conditions as congenial as possible, and as like as possible to the conditions which prevailed in the first place. So here we find ourselves in very similar surroundings . . .

I wear clothes; we produce them by thought, but I did not produce my own clothes.

Lady Barrett. Who did?

Sir William. A tailor. I might call him a producer of garments, but 'tailor' is a very good description. I am not clever or skilled in the production of suits, but others are, and they cannot do my work. Each one to his own trade for a certain time. My tailor may one day do my work, but for a considerable time after passing he is happier in his own.

I feel comfortable in a suit. Has anyone any objection to my having one? Yes, many will have, but they would have no objection to a white linen robe. There is the incongruity—the unreasonableness. I might have a white linen garment in which I should be most uncomfortable, but should be debarred from clothing most suitable to me.

Sir William. God helps those who help themselves—there is a lot of truth in it. God only allows us to help those who help themselves.

Communication is always permissible so long as it is not allowed to interfere with the spiritual, the mental and physical development of the individual while on earth.

> *Personality Survives Death: Messages from Sir William Barrett*, edited by his wife, 1937. Barrett died 26 May 1925

I ought to tell you first who I am for fear you might be under the impression that you are talking to Saint Mark, or some other great ones. I am S.C. and think it about time I dropped the *nom de plume* which gave me a following: namely, Mark Twain.

(Thank you. I know.)

I see so little to make me better comprehend what the meaning of it all is that I am not in the least tempted to mount a pulpit and preach to the lost. I only know that I am saved and that I have a few choice friends along with me and we are not worrying about the state of the rest of the world. It is most wonderful to be able to see so much at once. That is the one thing that stands out more clearly to me. It seems as if we had gained a double capacity to see. Do you understand what I mean by seeing?

(No, not exactly. Explain a little.)

Two worlds instead of one. We see double, in other words, and no one seems intoxicated either.

(Does the old physical world look as it did before passing?)

Sometimes it looks pretty much the same. It depends on where you float. Wall Street looks very much like—shall I say what I think—

(Yes.)

Inferno. It seems to have no saving grace as an atmosphere about it, but it always does look like that to a man who is not on the inside. I find a smoky atmosphere plenty good enough for me . . . Let's take a pipe and smoke away our trouble . . .

(Well, I hope it will not be one kind of smoking.)

I have not yet seen the sulphur pit, but I presume that there is one. Most of us would be glad of a chance to toss an enemy in on the sly, but so far I have restrained my desire and made a great effort to keep the peace and not to mar the joy of heaven.

> From a communication by Mark Twain (Samuel Clemens, who died in 1910) by automatic writing taken down by Mrs Chenoweth in February 1913

The Scottish medium, Helen Duncan, who died in 1956 at the age of 58 . . . was an uneducated woman of gross appearance whose manners and language were anything but ladylike. More seriously, both she and her husband–manager were almost certainly implicated in fraud . . . The witnesses with whom I have spoken or corresponded, all persons whose sanity I have no reason to doubt . . . all tell much the same story. They all speak of watching figures emerging from the cabinet or sometimes taking shape out of swirling masses of amorphous ectoplasm, sometimes they are of recognizable individuals whom the sitter had known in life, sometimes they engage in conversation, but, invariably, they soon disappear by sinking through the solid floor . . .

Eventually, Mrs Duncan made legal history by becoming the last person ever to be tried under the 'Witchcraft Act'. This was an archaic statute, introduced in the reign of George II, which stated that 'anyone pretending to exercise or use any kind of witchcraft, sorcery, enchantment or conjuration could be committed to prison for one year'. Her trial at the Old Bailey, in March 1944, became something of a *cause célèbre* in wartime London. It lasted seven days, capturing the headlines in the daily press, at the end of which the jury of seven men and one woman, with little hesitation, found her guilty and she was duly sentenced to nine months in prison. Her defence counsel, during the trial, made a bold offer to stage a seance for the benefit of the jury who, after all, knew nothing about such matters, but, although the judge was willing to give his permission, the jury turned down the offer.

JOHN BELOFF, *The Relentless Question: Reflections on the Paranormal*, 1990

One afternoon at my home in a North London suburb, three of us—Alan Parker, Andy Davey and I—were 'consulting' the ouija board. We were fifteen years old or thereabouts. The 'spirit' instructed us to contact somebody called Florence and provided us with a London telephone number. Andy—braver than Alan or I—made the call. He remembers, but is vague on this point, getting through to a garage. He asked to speak to Florence; there was an undeniable pause, then the voice at the other end said that Florence wasn't there, indeed she had passed away some months before.

Nothing more is remembered. Andy probably slammed the phone down straight away. Our feelings—a kind of joyful dread—may be imagined.

WILL SULKIN, in a letter to the editor, 1992

On the afternoon of October 24th 1917, four days after my marriage, my wife surprised me by attempting automatic writing. What came in disjointed sentences, in almost illegible writing, was so exciting, sometimes so profound, that I persuaded her to give an hour or two day after day to the unknown writer, and after some half-dozen such hours offered to spend what remained of life explaining and piecing together those scattered sentences. 'No,' was the answer, 'we have come to give you metaphors for poetry.' The unknown writer took his theme at first from my just published *Per Amica Silentia Lunae*. I had made a distinction between the perfection that is from a man's combat with himself and that which is from a combat with circumstance, and upon this simple distinction he built up an elaborate classification of men according to their more or less complete expression of one type or the other . . .

When the automatic writing began we were in a hotel on the edge of Ashdown Forest, but soon returned to Ireland and spent much of 1918 at Glendalough, at Rosses Point, at Coole Park, at a house near it, at Thoor Ballylee, always more or less solitary, my wife bored and fatigued by her almost daily task and I thinking and talking of little else. Early in 1919 the communicator of the moment—they were constantly changed—said they would soon change the method from the written to the spoken word as that would fatigue her less, but the change did not come for some months. I was on a lecturing tour in America to earn a roof for Thoor Ballylee when it came. We had one of those little sleeping compartments in a train, with two berths, and were somewhere in Southern California. My wife, who had been asleep for some minutes, began to talk in her sleep, and from that on almost all communications came in that way. My teachers did not seem to speak out of her sleep but as if from above it, as though it were a tide upon which they floated . . .

Whenever I received a certain signal (I will explain what it was later), I would get pencil and paper ready. After they had entranced my wife suddenly when sitting in a chair, I suggested that she must always be lying down before they put her to sleep. They seemed ignorant of our surroundings and might have done so at some inconvenient time or place; once when they had given their signal in a restaurant they explained that because we had spoken of a garden they had thought we were in it. Except at the start of a new topic, when they would speak or write a dozen sentences unquestioned, I had always to question, and every question to rise out of a previous answer and to deal with their chosen topic. My questions must be accurately worded, and, because they said their thought was swifter than ours, asked without delay or hesitation. I was constantly reproved for vague or confused questions, yet I could do no better, because, though it was plain from the first that their exposition was based upon a single geometrical conception, they kept me from mastering that conception . . .

The automatic writing and the speech during sleep were illustrated or accompanied by strange phenomena. While we were staying at a village near Oxford we met two or three nights in succession what seemed a sudden warm breath coming up from the ground at the same corner of the road. One night when I was about to tell my wife some story of a Russian mystic, without remembering that it might make her misunderstand an event in her own life, a sudden flash of light fell between us and a chair or table was violently struck.

Then too there was much whistling, generally as a warning that some communicator would come when my wife was asleep. At first I was inclined to think that these whistlings were made by my wife without her knowing it, and once, when I heard the whistle and she did not, she felt a breath passing through her lips as though she had whistled. I had to give up this explanation when servants at the other end of the house were disturbed by a 'whistling ghost', and so much so that I asked the communicators to choose some other sign. Sweet smells were the most constant phenomena, now that of incense, now that of violets or roses or some other flower, and as perceptible to some half-dozen of our friends as to ourselves, though upon one occasion when my wife smelt hyacinth a friend smelt eau-de-cologne.

YEATS, from introduction to *A Vision*, edition of 1937

Thomas Mann compares spiritualism to 'a Sunday afternoon diversion for the servants' hall', and quotes Herr Krall of Elberfeld, famous for his calculating horses (see pp. 400–1), as saying: 'If there are ghosts, then there is every reason why a man should pray for a long life; for there could not possibly be anything more insipid, childish, futile, confused, and pathetic than the existence of these creatures, to judge from their supposed manifestations.' But, Mann allows, a doubt lingers as to 'whether dignity and good taste are absolute criteria in the field of science, in the search for truth'.

Dr Freiherr Baron von Schrenck-Notzing (1862–1929), parapsychologist and specialist in nervous diseases, in Munich, used to entertain friends to evening sittings. After witnessing a demonstration of telekinetic phenomena and materializations, featuring a medium, Willy, and his spirit guide, Minna, Mann reflects:

No, I will not go to Herr von Schrenck-Notzing's again. It leads to nothing, or at least to nothing good. I love that which I called the moral upper world, I love the human fable, and clear and humane thought. I abhor luxations of the brain, I abhor morasses of the spirit. Up to now, indeed, I have seen but a few stray sparks from the infernal fires—but that must suffice me. I should like of course to hold, as others have held, a hand like that, a metaphysical delusion made of flesh and blood, in mine. And perhaps there might appear to me, as it has to others, Minna's head, above the shoulder of the sleeping Willy: the head of a charming girl, Slavic in type, with lively black eyes. That, however uncanny, must be a wonderful experience . . . After all, I will have another try or so with Herr von Schrenck-Notzing; two or three times, not more. That much could do me no harm; and I know myself, I am a man of ephemeral passions; I shall take care that it leads to nothing, and put the whole thing out of my mind for ever after. No, I will not go two or three times, I will only go once, just once more and then not again. I only want to see the handkerchief rise up into the red light before my eyes. For the sight has got into my blood somehow, I cannot forget it. I should like once more to crane my neck, and with the nerves of my digestive apparatus all on edge with the fantasticality of it, once more, just once, see the impossible come to pass.

MANN, from 'An Experience in the Occult', 1923; tr. H. T. Lowe-Porter

'Is there an Intelligence present?' Herr Albin asked, severely directing his gaze over their heads into vacancy. After some hesitation, the glass tipped and said yes.

'What is your name?' Herr Albin asked, almost gruffly, and emphasized his energetic speech by shaking his head.

The glass pushed off. It ran with resolution from one point to another, executing a zigzag by returning each time a little distance towards the centre of the table. It visited H, O, and L, then seemed exhausted; but pulled itself together again and sought out the G, and E, and the R . . . It was Holger in person, the spirit Holger . . . He was there, floating in the air, above the heads of the little circle. What should they do with him? A certain diffidence possessed them, they took counsel behind their hands, what they were to ask him. Herr Albin decided to question him about his position and occupation in life, and did so, as before, severely, with frowning brows; as though he were a cross-examining counsel.

The glass was silent awhile. Then it staggered over to the P, zigzagged and returned to O. Great suspense. Dr Ting-Fu giggled and said Holger must be a poet. Frau Stöhr began to laugh hysterically; which the glass appeared to resent, for after indicating the E it stuck and went no further. However, it seemed fairly clear that Dr Ting-Fu was right.

What the deuce, so Holger was a poet? The glass revived, and superfluously, in apparent pridefulness, rapped yes. A lyric poet, Fräulein Kleefeld asked? . . . Holger was disinclined to specify. He gave no new answer, merely spelled out again, this time quickly and unhesitatingly, the word poet, adding the T he had left off before.

Good, then, a poet. The constraint increased . . . Did Holger feel at home, and content, in his present state? Dreamily, the glass spelled out the word tranquil. Ah, tranquil. It was not a word one would have hit upon oneself, but after the glass spelled it out, they found it well chosen and probable. And how long had Holger been in this tranquil state? The answer to this was again something one would never have thought of, and dreamily answered; it was 'A hastening while'. Very good. As a piece of ventriloquistic poesy from the Beyond, Hans Castorp, in particular, found it capital. A 'hastening while' was the time-element Holger lived in: and of course he had to answer as it were in parables, having very likely forgotten how to use earthly terminology and standards of exact measurement. Fräulein Levi confessed her curiosity to know how he looked, or had looked, more or less. Had he been a handsome youth? Herr Albin said she might ask him herself, he found the request beneath his dignity. So she asked if the spirit had fair hair.

'Beautiful, brown, brown curls,' the glass responded, deliberately spelling out the word brown twice. There was much merriment over this. The ladies said they were in love with him. They kissed their hands at the ceiling. Dr Ting-Fu, giggling, said Mister Holger must be rather vain.

Ah, what a fury the glass fell into! It ran like mad about the table, quite at random, rocked with rage, fell over and rolled into Frau Stöhr's lap, who stretched out her arms and looked down at it pallid with fear. They apologetically conveyed it back to its station, and rebuked the Chinaman. How had he dared to say such a thing—did he see what his indiscretion had led to? Suppose Holger was up and off in his wrath, and refused to say another word? They addressed themselves to the glass with the extreme of courtesy. Would Holger not make up some poetry for them? He had said he was a poet, before he went to hover in the hastening while. Ah, how they all yearned to hear him versify! They would love it so!

And lo, the good glass yielded and said yes! Truly there was something placable and good-humoured about the way it tapped. And then Holger the spirit began to poetize, and kept it up, copiously, circumstantially, without pausing for thought, for dear knows how long. It seemed impossible to stop him.

MANN, *The Magic Mountain*, 1924; tr. H. T. Lowe-Porter

She said, 'I have been asking myself whether the current interest in the spirit-world is an indication that the Celts have the right view of these matters. For Swedenborg went into the world of spirits and saw, he says, successive states of being, all being purified, all with their own homes and temples and libraries in their own kinds. And of late there have been many moved to seek apparent messages from the debatable lands beyond the veil that separates this world from the next. I have seen a few small unexplainable acts, myself. Spirit-wreaths brought by unseen hands, shining white, of unearthly beauty. Messages tapped painfully out by little hands that found this mode of communication infinitely clumsy for their now-refined nature, and yet persisted, out of love for those left behind. Music played by invisible hands on an accordion placed under a velvet pall out of reach of all. Moving lights.'

I said, 'I do not believe that these drawing-room tricks have anything to do with religion. Or with whatever it is that we hear in our streams and fountains here.'

She seemed surprised at my vehemence.

'That is because you make the mistake of supposing that spirits dislike vulgarity as much as you do. A spirit may speak to a peasant like Gode, because that is picturesque, she is surrounded by Romantic crags on the one hand and primitive enough huts and hearths on the other, and her house is lapped by real thick moral dark. But if there are spirits, I do not see why they are not everywhere, or may not be presumed to be so. You could argue that their voices may well be muffled by solid brick walls and thick plush furnishings and house-proud antimacassars. But the mahogany-polishers and the drapers' clerks are as much in need of salvation—as much desirous of assurance of an afterlife—as poets or peasants, in the last resort. When they were sure in their unthinking faiths—when the Church was a solid presence in their midst, the Spirit sat docile enough behind the altar rails and the Souls kept—on the whole—to the churchyard and the vicinity of their stones. But now they fear they may not be raised, that their lids may not be lifted, that heaven and hell were no more than faded drawings on a few old church walls, with wax angels and gruesome bogies—they ask, what *is* there? And if the man in shiny boots and gold watch-chain or the woman in bombazine and whalebone stays, with her crinoline hoop-lifter for crossing puddles—if these fat and tedious people *want* to hear spirits as Gode does, why may they not? The Gospel was preached to all men, and if we exist in successive states, the materialists among us must waken in this world and the next. Swedenborg saw them sweat unbelief and rage like heaps of glistening maggots.'

'You move too quickly for me to argue,' I said sullenly enough, 'But I have read about table-turning and spirit rappings in Papa's magazines and I say it sounds like conjuring tricks for the credulous.' . . .

'One may conjure real daemons with drawing-room conjuring tricks,' said my father, meditatively.

A. S. BYATT, *Possession*; from Sabine de Kercoz's journal, 1859, describing a conversation with her cousin, the poet Christabel LaMotte

At the Edinburgh Playhouse another man came to his widow. He told me that she had not been with him at the end. 'I was alone when I died,' he said, 'but I'm glad. We said goodbye, and I knew I wouldn't see her again in this life.' Then he told me that she had some problem with her ear. 'Did you have attention?' I asked.

'I went to see about a deaf aid,' she replied, 'but I won't use it. It's in the house in the drawer.'

Then the husband said something quite funny to me. 'All that money wasted,' were his words, 'not only on her ears but on her teeth too.'

When I reported this comment, for some reason there were peals of laughter in the Playhouse, which may have disconcerted the lady because she said, 'That's nonsense.'

The husband then told me that he knew his wife very well. 'He is glad to have made everybody laugh,' I told her. 'He was a happy man and if he could crack a joke, he would. Are you happy now?' I asked.

I realized that I may have misheard his earlier remark about his wife's teeth, for he was now telling me that there was something wrong with her *feet*, but she denied this too.

'No,' I was able to say, 'he said it's not your feet, it's your shoes.' For some reason the audience went into almost hysterical laughter.

'Your husband is a real comedian,' I told the lady. 'He said you've got to have a hat not just for Sunday but for every day of the week.'

Then he returned to the subject of his wife's ear. It was the left one that gave her problems, and he insisted that she put the deaf aid in the correct place and not leave it in a drawer.

'I will,' the lady said. 'I am going to put it in my ear.'

DORIS COLLINS, *The Power Within*, 1986

A demonstration in Poplar
Another young lad who was killed in an accident seemed to think that the name of his favourite pub was all the information necessary to convince his sister that he was really there.

'Just mention the Green Man,' he said confidently.

And some messages seemed puzzling to me but made perfect sense to the recipients. At one point I got the name Proctor and not one but two ladies claimed it. It turned out they were the Proctor sisters, a bubbly duo full of fun.

'Well, this is very odd,' I told them, 'I've got a lady here, I'm sure it's a lady, but they're calling her Henry.'

The sisters collapsed into each other's arms all laughter and dimples. 'Yes, that's right. It's Henrietta, but Father always called her Henry.'

'And now I've got another lady but they're calling her George.'

The sisters could hardly speak for mirth. 'That's right,' they spluttered, 'Georgina!' and the whole theatre laughed with them.

Questions and answers at public demonstrations

Q. If you carry a kidney donor card and leave parts of your body to someone on earth, does it hinder your progression into spirit?

A. Oh no, love. Blimey, I hope they've got my parts parcelled and labelled! I've had so many bits and pieces taken away, love . . . It doesn't make any difference to us over there. My mother only had one eye. She lost it at birth, but when I saw my mother on the other side I couldn't understand what was different about her at first—then I realized she had two eyes.

They can put me in the dustbin when I've gone for all the difference it'll make to me. I'll be away.

Q. If you have more than one husband, who do you end up with?

A. If you loved them both equally you'd go to both because there is no jealousy. But if you didn't get on on earth you probably wouldn't want to see each other again, so you wouldn't. You go where the love is.

Q. If you have an animal put down, are you held responsible even if it was for the good of the animal?

A. No, love. I hope someone would do the same for me if I was suffering and never going to get well. But animals live on too and they are fit and healthy on the other side. You will meet your pets again.

Q. If they watch you from the other side, do they come into the room or do they watch you from somewhere else?

A. Are you worried about your privacy, love? There wouldn't be babies born if everyone thought like that. No, they respect our privacy. They come when you send out love. If you think, isn't this lovely, I wish so-and-so could be here to see it—they come.

DORIS STOKES, *Whispering Voices*, 1985. She has been described as number one in 'bringing mediums to the masses', and, by Jean Rook in the *Daily Express*, as 'a built-in telephone exchange to the Other World', though in outward appearance a 'plump, grey, permed housewife'. Of the supposed rivalry between her and Doris Collins, the two 'psychic superstars', Doris Stokes has said: 'Our styles are different . . . but there's certainly no need for us to "battle". There's more than enough work around to keep us, and goodness knows how many other mediums as well, fully occupied for the rest of our lives'

'I've always thought that you had a pretty notion of the creepy, but the mistake that you make is to imagine that creepiness is characteristic of the borderland. No doubt there are creepy things there, but so there are everywhere, and a thunderstorm is far more terrifying than an apparition. And when you get really close to the borderland, you see how enchanting it is, and how vastly more enchanting the other side must be. I got right on to the borderland once, here in this house, as I shall probably tell you, and I never saw so happy and kindly a place. And without doubt I shall soon be careering across it in my own person. That'll be, as we've often determined, wildly interesting, and it will have the solemnity of a first night at a new play about it. There'll be the curtain close in front of you, and presently it will be raised, and you will see something you never saw before. How well, on the whole, the secret has been kept, though from time to time little bits of information, little scraps of dialogue, little descriptions of scenery have leaked out. Enthrallingly interesting; one wonders how they will come into the great new drama.'

'You don't mean the sort of thing that mediums tell us?' I asked.

'Of course I don't. I hate the sloshy—really there's no other word for it, and why should there be, since that word fits so admirably—the sloshy utterances of the ordinary high-class, beyond-suspicion medium at half a guinea a sitting, who asks if there's anybody present who once knew a Charles, or if not Charles, Thomas or William. Naturally somebody has known a Charles, Thomas or William who has passed over, and is the son, brother, father or cousin of a lady in black. So when she claims Thomas, he tells her that he is very busy and happy, helping people . . . O Lord, what rot! I went to one such seance a month ago, just before I was taken ill, and the medium said that Margaret wanted to get into touch with somebody. Two of us claimed Margaret, but Margaret chose me and said she was the spirit of my wife. Wife, you know! You must allow that this was a very unfortunate shot. When I said that I was unmarried, Margaret said that she was my mother, whose name was Charlotte. Oh dear, oh dear!'

E. F. BENSON, from 'Roderick's Story', 1923

The case I allude to is that of an invalid woman [Eusapia Palladino] who belongs to the humblest class of society. She is nearly thirty years old and very ignorant . . .

This woman rises in the air, no matter what bands tie her down. She seems to lie upon the empty air, as on a couch, contrary to all the laws of gravity; she plays on musical instruments—organs, bells, tambourines—as if they had been touched by her hands or moved by the breath of invisible gnomes . . . This woman at times can increase her stature by more than four inches.

PROFESSOR ERCOLE CHIAI, from letter to Professor Cesare Lombroso, 1888

An American reporter, on the occasion of Eusapia's visit to his country in 1910, bluntly asked the medium if she had ever been caught tricking. Here is Eusapia's frank reply: 'Many times I have been told so. You see, it is like this. Some people are at the table who expect tricks—in fact, they want them. I am in a trance. Nothing happens. They get impatient. They think of the tricks— nothing but tricks. They put their mind on the tricks, and—I—and I auto- matically respond. But it is not often. They merely will me to do them. That is all.'

CONAN DOYLE, *The History of Spiritualism*

Conan Doyle had a sitting with a young medium he later refused to name, whose spirit control continually addressed him through a silver trumpet as 'Sir Sherlock Holmes'. When he declined to respond, the trumpet banged him impatiently. Finally, he shouted out, 'MY NAME, SIR, IS CONAN DOYLE!'

CHARLES HIGHAM, *The Adventures of Conan Doyle*, 1976; the incident took place in New York in April 1922

One of their [fake mediums'] activities is to produce what are known as apports, or small objects which they claim to bring from afar by psychic means. On one occasion the Hon. Everard Feilding, who was at the time research officer for the SPR, arranged a sitting with a reputed physical medium, of whom he had his doubts. She was unwise enough to leave him alone in her room beforehand and he took the opportunity to have a look behind the curtains. Attached to these he found a number of prawns, and round their necks he tied bows of pink ribbon with which he had had the foresight to come provided. Thus adorned the prawns duly appeared at his sitting, purporting to have been brought from the sea by psychic means.

ROSALIND HEYWOOD, *The Sixth Sense*

—Paddy Dignam dead? says Alf.

—Ay, says Joe.

—Sure I'm after seeing him not five minutes ago, says Alf, as plain as a pikestaff.

—Who's dead? says Bob Doran.

—You saw his ghost then, says Joe, God between us and harm.

—What? says Alf. Good Christ, only five . . . What? . . . and Willie Murray with him, the two of them there near whatdoyoucallhim's . . . What? Dignam dead?

—What about Dignam? says Bob Doran. Who's talking about . . .?

—Dead! says Alf. He is no more dead than you are.

—Maybe so, says Joe. They took the liberty of burying him this morning anyhow.

—Paddy? says Alf.

—Ay, says Joe. He paid the debt of nature, God be merciful to him.

—Good Christ! says Alf.

Begob he was what you might call flabbergasted.

In the darkness spirit hands were felt to flutter and when prayer by tantras had been directed to the proper quarter a faint but increasing luminosity of ruby light became gradually visible, the apparition of the etheric double being particularly lifelike owing to the discharge of jivic rays from the crown of the head and face. Communication was effected through the pituitary body and also by means of the orangefiery and scarlet rays emanating from the sacral region and solar plexus. Questioned by his earthname as to his whereabouts in the heavenworld he stated that he was now on the path of prālāyā or return but was still submitted to trial at the hands of certain bloodthirsty entities on the lower astral levels. In reply to a question as to his first sensations in the great divide beyond he stated that previously he had seen as in a glass darkly but that those who had passed over had summit possibilities of atmic development opened up to them. Interrogated as to whether life there resembled our experience in the flesh he stated that he had heard from more favoured beings now in the spirit that their abodes were equipped with every modern home comfort such as tālāfānā, ālāvātār, hātākāldā, wātāklāsāt and that the highest adepts were steeped in waves of volupcy of the very purest nature. Having requested a quart of buttermilk this was brought and evidently afforded relief. Asked if he had any message for the living he exhorted all who were still at the wrong side of Māyā to acknowledge the true path for it was reported in devanic circles that Mars and Jupiter were out for mischief on the eastern angle where the ram has power. It was then queried whether there were any special desires on the part of the defunct and the reply was: *We greet you, friends of earth, who are still in the body. Mind C.K. doesn't pile it on.* It was ascertained that the reference was to Mr Cornelius Kelleher, manager of Messrs H. J. O'Neill's popular funeral establishment, a personal friend of the defunct, who had been responsible for the carrying out of the interment arrangements. Before departing he requested that it should be told to his dear son Patsy that the other boot which he had been looking for was at present under the commode in the return room and that the pair should be sent to Cullen's to be soled only as the heels were still good. He stated that this had greatly perturbed his peace of mind in the other region and earnestly requested that his desire should be made known.

Assurances were given that the matter would be attended to and it was intimated that this had given satisfaction.

JAMES JOYCE, *Ulysses*, 1922

Mrs Eliza Ravenshaw of Malvern Link thus wrote to me in 1878, in reference to one of my volumes on the Supernatural: 'I was so much interested in the part called "Modern Necromancy". I am so glad you have written so strongly against it. I heard only a few weeks ago that a certain Spiritualist, before coming to stay with her sister-in-law (an acquaintance of mine), wrote to beg her brother and sister would sleep with their bedroom doors open during her visit, as she was so terrified at night by fears of devils coming to seize her. She had, as she averred, lately had a message from a deceased brother *begging her to destroy herself, as he wanted her in the Spirit-World.*'

LEE, *Glimpses in the Twilight*

The road to En-dor is easy to tread
　　For Mother or yearning Wife.
There, it is sure, we shall meet our Dead
　　As they were even in life.
Earth has not dreamed of the blessing in store
For desolate hearts on the road to En-dor.

Whispers shall comfort us out of the dark—
　　Hands—ah, God!—that we knew!
Visions and voices—look and hark!—
　　Shall prove that the tale is true,
And that those who have passed to the further shore
May be hailed—at a price—on the road to En-dor.

But they are so deep in their new eclipse
   Nothing they say can reach,
Unless it be uttered by alien lips
   And framed in a stranger's speech.
The son must send word to the mother that bore,
Through an hireling's mouth. 'Tis the rule of En-dor.

And not for nothing these gifts are shown
   By such as delight our Dead.
They must twitch and stiffen and slaver and groan
   Ere the eyes are set in the head,
And the voice from the belly begins. Therefore,
We pay them a wage where they ply at En-dor.

Even so, we have need of faith
   And patience to follow the clue.
Often, at first, what the dear one saith
   Is babble, or jest, or untrue.
(Lying spirits perplex us sore
   Till our loves—and their lives—are well known at En-dor) . . .

Oh, the road to En-dor is the oldest road
   And the craziest road of all!
Straight it runs to the Witch's abode,
   As it did in the days of Saul,
And nothing has changed of the sorrow in store
For such as go down on the road to En-dor!

     KIPLING, 'En-dor', 1914–19—?: 'Behold, there is a Woman that hath a familiar
     spirit at En-dor, 1 Samuel, 28, vii'

HIGH SPIRITS AND LOW

Some of the items printed here indicate that considerations of social class operate in supernatural contexts ('Excuse me, my lady') as in others, notwithstanding the Right Revd Mervyn Stockwood's intercession on behalf of the humble and unpretentious.

Some spirits, it seems, have a taste for spirits, or in the case of the more refined for the pure bouquet of vintage wines. A drop taken might account for the garbled transmissions received by Dickens's travelling companion. It is worth noting that Graves's 'Welsh Incident' was at the outset a riddle poem, along the lines of 'What am I?', the answer being anticipated in the original title, 'Railway Carriage'. The change invests the poem with altogether greater reach and suggestiveness.

The following anecdote would have sounded tendentious had it been placed in the preceding section, but here it can be thought to add innocently to the gaiety of nations, those of both this world and the other, as well as furnishing further evidence of how the natural and mundane mingles so readily with the supernatural and prodigious. At one of the lantern lectures which Conan Doyle gave in New York in 1922 the audience, overcome with awe, stood and prayed for several minutes in a silence broken by occasional sobs and cries. Then a strange, high-pitched whistle, eerie and unsettling, floated up to the ceiling. Someone on the podium called out, 'There is a spirit manifestation among you, is there not?', which provoked further hysteria among the audience, until Conan Doyle called for silence to be restored. A thin quavering voice then emerged from somewhere in the hall, and an old man, supported by a stick, rose to his feet. 'No!' he cried, 'It's not a spirit, it's my hearing aid!'

'Is it haunted?' I asked.

The landlord looked at me, shook his head, and answered, 'I say nothing.'

'Then it *is* haunted?'

'Well!' cried the landlord, in an outburst of frankness that had the appearance of desperation—'I wouldn't sleep in it.'

'Why not?'

'If I wanted to have all the bells in a house ring, with nobody to ring 'em; and all the doors in a house bang, with nobody to bang 'em; and all sorts of feet treading about, with no feet there; why, then,' said the landlord, 'I'd sleep in that house.'

'Is anything seen there?'

The landlord looked at me again, and then, with his former appearance of desperation, called down his stable-yard for 'Ikey!' . . .

'This gentleman wants to know,' said the landlord, 'if anything's seen at the Poplars.'

' 'Ooded woman with a howl,' said Ikey, in a state of great freshness.

'Do you mean a cry?'

'I mean a bird, Sir.'

'A hooded woman with an owl. Dear me! Did you ever see her?'

'I seen the howl.'

'Never the woman?'

'Not so plain as the howl, but they always keeps together.'

'Has anybody ever seen the woman as plainly as the owl?'

'Lord bless you, Sir! Lots.'

'Who?'

'Lord bless you, Sir! Lots.'

'The general-dealer opposite, for instance, who is opening his shop?'

'Perkins? Bless you, Perkins wouldn't go anigh the place. No!' observed the young man, with considerable feeling; 'he an't overwise, an't Perkins, but he an't such a fool as *that*.'

(Here, the landlord murmured his confidence in Perkins's knowing better.)

'Who is—or who was—the hooded woman with the owl? Do you know?'

'Well!' said Ikey, holding up his cap with one hand while he scratched his head with the other, 'they say, in general, that she was murdered, and the howl he 'ooted the while.'

DICKENS, from 'The Haunted House', 1859

One wintry night, at half-past nine,
   Cold, tired, and cross, and muddy,

I had come home, too late to dine,
And supper, with cigars and wine,
   Was waiting in the study.

There was a strangeness in the room,
   And something thin and wavy
Was standing near me in the gloom—
I took it for the carpet-broom
   Left by that careless slavey.

But presently the thing began
   To shudder and to sneeze:
On which I said 'Come, come, my man,
That's a most inconsiderate plan—
   Less noise there, if you please!'

'I've caught a cold,' the thing replies,
   'Out there upon the landing—'
I turned to look in some surprise,
And there, before my very eyes,
   A little ghost was standing! . . .

He said 'A flutter of alarm
   Is not unnatural, is it?
I really feared you meant some harm,
But now I see that you are calm,
   Let me explain my visit.

'The last ghost left you on the third—
   Since then you've not been haunted:
But, as he never sent us word,
'Twas quite by accident we heard
   That any one was wanted.

'A Spectre has first choice, by right,
   In filling up a vacancy;
Then Phantom, Goblin, Elf, and Sprite—
If all these fail them, they invite
   The nicest Ghoul that they can see.

'The Spectres said the place was low,
   And that you kept bad wine:
So, as a Phantom had to go,
And I was first, of course, you know,
   I couldn't well decline.'

'No doubt,' said I, 'they settled who
   Was fittest to be sent:
Yet still to choose a brat like you
To haunt a man of forty-two,
   Was no great compliment.'

'I'm not so young, Sir,' he replied,
   'As you might think—the fact is,
In caverns by the water side,
And other places that I've tried,
   I've had a lot of practice.

'But I have never taken yet
   A strict domestic part,
And in my flurry I forget
The Five Good Rules of Etiquette
   We have to know by heart.' . . .

And still he seemed to grow more white,
   More vapoury, and wavier—
Seen in the dim and flickering light,
As he proceeded to recite
   His 'Maxims of Behaviour'.

      LEWIS CARROLL, from 'Canto I', *Phantasmagoria*, 1869

Mr *Samuel Clark* hath published the Apparition to Mr *White* of *Dorchester*, Assessor to the *Westminster*-Assembly, at *Lambeth*. The Devil, in a light Night, stood by his Bed-side: He looked a while whether he would say or do any thing, and then said, *If thou hast nothing else to do, I have*; and so turned himself to sleep. Many say it from Mr *White* himself.

Mr *Mun*, Rector of *Stockerson* in *Leicestershire*, had a Daughter married to one Mr *Beecham*, Rector of *Branston* in *Rutland*; in whose House it was frequently observed, that a Tobacco-pipe would move it self from off a Shelf at one end of the Room, without any Hand. Mr *Mun* visiting his Son-in-Law, took a Pipe of Tobacco in that Room, and looked for some such Motion; but a great Bible, instead of a Pipe, moved it self off from a Desk at the lower end of the Room, and cast it self into his Lap. Whereupon he opened the Bible at *Gen.* 3. 15. saying, *Come, Satan; I'll shew thee thy Doom: The Seed of the Woman shall break the Serpent's Head. Avoid Satan.*

      BAXTER, *The Certainty of the Worlds of Spirits*

There's a delightful story of a spirited old lady—as plucky as she was old, it seems—who was told on a country visit that she was in a haunted room, and asked if she minded.

'Mind?' she repeated scornfully. 'Not a scrap. Why should I?'

She was assured that while the ghost was harmless enough, it took the unusual form of a very tiny man, a little fellow, hardly bigger than a gnome.

'But it very rarely shows itself,' her hostess explained. 'I've never seen it myself, though I've lived here many years. It's always my friends who have the luck.'

'Well,' snorted the plucky old lady, 'I'm one of your friends, so I hope I shall be lucky.'

She was. She locked her door, as against any possible tricks, and in due course climbed into bed and began to read. As she read, a movement caught her eye. At the far end of the room, out of the panelled wall, emerged a figure—an extremely diminutive little man. He came out into the middle of the room, plain as a leg of mutton. He skipped about a bit, as though dancing, hopping to and fro like a bird, but looking at her as he did so. His bright eyes never left her face. He watched; he seemed to study her. Then, abruptly, with a sudden rush, he darted across the room, took a springing leap upon her bed, reached out a tiny hand, snatched the wig off her head, shot down again, scuttled over the floor, and rushed up the face of the big cupboard like a shadow. Between the top of this cupboard and the ceiling there was a space of two feet. He perched himself there, sitting cross-legged, waving the wig to and fro in the air with a smile of great glee. And, as he did so, repeating over and over again in a high, thin, squeaky voice: 'Here we are! Here we are! All alone till morning!'

The plucky, high-spirited lady watched and listened for a few minutes and then turned out the light and fell asleep. Next morning she tried to persuade herself that she had dreamt the whole little episode but against this explanation was the fact that her wig still lay on the top of that high cupboard and that she had a rare old job climbing up with a chair to get it down again.

BLACKWOOD, from 'The Wig', radio talk, 1935

When Mr Hiram B. Otis, the American Minister, bought Canterville Chase, everyone told him he was doing a very foolish thing, as there was no doubt at all that the place was haunted. Indeed, Lord Canterville himself, who was a man of the most punctilious honour, had felt it his duty to mention the fact to Mr Otis when they came to discuss terms.

'We have not cared to live in the place ourselves,' said Lord Canterville, 'since my grand-aunt, the Dowager Duchess of Bolton, was frightened into a fit, from which she never really recovered, by two skeleton hands being placed on her shoulders as she was dressing for dinner, and I feel bound to tell you, Mr Otis, that the ghost has been seen by several living members of my family, as well as by the rector of the parish, the Rev. Augustus Dampier, who is a Fellow of King's College, Cambridge . . .'

'My Lord,' answered the Minister, 'I will take the furniture and the ghost at a valuation. I come from a modern country, where we have everything that money can buy; and with all our spry young fellows painting the Old World red, and carrying off your best actors and prima-donnas, I reckon that if there were such a thing as a ghost in Europe, we'd have it at home in a very short time in one of our public museums, or on the road as a show . . . But there is no such thing, sir, as a ghost, and I guess the laws of Nature are not going to be suspended for the British aristocracy.'

'You are certainly very natural in America,' answered Lord Canterville, who did not quite understand Mr Otis's last observation, 'and if you don't mind a ghost in the house, it is all right. Only you must remember I warned you.'

The day had been warm and sunny; and, in the cool of the evening, the whole family went out to drive. They did not return home till nine o'clock, when they had a light supper. The conversation in no way turned upon ghosts, so there were not even those primary conditions of receptive expectation which so often precede the presentation of psychical phenomena. The subjects discussed, as I have since learned from Mr Otis, were merely such as form the ordinary conversation of cultured Americans of the better class, such as the immense superiority of Miss Fanny Davenport over Sara Bernhardt as an actress; the difficulty of obtaining green corn, buckwheat cakes, and hominy, even in the best English houses; the importance of Boston in the development of the world-soul; the advantages of the baggage check system in railway travelling; and the sweetness of the New York accent as compared to the London drawl. No mention at all was made of the supernatural, nor was Sir Simon de Canterville alluded to in any way. At eleven o'clock the family retired, and by half-past all the lights were out. Some time after, Mr Otis was awakened by a curious noise in the corridor, outside his room. It sounded like the clank of metal, and seemed to be coming nearer every moment. He got up at once, struck a match, and looked at the time. It was exactly one o'clock. He was quite calm, and felt his pulse, which was not at all feverish. The strange noise still continued, and with it he heard distinctly the sound of footsteps. He put on his slippers, took a small oblong phial out of his dressing-case, and opened the door. Right in front of him he saw, in the wan moonlight, an old man of terrible aspect. His eyes were as red burning coals; long grey hair fell over his shoulders in matted coils; his garments, which were of antique cut, were soiled and ragged, and from his wrists and ankles hung heavy manacles and rusty gyves.

'My dear sir,' said Mr Otis, 'I really must insist on your oiling those chains, and have brought you for that purpose a small bottle of the Tammany Rising Sun Lubricator. It is said to be completely efficacious upon one application, and there are several testimonials to that effect on the wrapper from some of our most eminent native divines. I shall leave it here for you by the bedroom candles, and will be happy to supply you with more should you require it.' With these words the United States Minister laid the bottle down on a marble table, and, closing his door, retired to rest.

For a moment the Canterville ghost stood quite motionless in natural indignation; then, dashing the bottle violently upon the polished floor, he fled down the corridor, uttering hollow groans, and emitting a ghastly green light. Just, however, as he reached the top of the great oak staircase, a door was flung open, two little white-robed figures appeared, and a large pillow whizzed past his head! There was evidently no time to be lost, so, hastily adopting the Fourth Dimension of Space as a means of escape, he vanished through the wainscoting, and the house became quite quiet.

OSCAR WILDE, from 'The Canterville Ghost', 1887

When I went to bed last night I fancied that something ran in at my bedroom door after me from the gallery. It seemed to be a skeleton. It ran with a dancing step and I thought it aimed a blow at me from behind. This was shortly before midnight.

KILVERT, *Diary*, 23 January 1875

... a recent case, when a man was brought before a local magistrates' court for refusing to pay his rent, because his council-owned house had a ghost. Unfortunately for him, the magistrates ruled that ghosts could not be admitted to exist and, therefore, he could not refuse to pay rent on the grounds that his house was already tenanted. He lost his case.

TERENCE WHITAKER, *Yorkshire's Ghosts and Legends*

For reputation of the art
Each Ghost must act a proper part,
Observe decorum's needful grace,
And keep the laws of time and place;
Must change, with happy variation,
His manners with his situation;
What in the country might pass down
Would be impertinent in town.
No spirit of discretion here
Can think of breeding awe and fear,
'Twill serve the purpose more by half
To make the congregation laugh.
We want no ensigns of surprise,
Locks stiff with gore, and saucer eyes;
Give us an entertaining sprite,
Gentle, familiar, and polite,
One who appears in such a form
As might an holy hermit warm,
Or who on former schemes refines,
And only talks by sounds and signs,
Who will not to the eye appear,
But pays her visits to the ear,
And knocks so gently, 'twould not fright
A lady in the darkest night.
Such is our Fanny, whose good will,
Which cannot in the grave lie still,
Brings her on earth to entertain
Her friends and lovers in Cock Lane.

CHARLES CHURCHILL, *The Ghost*, 1762–3

Mr Hawker had a story of a Wellcombe woman whom he visited after the loss of her husband.

'Ah! thank the Lord,' said she, 'my old man is safe in Beelzebub's bosom.'

'Abraham's bosom, my good woman,' said the vicar.

'Ah! I dare say. I am not acquainted with the quality and so don't rightly know their names.'

BARING-GOULD, *The Vicar of Morwenstow*

My father gave me a lovely house in the park at Wilton. It was a 'folly' built in the eighteenth century, and had been moved from a bridge over the river Nadder to where it now stands. Later it was turned into a school and run by Lady Georgina Herbert, who married Lord Lansdowne . . . The purpose of the school was to educate the children of the employees on the estate. Lady Georgina didn't live very long and she is supposed to have drowned by falling into the river at the bottom of the garden, getting entangled in the weeds.

The school continued until the first socialist government put an end to privately supported free education . . . It was an enchanting place, situated in the middle of a wood carpeted with bluebells and primroses . . .

I love birds and couldn't understand why the ones I hung in a certain window always died. I said to Mrs Quinn, my housekeeper, 'I cannot think why those birds always die, Mrs Quinn.'

'Oh, Mr David,' she said, 'that's where the Lady walks in. It used to be the front door of the house, you know.'

I said: 'What lady, Mrs Quinn?'

'Mr David, you know perfectly well that Lady Georgina Herbert haunts this place and I often see her!'

'You often see her, Mrs Quinn?'

'Yes, indeed I do, Mr David.'

'What do you do when she appears?'

'Well, seeing as how it's gentry, I say: "Excuse me, my lady", and leave the room.'

DAVID HERBERT, *Second Son*, 1972

The famous Huxley (whose grandson occupies a leading position in the English literary world of today) relates that one of his patients no longer dared go out socially because often, on the very chair that was offered to her with a courteous gesture, she saw an old gentleman already seated. She was quite certain that either the gesture of invitation or the old gentleman's presence was a hallucination, for no one would have offered her a chair that was already occupied. And when Huxley, to cure her, forced her to reappear in society, she had a moment of painful hesitation wondering whether the friendly sign that was being made to her was the real thing, or whether, in obedience to a non-existent vision, she was about to sit down in public upon the knees of a gentleman of flesh and blood. Her brief uncertainty was agonizing.

PROUST, *Sodom and Gomorrah*, 1921

Monsieur Lazolet, an inspector of the Academy (with the degree of Litt. Doc.), had the curiosity to wish to see the Saint of Lumbres of whom everyone was talking. He paid him a secret visit with his wife and daughter. He was rather moved. 'I had imagined an imposing man,' he said, 'with manners and a presence. But this poor fellow has no dignity. He eats in the street like any beggar.' 'What a pity,' he added, 'that a man like that can possibly believe in the devil!'

GEORGES BERNANOS, *The Star of Satan*, 1926; tr. Veronica Lucas

We have also heard of a lady belonging to the aristocracy who gave herself up to communications with pretended spirits in tables and who, scandalized beyond measure at the unsuitable replies of her particular piece of furniture, undertook a journey to Rome to submit the heretical article to the chair of St Peter. She carried it with her and had an *auto-da-fé* in the capital of the Christian world. Better to burn her furniture than to court madness, and to say the truth it was an imminent danger for the lady here in question.

LÉVI, *History of Magic*

To the rational, common-sense Reformers of the later Middle Ages, the Church appeared to confuse the genuinely mystical with the silliest credulity . . . The Holy Blood at Hailes in Gloucestershire was the most popular of all shrines for West Country pilgrims: it did not reveal the Blood unless to the worthy, for— so Henry VIII's Commissioners reported—it was kept in a crystal vessel which was opaque on one side and could be turned round by its operator. The prize joke for the Reformers was the cult of Sir John Schorne, rector of North Marston in Buckinghamshire, who died about 1309. He was said to have conjured the Devil into a boot. The ensuing highly profitable racket was enlivened by a working model of the boot, which had the Devil popping up— supposedly the origin of the Jack-in-a-Box toy.

THEO BROWN, *The Fate of the Dead*, 1979. A note claims that the first phenomenon gave rise to the proverb, 'As sure as God's in Gloucestershire'

It is a general opinion amongst the lower orders, that the last buried corpse has to perform an office like that of a 'fag' in our public schools by the junior boy, or at a regimental mess by the youngest officer, and that the attendance on his churchyard companions is only relieved by the interment of some other person. The notion may seem too absurd, yet serious consequences have sometimes resulted from it, and an instance comes within my recollection where two funerals, proceeding to the same burial ground, arrived within view of each other, a short distance from their place of destination. Both immediately halted, and a messenger was mutually dispatched to demand precedence; their conference terminated in blows, and the throng on both sides, forsaking the coffins, rushed impetuously forward, when a furious contest ensued, in which some lives were lost.

CROKER, *Letters from the Irish Highlands*, 1825

There is a ghost
who devours handkerchiefs,
it accompanies you
on your voyage,
it eats out of the portmanteau,
out of the bed,
out of the bedside table,
like a bird
out of the hand,
many of them eaten up—
not all, not at one go.
With eighteen hankies,
proud sailor,
you set forth
on unknown seas,
with between eight and seven
you return home,
a grief to the housewife.

CHRISTIAN MORGENSTERN, 'Ghost', 1919

Virgins who died on the eve of marriage
Walk abroad with unassuaged desires,
High-minded moneylenders brush aside
All debts, while genial physicians
Scatter efficacious pills and potions,

And jolly drunkards share their jars of wine—
Such are the ghosts who move among the people.

Ours are of another tribe. Envious shades
Who hide the inkstone, rip the scrolls,
Pluck out the fine hairs from our brushes,
Suck up the midnight oil like vampires;
Who scribble nonsense on the *Book of Odes*,
Misnaming trees and flowers, birds and beasts,
Perverting allegories, confusing allusions.

For us, it seems, the undying company
Of rancorous rhymers and malignant critics,
Barbarous calligraphers, withered pedants—
Compared with us, how blest the common people!

TAO TSCHUNG YU (?18th century), 'Familiar Spirits'

. . . a wag recently wrote in a book review, 'an element of the supernatural is introduced when a reader finds the book he is looking for in the London Library'.

But almost everybody believes in the way, on those open shelves, that books seem mysteriously to offer themselves when you are thinking about a particular subject, though not many have had the experience of one of the library's more eccentric members who claimed that a book literally leaped out of the shelves and hit her. It was by the notorious practitioner in the black arts, Aleister Crowley.

[Suggestions Book] N. Tolstoy: Would it be possible for the Library to purchase James Reynold's *Irish Ghost Stories*—a classic of its kind—published *c*.1946? *Also* I still receive electric shocks from the light switches in the Occult section.

JOHN WELLS, *Rude Words: A Discursive History of the London Library*, 1991

There is still the ghost of a chance to win a chance of sleeping with a ghost at Castle Stuart, Inverness. Charles Stuart—who leases the castle from his distant relative Douglas Stuart, the Earl of Moray—decided that raffling off a night in the haunted turret bedroom would raise money for charity and lay the ghosts of a room that has not been slept in for 300 years. Speculation has it that the bedroom may be haunted by the Marquis of Montrose, who was hung, drawn and quartered in 1652. Tickets cost £1 each, and all proceeds go to the Cancer Research Campaign.

Victoria McKee, 'And Briefly', *The Times*, 16 October 1991

Sung Ting-po of Nanyang, as a young man, met a ghost one night as he was walking.

'Who are you?' he asked.

The ghost answered, 'A ghost.' It then asked, 'And who are you?'

'I am a ghost too,' lied Sung.

'Where are you going?'

'To the town of Wan,' was the answer.

'I'm going there too.'

They went along together for several *li*.

'Walking like this is too slow. Why not carry each other in turn?' suggested the ghost.

'A good idea,' agreed Sung.

First, the ghost carried him for several *li*.

'How heavy you are!' said the ghost. 'Are you really a phantom?'

'I am a new ghost,' answered Sung. 'That's why I am heavy.'

Then he carried the ghost, who of course had no weight at all. And so they went on, changing several times.

'As I am a new ghost,' remarked Sung presently, 'I don't know what we spectres have to fear most.'

'What we detest is men's spittle.'

They proceeded together till they came to a stream. Sung invited the ghost to cross first, which it did without a sound. Sung, however, made quite a splash.

'How come you make so much noise?' enquired the ghost.

'That's because I am a new ghost. I am not accustomed yet to wading through water. You mustn't blame me.'

As they approached the town of Wan, Sung threw the ghost over his shoulder and held it fast. With a screech, the ghost begged to be put down, but Sung paid no attention, making straight for the town. When he set the ghost down, it had turned into a sheep. He promptly sold it, having spat at it first to prevent it from changing into another form. Then he left, richer by one thousand five hundred coins.

Shih Chung commented on this at the time:

'Sung Ting-po did better than most,
Made fifteen hundred coins by selling a ghost.'

ANON., *Stories About Not Being Afraid Of Ghosts*, 3rd to 5th century; tr. Yang
Xianyi and Gladys Yang

'I'll have a wager with you,' said Buddha. 'If you are really so clever, jump
off the palm of my right hand. If you succeed, I'll tell the Jade Emperor to
come and live with me in the Western Paradise, and you shall have his throne
without more ado. But if you fail, you shall go back to earth and do penance
there for many a kalpa [a period estimated at 4,320 million years] before you
come to me again with your talk.'

'This Buddha,' Monkey thought to himself, 'is a perfect fool. I can jump a
hundred and eight thousand leagues, while his palm cannot be as much as
eight inches across. How could I fail to jump clear of it?' 'You're sure you are
in a position to do this for me?' he asked. 'Of course I am,' said Buddha.

He stretched out his right hand, which looked about the size of a lotus leaf.
Monkey put his cudgel behind his ear, and leapt with all his might. 'That's all
right,' he said to himself. 'I'm right off it now.' He was whizzing so fast that
he was almost invisible, and Buddha, watching him with the eye of wisdom,
saw a mere whirligig shoot along.

Monkey came at last to five pink pillars, sticking up into the air. 'This is the
end of the World,' said Monkey to himself. 'All I have got to do is to go back
to Buddha and claim my forfeit. The Throne is mine.' 'Wait a minute,' he said
presently, 'I'd better just leave a record of some kind, in case I have trouble
with Buddha.' He plucked a hair and blew on it with magic breath, crying
'Change!' It changed at once into a writing brush charged with heavy ink, and
at the base of the central pillar he wrote, 'The Great Sage Equal to Heaven
reached this place.' Then to mark his disrespect, he relieved nature at the
bottom of the first pillar, and somersaulted back to where he had come from.
Standing on Buddha's palm, he said, 'Well, I've gone and come back. You can
go and tell the Jade Emperor to hand over the Palaces of Heaven.' 'You
stinking ape,' said Buddha, 'you've been on the palm of my hand all the time.'
'You're quite mistaken,' said Monkey. 'I got to the end of the World, where I
saw five flesh-coloured pillars sticking up into the sky. I wrote something on
one of them. I'll take you there and show you, if you like.' 'No need for that,'
said Buddha. 'Just look down.' Monkey peered down with his fiery, steely
eyes, and there at the base of the middle finger of Buddha's hand he saw
written the words 'The Great Sage Equal to Heaven reached this place', and

from the fork between the thumb and first finger came a smell of monkey's urine. It took him some time to get over his astonishment. At last he said, 'Impossible, impossible! I wrote that on the pillar sticking up into the sky. How did it get on to Buddha's finger? He's practising some magic upon me. Let me go back and look.' Dear Monkey! He crouched, and was just making ready to spring again, when Buddha turned his head, and pushed Monkey out at the western gate of Heaven. As he did so, he changed his five fingers into the Five Elements, Metal, Wood, Water, Fire and Earth. They became a five-peaked mountain, named Wu Hsing Shan (Mountain of the Five Elements), which pressed upon him heavily enough to hold him tight.

WU CH'ENG-EN (*c.*1505–80), *Monkey*; tr. Arthur Waley

'You will excuse me,' said the gentleman contemptuously, 'if I am too much in advance of common humanity to trouble myself at all about it. I have passed the night—as indeed I pass the whole of my time now—in spiritual intercourse.'

'O!' said I, something snappishly.

'The conferences of the night began,' continued the gentleman, turning several leaves of his notebook, 'with this message: "Evil communications corrupt good manners." '

'Sound,' said I; 'but, absolutely new?'

'New from spirits,' returned the gentleman.

I could only repeat my rather snappish 'O!' and ask if I might be favoured with the last communication.

' "A bird in the hand," ' said the gentleman, reading his last entry with great solemnity, ' "is worth two in the Bosh." '

'Truly I am of the same opinion,' said I; 'but shouldn't it be Bush?'

'It came to me, Bosh,' returned the gentleman.

The gentleman then informed me that the spirit of Socrates had delivered this special revelation in the course of the night. 'My friend, I hope you are pretty well. There are two in this railway carriage. How do you do? There are seventeen thousand four hundred and seventy-nine spirits here, but you cannot see them. Pythagoras is here. He is not at liberty to mention it, but hopes you like travelling.' Galileo likewise had dropped in, with this scientific intelligence. 'I am glad to see you, *amico. Come sta?* Water will freeze when it is cold enough. *Addio!*' In the course of the night, also, the following phenomena had occurred. Bishop Butler had insisted on spelling his name, 'Bubler', for which offence against orthography and good manners he had been dismissed as out of temper. John Milton (suspected of wilful mystification) had repudiated the authorship of *Paradise Lost*, and had introduced, as joint authors of that poem, two unknown gentlemen, respectively named Grungers and Scadgingtone. And Prince Arthur, nephew of King John of England, had described himself as tolerably comfortable in the seventh circle, where he was learning to paint on velvet, under the direction of Mrs Trimmer and Mary Queen of Scots.

DICKENS, from 'The Haunted House', 1859

A European planter . . . having died in the jungles of the Malabar country of South-west India, was buried there by the people. Some years afterwards, a friend of the planter found the grave carefully fenced in and covered with empty whisky and beer bottles. At a loss to understand such an unusual sight, he asked for an explanation, and was told that the dead *sahib*'s ghost had caused much trouble and that no way had been discovered to lay the ghost until an old witch-doctor declared that the ghost craved whisky and beer, to which it had long been habituated when in the flesh and which were the real cause of its separation from the fleshly body. The people, although religiously opposed to intoxicants, began purchasing bottled whisky and beer of the same brands which the *sahib* was well known to have used, and, with a regular ritual for the dead, began sacrificing them to the ghost by pouring them out upon the grave. Finding that this kept the ghost quiet, they kept up the practice in self-defence.

W. Y. EVANS-WENTZ, footnote to foreword (1927), *The Tibetan Book of the Dead*

'Not that she saw the ghost—not she. What she saw was a bogie, not a ghost.'

'Why, what is the difference?'

'Immense! As big as that which separates the objective from the subjective. Anyone can see a bogie. It is a real thing belonging to the external world. It may be a bright light, a white sheet, or a black shadow—always at night, you know, or at least in the dusk, when you are apt to be a little mixed in your observations. The best example of a bogie was Sir Walter Scott's. It looked— in the twilight remember—exactly like Lord Byron, who had not long de-parted this life at the time Sir Walter saw it. Nine men out of ten would have gone off and sworn they had seen a ghost; why, religions have been founded on just such stuff: but Sir Walter, as sane a man as ever lived—though he did

write poetry—kept his head clear and went up closer to his ghost, which
proved on examination to be a waterproof.'

'A waterproof?'

'Or a railway rug—I forget which: the moral is the same.'

'No, they have not seen any more ghosts, sir,' replied Castleman scornfully
next day, 'and never need have seen any. It is all along of this tea-drinking. We
did not have this bother when the women took their beer regular. These
teetotallers have done a lot of harm. They ought to be put down by Act of
Parliament.'

LANOE FALCONER, Cecilia de Noël, 1891

> Midnight has come, and the great Christ Church Bell
> And many a lesser bell sound through the room;
> And it is All Souls' Night,
> And two long glasses brimmed with muscatel
> Bubble upon the table. A ghost may come;
> For it is a ghost's right,
> His element is so fine
> Being sharpened by his death,
> To drink from the wine-breath
> While our gross palates drink from the whole wine.

YEATS, from 'All Souls' Night', 1925

There was a party of witches and warlocks assembled in the refectory of a
ruined abbey, intending to have a merry supper, if they could get the materials.
They had no money, and they had for servant a poor bogle, who had been lent
to them by his Satanic majesty, on condition that he should provide their
supper if he could; but without buying or stealing. They had a roaring fire,
with nothing to roast, and a large stone table, with nothing on it but broken
dishes and empty mugs. So the firelight shone on an uncouth set of long
hungry faces. Whether there was among them 'ae winsome wench and wawlie'
is more than I can say; but most probably there was, or the bogle would
scarcely have been so zealous in the cause. Still he was late on his quest. The
friars of a still flourishing abbey were making preparations for a festal day, and
had dispatched a man with a cart to the nearest town, to bring them a supply

of good things. He was driving back his cart well loaded with beef, and poultry, and ham; and a supply of choice rolls, for which a goodwife in the town was famous; and a new arrival of rare old wine, a special present to the Abbot from some great lord. The bogle, having smelt out the prize, presented himself before the carter in the form of a sailor with a wooden leg, imploring charity. The carter said he had nothing for him, and the sailor seemed to go on his way. He reappeared in various forms, always soliciting charity, more and more importunately every time, and always receiving the same denial. At last he appeared as an old woman, leaning on a stick, who was more pertinacious in her entreaties than the preceding semblances; and the carter, after asseverating with an oath that a whole shipload of beggars must have been wrecked that night on the coast, reiterated that he had nothing for her. 'Only the smallest coin, master,' said the old woman. 'I have no coin,' said the carter. 'Just a wee bite and sup of something,' said the old woman; 'you are scarcely going about without something to eat and drink; something comfortable for yourself. Just look in the cart: I am sure you will find something good.' 'Something, something, something,' said the carter; 'if there is anything fit to eat or drink in the cart, I wish a bogle may fly away with it.' 'Thank you,' said the bogle, and changed himself into a shape which laid the carter on his back, with his heels in the air. The bogle made lawful prize of the contents of the cart. The refectory was soon fragrant with the odour of roast, and the old wine flowed briskly, to the great joy of the assembly, who passed the night in feasting, singing, and dancing, and toasting Old Nick.

THOMAS LOVE PEACOCK, *Gryll Grange*, 1860

'But that was nothing to what things came out
From the sea-caves of Criccieth yonder.'
'What were they? Mermaids? dragons? ghosts?'
'Nothing at all of any things like that.'
'What were they, then?'
      'All sorts of queer things,
Things never seen or heard or written about,
Very strange, un-Welsh, utterly peculiar
Things. Oh, solid enough they seemed to touch,
Had anyone dared it. Marvellous creation,
All various shapes and sizes and no sizes,
All new, each perfectly unlike his neighbour,
Though all came moving slowly out together.'

'Describe just one of them.'
                                'I am unable.'
'What were their colours?'
                                'Mostly nameless colours,
Colours you'd like to see; but one was puce
Or perhaps more like crimson, but not purplish.
Some had no colour.'
                                'Tell me, had they legs?'
'Not a leg nor foot among them that I saw.'
'But did these things come out in any order?
What o'clock was it? What was the day of the week?
Who else was present? How was the weather?'
'I was coming to that. It was half-past three
On Easter Tuesday last. The sun was shining.
The Harlech Silver Band played *Marchog Jesu*
On thirty-seven shimmering instruments,
Collecting for Carnarvon's (Fever) Hospital Fund.
The populations of Pwllheli, Criccieth,
Portmadoc, Borth, Tremadoc, Penrhyndeudraeth,
Were all assembled. Criccieth's mayor addressed them
First in good Welsh and then in fluent English,
Twisting his fingers in his chain of office,
Welcoming the things. They came out on the sand,
Not keeping time to the band, moving seaward
Silently at a snail's pace. But at last
The most odd, indescribable thing of all,
Which hardly one man there could see for wonder
Did something recognizably a something.'
'Well, what?'
                                'It made a noise.'
                                                'A frightening noise?'
'No, no.'
                'A musical noise? A noise of scuffling?'
'No, but a very loud, respectable noise—
Like groaning to oneself on Sunday morning
In Chapel, close before the second psalm.'
'What did the mayor do?'
                                'I was coming to that.'
                        ROBERT GRAVES, 'Welsh Incident', 1929

One time Tom . . . said he had got secret news by his spies that next day a whole parcel of Spanish merchants and rich A-rabs was going to camp in Cave Hollow with two hundred elephants, and six hundred camels, and over a thousand 'sumter' mules, all loaded down with di'monds, and they didn't have only a guard of four hundred soldiers, and so we would lay in ambuscade, as he called it, and kill the lot and scoop the things. He said we must slick up our swords and guns, and get ready. He never could go after even a turnip-cart but he must have the swords and guns all scoured up for it; though they was only lath and broomsticks . . . I didn't believe we could lick such a crowd of Spaniards and A-rabs, but I wanted to see the camels and elephants, so I was on hand next day, Saturday, in the ambuscade; and when we got the word, we rushed out of the woods and down the hill. But there warn't no Spaniards and A-rabs, and there warn't no camels nor no elephants. It warn't anything but a Sunday-school picnic, and only a primer-class at that. We busted it up, and chased the children up the hollow; but we never got anything but some doughnuts and jam, though Ben Rogers got a rag doll, and Jo Harper got a hymn-book and a tract; and then the teacher charged in and made us drop everything and cut. I didn't see no di'monds, and I told Tom Sawyer so. He said there was loads of them there, anyway; and he said there was A-rabs there, too, and elephants and things. I said, why couldn't we see them, then? He said if I warn't so ignorant, but had read a book called *Don Quixote*, I would know without asking. He said it was all done by enchantment. He said there was hundreds of soldiers there, and elephants and treasure, and so on, but we had enemies which he called magicians, and they had turned the whole thing into an infant Sunday school, just out of spite. I said, all right, then the thing for us to do was to go for the magicians. Tom Sawyer said I was a numskull.

'Why,' says he, 'a magician could call up a lot of genies, and they would hash you up like nothing before you could say Jack Robinson. They are as tall as a tree and as big around as a church.'

'Well,' I says, 's'pose we get some genies to help *us*—can't we lick the other crowd then?'

'How you going to get them?'

'I don't know. How do *they* get them?'

'Why, they rub an old tin lamp or an iron ring, and then the genies come tearing in, with the thunder and lightning a-ripping around and the smoke a-rolling, and everything they're told to do they up and do it. They don't think nothing of pulling a shot tower up by the roots, and belting a Sunday-school superintendent over the head with it.'

'Who makes them tear around so?'

'Why, whoever rubs the lamp or the ring. They belong to whoever rubs the lamp or the ring, and they've got to do whatever he says. If he tells them to build a palace forty miles long, out of di'monds, and fill it full of chewing-gum, or whatever you want, and fetch an emperor's daughter from China for you to marry, they've got to do it—and they've got to do it before sun-up next morning, too.' . . .

I thought all this over for two or three days, and then I reckoned I would see if there was anything in it. I got an old tin lamp and an iron ring and went out in the woods and rubbed and rubbed till I sweat like an Injun, calculating to build a palace and sell it; but it warn't no use, none of the genies come. So then I judged that all that stuff was only just one of Tom Sawyer's lies. I reckoned he believed in the A-rabs and the elephants, but as for me I think different. It had all the marks of a Sunday school.

MARK TWAIN, *The Adventures of Huckleberry Finn*, 1884

Christmas Eve is the ghosts' great gala night. On Christmas Eve they hold their annual fête. On Christmas Eve everybody in Ghostland who *is* anybody—or rather, speaking of ghosts, one should say, I suppose, every nobody who *is* any nobody—comes out to show himself or herself, to see and to be seen, to promenade about and display their winding-sheets and grave-clothes to each other, to criticize one another's style, and sneer at one another's complexion.

'Christmas Eve parade', as I expect they themselves term it, is a function, doubtless, eagerly prepared for and looked forward to throughout Ghostland, especially by the swagger set, such as the murdered Barons, the crime-stained Countesses, and the Earls who came over with the Conqueror, and assassinated their relatives, and died raving mad.

Hollow moans and fiendish grins are, one may be sure, energetically practised up. Blood-curdling shrieks and marrow-freezing gestures are probably rehearsed for weeks beforehand. Rusty chains and gory daggers are overhauled, and put into good working order; and sheets and shrouds, laid carefully by from the previous year's show, are taken down and shaken out, and mended, and aired.

He does love prophesying a misfortune, does the average British ghost. Send him out to prognosticate trouble to somebody, and he is happy. Let him force his way into a peaceful home, and turn the whole house upside down by foretelling a funeral, or predicting a bankruptcy, or hinting at a coming disgrace, or some other terrible disaster, about which nobody in their senses would want to know sooner than they could possibly help, and the prior knowledge of which can serve no useful purpose whatsoever, and he feels that he is combining duty with pleasure.

. . . the young man who woke up with a strange sensation in the middle of the night, and found his rich bachelor uncle standing by his bedside. The rich uncle smiled a weird sort of smile and vanished. The young man immediately got up and looked at his watch. It had stopped at half-past four, he having forgotten to wind it.

He made inquiries the next day, and found that, strangely enough, his rich uncle, whose only nephew he was, had married a widow with eleven children at exactly a quarter to twelve, only two days ago.

> JEROME K. JEROME, from 'Introductory', *After Supper Ghost Stories and Other Tales*, 1891

The emperor Frederic, father of Maximilian, invited a necromancer to dine with him, and, by his knowledge of magic, turned his guest's hands into griffins' claws. He then wanted him to eat, but the man, ashamed, hid his claws under the table.

He took his revenge, however, for the jest played upon him. He caused it to seem that a loud altercation was going on in the courtyard, and when the emperor put his head out of window to see what was the matter, he, by his art, clapped on him a pair of huge stag's horns, so that the emperor could not get his head into the room again until he had cured the necromancer of his disfigurement. I am delighted, when one devil plagues another. They are not all, however, of equal power.

> LUTHER, *Table-Talk*

One of the oldest instances I remark of persons raised from the ground without any one touching them, is that of St Dunstan, Archbishop of Canterbury, who died in 988, and who, a little time before his death, as he was going up stairs to his apartment, accompanied by several persons, was observed to rise from the ground; and as all present were astonished at the circumstance, he took occasion to speak of his approaching death . . .

In the last century, the reverend Father Dominic Carme Déchaux was raised from the ground before the King of Spain, the Queen, and all the court, so that they had only to blow upon his body to move it about like a soap bubble.

Pliny the Younger [*Epistles*] had a freed-man named Marcus, a man of letters, who slept in the same bed with his brother, who was younger than himself. It seemed to him that he saw a person sitting on the same bed, who was cutting off his hair from the crown of his head. When he awoke, he found his head shorn of hair, and his hair thrown on the ground in the middle of the chamber. A little time after, the same thing happened to a youth who slept with several others at a school. This one saw two men dressed in white come in at the window, who cut off his hair as he slept, and then went out by the same window; on awaking, he found his hair scattered about on the floor. To what can these things be attributed, if not to an elf?

St Martin, Bishop of Tours, being at Trèves, entered a house, where he found a spectre which frightened him at first. Martin commanded him to leave the body which he possessed; instead of going out (of the place), he entered the body of another man who was in the same dwelling; and throwing himself upon those who were there, began to attack and bite them. Martin threw himself across his way, put his fingers in his mouth, and defied him to bite him. The demoniac retreated, as if a bar of red-hot iron had been placed in his mouth, and at last the demon went out of the body of the possessed, not by the mouth but behind.

Augustine Calmet, *The Phantom World*, 1746; tr. Revd Henry Christmas

When he [Allan Bennett] was about sixteen, the conversation in the laboratory where he was working turned upon childbirth. What he heard disgusted him. He became furiously angry and said that children were brought to earth by angels. The other students laughed at him and tried in vain to convince him. He maintained their theory to be a bestial blasphemy. The next day one of the boys turned up with an illustrated manual of obstetrics. He could no longer doubt the facts. But his reaction was this: 'Did the Omnipotent God whom he had been taught to worship devise so revolting and degrading a method of perpetuating the species? Then this God must be a devil, delighting in loathsomeness.' To him the existence of God was disproved from that moment.

He had, however, already some experience of an unseen world. As a little boy, having overheard some gossip among superstitious servants, he had gone into the back garden and invoked the devil by reciting the Lord's Prayer backwards. Something happened which frightened him.

Having now rejected Catholicism, he took up Magick and at once attained extraordinary success. He used to carry a 'lustre'—a long glass prism with a neck and a pointed knob such as adorned old-fashioned chandeliers. He used this as a wand. One day, a party of theosophists were chatting sceptically about the power of the 'blasting rod'. Allan promptly produced his and blasted one of them. It took fourteen hours to restore the incredulous individual to the use of his mind and his muscles.

CROWLEY, *The Confessions of Aleister Crowley*

'Mr Brand is set to become the most successful medium in London. The evening began with table-tapping, which is quite usual, but by the end of the evening the spirits were speaking through his voice, a man and a woman coming through very distinctly.'

'Remarkable,' said Sergeant Cribb.

'Indeed, yes. They conveyed a message to me.'

'Nothing to do with your house being burgled?'

Miss Crush frowned. 'No. They are not concerned with worldly matters once they have gone over to the Other Side. It was to tell me that my late Uncle Walter is well content where he is. He made an unfortunate marriage, poor man, and my aunt frequently drove him to distraction. There was no mention of her in the message, although she followed him only two months after his going.'

'It's an extensive place, I understand,' said Cribb. 'If your uncle kept moving . . .'

'Quite so.'

PETER LOVESEY, *A Case of Spirits*, 1975

. . . the Master of Ceremonies, Harri Jenkins, valiantly continued, 'The stage appearance of The Marvellous Girl is a one-off. She has basically given up stage appearances. Instead she works selflessly at that healing centre, that wonderful healing centre, Metatron Hall in the Vale of Glamorgan. Um. It's the cause of the Blind that brings her here tonight. And my own personal interest in Metatron Hall. Ladies and Gentlemen, please welcome The Marvellous Girl and her marvellous mother.'

The audience applauded and, at once, Mrs Gibbs came on to the stage carrying a lit black candle which she placed on the black velvet cloth, followed by The Marvellous Girl who was wearing bow tie, tuxedo and shiny top hat. Her face had been powdered an unnatural white to emphasize her large, staring eyes. She stood behind one of the crimson chairs while her mother pronounced, 'When the angels descend to this world to fulfil a mission they wear the garments of this world and they take on the appearance of the people of this world. Otherwise they would not be tolerated here on this earth and we, in turn, could not endure them.'

Was Mrs Gibbs suggesting that her daughter was divine? I recalled my uncle's remarks about Sandra Gibbs that she was 'sort of insane'. Perhaps the mother was too?

The show began. It seemed that the slim, haunted-looking girl in disturbing top hat and in evening-dress suit owned psychokinetic and telepathic gifts. She, at first, did not speak, utter one single word, yet this somehow did not diminish her almost palpable charisma. The mother vocalized everything—quite a joky auctioneer's patter she had too—as Sandra Gibbs, in a kind of cataleptic trance, stared at the flickering lit candle with terrible concentration and made solid objects apparently dematerialize and rematerialize.

After about half an hour of this The Marvellous Girl was blindfolded and a few members of the audience were invited to clamber onto the stage. Each, in turn, was asked to write the name of some real, concrete object on the blackboard. One of my neighbours wrote down 'Tusker Rock', the young woman with streaky blonde hair that I had seen at Metatron Hall chalked up 'Niagara Falls', and Mrs Maddocks, our local wit, started to write the name of the village in Gwynedd fifty-eight letters long. She had got as far as 'Llanfairpwll' when May Gibbs stopped her saying that the village's name, Llanfairpwllgwyngyllgogerychwyrndrobwllllantysiliogogogoch, would be too easy for The Marvellous Girl. 'So give her something more difficult,' urged May Gibbs. After much laughter Mrs Maddocks wrote down, 'Lol, the shepherd' and again everybody laughed.

Sandra Gibbs stood very still, blindfolded, in front of the stage while her mother took a billiard cue and pointed to the words 'Tusker Rock'. 'Concentrate your minds,' commanded May Gibbs addressing the silent audience. 'Bring into your minds a vision of what is written here. Think, think of it, picture it.' She cleared her throat and mumbled something I couldn't hear, then added, 'Ye-es, let it float into your minds. It's coming, it's coming, that's right, into your minds and now it will be seen by The Marvellous Girl.'

The audience waited. The girl with the white powdered face opened her mouth as if to speak but uttered no word. The Sunset Lounge was quite silent.

Then, in an unexpectedly deep voice, The Marvellous Girl said, 'Tusker Rock'. And everybody applauded. The same routine was followed before Sandra Gibbs pronounced 'Niagara Falls' and then, with even greater hesitation and more patter from her mother, 'Lol, the shepherd'. Again everybody applauded.

Was this exhibition of telepathy somehow faked? Others followed in similar fashion. Did Mrs Gibbs' patter conceal a code? I suspected so. What did somewhat unnerve me was The Marvellous Girl's remarkable, eerie voice. Deep as a man's. And her clothes were like a man's. Was her evident charisma expressed in the mythic apprehension that man and woman once were one person, a god and goddess dwelling in one body?

'Now, another phenomenon,' May Gibbs solemnly announced after the show had lengthened to almost two hours. She placed a large glass vase on the black velvet cloth next to the one lit candle. 'The Marvellous Girl will now, by a further concentration of psychic energy, shatter this vase into a hundred pieces. She will not, I promise you, touch it.'

Seemingly more white-faced than ever, her eyes hardly blinking and conspicuous beneath her top hat, Sandra Gibbs stepped forward to stand a foot or two from the table. 'Silence, please, utter silence,' called May Gibbs who then raised her right foot on its heel before letting the sole slap down, up and down repeatedly on the floor to evince a regular pattern of noise.

'Slower,' The Marvellous Girl surprisingly objected. 'Slower. The same rate as my heartbeat.'

The foot tapped slower, tap tap tap, about seventy beats a minute, I reckoned. Meanwhile The Marvellous Girl, Sandra Gibbs, passed her hands back and forward horizontally, arms outstretched, above the vase. Suddenly, May Gibbs stopped tapping the floor, the candle flame, which had been increasingly flickering, inexplicably went out and there was a great crash behind me. One of the pictures on the wall had, for no evident reason, smashed down onto the floor. Everybody looked away from the stage over their shoulders and the woman next to me mumbled, 'They say when a picture frame falls down on its own there'll be a death in the family.'

The vase on the velvet cloth remained whole, unshattered. May Gibbs looked dismayed. 'Oh my God,' uttered the Marvellous Girl in her dark voice, 'I'm sorry. I'm sorry. I visited the Void. That was a malefic influence. I'm sorry.'

May Gibbs quickly took the vase away. She told a joke about how things can go wrong that made everybody laugh while Sandra Gibbs sat down again, unsmiling, somnambulistically, on one of the crimson chairs, hands on her knees, palms turned upwards.

'Yes, that picture is of Foxhunting and The Marvellous Girl is an anti-vivisectionist and a vegetarian,' May Gibbs declared.

DANNIE ABSE, from 'The Deceived', 1991

Not far from this town there was dwelling a wealthy churl that was somewhat fantastical, and given to believe every tale he heard, which churl's wealth whetted so the desire of this woman [Judith Philips], that she devised a subtle practice to have a share out of his coffers . . .

This Judith Philips one evening very late went into the back side of this man's house, where under a hollow holly tree she buried an angel of gold and sixpence in white money, and then returned home to her lodgings again for the night.

But the next day after, she walked by the churl's house . . . she told him, if he would be at some charge, she would bring him to great sums of gold and silver that was hidden about his grounds; to whom the man, being somewhat covetous, said, 'If I might first see something of thy skill, I will be at any charge thou wilt; but first tell me what thou art and from where thou camest.'

'I am,' said this Judith, 'an Englishwoman born, but come now from the Pope and know more of his mind than any woman in the world.' To confirm her words for truth, she took her oath upon the Bible how that she came from the Pope—which was true, for her husband's name as then was Pope; which being done, she took him by the hand and led him to the root of the hollow tree, where she caused him to dig till he found some gold (which was the angel) and the sixpence which the night before she closely hid.

This brought the covetous churl into such a conceit that he promised to give her whatsoever she desired, so that her promise might be performed. Then she demanded of him for her pains fourteen pounds, whereat he grumbled to lose so great a gub [amount] at one time, yet at last the hope of the treasure hidden under the tree made him to consent; and so with speed he gave this woman fourteen pounds in ready gold and silver. Then said this woman, 'Now must I have the largest chamber in your house behung with the finest linen you can get, so that nothing about your chamber but white linen cloth be seen; then must you set five candlesticks in five several places in your chamber, and under every candlestick you must put an angel of gold'—all which was done as she required. 'And likewise,' said she, 'you must also get a saddle and a bridle with two new girths thereunto,' all which the covetous churl performed in hope to attain to great wealth.

Then this Judith caused him and his wife to go into the yard, where she set the saddle on his back, and thereon girteth it fast with two new girths, and also put a bridle upon his head; all which being done, she got upon his back in the saddle, and so rid him three times betwixt the chamber and the holly tree. Then said this cozening quean, 'You must lie three hours one by another grovelling on your bellies under this tree, and stir not, I charge you, until I come back again; for I must go into the chamber to meet the Queen of Fairies and welcome her to that holy and unspotted place.'

So this churl and his wife were left quaking in the cold, casting many a long look for the coming of this woman. But she in the meantime took down all the fine linen cloths from the walls of the chamber and wrapped them up close in a bundle, and all the gold from under the candlesticks and put them into her purse; then putting herself into a fair white smock, somewhat disguised with a thing on her head all white, and a stick in her hand, she appeared unto him and his wife. Using some dalliance, as old wives say spirits with night-spells do, she vanished away, and again entered the chamber where her pack lay ready and so roundly went away, leaving the churl and his wife in their cold lodging.

ANON., *The Brideling, Sadling and Ryding, of a rich Churle in Hampshire*, 1595; ed. Barbara Rosen

A number of men there be yet living, who have been haunted by their wives after their death, about forswearing themselves, and undooing their children, of whom they promised to be carefull fathers: whereof I can gather no reason but this, that Women are borne to torment a man both alive and dead.

NASHE, *The Terrors of the Night*

It is the easiest thing, sir, to be done,
As plain as fizzling: roll but with your eyes,
And foam at the mouth. A little castle-soap
Will do't, to rub your lips; and then a nut-shell,
With tow, and touch-wood in it, to spit fire.
Did you ne'er read, sir, little Darrel's tricks
With the boy of Burton, and the seven in Lancashire,
Somers at Nottingham? all these do teach it.
And we'll give out, sir, that your wife has bewitch'd you.

JONSON, *The Devil is an Ass*, 1616

We have several times had to refer in this work to a custom of the Chinese of placing the graves in such a situation as they think will bring the occupants thereof happiness and comfort, and at the same time secure the prosperity of their ownselves, both in this world and in the world to come. In connection herewith we have mentioned certain theories, popularly styled *Feng Shui* . . . By *Feng Shui* the graves are turned into mighty instruments of blessing or punishment, the spirits of the ancestors, dwelling therein, being the divinities of the nation, with whose protection and goodwill all social happiness is intimately bound up.

The people are perfectly aware that geomancers are not only useful, but also dangerous. Indeed, these men can supply them with graves and dwellings which establish the prosperity of whole families; but they have also the power of plunging families into woe and misery by undoing graves and houses of good *Feng Shui* by their cunning artifices. The professors . . . frequently relate that, once upon a time, there lived a family, which was rendered very rich and prosperous by the influence of a grave sought out for it by a geomancer of great renown. He, on discovering this priceless spot, had become aware that it would cost him his eyesight if anybody were buried in it; and yet he had not hesitated to assign it to that family, on condition they should lodge, clothe and feed him to the end of his days, and give him a decent burial after his death. So he lived with them, quite blind, but happy, and free from worldly care, leading an enviable life of leisure and idleness. One fine day it came to pass that a kid belonging to the family fell into an open privy and was suffocated. The Chinese are a thrifty people, and even the wealthy classes are averse to throwing useful things away. Hence the family, as none of them chose to eat of the kid, resolved to cook it for the professor, who, being blind and not aware of the circumstance, would certainly enjoy the savoury food. This was done; but, unfortunately, a loquacious matron of the family told him in secret how ignominiously the others had abused his helpless condition. Our readers can guess the end of the story:— the professor without mercy destroyed the good *Feng Shui* of the grave by giving wrong advice regarding it, and so he brought the family back to the same dire poverty from which he had extricated it. We are not, however, told whether he recovered from his blindness, after having thus avenged himself.

J. J. M. DE GROOT, *The Religious System of China*, 1892 onwards

'Éliphas Lévi talked to me himself of this evocation,' said Dr Porhoët. 'He told me that its influence on him was very great. He was no longer the same man, for it seemed to him that something from the world beyond had passed into his soul.'

'I am astonished that you should never have tried such an interesting experiment yourself,' said Arthur to Oliver Haddo.

'I have,' answered the other calmly. 'My father lost his power of speech shortly before he died, and it was plain that he sought with all his might to tell me something. A year after his death, I called up his phantom from the grave so that I might learn what I took to be a dying wish.' . . .

'What did he say?' asked Susie.

'He said solemnly: "*Buy Ashantis, they are bound to go up*." I did as he told me; but my father was always unlucky in speculation, and they went down steadily. I sold out at considerable loss, and concluded that in the world beyond they are as ignorant of the tendency of the Stock Exchange as we are in this vale of sorrow.'

> W. SOMERSET MAUGHAM, *The Magician*, 1908; the character Haddo was based on Aleister Crowley, who reviewed the novel in *Vanity Fair* over the signature 'Oliver Haddo'

The death of Lord Carnarvon has been followed by a panic among collectors of Egyptian antiquities. All over the country people are sending their treasures to the British Museum, anxious to get rid of them because of the superstition that Lord Carnarvon was killed by the 'ka' or double of the soul of Tutankhamun . . .

Few of the parcels received at the Museum bear the senders' names. The owners, in their eagerness to wash their hands of the accursed things, have tried to keep their identity secret. Statuettes that peer out of the corners of slanting eyes are responsible for many cases of 'nerves' and the Museum is richer by several gifts of this sort—not much richer, however, for few of the pieces are valuable.

> *Daily Express*, 'Egyptian Collectors in a Panic', 7 April 1923

'A prophet is not without honour, save in his own country.' It is a hard saying, but a true one. In this land of ours the prophet, unless he be connected with the Turf, has an unenviable legal status. Witness the following stereotyped reply which it was the custom of a former Astronomer Royal, the late Sir

William H. M. Christie, to transmit to the numerous domestic servants and other persons of imperfect education who wrote to consult him upon matters relating to astrology rather than astronomy.

Sir or Madam,
    I am directed by the Astronomer Royal to inform you that he is unable to rule your planets. Persons professing to do so are rogues and vagabonds.
    I am, yours faithfully,

                                            —— (*Secretary*)

It was not always so, even at Greenwich. [John] Flamsteed who, as the first Astronomer Royal, founded in 1675 a brilliant and long-lived dynasty, performed the first official act of his reign by casting the horoscope of the Observatory. The calculation still exists—although he has written across it the sarcastic comment *Risum teneatis, amici?* (Can you keep from laughing, friends?). On another occasion he was made to appear, by an unfortunate coincidence, as one well-skilled in conjuration.

An old woman, no wiser than most of them, once called at the Observatory to enlist his aid in recovering a piece of property (by some accounts, a bundle of washing) which she had lost. Flamsteed, wishing to give her a lesson against believing in soothsayers, listened gravely to the details of the case, and having drawn a plan of her house and grounds, which he adorned with various fearsome symbols, directed her to search at a particular point which he had carefully selected at random. He intended, when she should call or write complaining of her fruitless search, to administer the lesson in question.

To his confusion, she informed him soon afterwards that she had found the bundle in the exact spot he had indicated. He ascribed the coincidence, in all seriousness, to the craft and malice of the Evil One.

            Lieut.-Commander Rupert T. Gould, *Oddities: A Book of Unexplained Facts*,
            1928

It is said that Mulla Nasrudin lived for five hundred years before he started to become ancient.

He used to sit at a crossroads, nodding himself to sleep and jerking awake again.

One day a countryman passing by said:

'What have you seen, Mulla?'

'I saw hundreds of invaders swarm up that valley yonder, sword in hand, they were. I had to rush down to repulse them.'

'Why did you not call me for help?'
'Who would have heard me? It was a hundred and forty years ago.'

                    Sufi story; in Raoul Simac: *The World of the Sufi*, 1979

I bought (I was too wealthy for my age)
A passage to the dead ones' habitat,
And learnt, under their tutelage,
To twitter like a bat

In imitation of their dialect.
Crudely I aped their subtle practices;
By instinct knew how to respect
Their strict observances.

The regions of the dead are small and pent,
Their movements faint, sparing of energy.
Yet, like an exiled Government,
With so much jealousy

As were the issue a campaign or Crown,
They hold debates, wage Cabinet intrigues,
Move token forces up and down,
Turn inches into leagues.

Long I was caught up in their twilit strife.
Almost they got me, almost had me weaned
From all my memory of life.
But laughter supervened:

Laughter, like sunlight in the cucumber,
The innermost resource, that does not fail.
I, Marco Polo, traveller,
Am back, with what a tale!

                    NORMAN CAMERON, 'A Visit to the Dead', 1942

My Uncle from the realms of Death
Returned to draw an earthly breath
And as he walked upon the heath
The wild wind whistled through his teeth.

He came unto a habitation
That was the centre of the nation
He knocked upon each house and said:
It is much better to be dead.

And when they stoned him from the door
He vowed he would come back no more.

STEVIE SMITH, 'Le Revenant', 1950

'Please,' his voice quavered through the foul brown air, 'Please, is that an omnibus?'

'Omnibus est,' said the driver, without turning round . . .

'Stop!' he shouted. 'Stop!' And then, being of a polite disposition, he glanced up at the painted notice-board so that he might call the driver by name. 'Mr Browne! stop; O, do please stop!'

Mr Browne did not stop, but he opened a little window and looked in at the boy. His face was a surprise, so kind it was and modest.

'Mr Browne, I've left my purse behind. I've not got a penny. I can't pay for the ticket. Will you take my watch, please? I am in the most awful hole.'

'Tickets on this line,' said the driver, 'whether single or return, can be purchased by coinage from no terrene mint. And a chronometer, though it had solaced the vigils of Charlemagne, or measured the slumbers of Laura, can acquire by no mutation the doublecake that charms the fangless Cerberus of Heaven!' So saying, he handed in the necessary ticket, and, while the boy said 'Thank you', continued: 'Titular pretensions, I know it well, are vanity. Yet they merit no censure when uttered on a laughing lip, and in an homonymous world are in some sort useful, since they do serve to distinguish one Jack from his fellow. Remember me, therefore, as Sir Thomas Browne.'

'Are you a Sir? Oh, sorry!' He had heard of these gentlemen drivers. 'It *is* good of you about the ticket. But if you go on at this rate, however does your bus pay?'

'It does not pay. It was not intended to pay. Many are the faults of my equipage; it is compounded too curiously of foreign woods; its cushions tickle erudition rather than promote repose; and my horses are nourished not on the evergreen pastures of the moment, but on the dried bents and clovers of Latinity. But that it pays!—that error at all events was never intended and never attained.'

'Sorry again,' said the boy rather hopelessly. Sir Thomas looked sad, fearing that, even for a moment, he had been the cause of sadness. He invited the boy to come up and sit beside him on the box, and together they journeyed on through the fog, which was now changing from yellow to white. There were no houses by the road; so it must be either Putney Heath or Wimbledon Common.

'Have you been a driver always?'

'I was a physician once.'

'But why did you stop? Weren't you good?'

'As a healer of bodies I had scant success, and several score of my patients preceded me. But as a healer of the spirit I have succeeded beyond my hopes and my deserts. For though my draughts were not better nor subtler than those of other men, yet, by reason of the cunning goblets wherein I offered them, the queasy soul was ofttimes tempted to sip and be refreshed.'

'The queasy soul,' he murmured; 'if the sun sets with trees in front of it, and you suddenly come strange all over, is that a queasy soul?'

'Have you felt that?'

'Why yes.'

After a pause he told the boy a little, a very little, about the journey's end.

E. M. FORSTER, from 'The Celestial Omnibus', 1911

I knew another man—let me see—forty years ago now—who took an old, damp, rotten set of chambers, in one of the most ancient Inns, that had been shut up and empty for years and years before. There were lots of old women's stories about the place, and it certainly was very far from being a cheerful one; but he was poor, and the rooms were cheap . . . He was obliged to take some mouldering fixtures that were on the place, and, among the rest, was a great lumbering wooden press for papers, with large glass doors, and a green curtain inside; a pretty useless thing for him, for he had no papers to put in it; and as to his clothes, he carried them about with him, and that wasn't very hard work, either. Well, he had moved in all his furniture, and had sprinkled it about the room, so as to make the four chairs look as much like a dozen as possible, and was sitting down before the fire at night, drinking the first glass of two gallons of whisky he had ordered on credit, wondering whether it would ever be paid for, and if so, in how many years' time, when his eyes encountered the glass doors of the wooden press. 'Ah,' says he. 'If I hadn't been obliged to take that ugly article at the old broker's valuation, I might have got something comfortable for the money. I'll tell you what it is, old fellow,' he said, speaking aloud to the press, having nothing else to speak to: 'If it wouldn't cost more to break up your old carcass, than it would ever be worth afterwards, I'd have a fire out of you in less than no time.' He had hardly spoken the words, when a sound resembling a faint groan, appeared to issue from the interior of the case. It startled him at first, but thinking, on a moment's reflection, that it must be some young fellow in the next chamber, who had been dining out, he put his feet on the fender, and raised the poker to stir the fire. At that moment, the sound was repeated: and one of the glass doors slowly opening, disclosed a pale and emaciated figure in soiled and worn apparel, standing erect in the press. The figure was tall and thin, and the countenance expressive of care and anxiety; but there was something in the hue of the skin, and gaunt and unearthly appearance of the whole form, which no being of this world was ever seen to wear. 'Who are you?' said the new tenant, turning very pale: poising the poker in his hand, however, and taking a very decent aim at the countenance of the figure. 'Who are you?' 'Don't throw that poker at me,' replied the form; 'If you hurled it with ever so sure an aim, it would pass through me, without resistance, and expend its force on the wood behind. I am a spirit.' 'And, pray, what do you want here?' faltered the tenant. 'In this room,' replied the apparition, 'my worldly ruin was worked, and I and my children beggared. In this press, the papers in a long, long suit, which accumulated for years, were deposited. In this room, when I had died of grief, and long-deferred hope, two wily harpies divided the wealth for which I had contested during a wretched existence, and of which, at last, not one farthing was left for my unhappy descendants. I terrified them from the spot, and since that day have prowled by night—the only period at which I can revisit the earth—about the scenes of my long-protracted misery. This apartment is mine: leave it to me.' 'If you insist upon making your appearance here,' said the tenant, who had had time to collect his presence of mind during this prosy statement of the ghost's, 'I shall give up possession with the greatest pleasure; but I should like to ask you one question, if you will allow me.' 'Say on,' said the apparition, sternly. 'Well,' said the tenant, 'I don't apply the observation personally to you, because it is equally applicable to most of the ghosts I ever heard of; but it does appear to me somewhat inconsistent, that when you have an opportunity of visiting the fairest spots of earth—for I suppose space is nothing to you—you should always return exactly to the very places where you have been most miserable.' 'Egad, that's very true; I never thought of that before,' said the ghost. 'You see, sir,' pursued the tenant, 'This is a very uncomfortable room. From the appearance of that press, I should be disposed to say that it is not wholly free from bugs; and I really think you might find much more comfortable quarters: to say nothing of the climate of London, which is extremely disagreeable.' 'You are very right, sir,' said the ghost, politely, 'it never struck me till now; I'll try change of air directly.' In fact, he began to vanish as he spoke: his legs, indeed, had quite disappeared. 'And if, sir,' said the tenant, calling after him, 'if you *would* have the goodness to suggest to the other ladies and gentlemen who are now engaged in haunting old empty houses, that they might be much more comfortable elsewhere, you will confer a very great benefit on society.' 'I will,' replied the ghost; 'we must be dull fellows, very dull fellows, indeed; I can't imagine how we can have been so stupid.' With those words, the spirit disappeared; and what is rather remarkable, he never came back again.

DICKENS, *The Pickwick Papers*, 1837

CHAPTER I

The sun was setting over Sloperton Grange, and reddened the windows of the lonely chamber in the western tower, supposed to be haunted by Sir Edward Sedilia, the founder of the Grange. In the dreamy distance arose the gilded mausoleum of Lady Felicia Sedilia, who haunted that portion of Sedilia Manor known as 'Stiff-uns Acre'. A little to the left of the Grange might have been seen a mouldering ruin, known as 'Guy's Keep', haunted by the spirit of Sir Guy Sedilia, who was found, one morning, crushed by one of the fallen battlements. Yet, as the setting sun gilded these objects, a beautiful and almost holy calm seemed diffused about the Grange.

The Lady Selina sat by an oriel window overlooking the park. The sun sank gently in the bosom of the German Ocean, and yet the lady did not lift her beautiful head from the finely curved arm and diminutive hand which supported it. When darkness finally shrouded the landscape, she started, for the sound of horse-hoofs clattered over the stones of the avenue. She had scarcely risen before an aristocratic young man fell on his knees before her.

'My Selina!'

'Edgardo! You here?'

'Yes, dearest.'

'And—you—you—have—seen—nothing?' said the lady in an agitated voice and nervous manner, turning her face aside to conceal her emotion.

'Nothing—that is, nothing of any account,' said Edgardo. 'I passed the ghost of your aunt in the park, noticed the spectre of your uncle in the ruined keep, and observed the familiar features of the spirit of your great-grandfather at his post. But nothing beyond these trifles, my Selina. Nothing more, love, absolutely nothing.'

The young man turned his dark liquid orbs fondly upon the ingenuous face of his betrothed.

'My own Edgardo!—and you still love me? You still would marry me in spite of this dark mystery which surrounds me? In spite of the fatal history of my race? In spite of the ominous predictions of my aged nurse?'

'I would, Selina'; and the young man passed his arm around her yielding waist. The two lovers gazed at each other's faces in unspeakable bliss. Suddenly Selina started.

'Leave me, Edgardo! leave me! A mysterious something—a fatal misgiving—a dark ambiguity—an equivocal mistrust oppresses me. I would be alone!'

The young man arose, and cast a loving glance on the lady. 'Then we will be married on the seventeenth.'

'The seventeenth,' repeated Selina, with a mysterious shudder.

They embraced and parted. As the clatter of hoofs in the courtyard died away, the Lady Selina sank into the chair she had just quitted.

'The seventeenth,' she repeated slowly, with the same fatal shudder. 'Ah!—what if he should know that I have another husband living? Dare I reveal to him that I have two legitimate and three natural children? Dare I repeat to him the history of my youth? Dare I confess that at the age of seven I poisoned my sister, by putting verdigris in her cream tarts—that I threw my cousin from a swing at the age of twelve? That the lady's-maid who incurred the displeasure of my girlhood now lies at the bottom of the horse-pond? No! no! he is too pure—too good—too innocent, to hear such improper conversation!' and her whole body writhed as she rocked to and fro in a paroxysm of grief.

But she was soon calm. Rising to her feet, she opened a secret panel in the wall, and revealed a slow-match ready for lighting.

'This match,' said the Lady Selina, 'is connected with a mine beneath the western tower, where my three children are confined; another branch of it lies under the parish church, where the record of my first marriage is kept. I have only to light this match and the whole of my past life is swept away!' She approached the match with a lighted candle.

But a hand was laid upon her arm, and with a shriek the Lady Selina fell on her knees before the spectre of Sir Guy.

CHAPTER II

'Forbear, Selina,' said the phantom in a hollow voice.

'Why should I forbear?' responded Selina haughtily, as she recovered her courage. 'You know the secret of our race?'

'I do. Understand me—I do not object to the eccentricities of your youth. I know the fearful fate which, pursuing you, led you to poison your sister and drown your lady's-maid. I know the awful doom which I have brought upon this house! But if you make away with these children—'

'Well?' said the Lady Selina hastily.

'They will haunt you!'

'Well, I fear them not,' said Selina, drawing her superb figure to its full height.

'But what place are they to haunt? The ruin is sacred to your uncle's spirit. Your aunt monopolizes the park, and, I must be allowed to state, not unfrequently trespasses upon the grounds of others. The horse-pond is frequented by the spirit of your maid, and your murdered sister walks these corridors. To be plain, there is no room at Sloperton Grange for another ghost. I cannot have them in my room—for you know I don't like children. Think of this, rash girl , and forbear! Would you, Selina,' said the phantom mournfully, 'would you force your great-grandfather's spirit to take lodgings elsewhere?'

Lady Selina's hand trembled; the lighted candle fell from her nerveless fingers.

'No,' she cried passionately, 'never!' and fell fainting to the floor.

BRET HARTE, from 'Selina Sedilia', 1865

BELIEVERS AND DISBELIEVERS
ON READING AND WRITING ABOUT
THE SUPERNATURAL

I MAKE no apology for including in this anthology so much by Dr Johnson: in him a stout unwillingness to be hoodwinked, whether by others or by himself, accompanied an 'elevated wish' for a greater degree of knowledge and certainty on a subject intimately related to a Christian's faith in the immortality of the soul.

The contention that disbelief in the appearance of spirits is the beginning of atheism will cut no ice today. In any case, the observation made some ninety years ago by a character in a story by Robert Hichens has occurred to many others: 'The devoutly religious, those who believe implicitly in the miracles recorded in the Bible, and who regulate their lives by the messages they suppose themselves to receive directly from the Great Ruler of a hidden World, are seldom inclined to accept any notion of supernatural intrusion into the affairs of daily life. They put it from them with anxious determination. They regard it fixedly as hocus-pocus, childish if not wicked.' Rather than appealing to the danger of infidelity, the supernatural's best defence, if defence there must be, against accusations of capriciousness, illogic, and futility can be summed up in Lamb's words, 'There is no law to judge of the lawless', a proposition we have met in diverse shapes and sizes.

We gather that belief in some aspects of the supernatural is widespread. According to a poll carried out for Channel Four Television in 1987, 60 per cent of people believe that telepathic communication is possible, 59 per cent that some houses are haunted, the same percentage that it is possible to dream of future events, while 45 per cent believe in reincarnation, and 30 per cent that we can receive messages from the dead. At the same time we are given to understand that there is widespread resistance to any such beliefs. Bernard Levin (*The Times*, 4 June 1992) talks of 'the extraordinary terror which seizes otherwise perfectly sensible people when the subject of the paranormal comes up'. He has formulated what he calls 'Levin's Question': 'If the paranormal does exist, and acts upon us without our knowing how the effect is made, *what would be so dreadful about it?*', and claims that by simply asking for an answer to the question he has 'repeatedly induced shaking rage in those who deny the paranormal'. Judging from the zealots on both sides, we would appear to be hopelessly trapped in Thomas Fuller's catch-22 of 1732: 'Superstition renders man a fool, and scepticism makes him mad.'

'To no one type of mind is it given to discern the totality of truth.' In choosing material for this book I have tried to steer a middle course between those whose minds are so firmly closed that nothing can get in and those whose minds are so wide open that everything has fallen out.

Elsewhere in the article quoted below, Virginia Woolf says that 'The great increase of the psychical ghost story in late years . . . testifies to the fact that our sense of our own ghostliness has much quickened. A rational age is succeeded by one which seeks the supernatural in the soul of man, and the development of psychical research offers a basis of disputed fact for this desire to feed upon.' If the definition of it thus implied is to be trusted, there has never been a wholly rational age. Much earlier Walter Scott spoke of 'that secret and reserved feeling of love for the marvellous and supernatural, which occupies a hidden corner in almost everyone's bosom'. As a corrective to the femininity of the extract from *Northanger Abbey* (should any be deemed advisable) we might cite Jenny Uglow's comment in introducing *The Virago Book of Victorian Ghost Stories*, that 'the experience of seeing a ghost pushes men into conventional female roles, timid, nervous, helpless'. One touch of the supernatural makes us all akin.

Scott is entertaining on the question of 'explanations', opining that, compared with Horace Walpole in *The Castle of Otranto*, Ann Radcliffe's one inferiority lay in providing at the end of her narrative natural causes for what had been offered as supernatural happenings, a practice he compares to Bottom the weaver's solicitous instruction that the player of the lion in the interlude should show half his face through the mask and spare the ladies' nerves by telling them plainly that he is Snug the joiner. In the *Quarterly Review* of May 1810 Scott returned to the point: 'We can believe, for example, in Macbeth's witches, and tremble at their spells; but had we been informed, at the conclusion of the piece, that they were only three of his wife's chambermaids disguised for the purpose of imposing on the Thane's credulity, it would have added little to the credibility of the story, and entirely deprived it of the interest.'

Prodigies, Henry James declares, should not come 'straight', but rather through 'the indispensable history of somebody's *normal* relation to something', for it is then that they are of most consequence. (His most famous ghost story, *The Turn of the Screw*, which alas defies excerption, bears out the thesis.) Certainly many of the finest writers have written engagingly on the supernatural, if we interpret that term broadly. It may well be true, also, that many of the best readers have found pleasure and food for thought in reading about it.

~

Dr Johnson on the subject

'That the dead are seen no more,' said Imlac, 'I will not undertake to maintain against the concurrent and unvaried testimony of all ages, and of all nations. There is no people, rude or learned, among whom apparitions of the dead are not related and believed. This opinion, which, perhaps, prevails as far as human nature is diffused, could become universal only by its truth: those, that never heard of one another, would not have agreed in a tale which nothing but experience can make credible. That it is doubted by single cavillers can very little weaken the general evidence, and some who deny it with their tongues confess it by their fears.'

JOHNSON, *The History of Rasselas, Prince of Abyssinia*, 1759

We talked of belief in ghosts. He said, 'Sir, I make a distinction between what a man may experience by the mere strength of his imagination, and what imagination cannot possibly produce. Thus, suppose I should think that I saw a form, and heard a voice cry "Johnson, you are a very wicked fellow, and unless you repent you will certainly be punished"; my own unworthiness is so deeply impressed upon my mind, that I might *imagine* I thus saw and heard, and therefore I should not believe that an external communication had been made to me. But if a form should appear, and a voice should tell me that a particular man had died at a particular place, and a particular hour, a fact which I had no apprehension of, nor any means of knowing, and this fact, with all its circumstances, should afterwards be unquestionably proved, I should, in that case, be persuaded that I had supernatural intelligence imparted to me.'

BOSWELL, *Life of Johnson*, 25 June 1763

BOSWELL: 'This objection is made against the truth of ghosts appearing: that if they are in a state of happiness, it would be a punishment to them to return to this world; and if they are in a state of misery, it would be giving them a respite.' JOHNSON: 'Why, Sir, as the happiness or misery of unembodied spirits does not depend upon place, but is intellectual, we cannot say that they are less happy or less miserable by appearing upon earth.'

28 March 1772

The subject of ghosts being introduced, Johnson repeated what he had told me of a friend of his, an honest man and a man of sense, having asserted to him, that he had seen an apparition. Goldsmith told us, he was assured by his brother, the Reverend Mr Goldsmith, that he also had seen one. General Oglethorpe told us that Prendergast, an officer in the Duke of Marlborough's army, had mentioned to many of his friends, that he should die on a particular day. That upon that day a battle took place with the French; that after it was over, and Prendergast was still alive, his brother officers, while they were yet in the field, jestingly asked him, where was his prophecy now. Prendergast gravely answered, 'I shall die, notwithstanding what you see.' Soon afterwards, there came a shot from a French battery, to which the orders for a cessation of arms had not yet reached, and he was killed upon the spot. Colonel Cecil, who took possession of his effects, found in his pocket-book the following solemn entry:

'Dreamt . . . Sir John Friend meets me' (here the very day on which he was killed, was mentioned). Prendergast had been connected with Sir John Friend, who was executed for high treason.

11 April 1772

Talking of ghosts, he said, 'It is wonderful that five thousand years have now elapsed since the creation of the world, and still it is undecided whether or not there has ever been an instance of the spirit of any person appearing after death. All argument is against it; but all belief is for it.'

3 April 1778

At Caen he is said to have had some preternatural intelligence of his father's death.

'The lord Roscommon, being a boy of ten years of age, at Caen in Normandy, one day was, as it were, madly extravagant in playing, leaping, getting over the tables, boards, &c. He was wont to be sober enough; they said, God grant this bodes no ill-luck to him! In the heat of this extravagant fit, he cries out, *My father is dead*. A fortnight after, news came from Ireland that his father was dead. This account I had from Mr Knolles, who was his governor, and then with him,—since secretary to the earl of Strafford; and I have heard his lordship's relations confirm the same.' *Aubrey's Miscellany*.

The present age is very little inclined to favour any accounts of this kind, nor will the name of Aubrey much recommend it to credit: it ought not, however, to be omitted, because better evidence of a fact cannot easily be found than is here offered, and it must be by preserving such relations that we may at last judge how much they are to be regarded. If we stay to examine this account, we shall see difficulties on both sides; here is a relation of a fact given by a man who had no interest to deceive, and who could not be deceived himself; and here is, on the other hand, a miracle which produces no effect; the order of nature is interrupted, to discover not a future but only a distant event, the knowledge of which is of no use to him to whom it is revealed. Between these difficulties, what way shall be found? Is reason or testimony to be rejected? I believe what Osborne says of an appearance of sanctity may be applied to such impulses or anticipations as this: *Do not wholly slight them, because they may be true: but do not easily trust them, because they may be false.*

> JOHNSON, 'Roscommon', *The Lives of the English Poets*, 1779; the closing reference is to Francis Osborne's *Advice to a Son*, 1656–8

Of apparitions, he observed, 'A total disbelief of them is adverse to the opinion of the existence of the soul between death and the last day; the question simply is, whether departed spirits ever have the power of making themselves perceptible to us; a man who thinks he has seen an apparition, can only be convinced himself; his authority will not convince another, and his conviction, if rational, must be founded on being told something which cannot be known but by supernatural means.'

> BOSWELL, *Life of Johnson*, 15 April 1781. Edmond Malone, who edited later editions, adds the footnote, that the subject occurs so frequently in the *Life* that the reader may suppose Johnson was very fond of such discussions, but in truth it was Boswell who delighted to talk about ghosts, and therefore took every opportunity of 'leading' Johnson to converse on the subject. But Boswell is nearer the mark in commenting (*Life*, 21 March 1772) that Johnson's 'elevated wish for more and more evidence for spirit, in opposition to the grovelling belief of materialism, led him to a love of such mysterious disquisitions'

Grim reader, did you ever see a ghost?
   No; but you've heard—I understand—be dumb!
And don't regret the time you may have lost,
   For you have got that pleasure still to come;
And do not think I mean to sneer at most
   Of these things, or by ridicule benumb
That source of the sublime and the mysterious:
For certain reasons, my belief is serious . . .

I merely mean to say what Johnson said,
   That, in the course of some six thousand years,
All nations have believed that, from the dead,
   A visitant at intervals appears.
And what is strangest upon this strange head,
   Is that, whatever bar the reason rears
'Gainst such belief, there's something stronger still
In its behalf, let those deny who will.

BYRON, Don Juan

He has been ignorantly misrepresented as weakly credulous upon that subject; and, therefore, though I feel an inclination to disdain and treat with silent contempt so foolish a notion concerning my illustrious friend, yet as I find it has gained ground, it is necessary to refute it. The real fact then is, that Johnson had a very philosophical mind, and such a rational respect for testimony, as to make him submit his understanding to what was authentically proved, though he could not comprehend why it was so. Being thus disposed, he was willing to inquire into the truth of any relation of supernatural agency, a general belief of which has prevailed in all nations and ages. But so far was he from being the dupe of implicit faith, that he examined the matter with a jealous attention, and no man was more ready to refute its falsehood when he had discovered it. Churchill, in his poem entitled *The Ghost*, availed himself of the absurd credulity imputed to Johnson, and drew a caricature of him under the name of 'POMPOSO', representing him as one of the believers of the story of a Ghost in Cock-lane, which, in the year 1762, had gained very general credit in London. Many of my readers, I am convinced, are to this hour under an impression that Johnson was thus foolishly deceived. It will therefore surprize them a good deal when they are informed upon undoubted authority, that Johnson was one of those by whom the imposture was detected. The story had become so popular, that he thought it should be investigated; and in this research he was assisted by the Reverend Dr Douglas, now Bishop of Salisbury, the great detector of impostures; who informs me, that after the gentlemen who went and examined into the evidence were satisfied of its falsity, Johnson wrote in their presence an account of it, which was published in the newspapers and *Gentleman's Magazine*, and undeceived the world.

BOSWELL, Life of Johnson, 25 June 1763

Could anything be more miraculous than an actual authentic Ghost? The English Johnson longed, all his life, to see one; but could not, though he went to Cock Lane, and thence to the church-vaults, and tapped on coffins. Foolish Doctor! Did he never, with the mind's eye as well as with the body's, look round him into that full tide of human Life he so loved; did he never so much as look into Himself? The good Doctor was a Ghost, as actual and authentic as heart could wish; wellnigh a million of Ghosts were travelling the streets by his side. Once more I say, sweep away the illusion of Time; compress the threescore years into three minutes: what else was he, what else are we? Are we not Spirits, that are shaped into a body, into an Appearance; and that fade away again into air and invisibility? This is no metaphor, it is a simple scientific *fact*: we start out of Nothingness, take figure, and are Apparitions . . . Ghosts! There are nigh a thousand-million walking the Earth openly at noontide; some half-hundred have vanished from it, some half-hundred have arisen in it, ere thy watch ticks once.

THOMAS CARLYLE, Sartor Resartus, 1833–4

A mother's sudden awareness that her distant son was drowning; a wife's vision of her dying husband; a man's consciousness that his friend was in desperate need; an apparition giving warning of danger; foreknowledge of an unexpected event; these were the kind of phenomena which aroused contempt in the majority and detached curiosity in but few. Yet they were sometimes reported by reasonable and educated persons, often enough indeed for a small number of open-minded men to doubt whether they could be attributed solely to chance, fraud, or fevered imagination. But they were not evidence, collected in a scientific manner . . . Moreover, it was not difficult to prove that many claims for so-called supernatural events were impostures, and natural contempt was aroused by the fact that these were—and still are—uncritically accepted by the many who, in Carlyle's bitter words, hunger and thirst to be bamboozled.

It is a natural instinct to revolt against the unknown, particularly against an unknown which has in the past been labelled abnormal, supernatural, uncanny, and has been associated with fraud and superstition throughout the ages. But a banknote is no less a banknote because there are forgeries.

ROSALIND HEYWOOD, *The Sixth Sense*

My friend Sir Roger has often told me, with a great deal of mirth, that at his first coming to his estate, he found three parts of his house altogether useless; that the best room in it had the reputation of being haunted, and by that means was locked up; that noises had been heard in his long gallery, so that he could not get a servant to enter it after eight o'clock at night; that the door of one of his chambers was nailed up, because there went a story in the family, that a butler had formerly hanged himself in it; and that his mother, who lived to a great age, had shut up half the rooms in the house, in which either a husband, a son, or daughter, had died. The knight, seeing his habitation reduced to so small a compass, and himself in a manner shut out of his own house, upon the death of his mother ordered all the apartments to be flung open, and exorcized by his chaplain, who lay in every room one after another, and by that means dissipated the fears which had so long reigned in the family.

I should not have been thus particular upon these ridiculous horrors, did I not find them so very much prevail in all parts of the country. At the same time I think a person who is thus terrified with the imagination of ghosts and spectres much more reasonable, than one who, contrary to the reports of all historians, sacred and profane, ancient and modern, and to the traditions of all nations, thinks the appearance of spirits fabulous and groundless. Could not I give myself up to this general testimony of mankind, I should to the relations of particular persons who are now living, and whom I cannot distrust in other matters of fact.

ADDISON, from *The Spectator*, 6 July 1711

What are we to think about magic and spells? The theory of it is obscure, the principles are vague, uncertain, and close to the visionary; but there are embarrassing facts, affirmed by grave men who have experienced them, or learned of them from persons like themselves: to believe them all or to reject them all seems equally wrong; and I dare say that, in this matter, as with all extra-ordinary things which fall outside the common rules, there is a middle way to be found between credulous souls and freethinkers.

JEAN DE LA BRUYÈRE, *Les Caractères*, 1688

It is not impossible to conceive, nor repugnant to reason, that there may be many *Species of Spirits*, as much separated and diversified one from another by distinct Properties, whereof we have no *Ideas*, as the *Species* of sensible Things are distinguished one from another, by Qualities which we know, and observe in them. That there should be more *Species* of intelligent Creatures above us, than there are of sensible and material below us, is probable to me from hence: That in all the visible corporeal World we see no Chasms, or Gaps. All quite down from us, the descent is by easy steps, and a continued series of Things, that in each remove differ very little one from the other . . . And when we consider the infinite Power and Wisdom of the Maker, we have reason to think that it is suitable to the magnificent Harmony of the Universe, and the great Design and infinite Goodness of the Architect, that the *Species* of Creatures should also, by gentle degrees, ascend upward from us, toward his infinite Perfection, as we see they gradually descend from us downward: Which, if it be probable, we have reason then to be perswaded that there are far more *Species* of Creatures above us, than there are beneath; we being in degrees of Perfection much more remote from the infinite Being of GOD than we are from the lowest state of Being, and that which approaches nearest to nothing.

JOHN LOCKE, *Essay Concerning Human Understanding*, 1690

We are too hasty when we set down our ancestors in the gross for fools, for the monstrous inconsistencies (as they seem to us) involved in their creed of witchcraft. In the relations of this visible world we find them to have been as rational, and shrewd to detect an historic anomaly, as ourselves. But when once the invisible world was supposed to be opened, and the lawless agency of bad spirits assumed, what measures of probability, of decency, of fitness, or pro-portion—of that which distinguishes the likely from the palpable absurd—could they have to guide them in the rejection or admission of any particular testimony?—that maidens pined away, wasting inwardly as their waxen images consumed before a fire—that corn was lodged, and cattle lamed—that whirl-winds uptore in diabolic revelry the oaks of the forest—or that spits and kettles only danced a fearful-innocent vagary about some rustic's kitchen when no wind was stirring—were all equally probable where no law of agency was understood. That the prince of the powers of darkness, passing by the flower and pomp of the earth, should lay preposterous siege to the weak fantasy of indigent eld—has neither likelihood nor unlikelihood *a priori* to us, who have no measure to guess at his policy, or standard to estimate what rate those anile souls may fetch in the devil's market. Nor, when the wicked are expressly symbolized by a goat, was it to be wondered at so much, that *he* should come sometimes in that body, and assert his metaphor.—That the intercourse was opened at all between both worlds was perhaps the mistake—but that once assumed, I see no reason for disbelieving one attested story of this nature more than another on the score of absurdity. There is no law to judge of the lawless, or canon by which a dream may be criticized.

LAMB, from 'Witches, and other Night-Fears', 1823

The general, or, it may be termed, the universal belief of the inhabitants of the earth, in the existence of spirits separated from the encumbrance and incapacities of the body, is grounded on the consciousness of the divinity that speaks in our bosoms, and demonstrates to all men, except the few who are hardened to the celestial voice, that there is within us a portion of the divine substance, which is not subject to the law of death and dissolution, but which, when the body is no longer fit for its abode, shall seek its own place, as a sentinel dismissed from his post. Unaided by revelation, it cannot be hoped that mere earthly reason should be able to form any rational or precise conjecture concerning the destination of the soul when parted from the body; but the conviction that such an indestructible essence exists, the belief expressed by the poet in a different sense, *Non omnis moriar*, must infer the existence of many millions of spirits, who have not been annihilated, though they have become invisible to mortals who still see, hear, and perceive, only by means of the imperfect organs of humanity . . .

These spirits, in a state of separate existence, being admitted to exist, are not, it may be supposed, indifferent to the affairs of mortality, perhaps not incapable of influencing them. It is true, that, in a more advanced state of society, the philosopher may challenge the possibility of a separate appearance of a disembodied spirit, unless in the case of a direct miracle, to which, being a suspension of the laws of nature, directly wrought by the Maker of these laws, for some express purpose, no bound or restraint can possibly be assigned. But under this necessary limitation and exception, philosophers might plausibly argue, that, when the soul is divorced from the body, it loses all those qualities which made it, when clothed with a mortal shape, obvious to the organs of its fellow men . . . But these sceptic doubts of philosophers on the possibility of the appearance of such separated spirits, do not arise till a certain degree of information has dawned upon a country, and even then only reach a very small proportion of reflecting and better informed members of society. To the multitude, the indubitable fact, that so many millions of spirits exist around and even amongst us, seems sufficient to support the belief that they are, in certain instances at least, by some means or other, able to communicate with the world of humanity. The more numerous part of mankind cannot form in their mind the idea of the spirit of the deceased existing, without possessing or having the power to assume the appearance which their acquaintance bore during his life, and do not push their researches beyond this point.

SCOTT, *Letters on Demonology and Witchcraft*

The author would say to pretended philosophy: Why seek to deny that which you cannot understand? Is not the unbelief which affirms in the face of the unknown more precipitate and less consoling than faith? Does the dreadful form of personified evil only prompt you to smile? Hear you not the ceaseless sobbing of humanity which writhes and weeps in the crushing folds of the monster? Have you never heard the atrocious laugh of the evil-doer who is persecuting the just man? Have you never experienced in yourselves the opening of those infernal deeps which the genius of perversity furrows in every soul? Moral evil exists—such is the unhappy truth; it reigns in certain spirits; it incarnates in certain men; it is therefore personified, and thus demons exist; but the most wicked of these demons is Satan.

LÉVI, *The History of Magic*

'But the ghost itself?' I said . . . 'What do you think of that?'

'I am afraid there is no possible doubt what that was. Its face, as I tell you, was a revelation of evil—evil and its punishment. It was a lost soul.'

'Do you mean by a lost soul, a soul that is in never-ending torment?'

'Not in physical torment, certainly; that would be a very material interpretation of the doctrine. Besides, the Church has always recognized degree and difference in the punishment of the lost. This, however, they all have in common—eternal separation from the Divine Being.'

'Even if they repent and desire to be reunited to Him?'

'Certainly; that must be part of their suffering.'

'And yet you believe in a good God?'

'In what else could I believe, even without revelation? But goodness, divine goodness, is far from excluding severity and wrath, and even vengeance. Here the witness of science and of history is in accord with that of the Christian Church; their first manifestation of God is always of "one that is angry with us and threatens evil".'

LANOE FALCONER, *Cecilia de Noël*

Life is the one pervading principle, and even the thing that seems to die and putrefy, but engenders new life, and changes to fresh forms of matter . . . If even man himself is a world to other lives, and millions and myriads dwell in the rivers of his blood, and inhabit man's frame as man inhabits earth, common sense (if your schoolmen had it) would suffice to teach that the circumfluent Infinite which you call space—the boundless Impalpable which divides earth from the moon and stars—is filled, also, with its correspondent and appropriate life. Is it not a visible absurdity to suppose that Being is crowded upon every leaf, and yet absent from the immensities of space? . . . In the very charnel-house is the nursery of production and animation. Is that true? Well, then, can you conceive that space which is the Infinite itself is alone a waste, is alone lifeless, is less useful to the one design of universal being than the dead carcass of a dog, than the peopled leaf, than the swarming globule? The microscope shows you the creatures on the leaf; no mechanical tube is yet invented to discover the nobler and more gifted things that hover in the illimitable air. Yet between these last and man is a mysterious and terrible affinity. And hence, by tales and legends, not wholly false nor wholly true, have arisen from time to time, beliefs in apparitions and spectres . . .

To penetrate this barrier, the soul with which you listen must be sharpened by intense enthusiasm, purified from all earthlier desires. Not without reason have the so-styled magicians, in all lands and times, insisted on chastity and abstemious reverie as the communicants of inspiration. When thus prepared, science can be brought to aid it; the sight itself may be rendered more subtle, the nerves more acute, the spirit more alive and outward, and the element itself—the air, the space—may be made, by certain secrets of the higher chemistry, more palpable and clear. And this, too, is not magic, as the credulous call it . . . magic (or science that violates nature) exists not;—it is but the science by which Nature can be controlled. Now, in space there are millions of beings, not literally spiritual, for they have all, like the animalculae unseen by the naked eye, certain forms of matter, though matter so delicate, air-drawn, and subtle, that it is, as it were, but a film, a gossamer, that clothes the spirit. Hence the Rosicrucian's lovely phantoms of sylph and gnome. Yet, in truth, these races and tribes differ more widely, each from each, than the Kalmuck from the Greek—differ in attributes and powers. In the drop of water you see how the animalculae vary, how vast and terrible are some of those monster-mites, as compared with others. Equally so with the Inhabitants of the atmosphere: some of surpassing wisdom, some of horrible malignity; some hostile as fiends to men, others gentle as messengers between earth and heaven. He who would establish intercourse with these varying beings, resembles the traveller who would penetrate into unknown lands. He is exposed to strange dangers and unconjectured terrors . . . I cannot direct thee to paths free from the wanderings of the deadliest foes. Thou must alone, and of thyself, face and hazard all.

BULWER-LYTTON, *Zanoni*, 1842

We college-bred gentry, who follow the stream of cosmopolitan culture exclusively, not infrequently stumble upon some old-established journal, or some voluminous native author, whose names are never heard of in *our* circle, but who number their readers by the quarter-million. It always gives us a little shock to find this mass of human beings not only living and ignoring us and all our gods, but actually reading and writing and cogitating without ever a thought of our canons and authorities. Well, a public no less large keeps and transmits from generation to generation the traditions and practices of the occult; but academic science cares as little for its beliefs and opinions as you, gentle reader, care for those of the readers of the *Waverley* and the *Fireside Companion*. To no one type of mind is it given to discern the totality of truth.

WILLIAM JAMES, *The Will to Believe*, 1897. He served as President of the Society for Psychical Research 1894–6

It is a field in which the sources of deception are extremely numerous. But I believe there is no source of deception in the investigation of nature which can compare with a fixed belief that certain kinds of phenomenon are *impossible*.

WILLIAM JAMES, from letter to Carl Stumpf, 1 January 1886

Spiritualism proposes as a dogma the inevitable amelioration of our species. The earth will one day become heaven, which is why this doctrine charmed the schoolmaster. Without being Catholic, it calls St Augustine and St Louis as witnesses; Allan-Kardec has even published fragments dictated by them which accord with contemporary opinion. It is practical, beneficent, and, like the telescope, reveals superior worlds to us.

After death the spirits are transported there in an ecstasy. But sometimes they descend to our globe, where they make furniture creak, join in our amusements, taste the beauties of Nature and the pleasures of the Arts.

Some of us, however, possess an aromal proboscis, that is to say, a long tube at the back of the head which mounts from the hair up to the planets and enables us to converse with the spirits of Saturn; intangible things are no less real, and from the earth to the stars, from the stars to the earth, there is a coming-and-going, a transmission, a continuous interchange.

Then Pécuchet's heart swelled with inordinate aspirations, and when night came, Bouvard surprised him at the window, gazing out upon those luminous spaces which are peopled by spirits.

Swedenborg made long journeys there. In under a year he explored Venus, Mars, Saturn and, twenty-three times, Jupiter. Moreover, he saw Jesus Christ in London, he saw St Paul, he saw St John, he saw Moses, and in 1736 he even saw the Last Judgement.

This is how he gave us descriptions of heaven.

You find there flowers, palaces, markets and churches, exactly as with us.

The angels, who were formerly men, inscribe their thoughts on tablets, chat about domestic or spiritual matters, and ecclesiastical offices belong to those who, in their terrestrial life, studied the Scriptures.

As for hell, it is filled with a nauseating stench, with hovels, foulness, persons shabbily dressed.

And Pécuchet racked his brains to discover what beauty there was in these revelations. They seemed to Bouvard the ravings of an idiot. Such affairs exceed the bounds of Nature! Besides, who knows anything about them? And they gave themselves to the following reflections:

Jugglers can delude a crowd; a man of violent passions inflames others; but how can the will by itself affect inert matter? A Bavarian, it is said, has caused grapes to ripen, M. Gervais has revived a heliotrope; someone with greater powers, at Toulouse, can disperse the clouds.

Must we admit the existence of a substance intermediary between the world and ourselves? Perhaps the od, a new imponderable, a sort of electricity, is nothing else? Its emissions explain the pale glow that magnetized persons think they see, the wandering fire in cemeteries, ghostly forms.

These images would not be an illusion, then; and the extraordinary gifts of persons who are possessed, like those of somnambulists, may they not have a physical cause?

Whatever its origin may be, there is an essence, a secret and universal agent. If we could get hold of it, there would be no need for prolonged effort. What takes centuries would develop in a moment: every sort of miracle would be practicable, and the universe would be at our disposal.

> FLAUBERT, *Bouvard and Pécuchet*, written 1872–80, left unfinished. The word 'od' was coined in the 19th century by Baron Karl von Reichenbach to signify a hypothetical force pervading nature and considered responsible for such phenomena as magnetism and hypnotism

The 'haunted house' has not yet become extinct even in the most enlightened and the most intellectual cities, nor has the peasant ceased to believe in the bewitching of his cattle. On the contrary, in this age of materialism—the inevitable consequence of rationalistic enlightenment—there has been a revival of the belief in spirits, but this time on a higher level. It is not a relapse into the darkness of superstition, but an intense scientific interest, a need to direct the searchlight of truth on to the chaos of dubious facts. The names of Crookes, Myers, Wallace, Zöllner, and many other eminent men symbolize this rebirth and rehabilitation of the belief in spirits. Even if the real nature of their observations be disputed, even if they can be accused of errors and self-deception, these investigators have still earned for themselves the undying moral merit of having thrown the full weight of their authority and of their great scientific name into these endeavours to shed fresh light on the darkness, regardless of all personal fears and considerations. They shrank neither from academic prejudice nor from the derision of the public, and at the very time when the thinking of educated people was more than ever spellbound by materialistic dogmas, they drew attention to phenomena of psychic provenience that seemed to be in complete contradiction to the materialism of their age.

These men typify the reaction of the human mind against the materialistic view of the world. Looked at from the historical standpoint, it is not at all surprising that they used the belief in spirits as the most effective weapon against the mere truth of the senses, for belief in spirits has the same functional significance also for primitive man. His utter dependence on circumstances and environment, the manifold distresses and tribulations of his life, surrounded by hostile neighbours, dangerous beasts of prey, and often exposed to the pitiless forces of nature; his keen senses, his cupidity, his uncontrolled emotions—all these things bind him to the physical realities, so that he is in constant danger of adopting a purely materialistic attitude and becoming degenerate. His belief in spirits, or rather, his awareness of a spiritual world, pulls him again and again out of that bondage in which his senses would hold him; it forces on him the certainty of a spiritual reality whose laws he must observe as carefully and as guardedly as the laws of his physical environment.

JUNG, from 'The Psychological Foundations of Belief in Spirits'

The other day a friend of mine attended a funeral. As the coffin was being lowered someone took a photograph of the mourners, and, when the plate was developed, the photograph of the man whose body was being buried appeared standing beside his wife. This was shown to the clergyman who officiated and he replied, 'Yes, I saw him standing there just as the photograph depicts it.' My friend then said, 'Well, you should tell your congregation that from the pulpit.' To which he replied, 'I would not dare; my Bishop would object.' Yet this same parson will preach about the disciples walking to Emmaus in company with an etheric man, whom they saw and spoke to, but he dare not say that he himself has seen one. Could anything exemplify better the present hopelessly illogical position of the Christian Church?

Spiritualists do not believe in miracles, or in the supernatural, or in anything contrary to nature. They believe in law and order in the universe, and they never talk about supernatural events or miraculous occurrences. When they refer to something occurring beyond our limited sense perceptions they refer to it as supernormal. No miracle, or supernatural occurrence, has ever taken place in the history of the universe, so far as our knowledge extends.

ARTHUR FINDLAY, Hon. Vice-President of the Spiritualists' National Union, past Chairman of The International Institute for Psychical Research, *The Rock of Truth*, 1933

Mr Hawker had a theory that there was an atmosphere which surrounded men, imperceptible to the senses, which was the vehicle of spirit, in which angels and devils moved, and which vibrated with spiritual influences affecting the soul. Every passion man felt set this ether trembling, and made itself felt throughout the spiritual world. A sensation of love or anger or jealousy felt by one man was like a stone thrown into a pool; and it sent a ripple throughout the spiritual universe which touched and communicated itself to every spiritual being. Some mortal men, having a highly refined soul, were as conscious of these pulsations as disembodied beings; but the majority are so numbed in their spiritual part as to make no response to these movements.

BARING-GOULD, *The Vicar of Morwenstow*

I want first to tell you quite shortly my theory about ghost-seeing, and I can explain it best by a simile, an image. Imagine then that you and I and every-body in the world are like people whose eye is directly opposite a little tiny hole in a sheet of cardboard which is continually shifting and revolving and moving about. Back to back with that sheet of cardboard is another, which also, by laws of its own, is in perpetual but independent motion. In it too there is another hole, and when, fortuitously it would seem, these two holes, the one through which we are always looking, and the other in the spiritual plane, come opposite one another, we see through, and then only do the sights and sounds of the spiritual world become visible or audible to us. With most people these holes never come opposite each other during their life. But at the hour of death they do, and then they remain stationary. That, I fancy, is how we 'pass over'.

E. F. BENSON, from 'The Bus-Conductor', 1912

On each of the six occasions just recorded, the writer had been rapt into a momentary communion with the actors in a particular historic event through the effect upon his imagination of a sudden arresting view of the scene in which this long-past action had taken place. But there was another occasion on which he had been vouchsafed a larger and a stranger experience. In London in the southern section of the Buckingham Palace Road, walking southward along the pavement skirting the west wall of Victoria Station, the writer, once, one afternoon not long after the end of the First World War—he had failed to record the exact date—had found himself in communion, not just with this or that episode in History, but with all that had been, and was, and was to come. In that instant he was directly aware of the passage of History gently flowing through him in a mighty current, and of his own life welling like a wave in the flow of this vast tide. The experience lasted long enough for him to take visual note of the Edwardian red brick surface and white stone facings of the station wall gliding past him on his left, and to wonder—half amazed and half amused—why this incongruously prosaic scene should have been the physical setting of a mental illumination. An instant later, the communion had ceased, and the dreamer was back again in the everyday cockney world which was his native social milieu and of which the Edwardian station wall was a characteristic period piece.

ARNOLD J. TOYNBEE, A Study of History, Vol. X, 1954

If the gibberings, the preposterous incivilities, and the unwholesome uproar committed in that house for ten unforgettable years by these unhallowed genii may be accepted as an argument tending to establish the continued existence of the individual after death, the seductions of futurity are scarcely increased to

> Exhausted travellers that have undergone
> The scorching heats of life's intemperate zone.

Such questionable intimations of immortality are hardly calculated to soothe us—

> When worn with adverse passions, furious strife,
> And the hard passage of tempestuous life.

Nevertheless, this singular history, taken in connection with others of its class, may to the impartial and philosophic mind hide a lesson of the highest import. M. Renan, in one of the very last of his many charming pages, troubled with doubts as to a future existence, whilst smiling at the superstition of the old-fashioned and orthodox hell, exclaims how glad he would be to be sure even of hell, a hypothesis so preferable to annihilation.

In the same way, may we not justifiably postulate this: that if we can prove the existence of spirits of a low or inferior order, then faith, analogy, and evolution, if not logic and conviction, can claim those of a progressive, a high and superior order? Is it not rational to suppose that the more debased and the most unhappy have the greatest facility in giving tangible proof of their exist-ence, under certain conditions imperfectly understood; whilst the purer and nobler souls find intercourse painful or impossible, but are yet occasionally able to achieve it in those picturesque and beneficent instances where their visitation is recorded, not only in the Old and New Testaments, but scattered all through literature; cases which possibly the many may still deride, but which others cherish as indications of the divine and proofs of immortality?

EDMUND PROCTER, Journal of the Society for Psychical Research, Vol. 5,
December 1892; concerning the haunting in 1835 of Willington Mill, Tyneside,
the home of his parents

We must perhaps be grateful to spiritualism for the fact that with its quaint messages from the Beyond, which suggest the spirits of deceased cooks, it satisfies the crude metaphysical craving to shovel down spoonfuls of, if not God, then at least the spirits, like some pabulum that, partaken of in darkness, slips icily down the gullet. In older times this craving to get into personal touch with God or any of the heavenly hierarchy—which allegedly happened when one was in the condition of ecstasy—in spite of the frail and to some extent weird forms that it took on did nevertheless give rise to an intermingling of a crude earthly attitude with the experiences that occurred in an extremely unusual and quite indefinable condition of intuitive apprehension. The metaphysical was merely the physical as it was projected into that condition, a mirror-image of earthly desires; for people believed they saw then whatever contemporary notions made them have a lively expectation of being able to see. Now it is, however, precisely the notions emanating from the intellect that change with the times and become incredible. If anyone were today to declare that God had spoken to him, had seized him painfully by the hair and drawn him up to Himself, or had slipped into his breast in some not entirely comprehensible but intensely sweet way, nobody would believe in these particular images in which he clothed his experience, least of all, naturally, the professional men of God, because they, as children of a rational age, have a thoroughly human fear of being compromised by hysterical adherents in a state of exaltation. The consequence of this is that one has either to regard experiences that were numerous and well-defined in the Middle Ages, as also in pagan Antiquity, as delusions and pathological phenomena, or to conjecture that they contained something that remains independent of the mythical terms in which it has hitherto always been expressed: that is to say, a pure core of experience that ought to stand up even to being investigated according to strict empirical principles and which then, it goes without saying, would constitute a matter of extreme importance long before one got to the second question as to what conclusions were to be drawn from this with reference to our relations to the supramundane realm. And while faith, having been organized into the system of theological reason, everywhere has to fight a hard battle against doubt and opposition from the rational attitude prevailing nowadays, it seems in fact that the naked fundamental experience—peeled out of all the traditional terminological husks of faith, detached from the old religious concepts—this fundamental experience that perhaps cannot even any longer be called an exclusively religious one, this experience of mystic rapture, has extended vastly and now constitutes the soul of that multiform, irrational movement which haunts the age in which we live like a nocturnal bird that has strayed into the daylight.

ROBERT MUSIL, *The Man Without Qualities*, Vol. II, 1930; tr. Eithne Wilkins and Ernst Kaiser

The passage from Revelation sent a frisson of accustomed delight through the frame of Mrs Papagay, who loved its sonorous booming and its lurid colours, scarlet, gold, white and the black of the Pit. She loved too, and had loved since childhood, all its strange visions and images, the angels rolling up the scroll of the heavens and tidying them away for ever, the stars falling out of the sky into the sea like a rain of golden fiery globes, the dragons and swords, the blood and the honey, the swarms of locusts and the hosts of angels, those creatures at once pure white and fiery-eyed, casting down their golden crowns around a glassy sea. She had asked herself often and often why everyone loved the ferocious St John and his terrible vision so, and had answered herself variously, like a good psychologist, that human beings liked to be terrified—look how they enjoyed the nastier Tales of Mr Poe, pits, pendulums, buried alive. Not only that, they *liked to be judged*, she considered, they could not go on if their lives were not of importance, of absolute importance, in some higher Eye which watched and made real. For if there were not death and judgement, if there were not heaven and hell, men were no better than creepy-crawlies, no better than butterflies and blowflies. And *if this was all*, sitting and supping tea, and waiting for bedtime, why were we given such a range of things guessed at, hoped for and feared beyond our fat bosoms confined in stays, and troubles with stoves? Why the white airy creatures towering, the woman clothed with the sun and the Angel standing in it?

A. S. BYATT, from 'The Conjugial Angel', 1992

We are astonished when we find someone who claims to believe that an evil spirit dwells in a certain oak tree, or that there is a God who hears our prayers and loves us. What can they mean? What are they up to, saying that these things are the case, when plainly, in all the ways they otherwise accept for things being or not being the case, these things are *not* the case?

Imagine someone from a tribe which had no notion of pictorial representation. Mightn't he be astonished when he came up against our belief that certain coloured smears on canvas 'showed' living people? He gazes at us in amazement as we are moved by one portrait, and amused by another. Don't we realize that human beings are complex structures of protein, and that most of the colours we are looking at on the canvas are not even organic?

The portraits are interesting to us precisely because they are done in paint instead of flesh. It's the same with the myths. Their discontinuity with experienced life, with normal logic—the fact that they are plainly done in another material—is what gives them their otherness.

I should like to say this: don't *worry* when you find yourself in the midst of a mythology. Relax and enjoy it! Sit in one mythology, and put your feet up on another! You'll still be tied up in *some* myth even if you get out of this one. And after all, you know how to enjoy fairy stories without translating wands into phalluses all the time, and handsome princes into members of the feudal oppressor class. (At least, I hope you do.) You can read a novel without wondering anxiously all the time whether it's true or false. You understand in what way it's true that Kuznetzov was at Borodino, and in what way it's true that Pierre was.

Live mythologies up to the hilt, like the old woman Sinyavsky writes about, who cries to her son when he tries to cut her toenails for her, 'How can you think of such a thing, Kostik! How can you? It's time for me to die. And how am I going to climb the mountain up to God without my toenails?'

MICHAEL FRAYN, *Constructions*, 1974

I wish, likewise, with all my heart, that Homer could have known the rule prescribed by Horace, to introduce supernatural agents as seldom as possible. We should not then have seen his gods coming on trivial errands, and often behaving themselves so as not only to forfeit all title to respect, but to become the objects of scorn and derision . . .

The only supernatural agents which can in any manner be allowed to us moderns are ghosts; but of these I would advise an author to be extremely sparing. These are indeed like arsenic, and other dangerous drugs in physic, to be used with the utmost caution; nor would I advise the introduction of them at all in those works, or by those authors to which, or to whom, a horse-laugh in the reader, would be any great prejudice or mortification.

As for elves and fairies, and other such mummery, I purposely omit the mention of them, as I should be very unwilling to confine within any bounds those surprising imaginations, for whose vast capacity the limits of human nature are too narrow; whose works are to be considered as a new creation; and who have consequently just right to do what they will with their own.

FIELDING, *The History of Tom Jones*, 1749

Should Latin, Greek, and Hebrew fail,
I know a charm which *must* prevail:

> Take but an ounce of Common Sense,
> 'Twill scare the Ghosts, and drive 'em hence.
>
> *Public Advertiser*, 5 February 1762; concerning the Cock Lane ghost

How loath were we to give up our pious belief in ghosts and witches, because we liked to persecute the one, and frighten ourselves to death with the other!

WILLIAM HAZLITT, from 'On the Pleasure of Hating', 1826

The *Scythians*, being a stout and a warlike nation (as divers writers report), never see anie vaine sights or spirits. It is a common saieng: A lion feareth no bugs. But in our childhood our mothers' maids have so terrified us with an ouglie divell having hornes on his head, fier in his mouth, and a taile in his breech, eies like a bason, fanges like a dog, clawes like a beare, a skin like a Niger, and a voice roring like a lion, whereby we start and are afraid when we heare one crie Bough: and they have so fraied us with bull beggers, spirits, witches, urchens, elves, hags, fairies, satyrs, pans, faunes, sylens, kit with the cansticke, tritons, centaurs, dwarfes, giants, imps, calcars, conjurors, nymphes, changlings, *Incubus*, Robin good-fellowe, the spoorne, the mare, the man in the oke, the hell waine, the fierdrake, the puckle, Tom thombe, hob gobblin, Tom tumbler, boneles, and such other bugs, that we are afraid of our owne shadowes.

SCOT, *The Discoverie of Witchcraft*

> England, a happy land we know,
> Where follies naturally grow,
> Where without culture they arise,
> And tower above the common size;
> England, a fortune-telling host
> As numerous as the stars, could boast;
> Matrons, who toss the cup, and see
> The grounds of fate in grounds of tea;
> Who, vers'd in every modest lore,
> Can a lost maidenhead restore,
> Or, if their pupils rather choose it,
> Can show the readiest way to lose it.

Gipsies, who every ill can cure
Except the ill of being poor,
Who charms 'gainst love and agues sell,
Who can in hen-roost set a spell,
Prepar'd by arts to them best known,
To catch all feet except their own,
Who, as to fortune, can unlock it
As easily as pick a pocket;
Scotchmen who, in their country's right,
Possess the gift of second sight,
Who (when their barren heaths they quit,
Sure argument of prudent wit,
Which reputation to maintain,
They never venture back again)
By lies prophetic heap up riches,
And boast the luxury of breeches.

CHURCHILL, *The Ghost*

Of all others, the oracle of *Apollo Pythius*, at Delphi, was the most celebrated; it was, in short, consulted always as a *dernier ressort*, in cases of emergency, by most of the princes of those ages.—Mr Bayle observes, that at first, it gave its answers in verse; and that at length it fell to prose, in consequence of the people beginning to laugh at the poorness of its versification.

FORSYTH, *Demonologia*

Owen Glendower.   At my nativity
The front of heaven was full of fiery shapes,
Of burning cressets; and at my birth
The frame and huge foundation of the earth
Shaked like a coward.
Hotspur. Why, so it would have done at the same season, if your mother's cat
had but kittened, though yourself had never been born.
Glend. I say the earth did shake when I was born.
Hot. And I say the earth was not of my mind,
If you suppose as fearing you it shook.
Glend. The heavens were all on fire; the earth did tremble.

Hot. O, then the earth shook to see the heavens on fire,
 And not in fear of your nativity.
 Diseased nature oftentimes breaks forth
 In strange eruptions; oft the teeming earth
 Is with a kind of colic pinch'd and vex'd
 By the imprisoning of unruly wind
 Within her womb; which, for enlargement striving,
 Shakes the old beldam earth and topples down
 Steeples and moss-grown towers. At your birth
 Our grandam earth, having this distemperature,
 In passion shook.
Glend.   Cousin, of many men
 I do not bear these crossings. Give me leave
 To tell you once again that at my birth
 The front of heaven was full of fiery shapes,
 The goats ran from the mountains, and the herds
 Were strangely clamorous to the frighted fields.
 These signs have mark'd me extraordinary;
 And all the courses of my life do show
 I am not in the roll of common men.
 Where is he living, clipp'd in with the sea
 That chides the banks of England, Scotland, Wales,
 Which calls me pupil, or hath read to me?
 And bring him out that is but woman's son
 Can trace me in the tedious ways of art
 And hold me pace in deep experiments.
Hot. I think there's no man speaks better Welsh.
 I'll to dinner . . .
Glend. I can call spirits from the vasty deep.
Hot. Why, so can I, or so can any man;
 But will they come when you do call for them?
Glend. Why, I can teach thee, cousin, to command the devil.
Hot. And I can teach thee, coz, to shame the devil
 By telling truth . . .

Mortimer. Fie, cousin Percy! How you cross my father!
Hot. I cannot choose: sometimes he angers me
 With telling me of the moldwarp and the ant,
 Of the dreamer Merlin and his prophecies,
 And of a dragon and a finless fish,

A clip-wing'd griffin, and a moulten raven,
A couching lion, and a ramping cat,
And such a deal of skimble-skamble stuff
As puts me from my faith. I'll tell thee what;
He held me last night at least nine hours
In reckoning up the several devils' names
That were his lackeys. I cried 'hum' and 'well, go to',
But mark'd him not a word. O, he's as tedious
As a tired horse, a railing wife;
Worse than a smoky house.

SHAKESPEARE, *1 Henry IV*, *c.*1597

'And perhaps, sir, as the room is big and draughty it might be well to have one of those big screens put round your bed at night—though, truth to tell, I would die myself if I were to be so shut in with all kinds of—of "things", that put their heads round the sides, or over the top, and look on me!' The image which she had called up was too much for her nerves, and she fled incontinently.

Mrs Dempster sniffed in a superior manner as the landlady disappeared, and remarked that for her own part she wasn't afraid of all the bogies in the kingdom.

'I'll tell you what it is, sir,' she said: 'bogies is all kinds and sorts of things — except bogies! Rats and mice, and beetles, and creaky doors, and loose slates, and broken panes, and stiff drawer handles, that stay out when you pull them and then fall down in the middle of the night. Look at the wainscot of the room! It is old—hundreds of years old! Do you think there's no rats and beetles there! And do you imagine, sir, that you won't see none of them! Rats is bogies, I tell you, and bogies is rats; and don't you get to think anything else!'

'Mrs Dempster,' said Malcolmson gravely, making her a polite bow, 'you know more than a Senior Wrangler! And let me say, that, as a mark of esteem for your indubitable soundness of head and heart, I shall, when I go, give you possession of this house, and let you stay here by yourself for the last two months of my tenancy, for four weeks will serve my purpose.'

'Thank you kindly, sir!' she answered, 'but I couldn't sleep away from home a night. I am in Greenhow's Charity, and if I slept a night away from my rooms I should lose all I have got to live on. The rules is very strict; and there's too many watching for a vacancy for me to run any risks in the matter.'

BRAM STOKER, from 'The Judge's House', published posthumously, 1914

If we balance against each other the advantages and disadvantages which might accrue to a person organized not only for the visible world, but also, to a certain degree, for the invisible (if ever there was such a person), such a gift would seem to be like that with which Juno honoured Tiresias, making him blind so that she might impart to him the gift of prophesying. For, judging from the propositions above made, the knowledge of the other world can be obtained here only by losing some of that intelligence which is necessary for this present world.

IMMANUEL KANT, *Dreams of a Spirit-Seer*, 1766; tr. Emanuel F. Goerwitz

Once upon a time, some people in India made a new Heaven and a new Earth out of broken teacups, a missing brooch or two, and a hairbrush. These were hidden under bushes, or stuffed into holes in the hillside, and an entire Civil Service of subordinate Gods used to find or mend them again; and every one said, 'There are more things in Heaven and Earth than are dreamt of in our philosophy.' Several other things happened also, but the Religion never seemed to get much beyond its first manifestations; though it added an air-line postal service and orchestral effects in order to keep abreast of the times and choke off all competition.

The Religion was too elastic for ordinary use. It stretched itself and embraced pieces of everything that the medicine-men of all ages have manufactured. It approved of and stole from Freemasonry; looted the Latter-day Rosicrucians of half their pet words; took any fragments of Egyptian philosophy that it found in the *Encylopaedia Britannica*; annexed as many of the Vedas as had been translated into French or English, and talked of all the rest; built in the German versions of what is left of the Zend Avesta; encouraged White, Grey, and Black Magic, including spiritualism, palmistry, fortune-telling by cards, hot chestnuts, double-kernelled nuts, and tallow droppings; would have adopted Voodoo and Obeah had it known anything about them, and showed itself, in every way, one of the most accommodating arrangements that had ever been invented since the birth of the Sea.

KIPLING, from 'The Sending of Dana Da', 1888; alluding to Madame Blavatsky and the Theosophical Society, founded by her and Colonel H. S. Olcott in 1875 and re-established in India in 1879

'History is full of little sects that make up their own style, part swagger, part mysticism. The Templars themselves didn't really understand what they were doing. On the other hand, there's always the esoteric explanation: they knew exactly what they were doing, they were adepts of Oriental mysteries, and even the kiss on the ass had a ritual meaning.'

'Do explain to me, briefly, the ritual meaning of the kiss on the ass,' Diotallevi said.

'All right. Some modern esotericists maintain that the Templars were reviving certain Indian doctrines. The kiss on the ass serves to wake the serpent Kundalini, a cosmic force that dwells at the base of the spinal column, in the sexual glands. Once wakened, Kundalini rises to the pineal gland . . .'

'Descartes's pineal gland?'

'I think it's the same one. A third eye is then supposed to open up in the brow, the eye that lets you see directly into time and space. That is why people are still seeking the secret of the Templars . . . Act like a lunatic and you will be inscrutable for ever. Abracadabra, Mene Tekel Upharsin, Pape Satan Pape Satan Aleppe, le vierge le vivace et le bel aujourd'hui. Whenever a poet or preacher, chief or wizard spouts gibberish, the human race spends centuries deciphering the message.' .

UMBERTO ECO, *Foucault's Pendulum*, 1988; tr. William Weaver

'When Mother was a girl, Elbert Hubbard [American essayist] was the household god. He could do no wrong . . . Well, to make a long story short, I guess you all know that Elbert Hubbard went down with the *Lusitania*. That night, for no reason whatsoever, Mother sat bolt upright in bed. It's not something she likes to talk about, but I know she thinks about it a good deal.'

'Does she believe in extrasensory perception?' Victor asked.

'First,' Irving said, 'let me ask you a question, which I'll put this way. Do you *not* believe in ESP?'

Victor gave this some thought before he spoke. 'No. The way I see it, it's just one of those things science hasn't caught up with yet.'

Irving seemed to find this acceptable, but contented himself with saying, 'As for Mildred, she has no choice but to believe in it.'

'Heavens,' Nadia said, 'you give me a shiver.'

Claire, however, scoffed. 'We have no such thing in France—the supernatural is exclusively an Anglo-Saxon preoccupation.'

'What about those ghosts at Versailles?' Victor asked.

'You know they waited two hundred years before appearing to some English spinsters, doubtless because they could find no French person gullible enough to believe in them. My house in Vermont was cheap partly because there is supposed to be a ghost in it—that of a virgin who likes to emit hair-raising groans. But I told the agent, "You do not frighten one nurtured on Descartes and Auguste Comte." '

JOHN ASHBERY and JAMES SCHUYLER, A *Nest of Ninnies*, 1969

I have always noticed a prevalent want of courage, even among persons of superior intelligence and culture, as to imparting their own psychological experiences when those have been of a strange sort. Almost all men are afraid that what they could relate in such wise would find no parallel or response in a listener's internal life, and might be suspected or laughed at. A truthful traveller, who should have seen some extraordinary creature in the likeness of a sea-serpent, would have no fear of mentioning it; but the same traveller, having had some singular presentiment, impulse, vagary of thought, vision (so called), dream, or other remarkable mental impression, would hesitate considerably before he would own to it. To this reticence I attribute much of the obscurity in which such subjects are involved . . . The consequence is, that the general stock of experience in this regard appears exceptional, and really is so, in respect of being miserably imperfect.

DICKENS, from 'To be Taken with a Grain of Salt', 1865

I have not made up my mind upon these subjects. When one can believe frankly in all the Church says, many things become simple, which otherwise cause great difficulty in the mind. The mysterious and wonderful then find their natural place in the course of affairs; but when a man thinks for himself, and has to take everything on his own responsibility, and make all the necessary explanations, there is often great difficulty. So many things will not fit into their places, they straggle like weary men on a march. One cannot put them together, or satisfy one's self.

MARGARET OLIPHANT, A *Beleaguered City*; the reflections of M. Dupin, the mayor

It is an old story, that men sell themselves to the tempter, and sign a bond with their blood, because it is only to take effect at a distant day; then rush on to snatch the cup their souls thirst after with an impulse not the less savage because there is a dark shadow beside them for evermore. There is no short cut, no patent tram-road, to wisdom: after all the centuries of invention, the soul's path lies through the thorny wilderness which must be still trodden in solitude, with bleeding feet, with sobs for help, as it was trodden by them of old time.

GEORGE ELIOT, *The Lifted Veil*

One further [Eton] College Pop debate may be noted, occasioned by A. E. Brooke's motion 'That we need not believe in ghosts'. It all depended, Monty [M. R. James] said, on what one meant by belief; for himself, 'he could not but believe in anything and everything when in bed'. Further, did not Mr Brooke's scepticism indicate a tendency to disbelieve in a future state, and indeed in the Bible itself? According to Monty, something like ten out of every hundred ghost stories had some basis of truth in them: they were dismissed simply because people did not like the idea of such things happening.

MICHAEL COX, *M. R. James: An Informal Portrait*, 1983

The tendency on the part of journalists to draw a strong and unquestioning demarcation line between everyday experience and the mystical—'freak news'— came home to me strongly as a result of a conversation I had at about this time with my paper's [*The Observer*'s] editor, Donald Trelford.

Trelford had recently published an article in the *Spectator* [4 April 1987] claiming that many years earlier he had seen the mysterious apparition of a schoolfriend one winter's afternoon in Coventry. He and his friend (they were both in their early twenties then) had agreed to meet under the town-centre clock-tower at six in the evening, after playing in separate rugby football matches. Trelford was waiting at the appointed hour, and eventually his friend came walking towards him on the crowded pavement. But instead of stopping he carried on walking and disappeared in the darkness. Baffled by this behaviour, Trelford returned home, where he discovered that his friend had been killed in a road accident earlier that afternoon. The article had not been written up as a curious paranormal episode for Hallowe'en or Christmas, but as a deeply felt reminiscence of a sadly missed friend; it was an eloquent, finely observed piece of unfinished business.

Not long after the publication of this story I had dinner with Trelford and asked him how he accounted for this experience. Had he seen a ghost? 'No! I don't believe in ghosts.' Had he been mistaken and seen a look-alike? 'No! It was definitely my friend.'

Eventually I said, 'But Donald, if it happened and you're not making it up, you surely have to account for it.'

'Well, it definitely happened,' he said with finality, 'and I *don't* have to account for it, and I *won't*.'

JOHN CORNWELL, *Powers of Darkness, Powers of Light*, 1991

During one of my various engagements in Paris Madame Sarah Bernhardt had witnessed my performance and was anxious to see one of my outdoor exploits, so, when we were both playing at the same time in Boston, out of good camaraderie I gave a special performance at my hotel, adding a few extra experiments for her benefit. As we were seated in the motor car on the way to my demonstration she placed her arm gently around my shoulder, and in that wonderful speaking voice with which she was gifted and which has thrilled thousands of auditors, but now stilled for ever, she said to me:

'Houdini, you do such marvellous things. Couldn't you—could you bring back my leg for me?'

I looked at her, startled, and failing to see any mischievous sparkle in her eye replied:

'Good heavens, Madame, certainly not; you cannot be serious. You know my powers are limited and you are actually asking me to do the impossible.'

'Yes,' she said as she leaned closer to me, 'but you do the impossible.'

We looked at each other; she, the travel-worn, experienced woman of the world; I, the humble mystifier, nonplussed and thunderstruck at the extraordinary, unintentional compliment she was paying me. Then I asked:

'Are you jesting?'

'*Mais non, Houdini, je n'ai jamais été plus sérieuse dans ma vie*,' she answered as she slowly shook her head.

'Madame, you exaggerate my ability,' I told her.

Not only are mediums alert to embrace every advantage offered by auto-suggestion but they also take advantage of every accidental occurrence. For instance, my greatest feat of mystery was performed in 1922 at Seacliffe, Long Island, on the Fourth of July, at the home of Mr B. M. L. Ernest. The children were waiting to set off their display of fireworks when it started to rain. The heavens fairly tore loose. Little Richard in his dismay turned to me and said:

'Can't you make the rain stop?'

'Why certainly,' I replied and raising my hands said appealingly, 'Rain and Storm, I command you to stop.'

This I repeated three times and, as if by miracle, within the next two minutes the rain stopped and the skies became clear. Toward the end of the display of fireworks the little fellow turned to me and with a peculiar gleam in his eyes said:

'Why, Mr Houdini, it would have stopped raining anyway.'

I knew I was risking my whole life's reputation with the youngster but I said:

'Is that so? I will show you.'

Walking out in front I raised my hands suppliantly toward the heavens and with all the command and force I had in me called:

'Listen to my voice, great Commander of the rain, and once more let the water flow to earth and allow the flowers and trees to bloom.'

A chill came over me for, as if in response to my command or the prayer of my words, another downpour started, but despite the pleading of the children I refused to make it stop again. I was not taking any more chances.

HARRY HOUDINI, *A Magician among the Spirits*, 1924

'I believe in such phenomena in a certain sense,' said Willie Cranmer, 'but I am not prepared to allow them a supernatural—in the more esoteric sense of the word—existence. By some unexplained means, certain places, certain things, become impregnated, kinetic, sensitized. How or why one room, one chair, even one WC, allows itself to be so impregnated is an utterly inexplicable mystery. One battlefield is "haunted"; a thousand are as placid as Port Meadow. Usually, I grant you, there is evidence that a potent emanation of some passion has at some time been released and operative in such disturbed areas, though not, I believe, by any means in every case. But the most singular thing to my mind about the supernatural is its caprice, its fortuitousness, its rarity—and indeed its essential lack of purpose . . .'

'I knew a house,' said George Dunbar, 'in which I would not spend a week alone for one thousand guineas. Not merely is it impregnated, it is dripping with horror and beastliness. It is dark and brooding and has—it seems to me—an evil life of its own. Everyone, I know, who has entered it has taken an immediate and increasing loathing for it. It has a shocking record of suicides—eight in thirty years, but I agree with Willie that I never got the impression that there was any mind or will animating those coughs one heard, the steps behind one, the dim, drawn faces one thought one saw at windows; and all the symposium of dread one experienced there. I mean that one was left convinced that there was no consciousness working in our space and time—these things seemed to be passing in and out of another dimension—that is vague, but just the impression I got. All these phenomena seemed quite purposeless, and therefore should not have been, as they were, frightening—puppets without strings—like the mechanical recording of a gramophone.'

'I think that's a better simile than mine,' said Cranmer. 'Once the record is made by the living it goes on long after the recorder is dead, repeating and repeating until it wears out, and there is evidence that the influence does wear out in certain senses. All such comparisons between affairs on one plane and on another are fallacious, but they help to clear the air of debate.'

'But someone has to put the record on,' objected Mr Partridge.

'I suggest it is never taken off,' replied Cranmer.

'What a typical ghost discussion it has been,' thought Mr Partridge, 'hopelessly inconclusive, tentative, vaguely disturbing, subjective, guesswork.'

H. RUSSELL WAKEFIELD, from 'A Peg on Which to Hang—', 1928

~

'But, my dearest Catherine, what have you been doing with yourself all this morning?—Have you gone on with Udolpho?'

'Yes, I have been reading it ever since I woke; and I am got to the black veil.'

'Are you, indeed? How delightful! Oh! I would not tell you what is behind the black veil for the world! Are not you wild to know?'

'Oh! yes, quite; what can it be?—But do not tell me—I would not be told upon any account. I know it must be a skeleton, I am sure it is Laurentina's skeleton. Oh! I am delighted with the book! I should like to spend my whole life in reading it. I assure you, if it had not been to meet you, I would not have come away from it for all the world.'

'Dear creature! how much I am obliged to you; and when you have finished Udolpho, we will read the Italian together; and I have made out a list of ten or twelve more of the same kind for you.'

'Have you, indeed! How glad I am!—What are they all?'

'I will read you their names directly; here they are, in my pocket-book. Castle of Wolfenbach, Clermont, Mysterious Warnings, Necromancer of the Black Forest, Midnight Bell, Orphan of the Rhine, and Horrid Mysteries. Those will last us some time.'

'Yes, pretty well; but are they all horrid, are you sure they are all horrid?'

'Yes, quite sure; for a particular friend of mine, a Miss Andrews, a sweet girl, one of the sweetest creatures in the world, has read every one of them.'

> JANE AUSTEN, *Northanger Abbey*, written between 1798 and 1803, published in 1818. A conversation between Isabella Thorpe and Catherine Morland; *The Mysteries of Udolpho* (1794) and *The Italian* (1797) are novels by Ann Radcliffe, and the titles listed by Isabella were real books published during the craze for 'Gothic' fiction

Mrs Radcliffe's popularity stood the test, and was heightened rather than diminished by *The Mysteries of Udolpho*. The very name was fascinating; and the public, who rushed upon it with all the eagerness of curiosity, rose from it with unsated appetite. When a family was numerous, the volumes always flew, and were sometimes torn, from hand to hand; and the complaints of those whose studies were thus interrupted, were a general tribute to the genius of the author. Another might be found of a different and higher description, in the dwelling of the lonely invalid, or unregarded votary of celibacy, who was bewitched away from a sense of solitude, of indisposition, by the potent charm of this mighty enchantress. Perhaps the perusal of such works may, without injustice, be compared with the use of opiates, baneful, when habitually and constantly resorted to, but of most blessed power in those moments of pain and of languor, when the whole head is sore, and the whole heart sick. If those who rail indiscriminately at this species of composition, were to consider the quantity of actual pleasure which it produces, and the much greater proportion of real sorrow and distress which it alleviates, their philanthropy ought to moderate their critical pride, or religious intolerance . . .

The public soon, like Macbeth, become satiated with horrors, and indifferent to the strongest stimuli of that kind. It shows, therefore, the excellence and power of Mrs Radcliffe's genius, that she was able three times to bring back her readers with fresh appetite to a banquet of the same description; while of her numerous imitators, who rang the changes upon old castles and forests, and 'antres dire', scarcely one attracted attention, until Mr Lewis published his *Monk*, several years after she had resigned her pen.

> SCOTT, *Lives of the Novelists*, 1821–4, 'Mrs Ann Radcliffe'

He [Johnson] once told me another accident of his younger Years . . . he was just nine Years old when having got the play of Hamlet to read in his Father's

Kitchen, he read on very quietly till he came to the Ghost Scene, when he hurried up Stairs to the Shop Door that he might see folks about him. This Story he was not unwilling to tell as a Testimony to the Merits of Shakespear.

HESTER LYNCH THRALE, *Thraliana: The Diary of Mrs Thrale*, 1776–1809

When we want to wonder there's no such good ground for it as the wonderful—premising indeed always, by an induction as prompt, that this element can but be at best, to fit its different cases, a thing of appreciation. What is wonderful in one set of conditions may quite fail of its spell in another set, and, for that matter, the peril of the unmeasured strange, in fiction, being the silly, just as its strength, when it saves itself, is the charming, the wind of interest blows where it lists, the surrender of attention persists where it can. The ideal, obviously, on these lines, is the straight fairy tale, the case that has purged in the crucible all its *bêtises* while keeping all its grace. It may seem odd, in a search for the amusing, to try to steer wide of the silly by hugging close the 'supernatural'; but one man's amusement is at best (we have surely long had to recognize) another's desolation; and I am prepared with the confession that the 'ghost story', as we for convenience call it, has ever been for me the most possible form of the fairy tale. It enjoys, to my eyes, this honour by being so much the neatest—neat with that neatness without which *representation*, and therefore beauty, drops.

We but too probably break down, I have ever reasoned, when we attempt the prodigy, the appeal to mystification, in itself; with its 'objective' side too emphasized the report (it is ten to one) will practically run thin. We want it clear, goodness knows, but we also want it thick, and we get the thickness in the human consciousness that entertains and records, that amplifies and interprets it. That indeed, when the question is (to repeat) of the 'supernatural', constitutes the only thickness we do get; here prodigies, when they come straight, come with an effect imperilled; they keep all their character, on the other hand, by looming through some other history—the indispensable history of somebody's *normal* relation to something. It's in such connections as these that they most interest, for what we are then mainly concerned with is their imputed and borrowed dignity.

HENRY JAMES, preface to *The Altar of the Dead, and Other Tales*, 1909

The fear which we get from reading ghost stories of the supernatural is a refined and spiritualized essence of fear. It is a fear which we can examine and play with. Far from despising ourselves for being frightened by a ghost story we are proud of this proof of sensibility, and perhaps unconsciously welcome the chance for the licit gratification of certain instincts which we are wont to treat as outlaws. It is worth noticing that the craving for the supernatural in literature coincided in the eighteenth century with a period of rationalism in thought, as if the effect of damming the human instincts at one point causes them to overflow at another.

Some element of the supernatural is so constant in poetry that one has come to look upon it as part of the normal fabric of the art; but in poetry, being etherealized, it scarcely provokes any emotion so gross as fear. Nobody was ever afraid to walk down a dark passage after reading *The Ancient Mariner*, but rather inclined to venture out to meet whatever ghosts must deign to visit him. Probably some degree of reality is necessary in order to produce fear; and reality is best conveyed by prose.

It would be a mistake to suppose that supernatural fiction always seeks to produce fear, or that the best ghost stories are those which most accurately and medically described abnormal states of mind. On the contrary, a vast amount of fiction both in prose and in verse now assures us that the world to which we shut our eyes is far more friendly and inviting, more beautiful by day and more holy by night, than the world which we persist in thinking the real world. The country is peopled with nymphs and dryads, and Pan, far from being dead, is at his pranks in all the villages of England. Much of this mythology is used not for its own sake, but for purposes of satire and allegory; but there exists a group of writers who have the sense of the unseen without such alloy. Such a sense may bring visions of fairies or phantoms, or it may lead to a quickened perception of the relations existing between men and plants, or houses and their inhabitants, or any one of those innumerable alliances which somehow or other we spin between ourselves and other objects in our passage.

VIRGINIA WOOLF, from 'The Supernatural in Fiction', 1918; reviewing Dorothy Scarborough: *The Supernatural in Modern English Fiction*

What first interested me in ghosts? This I can tell you quite definitely. In my childhood I chanced to see a toy Punch and Judy set, with figures cut out in cardboard. One of these was The Ghost. It was a tall figure habited in white with an unnaturally long and narrow head, also surrounded with white, and a dismal visage.

Upon this my conceptions of a ghost were based, and for years it permeated my dreams . . .

I am speaking of the literary ghost story here. The story that claims to be 'veridical' (in the language of the Society for Psychical Research) is a very different affair. It will probably be quite brief, and will conform to some one of several familiar types. This is but reasonable, for, if there be ghosts—as I am quite prepared to believe—the true ghost story need do no more than illustrate their normal habits (if normal is the right word), and may be as mild as milk.

The literary ghost, on the other hand, has to justify his existence by some startling demonstration, or, short of that, must be furnished with a background that will throw him into full relief and make him the central feature.

Since the things which the ghost can effectively do are very limited in number, ranging about death and madness and the discovery of secrets, the setting seems to me all-important, since in it there is the greatest opportunity for variety . . .

If there is a theme that ought to be kept out of the ghost story, it is that of the charnel house. That and sex.

> M. R. JAMES, from 'Ghosts—Treat Them Gently!', *Evening News*, 17 April 1931

Ghosts, it is advanced, either do not exist at all, or else, like the stars at noonday, they are there all the time and it is we who cannot see them . . .

At first sight it would therefore appear that the writer of ghost stories in this sense has unlimited material to his hand; but actually this is not so. All-the-time manifestations, pervading the whole of nature with a ghostly element, are for all practical purposes no manifestations at all. What the writer has in practice to investigate is the varying 'densities' of the ghostliness that is revealed when this surface of life, accepted for everyday purposes as stable, is jarred, and for the time of an experience does not recover its equilibrium.

Nevertheless his realm is no narrow one. True its Central Province is of strictly limited extent, but, as this provides only the class of story so plainly labelled 'ghost' that it cannot be mistaken for anything else, the spectre is apt to be swamped by the traditional apparatus that makes the stock illustration for the Christmas Number, and there is little to be said about this region except that here the ghostly texture is found at its coarsest.

But this place of shrouds and moans and bony fingers is surrounded by territory no less haunted than itself, and with far subtler terrors. This is the ghost-belt that never asserts its spectre, but leaves you in no doubt about his presence. Above all, only rarely is he seen, and I myself have never been able to understand why the unvarying question should be, 'Have you ever *seen* a ghost?' when, if a ghost cannot exist apart from visibility, his being rests solely on the testimony of one sense, and that in some respects the most fallible one of all. May not his proximity be felt and his nature apprehended in other ways? I have it on excellent authority that such a visitor can in fact be heard breathing in the room, most powerfully smelt, and known for a spirit in travail longing for consolation, all at one and the same time, and yet not be seen by the eye. And even short of signs so explicit as these, who at some time or other has not walked into a room, known and familiar and presently to be known and familiar again, but that for a space has become a different room, informed with other influences and charged with other meanings? Something has temporarily upset the equilibrium, which will be restored by and by. Much less dense, I take it, is the texture of the spirits that make this secondary zone their habitat, but ah, how much more shiveringly it gets to the marrow than do the groans and clankings of the grosser spook!

OLIVER ONIONS, from 'Credo', *The Collected Ghost Stories*, 1935

This story, which I admit to be in its brevity a fairly complex piece of work, was not intended to touch on the supernatural. Yet more than one critic has been inclined to take it in that way, seeing in it an attempt on my part to give the fullest scope to my imagination by taking it beyond the confines of the world of the living, suffering humanity. But as a matter of fact my imagination is not made of stuff so elastic as all that. I believe that if I attempted to put the strain of the Supernatural on it it would fail deplorably and exhibit an unlovely gap. But I could never have attempted such a thing, because all my moral and intellectual being is penetrated by an invincible conviction that whatever falls under the dominion of our senses must be in nature and, however exceptional, cannot differ in its essence from all the other effects of the visible and tangible world of which we are a self-conscious part. The world of the living contains enough marvels and mysteries as it is; marvels and mysteries acting upon our emotions and intelligence in ways so inexplicable that it would almost justify the conception of life as an enchanted state. No, I am too firm in my con- sciousness of the marvellous to be ever fascinated by the mere supernatural, which (take it any way you like) is but a manufactured article, the fabrication of minds insensitive to the intimate delicacies of our relation to the dead and to the living, in their countless multitudes; a desecration of our tenderest memories; an outrage on our dignity.

JOSEPH CONRAD, Author's Note, 1920, to *The Shadow-Line*

The ghost story appealed to serious writers largely because it invited a concern with the profoundest issues: the relationship between life and death, the body and the soul, man and his universe, the nature of evil. Like other forms of fantasy—myths, legends or fairy tales—it could be made to embody symbolically hopes and fears too deep and too important to be expressed more directly.

They no longer represented the vital links of a stable community with its dead, as ghosts had once done. Indeed, as if to emphasize their contemporary relevance more sharply, the spirits summoned by mid-nineteenth-century mediums were often those of Red Indian chiefs, who, conveniently enough, had few connections with an English past.

> JULIA BRIGGS, *Night Visitors: The Rise and Fall of the English Ghost Story*, 1977; the first extract refers specifically to 19th-century writing, the second contrasts the 'new' ghosts of psychic circles with the traditional ones

Let us, then, be introduced to the actors in a placid way; let us see them going about their ordinary business, undisturbed by forebodings, pleased with their surroundings; and into this calm environment, let the ominous thing put out its head, unobtrusively at first, and then more insistently, until it holds the stage. It is not amiss sometimes to leave a loophole for a natural explanation; but, I would say, let the loophole be so narrow as not to be quite practicable. Then, for the setting. The detective story cannot be too much up-to-date: the motor, the telephone, the aeroplane, the newest slang, are all in place there. For the ghost story, a slight haze of distance is desirable. 'Thirty years ago', 'Not long before the war', are very proper openings . . . For some degree of actuality is the charm of the best ghost stories; not a very insistent actuality, but one strong enough to allow the reader to identify with the patient.

> V. H. COLLINS, from introduction to *Ghosts and Marvels*, 1924

The returning dead are traditionally at home in mists and shadows, and we expect to meet them, if not in their native churchyards, then at least somewhere equally gloomy and isolated: in ruinous or long-empty houses, on lonely roads, wild moorlands, or dreary estuaries; among monastic ruins and other sites of ancient worship, in disused churches, overgrown gardens, decaying canals, and vanished railways; and we do not expect them before twilight. Yet more disconcerting are the ghosts permitted by their authors to intrude upon mundane concerns in broad daylight in hotels, suburban bungalows, or country houses, utilizing—when it suits them—our telephones and modes of transport. The critic Edmund Wilson, writing in 1944, expressed surprise that the ghost story was still alive and well in the age of the electric light: a decade later literary ghosts were still thriving. This adaptability was memorably described by L. P. Hartley [introduction to *The Third Ghost Book*, edited by Lady Cynthia Asquith, 1955]: 'Like women and other depressed classes, [ghosts] have emancipated themselves from their disabilities, and besides being able to do a great many things that human beings can't do, they can now do a great many things that human beings can do. Immaterial as they are or should be, they have been able to avail themselves of the benefits of our materialistic civilization.'

MICHAEL COX and R. A. GILBERT, from introduction to *The Oxford Book of English Ghost Stories*, 1986

I read the other day in a book by a fashionable essayist that ghosts went out when electric light came in. What nonsense! The writer, though he is fond of dabbling, in a literary way, in the supernatural, hasn't even reached the threshold of his subject. As between turreted castles patrolled by headless victims with clanking chains, and the comfortable suburban house with a refrigerator and central heating where you feel, as soon as you're in it, *that there's something wrong*, give me the latter for sending a chill down the spine! And, by the way, haven't you noticed that it's generally not the high-strung and imaginative who see ghosts, but the calm matter-of-fact people who don't believe in them, and are sure they wouldn't mind if they did see one?

EDITH WHARTON, from 'All Souls'', 1937

'An author has rights which the reader is bound to respect.'

'For specific example?'

'The right to the reader's undivided attention. To deny him this is immoral. To make him share your attention with the rattle of a streetcar, the moving panorama of the crowds on the sidewalks, and the buildings beyond—with any of the thousands of distractions which make our customary environment—is to treat him with gross injustice. By God, it is infamous! . . . You know what I mean,' continued the writer, impetuously, crowding his words—'You know what I mean, Marsh. My stuff in this morning's *Messenger* is plainly subheaded "A Ghost Story". That is ample notice to all. Every honourable reader will understand it as prescribing by implication the conditions under which the work is to be read.'

The man addressed as Marsh winced a trifle, then asked with a smile: 'What conditions? You know that I am only a plain business man, who cannot be supposed to understand such things. How, when, where should I read your ghost story?'

'In solitude—at night—by the light of a candle. There are certain emotions which a writer can easily enough excite—such as compassion or merriment. I can move you to tears or laughter under almost any circumstances. But for my ghost story to be effective you must be made to feel fear—at least a strong sense of the supernatural—and that is a different matter. I have a right to expect that if you read me at all you will give me a chance; that you will make yourself accessible to the emotion which I try to inspire.'

AMBROSE BIERCE, from 'The Suitable Surroundings', 1892

The sceptic does not mean the one who doubts, but the one who inquires and searches, as opposed to the one who asserts and supposes he has found.

MIGUEL DE UNAMUNO, from 'My Religion', 1924

ACKNOWLEDGEMENTS

The editor and publisher are grateful for permission to include the following copyright material:

Dannie Abse, from 'The Deceived', in *There Was a Young Man From Cardiff* (Hutchinson, 1991). © Dannie Abse 1991. Reprinted by permission of Sheil Land Associates Ltd.

Anon., from *The Brideling, Sadling and Ryding, of a rich Churle* . . . and from 'The Examination of John Walsh', in *Witchcraft* (Stratford upon Avon Library Series), edited by Barbara Rosen (1969). Reprinted by permission of Edward Arnold Publishers.

Anon., from *Stories About Not Being Afraid of Ghosts* (1961), translated by Yang Xianyi and Gladys Yang. (Foreign Languages Press, Beijing.)

Guillaume Apollinaire, from 'The Moon King', in *The Poet Assassinated and Other Stories* (1985), translated by Ron Padgett. Reprinted by permission of Carcanet Press Ltd., and North Point.

John Ashbery and James Schuyler, from *A Nest Of Ninnies* (Dutton, 1969).

Earl Clement Attlee, from *I Saw A Ghost* . . ., edited by Ben Noakes (1986). Reprinted by permission of Weidenfeld and Nicolson.

Beryl Bainbridge, from *The Birthday Boys* (1991). Reprinted by permission of Gerald Duckworth Ltd.

Paul Barber, extracts from *Vampires, Burial, and Death* (1988). Reprinted by permission of Yale University Press.

Dennis Bardens, from *Psychic Animals* (1987). Reprinted by permission of Robert Hale Ltd. (US rights: Scott Ferris Agency).

A. L. Barker, from 'The Little People', in *Any Excuse for a Party* (Hutchinson, 1991).

Winifred Beechey, from 'The Duke of Wellington, and Jane', in *The Reluctant Samaritan* (1991). Reprinted by permission of Oxford University Press.

Patricia Beer, from *Moon's Ottery* (1978). Reprinted by permission of Carcanet Press Ltd.

John Beloff, from *The Relentless Question: Reflections on the Paranormal* © 1990 John Beloff. Reprinted by permission of McFarland and Company Inc., Publishers, Jefferson NC 28640.

Sir Ernest Bennett, from *Apparitions and Haunted Houses* (Faber, 1939). Reprinted by kind permission of Mrs M. E. White.

Michael Bentine, from *The Door Marked Summer* (Granada, 1981).

Georges Bernanos, from *The Star of Satan*, translated by Veronica Lucas (John Lane, The Bodley Head, 1927). Reprinted by permission of Random House.

Algernon Blackwood, from 'The Wig', radio talk, 1935, and from 'The Little Beggar', in *Tales of the Uncanny and the Supernatural* (Hamlyn, 1962). Reprinted by permission of A. P. Watt Ltd., on behalf of Sheila Reeves.

Paul Bowles, from *Without Stopping: An Autobiography* (1972). Reprinted by permission of Peter Owen Publishers Ltd.

Julia Briggs, from *Night Visitors: The Rise and Fall of the English Ghost Story* (1977). Reprinted by permission of Faber and Faber Ltd.

K. M. Briggs, from *Pale Hecate's Team* (Routledge, 1962). From 'Traditional Invention in Ghost Stories', *The Folklore of Ghosts* (Boydell & Brewer Ltd., 1981). Reprinted by permission of A. P. Watt Ltd. on behalf of Katherine Law.

Andrew Brown: 'Aubergines reveal true faith to Muslim Pilgrims', from the *Independent*, 28 March 1993. Reprinted by permission of the *Independent*.

Rosemary Brown, from *Unfinished Symphonies: Voices from the Beyond* (1971). Reprinted by permission of Souvenir Press Ltd.

Theo Brown, from 'The Black Dog in Devon', in *Transactions of the Devonshire Association*, Vol. 91, 1959. From *The Fate of the Dead*, D. S. Brewer/Rowman and Littlefield (1979).

Anthony Burgess, from *You've Had Your Time* (Heinemann, 1990). Reprinted by permission of Sheil Land Associates Ltd.

Dino Buzzati, from 'The Count's Wife', in *Restless Nights* (1984), translated by Lawrence Venuti. Reprinted by permission of Carcanet Press Ltd., and North Point.

A. S. Byatt: from *Possession* (Chatto, 1990) and from 'The Conjugal Angel' from *Angels and Insects* (Chatto, 1992). Reprinted by permission of Random House.

Norman Cameron: 'A Visit to the Dead', from *Norman Cameron: Collected Poems and Selected Translations*, edited by Warren Hope and Jonathan Barker. Reprinted by permission of Anvil Press Poetry.

Angela Carter, from 'The Company of Wolves', in *The Bloody Chamber* (1979). Reprinted by permission of Victor Gollancz, and Penguin USA.

C. P. Cavafy: 'Nero's Deadline', in *C. P. Cavafy: Collected Poems*, translated by Edmund Keeley and Philip Sherrard (1975). Reprinted by permission of Random House and Princeton University Press.

Wu Ch'eng-en, from *Monkey*, translated by Arthur Waley (Allen & Unwin, 1942). Reprinted by permission of HarperCollins Publishers.

Norman Cohn, from *Europe's Inner Demons* (Chatto/Heinemann for Sussex University Press, 1975).

S. T. Coleridge: Letter to Mary Evans, 13 February 1792, from *Collected Letters of S. T. Coleridge*, Vol. I, edited by Earl Leslie Griggs (1956). Reprinted by permission of Oxford University Press.

Doris Collins, from *The Power Within* (Grafton, 1986).

V. H. Collins, from the introduction to *Ghosts and Marvels* (1924). Reprinted by permission of Oxford University Press.

Maurice Collis, from *Somerville and Ross* (1969). Reprinted by permission of Miss Louise Collis.

John Cornwell, from *Powers of Darkness, Powers of Light* (Viking Penguin, 1991).

Michael Cox, from *M. R. James: An Informal Portrait* (1983). Reprinted by permission of A. P. Watt Ltd; from introduction to *The Oxford Book of English Ghost Stories* (1988) ed. M. Cox and R. A. Gilbert. By permission.

Aleister Crowley, from *The Confessions of Aleister Crowley: An Autohagiography*, edited by John Symonds and Kenneth Grant (Arkana 1989, corrected edition first published by Routledge & Kegan Paul, 1971) © John Symonds and Kenneth Grant 1969, 1979.

Robertson Davies, from *World of Wonders* (1975). © Robertson Davies 1975. Reprinted by permission of Curtis Brown Canada Ltd.

William Dick and Henry Gris, from *The New Soviet Psychic Discoveries* (1978). © William Dick and Henry Gris 1978.

Emily Dickinson. Reprinted by permission of the publishers & The Trustees of Amherst College from *The Poems of Emily Dickinson*, Thomas H. Johnson, ed., Cambridge, Mass.: the Belknap Press of Harvard University Press, copyright © 1951, 1955, 1979, 1983 by the President and Fellows of Harvard College.

Dostoevsky, from *The Brothers Karamazov*, translated by Constance Garnett (Heinemann, 1932). Reprinted by permission of the publisher.

J. W. Dunne, from *An Experiment With Time* (Macmillan, 1927).

Umberto Eco, from *Foucault's Pendulum*, translated by William Weaver (Secker, 1988). Reprinted by permission of the publisher.

Michael Edwardes, from *The Dark Side of History* (Hart-Davis, 1978).

George Eliot: letter to Harriet Beecher Stowe, 24 June 1872, from *The George Eliot Letters*, edited by Gordon S. Haight, Vol. V (Yale University Press/OUP, 1956). Reprinted by permission of Yale University Press.

T. S. Eliot, extract from 'The Dry Salvages'. Reproduced by kind permission of Mrs Valerie Eliot, Faber & Faber Ltd., and Harcourt Brace Jovanovich Inc.

Susan Ellicott, from 'America Under a Spell', in *The Times* 21 October 1991. © Susan Ellicott 1991. Reprinted by permission.

Allan J. A. Elliott, from *Chinese Spirit-Medium Cults in Singapore*, in Monographs on Social Anthropology, No. 14, New Series, 1955, London School of Economics and Political Science.

Alice Thomas Ellis, from *The 27th Kingdom* (1982). Reprinted by permission of Gerald Duckworth Ltd.

Ann Faraday, from *Dream Power* (1972). © Ann Faraday 1972. Reprinted by permission of Sheil Land Associates Ltd.

Henri Fauconnier, from *The Soul of Malaya*, translated by Eric Sutton (1931). Reprinted by permission of George Allen & Unwin Ltd.

Arthur Findlay, from *The Rock of Truth* (Spiritualists' National Union Publications, 1933).

E. M. Forster, from 'The Celestial Omnibus', in *The Celestial Omnibus* (1911). Reprinted by permission of the Provost and Scholars of King's College, Cambridge.

Richard Francis, from *The Land Where the Lost Things Go by Olive Watson* (1990). Reprinted by permission of Carcanet Press Ltd.

Michael Frayn, from *Constructions* (Wildwood House, 1974). © 1974 by Michael Frayn.

Sigmund Freud, from 'The Uncanny', translated by Alix Strachey in *The Collected Papers*, Vol. IV (Hogarth, 1925). Authorized translation under the supervision of Joan Riviere. Published by Basic Books, Inc. by arrangement with the Hogarth Press Ltd., and the Institute of Psycho-Analysis, London. By permission.

Robert Frost, 'The Witch of Coös', from *The Poetry of Robert Frost* (Cape/Holt Rinehart & Winston, 1971). Reprinted by permission.

Gallican Liturgy, Form of Exorcism, translated by Jeffrey Burton Russell, in *Lucifer: The Devil in the Middle Ages* (Cornell University Press, 1984).

Théophile Gautier, 'The Actor' trs. Richard Holmes, in *My Fantoms* (Quartet Books, 1976).

Rumer Godden, from *A House With Four Rooms* (Macmillan, London/W. M. Morrow, New York, 1989).

Goethe, from *Faust: Part I*, translated by David Luke (1987). Reprinted by permission of Oxford University Press.

Oliver St John Gogarty, from *As I Was Going Down Sackville Street* (Rich & Cowan, 1937).

Arturo Graf, from *The Story of the Devil*, translated by Edward Noble Stone (Macmillan, 1931). © 1931 E. N. Stone.

Douglas Grant, from *The Cock Lane Ghost* (1965). Reprinted by permission of Macmillan Press Ltd.

Robert Graves: 'Welsh Incident' from *Collected Poems 1975*. Reprinted by permission of A. P. Watt Ltd., on behalf of the Trustees of the Robert Graves Copyright Trust.

Celia Green: account given by an informant in *Out-of-the-Body Experiences* (Hamish Hamilton, 1968). © Proceedings of the Institute for Psychophysical Research, Oxford, Vol. II. Used by permission.

Graham Greene, from 'All But Empty' (Heinemann). © 1949 Verdant S.A. Reprinted by permission of David Higham Associates.

Margot Grey: account by an elderly Cockney lady in *Return From Death* (Arkana, 1988).

Arthur Grimble, from *A Pattern of Islands* (1952). Reprinted by permission of John Murray (Publishers) Ltd.

Henry Gris and William Dick, from *The New Soviet Psychic Discoveries*. © 1978 Henry Gris and William Dick.

Alec Guinness, from *Blessings in Disguise* (Hamish Hamilton, 1985).

J. C. Hall: 'A Kind of Faith', from *Selected and New Poems 1939–84* (Secker and Warburg, 1985). Reprinted by permission of the author.

Paule V. Hampso, from *The Cat Lover's Journal* (1974–5). Reprinted in *Psychic Animals* by Dennis Bardens (Robert Hale, 1987).

Peter and Mary Harrison: 'Concerning Philip Harding of Milton Keynes', in *Life Before Birth* (Futura, 1983).

L. P. Hartley, from 'W.S.' in *Collected Stories of L. P. Hartley* (Hamish Hamilton, 1968).

Anthony Hecht: 'A Voice at a Seance', from *Millions of Strange Shadows* (1977). Reprinted by permission of Oxford University Press and Atheneum Publishers.

David Herbert, from *Second Son* (1972). Reprinted by permission of Peter Owen Publishers Ltd.

Zbigniew Herbert: 'Anything Rather Than an Angel', in *Zbigniew Herbert: Selected Poems* (1985), translated by Czeslaw Milosz. Reprinted by permission of Carcanet Press Ltd., and the Ecco Press.

Rosalind Heywood, from *The Sixth Sense* (Chatto, 1959). From *The Infinite Hive* (Chatto, 1964). Reprinted by permission of Random House.

Charles Higham, from *The Adventures of Conan Doyle* (Hamish Hamilton, 1976).

Susan Hill, from *The Woman in Black* (Hamish Hamilton, 1983). Reprinted by permission of Richard Scott Simon.

Christina Hole, from *Haunted England* (B. T. Batsford Ltd., 1940). From *Witchcraft in England* (Batsford, 1945).

Michael Holroyd, from *I Saw A Ghost . . .*, edited by Ben Noakes (1986). Reprinted by permission of Weidenfeld and Nicolson.

G. M. Hopkins, from *The Notebooks and Papers of Gerard Manley Hopkins* (1937), edited by Humphry House. Reprinted by permission of Oxford University Press.

Peter Hough and Jenny Randles, from *Spontaneous Human Combustion* (1992). Reprinted by permission of Robert Hale Ltd.

Michael Howard, from *The Occult Conspiracy* (Rider, 1959). Reprinted by permission of Random House.

Zora Neale Hurston, from *Tell My Horse: Voodoo and Life in Haiti and Jamaica* (Harper and Row, 1938). Copyright 1938 by Zora Neale Hurston © renewed 1966 by Joel Hurston and John C. Hurston. Reprinted by permission of HarperCollins Publishers Inc. and Farrar, Straus & Giroux.

Aldous Huxley, from *The Devils of Loudun* (Chatto, 1952). Reprinted by permission of Random House.

Brian Inglis, from *The Hidden Power* (Cape, 1986). © 1986 Brian Inglis. Reprinted by permission of Jonathan Cape and Curtis Brown London Ltd.

Shirley Jackson, from 'Experience and Fiction', in *Come Along With Me*, edited by Stanley Edgar Hyman (Viking, 1968).

W. W. Jacobs, from *The Monkey's Paw* (1902). Reprinted by permission of the Society of Authors as the literary representative of the Estate of W. W. Jacobs.

Ernest Jones, from *On The Nightmare* (Hogarth Press, 1931). Reprinted by permission of Random House.

Alan Judd, from *The Devil's Own Work* (HarperCollins, 1991).

Carl Gustav Jung, from 'The Psychological Foundations of Belief in Spirits', and 'Synchronicity: An Acausal Connecting Principle', in *C. G. Jung: Collected Works*, Vol. 8, translated by R. F. C. Hall. Reprinted by permission of Routledge and Kegan Paul.

Franz Kafka, from 'Unhappiness', in *Franz Kafka: Stories 1904–1924* (1981), translated by J. A. Underwood. Reprinted by permission of Little Brown & Company.

P. J. Kavanagh: 'Sometimes', from *Collected Poems* (1992). Reprinted by permission of Carcanet Press Ltd.

Maxine Hong Kingston, from *The Woman Warrior* (Allen Lane, 1977). Reprinted by permission of A. M. Heath & Co.

Arthur Koestler, from *The Roots of Coincidence* (Hutchinson, 1972). From *The Invisible Writing* (Hutchinson, 1954). Reprinted by permission of the Peters Fraser and Dunlop Group Ltd.

Heinrich Krämer and Jakob Sprenger, from *Malleus Maleficarum* (Hammer of the Witches) translated by Montague Summers (John Rodker, 1928/The Pushkin Press, 1948).

Evald Tang Kristensen, from 'Danish Legends', translated by Joan Rockwell in *The Folklore of Ghosts* (Boydell & Brewer Ltd., 1981), edited by Hilda R. Ellis Davidson and W. M. S. Russell. Reprinted by permission of the Folklore Society, London.

Manuel Mujica Lainez, from *The Wandering Unicorn*, translated by Mary Fitton (Lester & Orpen Dennys Ltd., Canada 1982/Chatto, 1983). Reprinted by permission of Random House. (US rights: Lester & Orpen Dennys.)

D. H. Lawrence, from 'Glad Ghosts' from *Complete Short Stories of D. H. Lawrence*. Reprinted by permission of Alfred A. Knopf, Inc., a division of Random House Inc.

Tanith Lee, from 'The Devil's Rose', reprinted in *Women of Darkness*, edited by Kathryn Ptacek (Tor Books, 1988). Reprinted by permission of the author.

Rosamond Lehmann, from *The Swan in the Evening* (Collins, 1967).

Primo Levi, from 'The Servant', translated by Raymond Rosenthal, in *The Sixth Day and Other Tales* (Michael Joseph/Simon & Schuster, 1990). © 1966, 1977 by Giulio Einaudi Editore s.P.a., Torino. English translation © 1990 by Simon & Schuster Inc. Reprinted by permission of The Penguin Group and Simon & Schuster Inc.

C. S. Lewis, from the preface to *The Screwtape Letters* (Geoffrey Bles, 1961 edition). Reprinted by permission of HarperCollins Publishers.

Peter Lovesey, from *A Case of Spirits* (Macmillan, 1975).

Andrew MacKenzie, from *Frontiers of the Unknown* (Arthur Barker, 1968). Reprinted by permission of A. M. Heath Ltd., on behalf of the Estate of the late Andrew MacKenzie.

Maurice Maeterlinck, from *The Unknown Guest*, translated by Alexander Teixeira de Mattos (Methuen, 1914).

Thomas Mann: entry for 22 May 1937, from *Diaries 1918–1939*, translated by Richard and Clara Winston (1983). Reprinted by permission of André Deutsch Ltd. and Harry N. Abrama, Inc.; from *Doctor Faustus*, translated by H. T. Lowe-Porter (London: Secker/New York: Knopf, 1949), from Three Essays, H. T. Lowe-Porter (Secker/Knopf, 1932); from *The Magic Mountain* trs. H. T. Lowe-Porter (Secker/Knopf, 1928).

Hilary Mantel, from *Fludd* (1989). Reprinted by permission of the Penguin Group Ltd. (US rights: A. M. Heath Ltd.)

Walter de la Mare: 'The Ghost', from *Motley and Other Poems* (Faber, 1919). Reprinted by permission of the Literary Trustees of Walter de la Mare and the Society of Authors as their representatives.

Saiichi Maruya, from *Rain in the Wind: Four Stories* (1990), translated by Dennis Keene. Reprinted by permission of André Deutsch Ltd., and Kodansha International Ltd.

W. Somerset Maugham, from *The Magician* (Heinemann, 1908). Reprinted by permission of the publisher.

André Maurois, from *Victor Hugo*, translated by Gerard Hopkins (Cape, 1956). Reprinted by permission of Random House.

Victoria Mckee, 'And Briefly', from *The Times*, 16 October 1991. © Victoria Mckee 1991.

Prosper Mérimée, from 'The Venus of Ille', in *The Venus of Ille and Other Stories*, translated by Jean Kimber (1966). Reprinted by permission of Oxford University Press.

Czeslaw Milosz, from *Unattainable Earth* (Ecco Press/Penguin, 1986), translated by the author and Robert Haas.

Robert Musil, from *The Man Without Qualities*, Vol. II, translated by Eithne Wilkins and Ernst Kaiser (Secker, 1954). Reprinted by permission of the publisher.

R. K. Narayan, from 'God and the Cobbler', in *Malgudi Days* (Heinemann, 1982). Reprinted by permission of Sheil Land Associates Ltd.

Imam Nawawi, from *Gardens of the Righteous*, translated by Muhammad Zafrulla Khan. Reprinted by permission of Curzon Press.

Harold Nicolson, from *Diaries and Letters 1930–1939*, edited by Nigel Nicolson (Collins, 1966).

Sean O'Faolain, from *The Irish* (Penguin, 1947). Reprinted by permission of Rogers Coleridge & White Limited.

Oliver Onions, from 'Credo', in *Collected Ghost Stories of Oliver Onions* (1935).

Harold Owen, from *Journey From Obscurity*, Vol. III (1965). Reprinted by permission of Oxford University Press.

John S. Peart-Binns, from *Bishop Hugh Montefiore* (1990). Reprinted by permission of Quartet Books Ltd.

Pliny the Younger: letter to Lucius Lucinius Sura, from *Letters*, Vol. II, translated by William Melmoth, revised by W. M. L. Hutchinson (Loeb, 1915). Reprinted by permission of Harvard University Press.

'Poltergeist Raid Puzzles Detectives', from *The Times*, 10 December 1990. © Times Newspapers Ltd. 1990. Reprinted by permission.

Marcel Proust, from *In Search of Lost Time*, Vols. I, IV, and V, trs. C. K. Scott Moncrieff and Terence Kilmartin, revised by D. J. Enright. Translation copyright 1992 Chatto & Windus/Rardom House, Inc. Reprinted by kind permission of Chatto & Windus, Random House Inc., and the Estate of Terence Kilmartin.

Radio 4: extract from a transcript of an interview between Richard de la Mare and Robert Robinson on BBC Radio 4 on 25 April 1973, the centenary of the birth of Walter de la Mare.

Charles Richet, from *Thirty Years of Psychical Research* (Collins, 1923), translated by Stanley De Brath.

Sogyal Rinpoche, from *The Tibetan Book of Living and Dying* © 1993 by Rigpa Fellowship. Reprinted by permission of HarperCollins Publishers Inc.

Gershom G. Scholem, from *Major Trends in Jewish Mysticism* (Thames & Hudson/Schocken Books, 1955). Reprinted by permission of Thames & Hudson Ltd.

Paul Seabright, from 'Is Life a Lottery?', in *The Times Literary Supplement*, 14–20 December 1990. © Times Newspapers Ltd. 1990. Reprinted by permission.

Peter Scupham: 'A House of Geraniums', from *Out Late* (1986). Reprinted by permission of Oxford University Press.

Raoul Simac, from 'Sufi Story', in *The World of the Sufi* (1979). Reprinted by permission of Octagon Press London.

Isaac Bashevis Singer, from 'A Little Boy in Search of God', in *Love and Exile* (Cape, 1984).

Robin Skelton, from *The Practice of Witchcraft Today* (1988). Reprinted by permission of Robert Hale Ltd. (US rights: Pacific Publishers Support Services.)

Eleanor Smith, from *Life's a Circus* (Longmans Green, 1939).

Stevie Smith: 'The Revenant', from *Collected Poems of Stevie Smith* (Penguin). By permission of James MacGibbon and New Directions, New York.

Ian Stevenson, from 'The Contribution of Apparitions to the Evidence for Survival', in *Journal of the American Society for Psychical Research*, No. 76, 1982.

Doris Stokes (with L. Dearsley), from *Whispering Voices* (1985). Reprinted by permission of Little Brown & Company.

August Strindberg, from *From an Occult Diary*, translated Mary Sandbach (Secker, 1965). Reprinted by permission of the publisher; from *Inferno*, translated Mary Sandbach (Hutchison, 1965). Reprinted by permission of the publisher and the author's estate.

Will Sulkin. Reprinted by permission of the author.

Montague Summers, from *The Werewolf* (1933). Reprinted by permission of Routledge & Kegan Paul.

P'u Sung-ling, from 'Lien-hsiang', in *Chinese Literature 3: Tales of the Supernatural*, translated by H. C. Chang (1983). Reprinted by permission of Edinburgh University Press.

Noël Taillepied, from *A Treatise of Ghosts* (1958) translated by Montague Summers (1933). Reprinted by permission of Fortune Press.

Keith Thomas, from *Religion and the Decline of Magic* (1971). Reprinted by permission of Weidenfeld and Nicolson.

Herbert Thurston, from *Studies* (Dublin, 1928), reprinted in *Ghosts and Poltergeists*, edited by J. H. Crehan (1953). Reprinted by permission of Search Press Ltd./Burns and Oates Ltd.

Arnold J. Toynbee, from *A Study of History*, Vol. X (1954). Reprinted by permission of Oxford University Press Ltd.

G. N. M. Tyrrell, from *Apparitions* (1943). Reprinted by permission of The Society for Psychical Research.

Peter Underwood, from *No Common Task: The Autobiography of a Ghosthunter* (Harrap, 1983). Reprinted by permission of John Johnson (Authors' Agent) Ltd.

Peter Vansittart, from *The Wall* (1990). Reprinted by permission of Peter Owen Publishers Ltd.

Russell Wakefield, from 'A Peg On Which To Hang—', in *They Return at Evening, Quality Court* (Phillip Allan & Co./Geoffrey Bles).

Derek Walcott: 'Le Loupgarou', from *Collected Poems 1948–84*. Reprinted by permission of Faber & Faber Ltd., and Farrar, Straus & Giroux Inc.

Chris Wallace-Crabbe: 'Trace Elements', from *Rungs of Time* (1993). Reprinted by permission of Oxford University Press.

Sylvia Townsend Warner, from her unpublished diaries, 24 September 1972. Reprinted in *Sylvia Townsend Warner* by Claire Harman. From *Kingdoms of Elfin*, (Chatto, 1977).

John Wells, from *Rude Words: A Discursive History of The London Library* (Macmillan, 1991).

Rebecca West, from *The Fountain Overflows* (Macmillan, 1957).

Terence Whitaker, from *Yorkshire's Ghosts and Legends* (Grafton/Collins, 1983).

T. H. White, from 'Soft Voices at Passenham', reprinted in *The Maharajah and Other Stories*, edited by Kurth Sprague (Macdonald, 1981). Reprinted by permission of David Higham Associates.

Nigel Williams, from *They Came From SW19* (1992). Reprinted by permission of Faber & Faber Ltd. (US rights: Judy Daish).

Colin Wilson, from *Beyond the Occult* (Bantam Press/Transworld, 1988). Reprinted by permission of Transworld Publishers Ltd.

Ian Wilson, from *The After-Death Experience* (Sidgwick & Jackson, 1987). Reprinted by permission of the author and the publisher.

Jean Moorcroft Wilson, from the introduction to *The Collected Letters of Charles Hamilton Sorley* (1990). Reprinted by permission of Cecil Woolf.

W. E. Woodward, from *The Gift of Life* (Dutton, 1947).

'World Cup Notebook: Unearthly Forces Rally to the Call', from *The Times*, 12 June 1990. © Times Newspapers Ltd. 1990. Reprinted by permission.

Chao Yeh (attrib): 'Princess Purple Jade', in *The Golden Casket: Chinese Novellas of Two Millennia* (Allen & Unwin/Harcourt Brace Jovanovich, 1965), edited by Wolfgang Bauer and Herbert Franke, translated by Christopher Levenson.

Robin Young: 'Call For Exorcism at Witch's Church', in *The Times*, 16 October 1992. © Times Newspapers Ltd. 1990. Reprinted by permission.

Every effort has been made to secure reprint permission prior to publication. However, in a few instances this has not been possible. If notified, the publisher will rectify any errors or omissions at the earliest opportunity.

INDEX OF AUTHORS AND
PERSONS MENTIONED

INDEX OF UNASCRIBED PASSAGES

OXFORD

MORE OXFORD PAPERBACKS

This book is just one of nearly 1000 Oxford Paperbacks currently in print. If you would like details of other Oxford Paperbacks, including titles in the World's Classics, Oxford Reference, Oxford Books, OPUS, Past Masters, Oxford Authors, and Oxford Shakespeare series, please write to:

UK and Europe: Oxford Paperbacks Publicity Manager, Arts and Reference Publicity Department, Oxford University Press, Walton Street, Oxford OX2 6DP.

Customers in UK and Europe will find Oxford Paperbacks available in all good bookshops. But in case of difficulty please send orders to the Cash-with-Order Department, Oxford University Press Distribution Services, Saxon Way West, Corby, Northants NN18 9ES. Tel: 01536 741519; Fax: 01536 746337. Please send a cheque for the total cost of the books, plus £1.75 postage and packing for orders under £20; £2.75 for orders over £20. Customers outside the UK should add 10% of the cost of the books for postage and packing.

USA: Oxford Paperbacks Marketing Manager, Oxford University Press, Inc., 200 Madison Avenue, New York, N.Y. 10016.

Canada: Trade Department, Oxford University Press, 70 Wynford Drive, Don Mills, Ontario M3C 1J9.

Australia: Trade Marketing Manager, Oxford University Press, G.P.O. Box 2784Y, Melbourne 3001, Victoria.

South Africa: Oxford University Press, P.O. Box 1141, Cape Town 8000.

OXFORD BOOKS

THE OXFORD BOOK OF ENGLISH GHOST STORIES

Chosen by Michael Cox and R. A. Gilbert

This anthology includes some of the best and most frightening ghost stories ever written, including M. R. James's 'Oh Whistle, and I'll Come to You, My Lad', 'The Monkey's Paw' by W. W. Jacobs, and H. G. Wells's 'The Red Room'. The important contribution of women writers to the genre is represented by stories such as Amelia Edwards's 'The Phantom Coach', Edith Wharton's 'Mr Jones', and Elizabeth Bowen's 'Hand in Glove'.

As the editors stress in their informative introduction, a good ghost story, though it may raise many profound questions about life and death, entertains as much as it unsettles us, and the best writers are careful to satisfy what Virginia Woolf called 'the strange human craving for the pleasure of feeling afraid'. This anthology, the first to present the full range of classic English ghost fiction, similarly combines a serious literary purpose with the plain intention of arousing pleasing fear at the doings of the dead.

'an excellent cross-section of familiar and unfamiliar stories and guaranteed to delight' *New Statesman*

OXFORD BOOKS

THE NEW OXFORD BOOK OF
IRISH VERSE

Edited, with Translations, by Thomas Kinsella

Verse in Irish, especially from the early and medieval periods, has long been felt to be the preserve of linguists and specialists, while Anglo-Irish poetry is usually seen as an adjunct to the English tradition. This original anthology approaches the Irish poetic tradition as a unity and presents a relationship between two major bodies of poetry that reflects a shared and painful history.

'the first coherent attempt to present the entire range of Irish poetry in both languages to an English-speaking readership' *Irish Times*

'a very satisfying and moving introduction to Irish poetry' *Listener*

THE AGES OF GAIA

A Biography of Our Living Earth

James Lovelock

In his first book, *Gaia: A New Look at Life on Earth*, James Lovelock proposed a startling new theory of life. Previously it was accepted that plants and animals evolve on, but are distinct from, an inanimate planet. Gaia maintained that the Earth, its rocks, oceans, and atmosphere, and all living things are part of one great organism, evolving over the vast span of geological time. Much scientific work has since confirmed Lovelock's ideas.

In *The Ages of Gaia*, Lovelock elaborates the basis of a new and unified view of the earth and life sciences, discussing recent scientific developments in detail: the greenhouse effect, acid rain, the depletion of the ozone layer and the effects of ultraviolet radiation, the emission of CFCs, and nuclear power. He demonstrates the geophysical interaction of atmosphere, oceans, climate, and the Earth's crust, regulated comfortably for life by living organisms using the energy of the sun.

'Open the cover and bathe in great draughts of air that excitingly argue the case that "the earth is alive".' David Bellamy, *Observer*

'Lovelock deserves to be described as a genius.' *New Scientist*

WORLD'S CLASSICS SHAKESPEARE

'*not simply a better text but a new conception of Shakespeare. This is a major achievement of twentieth-century scholarship.*' Times Literary Supplement

Hamlet
Macbeth
The Merchant of Venice
As You Like It
Henry IV Part I
Henry V
Measure for Measure
The Tempest
Much Ado About Nothing
All's Well that Ends Well
Love's Labours Lost
The Merry Wives of Windsor
The Taming of the Shrew
Titus Andronicus
Troilus & Cressida
The Two Noble Kinsmen
King John
Julius Caesar
Coriolanus
Anthony & Cleopatra

OXFORD POPULAR FICTION
THE ORIGINAL MILLION SELLERS!

This series boasts some of the most talked-about works of British and US fiction of the last 150 years—books that helped define the literary styles and genres of crime, historical fiction, romance, adventure, and social comedy, which modern readers enjoy.

Riders of the Purple Sage	Zane Grey
The Four Just Men	Edgar Wallace
Trilby	George Du Maurier
Trent's Last Case	E C Bentley
The Riddle of the Sands	Erskine Childers
Under Two Flags	Ouida
The Lost World	Arthur Conan Doyle
The Woman Who Did	Grant Allen

Forthcoming in October:

Olive	Dinah Craik
The Diary of a Nobody	George and Weedon Grossmith
The Lodger	Belloc Lowndes
The Wrong Box	Robert Louis Stevenson

ILLUSTRATED HISTORIES IN
OXFORD PAPERBACKS

THE OXFORD ILLUSTRATED HISTORY
OF ENGLISH LITERATURE

Edited by Pat Rogers

Britain possesses a literary heritage which is almost unrivalled in the Western world. In this volume, the richness, diversity, and continuity of that tradition are explored by a group of Britain's foremost literary scholars.

Chapter by chapter the authors trace the history of English literature, from its first stirrings in Anglo-Saxon poetry to the present day. At its heart towers the figure of Shakespeare, who is accorded a special chapter to himself. Other major figures such as Chaucer, Milton, Donne, Wordsworth, Dickens, Eliot, and Auden are treated in depth, and the story is brought up to date with discussion of living authors such as Seamus Heaney and Edward Bond.

'[a] lovely volume . . . put in your thumb and pull out plums' Michael Foot

'scholarly and enthusiastic people have written inspiring essays that induce an eagerness in their readers to return to the writers they admire' *Economist*

OXFORD REFERENCE

THE CONCISE OXFORD COMPANION TO ENGLISH LITERATURE

Edited by Margaret Drabble and Jenny Stringer

Based on the immensely popular fifth edition of the *Oxford Companion to English Literature* this is an indispensable, compact guide to the central matter of English literature.

There are more than 5,000 entries on the lives and works of authors, poets, playwrights, essayists, philosophers, and historians; plot summaries of novels and plays; literary movements; fictional characters; legends; theatres; periodicals; and much more.

The book's sharpened focus on the English literature of the British Isles makes it especially convenient to use, but there is still generous coverage of the literature of other countries and of other disciplines which have influenced or been influenced by English literature.

From reviews of *The Oxford Companion to English Literature*:

'a book which one turns to with constant pleasure . . . a book with much style and little prejudice' Iain Gilchrist, *TLS*

'it is quite difficult to imagine, in this genre, a more useful publication' Frank Kermode, *London Review of Books*

'incarnates a living sense of tradition . . . sensitive not to fashion merely but to the spirit of the age' Christopher Ricks, *Sunday Times*